Also by Marian L Jasper

FOR ALL TIME
First in the Liza Marchant Series

AGAINST ALL ODDS
Second in the Liza Marchant Series

NOW AND FOREVER
Third in the Liza Marchant Series

FOR BETTER OR WORSE
Fourth in the Liza Marchant Series

Marian L. Jasper

Fifth in the Liza Marchant Series

Copyright © 2021 Marian L. Jasper

ISBN: 978-1-922565-60-0
Published by Vivid Publishing
A division of Fontaine Publishing Group
P.O. Box 948, Fremantle
Western Australia 6959
www.vividpublishing.com.au

A catalogue record for this
book is available from the
National Library of Australia

Dedication

For Peter, who was my greatest fan and fiercest critic.

Introduction

Eddy Fuller travelled from Belfast to Jamie Edgeworth's home in Surrey. He was joining his sister to discuss all that they knew about Liza Marchant-Kelly-Edgeworth's life and hopefully they could piece together some of the gaps that had inexplicably occurred in her history. Ellie had finally managed to persuade Lord Edgeworth that Liza had not been a 'scarlet woman' as had been portrayed down time and now he was equally intrigued and was going to assist in finding the truth.

He had been astounded to find that the Edgeworth good fortune had been instigated by Liza and not his great, great, great grandmother, Evelyn. They both had the same initials; Liza's given names being Elizabeth Anna and Evelyn's being Evelyn Adeline. Nobody was sure that it was indeed a mistake as Evelyn had on many occasions laid claim to Liza's identity both to do harm and to take credit which she did not deserve.

With the introductions over and Eddy ensconced comfortably, dinner that evening was a very cordial affair.

"You still stick to the dining traditions then Jamie," said Eddy.

"Not really, but as there are three of us it's nice to sit comfortably to eat," said Jamie.

"Is this room as it would have been in the past?" asked Eddy.

"It naturally has been decorated a number of times, but I do like to keep it as it was. I have never found it to be too old fashioned; I have always found it to be very relaxing and convivial, but that does of course depend on the company," smiled Jamie.

"I can almost see it as it was in those days; there must have been some very elegant gatherings here," said Eddy.

"Yes, well I no longer insist that ladies withdraw to the drawing room, whilst the gentlemen enjoy their port and cigars," said Jamie. "I'm very pleased that you are both here as I need to put right some serious errors and I know that you are the only ones who can help with this."

5

After their meal they all went into the sitting room and Ellie pointed to the portraits of two people and asked if they were the ones that Jamie had referred to, especially as one looked a little worse for wear as it had apparently fallen from the wall on so many occasions no matter how well it was fixed.

"Yes, that's my ancestor and namesake, Jamie Edgeworth and that's Evelyn. There are no portraits of Liza, which with what you have found out is somewhat surprising, although I suppose any portrait could have been destroyed," said Jamie.

"What are you proposing to do tomorrow Ellie?" asked Eddy.

"I think that we should go to the local church because although I know they were not able to have a church ceremony my information is that the local vicar gave them a blessing and I would have thought that it would have been recorded somewhere. Also if she died here then she should be buried in the graveyard if not in your family's tomb. Of course there is always Belfast, but we have found no record of her burial there. There is also the outside chance that she was laid to rest in Benson, but I really think that is unlikely," said Ellie.

After breakfast the following morning they all made their way to the local church. They took very little notice of the gravestones although one in particular looked very well kept. They introduced themselves to the vicar who naturally already knew Lord Edgeworth and Ellie then explained their mission to find out all that they could about Lady Liza Edgeworth who it appeared had been obliterated from the Edgeworth family history.

"I believe that the clergyman of that time agreed to give the marriage a blessing although it was acknowledged that as Lord Jamie Edgeworth was divorced, they could not have a church wedding," said Ellie. "I also believe that it was in the year 1855 and that the vicar was one Reverend Bernard Collins."

The vicar quietly sat down on one of the pews and took a long time to answer and when he did it was indeed enlightening.

"When I took over this parish some years ago, I was handed a letter from the previous vicar, who in turn had been given letters from all earlier vicars," he said with a great deal of emotion. "In that letter it asked me to keep intact all letters and packages relating to the Edgeworth family which were placed safely in our vault. I was also asked to only allow access to those who wanted to know the truth regarding Liza Edgeworth and not the lies that had been spread about her. Also I was told that there was a diary or journal that the Reverend Bernard Collins had felt obliged to write and leave for future

6

generations. Before I feel that I can relinquish this responsibility I have to be absolutely certain that you are the ones who will handle all the knowledge correctly."

Ellie explained who she and Eddy were and the close association that her family had with Liza Edgeworth and the fact that she had been considered as a much-loved member of that family.

The vicar then looked closely at Jamie Edgeworth and said, "You have never shown any desire to set any records straight; why are you so interested now?"

"It is because I never knew that there were any records to set straight. If I had done, then we would not be having this conversation now. I believe that my family has been very remiss, and arrogant, in our assessment of Liza Edgeworth's role in our family and I am now desperate to ensure that she is acknowledged as an important part of my family's history and her soul laid to rest as it should be," said Jamie.

"Even now the people of this village have always tended her grave as they knew that she should be looked after as she looked after them. I have read some of the Reverend Collins' notes and after the death of your great, great, great grandfather she was outrageously moved from the family tomb by the other Lady Edgeworth with the instruction that she be placed in a pauper's grave with no headstone or notification of where she was. The people of this village took it upon themselves to rebury her with dignity and they still look after her, but she is not where she should be and I hope that in time you will lay her to rest in her proper place," said the vicar.

They were all looking at the vicar in horror and Jamie said, "You don't mean to tell me that she was moved so that she could not lay at rest with my ancestor. That is an absolutely evil act to carry out. Why didn't his son object because I know that he would not have been a party to such a terrible deed?"

"I'm afraid I don't know the answer to that. Perhaps when you read the journals you will understand it more fully," said the vicar.

Ellie was thoughtful for a while and then finally said, "She had foresight. She knew that it would happen; she told Evelyn that she would take a final revenge on her and that others would be appalled by her actions. She also said that in the future there were those who would put right the wrong, but she would be long gone by then. We are who she was talking about, aren't we?"

Eddy was gulping back tears and Jamie was trying to hide his annoyance, but they were both nodding in agreement.

"I will bring you everything that the Reverend Collins left for you and place it in your safe keeping. I believe that you are right and that the three of you will lay her to rest in her rightful place and set all the records straight," said the vicar.

All three seemed lost for words as the vicar disappeared and could be heard rummaging around at the back of the altar. He finally emerged and both Eddy and Jamie went to assist him as two of the items were rather large and had been wrapped very carefully, although they could see that several layers of protection of various dates had been used to keep them safe over the years. The letters and journal had also been wrapped with care. The vicar told them that the larger items were two portraits which had been thrown away with the instruction that they be burned, but the gardeners of the time took them to the village and they were finally placed in the safe keeping of the church.

They passed the Edgeworth tomb on the way through the churchyard to the car and Ellie stopped and called to them whilst pointing to a gravestone opposite. It was the one that was noticeably neatly kept and had fresh flowers in a vase. The only inscription on it was the name 'Liza'.

"We've found her Eddy; we'll do right by her now," said Ellie and Jamie nodded in agreement.

Back at the house the portraits were unwrapped and Ellie, Eddy and Jamie drew in their breath in shock; they had all seen that face before in their dreams; it was the beautiful, smiling, happy face of a very sparkling green eyed Liza and she appeared to be looking at them. When they opened the second package they were surprised as it was so unlike the other dour portrait of Lord Jamie Edgeworth. This one was of him with a smiling and contented face, one that was so full of love that it created happiness.

Jamie called for his housekeeper and asked her to get one of the gardeners to come in and help them.

Ellie smiled at him and said, "You're going to put them in their rightful places aren't you Jamie?"

"Yes, I am," he said. "Evelyn Edgeworth may have been my natural ancestor, but she has no place in this house. Liza Edgeworth should have had pride of place for all these years and I'm going to make sure that she is also laid to rest where she should be and that is next to my ancestor and namesake, Lord Jamie Edgeworth."

A short while later Ellie, Eddy and Jamie stood smiling up at Liza and Jamie Edgeworth and they could have sworn that they both had nodded their acknowledgement of the beginning of righting a very great wrong.

"I suppose you must be nearing the end of her life," said Jamie.

"Good heavens no!" exclaimed Ellie. "You must remember that we have just reached the great acknowledgement and acclaim that she and Jamie had received from the Duke of Berkshire regarding their charity and also that Queen Victoria was showing a great deal of interest in what they were trying to achieve. Prince Albert had expressed a desire to become a patron. So there is a great deal to read and research and I know that they both travelled to the American south at a very interesting and dangerous time. No, their adventurous lives are not over yet."

"From what you have already written it seemed that Liza was not too pleased with all the adulation that she and the family were receiving," said Jamie.

"I think that she was pleased with what it meant for the charity, but she was never happier than when she was with the villagers at their cricket matches and she never lost her love for the people of Benson who had made her so welcome before they knew who she really was. The children had loved the freedom that they had when they lived there, although that disappeared when Patrick died but she did make a happy life with Jamie Edgeworth; she loved him dearly and he her, it was just a little more restricting and necessarily so," said Ellie.

"Have you any information about the mysterious Uncle David that they had just found out about?" Eddy asked Jamie.

"Yes, there are quite a few references to him in some of the documents that I have. I think I'm right in saying that he was a vicar, and he scandalously ran off with the fiancée of Jamie's father. I believe that for many years his name was never mentioned to such an extent that most family members were surprised that he ever existed," said Jamie.

"It's just another interesting development that I will have to research. I seem to recall that David Edgeworth fell in love with the lady and James Edgeworth was only marrying her for her money. Apparently, she stood at the altar and refused to make her marriage vows. She was of course disowned by her family but finally made a happy life with David. I still have to find out what became of him and if he ever was accepted back into the family," said Ellie. "He also somehow managed to buy back the Edgeworth diamonds which had been pawned by Jamie's father over gambling debts and the mystery is how a vicar could afford to redeem them."

"Tomorrow I'll see what else I can find on him," said Jamie. "There are so many twists and turns in the history of my family. Until recently I thought I knew everything about us, but I've realised that I have known practically nothing. I'm really looking forward to finding whatever we can uncover; it's all very exciting for me."

Chapter 1

It was the morning after the Duke of Berkshire's dinner and Liza yawned and stretched out in Jamie's bed. He was still sleeping peacefully and much as she wanted to stay and rest with him, she knew that she had a great deal to do that day. Firstly she had to write to Wendell and let him know of the great good fortune that the charity would now receive from the Duke and his friends not only in money but also in patronage including Prince Albert. The Queen had said how appalled she was that such a charity was needed in her realm and she lent her support for it but understandably she could not show favour to one charity above another.

Liza slipped out of bed and made her way to her own room and started to get ready for the day. She heard the boys making their way down to the kitchen for breakfast and then Jamie put his head around her door.

"Good morning Liza," he said. "I didn't hear you leave this morning; you must have tiptoed away. How are you? Have you got over your bout of depression?"

"Oh Jamie, you know I wasn't really depressed, I was just being silly. You must admit though it would be nice to go here, there and everywhere without people treating us like royalty," said Liza.

"So you think we're treated like royalty, do you? I didn't treat you like royalty last night, did I? I don't think that royalty would have had the fun that we had in bed. You have to admit that we had no airs and graces and I hope you enjoyed it as much as I did," laughed Jamie.

"I enjoy everything that we do together Jamie," said Liza. "I hope we weren't too noisy. I would hate to think that we woke the household with our energetic endeavours."

"I suppose it wouldn't be the first time that the household have heard love making," said Jamie. "What are your plans for the day?"

"Firstly I must write to Wendell informing him of what is happening. He'll be so pleased. I know that he has handed over much of the running to Edward and Joseph, but he does worry about the financial side of the charity, so he will now have his mind put at rest," said Liza. "Then I must send somebody to find the Major and Hector and hope that they can call here later today or first thing tomorrow. We may be able to make even better improvements to the Home. We'll see what they have to say."

"I know what you're really dying to do," said Jamie. "You want to go and find out about my Uncle David, don't you?"

"Yes, don't you?" said Liza.

"Of course I do. Whilst you're writing your letters I'll go and see my mother and find out if she can shed any light on the subject. She has never mentioned my uncle, so I wonder if she has ever heard of him. Perhaps it all happened a long time before she came here. There was quite an age gap between her and my father so maybe some years had elapsed since the family rift. I'm surprised that some of the villagers had said nothing," said Jamie.

"Perhaps they daren't. Don't forget many of them were reliant on the estate for their welfare and when that's the case they get used to keeping their thoughts to themselves. Possibly with time the incident was forgotten," said Liza. "Also you must remember how they all kept quiet about your mother but always informed her about everything that you were doing."

By lunchtime Davis had been dispatched to arrange for the letter to be sent to Wendell and then carry on to the Ffoulks house with the message to both the Major and Hector to join them either that evening or in the morning. Liza arranged that their rooms were made ready just in case they should arrive that day.

Liza and Jamie then made their way to see the Reverend Collins. Miranda had been unable to shed any light on the mysterious uncle apart from knowing that Jamie's father had been engaged years before his marriage to her and it had been a subject that it had been wise not to refer to.

The Reverend was surprised to see them and even more surprised to know their reason for visiting him.

"What year are we talking about?" asked the Reverend.

"I suppose it has to be about fifty years ago that the marriage was meant to take place, so my uncle's birth date must have been around seventy years ago," said Jamie.

"I'm sure you're dying to find out all about your mysterious uncle, but you must appreciate that searching our records is going to take some considerable time, especially going back as far as seventy years. Also I'm not sure that our records were kept in very good order that far back," said Bernard Collins.

He could see the look of disappointment on Liza's face and smiled. "Don't worry if there is anything about David Edgeworth, we will find it. I think I'll ask young Derek Price to help. You probably know that he is very good at organising. I take it that you would have no objection to him delving into your family history."

"I know that he's very good at his lessons and I can believe that he would be happy looking through all the old dusty records," smiled Liza.

"I have no objection; whatever happened was a very long time ago and we would like to get to the bottom of this particular part of our history; so any help that you can give us would be much appreciated," said Jamie.

Liza and Jamie were therefore resigned to the fact that it would take a little while to research and find any reference to David Edgeworth, and although disappointed that they had no answers that day they were pleased that they had set in operation all that could be done to find him.

***

Much later that day the Major and Hector arrived. They had concerned looks on their faces but one look at a smiling Liza and Jamie allayed any fears that they might have had. They both had hastily packed overnight cases which were taken up to their rooms and Liza made them comfortable in the drawing room.

The Major and Hector were astounded by the news of not only the increase in fortunes for the charity, but also the fact that so many illustrious names wished to become patrons, which in turn would bring in even more funds.

"Tomorrow the Duke of Berkshire will be visiting us and I would like to have in place a few thoughts on how we can improve what we are already doing and also perhaps we could discuss where could be the best places to open further homes. One of these days it would be nice if our Homes are solely devoted to homeless children and not just those who have been abused," said Liza.

"I know that the lawmakers are devoting a great deal of time to writing legislation which will make the consequences for those who perpetrate child abuse much harsher, but that is going to take time," said Jamie.

"I've written to Wendell and I know that he and the Fuller family will be delighted that we no longer have concerns about funding for our charity, but today it is up to the four of us to try to put some plans in place to let the Duke know that we are quite capable of handling the good fortune that he and his friends are bestowing on the children," said Liza.

"Liza I am just a very small pawn in your organisation. I am indeed flattered that you should feel that you can consult with me over this matter, but I am only beginning to learn exactly what your charity is all about," said Hector.

"You do yourself an injustice Hector; we have all seen how dedicated you have been to arranging the best way forward for housing the children in the Ffoulks house and I am confident that you would be able to do the same in many establishments," said Liza.

"I too have only been in the employ of the charity for a relatively short time," said the Major. "You know that I do have many ideas on the running of the Home, but I have not yet thought further than what I am doing at present."

"Do you not feel that you would be capable of overseeing the running of several such establishments?" Jamie asked the Major.

"Of course that does depend on how many you are thinking of, but if you are going to get three or four up and running, one at a time, then I will be more than capable of handling them overall," said the Major. "It does also depend on how close their proximity is to one another."

Liza then turned to Hector, "well Hector, do you think that you would be capable of finding suitable establishments for us?" asked Liza. "More to the point, would you like to permanently work for the charity in many capacities and once the Ffoulks house is ready; would you be happy that your first role would be looking for the right properties?" asked Liza.

"You have a great deal of faith in me Liza; until recently I was an army man and I admit that I have never taken life seriously until now. I would like to work for the charity in whatever capacity is required," said Hector.

"It isn't just me who has faith in you Hector; Jamie does also, and I believe that the Major has relied on you a great deal," said Liza. "Am I right Major?"

"You are Liza; Hector has been invaluable in assisting and advising on the alterations to the Ffoulks house. I know that he would be an asset to the charity," said the Major.

"Good," said Jamie. "So over dinner we can discuss how we can utilise some of the money to hurry the completion of the Ffoulks house and possibly add further improvements which previously we would have had to leave."

Dinner that evening was full of lively conversation and by the end of it several plans were in place and they would be ready for the Dukes' visit the following day. The Major and Hector felt that they were going to be under scrutiny by the Duke but Liza and Jamie assured them that he just wanted to make arrangements regarding the funds and just have some idea how they were going to be spent.

"It isn't going to be an interview," laughed Liza. "He's very enthusiastic regarding the charity and wants to know how we are getting on with it. There's no need to worry about him; he's very sweet."

"Well," said Jamie. "He's 'very sweet' when you are around Liza."

"I wonder if he will be bringing Bella with him, or maybe his mother-in-law," said Liza.

"He didn't say he was bringing anyone with him, but he is a law unto himself," said Jamie.

"I would have thought that one of the Fullers would want to be at the meeting tomorrow," said the Major.

"Yes, that would have been ideal, but there was not enough time to get them here. They will be here in the next day or so because some of the money will also be going to improve the facilities in Ireland," said Liza.

"What about America?" asked Hector.

"I believe that what is being offered is to help this side of the Atlantic, but that is something that we will have to establish tomorrow. The American operation is run independently to this one, although each does help the other. As you know many of our children make good lives for themselves over in America and we help them to get work, some become bond servants and some are adopted into families," said Liza.

Both the Major and Hector became very enthusiastic regarding their ideas on how to improve the Ffoulks house until Jamie said that they had all better get to bed as they needed to be very alert the following day.

"How are you going to avoid the Dukes' advances tomorrow," Jamie asked Liza when they were alone that night.

"He will be here on business; it won't be a social occasion," said Liza.

Jamie laughed, "Oh Liza, you really are naïve. You know he will never miss an opportunity to try to persuade you to become his mistress."

"Surely not, but if he does then he is going to be disappointed yet again. You don't think he'll withdraw his funding if I refuse him?" asked a suddenly concerned Liza.

"No Liza, he wouldn't do that, besides his mother-in-law would have something to say about that," laughed Jamie. "Stop worrying and come here."

15

He pulled her over to him, kissed her on the head and gently lifted her into bed.

***

All their enthusiasm had not diminished overnight and as Liza was unsure whether the Duke would be arriving before or after lunch, she had to arrange for the kitchen to be prepared for both lunch and dinner.

The Duke arrived just prior to lunch and he was alone. He carried with him a banker's draft for monies that he had collected from all those who were at the dinner the previous week but in the future each patron would make their contribution directly to the charity and Liza made a mental note to consider employing a permanent bookkeeper to handle all the finances because up to that time either she or Edward had dealt with it.

Jamie made the introductions to the Duke.

"I am very pleased to meet you Major Styles; I was sorry to hear about your son. Sadly many good young men lost their lives at that time. I hear that you are doing sterling work for the charity, perhaps shortly you could give me some idea where you have got to with the Ffoulks house," said the Duke.

"Yes, I'd be delighted to, perhaps after lunch we can go into detail," said the Major.

The Duke turned to Hector, "Well young Mr Ffoulks, I understand that you are helping quite considerably in many aspects of the charity. I am very pleased that you have at last found your feet and now have some purpose to your life. I know that it's never very easy being a second son and finding that the army life is not what you thought it would be. Well done."

"Thank you, Sir, but my road back into usefulness is down to Lord and Lady Edgeworth and Major Styles. Also the fact that I truly enjoy what I am doing, which is helping those less fortunate than I," said Hector.

Liza looked at Hector and felt very proud of him as he had come a long way since his return from Portugal.

Lunch was served and the Duke seemed to want to talk about all but the charity. Jamie smiled across to Liza as she skillfully avoided the propositions made to her. Hector was grinning broadly, and the Major had a raised eyebrow. At the end of the meal the Duke said how much he had enjoyed his lunch.

"Not only have I enjoyed the food but once again I have very much enjoyed meeting my verbal match in you Liza. I must compliment you on your choice of wife Jamie; if only all such wives were as loyal and faithful as yours and also as happy," said the Duke.

"Yes I'm a very lucky man," said Jamie once again smiling at Liza.

"And I'm a very lucky lady," said Liza.

"Before you give me some idea of your plans for the future, the Dowager Lady Redfern has given me a list of functions that you are invited to. Normally you will receive your own invitations but she has organised this on your behalf, or really on behalf of your charity, and hopefully you will be free to attend most, if not all of them," said the Duke.

"Thank you, and I'll thank the Dowager personally and of course I will respond to each invitation," said Liza and Jamie noticed that although she was smiling that smile was not reaching her eyes. He knew that she was thinking that this was the beginning of a life that she had never wished for.

"I'm not here to question you on how you will be spending the funds; I know you will spend it wisely, but it would be good to hear some of your ideas and put to you some of my thoughts," said the Duke.

They discussed the fact that the Ffoulks house could now finish earlier than expected and they would look towards purchasing other properties. Improvements could also be made to the Irish Homes and perhaps they could also buy another one.

"You haven't mentioned your American operation; will you not be utilising some of the funds for that?" asked the Duke.

"We were not sure that the funds were for that purpose," said Liza cautiously.

"Liza the funds are for you to spend where they are most needed, be it here, Ireland or in America. You don't have such a large operation there, do you?" he asked.

"We do concentrate on arranging new lives for some of our children from here, but at one time we were getting inundated with new born babies left on our doorsteps and sadly we had to start turning them away as we had run out of room. The articles of our charity stipulate that it is solely for abused children or those who are in danger of abuse. However the President realised how desperate we were getting and made arrangements to find premises for such children," said Liza.

"That must have been a hard decision for you Liza," said the Duke. "How did you manage to keep them away from your Homes; it must have been difficult to distinguish between those who were abused and those who were just abandoned?"

"We had to use security guards and they were not happy about such duties, but they appreciated that we really had no choice," said Liza.

"I'm impressed that the President has become involved. I did not think that the country was financially able to make much of a contribution," said the Duke and both Liza and Jamie made no comment, and the Duke smiled acknowledging that they kept such confidences.

The Major stepped in by saying that he understood that the American government were also discussing legislation that would make sentences much harsher for those who perpetrated such crimes, as were the English Parliament.

"That's good," said the Duke. "You have most certainly achieved a great deal in a relatively short space of time. So you will now be looking for further Homes for the children; I may be able to help you there. I know of one or two properties that will soon be placed on the market. I do not wish to divulge the names of the owners of the properties, but I will contact them and give them the option to get in touch with you should their intentions be serious."

"That would indeed be helpful and initially Hector would visit them to assess their suitability but of course we would be discreet," said Liza.

The Duke looked at Hector quizzically, "I did not think that you had much experience in that field Hector?"

"With all due respect Sir, I know what would convert to provide adequately for the children and now that we have no problems regarding funding it will be a much easier task than we have had at Ffoulks house where we had to watch how every penny was spent and cut some corners where necessary. I am not saying that we must throw the money away, but we can now create a much more comfortable environment for the children. However, no matter how much money we have there is no point in taking a property which would be totally inadequate for its purpose," said Hector.

"My apologies Hector, I stand corrected," smiled the Duke.

The Major nodded and said, "Hector has become a very important member of our team and even more so now with the expansion that we are planning."

18

Liza and Jamie also nodded both thinking how well the Major and Hector worked together and respected one another. As the afternoon wore on Liza invited the Duke to stay for dinner.

"I would love to Liza, but I must return and report to my wife and mother-in-law, who you will appreciate are extremely interested in what you are doing," he replied and shortly after he took his leave.

When Liza and Jamie returned after seeing him safely into his carriage, the Major and Hector were discussing the afternoons' events.

"I don't believe that the Duke thinks that I am up to the tasks in hand," said Hector.

"I know that the Duke likes to test some people Hector," said Liza. "I believe you stood up to his questioning well and he realised that you knew what you were talking about."

"It's interesting that he may know of some properties which may be available to us," said the Major. "It really has been an enlightening afternoon and tomorrow Hector and I will return to the Ffoulks house and expand on the work and hopefully bring forward the day that it can open."

"We are all going to be very busy for the foreseeable future," said Jamie. "It seems that Liza and I will be on a never-ending round of entertainment whilst you, Major, and Hector will be doing all the work."

"I don't envy you and Liza," said the Major. "I can also see that Liza is not altogether happy with the prospect of endless socialising and I'm not so sure that you are either Jamie. I know that you appreciate that it has become an important part of promoting and gaining funds for the charity."

"When are you both going to have the time to run your other businesses?" asked Hector.

"As you know Peter Fuller is a very efficient businessman and Edward and Joseph are very dedicated. I have many people working well for both companies and my interests in America are already under control. However I do feel that the time has come for us to have a secretary working for us here, and perhaps also someone who is an accurate bookkeeper," said Liza. "It is something that Jamie and I will have to discuss."

"We also have our boys to think about," said Jamie. "They need to spend time with us, and we must make sure that they do not suffer because we are concentrating on other children. I know that it is wonderful what has been offered for the charity, but it has put us both on permanent show and that is a direction that neither of us really wanted. We will, however, rise to the occasion but we will try to organise it so that we do have some time to ourselves."

"That is very important," said the Major. "I can see that you could be in danger of working yourselves into the ground but to the outside world it will appear that you are always out and about enjoying yourselves. I know how tiring functions can be and you do have so much more to do than wining and dining."

The boys could be heard going down to the kitchen for their supper and Liza excused herself and made her way down to see them. They were full of life as always and just being with them for a few minutes put Liza in a happier mood. After a short while she left them to enjoy their meal without her and made her way up to her bedroom to rest and bring some order to her thoughts.

A while later Jamie found her resting on her bed; she was already dressed for dinner. As he came into her room she turned and gave him a smile that would always melt his heart. She sat up and gestured for him to come and sit with her. He sat and put his arm around her.

"Well Liza, you were right, we have a difficult and busy job to do now. The thought of it didn't frighten me until now. Over the next few months, if not years, we will have very little time to ourselves but we must take every opportunity that we can to be with our boys and grab every moment we can for us to be alone," said Jamie.

As if on cue the boys knocked and when told they entered. They wanted to know if it was true that the Queen was coming to visit them.

Liza and Jamie laughed. "It's amazing how stories get exaggerated," said Liza. "No the Queen will not be visiting us; at least we don't think so. The Queen has shown some interest in our charity and Prince Albert wishes to become a patron, as do many influential people. You know that means that we will be able to help a great many more children than we have been able to so far."

"May we visit the Ffoulks house to see what is being done there?" asked John.

"Of course you can," said Jamie. "Are we free this weekend?" he asked Liza.

"I don't yet know. I haven't had a chance to see the list of invitations that Lady Redfern has organised for us. I would like us to go with you, but if we are busy, I'll ask Mr Reece and April to take you," said Liza.

"It would be better if you went with us," said James.

"I know it would James, but the entertainments which have been organised for us are to help with raising money for the charity, so I'm afraid we cannot refuse the invitation, but you heard what your mother said; she has yet to see what has been planned for us and we may well be free to be with you," said Jamie.

Matthew just looked, smiled, and nodded. He seemed well aware that it was a situation which was not of their choosing.

The boys went off to their room and Jamie turned to Liza and said, "We're neglecting our boys already. We married so that we could be together and have our boys with us. In a way I now think that I understand why you were so upset the other evening; our comfortable and cosy life is altering and I'm not very happy about it."

"We must make sure that we keep some time just for us and our family. If there is an invitation for this coming weekend I can refuse it because it is such short notice that I can plead a prior engagement, which will be true as we do have a prior engagement with our boys," said Liza.

Miranda and Lucinda were joining them that evening for dinner and the talk around the table was lively and it eventually got on to the mystery surrounding Jamie's Uncle David.

"You're going to have to spare some time searching for him," said Lucinda. "Have you really never heard of him before?"

"No I haven't and neither has my mother," said Jamie.

"It's all very exciting," said Hector. "Where are you going to start looking?"

"We've already started. We have the Reverend Collins looking in the parish records; his birth must have been registered, but we don't know exactly when he was born. There may well be some note of the abandoned wedding," said Jamie. "Young Derek is going to help with the investigation. We think that he'll enjoy doing that."

"She must have been a very brave woman to stand there and refuse to marry your father," said Lucinda. "I suppose we have to look at the fact that if she had made her vows none of us would be sitting here today."

"You're right Lucinda," said Jamie. "My mother would not have married my father and therefore I would not have been born and James would not have been born. If I had not been born then Liza, Matthew and John would not be here. You are all here because my mother and I are here; it's very strange to think of it in that way."

"Do you think that we will be able to go to Belfast for Easter as we usually do? You now have so many commitments that it may be difficult for you," said Miranda.

"I am determined that we will be there for Easter and we also have to remember that it will be Adam and April's wedding when we return," said Jamie.

"I know that the invitations that we may have are very important for the charity, but I believe that those concerned will appreciate that we already have commitments but we will attend as many as we can," said Liza.

"I shall be attending their wedding," said Hector. "I'm looking forward to it."

Liza and Jamie smiled at him as they knew that he had invited himself to the event and they still doubted that Adam and April knew that he was going to attend. Adam's sister, Estelle, was his reason for wanting to be there.

"You know that Estelle would be quite capable of helping you with all your paperwork Liza," said Hector.

"I know she could Hector, but she is a teacher and will be working with the children at the Ffoulks house shortly and I will need someone who will be with me on a permanent basis," said Liza.

"I suppose you're right; you really need someone who won't be leaving you in a few weeks," said Hector.

"Lucinda and I can help you until you find someone suitable," said Miranda.

When they all finally made their way to bed Liza found that it was a time of reflection for her. April had helped her to get ready and when she had left Liza sat at her dressing table gathering her thoughts. That night Jamie came into her.

"Are you not coming into my bed tonight?" he asked.

"I'm sorry Jamie I was deep in thought; have I been sitting here for a long while?" she asked.

"Yes for a while. I think I'd like to join you in your bed tonight. Would you like that?" asked Jamie.

"I want to be wherever you are Jamie and you are more than welcome to come into my bed tonight," said Liza.

"We are not going to let anything stop us from enjoying ourselves, and nothing is going to stop us looking after our boys properly. The charity will take second place in our lives, important as it is," said Jamie.

They both climbed into Liza's bed and took great comfort in one another. Liza lay back at one stage and made a silent promise that she would care for

Jamie and her family above all else. Finally she slept more contentedly than she had done for some days.

***

Liza was sitting at her desk and smiling the next morning. She had read the Dowager Lady Redfern's letter which accompanied all the invitations to functions and realised how wonderfully efficient she was. Jamie called her saying that the Major and Hector were about to leave so she went to bid her farewells to them.

"You're looking much happier than you were last night," said Hector, who suddenly realised that he may have sounded rather tactless in his approach.

"I am Hector. I've discovered just how efficient Lady Redfern is; she has organised the necessary functions which should fit in well with our prior commitments," said Liza.

"Well that's very thoughtful of her," said the Major. "We'll see you and the boys at the weekend. Will you be staying overnight?"

"We hadn't planned to, but we will of course see Anthony and Diana while we are there. Perhaps you will tell them that we are going to visit the Home," said Liza.

"You know that you only have to turn up on their doorstep. Your rooms are always ready for you, as are theirs here. Of course little Thomas would be delighted to see 'Maffew'," laughed Hector, "although I am not so sure that 'Maffew' would be as delighted to see him."

"Thomas does seem to do exactly as Matthew tells him," said Liza, "which could be either a good thing or a bad one."

"Matthew deals with him very well, and so do the other boys. I don't think that he will go far wrong with their influence," said the Major.

"It's very kind of you to say so," said Jamie.

The Major and Hector climbed into the carriage and went on their way back to the Ffoulks house. Jamie and Liza went back into the house and Jamie asked Liza what had made her so noticeably happy. "It was obviously something that was in Lady Redfern's letter."

"Yes, she has written that she realises that we would not be available at short notice, although Lord Carlton would like us to attend dinner next week as many patrons will be in attendance and they would like us to talk to them about the origins of the charity and of course how it will now progress," said Liza.

"Why would that make you so happy?" asked a confused Jamie.

"That hasn't made me happy; it's something that I really would rather not talk about, but I suppose that as all the guests at Lord Carlton's are now our sponsors then they deserve an explanation. What has pleased me is the fact that Lady Redfern has gone to the bother of finding out what our normal routine is and nothing has been planned following Lord Carlton's dinner until we return after Easter and then there is only one event between our return and Adam and April's wedding. It means that I don't have to write too many letters of apology and all the other invitations have been organised in areas close to one another and thankfully not every week. I really could use Lady Redfern as a secretary," laughed Liza.

"Does that mean that you won't need someone to assist you?" asked Jamie.

"It would be someone to assist us Jamie, not just me," said Liza. "I think that Lady Redfern realised that we are not yet in a position to organise ourselves efficiently until after Adam and April's marriage. I wonder how she was aware of their wedding. Of course she has proved before that she has contacts everywhere."

"It's a shame that Estelle Reece will be going to the Ffoulks house," said Jamie. "As you say though she is really a teacher and it is probably what she is best at. It's also a pity that Derek is still too young as I believe he is very good at organising."

"You're right Jamie, both would be excellent, but I will have to look elsewhere for a secretary. It would be ideal if someone could be working for us ready for when we return after Easter," said Liza. "Something always falls into place with us so I'm not too worried."

"Will we stay with Anthony and Diana this weekend? The boys will enjoy it and so will little Thomas," said Jamie.

"We'll go prepared as we will be able to spend more time at the Home if we are there for the night. I'll get a note to Diana to make sure we are welcome," smiled Liza. "I must now also write to Lady Redfern thanking her for all she has organised for us."

Liza then spent many hours sorting out the dates of functions and responding to invitations. When she had finished, she then studied a report on the progress of the building of the Marchant & Fuller steamship. She looked at all the correspondence on her desk and shook her head. *Hector was right*, she thought, *when am I going to have time to concentrate on my business and more importantly when am I going to find time for my family?*

She had not realised that Jamie had quietly come into the study and had been watching her as she worked. "There has to be a way that I can help you Liza," he said gently.

She looked around startled. "I don't know Jamie; I really wish that I did. It's a long time since I felt unable to cope with all that seems to be landing on my desk. I'm sure it will ease, and I must concentrate on getting someone to deal with much of my correspondence leaving me to make decisions and giving me time for my family."

"You have felt like this before then Liza. I did not know that. You have always seemed very much in control of all that is asked of you. When was that?" asked Jamie.

"It was some years ago, just after dear Danny died and Angus had killed himself because of it. Matthew wasn't quite one-year-old then. Poor Kathy and Joe went to pieces and I ended up running the store as well as trying to sort out the legal problems of the townspeople. I had no time to spend with my son; I seemed to be on call morning, noon and night. The people expected me to be able to solve every problem and have an answer for everything. The only way that it eased was when I collapsed on the sidewalk," said Liza.

"Were you also dealing with some of the Marchant & Fuller business at that time?" asked Jamie.

"Yes, I was helping to set up the banking section and I was also teaching English to German and Italian families, but what is concerning me now is the fact that what is expected of me is so much bigger," said Liza.

"I have never known you doubt yourself before Liza. I believe that you will handle all that's asked of you beautifully but to do that you will definitely need someone who is reliable to work with you," said Jamie.

"Jamie, your workload will also increase considerably. There will be many functions which will be men only affairs so any assistant will be needed by both of us," said Liza. "I think we will have to take up your mother's and Lucinda's offer of help; they will be able to deal with all the replies to the various invitations and that will leave me free to deal with my business and you to deal with your business. So you're right Jamie, we will both handle everything beautifully."

There was chatter and the sound of the boys making their way down to the kitchen for their supper and both Liza and Jamie smiled. "Everything is still very normal here and I don't think that it's going to change," said Jamie.

"I'm going down to see the boys and find out what they are having for supper," said Liza.

"I'm coming with you," said Jamie. "Do you think they will appreciate us spending time with them during their supper?"

"We won't spend all their supper time with them, but we have ignored them quite considerably over the past few days and I want them to know that they are not forgotten," said Liza.

The boys were delighted to see them and spent a long while telling them what they had been doing and how much they were looking forward to going to the Ffoulks house and possibly staying with Anthony and Diana overnight. Liza and Jamie then left them to enjoy their supper without the restrictions that they thought parents imposed.

The next morning a note arrived from Diana telling them that she looked forward to seeing them over the weekend.

Chapter 2

Shouts of 'Maffew' could be heard as their carriage pulled up in front of Anthony and Diana's house and Matthew had a resigned look on his face.

"Never mind Matthew," said Liza. "We will be meeting the Major at the other house shortly and I doubt that Thomas will be accompanying us there."

"Don't worry Matthew," said James. "We'll help you with him, won't we John?"

Diana and Anthony came down the steps to greet them followed by little Thomas who was grinning and jumping up and down as he held tightly onto Rose's hand.

"You look just as excited as little Thomas," said Liza to Diana.

"I am," said Diana. "We've received an invitation."

"Really," said Liza. "You must tell me all about it."

"As if you didn't know," said Diana smiling.

"No, I don't but I think I can guess, but let's go in and you can show me what you have," smiled Liza.

Anthony was also smiling happily and whilst the boys were occupied with Thomas, Diana pulled out an invitation from Lord Carlton to the function on the following week.

"I don't know what you both did, but I want to thank you for getting us included at Lord Carlton's dinner," said Anthony.

"I wish I could lay claim to that," said Jamie, "but I believe it was something that Liza said to Bella."

All eyes turned to Liza who brushed off their thanks. "It was really nothing," said Liza. "I just told them the truth and shall we leave it at that."

"Alright," said Anthony smiling, "if that's what you want, but we are grateful."

For a short while Liza and Diana discussed what they would be wearing to Lord Carlton's dinner and then Jamie, Liza and the boys left for Ffoulks house and they spent the rest of the day inspecting all the work that was being carried out there.

When they returned to Anthony and Diana's house, the boys went straight down for supper and little Thomas went proudly with them and Matthew could be heard encouraging him to eat his food 'like a big boy'.

Liza and Jamie went up to their room to rest for a short while before getting dressed for dinner when Hector and the Major would be joining them as well as Rose.

The conversation was lively over dinner. Hector and the Major were very animated about all the added improvements that were now being undertaken.

"I understand that you are giving a talk on the origins of the charity," said Hector to both Liza and Jamie.

"Well we'll be answering a few questions," said Jamie.

"That's not according to Lord Carlton's invitation, apparently you are the evenings' entertainment," said Hector.

"We haven't seen an invitation, we received ours through Lady Redfern and all she said in her letter was that there would be a number of the charity's patrons there and they wanted to know something of how the charity started," said Liza.

"It requests the pleasure of our company for dinner which is to be followed by an interesting talk by Lady Liza Edgeworth on the origins of her children's charity," said Anthony.

"Oh," said Liza with a frown. "I don't usually go into details about that."

"You only have to tell them as little as you want," said Rose, "but I know that a legend was born at that time and I suppose that it is what they want to learn about."

"Unfortunately that has piqued their imagination and of course it is only natural that they want to know more," said the Major.

"I may have to disappoint them in that," said Liza quietly.

All those around the table were now silent and thoughtful. Jamie looked at Liza with concern as he could see that she was close to tears.

Hector was the first to break the silence. "I have heard several reports of a tall American soldier appearing on occasion and helping children to safety; I presume that it's a myth but that is probably the legend that they want to hear about."

"He would not have wanted to become a legend; he would have been mortified to know how he is now regarded. He was a soldier and that was all he ever wanted to be," said Liza.

At last realisation dawned on Hector as he saw the pain showing on Liza's face and Jamie's old familiar look of aloofness. "I'm so sorry; I've obviously opened up old wounds."

Liza suddenly smiled and said. "Please don't trouble yourself Hector; all it has done is bring back a little of the past and it is something that I will have to prepare for when I make my presentation at Lord Carlton's function. It was how the charity started so I shall now be ready for all that is asked of me that evening. Jamie was around at that time, so we will be able to pool our memories and make our talk as interesting as we possibly can."

The Major was looking at Hector with some annoyance and he would tell him later that it would have been a good idea to study the past of those that he now worked for and that he would also attempt to give him some lessons in tactfulness.

"Are you alright Liza?" asked Diana.

"I am thank you Diana," said Liza. "We have all become a little maudlin which is not what we should be at this lovely friendly gathering. We still have to finalise what we will be wearing for the event and we must work out whether you will be staying with us for that night or whether we will be here with you. What do you think Jamie? Are we nearer to Lord Carlton's or are Anthony and Diana?"

Liza smiled and held Jamie's gaze until his eyes softened and he realised that she was talking with her eyes and they told him that she loved him and that the past was the past. The tension around the table eased and the talk turned to the boys and Thomas as well as how the Ffoulks house was progressing and how it was now going to be even more comfortable for the children.

When Liza and Jamie were in their room that night, Liza turned to Jamie and laughed, "Do you know Jamie, I believe that Hector and Edward would get on well together as neither of them appear capable of saying much without creating embarrassment."

"Yes, you are right; Hector does seem to be a little tactless on occasion. I often wonder if he enjoys making people feel awkward," said Jamie.

"I think that he did at one time gain pleasure from such actions, but he has changed and I know that he cares for our family a great deal and would do nothing to hurt any of us," said Liza.

"I noticed that the Major appeared annoyed with him and no doubt he'll have a quiet word with him. He has taken him under his wing and Hector shows that he has a great deal of respect for the Major. They work well together," said Jamie.

Liza climbed into bed and smiled at Jamie.

"Are you sure you want me tonight Liza?" asked Jamie.

A look of hurt crossed Liza's face. "Are you always going to feel this way whenever Patrick is mentioned? I thought that we had got through that and come out very strongly on the other side. I'm not going to apologise for my past as I have nothing to be ashamed of. I said to you once before that I hoped that you had never felt anything but loved by me. I don't want to keep fighting this battle Jamie," said a very weary Liza.

She lay down in bed and turned her back on Jamie. A short while later she felt him climb in next to her and then lie very still. "I'm pleased that we don't have separate rooms in this house because if we did, I wouldn't be able to get near you and tell you how sorry I am. I know that you show your love for me in every way, but sometimes I feel that your mind is elsewhere, and I felt that this evening," said Jamie.

She stayed with her back to him and said, "I cannot be held responsible for what you feel. I think I am going to refuse to attend Lord Carlton's function because it is going to open up old wounds for us both and I am not prepared to have my loyalty questioned by you yet again."

"It would be nice if we did not have to go to the function, but you know that it would be impossible and it would do untold harm to the charity," said Jamie.

"I said that I wouldn't go, I did not say that you should not attend; you can do just as good a job as I, probably even better after all they are your class of people, not mine; I'm from very humble stock," said Liza.

"Please turn around Liza; I can't apologise to the back of your head and you can't see how sorry I am and how much I love you and want you; and I wouldn't care if you came from a family who lived in a mud hut, you are Liza and that's all you need to be," said Jamie.

"If I turn around are you still going to have that aloof look on your face, because I don't want to see it," said a sulky Liza.

"Oh Liza," said Jamie, "even in the midst of a disagreement you still make me smile. No I haven't an aloof look on my face, I hope that all I have on my face is love, but I don't know because I can't see myself. Let me see your face as I'm sure you will be pouting just like Matthew."

As he said that Liza realised that she was pouting and then she laughed and turned, and their difference of opinion was over. Jamie engulfed her in his arms and breathed a great sigh of relief.

Liza looked into his eyes and said, "Never doubt me Jamie; you will never have any reason to, and if our dinner at Lord Carlton's is going to be too difficult for you then I suggest that you feign illness, or I do."

"No, we'll face it together and tell them what they seem to need to know. We'll show them a united front, which is what we have, and we'll end up making lots of money for the charity; it will be a small price to pay for the poor, unfortunate children," said Jamie.

"We have nothing to attend for a while after Lord Carlton's function so we will be enjoying a family Easter in Belfast and then April and Adam's wedding. We'll have a wonderful time and we'll appreciate that it could be a while before we have other such times," said Liza.

***

Sunday was a pleasant day and Anthony and Jamie helped the boys with their bowling and batting skills telling them that they wanted them to be in good shape when the cricket season began. Diana and Rose spent a while watching them and trying to tell little Thomas what it was all about and Liza went with the Major and Hector back to the Ffoulks house and discussed in detail how the kitchens and dining areas were now going to be laid out.

"My lack of cooking expertise has become legendary. Major, I wonder if your cook would mind spending a little time here to see if we are making the best use of the facilities," said Liza.

"Yes it would be useful to have the thoughts of someone who is used to a kitchen. Also I believe that my cook is quite good friends with your cook Hector, I think that they could pool their ideas," said the Major.

"She's not my cook Major, she's Anthony's and Diana's, but their kitchen does seem to run very smoothly, so I'll suggest it when I return, or you can Liza," said Hector.

As they returned to Anthony and Diana's house, they saw a messenger leaving.

"That's unusual for a Sunday," said Hector. "It must be important; I hope it's not bad news."

Hector sprinted up the steps and was met by a smiling Anthony. "It would appear that you have an invitation to Lord Carlton's function next week Hector. Not that I have opened it, but it looks the same as ours. There's also one for you Major."

"Lord Carlton has obviously realised just how important you are to our organisation," smiled Liza.

Both Hector and the Major were studying their invitations as afternoon tea was brought in. Rose was escorted in by the boys with little Thomas tiredly trailing behind them.

"The invitation stipulates the pleasure of Mr Hector Ffoulks and guest," smiled Hector.

"Yes, mine is the same," said the Major.

"Liza, would you mind if I came back with you this afternoon as I would like to see Estelle and ask her to accompany me to the function next week," said Hector.

There was an intake of breath from Rose and Anthony frowned at his brother. "You're putting Liza and Jamie in an awkward position Hector," he said.

"Why? They have no objections to my association with Estelle. It's only our mother who thinks she's not good enough," said Hector. "Don't worry Jamie I'll ride over now and get back tonight."

"You're always welcome at our house Hector, you know that, and it would be dangerous for you to ride all that way and return late at night," said Jamie. "Whether what you are contemplating is wise is another matter, but only you can sort that out."

"Thank you, Jamie; I'll organise my overnight case. I'll be back as soon as I can tomorrow morning Major," said Hector as he disappeared to his room, calling to his valet as he went.

It was very quiet in the room with the boys looking at one another awkwardly until Liza told them to choose what cake they would like with their tea.

"Hmmm," said the Major.

"I don't dislike Miss Reece," said Rose quietly and Liza hoped that the boys weren't listening although they did seem to be concentrating intently on the cakes in front of them. "I just don't think she's right for Hector. She's a teacher, isn't she Liza?"

"Yes, she is Rose, and she's very intelligent. I know that she's going to be an asset to the Home," said Liza.

The Major suddenly said, "My invitation also requests that I bring a guest; would you be kind enough to accompany me, Rose. I'm sure you have been to functions such as this before and I should be grateful if you could make sure that I am suitably attired and assist me with any conversations that I may be drawn into."

"Oh Major, I would be delighted and I'm sure you really don't need my assistance with anything, but it's kind of you to ask," said Rose.

Jamie and Anthony were looking everywhere but at Rose and the Major and Diana and Liza were pretending not to have heard what the Major had said. The boys, of course, were more interested in their cakes than what the adults were saying, and little Thomas had fallen asleep on a couch.

Well done Major, thought Liza, *that has diffused the situation. I wonder what Jennifer is going to say.*

It was a little crowded in their carriage back home, but Hector said very little about Estelle in front of the boys and when they arrived, they were delighted to find that Peter had made the journey to see them. Mrs Frances had organised his room and now she had to organise another room for Hector.

"Peter I'm so pleased to see you; I've had to make so many decisions without consulting with you or Wendell. I hope they have been the right ones. Jamie has been so supportive and the Major and Hector are really working so hard, but to have you here, even if it's just for a couple of days is such a relief," said Liza.

"Why Liza," said Peter, "this is so unlike you; you're normally so sure of yourself."

"Yes, I know, but this is the first time that I have had to deal with a situation like this. The money I know we can spend wisely, it's just the exalted circles that I now am expected to move in concern me," said Liza.

"Liza, I know you'll carry it off beautifully; nobody other than Jamie and I will ever know how you really feel," said Peter. "What's Hector doing here?"

"He's come to ask Estelle to accompany him to Lord Carlton's function on Thursday," said Jamie.

"Will you be able to stay for that Peter? Apparently most, if not all, of our new patrons will be there and they want to know the origins of the charity and they've asked us to speak about it. If you can I'll get a note to Lord Carlton telling him that you are here, he knows that you helped start the charity," said Liza.

"Yes, I'll be staying until next weekend. We have a great deal to sort out now with the charity and I have one or two things to discuss with you about Bradley & Company as well as Marchant & Fuller," said Peter. "Who's Estelle?"

"Estelle is Adam's sister; she will be teaching at the Ffoulks home," said Liza.

"Ah, I suppose that is not sitting too well with Rose," said Peter.

The boys came in to say goodnight to everyone and John's face was a picture of happiness seeing Peter and knowing that he would be staying for some days.

A light supper was organised for later and Hector joined them, but he did not look very happy.

"It would appear that Miss Reece does not wish to go to the function with you Hector," said Jamie much to the surprise of Liza who thought that it was rather tactless of him.

"Can you persuade her Liza? She says that she would feel out of place at such a gathering and that she has never owned clothes that would be suitable for such an event," said Hector.

"I don't think I should enter into this situation; it really is between you and Estelle only," said Liza.

"But you must have an opinion; I know that she would not be out of place and I know that you think the same," said Hector.

"I normally keep my opinions to myself Hector and also my thoughts. As I've already said, this is between you and Estelle. All I will say is that it could be quite daunting for her to be surrounded by the sort of people who will be at the function; I know that I feel daunted by it and I've met many of them before," said Liza.

"If it's really just the clothes, you'd be able to help her with that, wouldn't you Liza," said Hector.

"Hector, for heaven's sake, please will you leave Liza alone. She's told you that you must sort it all out with Estelle and if you do then you know that Liza would make sure that she looks how she should," said Jamie.

Hector ate very little supper and then excused himself and they knew that he was going to attempt to persuade Estelle yet again to go to the function.

"Do you think he'll manage to get her to agree?" asked Peter.

"It won't be for the want of trying," said Jamie.

34

"I hope she does agree. She has been a very good influence on him, as has the Major. I think that Rose is wrong. I know that she would prefer that Hector marries someone with a title, but Estelle is a really nice person and would look after Hector so well. I'm sure they would be very happy together, but it is very early days of their relationship," said Liza.

"You really don't need Hector's romantic problems on your shoulders along with all else that's going on now," said Jamie.

"They're not my problems Jamie; I'll say it again, it's down to them to sort themselves out," said Liza.

"Are you free tomorrow Liza; I have a great deal to discuss with you," said Peter.

"Yes, my only definite task tomorrow is to write to Lord Carlton about you," said Liza.

"We also have to talk about the charity, and I hope that you are also free Jamie," said Peter. "My father has many thoughts on how some of the money could be spent. He's delighted that at last people recognise how serious the problem of abused children is. It seems strange that Binky's attempt to hurt John and then have you attacked Jamie, has made all this possible. It's a classic case of good coming out of evil."

"I'm glad to hear that Wendell is using his brains well. I presume he is still not going into the office," said Liza.

"No, but he has set up an office at home. He always had a small one, but he has now commandeered a larger room. However, my mother doesn't let him work late and we don't let him take on too much," said Peter.

"He wouldn't be happy being idle," said Liza. "How is Brendan getting on?"

"He's doing very well. We're still smoothing out some of the rough edges, but he is very dedicated and much brighter than he first appeared. We're very pleased with him," said Peter.

"When are you going to write your speech Liza?" asked Jamie.

"I believe that it is down to the two of us to be the entertainment for the evening Jamie," said Liza, "so you must let me know what you are intending to talk about, as we don't want to end up telling the same stories."

"Now I know you are being sarcastic; you are well aware that it is you that they want to hear from, not me," said Jamie.

"Well," said Liza. "I shall answer your question with a question. When have you known me to write a speech?"

"I never have, but this is quite a different function and I would have thought that you would at least need some notes," said Jamie.

"No, I need no notes. I don't know what we will be asked, and you can't prepare for that. The story of the beginning of the charity is emblazoned in my mind, so I need nothing to refer to. I'll just have to take it all as it comes, and so will you Jamie," said Liza smiling at Jamie's horrified face.

"It's lucky that I'm here as I can fill in any gaps that there may be, especially as far as finances are concerned," said Peter.

Hector returned with a sullen look on his face and they felt it prudent not to ask him how he had fared in his attempt to persuade Estelle to accompany him to the function.

"I'm just going to check on the boys," said Liza. "I'll be back shortly."

As she made her way up the stairs, Estelle was making her way back to her room and she stopped and asked if she could see Liza for a moment. Liza nodded and joined her in her room.

"You must know that Hector has asked me to accompany him to the function on Thursday, but I do not feel comfortable in accepting. I know that his mother is disappointed that he has shown an interest in me and I know that she will be attending. Also the people who will be there are amongst the highest noblemen of our country and I would feel very out of place in such company and finally . . . ." She said but Liza cut her off.

"Please don't say that finally you have nothing to wear because you know that I would not let you attend such a function improperly attired," said Liza.

"I was going to say something similar," said Estelle.

"If you were to take Hector out of the picture and his mother of course, would you be happy to attend?" asked Liza.

"I would still feel somewhat intimidated, but I shall be looking after the children and I would find the evening so interesting and informative. Hearing about the origins of the charity and how it has since evolved would give me a greater understanding of the task that is expected of me. Also, to see how so many people are concerned for the children would give me a great deal of hope for the future," said Estelle.

"So, if you were to come as a guest of mine and his Lordship as well as of Peter Fuller would you find it easier to make up your mind?" asked Liza.

Estelle frowned and thought for a moment, "How would that work?"

"The Ffoulks' are coming here to stay the day before and the Major and Hector will be arriving at lunchtime. We will all be travelling to Lord Carlton's together and the Major and Hector have been invited because they work for the charity as do you. If you do decide to attend, I cannot say who you will be seated next to, but you can be assured it will be with our party. It could be Peter Fuller, the Major, Anthony Ffoulks or even Hector," said Liza.

"You make it sound very easy. I'll think about it and let you know tomorrow. Could you advise me on what I should wear if I decide to attend?" asked Estelle.

"Of course I'll help you with that but do think about it seriously and you know that his Lordship and I would be delighted to see you there," said Liza.

Liza left her and made her way to the boys' room. She could hear them talking and when she looked in on them, they were all comfortably in their beds. She smiled and said goodnight to them and they chorused goodnight back to her with John adding how nice it was to have his Uncle Peter with them for a few days.

"I'm sure he will be spending some time with you all, although we do have a great deal of work to get through tomorrow, but he will be here until the weekend," said Liza and she then made her way back down to the sitting room.

"I believe that I have wasted my time coming here today," said a very despondent Hector.

Liza said nothing and Jamie looked at her closely. "Have you found a solution to Hector's problem?" he asked.

"I may have done, but it is down to Estelle to make the final decision," said Liza. "My suggestion to you Hector is to leave her to make up her own mind and I think that it would be foolish of you to ask her again; it could make her dismiss attending out of hand."

Hector frowned and said, "I'll take your advice Liza, but could you tell me what you have suggested?"

"Estelle is an integral part of our charity in that she will be undertaking teaching duties and she should therefore consider whether she would like to be included in some of the diverse functions that will probably be held now and in the future. So I will say it again Hector, you must leave her to make up her own mind as she will be mixing in company that she has never met before and it is rather daunting for her. She sees it as a major decision that she has to make, so please don't try to impose your own will on her Hector," said Liza.

"Thank you, Liza, I hope she decides to attend but you're right I could do more harm by trying to insist that it's a good idea for her to be escorted by me," said Hector.

"She will be escorted by any one of us if she decides to join us," said Liza. "Now can we talk about something else?"

***

Hector left early the next morning and he had taken Liza's advice and did not try to persuade Estelle any further on the subject of the function.

Before Liza's meeting with Peter and Jamie she sat at her desk and wrote to Lord Carlton to inform him of Peter's arrival and request that he be included in the Thursday gathering. She was very surprised to have a visiting card handed to her announcing that the Dowager Lady Redfern was waiting in her carriage. Liza sent word for her to be shown into the drawing room and also asked the butler, Harper, to find Jamie.

Liza greeted Lady Redfern telling her that it was a pleasure to see her, although somewhat unexpected.

"My apologies Lady Edgeworth but I am on my way to the Palace and felt that I should talk to you about Lord Carlton's forthcoming event," said Lady Redfern.

By this time Jamie had entered the room and he greeted her warmly whilst also saying that it was an unexpected pleasure.

"I was just saying to your wife that I needed to talk to you about the function on Thursday," she said to Jamie. "There will be a special guest there and I felt that I should let you know beforehand. One who will want to keep their identity a secret and hopefully will not be seen or recognised by anyone there."

Both Jamie and Liza realised who she was talking about and they said that they understood what she was saying and that nobody in their party would be aware of the honour that was being shown to the charity.

"I felt that you should know, although I believe that should you have only realised on the night you would be concerned and feel that you must leave out some of the details of your talk but you should not. Your story needs to be heard if we are to do anything to stop this appalling trade as well as help the children already in your care. Their Majesties want to hear everything from the beginning of your involvement," said Lady Redfern.

"I presume they will not be at the dinner," said Jamie.

"They will join us later and will be sitting behind a curtain, although Prince Albert is known to be a patron," said Lady Redfern.

"I was writing to Lord Carlton because Peter Fuller has just arrived from Belfast and would naturally like to be included in the event," said Liza.

"Don't you worry about that Liza," said Lady Redfern, "I'll get an invitation sent to him this afternoon, which will include a guest. You may tell him who our likely guests will be after all he is an integral part of the Marchant & Fuller charity. He isn't married, is he?"

"No, not yet but we often wonder whether he is married to the company. He is a very clever and dedicated businessman and has taken over from his father so well. He is now the Managing Director of Marchant & Fuller, although his father has retained the Chairmanship," said Liza.

"I must get on my way to the Palace now and I look forward to seeing you on Thursday. None of the guests are expecting the evening to be full of fun and laughter, but they are expecting it to be an interesting and informative event," said Lady Redfern.

She took her leave of them saying that an invitation for Peter would be with them by the end of the day. Miranda and Lucinda were in the hallway as she was leaving and she said how wonderful it was to see Miranda after all these years, and then she was gone on her way to the Palace.

Peter appeared asking if it was Lady Redfern who had just visited. "Yes," said Jamie, "An invitation for you will be here by this evening."

"Surely she didn't call around for that. She had no idea that I was here," said Peter.

"It was just to do with how everything was to be organised," said Liza.

Peter realised that neither Liza nor Jamie wanted to say what had been discussed with Lady Redfern whilst Miranda and Lucinda were within hearing.

"I'll be with you shortly Peter, but I must find out if Estelle has made up her mind about the function because if she has I must make sure that she will be properly attired, which will mean that one of my dresses will have to be altered as she is a little taller than I am," said Liza realising that she had made an unnecessary explanation.

Miranda and Lucinda did not seem to notice that Liza and Jamie were keeping something to themselves. Liza smiled and then made her way to find Estelle who was working at the back of the school room organising what she would need when the Ffoulks Home finally opened.

Estelle quietly joined Liza and they made their way to Liza's bedroom. "I really don't wish to push you for a decision but if you do wish to attend then we must choose a dress for you and as you are taller than I am some alterations will be necessary."

"I didn't expect you to lend me one of your gowns; I thought that April and I could add some embellishments to one of my afternoon dresses," said Estelle.

"Well, if you would prefer to do that then I'm sure it would look very pretty," said Liza.

"Oh no, I wouldn't prefer to do that, I just thought that I had no option," said Estelle.

"I'll show you what I shall be wearing and also what I wore at the last event, as I know that most ladies have very long memories as far as gowns are concerned and I'm sure you wouldn't want it known that you are wearing one of my dresses," said Liza. "Just get April to help you choose from any of the others and I know that you both will be able to successfully make any alterations necessary. Choose one that has matching accessories; April will know what to sort out for you."

Estelle thanked her profusely and said how she was now looking forward to the event although she still had some reservations.

"I'm pleased that you will be joining us; it's right that you are as it is an evening that will be devoted to the charity and we will all be with you," said Liza. "I must go now; I have a great deal of business to sort out today. Go and find April to help you."

She then joined Jamie and Peter in the library. "Well Liza, you both certainly have moved up into the highest echelons of society."

"So have you Peter; they will be well aware of who you are," said Liza.

"I thought that I would ask your mother to be my guest; would you have any objections to that?" said Peter.

"I'm sure she would be delighted. Of course we would have no objections," said Jamie.

"I just wondered whether you would be happy with her hearing what you will be talking about," said Peter.

"There is nothing for us to be ashamed of," said Liza. "You can ask her at lunchtime; she will be here then."

"Will you be tempering your talk under the circumstances?" asked Peter.

"Lady Redfern says that we should not," said Liza.

The rest of the morning was spent discussing all the new ideas for the charity and how Jamie's estate was faring as well as his land in Ireland that was rented by Bradley & Company. At lunchtime Peter asked Miranda to accompany him as his guest to the function at Lord Carlton's house and she was delighted to accept and that led to a conversation about which dress she should wear. When lunch was finished, she and Lucinda went to the Dower House to arrange what Miranda would be wearing.

Peter and Liza spent most of the afternoon on Marchant & Fuller business and finally Peter went to see the boys which left Liza free to rest before dinner.

***

Anthony, Diana, Rose and little Thomas and his nurse arrived the day before the function and they settled into their usual rooms. Rose was looking forward to staying with Miranda and Lucinda as she had in the past. Hector and the Major would be arriving the following morning.

The main question around the dinner table that evening was what Liza and Jamie would be talking about the next day. "Have you written a speech?" Diana asked.

"No, I know the history of the charity and why it was needed so I don't need notes for that. How each Home is run can be answered easily. What happens to the children in our care is common knowledge to many as are our links to America. How Ffoulks House is coming along will probably be asked about and if it isn't, I will talk about it and lastly, I must talk about our plans for the future now that we have extra funds. Lady Redfern said today that nobody was expecting it to be all fun and laughter, but I will try to make it as light-hearted as possible without being flippant," said Liza.

"Will you be talking also Jamie?" asked Rose.

"I think that I may have to answer some questions but as Liza has said, you can't prepare for what you don't know you are going to be asked. I do however know how the charity works and who works within it, so I should have no problems, although I believe that they are more interested in some of the legends that are currently surrounding the origins of the charity and only Liza will be able to answer those," said Jamie.

It became very quiet around the table as everyone there knew that the main legend referred to Patrick.

41

Suddenly Liza said, "Yes that is going to be difficult, but if that is what they want to hear then I'm afraid I will have to touch on it."

"Yes you will Liza. These people are giving a great deal of money to help all the children in our care and until fairly recently they had no idea that the charity was necessary," said Peter. "I believe that they have been appalled by what they have been hearing and I'm sure that they are interested in exactly how you became aware of the problem and how you have since been working towards solving it."

"We have all been working towards solving it Peter, not just me," said Liza.

"You were the first one to recognise just how much of a problem child abuse was; so I'm afraid you are therefore the one who is looked towards to inform them of the charity's history and how it is now progressing," said Jamie.

When the ladies had retired Anthony asked if Liza was going to be able to handle what was being asked of her.

"She will," said Jamie. "She won't be happy doing it but really that is because she thinks that part of what she will be talking about will hurt me. I know that it was Patrick who helped the first children in our care and that he has become a legend which naturally intrigues people."

It was decided that they all have an early night as they would have a busy time the following day. When Liza and Jamie were in bed together that night Jamie told her that she must not worry about what she would be saying the next day. He knew that she loved him and mentioning what has now become the legend of Patrick was necessary. He hoped that it would not upset her too much because he knew that she did not wish to dwell on the past.

"It's how the charity originated and that is what they want to hear," said Liza and she snuggled up to Jamie and he sensed that she needed his love very much that night.

***

The Major and Hector arrived early the next morning and Hector was delighted to learn that Estelle would be attending the function. Liza warned him that she was attending because she was to be the teacher at the Ffoulks home and therefore was entitled to join them in her own right.

"Yes, of course Liza. You always know a way to sort out a problem, don't you?" he said smiling.

"Show her the courtesy of letting her know that she has every right to be there and that she would be attending even if you weren't," said Liza.

"Yes, of course Liza," he said yet again.

"I'm inviting Estelle to join us for lunch, and I don't want you to crowd her Hector. Luckily your mother will be lunching at the Dower House, so there won't be too much of an awkward situation for her. At least the Major will be here which will make her feel more at home," said Liza.

"I know you're right Liza," said Hector. "I really do like Estelle. In fact I know that it is more than just like. I think what you are saying is if I push her too hard then I could lose her altogether."

"Yes that is precisely what I am saying and that would be a shame as you seem to be good for one another," said Liza.

"I thought you might have reservations because of her background," said Hector.

"You don't know me very well then Hector. I have no class prejudices, after all I come from very humble beginnings," said Liza.

Estelle shyly came into the dining room at lunchtime and Hector smiled at her but the Major stepped in and guided her to the table.

Liza said that she believed that they all knew Estelle, and everyone smiled and nodded. The Major sat her next to him and Anthony placed himself on the other side of her. Hector made sure that he sat opposite her. She joined in very well and Liza felt that she would be an asset at the function that evening.

Chapter 3

They took three carriages to Lord Carlton's house. Liza, Jamie, Peter and Miranda were in one; Anthony, Diana, Hector and Estelle were in the second one and the small carriage had just the Major and Rose.

Liza was wearing an attractive green outfit edged in silver and she wore the Edgeworth emeralds to compliment it. Estelle had chosen a very pretty yellow dress which had matching accessories and it suited her colouring beautifully. She had edged the hem with two layers of white lace and had also added it around the neckline and edged the sleeves with it. It looked as if it had been made that way. Liza had given her some pearls to wear that evening which finished the outfit off to perfection. Hector found it difficult to keep his eyes away from her.

Lord Carlton and the Dowager Lady Redfern greeted their guests and they moved through to a large drawing room where they were made welcome by the Duke of Berkshire and Bella. Jamie introduced Peter and Estelle to them as they were the only ones not already known to them, although the Duke did say that it had been a very long time since he had seen Jamie's mother and he in turn then introduced her to Bella, along with the Major whom she had not met before.

When all the guests had arrived, the large doors were opened onto the dining room which was furnished with many tables, each seating eight people. One table was set on a dais at the far end of the room and Liza and Jamie were escorted to their places at that table. They were joined by Lord Carlton and Lady Redfern, followed by the Duke of Berkshire and Bella. Finally, and much toLiza and Jamie's pleasure, Peter and Miranda were escorted to their table.

On a table to the right of them were the rest of their party plus a young couple that Liza did not recognise. Jamie was frowning as if he was trying to recall a name. Bella was seated next to him and leaned over and said, "I can see you're puzzled Jamie; that's Lord Randolph Langston and his sister Lady

Penelope. We thought they would be comfortable at that table as both Anthony and Hector must surely remember him."

"Was he not the youngest of the three Langston boys? Obviously something terrible has happened to his older brothers," said Jamie.

"Yes, the oldest of them died last year in a riding accident I believe and Harold, who was in the army had already been killed in the Crimea, therefore Randolph inherited the title, which I do not feel that he is comfortable with. We persuaded him to attend this evening; he is not very happy with joining in functions. His sister helps him a great deal," said Bella.

"That's very sad," said Jamie.

Liza watched as both Anthony and Hector were introducing Lord Langston and his sister to the other guests at the table. She saw something in his eyes that made her uneasy and then it dawned on her; she had seen that look in the eyes of many of the children in the Homes and she had most certainly seen it in John's eyes when he had first come to her and now only occasionally. *Lord Langston has been abused,* she thought.

Lady Redfern had been watching her from across the table and she stood up and came around to her, "You look concerned Liza," she said, "I realise you are very astute and I would just inform you that Binky attempted to make Lord Langston one of his special friends; I am not sure whether he succeeded. We felt it important for him to attend this evening, not to remind him, but to make him very aware that he is not alone."

Liza nodded, "Yes it could go either way, but hopefully it will help him."

Everyone was now seated and the large double doors to the drawing room were closed. Liza looked around and saw that there were just six tables and thought that talking to less than fifty people was not too daunting. She had spoken to more at her own fund raisers.

The dinner was superb, and the wine was flowing but both Jamie and Liza drank very little as they felt that they needed to keep their wits about them. Liza glanced across to Diana and she was enjoying fruit juice and Estelle was not showing signs of shyness even though Rose was also on that table. Hector was smiling happily, and Lord Langston and his sister seemed quite relaxed. The Major looked very contented and Liza thought how wonderful it was that he was now part of their organisation. Rose was now talking to Estelle and seemed to be enjoying the experience. It was all going very well.

The tables were cleared and the double doors to the drawing room were opened and they were all surprised to see a number of people standing and waiting quietly. Chairs were brought in and placed between the tables as well as lined up at the back of the dining room. Liza saw that there were at least another fifty people waiting to enter the room.

"You look surprised Lady Edgeworth," said Lord Carlton. "I thought you knew that others would be joining us after dinner."

"Yes, but I had not expected so many," smiled Liza.

Jamie looked a little concerned but not as concerned as Lady Redfern who had noticed someone who she did not feel should be there, she whispered to Lord Carlton and then to the Duke of Berkshire and they nodded and she left the table and made her way towards those who were waiting to be seated. What Liza and Jamie did not realise until much later was that Evelyn had arrived with one of Binky's old friends. Nobody knew whether she stayed or not but if she did she remained out of sight and if it had been her intention to disrupt, she had not been given the opportunity.

People were being shown to their seats and given refreshments and when they were all settled Liza expected Lord Carlton to welcome everyone and explain the reason for the gathering, but nothing seemed to be happening. Liza and Jamie looked at one another and both realised that they were obviously waiting for the special guests. Lady Redfern had left the table and finally there was movement behind the wall drapes and Lady Redfern returned to them. Lord Carlton called the room to order.

"I would like to thank you all for attending this evening and I know that unlike our usual gatherings the motive behind this one is serious and disturbing," said Lord Carlton. "Sadly children are being abused at an alarming rate and tonight we have with us those who try to save these children and attempt to guide them towards a safe and happy life, as well as campaigning to increase the punishments for those who perpetrate such crimes against these poor defenseless children."

"Lord and Lady Edgeworth and Mr Peter Fuller started the charity for abused children, and they are with us tonight to tell us the origins of that charity and answer any questions you may have," continued Lord Carlton. "Lord Edgeworth may we ask you to open the proceedings?"

"Certainly Lord Carlton," said Jamie. "But I would like to point out that although my involvement with the charity was in its early days, I cannot lay claim to creating it so I will hand you over to the person who originally saw the need to help these children and that is my wife, Lady Liza Edgeworth."

Liza stood and looked slowly around the room and then smiled and everyone in the room felt that she was smiling at them.

"Firstly I feel that I must make some important introductions; Lord Carlton has already told you how important our Peter Fuller is to the charity as he was with me on the day that we realised that a problem existed and we felt that Marchant & Fuller would be able to set aside funds to help in that respect, although we could not have envisaged just how large a problem it was going to be. Shortly after Lord Jamie Edgeworth allowed us the use of one of his properties near Belfast to house these poor unfortunate children and lent his name as patron to the charity."

"We have raised funds in many areas, but I will come to that later. We now have many people who give their time and energies to help in what we try to achieve and I would like to introduce you to Major Wilfred Styles – please stand Major – who is organising all that is necessary to house the children in the new Home which is currently being refurbished to accommodate many of the unfortunate little ones. Thank you Major. We also have the Honourable Hector Ffoulks whose help has been invaluable in this project. Please stand Hector. Thank you. We also have with us tonight Miss Estelle Reece. I believe many of you know my views on education. Miss Reece will be spending her time teaching the children to at least read and write and hopefully they will have a rudimentary understanding of arithmetic. She is capable of far more, but we have to realise that most of the children will be coming to us with no knowledge of such teachings. Please stand Estelle. Thank you. The Home that we are currently setting up was previously owned by Lord Anthony Ffoulks and he has graciously arranged that we acquire it. Please stand Anthony. Thank you. "

"There are so many others that I could mention, but I would be here until tomorrow, suffice to say that we have many dedicated helpers and of course we also have all of you who are now so very important in assisting us to help the vulnerable in our society," said Liza.

It took a moment for everyone to digest and acknowledge those she had highlighted.

"I know that there are questions that you all want answered and I hope that you will appreciate that some of them will be difficult for me, but you have a right to know everything about the charity that you are so generously supporting," said Liza bracing herself for what was to come. She turned and smiled at Jamie and he smiled and nodded back to her and his look told her to hold nothing back for his sake.

The Duke of Berkshire took the lead, "Legends have built up around the origins of the charity Lady Edgeworth and I know that all here would like to know the truth or otherwise of such legends."

"I believe that all I can do in that respect is to tell you about the day that it was realised that child abuse was so rife and I will attempt to recall it to the best of my ability," said Liza. "It was seven years ago, and I was at the time married to Patrick Kelly, who was a lieutenant in the American Army. We were in Belfast and he had made contact with family and old friends. It is essential that I cut the story short, but one day an old friend came to us because a child who should have been in the care of a childminder had gone missing and the word was that he had been sold to a person of dubious character. The details of why the child was in care are immaterial but help was needed and Patrick decided that it would be best to don his Army uniform as he felt that it would carry more weight in a difficult situation."

Liza stopped for a moment to let the scenario sink in so that the audience could perhaps realise how the legend had come about.

"Whereas I and many others had no knowledge of the appalling things that were happening to children in the world, Patrick had seen, heard and had to deal with many despicable occurrences in his army life and he was apparently under no illusions. He and his friend went to the childminder and much as he did not believe in striking a woman, he had no compunction in doing so in defense of a child. He managed to gain the address of where the child was, and he made his way there."

"On arrival he pretended to be interested in buying the services of this child; his friend was horror struck but managed to keep up the pretense and hold onto his stomach. I was told that they were shown into a room and three children were paraded in front of them. One crying bitterly, the other two resigned to what they thought was about to happen to them. The following details are rather sketchy, but apparently the owner of the establishment was knocked unconscious and Patrick and his friend persuaded the children to go with them and they ended up at my front door."

There was silence in the room and everyone seemed to be holding their breath and waiting for Liza to continue.

Liza took a deep breath and continued, "The young boy went to his family and the other two were taken in by the local doctor until a better place could be found for them. The following day there were two children on our doorstep asking for the 'tall American soldier'. How they had heard about him was a mystery to us as well as how they knew where he lived. The next day there were three of them, all asking for 'the tall American soldier'. Very few days went by when we did not find children on our doorstep asking for the 'tall American soldier'. They risked everything to get to him. He was somebody to aim for; he gave them hope. He still does even though he died five years ago."

Once again there was silence in the room and Liza could no longer hold back her tears, she turned away from the audience and took a short while to compose herself. When she turned back her smile was securely in place.

"That day the legend was born. He is still the aiming point for many here in England, in Ireland and also in America. He would have hated the adulation although he would have dealt with it for the sake of the children, but he was a soldier and wanted nothing more. There are children who believe that they see him now and I am convinced that if you want something badly enough you will see what you want to see. We do not disillusion them, most of them do not know that he is dead; we find that it gives them the courage to break away from their miserable lives and look for something better. Even in death he is doing a very important job."

Liza again had to blink back her tears as did one or two in the audience.

"At that time we formed the Marchant & Fuller charity for abused children and for those who were in danger of abuse and our immediate problem was finding premises large enough to house the number of children who had come into our care. The good doctor was running out of room, but Lord Edgeworth came to the rescue by offering his original family home in Belfast. It was the answer to our prayers. It needed some renovation but most of that was undertaken by the older children under the watchful eyes of local tradesmen who gave their time freely. Sections of garden were devoted to growing vegetables and a few animals were purchased."

"A percentage of the Marchant & Fuller profits went to the charity; it still does, but it was not enough and so we embarked on a series of fund raising functions and our first was held in New York and the people were very generous; we raised enough to open another Home in Ireland but part of our mission in New York was to find suitable places for some of the children through adoption, bond servitude or suitable employment and in that we were successful. Many of the charity's organisers are skilled enough to ensure that the children and young adults went to good homes and were not taken advantage of."

"Our reputation preceded us, and we found that children started looking for us in New York and we found it necessary to acquire Homes there also. However, we have to police those Homes carefully as mothers are leaving their new born babies on our doorsteps and our charity's articles stipulate that it is solely for the abused and those who are in danger of abuse and that is apart from the fact that those Homes are already overcrowded."

"We are increasingly finding that some of our older children have risked all to bring little ones safely to us and we are shocked at the ages of some of them. They are little more than babies and we are disgusted that there is obviously a market for such abuse and that people take pleasure from it. I know that both here and in America legislation is being formulated to increase the penalties for those who perpetrate such abuse and I pray that it will not be too long before such a law is enacted."

"I believe that you will all now understand how the charity came about and also how the legend of the 'tall American soldier' was born. I realise that there are many questions that you would like answered and we will do our best to enlighten you, so please feel free to ask us whatever you have in mind," said Liza and she smiled all around the room and sat down.

Lord Berkshire and Bella clapped which led to the whole room following suit as they realised that it had been a particularly hard speech for Liza to make. Jamie leaned over to her and kissed her lightly on the cheek and murmured "Well done; I know that wasn't easy for you."

Lord Carlton and Lady Redfern nodded their approval and Peter was showing his concern. Miranda appeared a little emotional as she had not before heard the complete story of the origins of the charity, although she did know that the 'tall American soldier' was Liza's previous husband.

Lord Berkshire started the questioning by asking how the charity saw the future. Peter came in on that answer saying that with the increase in the funding they would now be able to set up further Homes and attempt to educate the children so that they could become useful members of diverse communities. They wanted them to have trades and so they would now be able to train them adequately for their futures. "I know that we all would like our charity to become unnecessary and we hope that one day that will be the case; when and if that day arrives, we will use our Homes and experience to care for all homeless children, but sadly that is a long way in the future, so we now have to do our best for those who are in our care and those who are coming to us on a daily basis."

Many questions were asked and answered, including how they managed to police the orphanages in New York which Liza answered telling them that they had to use the Marchant & Fuller security firm which even their employees were reluctant to carry out, but they realised that it was unfortunately necessary. "It is quite easy to distinguish between those who just want to discard their children and those who genuinely need help."

She was asked how they distinguished between them and she answered that the genuine ones were mostly young girls who were all but children themselves and they usually came with toddlers who they were attempting to protect. "We have been fooled on occasion, but that rarely happens. If you saw the look of fear in the children's eyes you would know that they genuinely needed help."

Many wanted to know details of how the bond servant system worked and Liza explained how the contracts had been meticulously drawn up by Mr Charles Enderby who was a friend to the charity and double checked by lawyers. Liza went on to say how important it was for everyone to be able to read and write as she had come across families who had unwittingly made their mark on documents which meant that not only were the parents indentured for seven years, but their children also, and their children's children as well and they would all be in servitude until the last child had served seven years from the age of seven. "In other words," she said, "they would have been slaves for the rest of their lives. The documents were perfectly legal with no get out clause. When the families realised what they had signed they were prepared to kill themselves and their children. Luckily the perpetrator of the deception changed his mind."

Lord Berkshire noticed a smile of triumph on Liza's face. "How did you manage that Liza?" he asked also with a smile.

"I blackmailed him," she answered smiling happily. "And no, don't ask me how. That's between him and me."

This raised a laugh from those near to them and Jamie realised that she was talking about Charles Enderby who had therefore turned over a remarkably new leaf.

People were now beginning to mingle. The Major was talking to people at the next table and Rose had seen an old acquaintance nearby. Hector and Estelle were talking animatedly to Lord Langston and his sister. Bella had gone over to speak to Diana and Anthony excused himself and made his way towards Jamie. Liza was talking to Lord Carlton. Lady Redfern stood and was about to make her way towards where Liza assumed the special guests were sitting when a rather affected voice shouted, "I have a question for Lord Edgeworth."

Jamie looked up and recognised the voice from his university days as someone who had become one of Binky's friends and he knew that it was not going to be a friendly question.

Lady Redfern now started to make her way towards Binky's friend but not before he asked his question.

"Lord Edgeworth, I would not think that it was right for someone like you to have such a high profile in a charity such as this."

"And why might that be?" asked Jamie. The Duke of Berkshire put a hand on Jamie's arm intimating that it would be better not to engage in such a conversation. Lady Redfern had nearly reached the man.

"Because as it is illegal in this country to have two wives, you are therefore living in sin with the woman called Liza, you are hardly an example of clean living to be showing to the children that you say are in your care," said the man.

It had been a long time since Liza had seen such a look of fury on Jamie's face. Lord Carlton and the Duke of Beresford put restraining hands on Jamie. "We will deal with this Jamie," said Lord Carlton.

Lady Redfern was now talking quietly to the man whilst beckoning security guards to take him away. Hector suddenly appeared next to her and said, "You are a fine one to talk, I remember you attacking and abusing the younger boys at university. I thought I recognised your face and it's come to me now. There were two or three of you who had a perverted view of what new boys were all about. Ah, I see you are leaving now."

The man was now being unceremoniously removed from the premises. Lord Langston had joined Hector and the look on his face was one of pure hatred. "I will help to take him outside," he said as if he had been waiting all his life for this opportunity. Hector looked at him and said that he would help him, and Lady Redfern smiled and nodded to him. She then moved towards where the special guests were seated.

There were a few murmurings in the room and Liza stood and addressed the guests.

"I would like to assure you all that Jamie Edgeworth and I are indeed married and have been for three years," smiled Liza.

"Well nearly three years," corrected Jamie.

"Ah, so you remember when our anniversary is," laughed Liza.

"Would I dare forget?" smiled Jamie, although Liza could see that he was still annoyed by the words of Binky's friend.

It did however create some amusement amongst the guests. Miranda and Peter looked upset and Liza smiled at them reassuringly.

Lord Carlton and the Duke of Berkshire were making their way back to the table, as was Bella. Lady Redfern was still not in sight.

Liza stood again. "There are many wonderful sides to running a charity such as this. We see the children coming to us hurt and broken and within a short while they start acting like normal children. To see them laugh at last is exciting; to hear them attempting to read fills us with pride for them. To be able to wipe away their tears and tell them that they are safe brings forward an emotion that is indescribable. But with that enjoyment and satisfaction comes a price that we often have to pay, and that you have all witnessed tonight. We do not let the unfounded words of others stop us from doing what is right; how is it said Jamie? Ah yes, 'we have to take it on the chin' and we do that willingly."

She was applauded and Jamie once again smiled and said, "Well done Liza."

Hector and Lord Langston could be seen returning to their places, both attempting to cover their knuckles with serviettes. *They'll need some bathing when they get home,* thought Liza.

"Lady Edgeworth," said someone at a nearby table. "Is it true that you have been shot at?"

Liza could see that Jamie's shoulders were stiffening and she was silent for a moment. "It is amazing how stories get around. Yes, it is true that a bullet missed me, it was an accident and I was in the wrong place at the wrong time. I'm afraid it was not as dramatic as you have just made it sound," smiled Liza.

"You have both been in danger because of your involvement in helping the children, haven't you Lady Edgeworth," said Lord Carlton who Liza realised was trying to take the guests minds away from Binky's friend's accusation. "Do you mind telling us about your scrapes with death?"

"I did not realise that this was known, but no I don't mind telling you if you really think that it is of interest," smiled Liza. "What everyone must appreciate is that with each child we have in our care, their owners, if you can call them that, have a little more of their income taken away. When we were last in New York two older girls came to us with a very small child. We took the little girl into the care of our orphanage and spirited the two older girls away to one of the southern States. This apparently left the 'owner' with no income. I was attacked with a knife as we waved the girls off at the docks and my very close friend, Zelma, placed herself between the woman and myself and was wounded. Our chief of security wrestled with the woman and was himself stabbed. Luckily neither was seriously hurt but it made us realise that we could easily be targeted by those whose livelihoods we were ruining."

"I suppose it has made you both far more vigilant than others need be," said Lord Carlton. "However, I don't believe that Lord Edgeworth was vigilant enough when he was in Belfast last year."

"I'm not sure that it could be blamed on the charity," said Jamie. "Two ruffians set about me for reasons which have never really been clear; for me also it was a case of being in the wrong place at the wrong time. But we do take a great deal more care for our safety and that of our family than others may have to."

The Duke of Berkshire and Bella breathed sighs of relief and both Jamie and Liza realised that Lord Carlton knew nothing of Binky's predilections.

Further refreshments were then brought around and after a short while Lady Redfern returned. She leaned over to Jamie and Liza and said that their special guests had only just left; they were going to leave earlier but found that it had become more interesting and entertaining as the time went on.

Many questions were asked of all those from the charity and they were all mingling with the guests. The awkward situation with Binky's friend was forgotten and everyone seemed to be in a very happy mood. Pledges were made and finally Lord Carlton stood and called everyone to order. He thanked Liza and Jamie and then everyone in their party by name and then thanked all the guests and finally those who had decided to support the charity.

They were the last to leave and by the time their carriages came to the door they were all delighted to climb aboard so that they could relax on the journey home. It had been a successful evening, but very tiring. Peter asked who the annoying gentleman was and just nodded when told that he was one of Binky's friends.

Wearily they arrived home and went into the drawing room for a nightcap and to discuss the success of the evening.

"I think that you both handled that awkward situation very well," said Rose. "It does annoy me that there are people who try to belittle the work that you do. He could have done untold harm to the charity. Do you know who he was?"

"I believe that he was one of Binky's friends," said Anthony.

"I noticed that Lady Redfern had already had words with him and the lady he was with; she seemed to disappear after that," said Estelle.

"I'm surprised that he was with a lady," said Hector. "That was never his preference. I didn't see anyone with him. Who was she, does anyone know?"

The Major pursed his lips, Diana looked down, Anthony appeared embarrassed and Peter just raised his eyebrows. Liza was sitting listening but with her eyes closed so she did not see any of the reactions, but Jamie did. "I think I know what you aren't telling me," said Jamie quietly. Liza's eyes shot open and she said, "Surely not!"

"I'm afraid so. My previous neighbour accompanied that man and whatever Lady Redfern said to her made her disappear. Whether she stayed hidden or left, I have no idea. I breathed a sigh of relief that the situation had been dealt with prior to your talk," said the Major. "I thought that the gentleman had also left as I did not see him again until he tried to make things awkward for you both."

For the second time that night Liza saw a look of fury cross Jamie's face. "I told her what the consequences would be if she ever tried to harm you again Liza and she tried it once more tonight."

"I'm pleased that I didn't know she was there; I know that Lord Carlton would not have invited her. I suppose her partner was the one to be invited but she should not have agreed to accompany him. It must have been very embarrassing for her to be told to leave," said Liza. "She'll blame me for that."

"Well," said Hector. "You've got to admire her nerve."

"That's not how I would put it," said Jamie. "I do despair at her vindictiveness and stupidity. I'll make sure it never happens again."

"Jamie, you must not forget that the man was a very close friend of Binky's and he may blame us for Binky's need to disappear. If he has a similar character to Binky's then I'm surprised he did not plunge a knife into either of us," said Liza. "It may not have been Evelyn who instigated what that man said."

Silence followed as they all stared at Liza, mostly in disbelief. Peter was first to break that silence. "I have known you a great many years Liza and have always admired your business acumen, but what my parents say about you is so true. Your naiveté is astounding, but it makes you what you are." He shook his head smiling.

Estelle looked at Hector for some form of clarification over what was being discussed; Rose saw the look and whispered to her that she would enlighten her later.

"Oh my Liza," said Jamie. "I really do despair over you. You know that Evelyn will always try to hurt and demean your actions, but you still try to see the best in her. There is no best in her and the sooner you realise that the better it will be for you. I will sort Evelyn out once and for all. We gave her yet another chance to get on with her own life and leave us in peace, but there she was again trying to make life difficult for us."

"Well," said Miranda. "If it was at her instigation, she did not get what she wanted; I thought that you both handled it extremely well, especially you Liza by reassuring everyone that you were indeed married and I thought it was a stroke of genius making a joke out of Jamie remembering your anniversary."

"Yes, Jamie and I do work together well," smiled Liza.

"That comes from being such a close couple," said Diana with some sentimentality. "I'm sure that you know each other's thoughts."

"I believe that we achieved a great deal this evening, and those who now support us had a right to know the origins of the charity," said the Major. "It made them understand how it has already built from very humble beginnings and I know that most were under no illusions about how much time, energy and money you personally put into whatever is needed for the children and those demands are becoming greater. One day Liza, if you had to go on that way, you would have run out of money."

"Well, we don't have to worry about that now, do we?" said Liza.

"If you ladies are ready, I'll show you to the Dower House," said the Major to Miranda and Rose.

"Yes, it's been very tiring for us all," said Jamie. "We'll wait for your return Major."

"I'm sure Lucinda will be waiting up for us. She'll be anxious to hear how we all got on tonight," said Miranda.

All but Liza, Jamie and Hector made their way to their various rooms.

"Randolph Langston wants to get rid of his family home," said Hector suddenly.

"Is it far from here?" asked Liza.

"About twenty-five miles," said Hector. "I've never been there so I don't know what it is like. I believe he was placed at our table tonight for two reasons. I'm sure you were under no illusions that he had a troubled youth. If I could see it in his face, then I'm doubly sure you both could."

Both Liza and Jamie nodded. "Binky and his friends got to him then?" said Jamie. "Liza was accused of naiveté this evening, but mine was astounding when Anthony and I were with him at University. Neither of us saw what you had realised, Hector, and you are much younger than we are."

"He never tried anything with those in his year or those older than he was. His targets were the younger boys and unfortunately, he and his friends found some success with the likes of Randolph Langston. Randolph gave that chap a good thrashing tonight; I had to pull him off. All his pent-up feelings came to the fore. It has probably helped him," said Hector.

Liza went over to Hector and took his right hand in hers and studied his knuckles. "It seems to me that Lord Langston was not the only one to take revenge on Binky's friend. You need to bathe your hand, Hector; it looks rather painful."

"It was worth it Liza. I'm fine, there's nothing that won't cure itself," said Hector. "Would you like me to visit Lord Langston and see exactly what his house is like?"

"There's no need to rush, but yes it would be a good idea. It may not be what we are looking for, but there's only one way to find out," said Liza.

By that time the Major had returned. "I presume you have been talking about Lord Langston. That's one unhappy man. His sister is very caring of him but he's in a situation not of his choosing and I wonder whether he will ever be comfortable with his title."

"Hector will see if his property is what we are looking for," said Liza.

"I realised that Lady Redfern had placed him on our table for a reason, but I thought it was for a different reason," said the Major.

"I think that it was for two reasons Major," said Jamie. "The first was so that he could realise that he was not the only person to have had an abused childhood and the second was probably because she knew that he wanted to move from his property. She obviously thinks that it would be ideal for us."

Later when Liza and Jamie were alone, they discussed the events of the evening. "I told Evelyn that there would be no second chances," said Jamie. "She vowed that she would do nothing further to hurt this family and I relented in my decision to withdraw her income if she did not move from this country."

"If Estelle hadn't mentioned that a woman was with that man, then we would never have known that she was there. Admittedly she should have had more sense than to accept an invitation for this evening, but I do wonder if the awkward situation was instigated by Evelyn or by Binky's friend. She may not have known what he was going to do," said Liza.

"I really do wonder about you sometimes Liza. What was she doing with Binky's friend? She knew what he was like and she was bound to know how close he was to Binky. She knew that the function tonight was solely to do with the charity and that the origins were going to be discussed and that as you started the charity you would naturally be speaking about it. Also, as the charity was designed to rescue abused children, why was she with somebody who abuses children? At best she has been incredibly stupid and at worst she wanted to create untold trouble for us," said Jamie with some annoyance.

"I know you're right Jamie, but she has already been made to look stupid because Lady Redfern told her to leave. That must have been very embarrassing for her," said Liza.

"Why are you defending her Liza? She has never done anything to help you; she has always done the opposite," said Jamie.

"Because I have you and she doesn't. I have a wonderfully happy life with you and Matthew and John and also with her son. It must be very difficult for her. She also has a daughter and I feel responsible for that," said Liza.

"You can't possibly be held responsible for her daughter," said Jamie.

"I organised the adoption for her," said Liza quietly.

"Don't worry Liza; I'll sort it all out with Evelyn. She won't be bothering us again," said Jamie. "I'm very tired tonight Liza, do you think you could do without my body tonight?" And he laughed at the expression on her face. "Oh alright, I'll get up the energy somehow."

Chapter 4

The Major and Hector left early the next morning, but Hector was to return later in the week and then travel on to Lord Langston's property to see if it would be suitable for their needs.

Anthony, Diana and Rose left after lunchtime. Little Thomas had enjoyed himself in the company of the boys, especially Matthew and he could be heard shouting his farewells all the way down the driveway.

Peter was the final guest to leave with Liza very sorry to see him go and then Jamie ordered his carriage and told Liza that he would see her later, but he was not sure how long he would be.

"Do you really have to go Jamie?" asked a very unhappy Liza.

"Yes, I do. This has to be sorted out once and for all. I thought we had come to an amicable agreement, but Evelyn seems incapable of keeping her word. We can't go on looking over our shoulders waiting for her next evil scheme. We have enough to worry about keeping us all safe from others who would much rather we were not around," said Jamie.

"Please be careful Jamie. I don't think that she is going to stick a knife in you but isn't it better to have her within our sights than scheming behind our backs. Don't forget that it was all handled very well last night and we don't have to pretend to have a united front because that is exactly what we have," said Liza. "I love you Jamie Edgeworth and I know you love me. She is immaterial to us; she just seems to come to the fore on occasion and she doesn't worry me."

"No, it's not fair that you are constantly put through this awkwardness. It's not your fault that I always wanted you and never really wanted her. I'm going to sort it all out now before anything truly gets out of hand," said Jamie and he kissed her and went out to his carriage.

Liza spent the rest of the day dealing with correspondence and when she had finished, she went to find April to make sure that she had everything that she needed for her wedding. She and Adam would be going away for a few days afterwards and Adam was keeping very quiet about where their honeymoon destination was to be. They would be borrowing the small carriage and when they returned, they would be moving into two larger rooms in a different wing of the house. They would be using one room as a lounge and the other as their bedroom. They were in the process of furnishing them as they wished, and April was excited at the prospect that they would have their own lounge.

Estelle would be moving to the Ffoulks Home soon after the wedding and she was very busy preparing for the lessons that she would be giving to the children. She was under no illusions as most, if not all, of the children would be illiterate; her job was not going to be easy. Liza called in to see her and they discussed the previous evening's events.

"I presume you know that Hector is going to be at Adam and April's wedding," said Liza.

"So he has told me. I'm not sure that either Adam or April realise that he is going to be a guest. I suppose there is no harm in him just turning up on the day," said Estelle.

"Hector is a law unto himself, I'm afraid, but his heart is in the right place," said Liza. "I was pleased to see that you seemed to get on quite well with his mother."

"Yes, I was quite surprised that she seemed to warm to me," said Estelle. "The evening was not as awkward as I had expected it to be and apart from that obnoxious man, I thought that everyone there was very kind and pleasant."

Liza then went in to see the boys and asked them how they had survived little Thomas' visit. They all smiled, and John said that he thought that he was getting more like 'Maffew' every time he saw him, which brought a howl of displeasure from Matthew.

"He absolutely adores Matthew," said James, "which means that he does everything that Matthew tells him, so we don't get too bothered by him as Matthew gets him to sit quietly on occasion and he's quite happy as long as he's sitting next to Matthew. He is rather sweet really and is a very happy little boy. He's having a much nicer childhood than I had at his age. I remember not seeing anyone but adults for a long time."

The other two boys laughed, and John said that if he was trying to make them feel sorry for him, he was mistaken and he added that he knew that he had seen Matthew from a very early age.

"Yes, but that was only at holiday times, the rest of the time I was here alone. I used to really look forward to the holidays because 'mummy Liza' as I used to call her, let me do things that I would not be allowed to do any other time," said James.

"I didn't think that I was that lenient with you," said Liza. "You didn't need telling off."

"Oh, there were lots of things that you pretended not to notice," said Matthew. "There was nothing serious, but we used to enjoy eating with our fingers, and of course you must remember our so-called nightmares which meant that you let us get into bed with you. You knew that we didn't really have nightmares, didn't you?"

"Well, I had my suspicions about them," smiled Liza. "Yes, we had nice times then, and we still do, it's just that you're that much older so your happy times are different. We'll soon be starting our cricket matches again. I suppose you'll be taking Derek's runs for him again John."

"Yes, that seems to work. I wonder if he'll still be falling over each time. He's walking so much better now, but he's still not like the rest of us," said John sadly.

"That was my so-called mother's fault; she could have helped him, but she didn't," said James bitterly.

"Who told you that?" asked Liza.

"Oh, I heard somebody talking about it. They said that Derek's mother came to her for help but she ignored her and went away and that's why Derek can't walk properly," said James.

"That's not necessarily true James. Nobody is sure that Derek would have walked properly if he had have had help earlier. If you have to blame anybody you must blame his father who injured him in the first place," said Liza. "I think that he has done wonderfully well in the short time since the specialist came to see him, and his family are so dedicated in helping him with his exercises and you all help him as well. He's become one of you and that's lovely to see."

It was then time for the boys' supper and off they went to the kitchen to find out what they would be eating that evening, they always enjoyed being surprised by what they had and Mrs Lambert never let them down.

Liza was becoming quite anxious as Jamie had been gone for some while and she would have liked to have seen him safely home by that time. Slowly she went up to her room to change for dinner and when she was nearly ready she heard Jamie's carriage arrive and she breathed a sigh of relief.

Jamie came to find her; he looked tired and she could see that a frown was not leaving his face. She looked closely and could see a small cut on his cheek, and she waited for him to tell her the outcome of his meeting with Evelyn. He came over to her and put his arms around her and she could feel the tension in him but then slowly he relaxed as he remained holding her.

"I can see that your meeting did not go too well Jamie," said Liza gently. "Do you want to tell me about it now, or do you want to try to relax and tell me later in your own time?"

"She will be leaving the country for quite some time," said Jamie wearily. "Some of the things that she said are still ringing in my ears. I think I'll just go and lay on my bed; can dinner be held up for a while?"

"Of course it can," said Liza. "Your mother and Lucinda were not joining us this evening; it is just the two of us tonight."

"Good," said Jamie, "I will tell you later but for now I just want to rest; will you tell Roberts to come in say an hour; not that I really need him to help me."

"No Jamie, I'll get some food sent up to my room. You don't need to change; you can stay as you are or get into your dressing gown. I'll tell Roberts not to bother you; I'll come back and help you and then we can just go across the corridor for the evening," said Liza.

She helped him out of his coat and realised that he was in pain, but he brushed off her concern. She then removed his boots and he went into his room and stretched out on his bed, while Liza went off to make all the necessary arrangements.

As she was making her way back up to her room she found James standing in the hall looking concerned.

"Has my father been hurt?" he asked. "He looked as if he was in pain. Has she hurt him?"

"I don't know what has happened James," said Liza. "Your father hasn't told me yet, but he seems very tired and is resting at the moment. Would you like me to find out if you can see him? He may be asleep, but I'll let you know. Wait there and I'll see how he is."

Liza tapped lightly on Jamie's door and entered before he could answer. He was lying on his bed staring at the ceiling. "How are you Jamie? Do you feel up

62

to seeing James? He's very concerned about you. He saw you coming home, and he asked if you had been hurt. I don't think the other boys realise."

Jamie sat up and Liza damped a handkerchief and wiped the small amount of dried blood from his cheek. She gently touched his arm which caused him discomfort. "You had better let him come in," said Jamie and Liza got up and opening the door found James standing outside. Liza smiled at him reassuringly and said that his father would like to see him.

What was said by Jamie to James was between the two of them but when James came out he looked much happier and said to Liza that she was the only mother he wanted and that he loved her more than anyone else in the world along with his father and brothers. He went towards the boys' room and Liza noticed that both Matthew and John were peeping out and waiting for him. *So the other boys did know, I should have guessed,* she thought.

Mrs Frances and one of the housemaids came up with their supper trays and placed them on tables in Liza's room. Liza went into Jamie's room as he was taking his shirt off and he couldn't hide the large bruise that was appearing across his right forearm.

"Oh Jamie, what on earth has happened?" said Liza.

"I got that defending myself. I felt like hitting her, but I didn't," said Jamie as Liza helped him into his nightclothes and dressing gown and when he was ready Liza put her arms around him and her head on his chest and she cried. Jamie kissed her on the head and said, "I thought you were meant to be comforting me Liza, rather than me comforting you," and Jamie smiled for the first time in many hours.

Liza dried her eyes, smiled, and took Jamie's hand and led him into her room for their supper.

***

Earlier that afternoon Jamie had driven up to Evelyn's house and after knocking loudly, the door was opened by her housekeeper and Jamie walked straight in past her. She mumbled that Lady Edgeworth was in the dining room and he found her sitting at her table alone. She looked up startled.

Jamie looked down on her and she was unnerved by the look of hatred in his eyes.

"What are you here for Jamie? Haven't you already made me look foolish in the eyes of your high and mighty friends? Have you come to gloat?" said Evelyn.

"The only person who made you look foolish was you Evelyn," said Jamie through gritted teeth. "Why did you turn up last night with that obnoxious person? You must surely have had more sense than to accept an invitation to the function, so you must have been there to disrupt the evening and once again hurt Liza. I told you what would happen if you ever tried to do her damage and you've tried to do it again."

"I've done nothing to hurt her; it was nothing to do with me. I was invited to the function by the Honourable Archie Goodman and I understood that it was going to be a very interesting evening," said Evelyn.

"Are you really that stupid Evelyn? You know that Archie Goodman was a very close friend of Binky and had exactly the same leanings and even if you didn't know that, you should not have accepted an invitation to a function which was purely for Liza's charity. You just wanted to create embarrassment for us both," said Jamie.

"Well both you and Liza created a great deal of embarrassment for me. Binky's mother told me in no uncertain terms that I was not welcome, so you and Liza managed to have me turned away," said Evelyn bitterly.

"You are wrong Evelyn; neither Liza nor I knew that you had been there until we were told after we returned home; so you can't blame us for that. But if I had known I would have had you ejected, I can assure you of that," said Jamie.

"I don't believe you Jamie; you would do anything that Liza told you and I know that she also told Binky's mother to make it clear that I was not welcome to her cosy chat to people who she can also twist around her little finger," snarled Evelyn.

"You're wrong Evelyn, but I don't really care what you believe; I'm telling you that you are going to leave us alone and that's because you won't be living in this country. You've broken your promises to us on so many occasions, so you have run out of chances. I'll be selling this house, so I suggest that you make your arrangements to move. You'll have a month to get organised and I never want to see you again," said Jamie.

"You know that Liza won't approve of that; I'll just go to her again and she'll make you change your mind. She's very weak where children are concerned," said Evelyn with a triumphant smile on her face.

"You had better not try that trick again and I can tell you that it didn't work last time and it won't work this time. Liza never persuaded me to change my mind; all she did was repeat what you had said. I was the one foolish enough to believe that you deserved another chance. I am not going to allow you to try again to demean what Liza is doing to help abused children, so make your arrangements to leave," said Jamie.

"Everybody thinks that she is so good, but I can see through her. You can't possibly compare her to me. She has no class. She wormed her way into your affections and took you away from me," said Evelyn whose voice was getting increasingly high pitched. "She has no right to be mixing with people such as the Duke of Berkshire and Lord Carlton; that should be me. I could help you far more in those circles. She's a witch who puts spells on people and especially on you Jamie. You really must get rid of her; she has done you no good."

"What are you talking about Evelyn? Have you lost your senses? Don't you dare belittle Liza in that way. You cannot possibly believe that you could step into her shoes. You have never thought of anyone but yourself. Why do you think Lady Redfern told you to leave? It wasn't just for our sake; it was because she did not want you at the function and neither did the Duke nor Lord Carlton. Your reputation preceded you. You were an embarrassment to them and all those in their so-called class," said Jamie.

Evelyn started screaming at him, "I can do everything that Liza does, and better because I have more class than she does."

"Evelyn, you have no class whatsoever. You are delusional. How you could turn up at a function to raise money for a charity for abused children with a man who abuses children is beyond belief and you have now done that twice. Don't forget what Binky tried to do to our John and you were his guest then and sleeping with him in my house. Lady Redfern was well aware of that and of course she was also well aware of what Archie Goodman's perverted leanings were. The Duke of Berkshire is her son-in-law and very close to her, so you can't believe that he knew nothing," said Jamie.

"They wouldn't think that I have anything to do with that way of life," said Evelyn dismissively.

"What else would they think; twice you have been partnered by people who sexually abuse children and at functions to raise money for the charity that helps those poor unfortunate children. I always thought that you had some sense, but you have shown very little recently. It would do you good to go away and start a new life elsewhere; it would also help your daughter to be in an environment where her mother's reputation will not damage her," said Jamie.

"You know that I could have done all the things that Liza has done and better. I could still be close to you Jamie. Don't forget that in the eyes of the church we are still married, so I could move back with you and no eyebrows would be raised. We could have a good life together; we had a good marriage before you heard that Liza had come back to life," said Evelyn.

"Are you mad Evelyn? We never had a good marriage. We ignored one another as much as possible and you found comfort in other men's arms. Besides I would never give up my Liza for the likes of you. You are no good Evelyn; you are selfish. You think of nobody but yourself. Instead of stopping to help someone you would walk right past them without a second glance. You would never have thought of helping an abused child, you would have turned your nose up at them and treated them as abnormal. You are not a patch on my Liza. Just go and leave us to our happy life and hopefully you can find some happiness elsewhere. I have reached the point when the sight of you disgusts me," said Jamie and he foolishly turned his back on her.

He heard an angry scream and was lucky enough to turn and he managed to fend off a blow from a heavy candlestick which Evelyn was aiming at his head. He caught the full force on his right arm and a corner reached his cheek and made a small cut.

Evelyn flew at him trying to scratch his eyes and he pushed her away, but she continued screaming and accusing him of terrible things. He could not calm her, so he called for her housekeeper to fetch a doctor. Her daughter's nurse rushed into the room and she managed to quieten her a little, but she was still shouting threats to him, to Liza, to the boys as well as anyone associated with them.

Jamie waited until the doctor arrived, but he was shaken. He had never seen Evelyn other than very cold and controlled. He ensured that her daughter was well cared for and that the servants were not too distraught, and he then climbed into his carriage and Davis drove him home. He just wanted to get back to his Liza and his family and shut out the nightmare that he had just witnessed.

***

Jamie was now sitting with Liza and toying with his supper. He had told her nothing of the events of the afternoon apart from the fact that Evelyn would be leaving the country. She sat silently trying to eat her supper, but she had no appetite. Eventually she knew that Jamie would tell her what had happened, all she could tell was that it had been a violent confrontation.

"James seemed a great deal happier after you had spoken to him," said Liza, hoping that it would make Jamie talk to her.

"Yes, he seemed better," said Jamie.

"You have said to me that there is nothing that I cannot tell you; it is the same for you Jamie; you can tell me anything and I will understand," said Liza.

"I know you will Liza," said Jamie. "But I can't talk about it now, it's enough that you know that the meeting was quite horrendous, and it has left me shaken and all I wanted to do was get home to you. You are already bringing some sanity to an otherwise insane afternoon."

"Are you going to let me have a proper look at your arm?" smiled Liza.

"You can have a proper look at everything that I have later, if you like," said Jamie.

Liza smiled and gradually through the course of the rest of the evening Jamie told her what had happened with Evelyn.

"Where will she go?" Liza asked Jamie.

"I have no idea and I could not care less. She has a month to find somewhere and move her possessions out of that house. She has friends and she has relatives, so she will have some place to go," said Jamie.

"Her relatives really don't want anything to do with her or her daughter and I believe that she now has very few friends. She has associated with some gentlemen of dubious character recently, so her reputation has become a little tarnished. I'm sure if she can find somewhere to stay for a while she will eventually be accepted back. Hopefully she will see it that way for the sake of her daughter. I worry about how all this will affect little Melanie; it's always the children that suffer the most," said Liza.

"Evelyn said that you wouldn't approve of my insisting that she leaves the country because of her child. She said that you were weak where children were concerned and that she would see you and get you to change my mind as you did last time," said Jamie.

"I didn't get you to change your mind. I know that we discussed what she had said, but I didn't persuade you, I wouldn't do that. Whatever you decide about Evelyn is entirely what you feel is best for everyone. You know that my only reservation is that sometimes it's better to know the whereabouts of a troublesome person," said Liza.

Jamie looked at her and laughed, "Oh Liza, you do make me feel better. A troublesome person you say, I think that is such an understatement. What will you do if Evelyn comes to visit you as she did last time?"

"I will make sure that you are with me; I will not talk to her without you," said Liza. "It would be very unfair of her to expect that and besides I've seen how she has hurt you; I don't want to be hurt; I will need you to protect me. James won't be happy if she comes here; he hasn't forgotten what she did last year. The boys still sometimes refer to his kidnap. I think that the word troublesome is quite accurate really."

"I'd call it evil, and the sooner she has gone from this country the better," said Jamie.

"I believed her when she promised never to bother us again," said Liza. "I am naïve, aren't I?"

"Yes, you are on occasion, but Peter was right when he said that it makes you what you are. I do love you Liza; you make me very happy and you also make me laugh, which I needed tonight. I'm very tired so I think I'll go to my room. I trust you'll join me," said Jamie.

"I'll get these dishes cleared away first and check on the boys and then I'll get ready and come into you. Do you need me to help you with anything? Is your arm bothering you very much?" asked Liza.

"It's only painful if I touch it, so I'll try not to touch it. I'll be waiting for you my Liza. We'll forget about Evelyn tonight and worry about her again tomorrow. No doubt you'll come up with an alternative solution for me to consider," said Jamie and he yawned and made his way to his room.

***

Jamie and Liza were up early the next morning. Jamie's arm was a little stiff and a small bruise had appeared around the cut on his cheek. Miranda appeared as they were breakfasting.

"I was very worried about you yesterday Jamie, and I can see from your cheek that I had every reason to be concerned," said Miranda.

"I'm sorry Mother, I should have let you know that I was back safely, but all I wanted to do was get home to Liza and calm down. It was a very difficult meeting with Evelyn and in the end I had to arrange for a doctor to see her as she seemed to lose her mind for a while," said Jamie.

"Is she going to leave the country for a while? It would be best for everyone if she did and especially for her daughter. She has been associating with known deviants and that won't do her reputation any good. Many people saw who she arrived with the other evening and knew that he was trying to make

68

life difficult for you both and it was also designed to damage the charity. Some saw that she was asked to leave by the organisers of the function. By trying to harm you she has harmed herself; yes it would be better if she left. Somebody should advise her about what is best for her," said Miranda staring at Liza.

"Oh no, you can't mean me," said Liza. "She takes no notice of what I say as is obvious from everything that she has done. She agrees with me and then does exactly the opposite. She'd probably scratch my eyes out anyway."

"Evelyn has told me in no uncertain terms that Liza is not her favourite person," said Jamie. "I would not want Liza to have to deal with her as she is particularly unstable at the moment. I've told Evelyn that she has a month to find somewhere else to live, so it's up to her to sort out her own life, not Liza."

Miranda left after a short while and Jamie was getting ready to go to his lawyer and arrange for the sale of Evelyn's house. Liza had some correspondence to check and was in the process of replying to various invitations when Harper came in with a letter for her. It was from Evelyn:

My dear Liza,

I made such a terrible scene yesterday when Jamie came to tell me that he wanted me to leave the country.

I can understand why he wants this; I have done some very foolish things because of the jealousy that I have always felt towards you. I have tried to stop such feelings but have not found it easy.

You helped me through a difficult time in the past and I would greatly appreciate your advice concerning my future and that of my daughter. You always have the ability to solve problems and I truly feel the need to talk to you now.

I know that it is a great imposition on my part, but I would appreciate it if you could visit me. I do not think that I would be welcome visiting you. Of course I know that you will tell Jamie of my request as I know you and he have no secrets.

I am now always at home as I no longer receive invitations from those who I considered my friends at one time.

Leaving here I know is the only answer and your advice concerning my final destination would be very helpful.

With regards,

Evelyn

"Did I hear a carriage arrive Liza?" asked Jamie as he was on his way out.

Liza looked up at him and nodded and he could tell from her face that she was not pleased and then he noticed the letter in her hand.

"Is it bad news Liza?" he asked coming further into the room.

"It could be considered such," she said as she held the letter out for him to read. He looked at her in disbelief.

"I cannot believe that she has yet again asked for your help when she is in trouble. Surely you're not thinking of doing what she asks," said Jamie.

"No I'm not Jamie. There really is nothing I can do to help her, but I am concerned for her daughter. I'm sure she won't end up on the streets. She says that she has no friends but I'm sure that's not true; she has always been surrounded by people. I remember when she was in Belfast a few years ago she turned her back on Felicity who was, as always, making trouble for me and was talking to many guests quite familiarly and they seemed very pleased to be with her," said Liza.

"Good, I'm glad you've made that decision. She is not your problem," said Jamie and he kissed her and said that he would be back in time for lunch.

"Your mother and Lucinda will be joining us," said Liza.

Evelyn's letter had annoyed Liza. It had put her in an awkward position as it was not in her nature to refuse help for anyone who needed it. She was also worried about Melanie as she had arranged hiding Evelyn's confinement, having spirited her away to one of her farms in Wales to await the birth. She had then organised the theoretical adoption and official documentation to save Evelyn's reputation and take away the stigma of illegitimacy for her daughter. She felt that she had a responsibility towards the child if not Evelyn.

She knew that Jamie would not have been pleased if she had agreed to visit Evelyn and she really did not want to, but her conscience kept reverting to the welfare of little Melanie.

Over lunch the situation was discussed, and Lucinda expressed outrage that Evelyn had turned to Liza for help yet again. Miranda was quiet on the subject, but Jamie also said how much of an imposition he felt that it was.

"It is the child that concerns you, isn't it Liza?" said a very understanding Miranda. "We are under no illusions about the circumstances of her birth. I know you have never divulged your involvement in how that came about, but gossip became rife and within our family the truth seemed obvious. You saved Evelyn's reputation then and I know it was mainly for the sake of her child and that's why I think you should do it now."

70

Jamie and Lucinda stared at Miranda in disbelief, but Liza smiled as she realised that she and Miranda were very alike.

"What makes you think that I would have a solution to her problem which would suit everyone?" asked Liza quietly.

"I know you have," said Miranda. "You have had since yesterday to think about it, and I know that you probably put it to the back of your mind until you received Evelyn's letter and were asked for help."

"I was just thinking how alike you and I are Miranda," smiled Liza.

"Liza you can't go to see her," said Jamie. "She's dangerous. She has only ever set out to hurt you and now she has shown that she would do you physical damage. If she could hurt me, God knows what she could do to you."

"She will do nothing Jamie," said Miranda, "because I'll be with her. I have yet to meet my grandson's step-sister and my being there will be a surprise for Evelyn."

"I don't think that either of you are being sensible," said Lucinda. "You're thinking of putting yourselves in great danger, all for the sake of someone who will never appreciate what you do for them."

"They may not appreciate it Lucinda but is it not better to know where someone like Evelyn is rather than have to keep wondering when she might appear and do you harm," said Miranda. "Also her reputation should be allowed time to heal and then perhaps her daughter will be accepted in the right circles, after all her daughter didn't ask to be born."

"I would like to forbid you to go Liza, but I know I have no power to do so. I'm just asking you not to go; she's not worth getting yourself hurt for," said Jamie with some passion.

"Do you really think that she is planning to hurt me?" asked Liza.

"She lost her temper with me yesterday. I have never seen her lose control before and it became very vicious and honestly quite frightening," said Jamie. "I managed to stop her hitting my head with a heavy candlestick, you would not be able to stop her; you wouldn't be strong enough."

"If you really think that she is that dangerous, then of course Liza shouldn't go," said Miranda. "But I will go in her place. You must not forget that Liza went to a great deal of trouble to hide the origins of Melanie, not for Evelyn's sake but for the child's sake and I would think that it carries some responsibility with it."

Lucinda was no longer entering into the conversation; she had only ever heard sketchy rumours about Evelyn's daughter and it now dawned on her that Liza had manipulated the situation to give legitimacy to the child and in doing so had saved the reputation of the mother. It was very clever, but Evelyn seemed to hate her for it. It did not seem logical to Lucinda.

Liza was also quiet. If she said anything it may confirm what Miranda was saying and it was a secret that should be kept.

Miranda smiled and said, "I have only put into words what many people think, although not many would believe that you were involved. You have not broken a confidence, Liza."

Jamie looked closely at Liza and said, "you are planning to go aren't you Liza? I told you once before that you will never be thanked by Evelyn for what you do for her. I will come with you, but I will not go into the house, I will stay in the carriage. Are you determined to also go Mother?"

"I'll go alone," said Liza suddenly. "I know she will not harm me; I'm afraid that she does need me and what we have to discuss is private and the only person who will know outside the two of us is Jamie. With all due respect to you Miranda, she does not know you and she will not feel comfortable baring her soul in front of you, but I do appreciate what you were prepared to do."

"You can see her alone Liza, but I'm coming with you. I won't come into the house unless you make it clear that you need me. However, I am determined that she is leaving and more importantly she must let us live our lives in peace, so please don't try to countermand my decision," said Jamie.

"I would never do that Jamie, but I have a feeling that she went one step too far the other evening and she may also have alienated all in her household," said Liza. "It will be a great relief to me that you are coming with me Jamie, and I do realise that it would be better if Evelyn isn't confronted by you again."

"I am so annoyed at Evelyn; she said that she would get me to change my mind through you and your concern for children. She is using her own child to manipulate me through you; I'm aware of it and I know you must be too, but of course you don't feel that you can take the chance as we may be wrong and she does genuinely need help. I would much rather leave her to sort out her own problems; my duty towards her was over when she wanted me to tell to the outside world that the Count's child that she was carrying was mine," said Jamie.

"She really has created a great many problems for you but remember Jamie that she still carries your name and she is likely to have that for the rest of her life. She could drag the Edgeworth name through the mud, so it may be just as well for you to put her somewhere out of harms' way and keep her there for some time," said Miranda.

"When do you want to go Liza?" asked Jamie.

"I think we should leave shortly; I have a feeling that sooner rather than later would be wise," said Liza.

"You should act on your instincts," said Miranda and it brought to the fore memories of Peter saying the same thing and she had not taken his advice and suffered for it, but this time it was on behalf of someone else.

It took them just over an hour to drive to Evelyn's house and with some trepidation Liza approached her front door; Jamie watched her carefully from the carriage and Davis was also aware of the tension in this visit. He had seen how Jamie had been hurt the day before and he wondered why Liza was going into the house alone. He knew that there had to be a good reason for it, but he was watchful as he had not forgotten what had happened to young James at the hands of his mother.

Liza knocked loudly on the door, but nobody answered it. She waited a while and then knocked again and once again there was no reply, so she pushed at it and it opened. Cautiously she moved into the hallway calling out for Evelyn as she went. She heard a noise in one of the rooms and made her way towards it. Her heart was in her mouth as she wondered whether this was a rouse on Evelyn's part to do her harm.

She called her name again and Evelyn's voice asked if it was Liza.

"Yes Evelyn, I've come as you asked," said Liza as she pushed open the sitting room door and found Evelyn sitting looking rather dishevelled.

"I knew you would. I knew you would try to help me," said Evelyn and Liza could recognise the look of panic in her eyes and knew that it was genuine.

Liza heard a slight sound in the hall behind her and knew that Jamie was watching over her; he must have seen that nobody had answered the door and was naturally concerned. Liza was grateful that he was there but knew that he would not make his presence known to Evelyn.

"Evelyn you certainly don't look yourself. Where is Melanie? Where's all your staff?" asked Liza.

"I no longer have any staff, apart from Melanie's nurse. All the others have walked out, and I suppose I can't really blame them," said Evelyn.

"Is Melanie here? Is she safe?" asked Liza who was getting increasingly concerned.

"Yes Liza, she's safe; I would do nothing to hurt my daughter," said Evelyn.

Liza held back the comment that everything that she had done recently had hurt her daughter but felt that this was not the right time to criticise.

"What is it that you would like me to do for you Evelyn?" asked Liza.

"I would like you to hide me away as you did in the past. I have ruined all that you did for me to protect my reputation and that of my child. People don't know the circumstances of Melanie's birth, so I can still salvage something for her, but I have associated with known child abusers and I don't even have the excuse that I didn't know of their leanings. Lady Redfern made it quite clear to me that through my friendship with both her son and Archie Goodman I was not welcome at a function promoting a charity for abused children and to associate with those who are child abusers must make me just as culpable as they are. She also told me that she realised that I was only there to create embarrassment for you, and she was right about that, but not about my support of child abusers. There were many there who could see that I had been ejected and heard the reasons why," said Evelyn.

"Oh Evelyn, you have made life so difficult for yourself. You were so different when you were at the Welsh farm. You seemed to get on so well with everyone there and you became yourself instead of someone that you thought you should be," said Liza.

"You are right Liza. One of the happiest times in my life was when I was there, the whole family made me so welcome. They made me forget the reason why I was there; I became one of them and for the first time felt that I belonged somewhere. Do you think that I could go back there for a while? I'm sure it would help me to get my life back in order," said Evelyn.

"You know that it's impossible to recapture the past successfully. I really don't think that it would be wise to go to the farm, but I do have a property in the village that is sitting idle at present. It's near enough for you to renew your friendship with the Evans' and especially Dilys and Carys; they will be very pleased to see you and Melanie. Have you kept in touch with them?" asked Liza.

"Yes, I have, but not as regularly as I should have done. Is it possible that I could go there for a while? Won't Jamie want me to leave the country? He was most insistent yesterday. Is the house nice? I think I know it; it's the one as you go through the village and past the little dressmakers, isn't it?" said Evelyn who was beginning to sound a little enthusiastic.

"Jamie had every right to be insistent that you left and more importantly that you left us alone and stopped trying to make difficulties for us, but as far

74

as you going to Wales, I don't believe that he would object too readily. As far as the house is concerned, it has just recently been cleaned and decorated. There's no furniture in it and it is smaller than this one, although it's not cramped. It has a dining room and sitting room on the ground floor. The kitchen is in the basement as is the housekeeper's room, although there is no housekeeper at the moment. It has two fairly large bedrooms on the first floor and three smaller ones on the second floor. The garden is a little small but neat and the house has a low wall surrounding it and gates lead up a small drive to the front door," said Liza.

"It sounds very nice Liza. I could take my own furniture. Would it fit in?" asked Evelyn.

"Well, you might have to sacrifice one or two pieces, but overall, your essential furniture would fit well. Would your nurse be prepared to go with you, do you think?" asked Liza.

"I don't know; she has looked after Melanie very well and does think a great deal of her but I have treated her very badly and she has said that she will stay until I can find someone else to take over her duties," said Evelyn.

"It's not an insurmountable problem; I'm sure that Dilys and Carys would help you out as far as Melanie is concerned and all you would need is a housekeeper. It would mean a complete change of lifestyle for you, but it may be just for a year or two, or perhaps less," said Liza.

"I would like to do that Liza; I truly need to go away. Jamie was right that I should leave the country, but his reasons were very different to mine," said Evelyn.

"If you are serious about doing this Evelyn, then we will have to get organised because the sooner you leave the better for you. We'll have to arrange hauliers for your furniture. Have you enough trunks for yours and Melanie's clothes. Would it be possible to get staff to help with your packing?" asked Liza.

"I don't know where to start Liza. Do you think that Jamie will approve of what you are doing?" asked Evelyn.

"I hope that he will as you are leaving and where you are going is far enough away to give us some peace," said Liza rather scathingly. "I presume you will revert to the name Carson when you are there. You were known as that in the village as well as the farm, so it would be advisable to use it again."

"I suppose that would be best. I think that Melanie's nurse could know who would be prepared to help with packing. They would probably be pleased to help if they know I am leaving," said Evelyn unhappily.

"It's too late to feel sorry about that; let's just concentrate on what has to be done. Firstly I would suggest that you make your peace with Melanie's nurse as she could be a tower of strength at this time and secondly it would be a good idea if you tidied yourself up; you don't want your daughter, or anyone else, to see you looking unkempt. Even if you feel that your reputation has been tarnished, it's no excuse to let yourself go. Or is it that you have forgotten how to dress yourself correctly?" said Liza sharply.

Evelyn was about to make a scathing retort but thought better of it. She had to admit that Liza was right and the last thing she should do was appear less than well dressed and she was quite capable of looking after herself.

"I will have to get to the Marchant & Fuller hauliers tonight to arrange for them to pick up your goods tomorrow. If we can get you some help now, do you think you could be ready by tomorrow?" asked Liza.

"Would I have to travel with the hauliers?" said Evelyn.

"Oh, I think that we could arrange a more comfortable journey for you than that," smiled Liza. "We'll have to find you somewhere to stay for a couple of days whilst your furniture is being transported. Will you go and tidy yourself now and ask Melanie's nurse what she can do to help. Jamie is here Evelyn; I believe he is in the hall. I'll ask him to join us if you have no objection."

"I thought you had come alone," said a frowning Evelyn.

"You said it yourself; Jamie and I have no secrets. He may have heard what we were discussing, or he may not have done, but if we can all talk calmly then we will come up with the best solution to your problem. It would however be a good idea to ask the nurse to get as much help as she can right away," said Liza.

They left the sitting room together and found Jamie waiting in the hallway. Evelyn nodded to him and made her way up to see the nurse. Liza ushered Jamie into the sitting room and told him what she and Evelyn had been discussing.

"I had heard some of what you were saying and much as I would have preferred her to go to France or some other country across the sea, Wales will be good enough to start with. If she at last keeps to her word and leaves us in peace, then I have no objection to her making a life for herself and her daughter there. I didn't know you had a house there Liza," said Jamie.

"You knew I had interests there; it was all part of Bradley & Company buying property in the area a long time ago. The tenants have left, and I had the place cleaned and decorated ready to rent out again, so it has all worked out well really," said Liza.

"Do you think that she will be accepted back there?" asked Jamie.

"If she acts as she did when she was there before then she will have a better life for herself and her daughter. Eventually she can return but as long as she doesn't smash her way back, she will be accepted. She is a very unhappy lady Jamie, she needs a great deal of support at this moment in time and I know you are going to say that her problems are of her own making, and you are right. It doesn't stop them being any the less serious," said Liza.

"I will go along with what you are planning Liza, but I believe that you will regret it," said Jamie. "You have never been thanked by Evelyn for anything that you have done to help her. I do realise that you are really only doing this for her daughter."

"Yes, you're right, but if I was in trouble it would be nice if somebody tried to help me; and you did that for me Jamie on many occasions," said Liza.

The nurse knocked and entered with Melanie. "I'm not too clear on what I am meant to be doing Lady Edgeworth. Can you tell me what is happening please?"

"Lady Evelyn is moving her household and she is hoping that you could find enough people to help with organising this move. I hope that I shall be able to arrange hauliers to collect her furniture and trunks during the course of tomorrow," said Liza.

"Yes, I'm sure I'll be able to get people to help her leave," said the nurse and neither Liza nor Jamie commented on the implication of what she had said.

"Would you like to leave Melanie with us whilst you organise some help?" asked Liza.

"Thank you, Lady Edgeworth; I only have to go around the corner where the housekeeper is staying and she will tell the rest of the staff. It won't take me long," said the nurse.

Liza smiled at Melanie and she seemed a little shy, but not frightened. Unfortunately there was no mistaking who her father was. Jamie drew in his breath but said nothing. Liza sat down and the nurse led Melanie over to her and after a very short while she was sitting on Liza's lap and smiling happily up at her. The nurse left and both Liza and Jamie hoped that her mission would be successful.

Within half an hour the sounds of people could be heard moving around the house and Jamie and Liza smiled at one another. "So the nurse has managed to get the help that's needed," said Jamie.

Evelyn came in and frowned when she saw Melanie nestling on Liza's lap. "I see you managed to get the staff back and my daughter seems quite comfortable on your knee."

"Yes her nurse went to round up your staff Evelyn," said Jamie. "And I'm quite sure that little Melanie would be just as happy sitting on your knee."

"We'll leave you now Evelyn as I have to organise the hauliers, but please help your staff and tell them what you want to keep and what you will leave behind. Anything that you're not sure about can be left and sent on to you should you need it. We'll store any furniture that you can't take," said Liza.

"I have to say Evelyn that I'm not entirely happy with the situation, but if you settle well where you are going it will suit all our purposes. I hope that this will be a new start for you and your daughter and that we will never again have to watch our backs," said Jamie.

"I'll come back tomorrow to see how you are getting on if you would like," said Liza.

Jamie frowned at this, but Evelyn said that she would appreciate any help that Liza could give.

"We'll have to think of somewhere for you and Melanie to stay for the next few days whilst your furniture is on its way to your new home. Will your nurse be travelling with you?" asked Liza.

"I don't know; she hasn't said," said Evelyn.

"For God's sake Evelyn," said Jamie. "Why don't you ask her? You really don't know how to talk to anyone do you?"

"Of course, I'll ask her," said Evelyn. "It is all rather daunting."

"You know all the people where you are going. When I set up my own house in Benson, I found it quite exciting. I enjoyed placing all my furniture and then moving it around. Sleeping for the first time in my new home was wonderful and then when Matthew arrived it became a house full of fun and laughter. You should have that Evelyn; you and little Melanie will have a very happy time settling in," said Liza.

"You and I are very different Liza. You found that fun, I will find it inconvenient. I shall be happy when everything is in place. I'm sure Melanie will find it entertaining," said Evelyn.

They left and, on the way, home called in at the local branch of the Marchant & Fuller hauliers giving them the necessary instructions.

"And where were you thinking of letting Evelyn stay when she can no longer be in her house? Surely not with us," said Jamie as they continued their journey.

"It did cross my mind but I decided against it, especially as it would upset James so much as well as the other boys, and instead she will have to stay at one of our hotels on the way to Wales. I'll have to get a letter of instruction quickly to the Evans' and also the local lawyer who deals with my properties, so I will have to write those tonight and get them on their way first thing tomorrow. I must also write another instruction letter for Evelyn to take to our hotels," said Liza, who was really thinking aloud.

"I suppose the alternative to all that is if you were to travel with her," said Jamie. "No doubt you have thought about that also. That's what you did when she went there to have Melanie, isn't it?"

Liza frowned and said nothing.

"Come on Liza, even Evelyn mentions the circumstances of Melanie's birth. I think that you and I have got past the stage of keeping her illegitimacy quiet," said Jamie. "It isn't as though either of us will shout about it to anyone else."

"I would have enjoyed seeing Evelyn and Melanie settled in the house; I find setting up home exciting and I would have liked to have seen the Evans' again. Dilys and Carys will help to find a housekeeper and anything else she needs. Do you know, she got on really well with them which surprised me," said Liza.

"You must let me know how much rent you expected to get from the house," said Jamie and Liza looked at him questioningly.

"Evelyn is still my responsibility, although I had said that I was going to stop financing her, but she is not your responsibility and it would be unfair of me to expect you to start funding her," said Jamie.

"It's good of you to think that way, but I do feel that I have a certain responsibility towards little Melanie, and I wasn't looking for rent under the circumstances. She is going to have a hard-enough time paying for staff as well as food," said Liza.

"No matter what I said to her the other day, I can see that she needs help and she has come down from her 'high horse'. I'm getting sentimental, just like you, and I won't let either of them starve. Her needs will be less as she only wants a housekeeper and someone to occasionally look after Melanie and perhaps a cook if the housekeeper cannot double as that. That is a lot less than she has currently, so I can afford to pay you a little rent," said Jamie.

"Well, whatever you are comfortable with Jamie; you know that I'm not asking for anything," said Liza.

***

They were late back, and Miranda and Lucinda were anxiously waiting for them.

"We're relieved to see that you have arrived with no further injuries. James has been very upset and even Matthew and John could not put his mind at rest. April and Adam did a wonderful job keeping them occupied as much as they could," said Miranda.

"I think that we had better go and see them before we do anything else," said Jamie and both Miranda and Lucinda nodded their agreement. "I think you both deserve to know what is happening with Evelyn and we'll tell you over dinner."

The boys were in bed, but it was obvious that they were not going to rest until they knew that their father and mother were safe and not hurt at all. Adam and April had been with them, but they made themselves scarce when Jamie and Liza came into the room. They both smiled their thanks to them.

All three boys sat up in bed looking expectantly at Liza and Jamie.

"Your mother and sister are moving away James and we are helping her to do so," said Jamie starkly. There was no other way to tell him.

"She's not my mother or my sister," said James petulantly.

"No matter what you think and no matter what you say, she is your mother and Melanie is your half-sister. I know you wish it otherwise, but it is a fact," said Jamie.

"James has been very upset, and we all have been worried about you both," said Matthew, once again becoming the leader of the group.

"I know, I didn't mean to be harsh with you, but we all have to accept that they are part of our lives and we must do the best we can for everyone," said Jamie. "That is why your mother, Liza, has organised their immediate move to another part of the country, which is far enough away so that none of us need ever be bothered again."

"We would not ban you from seeing your mother if that is what you want James, and if you do at some time want to get in touch with her then we will arrange it for you," said Liza.

80

"I don't want to, but I understand what you are saying. I'm pleased that we don't have to worry any longer," said James and Matthew and John nodded their agreement.

"When is she leaving?" asked James.

"Tomorrow; everything is being organised for then and I'm afraid I will have to go and help again, but don't worry, I will not be alone," said Liza, really not knowing if Jamie was going to accompany her, but felt that he probably would.

"I am so pleased that you are all my sons now," said Jamie. "You've made my life full of love and purpose. You now have nothing to worry about, but

both your mother and I do appreciate how concerned you were for us and how well you looked after one another. Sleep well boys and we'll see you tomorrow morning."

They both then went to their rooms and quickly changed for dinner and when they went to the dining room Miranda and Lucinda looked up expectantly and during the course of dinner they learned what had happened and what the result was to be for Evelyn.

"Were you thinking of going with Liza tomorrow Jamie?" asked Miranda.

"Neither of us wanted to go again, but it is necessary and I wouldn't let Liza go by herself, although Evelyn does seem to have calmed down considerably," said Jamie.

"I would really like to go with you tomorrow Liza," said Miranda. "I know I could help but also I would like to meet little Melanie and perhaps I could look after her whilst everyone else is busy."

"Certainly I have no objection," said Liza. "However I do wonder whether it could cause embarrassment to Evelyn as you met her previously under awkward circumstances. What do you think Jamie?"

"I can see no harm in it," said Jamie. "I'm sure that she would get over any embarrassment quickly once she realises how kind you are Mother," said Jamie.

"When we have sorted Evelyn out, we must then think about our trip at Easter and then it will be April and Adam's wedding," said Liza. "We will then have the opening of Ffoulks House, and Hector is inspecting the Langston house so we will have that to think about, and along with all that we must try to find your Uncle David."

"Perhaps 'Uncle David' doesn't want to be found," commented Jamie.

"Well, we won't insist that he sees us if that's the case," said Liza.

"I'm sure if you find him, or his children, that they would want to see you," said Lucinda. "I have no family, although you are all my family now, but if a long lost relative suddenly appeared in my life, I would be delighted to see them."

With dinner over Liza sat down and wrote her letters to the Evans family, her lawyer and one for Evelyn to show at the Marchant & Fuller hotels. She finally went up to her room and was surprised to find Jamie waiting there for her.

"I told April not to wait for you. I thought that I could get you ready for bed," smiled Jamie. "You look tired."

"So do you Jamie," said Liza. "It has been a very tiring day."

He helped her out of her dress, smiling as he did so. She stepped out of the rest of her clothes and looked up at him with an excited look in her eyes.

"Your eyes tell me everything Liza. I know what you want and it's exactly what I want too. We always manage to make one another happy no matter what other people try to do to us, and we enjoy our time in bed. We are so much luckier than others but there was a time when I thought otherwise," said Jamie.

"You need a great deal of love tonight Jamie. You have had to deal with a very difficult situation, and you have done it very well," said Liza as she pulled him towards her bed.

"No, you have dealt with it; I lost my temper with her and made matters worse," said Jamie.

"That's not right Jamie, Evelyn lost her temper and you managed to control yours, which cannot have been easy. You said yourself that you had never seen her other than controlled before. You made the right decision and that was that she had to leave; all I have done is found an alternative place for her to go. Your decision has not been countermanded; we have just put her out of harms' way in a place where she and her daughter will be accepted," said Liza.

Jamie smiled at her and swept her up and placed her on the bed and climbed in with her. They both needed love that night and as always, they managed to wipe away their worries of the day.

***

Evelyn's house was in uproar when Jamie, Liza and Miranda arrived the following morning. They had to give Evelyn her due; she was helping to pack and at the same time telling the hauliers which pieces of furniture to take and which to leave. She turned and caught sight of them, "I'm pleased you're both here; perhaps you could help me get some order out of this chaos?"

She looked questioningly at Miranda and Jamie stepped forward and told her that his mother was willing to help and perhaps she could look after Melanie as everyone was going to be busy.

Three hauliers' wagons were parked at the front and Evelyn was being quite sensible when choosing what she was taking, and Jamie assured her that whatever she left behind he would either send it onto her or store safely.

"Will your nurse be staying with you Evelyn?" asked Liza.

"She has promised to stay with me until I can find a replacement and then she would like to return. I will of course give her an excellent reference; I think she will miss Melanie, but she feels that she should now make a change," said a very calm Evelyn.

"I'm sure both Dilys and Carys will help out in that respect until you can get a permanent replacement. The people in the village will help with any other staff that you may need," said Liza.

By mid-afternoon the wagons were full and Evelyn, Melanie and the nurse were ready to leave. Jamie had hired a carriage to take them all the way to their new life and they would be stopping at the first hotel for two days before continuing their journey, when they would have one more overnight stop and this meant that they would arrive soon after the furniture wagons.

"You have arranged everything very well for me," said Evelyn just stopping short of thanking them.

The nurse came in and said that she had to get Melanie ready for the journey and Liza asked her to get in touch when she returned as there may be work for her at the Ffoulks House if that type of work would be of interest to her. She thanked Liza and said that she would bear it in mind on her return.

Miranda had kept Melanie occupied throughout the day and had enjoyed doing so, and then finally they were all ready to leave and Liza gave Evelyn the letter to show to the various hoteliers. Jamie helped them into their carriage, and they left without a backward glance, leaving Jamie, Liza and Miranda to close the house. They breathed a sigh of relief and prayed that it was the last that they would hear of Evelyn for some time. They were under no illusions that she would come to the fore sometime in the future but for now they were looking forward to a time when they did not have to worry about any of Evelyn's attempted disruptions.

"I can see why you married her Jamie," said Miranda. "From a distance, on occasion, I thought she was Liza, but when she was near there was no doubting who she was. She has a harsh look and that may not be of her own making. Jamie you were very wrong to marry her; you tried to make believe that she was Liza and Evelyn realised that. I cannot condone all the things that she has tried to do to you both, and especially to you Liza, but I can understand it and I believe you can also and that is why you help her."

"She did create a problem between Liza and her first husband long before our marriage, but in her defence she was trying to help Liza's stepson who had got himself into difficulties gambling and I can only lay claim to the fact that he was trying to keep up with me at the time," said Jamie.

Miranda looked at Liza and had tears in her eyes, "I now truly understand your compassion for her Liza but she does have evil intents and you will always have to watch out for her, especially when she has been alone and only has her thoughts to occupy her mind."

"That's why you wanted to come with us today, isn't it?" said Liza. "You needed to know why she has such vindictiveness towards us."

"I also have some compassion for her," said Jamie. "When I was told that Liza was dead, Evelyn brought me back from the brink. I was under no illusions that all she really wanted was a title and she also knew that I wanted an heir. That was our bargain, but I never loved her and she never loved me; we tolerated one another, and it is true that our marriage went from bad to worse when I learned that Liza was still alive. Even though she was across the Atlantic and eventually was happily married to someone else, I still loved her and Evelyn knew that. You are right Mother, from a distance, or with your eyes half closed, you could imagine that she was Liza and there were many occasions when I did that. It must have been very degrading for Evelyn and eventually we both hated one another and Evelyn did everything she could to hurt Liza, she still does and that I cannot allow."

"I know that it has been said before, but you know that she will never thank you for all that you have done for her. I feel that you have both done enough to vindicate past actions, but she will never see that. She does not have a forgiving nature," said Miranda.

Lucinda came out of the Dower House to greet them as they brought Miranda home, and they carried on to the main house and were surrounded by the boys as they walked in the front door all wanting to know if James was now safe and would not be 'kidnapped' again.

"You know that your mother just had a strange thought in her head when she 'kidnapped' James, as you call it. I know it was frightening for you at the time, but she is very sorry about it now and realises that it was a silly thing to do," said Jamie not really believing what he was saying.

"Yes it's all over now and will never happen again," said Liza.

"Has she really gone away now?" asked James.

"Yes, she's gone but you know that if you ever want to see her and your sister again you only have to tell us and we'll arrange it for you," said Liza.

"You're always saying that, why do you do that? Don't you want me to stay with you?" asked a sullen James.

"Don't be silly," said Matthew. "You know our mother only wants to be fair to everyone; she doesn't really want you to go to her, but she has to make sure you're happy about that."

Liza and Jamie looked at Matthew realising that he was wise beyond his years.

"Yes, that's exactly right," said John. "So, stop worrying and let's go and see what's for supper."

"Good idea," said James who appeared to have forgotten his concerns and off they all went to the kitchen.

"We've said it before," smiled Jamie, "nothing gets in the way of those boys' stomachs."

"Do you think that we have solved the Evelyn problem Jamie?" asked Liza.

"Probably we have for a while, possibly a long while although from what you said some time ago; she will come back to haunt us, but we won't be around to see it," said Jamie.

Liza frowned at him and a vague memory came to her, but it wasn't clear.

"You don't remember, do you? Never mind, perhaps it's just as well if you can't recall one of your dreams," smiled Jamie.

"I have a feeling that it could have been a nightmare," said Liza still trying to remember a premonition.

They dined together that night and enjoyed their own company and they both shared a sense of relief as they knew they had done the best for Evelyn and Melanie even though it would never be thought as such by Evelyn.

"Is the house that she is going to as nice as you said Liza?" asked Jamie.

"It is a very friendly house Jamie. It's not unlike my house in Benson only much bigger. It could be made quite elegant with the right furniture and furnishings which I'm sure Evelyn will put in place. She will be very comfortable there and so will Melanie. The Evans' are a wonderful family and they will make sure that she has everything that she needs. She won't have to hide away there, she will be accepted by everyone and the only person who could make life awkward for her is Evelyn herself and I do hope that she grasps this final opportunity with both hands," said Liza.

"She did rather put herself out on a limb and through trying to make our lives difficult she succeeded in making her own more difficult," said Jamie. "You have had to put up with a great deal since you married me."

"It started a long time before our marriage Jamie, you know that. It started when you were first engaged to her and has carried on at various times since then. Do you know that she tried to seduce Patrick and it must have been galling for her when he turned her down? So she had a husband who was showing that he wanted someone else and she offered herself to someone who refused her charms also because of someone else, and that someone else in both cases was me. You must understand her dislike of me, but she has done some very stupid things to try to get even. It's a shame that she couldn't just make another life for herself; there has to be someone out there who could love her," said Liza.

"She would hate to know that we both understand her so well," smiled Jamie, "and now my mother does also. Oh! She would be so unhappy with us all knowing how she ticks."

"I feel very relaxed tonight and we have no functions to attend until after Easter. I can get organised for Easter in Belfast and have plenty of time to make sure that April and Adam's wedding is going according to plan, although I promise I won't interfere with what they have in mind. We are going to have a very busy time afterwards though, so let's enjoy this quiet time whilst we have it," smiled Liza.

Chapter 5

Two weeks before they were due to leave for Easter in Belfast, the Reverend Collins called and he was smiling broadly. He had with him a register of births and a letter from the Bishop's office.

Luckily Jamie was at home that morning and he appeared just as excited as Liza. "Well Reverend, what have you got to tell us; it looks like good news from your face," said Jamie.

"Derek has been meticulous in searching through our records and he finally found the entry for the birth of your Uncle. He was three years younger than your father and his full names were David Charles William Edgeworth. There was also an entry relating to a marriage, but that was crossed out. The marriage was not going to take place here but was to be held in the lady's hometown in Hertfordshire," said Bernard Collins.

"I still find it difficult to believe that my uncle has been wiped out of our family records so completely, even if he did take away my father's fiancée. I should have thought that there would have been some record of his birth," said Jamie.

"What happened to him after the family rift?" asked Liza.

"As you know he was already a man of the cloth. He had not gone against any commandment, he was allowed to fall in love but it was embarrassing to both the family and the church that the lady in question had refused to take the marriage vows to your father in front of the whole congregation and instead preferred to have a life with his brother in virtual obscurity, and very happy they were together by all accounts," said Bernard.

"Where did they end up?" asked Jamie.

"He became the vicar of a country parish near Truro in Cornwell, and according to my information from the Bishop's office he is still there but has retired and a younger man has taken over the main duties of the parish. I believe he is now a widower, but I have no record if there are any children from the union," said Bernard.

"We must go and visit him," said a very happy Liza.

"Perhaps we should write to him first," said Jamie.

"Yes, I think that would be a good idea, after all you don't want to turn up on his doorstep and give him a shock," said Bernard smiling at Liza's enthusiasm followed by her obvious disappointment at not dropping everything and rushing off to Truro.

Jamie started his letter to the Reverend David Edgeworth when Bernard had left. He began it several times but finally he decided just to introduce himself and say that he had only recently been made aware of the fact that he had an uncle and that he would be delighted if it were possible for them to meet in the not too distant future and that he would therefore be pleased to hear from him.

"It would have been nice to surprise him with a visit," said Liza.

"Such a surprise could kill a man of his age," smiled Jamie.

"How old is he Jamie?" asked Liza.

"He's sixty-seven now; my father would have been seventy this year. He was just fifty-five when he died, which was quite young really. I suppose it was the result of a debauched life," said Jamie.

"You've done very well Jamie, you could so easily have followed in his footsteps and you were quite young to take over the title and all the responsibilities that it entails," said Liza.

"It wasn't until he died that I discovered just how much debt he was in. The estate had gone to virtual rack and ruin and it took me a long while to redeem some of the family jewels and silver and as you know I didn't manage to get it all back. I had to sell several properties, but I did get the farmland around this house back into some profit," said Jamie.

"I know that you had to sacrifice bringing Ireland back into proper operation to concentrate all your efforts over here; you had to make some very difficult decisions but they were the right ones," said Liza.

"Then I had an offer from some company called Bradley & Company," laughed Jamie, "and you didn't think that I would know that it was you. That gave me the opportunity to put my house completely in order. I have a great deal to thank you for Liza."

"You have to know that I was always in it to make money Jamie. I did you no favours. I treated you no differently to others, but you were special as at the time you were my largest investment and we all have done well out of the arrangement," said Liza.

"My uncle should be pleased with how we have progressed. He was here when my father and grandfather were gambling away the Edgeworth fortune. He will see quite a change in the place if he ever visits," said Jamie.

"I do hope that he does. It would be quite exciting," said Liza. "Your mother should be interested to meet him, although you could say that he was the cause of her downfall."

"You're right, if he hadn't run off with my father's fiancée then she would not have married my father," said Jamie.

"Well, I'm glad that he did otherwise you wouldn't be here and I wouldn't have the pleasure of being married to you," smiled Liza as she gave him a kiss on his head.

They felt that they had done all they could to reunite Jamie's uncle with the family and all they could do now was wait for a reply which they hoped would be forthcoming.

Two days before they were due to leave for Belfast, they received a letter from David Edgeworth. He wrote that he was pleased to have heard from Jamie and would be delighted to renew his acquaintance with his family and asked what suggestions were proposed for such a meeting. He added that he had over the years had news of how the Edgeworths were faring and was pleased that the family were now well settled.

Jamie immediately dashed off a reply telling him that they were travelling to the family home in Belfast for Easter but would like to make arrangements to meet up on their return.

They were all excited that another member of the family had been located, especially the boys who said that they hoped he was good at cricket. Miranda was intrigued by him and commented on how brave both he and his wife had been to stand up to the might of the Edgeworths. Lucinda wondered if he would be as good looking as Jamie, to which Jamie just raised his eyes.

Liza wondered how difficult it would be to get to Truro and started mapping out in her mind how long it would take and what hotels they could stay at on the way.

"Are April and Adam coming with us this Easter?" asked Lucinda.

"April is," answered Liza. "I did suggest that she stays to put the final touches to her big day, but she says that everything is well organised, and she will have two weeks after we return to prepare. Her dress is ready and the whole village is making sure that everything is in order. I have tried not to interfere as I know that April wanted to show that she and Adam could organise it all by themselves. She enjoys going back to Belfast; it was where her happy life began."

"What will Adam do whilst you are away?" asked Miranda.

"He'll be making sure that his surprise for their honeymoon is perfect. He'll also probably be organising lessons for the boys during his absence, which will not be pleasing to them," laughed Liza.

***

Easter passed pleasantly in Belfast. Amelia was getting very excited about the birth of her first grandchild and much as she was getting excited, Edward was beginning to panic and his worry about Nicole stemmed from the problems that he had heard that Liza had experienced when she had little Meg.

"You don't want to believe everything that you hear Edward. I'm still alive so your fears are unfounded and don't forget that I had no problems having Matthew it was only because I was badly hurt when I was attacked that I had difficulties. Nicole is young and very healthy so I know that she will come through the experience with flying colours," said Liza.

Amelia and Wendell were intrigued by the fact that Jamie had found his long-lost uncle and that they were going to arrange a meeting in the not too distant future.

"I suppose you and Jamie will be travelling to Truro soon after your return to Surrey," said Wendell.

"We just have one function for the charity before April's wedding and then we have several afterwards," said Liza. "So I really don't know when we can get to meet him."

"I can see that the world that you have been thrown into isn't sitting easily on your shoulders Liza," said Wendell. "I suppose you're worried about leaving the boys on too many occasions."

"It's something that we will probably get used to," said Liza not too convincingly.

"Liza enjoys a good function," said Edward cheerily.

"Not as many as she and Jamie are going to have to attend. I'm afraid you are high up on the list of essential guests at many a function now and I know you won't be able to refuse too many. It's not the direction that you wanted your lives to follow, is it?" said Wendell.

"No," said Jamie. "We have been very happy not being centre stage, but it is now expected of us. We are however determined that our boys will not suffer, and they are lucky that they have each other and my mother and Lucinda to watch over them. April and Adam also look after them wonderfully, although it's not the same as having your parents around."

"I suppose we will also be expected to attend some functions; I'll have to refuse until after our baby is born. It will be very entertaining, I'm sure Nicole will enjoy them as much as I will," said Edward happily.

"Yes, I'm sure you would enjoy them if you were ever invited," said Wendell somewhat sarcastically.

"Do you think that we will be invited to some of the grand functions?" asked Amelia.

"I'm sure we will be Amelia," said Wendell, "but if it meant travelling to England too often then I'm afraid I would have to decline."

"So you would have to send one of us instead," said a still happy Edward.

"Do you think that the Queen will be at some of them?" asked Amelia.

"I doubt whether she will, but I believe that Prince Albert will be. Lady Redfern has said that the Queen cannot favour one charity over another, but the Prince can," said Liza.

"That would be so exciting; could you arrange an invitation for all of us Liza?" asked Edward happily.

"I doubt that either Jamie or I have the influence over the various hosts as much as you think," smiled Liza.

Wendell just raised his eyes to heaven and Liza knew that he was wondering how he had fathered such a son, but everyone loved Edward and appreciated his enthusiasm. Nobody liked to inform Edward that if any of the Fullers were invited it would be Wendell and Amelia and, in their absence, Peter would step into that role.

Chapter 6

Whilst Liza, Jamie and the boys were enjoying their Easter break in Belfast, the regular stagecoach arrived in the Edgeworth town and out stepped a distinguished looking gentleman who turned and helped down a woman in her mid-forties. They made their way to the inn and booked two rooms; Mr Rogers asked how long they would be staying, and the gentleman said that it would be a few days and that they were undecided just how long they would be there. Mrs Rogers showed them up to their rooms and when she returned, she made it known to her husband that the man had to be an Edgeworth as he looked similar to the current Lord Edgeworth. Mr Rogers looked in the guest book and saw that his wife was correct and under their roof they had the Reverend David Edgeworth. They had no idea who the woman was but later that day they heard her refer to the man as 'father'.

"What are you going to do this afternoon Father?" asked Grace Pointer.

"I thought that I would call in at the local church and meet the current vicar. He won't know who we are so he could be quite forthcoming about the Edgeworth family and whether we were wise in visiting now," said David Edgeworth.

"You know my feelings on coming when you knew that the family would be away," said Grace.

"I told you that I wanted to find out whether we would truly be welcome by my nephew, and more importantly his current wife. I believe that she has more of a say in the affairs of the estate than should be the case. I am also concerned as I know that Jamie is a divorced man and therefore in the eyes of the church, he should not have gone through a form of marriage with the woman referred to as Lady Edgeworth," said David.

"I think you should be open minded Father. I know it's difficult for you because of your calling but you knew the circumstances before you decided to visit," said Grace.

"I didn't want us to be put in a position of having to meet the family if we do not feel comfortable doing so," said David.

"You'll find it strange seeing the place after all these years," said Grace.

"Yes, I wonder if it has changed much. I suppose it must have done, after all it is almost fifty years since I was here," said David.

"I hope that you decide to stay until the family return from Belfast. I would like to meet my cousin; it would be nice to have a family," said Grace. "I think Mother would be pleased that you have made your peace with the family."

"We'll see Grace; they may not wish to be associated with us," said David.

"Really Father," exclaimed Grace. "Remember that they took the first step and wrote to you wanting to renew the family acquaintance, so I think you are being unnecessarily cautious. I think we should definitely stay and meet them, after all what have we got to lose?"

"You are right Grace; we have absolutely nothing to lose. If we don't enjoy their company and they ours then we return to Truro as we planned and I have had the pleasure of showing you all my old haunts," said David.

Later that day they made their way to the church where the Reverend Collins was discussing with Adam the arrangements for his wedding to April. They both looked up as David Edgeworth and Grace Pointer entered the church. Bernard immediately recognised who he was and moved to greet the pair.

"Welcome Reverend Edgeworth," said Bernard as Adam turned and looked closely at David.

"I would not have thought that you would have known who I was," said a surprised David.

"There is no mistaking the Edgeworth features. I'm afraid the family are away in Belfast and won't be back for a couple of days. Were they expecting you?" asked Bernard.

"No, I thought that we would take advantage of the opportunity to look around without drawing attention to ourselves," said David.

"Have you somewhere to stay Sir?" said Adam. "If not, I know that Lady Edgeworth would want you to be comfortable in rooms in Edgeworth House and I can easily arrange that for you both."

"That's kind, but we are already booked in at the Inn. May I ask who you are Sir," said David.

"My apologies Sir; I tutor the Edgeworth boys and have done for a number of years now," said Adam.

"I see," said David. "This is my daughter, Grace. She is a very good travelling companion and has wanted to see where I grew up for some time now."

"Well, you have saved Lord and Lady Edgeworth a journey. I know that they were planning to visit you soon after their return, in fact if Lady Edgeworth had had her way, she would have travelled to see you once she heard that you were willing to meet up, but she was advised to wait until they contacted you again with a few dates which they hoped would be convenient to you," said Adam.

"Lady Edgeworth you say, I would have thought that she would have only shown a passing interest," said David.

"Good heavens no! Lady Liza was very excited when she heard that you were still alive," said Bernard. "In fact, neither his Lordship nor her Ladyship knew of your existence until a few weeks ago and when they learned they immediately came here to ask for my help in finding you, which I was pleased to do," said Bernard Collins.

"They could have seen my name in the family Bible or on a birth certificate. There were many documents carrying my name," said David dismissively.

"Unfortunately your name was obliterated completely from the Edgeworth family history and we had to study the church records extensively to find notification of your birth. It was only by a chance reference to you at a function that they were attending that they discovered your existence," said Bernard Collins who was detecting a certain amount of antagonism in Reverend David Edgeworth.

"I see," said David. "When I heard from my nephew, I thought that he had just made excuses about not knowing of me or he had just been too busy or disinterested to look up the family records; it did not occur to me that I had been wiped out of our history."

Both Adam and Grace were looking puzzled and Adam excused himself saying that he would see Bernard later and he left them to talk privately about why the Reverend David Edgeworth seemed to have been the 'black sheep of the family'.

"Father," said Grace. "I believe that there is something that you have not told me."

"I did not think that what I did would have hurt my brother unduly; he was not a man to have very great feelings for anyone other than himself, but I suppose I humiliated him and he would find that hard to accept, as would my father who would also have to face those he thought of as friends and who he felt were probably laughing at him," said David.

94

"What did you do Father?" asked Grace. "It must have been something very grave to make them obliterate you from all records. What was it?"

The Reverend David Edgeworth said, "I married your mother," and he was smiling at a memory.

Bernard Collins smiled and nodded as he knew the family history. "Please, come into the vicarage and have some refreshments; I will leave you to talk as it would appear that you have much to discuss."

"Thank you," said David. "Yes, I believe the time has come to tell my daughter why we live in Truro and have had no contact with the Edgeworths here in Surrey."

Bernard showed them to the vicarage, gave them tea and biscuits and left them alone. David Edgeworth told his daughter everything about his love for her mother and how he had taken her from his brother at the altar. He told her how brave her mother had been by refusing to make her marriage vows to James although she had been dragged to the church by her father. He told her how he still loved her mother and that her death nearly two years previously had not changed his feelings. He missed her every day and would do so until the day he died.

"You should have told me before we came here. I can see why there was such a rift in the family, but you are right, my mother was very brave. Do you think that my cousin knows the story?" asked Grace.

"As it was so long ago and I had never been mentioned, the probability is that he doesn't know," said David.

"I would think that it wouldn't matter if he did know as his father obviously married someone else and he is the result of that union," said Grace.

"My brother and father were cruel men and I wonder whether my nephew has the same traits. It would be difficult for him not to have as he must have been influenced by them," said David.

"I can see why you wanted to come here whilst my cousin was away; you wanted to make enquiries about him before you had a face-to-face meeting and you wanted to protect me from any unpleasantness. The Reverend Collins seems to know the family well and the tutor seemed to think that we would be made very welcome," said Grace.

"It was not really his place to offer us accommodation, although he seemed very confident that he was doing the right thing," said David.

"Reverend Collins said that Lady Liza was excited and wanted to meet you as soon as possible; she sounds quite nice," said Grace.

"I'm not sure how she fits into the Edgeworth picture; I just know that she seems to have a great deal of influence over what happens in the family and I'm not sure that it's such a good thing," said David.

"I don't think you can pass judgement yet; we have only been here a few hours and have a great deal more to look at and to hear," said Grace. "I have a feeling that you are going to be pleasantly surprised."

They thanked Bernard Collins for his hospitality and made their way back to the Inn where Mrs Rogers told them that she was pleased to meet members of the Edgeworth family. She knew how pleased Lord and Lady Edgeworth would be when they returned, and she carried on that the whole village would be pleased as once they were back the cricket matches would start again and they all enjoyed those Sunday afternoon gatherings.

"That sounds interesting," said David. "I see that there is a new green here, how long have the matches been held?"

"Ever since Lady Liza came here but this will be the first year that we will use the new green, we always used the grounds of Edgeworth House before. It's good fun; Lady Liza used to take the runs for young Derek Price as he couldn't walk, but he could bat a good ball, but her young son John now takes those runs for him. We've formed an Edgeworth team and we're now challenging other villages, so we're going to have to get in a great deal of practice," said Mrs Rogers.

As they made their way up to their rooms to change for supper Grace said, "I told you not to pass judgement; Mrs Rogers seems very happy with Lady Liza and so it would seem that many of the villagers are also. I'm really looking forward to meeting them and I hope you are also Father."

Over the next two days the Reverend David Edgeworth and his daughter Grace Pointer met many villagers and spent some time with Bernard Collins and bumped into Adam on a few occasions and the day that Liza, Jamie and the family were due back from Belfast, Grace was feeling excited and she could tell that her father was feeling the same way.

***

As always chaos surrounded the arrival of the family back from their stay in Belfast. The boys rushed back up to their room and could be heard pulling out toys and games that they hadn't seen for a few weeks. April was about to start unpacking when Liza told her to go and see Adam, after all they had been separated for some weeks and she was sure that they had missed each other.

Jamie watched as all were rushing around him and he retreated to his study and hid behind his newspaper. A short while later Adam knocked and entered.

"Excuse me Sir," he said, "but you may not have heard that your uncle arrived in the village two days ago. He has his daughter with him and they are staying with Mr and Mrs Rogers at the Inn."

Jamie was momentarily lost for words. "They should be staying here, why are they at the Inn. Mrs Frances should have arranged for their stay here."

"I spoke to him on the day he arrived, and I knew that you would want them here, but he refused the offer. He probably felt that it would be an imposition without a proper invitation from you or her Ladyship," said Adam.

"You did right in offering Adam. I wonder why he came when he knew we would be away. No matter, I must tell Liza and then go and see him myself," said Jamie and he went off calling for Liza.

Liza's reaction was the same as Jamie's, "Why did he come when he knew we weren't here? You say he has his daughter with him. Wonderful! I'll arrange for two rooms to be made ready for them. Surely he's not going to refuse our hospitality."

"I must go and find them," said Jamie. "Warn the boys to be on their best behaviour."

Liza looked at him and he knew that he really had not needed to say it. "I suppose it's best if you go alone. I hope they come back with you."

Jamie quickly freshened up and changed and took the small carriage into the village, arriving at the Inn well before lunch. He bounded in and Mr Rogers greeted him.

"I understand that my uncle and cousin are staying with you Mr Rogers, are they in at the moment?" Jamie asked.

"They are in our lounge your Lordship; shall I call them?" asked Mr Rogers.

"No, just show me the way, thank you Mr Rogers," said Jamie and he wondered whether he was feeling excited or worried; perhaps it was both.

In the lounge he saw someone who looked not unlike his father and he drew in his breath, and with him was a very pleasant looking woman. The man looked up from his newspaper and for once Jamie was lost for words and the man appeared the same. The woman came to the rescue and said, "I believe that you must be my cousin Jamie." She smiled and moved towards him, putting out her hand to shake his.

Her father seemed to come to life and he also stood and moved towards him. "Jamie," he said. "Oh my, you are very like your father, although I am hearing good things about you. I am so pleased that we are meeting at last."

Jamie finally also came to life. "I'm afraid that I had no idea of your existence until a few weeks ago, otherwise I would have tried to make contact sooner. Welcome home Uncle and of course my cousin also. It's a wonderful feeling to know that I do have more family than I thought."

"I had better introduce myself. My name is Grace and I am very pleased to meet you Cousin Jamie. I have been looking forward to this for a long while," said Grace.

"I'm sorry but I didn't know of your existence until today, but I'm very happy that you are here, Cousin Grace," smiled Jamie and she could see her father in him. "I trust you will both be coming home with me; I know that Liza is very keen to meet you. She has arranged rooms for you both, please come and meet her and our boys. My mother also will be delighted that you are here."

"We have no wish to impose on you Jamie; we are quite comfortable here, of course we would be delighted to meet all your family," said David Edgeworth and Jamie detected a reticence in him.

"It is no imposition Uncle, and Liza will be so disappointed if you don't take up our offer and it is after all your family home," said Jamie cautiously.

"Of course it is Jamie," said Grace. "Come on Father, let's pack our cases and thank Mr and Mrs Rogers for their hospitality and go and meet all our family at last."

"Yes, you are right Grace; I'm just being silly," said David.

"I suppose it could bring back some unhappy memories for you," said Jamie. "The house has changed over the years and it is now a very happy and comfortable home and that is thanks to my wife."

Mr Rogers helped them with their luggage, and it wasn't long before they were on their way to Edgeworth House. Miranda and Lucinda had already arrived, and Liza was making sure that the boys were neat and tidy, much to their annoyance. Mrs Frances had organised the rooms for their guests, although nobody really knew whether they would be staying or not. Mrs Lambert had been warned that they would probably have house guests for the next few days.

Jamie drew the carriage up to the steps and Liza was waiting for them. "Welcome," she said as she ushered them into the house and into the drawing room where Miranda and Lucinda were waiting. Jamie followed them into the room and made the necessary introductions.

"I'm so pleased that you are both here," said Liza. "There must be so much for you to catch up on. I hope you will be staying a long while."

"Thank you, Liza, you've made us very welcome, hasn't she Father?" said Grace trying to bring her father into the conversation. He had been strangely quiet and seemed to be studying Liza and trying to make up his mind about something.

"Yes, thank you. I'm sure we'll be very comfortable in Jamie's house," said David.

Jamie frowned and felt that this had been a snub to Liza, but she appeared not to notice, although Jamie doubted that she would not be aware of it.

The boys knocked on the door and entered and Jamie took it upon himself to introduce them to David and Grace and she said how pleased she was to meet them.

Matthew smiled and said to Grace, "I believe you must be our second cousin," and he turned to David and said, "and you are our great uncle."

"No, I'm James' great uncle, not yours," said David.

There was silence in the room momentarily until James said, "No you're wrong, we are now brothers, so you are an uncle to all of us."

David was about to argue the point, but he saw Jamie's face and thought better of it.

Liza smiled sweetly and asked the boys if they had yet had their lunch. "Not yet" was the answer, so she suggested that they go to the kitchen and enjoy whatever it was that they were having. They said goodbye and left although it had previously been arranged that they join the adults for lunch, but they were all astute enough to realise that they would have a happier time down in the kitchen.

Jamie was beginning to regret that they had ever contacted his uncle as it was becoming very obvious that he did not like Liza, or Matthew and John and he was not prepared to see any of them hurt.

Grace was totally different; she was very friendly towards Liza and was asking a great many questions of Miranda and Lucinda.

"Lunch will be served soon, would you both like to be shown to your rooms so that you can freshen up before the meal?" asked Liza.

"Thank you, Liza, that would be ideal. Come on Father," said Grace and when they neared their rooms she said that she would call for him shortly. She quickly tidied herself and then knocked on his door and entered when he answered.

"What are you thinking of Father?" she asked. "You are being rude to Liza and you have no reason to be. You were also sharp with the boys. No matter how much this used to be your family home, it is no longer, and you are now a guest in this house. I would have expected that at least you could be civil towards your hosts."

"I was just stating the obvious; this is Jamie's house, it is not Liza's, and it is only James who is our relative not the other two boys," said David.

"Well it was unnecessary to state it," said Grace. "You must realise that the boys are very close, you upset one you upset all three, not to mention Jamie and Liza by doing it, and I don't think that either Miranda or Lucinda were too happy with what you said. Please don't alienate our family any further."

"I don't think anyone noticed; well may be Jamie did, but Liza didn't," said David.

"Liza is far more astute than you are giving her credit for. She is a mother and knows when her children are being hurt and I know she was well aware of your snub towards her. The boys realised that you didn't want them around and Liza skillfully changed where they would be lunching as they were originally going to be with us, and they took her lead and left without an argument. You haven't done very well for your first visit to your old home. I'm so annoyed at you Father. I thought you had more compassion for people than you are showing to your own family. Why is it that you dislike her?" asked Grace.

"I find that I am uneasy with the legitimacy of their marriage. Jamie still has a wife somewhere in England and Liza has been married so many times that it's suspicious that each of her husbands have died. I wonder whether there is something sinister behind her marriage to Jamie," said David.

"You're seeing difficulties where there are none and you are really annoying me. So come on and get ready to go down to lunch and try to enjoy the company of your only relatives. I'm not going to allow you to ruin this visit for me," said Grace.

"I think that I am also finding it difficult as I can really see my brother in Jamie, but it is only in his looks, his character seems to be very thoughtful of others. I do wonder what happened in his first marriage, but it does seem that she was not well liked in the village, whereas Liza is. However it often takes two to make a bad marriage as it takes two to make a good one. I promise I won't let my prejudices ruin your time here and I will keep my own counsel on Jamie and Liza's marriage as well as her sons," said David.

"They are no longer her sons, Father, you were told in no uncertain terms by young James that they are brothers and are therefore now both Jamie and Liza's sons. Young James certainly put you in your place," said Grace.

David smiled and said, "Yes he did, didn't he? Shall we go now otherwise we will be late for lunch?"

Liza greeted them warmly as they entered the dining room; Jamie was a little more cautious but soon relaxed as the conversation around the table turned to David's early life and his subsequent life in Truro.

Jamie broached the subject of his marriage, "I have been told what happened between you and my father all those years ago. It was the Dowager Lady Redfern who told us why there was a rift; in fact it was at the Duke of Berkshire's dinner that we were informed that I had an uncle, up until that time I had no knowledge of you. Even my mother did not know, did you Mother?"

"I only knew that Jamie's father had been engaged before my time, but it was not wise to question him about it; he could be a violent man and not necessarily over anything as important as losing a fiancée so I never made it my business to find out. Of course when I left here, I only worried about leaving Jamie; I had no interest in finding out about his father's previous life," said Miranda.

"I understand that it is only relatively recently that you have managed to come back into the family Miranda. Did you not think about returning after the death of my brother?" asked David.

"By that time too many years had passed, and I know that my name had been blackened to my son, so I just watched him from afar. It was only when Liza recognised something in me that reminded her of Jamie and young James, that she realised who I was. That was at their wedding and Mr and Mrs Rogers had sneaked me in so that I could see Jamie married. Liza tossed her flowers directly at me; I couldn't miss them. She sought me out but promised that she would say nothing to Jamie, which was what I wanted, but she introduced me to my grandson and that put the icing on the cake for me that day," said Miranda.

"If Liza was going to say nothing to Jamie, how are you here now?" asked a puzzled Grace.

"It dawned on Jamie who I was some days later. I believe that he suddenly caught sight of James and he was reminded of the lady who caught the flowers and put two and two together," said Miranda.

"I asked Liza to find out more and eventually she got my mother's address from Mr and Mrs Rogers and visited her and somehow she persuaded her to come and live with us. I'm very happy that she did, and so are all her grandsons," said Jamie pointedly.

"Are you also a relative Lucinda?" asked Grace.

Liza quickly butted in, "She is now; she is part of our family and we love her dearly." And this, of course, made Lucinda cry.

"I've told you before Lucinda, don't drink if it makes you cry and there's only one cure and that's to have another glass of wine," said Miranda much to the amusement of everyone around the table, including David.

Liza decided that she would go for a walk around the grounds after lunch and invited others to join her. "I'll see if the boys want to come with us," and she went to see them. They had several questions about their Uncle David and John commented that it seemed that Uncle David didn't like them.

"He may not be used to seeing so many boys at one time," said Liza.

"He should do as he's a vicar and must meet many children," said Matthew.

Grace joined them on their walk. Miranda and Lucinda made their way to the Dower House and the others carried on around the grounds.

"I notice that you wear a wedding ring Grace, but I sense that your husband is no longer with us," said Liza.

"You're right; he was killed right at the beginning of the war, just before Christmas in 1853. He was an army lieutenant and we were married eighteen years when he died," said Grace. "We had a very happy marriage Liza; our only regret was that our two children didn't survive and especially now that he is not with me; they would have been a great comfort to me."

"I'm sorry Grace," said Liza. "Sometimes life just isn't fair. I suppose you look after your father now that your mother has gone."

"I moved back with them soon after Geoff died. My mother was unwell for quite some years before she died, and my father and I looked after her together. I only learned the other day that my mother was engaged to Jamie's father and that she left him at the church. It must have been very embarrassing for him and I can now understand why there has been such a rift in the family," said Grace.

"From what I am told about Jamie's father I don't think that embarrassment came into it; he was more upset that he was losing out on your mother's dowry and his father felt the same. I think your mother had a lucky escape; unfortunately Miranda was not so lucky. She had a very unhappy time with him," said Liza.

"Mr and Mrs Rogers told us how they had kept in touch with her and somehow she managed to follow what Jamie was doing throughout most of his life. She and Lucinda seem very happy; it's good that life has turned out so well for them now," said Grace.

"Yes, and the boys love them, although they are prone to playing jokes on them; nothing too harmful, and I believe that both Miranda and Lucinda look forward to pitting their wits against them," smiled Liza.

"You've had your share of difficult times, so I understand," said Grace.

"Yes, life hasn't always been easy, but Jamie and I are very happy and very settled together, and the boys love being 'brothers', they look out for one another and their greatest pleasure is that they sleep in the same room. They could each have a bedroom, but they refuse and are more contented in one big room. Their friend Si will be coming to live with us next year and they already have his bed in place," said Liza.

"Who's Si?" asked Grace.

"He's the son of my next-door neighbour and the lawyer in the town where I used to live in America. He and Matthew grew up together and when John came to me, they became a gang of three. He's coming to live with us so that he can finish his education here along with our boys," said Liza.

"They'll be quite a handful; I wish you well with that," laughed Grace.

"I'm sure we'll cope; they virtually look after themselves anyway," said Liza. "How long do you think you would like to stay Grace?"

"I have no commitments, but Father may want to return soon, although he really has nothing to go back for. There's a young clergyman in the parish now and Father just takes services on occasion, but he won't leave Mother. He sits in the churchyard and talks to her often; they had a true love match. He's become more questioning of his faith since she died; he really would have liked to have gone with her. I think that if I hadn't been around him, he would have starved to death. Jamie's letter gave him something to think about and I know that he was anxious to show me where he grew up and where he met Mother," said Grace.

"We're not anxious for you to leave; you are family and that's very importantto us," said Liza.

"You really mean that, don't you," said Grace, "Even though my father has treated you the way he has. I know you are well aware that he seems to want to make life difficult for you and your boys."

"He may want to, but he won't succeed in upsetting me or the boys. If he succeeds in upsetting Jamie on our behalf, well, that's another matter and will be between him and his nephew. I know Jamie will not allow anyone to hurt us, no matter who they are," said Liza. "Let's hope that we'll all come to a happy understanding."

The boys decided that they would like to visit their grandmother for a while and Liza nodded her consent. "I know they are hoping for cake and lemonade there. Both Miranda and Lucinda always have something in readiness for them. It amazes both Jamie and I just how much they are capable of eating. They'll be back shortly and go straight down to the kitchen to see what they are having for their supper."

"Don't you organise their meals?" asked Grace.

"Of course I know what they are having over the course of a week, but I keep quiet about it and they believe that Mrs Lambert dreams up their various meals. They eat what they are given and the only detrimental comments that I have heard are that they prefer one meal to another. It teaches them not to be fussy over food and they understand that they are lucky as many children have very little to eat," said Liza.

"I believe you have something to do with a children's charity; Mr and Mrs Rogers were not very forthcoming over that," said Grace.

"Yes, well we try to help in whatever way we can," said Liza and Grace decided not to question her further.

They made their way back to the house and Grace said that she should unpack hers and her father's belongings, but Liza told her that it would have already been done for them.

"I'm not used to being waited on," smiled Grace.

"You should make the most of it whilst you are here," smiled Liza.

***

Jamie invited David to join him in the library whilst Liza was showing Grace around the grounds.

"Firstly, Uncle I would like to reiterate that I am delighted to have found yet another long lost relative, in fact two of you. Cousin Grace seems an extremely pleasant lady and appears to enjoy the company of my wife and sons, unfortunately you do not seem to have the same kind feelings towards them," said Jamie. "Do you have a particular reason for your dislike?"

"Liza is not easy to dislike," said David quietly. "Your son is the next Lord Edgeworth; you have no other sons. What happens if your son dies, God forbid, would one of the other two feel that they should take his place? There are no other male offspring yet. Even my daughter's two boys died shortly after their birth. Which one of your wives would inherit the title? That is assuming I do not outlive your son. In my world Jamie, it would have to be your first wife and her closest male relative would become the next Lord Edgeworth."

Jamie stared at his uncle in horror. "Why would you think that Evelyn's family would inherit the title? In the eyes of the law I am married to Liza, and she would inherit from me and her son, Matthew, would therefore be next in line."

"The Church and the State are very close, and it could take years for the case to be heard and cost thousands to prove. Why did Evelyn divorce you, was it because of Liza?" asked David.

"I hardly know you Uncle, and I'm not prepared to lay bare my private life until I know you better, if then. I will just say that I allowed Evelyn to divorce me to save her reputation and that was before Liza was here and before her last husband was killed. However, I will just add that I have loved Liza since I first saw her when she was just seventeen years old, and my love for her has never wavered. So in answer to your question, in a way Liza was the reason for my divorce. Evelyn always knew of my love for her which naturally soured our marriage and made her do some very silly things," said Jamie.

"I see. Thank you for telling me that; I am sure there is much more that eventually I shall become privy to, but for now I will give you both the benefit of the doubt and just hope that there are no ulterior motives behind why Liza married you," said David.

Jamie drew in a deep breath. "I hope you are not inferring that Liza would marry me for my money or that she was trying to do away with us for the sake of her son. If you are then it is an insult that I would find difficult to forgive. Let me make just a few facts clear to you, and they are facts that Liza would not brag about, but I will break what she would deem a confidence on this one occasion. Liza is richer than you, I, or anyone else that I know. She is possibly on a level with Lord Carlton, the Duke of Berkshire and possibly even the Queen as far as finances are concerned. She works hard for both her companies and has improved their trade with her business acumen. My recent good fortune was through her investment in my lands and the improvements to my homes, both here and in Belfast, are totally down to her. Her two boys will not even inherit the company that her first husband left her as she feels that it is not their entitlement, which is why she set up her second company for them to inherit."

It was obvious to David that he had crossed the line with Jamie and that he had not done his homework as far as Liza was concerned.

"I am suitably reprimanded, and I apologise for any offence I may have given. However, I am still concerned at the legitimacy of your marriage and just who will inherit in the unlikely event of young James' untimely demise," said David.

"You have given me much to consider but I have immediately thought of a solution as I will not allow Evelyn or any of her family to get their hands on the Edgeworth title or estate; she is not suitable and would never handle the responsibility correctly and she most certainly does not deserve it. I will just say one more thing Uncle; I will not tolerate any unpleasantness aimed towards my Liza or any of my sons, be it from family or friends. I trust that I make myself clear," said Jamie adamantly.

"Perfectly Jamie but I hope that you understand why I have been concerned," said David and then he smiled. "Surely you didn't marry Liza for her money." He then laughed and Jamie joined him in that.

"No Uncle, I didn't marry Liza for her money; in fact I signed a document relinquishing all rights to anything that she has both now and in the future. I have become quite self-sufficient in recent years and need nothing else," said Jamie.

"That's good to hear; you are very unlike your father and grandfather," said David.

"I was heading down that road but when I saw the state that my father had left this family in through his gambling habits I pulled back into the real world and had to make some sacrifices to get this place back into profitability. Unfortunately it was to the detriment of the Irish lands but that was when Liza was buying and renting property through her company in Ireland. We negotiated a deal and now my Irish lands are rented to her and I have a share of the profits," said Jamie.

"That must have been organised some time ago," said David.

"Yes, I believe that was nearly seven years ago," said Jamie.

"That was also before her previous husband died. What are her companies called, I may have heard of them," said David.

"She's a large shareholding partner in the shipping company Marchant & Fuller and she completely owns Bradley & Company. I would think that it would be difficult for you not to have heard of at least one of them if not both," said Jamie.

David started laughing again, "and I thought she could be after your money and title." He carried on laughing for a while. "You say that you have known and loved her since she was very young. Why didn't you marry before?"

"She was married to James Marchant then; she was very young when she was married to him," said Jamie.

"Of course, I remember when he died; it was at sea wasn't it? She must have still been very young then. Why didn't you pursue her then?"

"I did, and I made the biggest mistake of my life. I insulted her with a particularly unseemly suggestion, and she would have nothing to do with me for some time. You must have heard how she was missing for two years. We were told that she was dead and I went to pieces; I felt that life was not worth living which was when Evelyn came to the fore and we made a bargain, I wanted an heir and she wanted a title. When Liza was eventually found she made her life in America as she felt she would not be accepted back in her home. I'm afraid that Evelyn did something very foolish against her, and it was not the first time that she had attempted to take her identity, but I will say no more on that subject."

"So, you were already married when Liza was free. You should never marry someone as second choice and to me it would appear that you married Evelyn on the rebound. That was not the basis for a good marriage. Did Evelyn know how you felt?" asked David.

"Unfortunately she did and her hatred of Liza has often known no bounds; even though she found comfort in many a man's arms she schemed against both me and Liza, even when Liza was still in America and happily married to Patrick, but he died in her arms over five years ago. He was a lieutenant in the American Army and was killed by someone with a grudge. It took Liza a very long while to get over his loss and sometimes I wonder whether she really has," said Jamie.

"It is difficult for anyone to get over such a loss Jamie. It must have been very traumatic for her and there will always be a memory which will come to the fore when someone makes an innocent comment, and I'm afraid that is something that you will have to live with. I have seen the way she looks at you, which I now believe to be genuine, and I have certainly seen the way you look at her. You will both work your way through any sad memories together, but I am still concerned about your marriage," said David.

"Liza is accepted in all social classes as my wife and is indeed Lady Edgeworth, so I would suggest that you let me worry about the legitimacy of our marriage and you just enjoy renewing your acquaintance with the house and the people of the town," said Jamie.

Chapter 7

Jamie found Liza in with the boys who had twisted their grandmother and Lucinda around their little fingers and eaten some very messy cakes, the result of which was their shirts covered in diverse colours of icing. She was telling them that they were worse than when they were eating ice cream in Italy.

April was trying to make them wash their faces and finding clean shirts for them. Jamie stood in the doorway and smiled at his family in amusement. "Liza, I need to see you for a minute," he said as she looked up and could see that he was serious even though he was smiling.

She followed him into his bedroom and sat on his bed waiting for him to tell her what was on his mind.

"You obviously have something serious on your mind; was it something your uncle has said?" asked Liza.

"Yes, it is Liza and the outcome is that I would like to adopt your boys. I'll explain why it is so important," said Jamie.

Liza was sitting staring at him with a slightly open mouth, but she let him carry on without comment and he told her of his conversation with his uncle and the worries that he had over the heritage of the Edgeworth title whereby Evelyn's nearest male relative could become Lord Edgeworth should James die young and childless.

"I would want your boys to inherit that title Liza, firstly Matthew as he is your natural son and should he have no children then young John should become Lord Edgeworth as he is your nephew by marriage, and the only way that could be is by them officially being my sons," said Jamie.

"I know that neither of them were Patrick's sons, but they always thought of themselves as such and I feel that by doing what you are suggesting is wiping Patrick finally off the face of the earth and taking my boys' identity away from them. I understand your reasoning, but I would like to think about it and eventually discuss it with both Matthew and John. They are both intelligent enough to appreciate the honour that you want to give to them, but we have all been happy with the way things are. You must also consider young James' feelings on the subject; he is your natural son and should also be consulted," said Liza.

"Of course they should be consulted, but would you be happy with them having the Edgeworth name?" said Jamie.

"I'm very proud to have your name Jamie and I'm sure that both Matthew and John would be if they choose to officially become your sons. I can understand your reasoning and I certainly don't think that Evelyn should have any influence over your estate; she would only handle it with vindictiveness and possibly so would any male heirs that she may have. Does she have any brothers, or cousins?" said Liza.

"I have no idea of her family background; I knew her parents and I don't think she had any brothers, but I seem to recollect a couple of cousins at our wedding. Of course her daughter could have children by that time, and they could be boys, so I feel that I must do everything I can to keep the estate within our family and this is one way of doing it. But the more I think about it, the more I like the idea of having two more sons with my name regardless of the reason why," said Jamie.

"I believe that when they have had time to think about it, they will be as proud as I am to carry your name and the responsibilities that go with it. It's just a little sudden and they should be given time to talk about it together," said Liza. "I hope you're not disappointed that I haven't jumped at the chance for the boys, but it is a major decision for you and for them."

"No, I'm not disappointed, I would expect you to be cautious for everyone including me," smiled Jamie.

"When do you think we should broach the subject to them? I suppose you would like to set this in motion sooner rather than later," said Liza.

"I don't think that today is the right time, perhaps when we have slept on it and thought of all the answers that we must be prepared to give to their questions, as I know that there will be many of those," said Jamie.

"So sometime tomorrow or perhaps Monday, because I believe they have in mind to visit Derek after church tomorrow. Then I think that cricket practice is high up on their itinerary after being allowed to join us for Sunday lunch," said Liza.

"Perhaps it would be a good idea when they are ready for bed tomorrow. I know that it is a time when they talk amongst themselves and sort out many of their perceived problems and then they will have all their questions ready by the next morning," said Jamie.

"As you say, we will also have time to think about it. I like being an Edgeworth and I'm sure that the boys will also, but I really don't want them to forget Patrick and what he did for them. He helped me bring them up at a very crucial time in their lives and sadly they saw him die, which has obviously left a mark on them. I know that you love them as you do James and I think you have to be prepared for some awkward questions," said Liza.

"They already think of themselves as brothers; it's just one step further for them but it's not such a big step for me," said Jamie.

"Before we suggest this step to the boys, there are one or two things that you should know, and they are difficult for me to tell you," said Liza.

"Liza there is nothing that I need to know; both your boys are well balanced, affectionate and are definitely a credit to the way you and Patrick brought them up. Since being with us they've brought fun and laughter to the house and James loves them just like brothers and I love them dearly," said Jamie.

Liza was quiet for a while and then said, "It's about John's parentage because you will be taking on someone with a difficult background."

"I have always believed that he was your first abused child which set you on the road to setting up the charity. I'm right, aren't I?"

"Yes, you're right, but I realised that you knew that. You need to know that his father and grandfather were one and the same and please believe me when I say that it was through no fault of Sally. She was not protected when she was a child and she ended up pregnant. Michael met her and they married but she dare not tell him about her son, so she arranged a child minder and you know the rest as far as John is concerned," said Liza.

Jamie was frowning and Liza thought that he may want to change his mind, and she also worried that he may look differently on John, however she felt that she had no option but to tell him who John's father was before he gave him the Edgeworth name and all that went with it.

Finally Jamie said, "It makes no difference; I always knew that there were reasons why you had never told me of John's background. You and Patrick did a really good job with him; he must have been quite a challenge to you both. He's a lovely boy Liza and he has both feet firmly on the ground, but I have a feeling that there is something that you are not telling me."

"No, Jamie, that's all that I know about John and I'm pleased that you still want him because he will be very honoured to have a proper surname and especially the Edgeworth name," said Liza.

"No doubt you will tell me the rest of the story at some time in the future, because I know that you are holding something back," said Jamie.

"I promise you it was nothing to do with John, it was more to do with Patrick's stepfather and something that I would prefer not to remember," said Liza as a shiver went up her spine.

Jamie put his arm around her shoulder and said, "you don't have to tell me anything more, but you know that when you are ready there is nothing that I can't help you with."

"Thank you, Jamie," said Liza and she changed the subject. "Your uncle has certainly given you food for thought; I wonder if he will approve of your solution to the problem. I know he doesn't approve of me, so why should he approve of my boys?"

"He does like you and the boys; he's just concerned about the legitimacy of our marriage and the future of the Edgeworth heritage. I find it strange that he is so worried about it as he has been away for so long and has no claim on it," said Jamie.

"Don't forget that he felt it important to reclaim the Edgeworth diamonds, so the Edgeworths do mean a great deal to him and the future of the family seems uppermost in his mind," said Liza.

"I still wonder where he got the money to redeem them; I wonder if his wife finally got her dowry. What was her name?" asked Jamie.

"I would have thought you would have known that Jamie," said Liza.

"I didn't think to ask," said Jamie.

***

Dinner that evening was much more relaxed than anyone had thought it would be. David was now showing a great interest in the whole family, but particularly in Liza and the boys. Grace seemed delighted with the change in the atmosphere.

Miranda and Lucinda asked him endless questions and finally they discovered his wife's name and it was Holly.

"That's a lovely name," said Liza. "Was there any significance behind it?"

"Yes, she was born on Christmas Eve and her mother insisted that it was appropriate, although I believe that her father was not quite so convinced. I am told that her refusal to marry my brother was blamed by her father on her 'un-Godly' name, as he called it," said David.

"Is it an un-Godly name? It doesn't seem so to me," said Lucinda. "I think it's very pretty and it probably suited her well."

"It did," said Grace. "Even when she was very ill she remained very pretty."

"Well," said Jamie "you obviously take after her Grace."

Everyone smiled indulgently at Jamie and Grace.

"I'll be going to church tomorrow; I believe the service is at ten o'clock. Will anyone be coming with me?" said David.

"We all will be David," said Liza and David looked surprised. "The boys will meet with some of their friends afterwards for a short while. Then it's lunch followed by cricket practice. Let's hope that the weather holds."

"You are Roman Catholic aren't you, Liza?" said David with a frown.

"There is no secret to the fact that I was in a place where the only religion was a form of paganism and when I came out of that nightmare I found myself in a town whose only church was a nondenominational one and my theory was that it was better to follow some Christian religion than no religion at all, and I carry that through to today. I would therefore say that I am neither Roman Catholic nor Church of England or any other religion. I am my own person and my religion is 'do unto others as you would have them do unto you', and 'love thy neighbour'," said Liza without sounding as if it was an excuse not to follow her original beliefs.

David looked at her and said, "Well said Liza, I wish there were more people like you. My life would have been much easier."

Jamie was smiling at her proudly; she had stood up to David's test on religion and seemed to have passed with flying colours. Miranda and Lucinda were also smiling and they each wondered if they would have been able to stand up to David on this test of religious beliefs. Now, if they were asked, they only had to say that they thought the same as Liza.

Grace was annoyed at her father and felt that he should not have questioned Liza's beliefs at the dinner table, or anywhere else for that matter.

"And your boys Liza," said David, "Have they been baptised?"

"Of course they have," said Jamie tetchily.

"Father," said Grace. "Do you think that your childhood home has changed much?"

David frowned and then realised from the look on his daughter's face that the subject most definitely should be changed.

"Yes, it has changed Grace, and for the better. It was rather dull and intimidating in my day; it feels much happier now and my room is very warm and inviting. Thank you, Jamie, for making our stay so comfortable," said David.

"There's no point in thanking me Uncle," said Jamie. "I believe you are well aware that Liza has made this house into a home."

Once again Jamie was regretting contacting his uncle. He was already heartily fed up with his uncle's unnecessary remarks against Liza and her boys and he had only been with them less than a day.

Miranda and Lucinda were looking embarrassed and Liza just stared ahead but Grace was showing how annoyed she was with her father. She had been looking forward to meeting her cousin and his family and seeing her father's childhood home and he was making it impossible for them to stay for any length of time. The thought of returning to Truro so soon did not please her and they really were not altogether welcome there as her father had virtually retired from his parish and it was only by the goodness of the current vicar that they had rooms in the vicarage. She had hoped that there would be a place for them somewhere in the village here in Surrey, but her father was making that a hopeless dream.

"Tomorrow, after the service, the boys will be spending a little while with their friend, Derek," said Liza desperately attempting to move onto another subject. "And then after Sunday lunch they are hoping to get some cricket practice in. I know the people from the village will also be practicing on the new cricket green. Jamie and I will be going then; perhaps you would like to join us."

"Yes, we will," said Miranda.

"I'd like to join you also if I may," said Grace ignoring her father.

After dinner David decided that he would like an early night much to everyone's relief.

Grace came and sat with Liza, "I'm sorry Liza. I don't know why my father is being so difficult. I had thought that he would enjoy his time here as he seemed so pleased when he received Jamie's letter. I was surprised when he decided to visit before you had returned from Belfast, but understood that he wanted to find out whether he would be truly welcome and he did say that it would be better to speak to people who knew you both first just in case you were really unapproachable."

"Please don't worry Grace; I'm sure he's just finding it difficult adjusting to being back in his old home," said Liza.

"You're very kind Liza, but I have never known my father to be so disagreeable," said Grace.

"I'm sure he has his reasons but let's not worry about it," said Liza. "Do you think you will enjoy watching the cricket tomorrow?"

They all discussed the events of the following day until Lucinda said that she was tired, and Jamie took a lantern and showed the ladies to the Dower House.

Grace went to her room and Liza checked on the boys and then made her way to her bedroom where April was waiting for her. She heard Jamie go into his room and Roberts followed him in. Liza knew it would be at least half an hour before Roberts would leave and so she lay on her bed and waited.

Liza got up when she heard Roberts wish Jamie a good night and as she crossed the hall Jamie's door opened and she smiled up at him, "Am I that predictable?" she asked.

"At this time of night, yes you are," said Jamie. "It's been a very long day for us, hasn't it? I am getting heartily fed up with my unpleasant uncle. I had thought that we had come to an understanding this afternoon, but he seems to have reverted to his dislike of you. I told him earlier that I would not tolerate anyone hurting you or the boys whether it's family or friends, so I am going to ask him to leave tomorrow."

"That's a shame. Your cousin Grace is very nice, and she says that she can't understand why her father is acting awkwardly as it is not normally in his nature. He must have his reasons," said Liza as she climbed into Jamie's bed and made herself comfortable.

"I have a few thoughts on why, and I dare say you have also," said Jamie, "but I'm not going to let it bother me tonight, I have better things to think about and do."

***

The Reverend Collins gave a good sermon the next morning and part of it was to welcome the Reverend Edgeworth back to his place of birth and to his family and he trusted that he would be with them a long while. *Not if I have anything to do with it,* thought Jamie.

After the service Bernard asked Liza and Jamie if they'd had a good trip to Belfast and the boys were chatting to Derek and the other children of the village. David was watching them intently. Suddenly John ran off and a short while later he was back with Derek's wheelchair and Derek climbed in and all the boys went off towards the cricket green bouncing him across the uneven ground, running and laughing.

"I gather that the young boy in the wheelchair is the one that John takes the runs for in cricket," said David to Jamie and Liza who were still talking to Bernard.

Jamie nodded and Liza said, "They are great friends. Derek comes to the house and has lessons with the boys; he's very bright, in fact he helped Bernard find you in the church records."

"He seems a very happy boy despite his disability and your boys are kind to him," said David.

"They're not kind David," said Liza. "They just accept him as he is, and they adapt to his needs. They don't think of him as disabled; they just know that he is limited in what he can do, and they allow for that. They also don't give him any quarter in what they know he is capable of doing. You'll see that this afternoon if you come to the cricket practice."

"I'll be there," said Bernard. "I think there's going to be quite a turnout now that you're back. Everyone seems to have been waiting for your return and I know the whole village are looking forward to April and Adam's wedding."

"I think they are going to be surprised at the number of people turning up for their marriage. I think I'll have to double on what they thought they would have for their reception," said Liza.

"Who are April and Adam?" asked David.

"You've already met Adam," said Jamie. "He teaches our boys and Derek. April looks after them and also my wife. She's been with us for years."

"You're organising their wedding reception then?" said David.

"No, they're doing all that themselves, but I don't think that they realise just how many people will be coming to see them married, so I'll just make sure that we have enough for everyone," said Liza.

Jamie was now looking for the boys and they suddenly appeared bumping Derek along in his wheelchair; they drew to a halt and Liza went over to them and asked Derek how he was getting on and how well he had done in helping to find their Uncle David. He got out of his wheelchair and Matthew handed him his walking sticks and he proudly showed Liza how well he was now managing to walk. She congratulated him on his achievement and said that she would see him again later at the cricket practice.

Liza and Jamie decided to walk back with the boys, whilst the others were going to return by carriage. Miranda and Lucinda smiled indulgently as they watched the boys running along and talking to Liza and Jamie loudly and excitedly about what they would be doing that afternoon.

The boys called out as the carriage passed them and everyone but David waved and called back to them and David said, "Those boys are unruly and out of control, especially those two of Liza's. They need some discipline and should be taught some manners."

"Father," exclaimed Grace, "All of those boys are perfectly well behaved; you know you have no reason to think otherwise."

Miranda and Lucinda were incensed by David's comments.

"You are talking about my grandsons David and they have never treated you with anything other than respect. Their behaviour has always been a credit to their parents, and I believe that it is about time you stopped trying to make trouble in this family," said Miranda.

Lucinda was nodding her agreement.

"Only one is your grandson, Miranda; the other two are nothing to you and you should not treat them in the same way," said David.

Once again Grace exclaimed, "Father."

"They are all my grandsons; I love and admire them all equally and I think it best that we stop this conversation now before something is said that we both regret," said Miranda and the rest of the journey was in silence.

The carriage stopped at the Dower House and David attempted to help both Miranda and Lucinda down.

"No thank you," said Lucinda, "we are quite capable of getting ourselves out of the carriage. We'll see you at lunch Grace."

Back in the carriage Grace turned on her father, "How could you say such things. Why are you doing this? Why are you trying to alienate everyone in your own family? They have done nothing to hurt you; if anyone hurt this family it was you and Mother."

"Don't you dare criticise your Mother. She didn't want Jamie's father; she was being forced into a loveless marriage and she wanted a better life than that. You certainly can't blame her for that," said David.

By that time they had reached the house and both went up to their rooms to freshen up before lunch. Grace was seething but she hoped that her father would be in a better frame of mind during lunch. She now had no doubt that they would be leaving shortly to go back to Truro, and it was not a prospect that she was looking forward to. She had only been here a day but she felt very much at home. The whole family had made her feel welcome and her father had thrown that kindness back in their faces. All she could see in her future now was living in rooms and looking after her father until he died and then she would be alone. Here she had family that she previously knew nothing about, and she liked them, and they seemed to like her. She really could not understand her father's attitude, it was so unlike him. He had always been kind, gentle and considerate of others.

Sunday lunch was meant to be a happy family affair but immediately Liza and Jamie noticed an atmosphere between Miranda and David, and possibly Lucinda also. Grace was also very quiet, but the boys appeared not to notice the tension around the table, although Liza doubted that they were insensitive of it, but they carried on as if nothing was untoward, however they only answered when spoken to. They said that they were looking forward to the cricket practice that afternoon and John was saying that Derek had again asked him to take his runs for him.

As John was talking David butted in, "You should keep those boys quiet during mealtimes, especially that one, Liza," and he indicated towards John.

Liza turned and snapped at him, "I do not need to be told how to bring up my sons in my own home. It is none of your business, so kindly keep your nose out of our affairs."

Her eyes flashed the most vivid of greens and David recoiled at their intensity. Jamie turned to his uncle and said, "In my study, now Uncle."

"I haven't finished my lunch yet Jamie," said David.

"You have now," said Jamie. "I said, in my study." He stood and waited for David to follow suit, which he did.

The boys looked upset and Liza moved over to them and said that perhaps they would like to go down to the kitchen to see what lovely sweets Mrs Lambert had for dessert.

"I'll take them down Liza," said Lucinda. "I think you are needed here."

Miranda had gone to Grace who was quietly shedding a tear and trying to apologise for her father.

"It's because he can't leave your mother isn't it?" said Liza.

Grace looked up and said, "I hadn't thought of that. Good heavens, you're probably right."

They could hear Jamie's voice raised and part of what he was saying was that he wanted his uncle to leave as soon as was practical.

"I'll see what I can do to ease the situation, although Jamie will not be pleased that I am butting in," said Liza and she drew a deep breath and made her way towards Jamie's study. She tapped gently on the door and entered.

Jamie looked up and did not appear pleased to see her. "I'm sorry to interrupt you but I felt that I would like to make one or two comments before your uncle leaves if I may," she said.

"Of course you may Liza; this unpleasantness has affected you very much," said Jamie gently.

"First of all I want to assure you how happy I am with you Jamie and I want your uncle to realise that there is nothing that we cannot tell each other. You know that there have been times in my life when I have been so very unhappy and one of those times was when I had to leave Patrick and my daughter in the graveyard in Benson. It was the hardest thing that I have ever had to do, and even now the thought of them lying there without my being able to visit them pulls at my heart strings," said Liza.

David was watching her closely and Jamie was gently reassuring her that he knew that she had realised what his uncle's problem appeared to be.

Liza carried on, "If I could have brought them back with me, it would have helped me through one of the worst times of my life and even now I would feel the comfort of having them near, but it was too far to be practical and I know that the people of Benson look after them for me."

Jamie smiled at her, "You're not upsetting me Liza, I know how you feel and of course we both felt that there were reasons why my uncle wished to stay aloof from us."

"You are both very astute," said David quietly. "I did not realise that you had lost a child Liza."

Liza looked at him and tried to make up her mind whether to tell him more and decided that she would carry on.

"I buried my first husband, my son and stepson in Belfast and I am lucky because I can visit them on a regular basis and when I do I sit for a while and quite often talk to them. Others may think that I am crazy doing that, but I believe that you know that it helps because nobody should be forgotten, even when you have made a new and happy life for yourself and your children. My boys talk to Patrick, especially on the anniversary of his death, but you've seen them, and you must admit that they are very happy and well balanced."

"You have not had an easy life, Liza. I'm sorry I added to it," said David.

"I haven't told you this to gain sympathy. Both Jamie and I want you to know that we understand that you would find it difficult to leave Holly, if that has been your reason for attempting to upset us. I'm sure that Grace wishes to start a new life, but she will not do that without you. I can sense that she would like to start that new life here with those she now considers family," said Liza.

"We would not impose on your hospitality; we would find our own accommodation in the village, but you are right, I can't leave my Holly, I just can't do it. If Grace would like to live here then I will encourage her to do so and assure her that I will do perfectly well on my own," said David.

"She won't leave you," said Jamie. "We do not know her very well, but we know her enough to realise that she will never leave you. You have been a comfort to one another and that will continue. One of you will have to make a sacrifice and at this moment it would appear that it will be Grace."

"Can you not bring Holly with you?" asked Liza and both David and Jamie seemed shocked at the suggestion.

"Surely that's not possible," said Jamie.

"I can't dig her up, that would be disrespectful," said David.

"It would not be disrespectful if it is handled correctly," said Liza. "She is an Edgeworth and should be laid to rest here, as should you when your time comes."

"With all due respect to you both; even if what you are suggesting is possible, I would not have my Holly resting in the Edgeworth mausoleum; it would not be right to have her in the same place as your father, Jamie," said David.

"No, but there would be room for you both nearby," said Jamie. "You seem to be giving the suggestion some consideration."

"It would be too costly, no it's best to leave things as they are," said David.

"If it could be organised to your satisfaction, would you consider moving here to be with your only family?" asked Jamie. "Also I would need your assurance that you would no longer try to belittle either Liza or any of our boys."

"It would do Grace a great deal of good to start afresh here. I don't know whether she would approve of moving her mother and we really don't have the money to do so," said David.

"Please don't worry about the cost; I can undertake that," said Liza.

"I can't let you do that, Holly is my responsibility," said David.

"Please stop arguing; if you would like her moved so that you could visit her then I will do that for you. When my time comes I will probably be the richest person in the graveyard and there is absolutely no point to that, so I might as well put some of my money to good use and there could not be a better use for it," said Liza.

"I must talk to Grace, but I believe she will feel unsettled at the prospect of her mother being disinterred," said David.

"I understand that Grace's husband was killed a few years ago. I am sure that if she could discover exactly where his body had been placed, she would want him disinterred and brought back and placed where she could watch over him, said Liza.

"You are right Liza," said David. "It has been a very difficult time for Grace as it took a long while for her to accept that he was dead because she could not lay him to rest. There was only one thing worse than his passing and that was not being able to bury him. I must apologise to you both, and to the whole family, but I realised when I arrived that I did not want you to like me. I wanted to go away with the knowledge that I was not welcome here and I strived to make that a fact."

"Both Liza and I could see that Grace was amazed at the way you were acting and we believed that there had to be some strange reason for it, but I meant what I said Uncle; I will not tolerate anyone creating distress for my wife or my sons, or anyone else in my family," said Jamie.

"I understand completely. I must now go and talk to my daughter; she must be so annoyed with me," said David.

"I believe that she knows and understands a great deal more than you think," said Liza.

He left the study to find Grace who had gone to her room. Jamie and Liza were thoughtful for a short while and Jamie smiled and said, "Where are we going to house my troublesome uncle? I suppose we have enough room in the house. Our family are certainly increasing at an alarming rate." He smiled with resignation.

121

"He may decide against moving here and more to the point, moving Holly to the churchyard. Grace may be appalled by the thought of digging up her mother and moving her," said Liza.

"I think that Grace would be more amenable to bringing her mother here. I wonder if we could make the gatehouse more habitable for them. It hasn't been lived in for some years but it's not falling down," said Jamie.

"I've never studied it too closely; all I've done is made sure it looks presentable and that the gardens look neat and tidy. How many rooms does it have Jamie?" asked Liza.

"I hate to admit that I really don't know; I've never been inside. I'm trying to remember the last people who lived there. I wonder why we stopped using gatekeepers," said Jamie.

"It's probably because you don't close your gates into the property," smiled Liza.

"It's more likely because my father ran out of money to pay the wages," said Jamie.

"Has it really been that long since the house was lived in? I suppose it's not much longer than when the Dower House was previously used," said Liza.

"I don't think that it was as well-furnished as the Dower House; you have to remember that it was very much a working man's home," said Jamie.

"We could look at it on our way to the cricket practice later this afternoon," smiled Liza.

"Liza, we don't know whether they would want to live there yet," said Jamie.

"Well, we should know the dimensions of what we would be offering them should they want it. It may be totally unsuitable. I'm not saying that we have to stay there for very long, but it would be good to know how many bedrooms it has and what the living facilities are like. Really what I am saying is we ought to take a very brief look to see if it could be made habitable, which it should be regardless of whether your uncle and Grace would want it," said Liza.

They found the boys sitting quietly in the drawing room with Lucinda and Miranda and Liza asked them if they had enjoyed their dessert and they had.

"You should get ready for your cricket practice," Jamie said to the boys. "Are you going Mother?"

"Yes, Lucinda and I would like to catch up with some of the people from the village," said Miranda.

"Liza and I have a few items to sort out before we join you, so we'd be pleased if you could go with the boys," said Jamie. "Off you go boys; we'll see you down at the pitch shortly."

The boys disappeared up to their room to change for the afternoon's event.

"Have you sorted everything out with David?" asked Miranda.

"As much as we can for the moment, but only David can really sort out what he wants," said Liza.

A short while later the boys quietly came down the stairs in their cricket outfits, carrying their bats and they went off for the afternoon with Miranda and Lucinda and shortly afterwards Adam and April made their way towards the cricket green.

"I don't think I have ever known the boys act so quietly," said Jamie. "It seems that my uncle has had a good effect on them."

"You wouldn't want to see them like that too often, would you?" said Liza.

They presumed that David was making his peace with Grace and they would hear the outcome later. They walked down the drive towards the gatehouse and Jamie had to push heavily on the door as it had not been opened in years. The outside looked in good order, but the inside was in great need of renovation. There were three rooms downstairs, one could be a dining room and another could be used as a sitting room. The third room was off the dining room and would make an adequate kitchen. There were two relatively large bedrooms on the first floor and one small room which could be used as a washroom. All the furniture had to be thrown away as it was all damaged and useless.

When they had looked around Liza stood in the dining room and Jamie asked her what she thought. "It's very similar to my house in Benson, but I believe it is slightly bigger. If you can see past the state that it is in, it is big enough for David and Grace; I doubt that it's bigger than the vicarage they had in Truro. They could always live with us as you said earlier, but I think that they really want to be independent and much as this is on your land, I'm sure that they would feel that they are not taking advantage. I have a feeling that he will want to pay rent, so you will have to handle that as you see fit."

Jamie asked Liza if she thought that David would agree to bring Holly to the local churchyard. "I know that he won't leave her behind. I don't suppose he would want to watch her disinterment, but a good undertaker would handle it with care and Bernard would make sure that she is laid to rest with dignity."

They made their way to the cricket green and could hear the shouts of everyone there. It was Derek's turn as they arrived and once again Adam was ensuring that he stood upright when he batted and John was waiting to take the runs for him. As Jamie and Liza were cheering Derek on, David and Grace came up behind them and they were both fascinated by what was happening.

"That's wonderful," David muttered, and Grace was watching with great interest.

Liza turned and smiled, "I hope Adam doesn't get too bruised. He wouldn't look too good covered in cuts and bruises on his wedding day."

"Will you both have time to see us later," asked David.

"Of course we will Uncle. You both look a great deal better," said Jamie. "I'm glad you've come to enjoy the cricket."

Mr and Mrs Lambert and Mrs Frances arrived with baskets of food, although the villagers had brought their own but they always looked forward to the extra goodies that Edgeworth House provided. Liza went off with April and Estelle to help set out what had been brought and they could be seen laughing with the children who always gathered around to see what was on offer. Grace moved over and offered to help, and her offer was accepted.

Everyone stopped what they were doing as Derek had hit a massive shot and John was making numerous runs. Adam was picking himself up and helping Derek to his feet and they were laughing whilst brushing themselves down. Finally a cheer went up, but John was not run out and Derek and Adam positioned themselves ready for the next ball to be bowled. Derek swung his bat attempting to hit the ball, but he missed and it knocked the wicket and he was bowled out. Once again Adam and Derek picked themselves up and James ran over with Derek's walking sticks. Derek, Adam, John and James walked off to the cheers of everyone there.

"That young lad has a great deal of courage," said David to Jamie. "Was he born that way?"

"No, unfortunately he had an abusive father who used to beat his mother. He screamed too loudly when his father was hitting her and his father threw him onto an iron fire grid and damaged his spine and pelvis. He was three or four at the time and it's only relatively recently that he has managed to survive without being pushed around in a wheelchair. Although as you saw this morning, he uses it when the boys want to get him somewhere quickly," said Jamie.

"His father doesn't seem to be around now," said David.

"A week after Derek was hurt his father was drunk and fell off a cart breaking his neck. Many in the village say that it was poetic justice, but it was a pity that it didn't happen a week earlier," said Jamie.

"You have him learning with your boys; is there a special reason for that?" asked David.

"He's much brighter than others of his age and that's because for many years all he had for entertainment were books. He is very well read and, in many ways, too bright for the local school. The teacher there could not spend the time educating him separately, but Adam has the time and the inclination. Derek is going to eventually be a very useful member of our society," said Jamie.

"But what will he do Jamie? There is limited work in the village for academics and he may be too well educated to fit in," said David.

"I wouldn't worry about that too much Uncle," said Jamie. "I know Liza has something in mind for when the time comes."

"Of course she has, I should have known," said David. "She likes happy endings, doesn't she?"

"Yes, and she hasn't had too many of those," said Jamie quietly.

"She has one now Jamie," said David. "Although it's not an ending, it's really a beginning. She will never forget the past, but she loves the present and is looking forward to the future. You are very lucky Jamie and so are Liza and the boys. This is a very happy house, much happier than in my day. I'm sorry that I made a dark cloud hover over it."

"I think that the boys will be a little wary of you for a while, but I'm sure you will be able to win them over," smiled Jamie.

"Cricket is very important to the boys, and the village, isn't it?" said David. "Would anyone mind if I joined in?"

"I believe everyone would be delighted; why not see if you can borrow one of the boys' cricket bats," said Jamie and he called Matthew over to them and asked if David could borrow his bat. Matthew stared at Jamie for a minute and then nodded. He came back with his bat and handed it to David.

"Thank you, Matthew, I'll treat it with care," said David. "Do you think it's possible for me to bat next?"

"I'll go and arrange it for you," said Matthew as David took off his coat and rolled his sleeves up.

Mr Lambert and Mr Rogers were seen listening to Matthew and then in unison they all looked at David. Mr Rogers beckoned him over and after a short conversation David moved across to the wicket. Liza and Grace stopped what they were doing to watch.

"I hope he doesn't have to take too many runs," said Grace. "He's not getting any younger and it is a year or two since he played."

"I'm sure he'll do very well; however I'll give you some liniment to rub on his aching limbs," laughed Liza.

He did do well for his age and everyone cheered him on, including the boys, and when he was bowled out, he received loud applause and many pats on the back. He spent time talking to everyone and by the time that the practice matches were over he had become a very popular figure.

Liza and Jamie were standing together watching David talking to many of the villagers. "I wonder if they are asking him to join the cricket team?" said Jamie.

"I hope he doesn't," said Grace who had joined them. "He's not a young man, and that really is a much younger man's game."

"Yes, you're right, but I think he is going to become their number one supporter," smiled Liza.

"I believe that we would like to talk to you both later," said Grace.

"Of course, but we have an appointment with our boys first and that could take a little while," said Jamie. "We'll see you at supper time. My mother and Lucinda won't be with us this evening so we can talk openly then."

"After this afternoon's food offerings I cannot believe that you are suggesting supper," said Grace.

"That's true as far as we are concerned, but the boys will go back and straight down to the kitchen to see what Mrs Lambert has for them; I am always amazed at their capacity for food, but they never put weight on," said Jamie.

"They run it off; they're always active which keeps them healthy," said Liza. "We'll have a very light snack for supper which you don't have to eat if you don't want to."

They called the boys and they all walked back to the house, notably with David limping a little. Miranda and Lucinda had yet to forgive him, as had the boys although they were not quite as wary as they had been.

The boys went to their room to change from their cricket clothes and wash their hands and faces before going down to the kitchen for their supper. David went to his room and Liza found the liniment for Grace to rub on her father, much to Jamie's amusement. Liza went to the kitchen to arrange a light supper for later.

By the time Liza and Jamie had changed out of their day clothes, the boys had finished their supper and were making their way back to their room.

"I was wondering whether to talk to the boys in the drawing room rather than their room," said Jamie.

"They are very comfortable in their room; they sort out any problems they have in that room. It's where they go when they have been upset and if one is in trouble the others gather with him there. What we have to talk to them about is a matter that they will think about and discuss in that room. No matter where we talk to them, they'll retreat to that room to sort it all out together," said Liza.

"So we may as well talk to them there," said Jamie.

"Do you know what you are going to say?" asked Liza.

"No, I'm going to take a leaf out of your book and see what comes to me at the time," said Jamie and they gathered themselves together and made their way to see the boys.

They all looked up as they walked in. "You've got something to tell us, haven't you," said Matthew.

"Yes, Matthew," said Jamie. "You're as perceptive as always."

All three boys sat on one bed and Liza and Jamie pulled up chairs facing them.

"You know that you are all sons to me," said Jamie. "You have said that you became brothers when your mother and I were married."

They all nodded in unison, still looking wary.

"Well Matthew and John, I would like to officially adopt you and give you the Edgeworth name. I know that this is a big step for you, and I would like you both to think about it, and I would also like James to consider what it means to him. I will do nothing until I know what your reaction to this is, but I would also like to say that it is something I would very much like to happen. I already love you and consider you as my sons, but you have to be really happy with what I am suggesting, as does James," said Jamie.

"When you and our mother married you said that we didn't have to forget our Daddy, does it still mean that we can remember him whenever we want?" asked John.

"Of course you must remember him," said Jamie. "He was a very big part of your lives; he was also part of James' life. He loved you all very much and I certainly don't expect you not to still love him and talk about him whenever you want to."

"I believe it's a good idea," said Matthew. "I don't know what to call myself. I know that my real father was Matthew Bradley, although he had the Indian name White Wolf, and I know that he died before I was born. I was never known as Bradley; my birth certificate has the name Marchant on it but in Benson I was known as Matthew Kelly, although he wasn't really my daddy. He loved me as if he was though and now people see me as an Edgeworth and sometimes I'm called Matthew Edgeworth, so it would be nice to finally have just one name."

Liza and Jamie were staring at Matthew trying to digest what he had just said. "I didn't know that you were so confused Matthew," said Liza with dismay.

"I know who I am," said Matthew, "I'm your son Mum, and I'm me and at the moment I'm Dad's stepson and James' stepbrother, but I don't know who I am to John. It would be nice to know that he has become my real brother."

Once again Liza and Jamie stared at Matthew and wondered at his logic.

"I would like a proper name, but if having a proper name meant that I had to forget Daddy Patrick's love for me then I wouldn't want it. As you've said that I don't have to forget that, I think I would like to be an Edgeworth. I don't know who my father was; I know who my mother is, but she found that she couldn't love me. I don't know what her name was when she had me; I know that she is a Phelan now and of course I was known as Kelly, as Matthew was. I like the thought that both James and Matthew will be my real brothers," said John.

"Both you and Matthew make me very happy that you would like my name but does that mean that you are also happy with me as a father?" said Jamie.

"Of course they are Dad," said James. "They wouldn't want the Edgeworth name if they didn't want you and me also. They could take any of their other names if they didn't like you. I know you are concerned that I might not like having to share my title when you die, but I'm not worried about that; I already like having them as my brothers and I think it's good to make it official."

"Both your father and I thought that you might need time to consider it, but it seems that you all have already made up your minds and very quickly," said Liza. "James, you would still become Lord Edgeworth as you are the eldest.

Should you not eventually have children then one of the others would inherit the title or their sons if they aren't around, but that is a long, long way off."

"We'll leave you to talk amongst yourselves now and if you are still as happy about it tomorrow morning, I will see my lawyer and set the adoptions in motion. You've no idea how happy you all have made me feel," said Jamie.

"I would like to be adopted by Mum Liza," said James.

"To adopt someone like yourself James, firstly you have to have permission from both parents. I don't think I need to say any more," said Jamie.

"That's a pity," said James. "She'd never give her permission for that. I still have you Dad, and Mum has looked after me since I was a little boy. The other one's not my mother, you are Mum and perhaps one day you will be able to adopt me, but until then I'm happy that I now will have real brothers and that they are yours."

Liza and Jamie left them to sort their thoughts out and as they were making their way down the stairs, they heard shouts of "Hooray" and "Wonderful".

"Do you think that they already knew what we were thinking?" Jamie asked Liza.

"No but it's obvious that it is something that they all wanted; perhaps they had thought about it themselves. Would you really have to get Evelyn's permission as you have custody of James?"

"I would probably eventually win any case that Evelyn is bound to bring but I do not wish to fight over James. Anything that upsets us is bound to create upset for James and Matthew and John; we would not be able to keep such antagonism to ourselves. James is very happy as things are and especially now that he is going to have official brothers," said Jamie. "Perhaps once we get Matthew and John under my wing, I may be able to blackmail Evelyn should she object to your adopting James but let's put first things first."

Liza smiled up at Jamie and said, "Now we must sort out the problems of the newest members of our family."

"Does it ever end Liza?" asked Jamie.

"I believe I have been asked that on many an occasion," smiled Liza as they entered the drawing room and found David and Grace waiting for them.

"Did the boys enjoy their day?" asked David opening the conversation.

"Yes," said Liza. "They always enjoy meeting up with their friends after being away for a while."

"Well Uncle," said Jamie. "Have you had time to think about coming to live back with your family?"

"I naturally have several reservations," said David. "I know that Grace would like to start a new life here, and she needs to be with people who are full of life and not looking after someone like me who only has a few years left, if that. And what will become of her when I've gone, she has no friends in Truro, she has been too busy firstly looking after her mother and then looking after me to make friends. Her married life was an army life and when her husband died, she then lost any friends that she had."

"Father," exclaimed Grace, "I hope you are not advocating that you leave me here and go back to Truro alone because if that is the case you are terribly wrong. I am quite happy being with you and I do know people in Truro."

Jamie and Liza were letting David and Grace resolve their differences without interfering.

"Yes, you do know people in Truro, but you have no real friends there. Here you have family and I know that you will be included in everything that happens and you will be cared for," said David.

"No, I'm not leaving you," said Grace who was now very near to tears. "Besides I can't live on the charity of Jamie and Liza, which is what you are suggesting."

"Oh, I have a way of sorting that out," said David. "No if Jamie and Liza are happy to have you here, then that is what you must do."

"Uncle, you know that we would be more than happy to have Grace with us, but we would like to have you with us also. We know that you are reluctant to leave Holly behind, but you know that we can solve that problem. Have you discussed the possibility of bringing her here with Grace?" asked Jamie.

"Only in passing, I don't think that Grace thought it was a serious option," said David.

"And if it is a serious option, would you move back to your old home David?" said Liza.

"Are you saying that we could really bring my mother's body here to the churchyard? Is that possible?" said Grace.

"Yes, it is possible, and it would be done with great care and dignity and she would be laid to rest where she should be, after all she was an Edgeworth," said Liza.

"I told you I wouldn't want her in the Edgeworth crypt. It wouldn't be right to place her near Jamie's father," said David.

"So you have discussed it seriously, why didn't you tell me?" said Grace in annoyance.

"You haven't answered Liza's question Uncle," said Jamie. "If you are happy to bring Holly back here would you both like to live here?" said Jamie.

"Yes, I would like that, but I think that it would be better to rent some rooms in the village and I could help out at the church on occasion. I believe that living under the same roof would be a mistake. This is your house Jamie and if I came to live here, I know that I would start acting as if it were mine," said David.

"Liza and I had a feeling you would say that, so we have an alternative that you may like to consider. The gatehouse has not been used in years, but we looked at it earlier today and although it needs renovation it is large enough to accommodate you both easily. If you are interested, then we can go there tomorrow and you can let us know what you think. Of course you will have to see beyond the state that it is in at present but regardless of whether you take it or not we are going to make it habitable once again," said Jamie.

"It looks very pretty from the outside," said Grace.

"I'm afraid that's as far as the renovations have reached," said Liza. "It needed to look nice as you come through the gated area."

"I seem to remember that there was a family living there in my day. I think that there were about five children all under that roof. How many bedrooms does it have?" asked David.

"It has two large rooms upstairs and one smaller one. It has a sitting room and a dining room with a kitchen and a washroom off. It's not too small, in fact it's quite roomy," said Liza. "But it really is very messy at the moment. If you are interested perhaps you could look at it and see what you would like us to do with it."

"Father, this seems to be an ideal solution. We will be very near our family but will be looking after ourselves and we will have Mother with us. Please say that we can do this," said Grace, who was once again near to tears.

"How will we arrange to get my Holly here?" asked David quietly.

"I will go to see our local undertaker and arrange everything with him. I think that it would be better for him to deal with it rather than one local to Truro, also I want to have a word with Bernard to arrange for a suitable resting place for Holly and I hope you will come with me to choose the plot," said Liza.

"I would prefer not to go to the undertaker with you, if you don't mind. I really don't want to know how it will be dealt with," said David.

"Of course," said Liza. "Will you need permission from your current vicar to remove her? Or is that really down to you and nobody else?"

131

"It is my decision to make," said David.

"I'll tell our undertaker to make all the necessary arrangements and not to bother you with them. When did she die David?" asked Liza.

"Just over eighteen months ago," said David.

"I think we should go into supper now," said Liza. "And we can discuss the future and you both have to think about what you are going to bring with you. I'm excited that you are going to be with us, and I cannot believe that I only met you the other day, I feel as if I have known you all my life."

"We have very little furniture to bring, but we do have many personal possessions. My Mother loved pretty things; when the new vicar moved in we had to pack up most of her things, so they are ready to move, as are our books," said Grace excitedly.

"We want to get the renovations started as soon as possible so perhaps we could go to the gatehouse early tomorrow and then I'll go into the village later," said Liza.

"I'd like to go tonight," laughed Grace, "but of course it's too dark now."

The rest of the time around the table was Grace planning her new life and her father looking on happily for at last his daughter had a future and she would be well looked after when he was no longer around.

They were all tired after a busy day and Grace said that she wanted an early night as she wanted to be up early the next day to see the gatehouse.

"We told you that it is not in a very good condition as yet," Jamie said to Grace smiling.

"I know, but that doesn't matter. I've lived in some appalling places with my Geoff being in the army, I'm sure it will look like a palace compared to them," said Grace.

David was smiling at his daughter and shaking his head at the same time. "I believe we will be moving into the gatehouse no matter what it is like," and he then laughed and guided Grace up the stairs to her room.

Jamie and Liza followed shortly and when they were both in Jamie's room he said, "How are we going to arrange for Holly to get here. You made it sound so easy, but I know it will be more complicated than it appeared."

"I don't think it will really be that difficult, but it does concern me that the undertakers may not be able to handle it with as much dignity as we would hope for. I think I will have to ask Grace what type of coffin she was buried in; I can't ask your uncle that question," said Liza.

"Of course, if it was a type of soft wood it could have started breaking up even though it has only been eighteen months," said Jamie thoughtfully.

"That's very macabre, but true. No matter what though, Holly Edgeworth is coming home with or without a decent box," said Liza. "But David will never know."

"Let us hope that it was mahogany. I've said that I will go with you tomorrow and then I'll go onto my lawyer. I suppose you will eventually have to sign documents agreeing to my adopting both Matthew and John. I presume there will be no difficulties with John," said Jamie.

"No, I arranged that John became mine when I was in Belfast after Patrick died, but I will inform Sally out of courtesy," said Liza.

"It scares me to think of the life he would have had if you and Patrick hadn't found him and taken him in. He would probably be dead by now," said Jamie. "He's very artistic, isn't he? He has a great deal of talent in that area."

"He's not as academic as James and Matthew, but he keeps up with them quite well. Each has their own strengths," said Liza.

"It seemed very important to them to have a name; I hadn't realised that they didn't think that they had proper names. I hope that didn't hurt you Liza," said Jamie.

"I'm just upset that I hadn't realised their need to have what they term a proper name. They have always been mine and I didn't think further than that, but they are very happy about it now," said Liza.

"I believe that I will be able to persuade Evelyn to allow you to adopt James, as long as you are happy to do so," said Jamie.

"Of course I am; I have thought of him as my son for a long time now. Evelyn told me that she also thought of him as my son, but we won't dwell on the reasons why she thought that," smiled Liza. "Are you going to call out my name when you are in the throes of passion tonight Jamie? Or will it be Evelyn that you are thinking of?"

Liza was laughing and Jamie said, "I try never to think of Evelyn and most certainly she will not be on my mind when I ravish you tonight, so get ready for me Lady Edgeworth; you're going to enjoy this."

"I'm sure I'm going to," laughed Liza.

Chapter 8

Grace was in raptures when she visited the gatehouse with her father and Liza the next morning. Mr Lambert had already started organising the clearing of the house and it was looking marginally better than it had done the day before.

"Are you going to be happy living on the edge of the estate?" Liza asked David when Grace was looking at the bedrooms for the second time.

"It's perfectly safe here Liza," said David. "We won't be too far away from the Dower House and it's only a five-minute walk to the main house. I see there's a stable at the side which has room for a small carriage as well as a horse. I don't have that at the moment, but I'm sure I can arrange that when we are here and that will make us very independent."

"I realise that it's very important for you to live your own lives, but you mustn't totally cut yourselves off from the rest of us. Sunday lunches are always a family gathering as well as some other mealtimes, but you don't have to wait just for a mealtime to come up to the house," said Liza.

"I know that Liza, but you can see how happy Grace is planning what she can do here. She has rarely had a permanent home since before her marriage; she moved around a great deal with Geoff and when he died, she came back to us. Holly was already quite ill, and I had to arrange to have help with running my parish, so a vicar and his wife moved in, and rightly so. Since then they have had a son and they are having another child soon and of course the vicarage necessarily became theirs rather than ours," said David.

"I believe it was totally unnecessary of us to say that she had to look past the current state of this place; I think she would move into it as it is," laughed Liza.

"We will have to think about travelling back to Truro to organise our move. We don't have very much to bring with us, and I'll have to hire a cart for our possessions," said David.

"I can organise that for you David; we do own a haulage company. I'll get in touch with the depot nearest to you and when you are ready, send them a note and they'll arrange everything for you. Don't look like that David"

134

exclaimed Liza, "it's one of the perks of owning a large company. I'll also give you a letter to the two hotels on your route back to Truro and they will accommodate you both ways."

"You're doing too much for us Liza; we are not without funds," said David.

"Good, that means that you are able to look after yourselves when you finally settle back here, but in the meantime take advantage of what is being offered. The hotels keep rooms especially for me and the Fuller family and as nobody will be using them at present you may as well rest comfortably on your journey," said Liza.

"Father," said Grace who had come back into the room. "I think that until we are settled here we will need all the help that we can get. When we are here we will be able to do what we like, when we like and how we like, so stop fighting Liza and swallow your pride for a few weeks."

"Well said Grace," smiled Liza. "Have you got everything sorted out in your mind? You must tell me what you are bringing and I will arrange the rest, but it is quite convenient that we have plenty of room at the main house until this place is in order, so you don't have to stay too long in Truro, you can get everything that you need and come straight back."

Jamie drove up in the carriage to pick Liza up and go into the village, but on the way they were going to stop at the church to meet Bernard so that David and Grace could sort out a suitable plot for Holly. Liza had already told him what they had in mind and Bernard felt that it was good that Holly was being brought home and laid to rest where her family could visit her.

Whilst they were walking around the churchyard Liza pulled Grace to one side and asked her about her mother's coffin. Apparently it had been made of a hard wood and when Liza suggested that hopefully it was mahogany Grace said that she thought that it was, but she was not going to ask her father such a question. She was under no illusions as to why Liza was asking. Liza also wanted to know if there was a headstone and when Grace said that there was Liza said that she would arrange for that to be brought also.

They chose a beautiful plot for Holly and there would also be room for David when his time came. It was near the Edgeworth crypt but on the opposite side of the pathway and David was going to have a seat made next to it.

With that organised David and Grace were going to walk back to the house, stopping at the gatehouse on the way, and Liza and Jamie would then carry onto the village, firstly to see the undertaker and then onto Jamie's lawyer to set in motion his adoption of Matthew and John.

The undertaker naturally wanted as much detail as possible about what he was being asked to carry out. He said that he and an assistant would make the journey and give as much dignity as possible to Mrs Holly Edgeworth. He asked about the coffin and all Liza could tell him was that it was believed to be mahogany and it was only just over eighteen months since the death. They would also attempt to bring the headstone back in one piece. Liza and Jamie cringed at the price, but it was a very large task and a long journey for them. They would be informed when they were to set out as they did not know when David and Grace would be returning to Truro.

Their visit to the lawyer was successful; it was going to be an easy task as Liza was Matthew's mother and John had been legally adopted by her. It was just a matter of paperwork and finalisation in the courts.

"So our next step is to get James adopted by you. It may be a little prolonged, but we will achieve it and he will be so pleased when it happens," said Jamie.

They made their way back home in time for lunch and they found Miranda and Lucinda in the drawing room with David and Grace. They had obviously made their peace and were chatting excitedly about the gatehouse.

"Oh Jamie," exclaimed Lucinda, "Isn't it wonderful that you now have all your family around you and to think that you didn't know your mother until three years ago, and you also had no idea that you had an uncle until just weeks ago. By finding him you also found a cousin that you didn't know existed. It's so marvellous that I think I'm going to cry."

"Don't you dare do that Lucinda," said Miranda. "I know it's all very wonderful but there's no need to cry over it, you're meant to smile and be happy for everyone."

"But I am happy for everyone, that's why I'm crying," sniffed Lucinda.

Jamie and Liza stared at her resignedly, Miranda tut-tutted, David looked puzzled and Grace laughed out loud.

"I think I'm really going to enjoy being amongst you all," laughed Grace. "You're all going to make my life very happy and I think it is also going to be full of laughter."

At Grace's comments Lucinda sniffed and made a slight sobbing sound and Miranda raised her eyes up to heaven.

"I hope you are all staying for lunch," said Liza. "I think that the boys should also join us so that we have all our family around the table. It's a momentous day for us today."

"Oh," said Lucinda. "I'll go back to the Dower House and see you later."

"Liza said we should have all the family with us Lucinda; you are just as much family as we all are," said Jamie. "Oh no, don't start crying again."

Liza was finding it difficult not to laugh, as were David and Grace. Miranda was frowning and Jamie was staring into the distance.

"I think I'll tell Mrs Frances that we are all in the dining room for lunch," said Liza with a laugh in her voice.

"I'll just go and see if the boys have finished their morning lessons," smiled Jamie.

"I'll just take a minute to freshen up," said David.

"Do pull yourself together Lucinda," said Miranda. "You know you've always been thought of as one of the family, so why should it upset you today? What will everybody think of you? Don't let the boys see you like this."

"Of course, you're right; this is a happy day. I don't know why I cry when I'm happy," sniffed Lucinda.

Jamie reappeared with the boys, who were in high spirits as they knew that their adoptions were now underway and James had been told that when Matthew and John had been sorted out, steps were going to be taken to try to make Liza his true mother. They had asked Jamie if they could mention it at lunch and were told that they were to leave it to him to announce it and they could join in afterwards.

They were giggling conspiratorially as they entered the drawing room with Jamie, and Liza arrived from the kitchen.

Lucinda was now smiling; she always found that the boys made her smile. David came in and the boys looked at him warily and he smiled at them and asked them what they had been doing that morning. Matthew was the spokesman and said what Adam had been teaching them.

Grace was smiling at everyone but especially the boys; she liked them and could see that each had his own character and more importantly they cared very much for each other.

"Liza and I have an announcement to make to our family," said Jamie. "This morning we set in motion the process of my legally adopting John and Matthew; once that is completed, they will officially be Edgeworths and entitled to all that involves. When that is finalised, we are then going to attempt to make James legally Liza's son. It tidies up our family beautifully and the boys are very happy about it."

David looked at Jamie and raised an eyebrow but said nothing. He turned and smiled at the boys and told them how pleased he was for them.

"I've always felt that they were yours Jamie," said Miranda. "You've always treated them as your own, just as Liza has always treated James as if he was hers. It's wonderful that you will now make it legal. I hope that you will be able to persuade Evelyn to agree, I'm sure that you will be able to."

"Do you think that she will do that?" Lucinda asked Miranda quietly.

"Oh yes, I'm sure she will," said Miranda with meaning. She knew that Jamie had a hold over Evelyn and although she may argue initially, she would have no option but to agree in the end.

Lucinda thought about it and then nodded. Grace noticed this and surmised that there was more to Jamie's divorce from Evelyn than met the eye and no doubt she would find out about that at some time in the future, but she was intrigued, as was David but he was better at keeping his thoughts to himself.

The boys all started talking at once until Jamie called them to order and said that perhaps they should go through to lunch but the boys would be allowed to talk over the meal as it was such an exciting day for them, but they were not to shout or all talk together.

Jamie, as always, was at the head of the table and Liza sat on his left side and Miranda on his right with James sitting next to her. Lucinda sat next to James and John was the other side of her. David was beside Liza and he had Grace next to him with Matthew next to her. They were all positioned very cosily.

David opened the conversation by saying how well behaved the boys were and he followed by commenting that they all seemed very close in age. Before Jamie or Liza could answer Matthew piped up, "James is the eldest by just two months, John is next; his birthday is in May. I'm the youngest by a year. So we have birthdays in March, April and May."

"I wouldn't have thought that you were the youngest Matthew," said David.

"Well, we've all been together since before we went to school and we have the same lessons, so there's no difference in us now," said John who seemed no longer wary of David.

Miranda had a happy smile on her face, she loved being with her grandchildren and up to a few years ago she would not have believed that she would be in this situation. "It's all very exciting for you boys, you all look very happy about it."

"Yes we are, Grandmother," said James very politely but with a twinkle in his eye. "Matthew and John have said that they will be proud to have the Edgeworth name and I'm pleased that they are going to be my real brothers, but as soon as my father and mummy Liza married we became brothers, but it's nice that it's going to be made official."

"It's nice for you to have brothers James," said Grace. "You all seem to get on so well together, and I've noticed that you watch out for one another."

"I have a very nice family now; it's much better than it was before, and I want mummy Liza to be my proper mother. She has been really since I first knew her when I was a very little boy; I remember her looking after me when the other one went missing," said James.

"James," interrupted Liza. "Did you know that Uncle David and Cousin Grace are coming to live here?"

The three boys stopped eating and stared from David to Grace with puzzled looks on their faces and of course it was Matthew who spoke first. "I didn't think that you liked being here."

"I didn't really know you and I was naturally a little nervous of meeting you all but I find that I like you all very much and I know that I will enjoy being part of the family, which as you know is my family as well," said David.

"My father and I have decided that we would be very happy here and we will be living in the gatehouse, which is being renovated now. It will be just right for us and you all will visit us regularly I hope," said Grace.

"Hmmm," said John. "Once you move in there, we'll be able to come and see you and have cakes with you. That will be good; we go to the Dower House and have tea and cakes there, so it will be another place for us to visit."

"Yes, that will be good," said Matthew. "When are you moving in?"

"There's quite a lot of work to do on the house, but there's room for both your uncle and cousin here until it's ready," said Jamie. "When are you planning to go back to Truro to collect your belongings?"

"Grace and I thought that we would wait until after the weekend. We have a few things to organise here before we leave, and we'd like to meet up with all the villagers again. I presume you will be having another cricket practice on Sunday if the weather is good. It's such a wonderful event to meet with everyone," said David.

"The new children's home is being opened in five weeks' time. I hope you'll be here for that," said Liza.

"Once we are in Truro it will only take about a week to ten days to arrange everything for our move, so we should be back in around three weeks," said Grace.

"You must tell me about what you are doing with the children's home; I presume that you sponsor it in some way," said David.

"Yes, that's right," said Liza as the boys grinned, as did Miranda and Lucinda. "We have to attend a function for it on Thursday, so I'm afraid you'll be left to your own devices on that evening."

Lucinda smiled and said, "Don't worry David; we will look after you then."

When lunch was over the boys asked to leave the table and they each thanked the adults for their company at an interesting lunch. Liza and Jamie nodded and smiled their approval at them, and they disappeared back to their schoolroom.

"You both can be very proud of those boys," said David. "It's very sensible what you are doing in adopting them, Jamie; it solves a potentially large problem."

"Well Uncle, regardless of the heritage problem, I'm delighted to do it. All our conversation of the other day did was to make me realise that although I considered them mine, I wanted them to be recognised as such. Liza and I did not know that they needed to find an identity and they are really happy that they will now be known by the name Edgeworth. It has all worked out very well," said Jamie.

"James seems to need Liza to become his legal mother. I hope that you are able to bring that about for him," said Grace.

"That's just going to take a little longer to achieve, but I know that it will happen," said Jamie.

David and Grace asked nothing further on the subject as they realised that there were probably difficulties that as yet they had no knowledge of.

***

The work on renovating the gatehouse was progressing well. All the old furniture had been removed and where necessary the walls and doors were being renewed. It was now very much an empty shell, but Grace loved it. She, Liza, Miranda and Lucinda discussed what was needed to make it a home and also what she would be able to bring from Truro which really was very little in the way of furniture.

"Father would want to pay for any furniture that you have to supply Liza," said Grace.

"I had no furniture when I came here, and Jamie and Liza furnished the Dower House for me. There were some pieces in the house but very little to make me comfortable and gradually my house became a home, especially when Lucinda moved in. Some of the pieces that I had were put to one side because Lucinda brought much of her own furniture with her, so I know that Liza has stored many items which are not currently in use," said Miranda.

Liza smiled at her and wished that she had thought of that herself. "Yes, that's right, so maybe the only main items which could be essential would be beds for you and your father. I believe we have tables and chairs stored somewhere."

Miranda and Lucinda knew that Liza was stretching the truth and possibly Grace knew it also.

"We do have bed linen, curtains and table linen, but we are a little short on cooking utensils. We have tea and dinner sets and I hope we can get them here in one piece," said Grace.

"I think that the best idea would be for you to borrow what you need from the main house until you can get exactly what you want," said Liza.

"Good heavens," said Grace, "what's that noise?"

A very heavily ladened cart had drawn up outside and two men jumped down and started struggling in with pieces for an oven.

They stood and watched as the pieces were gradually unloaded. Grace gasped, "That looks really modern. I thought I would have to clean up the old one; I'm sure that would have been good enough."

"It adds value to the property Grace, and I think you would have had great difficulty using the old oven; it seemed like a death trap to me," said Liza. "Anyway, shall we let the men get on with their job?"

On the way back to the main house Grace told Liza that she knew that they were all allowing her father to keep his dignity.

"That's not strictly true," said Liza. "This was his home for a number of years, so he is entitled to have a comfortable place to live, and really the gatehouse is not very salubrious in comparison to his previous home."

"Since my mother was taken ill and I moved back to help father with her, we had to be squashed into two small rooms so that the new vicar and his wife and eventual family could have the vicarage. I am not complaining about that situation, it was necessary, I am just saying that the gatehouse is absolute luxury for us. It is actually better than the whole of the vicarage, not necessarily in size but in its facilities. We are going to be so comfortable there. I am just sorry that my mother can't see it," said Grace.

"She can see it Grace; you know that she watches over you both and she is happy that she will be moving with you," said Liza quietly.

Grace stopped and looked strangely at Liza and Miranda came up and said, "Liza sees things that others do not Grace. She will be right about your mother."

Miranda and Lucinda made their way to the Dower House while Liza and Grace carried onto the main house. Jamie drove up with his uncle as he had been showing him how the estate was progressing.

Once inside Liza excused herself telling them that she had correspondence that she had to attend to and she went into her study and looked at the pile of documents that she had to deal with. She had not had a chance to look at them since she had returned from Belfast. She had the feeling of being overwhelmed again but knew that the only way she was going to be able to handle it was to sort it into sections. All correspondence from Benson she placed together, as she did also with Marchant & Fuller's American letters. Italian documents were next followed by Bradley & Company letters regarding Wales and Ireland. The Charity came next and lastly she looked at all the letters which were obviously invitations to various functions. She sat back and wondered where she should start.

Jamie quietly went into her study and coming up behind her put his arms around her. "You look a little swamped with paperwork Liza, is there anything I can help you with?" he asked.

"I've sorted it all into different sections, but I really don't know where to start, I think I need to quickly look at what invitations we have and see if we are available for any of them. I think I'll ask your mother and Lucinda to write and accept or decline once I've checked in the diary."

Jamie helped her open the invitations, noting the dates and looking at the diary. They worked their way through them and Jamie said that he would take them to his mother and Lucinda and ask them to reply to them.

David and Grace were in the drawing room when Jamie came from the study. "You look concerned Jamie," said David.

"I do get concerned when Liza has to work so hard. She's overwhelmed by paperwork today. Her workload has increased considerably since the charity has grown. The time has come for us to employ a secretary especially now that we have to attend so many functions, which Liza is not pleased about, but it is necessary for us to be seen at as many as possible as that is where the vast amount of money comes from to keep the children housed and fed."

"We've heard you mention the charity a few times; what does it cover?" asked Grace.

"It's one that Liza and Wendell Fuller started a few years ago when she discovered how many children were being sexually abused. She helped rescue three children from appalling circumstances and then found children turning up on her doorstep desperate for help. It is a long story, but we are now lucky as all the work has been noticed by people such as the Duke of Berkshire, Lord Carlton, the Dowager Lady Redfern and even Prince Albert. We have many great names sponsoring the charity now, but of course because of that we have commitments such as the function that we are attending on Thursday and I have all these invitations that I am taking to the Dower House to ask my mother and Lucinda to write the replies," said Jamie. "Liza will now be able to deal with all her business correspondence and that is also quite considerable."

David looked at Jamie and frowned, "It's a great deal bigger than I thought. I believed that you just attended functions and gave something towards whatever charity the hosts were sponsoring, I didn't realise that everything surrounds your charity and that you aren't just sponsors, in fact you are the charity. You say that it is for abused children; I had not realised that there was such a problem."

"I'm afraid it is far more serious than anyone realised and all we can do is set up homes for these children and when they become less traumatised we arrange for them to go to America either to work in reliable homes, or adopted into homes and lastly they can also become bond servants but we have made sure that such servitude is correctly handled. When you have been with us a while you will see exactly what we do, but as you know we are opening another home shortly and if you are able to return before that time then you will meet many of the people who help us," said Jamie.

"I think that there is a great deal that I can do to help," said David. "I have come across such children, but not in the numbers that you have to deal with, and I promise you I will not push religion at them. I would like to help to care for them."

"And I can also help," said Grace. "I will start now. Give me those invitations and I will go and work with Liza. It's the least I can do, and I know that I will enjoy doing that. I'm very good at correspondence and I know that I will be able to ease the pressure on Liza if she will let me."

"As I said Liza is going to employ a secretary, although she has had no time to do that yet. She does have in mind to employ Derek when he is old enough, but she needs help now. Actually we both do," said Jamie.

"Well if it is agreeable to you both I would like to undertake that work. I will only be away for about three weeks and when I return, I can regularly assist you both," said Grace.

Jamie smiled and went to see Liza and tell her that it appeared that they had found their secretary and that Grace was going to help her immediately. Liza looked up relieved and said that they must work out a salary for Grace.

"I don't think that she wants a salary, but I know that you think differently, and rightly so," said Jamie.

"She either takes a salary or she doesn't work for us," smiled Liza, "but I will tell her what I told the Major and that was that what he did with his salary was entirely up to him."

"I'll send her in and let you sort out the terms," smiled Jamie. "You said that something would turn up."

Grace came in and she started work immediately having first agreed terms, although initially she didn't want to take a salary, but she relented in the end and they worked well together for the rest of the afternoon.

A short while before dinner Hector arrived having spent a couple of days with Randolph Langston and his sister, Penelope. Liza immediately called Mrs Frances to make sure that his room was ready.

"Do you think that their house is suitable for our needs?" Liza asked Hector.

"It's about the same size as the Ffoulks house, but it's much brighter to start with. It could easily be adapted for what we need however the kitchens want a major refurbishment. Some of the bedrooms could be knocked into one, but any staff quarters need very little alteration. The grounds around the house are already well kept and there is an enclosed kitchen garden which would be very useful. It also has the advantage of another house in the grounds, rather like your Dower House, which is probably what it was previously used for. It's going to be within our price range, but it will be up to you and possibly Peter Fuller to finalise any negotiations over that. Overall it could be a good investment and it won't cost as much to put in order as my old house has," said Hector.

"Where will Lord Langston and his sister move to?" asked Liza.

"There was a suggestion that they move into the Dower House, but I don't think that it would be a very good idea. I think that any property within the grounds should only have charity staff living there as it would be difficult to have others coming and going whenever they wanted. Not that you would be locking the children in, but we would have to have some control over those leaving and more importantly those entering," said Hector.

"Thank you, Hector, it seems that you have found us another ideal place," said Liza. "You'll be meeting Jamie's uncle and cousin later; they will be with us permanently soon; we're really excited about it."

"You seem to be gathering increasing numbers of family around you Liza," smiled Hector. "Is Estelle here?"

"I believe she is; she is preparing for her move to the Ffoulks house; she may still be in the schoolroom," said Liza.

"I'll see if I can find her and then go to my room and freshen up before dinner," said Hector.

Soon after Hector had left, Jamie and his uncle arrived, and Jamie was pleased to know what Hector thought of Lord Langston's house. "I'm glad that you will be meeting him," Jamie said to his uncle. "He has a heart of gold but keeps it well hidden, and the art of tactfulness seems to have passed him by."

"It sounds as if he is quite a character," said David.

"Yes he is but he does hide his feelings behind a façade of over cheerfulness. He came home from the war slightly wounded in body, but the wounds of his mind went much deeper. I hope that he doesn't say anything that would upset Grace because Jamie is right when he said that tact is not his strong point," said Liza.

"Grace will understand that," said David. "Where is she by the way?"

"She's still working," smiled Liza, "and I would have been if Hector hadn't arrived unexpectedly."

"You keep a room for him then," said David.

"Yes, he comes and goes between here and his brother's house quite regularly," said Liza.

"Have April and Adam realised that Hector is going to their wedding?" asked Jamie.

"Well Estelle knows, but I have no idea whether she has told them, or whether Hector has either," said Liza. "I also believe that many of the people from the village are preparing to see them married and I do wonder whether they have organised enough refreshments for everyone."

145

"No doubt that as you and Mrs Lambert have realised the problem you are prepared to make sure everything is well covered," said Jamie.

"Yes, nobody will have to go without," said Liza, "but I don't want to take their plans away from them."

"Not many employers would be so considerate of their staff," said David.

"April and Adam are very special. They both look after our boys wonderfully well and the boys think a great deal of them," said Liza.

The boys were always pleased to see their Uncle Hector; they knew that he liked Estelle and was always trying to get her to go places with him. They also liked the fact that he always created problems by saying the wrong thing, but they knew that he never meant to hurt anyone, he just managed to 'put his foot in it'. They also knew that he was very fond of children but tried to hide it from everyone.

Hector bounded into the schoolroom shouting 'hello' to the boys and then grinning at Estelle who looked up not knowing whether she felt pleased or sorry at this intrusion. Adam looked at him with resignation. He knew that the boys would no longer be interested in what he had been telling them, so as it was nearly the end of school time, he told them to pack away their books and go and enjoy themselves.

They surrounded Hector asking various questions which he answered with patience. He really wanted to speak to Estelle, but the boys were making that impossible and both she and Adam smiled at Hector's slight frustration.

"Isn't it your supper time?" Hector asked the boys hopefully.

"No, not yet," said Matthew. "Will you be staying for the weekend? We've got a cricket practice on Sunday and I'm sure it would help you play better."

"Thank you, Matthew," said Hector. "You always manage to boost my confidence."

"That's alright," said Matthew not realising Hector's sarcasm.

"No, I can only stay tonight; I have a great deal to do before the Ffoulks house is ready for the children and we only have just over a month to finalise everything," said Hector. "I also have to finalise a few jobs before I return for your wedding Adam."

"Shall we go and see if supper is ready?" asked James. "We'll see you after supper, won't we Uncle Hector?"

"Of course," said Hector as he smiled and watched them leave the school room. He turned towards Estelle and asked her to take a walk with him. Adam looked up and wondered where the relationship was leading and hoped that it would not end in heartbreak for Estelle. He was also going to ask Estelle whether she knew that Hector was planning to be at his and April's wedding and he was beginning to worry as most of the villagers seemed to be saying that they would also be attending his wedding.

"I'm sure Liza wouldn't mind if you joined us for dinner tonight," Hector could be heard saying to Estelle.

"Hector, I work for the charity and therefore work for Lord and Lady Edgeworth. I do not want to join you for dinner. I am not comfortable with that situation. I know that Lady Edgeworth would not mind, but I would mind. When I am at Ffoulks house, that will be a different matter, everyone will be eating together."

Hector had to accept what Estelle said, but told her that he would like to meet up with her after dinner and she had no objection to that suggestion.

Just before dinner Hector joined everyone in the drawing room and was introduced to David and Grace.

"It's wonderful that Jamie has so many relatives appearing out of the woodwork," said Hector in his normal tactless way, but as David and Grace had been warned they took no offence.

"Yes, it is wonderful, isn't it, and it's even more wonderful that we will be living here," smiled David.

"When will you be moving here?" asked Hector.

"In about three weeks' time," said Grace. "We'll be living here until our house is ready for us."

"Oh, I had assumed that you would be under this roof; where will your house be?" asked Hector.

"We're moving into the gatehouse," said Grace.

"Really, isn't that a little cramped and really designed just for workers. I would have thought that Jamie would have put you somewhere better," said Hector.

By this time both David and Grace were smiling broadly. "It's what we wanted Hector. The alternative was for us to find a couple of rooms in the village but both Liza and Jamie would not hear of that and so they came up with this suggestion. It makes us independent but very near our family. You should come and view the place tomorrow before you leave," smiled David. "I think you will be suitably impressed with the way it is being renovated."

"Of course, you're a vicar and are probably used to not very salubrious surroundings," said Hector.

"Oh we're used to salubrious surroundings Hector," smiled Grace, "and when you see the gatehouse tomorrow, I believe you will see that we will be living very well."

"Naturally, Liza wouldn't let you live in a hovel; I should have known that," said Hector. "I look forward to seeing your new home tomorrow."

Liza and Jamie were sitting listening to Hector working his way out of his tactlessness without realising it.

Luckily Harper came in to say that dinner was served.

"Are your mother and Lucinda not joining us tonight," asked Hector.

"No they quite enjoy dining at their own house on occasion although I'm sure if they had known you were here they would have altered their arrangements. However, you will see them tomorrow before you leave no doubt," said Jamie.

"I asked Estelle to join us for dinner," said Hector. "I knew you wouldn't mind, but she refused. She said that she would be able to when we are all at the Ffoulks house as everyone would be eating together."

"I know that she has a great deal to do before she goes to the Ffoulks house to get ready for the first influx of children," said Liza.

David and Grace were smiling broadly, and Liza was so pleased that she had warned them of Hector's often thoughtless comments.

Jamie then defused the situation by asking Hector what he thought of the Langston House, who then proceeded to describe it in detail, which then became the main topic of conversation and they all did find it extremely interesting and enjoyed Hector's enthusiasm for it.

When the evening was finally over and Liza and Jamie were in bed, Liza suddenly started laughing. "I know," said Jamie. "It's Hector, isn't it? I'm glad we warned my uncle and Grace about him."

"When you and Anthony got him out of Portugal, he seemed so ungrateful and thoughtless of anyone but himself. He has shown us the other side of him, which is really very caring, and he would do anything for his family and our family also. I do wonder if he really knows how tactless he is, or if he does it on purpose," said Liza.

"If he's anything like Edward then he doesn't realise it, but I often doubt that he is so oblivious of his comments. Anyway as my uncle says, he is quite a character and does make life interesting," said Jamie.

Jamie turned onto his left side and looked at Liza lying with her eyes closed smiling happily and he was transported back twenty years and all he could see was the seventeen-year-old as he had wanted to see her all those years ago. He wondered what his life would have been like if he had not made the grave mistake of insulting her soon after she had been widowed for the first time; perhaps he would have spent the last sixteen years being as happy as he was now, instead of the misery that he had put himself through because of his stupidity.

Liza opened her eyes and saw him watching her and he seemed concerned. "What's the matter Jamie, has something upset you?" she asked.

"No Liza," said Jamie. "I was just thinking about all my lost years."

"There's no point in dwelling on what might have been; we are now in the present and have a lot of future to look forward to and I have a good idea of how I can make the present very happy for you," said Liza.

***

Hector was quite enthusiastic when he visited the gatehouse with Liza and Grace the following morning.

"This is going to be a very nice place to live," he said. "I knew that Liza wouldn't put you in a dingy dirty place, but I would much rather have rooms in the main house and be waited on hand and foot. Anyway I must get on my way; I'll be back in a week ready for Adam's wedding, if that's alright with you."

"It's not whether it's alright with me Hector; it's whether it's alright with Adam and April. Have you been invited?" asked Liza.

"Of course I have Liza," smiled Hector. "They know I'm attending."

"Do they? If they do then I'll see you next week," said Liza.

He left and Grace turned to Liza and asked if Adam and April really knew that he was going to their wedding.

"They probably know, but I doubt that he had been invited. I suppose they will cope with him; they've also got to cope with the number from the village who will be turning up," said Liza.

"You're at a function tonight. Have you sorted out what you will be wearing?" asked Grace as they walked back to the house.

"Yes, it's all sorted. April has been working on it for a couple of days," said Liza.

"Is it new then?" asked Grace.

"No, but it needed altering and adding to slightly; it's one I wore in America, so nobody here will have seen it before," said Liza. "As it's over two hours to get there we have been invited to stay the night, so we'll be leaving soon after lunch and won't be back until after lunch tomorrow."

"I suppose April will be going with you," said Grace.

"Yes and Roberts also. Jamie's mother and Lucinda will be spending the afternoon and evening at the main house. Adam and Estelle will make sure that the boys behave themselves," smiled Liza.

"I don't think that your boys need to be reminded how to behave," said Grace. "I'll also look after them Liza."

"I know you will Grace; they'll gang up against you and play tricks on you. They do it when anyone tries to look after them for the first time. April never told me what they did to her, and neither has Estelle. I'm not sure that they played any prank on Adam, but I wouldn't be surprised if they did," said Liza.

"Thank you for warning me; I'm sure I'll rise to the occasion," laughed Grace.

Chapter 9

It was raining when they left for Lord Fountain's function. They were taking two carriages, one for Liza and Jamie and one for April, Roberts and their carefully packed clothes.

Before they left Jamie had asked Liza what she intended wearing that evening. She had smiled and told him that it was the green dress which was covered in silver netting. "So it will be the emeralds for tonight's event," he said and disappeared into his room and she heard him opening his safe.

He always seemed pleased to see her wearing the Edgeworth jewels and she was very proud to do so and happy that he thought her worthy of them.

It took just over two hours for them to reach the Fountains' house and it was indeed magnificent. It took them nearly half an hour to go up the driveway to the front door.

"Have you been here before?" Liza asked Jamie.

"No, I haven't. It makes our place look positively tiny," said Jamie. "I have met both Edgar and Lucille Fountain on a couple of occasions and they were at Lord Carlton's function, although I believe they had to leave soon after your speech, so you probably weren't introduced to them."

"I wonder who will be here that we know," said Liza as their carriage drew up to the steps at the front door. Servants rushed down to open the door and help both Liza and Jamie to the ground. Their second carriage with April and Roberts was directed towards the back of the house, and when Liza and Jamie were safely on their way up the steps, Davis was also directed to follow the other carriage.

They were shown into a drawing room and were warmly greeted by Lady Lucille Fountain who apologised for her husband not being there for them, but he would be joining them shortly. Refreshments were brought in and they were shown to comfortable chairs and it was only then that they noticed the Dowager Lady Redfern and Lord Carlton talking to a number of guests. She looked across and smiling came over to them.

"I'm so pleased to see you both; there are going to be a number of people who you have already met and one or two who have already expressed a wish to be introduced to you. I presume that Jamie has introduced you to our hostess," said Lady Redfern.

"Yes, he has. Will your daughter and the Duke be with us tonight?" asked Liza.

"They will but they won't be arriving until later," said the Dowager.

Several guests came to greet them and after a short while Lady Fountain arranged for them to be shown to their rooms. Liza thanked her and a servant led them up the stairs. They looked at one another having noted that Lady Fountain had said 'rooms' and they assumed that they would not be sleeping together that night. However they were wrong as they were shown into a suite of rooms where April and Roberts had already unpacked their clothes.

Liza laughed and said, "I think we may be quite comfortable here."

As they were looking around there was a knock on the door and the housekeeper had come to tell them that afternoon tea would be served in the small dining room in an hour. Liza thanked her and she left.

"I wonder where the small dining room is," said Jamie.

"No doubt we'll find that somebody will be lurking around just waiting for us to emerge and we'll be gently guided towards our afternoon tea," smiled Liza.

The Duke of Berkshire and Bella had arrived by the time Liza and Jamie found their way down to the small dining room. Bella came over and greeted them like long lost friends and Jamie was whisked away by the Duke of Berkshire and Lord Carlton who were guiding him towards Lord Fountain.

Lady Redfern came to join Liza and Bella. Lucille Fountain also made her way towards them. "We would like to ask you something Liza," said Lady Redfern.

"Certainly, what can I do for you?" asked Liza.

"We know that you are opening the Ffoulks Home in around three weeks' time and we would like to be there to see how it is run and more importantly to be able to help with the first arrivals," said Lady Redfern.

"We also know that you and your staff are going to be under a great deal of pressure on that day and we would like to be of some use," said Lucille Fountain.

Bella was saying nothing and Liza wondered whether she was really interested in helping. Liza was thoughtful and finally said, "I appreciate what you are asking but I must be quite blunt, and I have no wish to upset anyone.

We cannot have the children treated as objects of interest; we would hate them to feel that they are on show. We want them to come into the Home and are made to feel that it is precisely that, a home where they can feel comfortable and have some privacy."

"I'm glad you have said that Liza," said Bella, "it is exactly what I said to my mother and Lucille when they first thought of the idea. Gone are the days when people climbed ladders to stare down at the poor and insane and I felt that this suggestion was only marginally better than that."

Liza smiled at Bella and was pleasantly surprised at her reaction. Lady Redfern and Lucille Fountain also smiled.

"Yes, we know just how you felt Bella and it does you credit, as it does Liza, but let me explain something to you both. We would not be there to gawp at the children, although I have a feeling that we are going to be shocked by what we see. We truly want to help with settling them into their new home. We are not going to push our titles into their faces, they will not know who we are and we are quite capable of helping them wash, dress, eat, drink and hold their hands to comfort them as, although they are coming to a better place, it will still be very traumatic for them," said Lady Redfern.

Liza stepped back and looked at them from top to toe and each lady frowned wondering what she was doing.

"You are at present wearing your afternoon dresses, and they are very nice and expensive. No doubt you would be intending to wear something similar when you would like to meet the children. That would set you apart from everyone else. You would need to wear clothes which are more allied to what your housekeepers are wearing, and large overalls would be essential. Nobody must look better than anyone else on that day; the children must not feel intimidated by anything that they see or hear," said Liza.

"I was told that you would speak your mind Liza," said Lucille Fountain. "And that you would champion the cause of the children above all else, even if you upset others but I would like to assure you that you have not upset me and I understand perfectly what you are saying. If we manage to borrow our housekeepers' clothes, don't speak with voices which are too upper crust and promise not to show disgust at how these poor children will probably arrive, would you let us help you?"

"You must also promise not to cry in front of the children, because I can assure you that you will feel like doing that. Show them love and care but keep to yourselves how disgusted you are when you see how badly these children

153

have been treated. When you realise what they have been subjected to you will want to cry and if you do you must go where they cannot see you. You will be there to settle them in not weep over their sores," said Liza. "Each one will have to be examined by our doctors and that could be a difficult process as they will wonder what is happening to them, but firstly food will help to relax them."

"From that I gather that you will not reject our help," smiled Bella. "May we come to see the Home before the children arrive as it would be useful to know where everything is and how we can best help."

"Of course, I'll be in touch with you over that, but I would think that a couple of days before the children are due to arrive would be a good time. However, you may all have prior engagements so you must let me know when you are free," said Liza.

Bella and Lucille moved away leaving Lady Redfern with Liza and it was obvious that she had something which was private to add to the conversation.

"Thank you, Liza but I think you probably realise that I have been asked to see what will happen at the Ffoulks house when the children arrive. Their Majesties are very concerned about the situation with abused children and I will be able to report back to them. I know that some of the sights I will see will not be pretty, but they want to know what these poor children are like and how they have been treated. They would prefer to see for themselves, but of course that is not possible," said Lady Redfern.

"I understand and unfortunately I believe that their Majesties will become quite shocked by what you will have to tell them," said Liza.

"I have been instructed to pull no punches when I report back," said Lady Redfern. "By the way, I understand that Evelyn Edgeworth has disappeared off the face of the earth. She did herself no favours with her association with certain types of people. I also hear that she was assisted in her disappearance by someone who is not standing too far away from me."

Liza looked at her trying not to show her shock at Lady Redfern's knowledge of the situation.

"Don't worry Liza," she said. "Your secret is safe with me and of course those who have already surmised your involvement in her disappearance. You are well known for not wanting the sins of the parents being visited on the children so it was not difficult to work out that you were the one person who would help her. Many believe that you must be slightly deranged to do anything to help her, but of course you are you so that answers everything. Ah, here comes Jamie, no doubt to rescue you from me."

Liza just smiled at her rather uncertainly and Lady Redfern moved away laughing as she went.

"What's the matter Liza, you look shocked," said Jamie.

"She knows that I helped Evelyn disappear; I don't know how she knows that Jamie," whispered Liza.

Jamie looked surprised but then said, "Staff don't necessarily keep their thoughts to themselves and certainly not if they have been treated badly and you know that Evelyn was never very caring of her staff."

"Yes, I suppose you're right," said Liza and she then went on to tell him that Lady Redfern, Bella and Lucille Fountain were offering their help with settling the children into Ffoulks house and she continued to tell him that it was a request that had come from a higher authority.

"You are therefore going to have to watch the ladies closely so that they don't upset the children by looking down on them and treating them like second class citizens," said Jamie.

"Yes, I've already told them how to behave," said Liza innocently whilst Jamie stared at her in horror.

"You've told them how to behave?" Jamie spluttered.

"Of course I have; the children have to be treated in a certain way and I cannot have anyone lording it over them; they have to be put as ease as much as possible and not gawped at as freaks," said Liza.

Jamie asked how the ladies had reacted to her instructions and was just as surprised as Liza at the fact that Bella had already told her mother and Lucille that she felt the children should not be regarded as a side show.

It was then time for them to go to their room to rest before getting ready for the evening. When they were dressed Jamie helped her with the Edgeworth emeralds and he stood back and told her how beautiful she looked and how her eyes sparkled more brilliantly than the jewels. Liza smiled up at him and told him that he was a flatterer.

Dinner was very pleasant and when it was over, they moved into the very large drawing room where an orchestra was playing and Lord and Lady Fountain were greeting further guests. Liza and Jamie were being approached by many people wanting to know how their charity was progressing and those who did not already contribute towards it were making offers and handing them their cards so that they could be contacted to finalise their pledges.

As the evening progressed both Liza and Jamie were popular figures and they were rarely without a dance partner and finally at the end of the function they made their way wearily to their rooms where April was waiting for Liza and Roberts for Jamie.

When April and Roberts had left Jamie made his way over to Liza. "We will be attending a number of functions like this one in the future and we will have to stay away from our home for many of them. I hope that you will agree to our making love in as many different beds as possible in the foreseeable future and we are going to have great fun doing it," he said as he sat on the side of the bed and pulled off his nightshirt. He took Liza's hand and she stood in front of him. He reached up and gently slid her nightdress from one shoulder and then the other until she was standing there naked. He pulled her onto him and they both lay on the bed together and he immediately started fondling her which he knew would make her very happy. Neither of them heard a door gently opening; they were too preoccupied with their own means of enjoyment.

***

April brought breakfast up to Liza the next morning whilst Jamie was eating with the gentlemen in the dining room. He knew that he would have to excuse himself from the table shortly so that he could get to Liza in time to wipe her chin as she was bound to have dribbled some of her breakfast down it. He enjoyed carrying out this chore for her and he was never sure that she didn't do it on purpose.

Liza looked up as he came into the room and grinned as he took her serviette and mopped up a trickle of butter from her chin. "When do you want to leave Jamie?" asked Liza.

"I think I'd like to be home by lunchtime, so I suppose we will have to leave at around eleven o'clock," said Jamie.

"I'll be ready by then. I'm sure April will be glad to get back as I know she has a great deal to do before next week," said Liza as she slid out of bed.

At ten o'clock Liza made her way down the stairs to the drawing room where she was greeted by Lucille and Lady Redfern. Bella had yet to emerge from her room.

"I hear that you will be having company at Ffoulks house when the children arrive," said Lord Carlton to Liza.

"Yes, they have kindly offered to help, and the children will need a great deal of care and kindness when they arrive. They are bound to be a little scared and disorientated and a few extra friendly faces will greatly help," said Liza.

Lucille asked Liza to confirm the exact times and dates that they would be needed and with a smile she promised not to overdress for the occasion.

Liza and Jamie were taking their leave and thanking their hosts for a wonderful evening and superb hospitality and Liza said that she looked forward to seeing Lucille again shortly. As she turned, she caught sight of April's frightened face looking into the drawing room, accompanied by Roberts. Several others in the room were looking surprised and as Liza made her way towards them, the Fountain's butler entered and went to Edgar Fountain and whispered in his ear.

"What's the matter April?" asked Liza and by that time Jamie had joined her and was looking quizzically towards Roberts, who guided them out into the hallway.

"I hate to tell you this Sir" said Roberts, "but we are unable to locate her Ladyship's jewellery."

"You know that I placed it safely in the locked cabinet in our rooms," said Jamie. "I did hand you the key this morning, didn't I Roberts?"

"You did Sir, but it was already unlocked and there was nothing but the open jewellery case inside," said Roberts.

Lord Fountain then joined them saying that he had just heard that the Edgeworth emeralds had been misplaced. Jamie said that they would go to the rooms and thoroughly search for them and Liza instructed April and Roberts to go through whatever packing they had done just in case they had fallen into the trunks, although she really knew that it would not be logical for that to have happened. The open jewellery case really proved that.

April was beginning to look very sick and Liza placed a hand on her shoulder and told her to calm down as there would probably be a very simple explanation.

Roberts and April unpacked every piece of clothing whilst Liza and Jamie looked in every drawer and cupboard, but they knew that they were wasting their time and this was proved to be true when Lucille came into their room to tell them that they were not the only ones to lose their jewellery.

By now Liza was feeling very sick and she prayed that she would not lose her breakfast in front of all those in their rooms. She was upset by the loss of the

Edgeworth emeralds, but she was more upset by the fact that Jamie had worked so hard to redeem them after his father had pawned them because of gambling debts.

There was a look of fury on Edgar Fountain's face which then turned to embarrassment and he started apologising for something that he had had no control over, but Liza could understand that for if it had happened in their house she would have felt exactly the same.

April was standing and looking very pale and Roberts was picking clothes up and putting them down again.

"Just carry on repacking our trunks April and Roberts will help you," said Liza who felt that they both needed to be occupied.

"Who else has lost jewellery?" asked Jamie.

"The Duke and Duchess of Berkshire and we have also," said Edgar Fountain.

"Surely all yours would be kept in a safe," said Liza.

"It normally is, but my wife left what she was wearing last night on her dressing table. My wife's jewellery, although valuable, does not carry the history of yours Lady Edgeworth," said Edgar Fountain. "I am so sorry that this has happened. Tell me, how reliable are your staff?"

Liza stiffened and Jamie bristled with indignation. "We trust our staff with not only our lives but those of our children. They have both been with us for a number of years and they are as honest as the day is long. I do not like your intimation that they may be thieves," said Jamie quietly.

Liza went back into the room where April and Roberts were working together. April was crying and Roberts could be heard telling her that she must not worry as nobody would ever think that she was to blame.

"Have you nearly repacked?" Liza asked.

April quickly mopped her eyes and nodded, and Liza smiled at Roberts. "I'm sure it will all be sorted out shortly," she said.

"April's worried that people will think that she has something to do with the disappearance of your jewels," said Roberts.

Liza smiled and said, "We all know that April would never do anything like that. It must have happened when nobody was in the rooms this morning and we are not the only ones to have lost items. We are still hoping to be able to leave shortly so please make sure we're ready."

Jamie was already in the drawing room and he naturally looked annoyed, but he beckoned her to come over to him.

"How is April and of course Roberts?" he asked.

"April is still a little upset and Roberts is looking after her," said Liza. "What do you think we should do now Jamie?"

"Unfortunately there is very little that we can do now. Lord Fountain has called in a professional team of investigators and they will be here shortly. They will want to ask questions of all the staff so we will have to stay until they have seen April and Roberts," said Jamie.

Liza pursed her lips. "I would have thought that we should all be questioned. After all I know what time I left our rooms and who I may have seen on my way down here and you must have some information if only to establish who was where and when. It's true that staff members are probably more observant than the rest of us because they move around in a place like this more than we do. Also I don't like the inference that the thieves could only be servants. This house has had many unfamiliar faces within it and it would therefore be easy for a stranger to enter without anybody realising it."

"You're right Liza," said Lady Redfern who was standing nearby. "There are many people I have seen who I have assumed should be here, but who would really know?"

The investigators arrived and after talking to Lord Fountain they wanted to see Jamie, who unfortunately could give them no significant information. They seemed determined to only ask questions of the men in the household and then decided to interview all members of the staff, starting with April.

Having been summoned from her duties, April arrived nervously, and Liza smiled at her reassuringly and went with her into the study where interviews were being held.

"You are Lady Edgeworth," stated a rather gruff gentleman. "We don't need to see you; we just want to interview your maid."

"I'm surprised that you don't wish to see me Sir, after all it is the Edgeworth emeralds which have been stolen and it was me who left the room and obviously therefore allowed whoever the thief was to gain entry with no one to stop him. Do you not wish to know if I saw anyone near my rooms at that time?" said Liza.

"Oh well, did you?" asked the investigator patiently.

"As it happens, no I didn't," smiled Liza.

By this time April was becoming more ill at ease.

"I see, well we don't need you any more Lady Edgeworth," said the investigator

159

"You may not need me Sir, but April does and I will not allow her to be intimidated by you, so I shall stay whilst you talk to her, just as Lord Edgeworth will stay whilst you interview his valet, Roberts," said Liza.

"Your maid was closest to where the jewels were, so she must know something about them," said the investigator.

April was now looking decidedly sick, so Liza stepped in yet again.

"Tell me April," said Liza. "How and when did you realise that the jewels were missing and try to remember who you saw on your way to our rooms this morning?"

"Lady Edgeworth, you have no experience in interviewing suspects, please leave it to me," he said.

"You are wrong Sir, I believe I have more experience in such matters than you do, so please let me carry on without interruption," said Liza.

April told of how she saw a couple of people in the corridor near the rooms, but she had seen them the night before and believed that they were employed by one of the house guests. She carried on that she was packing all Liza's clothes and possessions as was Roberts with Jamie's. When they had nearly finished Roberts went to what should have been a locked drawer to remove the jewels and pack them away safely. He found that the drawer had already been unlocked and the jewel case was open and empty and that was all she could tell him.

"You had the keys to that particular drawer, who else had them?" asked the interviewer.

"I didn't have any keys," said April. "Roberts was given the key by His Lordship."

"I presume that Lord Fountain had duplicate keys to all such safety drawers," said Liza. "I know that Lord Edgeworth just had one key which, as April has said, was given to Roberts this morning."

"I am sorry Lady Edgeworth, I do not wish to be rude, but I am trying to interrogate your maid and you are not helping," said the interviewer.

"Well Sir, you are not doing a very good job. It seems to me that you wish to find someone to blame whether or not they are to blame. I think we have finished here, and I now need April to finalise arrangements for us to leave," said Liza.

"You can leave your Ladyship, but she can't. I'm having her room searched at the moment, and even if we do not find any jewellery, we know that she has therefore passed it onto an accomplice. I'm surprised that you wish to associate with her under the circumstances," he said.

"I'm sorry April, I seem to have made matters worse, but please don't worry you know that I will not let anything happen to you, I promise you that," said Liza.

The interrogator, Isaac Flood, then said, "I want her securely locked in a room," and he called one of his men into the room.

"You are not going to do that," said Liza. "I am going to call in my own security division. I do not care who you are and how you are employed by Lord Fountain, I will have my own team here to investigate and I will have them here within hours. We will not leave the premises, so there is no need to 'lock up' April. I think in the meantime it would do you well to try to determine just who the thieves are because I know that they are not April or Roberts, and I doubt whether they would be any of the servants of the other guests. They value their jobs too much. You can leave April in my care and my word is good enough for all else here, I therefore presume that it is good enough for you."

"Lord Fountain will not bow to your request for your own security team. Who are they by the way?" the man asked with a smirk.

"They are the security division of Marchant & Fuller; I presume you have heard of them," said Liza.

"Everyone has heard of them," laughed Isaac Flood. "What are they to you?"

"They work for me. That's all you need to know. We are leaving this room now and I don't expect any arguments," said Liza.

Isaac Flood stared at Liza for a moment and realisation dawned on him. "You're Liza Marchant."

"I'm now Lady Liza Edgeworth, and I don't want you to forget that," said Liza and she walked with April out of the study and quickly they made their way to where Jamie was standing with Lord Fountain.

"I'm sorry Edgar but I am calling in my own security division to handle this debacle. I don't wish to belittle what you have tried to do to solve this situation, but your security investigator will not bring this problem to a happy conclusion. If this upsets you then I am sorry, but I am not going to have an idiot interview any more of my staff," said Liza with annoyance. Jamie stared at her and he did not know whether to be pleased or embarrassed.

Roberts was hovering not knowing what to do and Liza called him over, she looked at Jamie and he knew that she was asking his permission to carry out what she felt was essential and he nodded and smiled at her.

"Roberts, I want you to find Davis and our second coachman, Hendry, and I want one to go to the Marchant & Fuller offices in South London. I will write a letter to them, but I want experienced interrogators here as soon as possible. I also want Hendry to go to our house in Surrey and bring Adam Reece here. I will also write a note to him whilst they are getting organised," said Liza.

"May I use your study please Edgar. I need to write these notes quickly and when I have done that, I will apologise profusely to you for taking over the situation in your own home, but I have loyal employees who have been incorrectly accused of something that they would never do. I would also like to suggest that nobody leaves your house until my people get here, although I have a feeling that this has already been allowed," said Liza.

Jamie came over to her and said, "Liza this is not your house and you can't order people around in their own homes."

"I know that Jamie, but I cannot allow our staff to be accused by idiots who just want to show that they are doing a good job when they are doing nothing of the kind," said Liza.

Liza could see that Edgar Fountain was bristling with indignation, but she was suddenly aware of Lady Redfern beside her and Lucille Fountain joined her, and Bella slowly made her way towards her. Lord Carlton and the Duke of Berkshire were nodding their agreement to what Liza had said. Lord Edgar Fountain had no choice but to agree to Liza's requests and he showed her to his study and she ushered April in with her.

"I must write these notes April, but when I have done that you will go nowhere without either His Lordship or me, or perhaps Roberts. I am not going to have you alone at any time," said Liza.

"I haven't taken anything," said a very unhappy April, who was trying to mop up her tears.

"April, I know you have taken nothing; his Lordship knows that also, as does Roberts and just about everyone else here. The only one who wants to make his life easy is Isaac Flood who really has no idea how to conduct an investigation. Unfortunately it may well be that the perpetrators have long since left this place and if that idiot had stopped people leaving earlier then we could have had our possessions back with us by now; or it could have been discovered who had left taking their ill-gotten gains with them. He is wasting a

162

great deal of time and I am not going to allow that to go on much longer," said Liza.

"Thank you," said April.

Liza looked at her and smiled, "April, there is no need for you to thank me. Sit down and let me get on with my correspondence."

Firstly Liza wrote to her head of security at the docks south of the River, telling him of the situation at the Fountain House and requesting that he immediately make his way to them with a number of experienced men to take charge of the situation.

Her next letter was to Adam and she told him that April really needed his support at this moment and that he was to leave all in the hands of Estelle, Grace and David and organise that Miranda and Lucinda come to the main house to keep everything running smoothly.

Davis and Hendry were hovering at the main steps waiting for their instructions and when Liza had finished her letters, she went to them both and told them how urgent their missions were.

"April would never do anything wrong," said Davis. "What they are saying about her is totally untrue. It is not in her nature to be dishonest. There were many people milling around yesterday and even the permanent staff had no idea just who they were. Don't worry your Ladyship we'll get the help you need as soon as possible. I'll go to the docks, and Hendry will get Mr Reece and make sure all is well at the house."

"Thank you, Davis, you have always been loyal and caring to our household. I don't forget what you did in the past for young Master James and I know that Hendry is just as loyal," said Liza and they climbed aboard their two carriages and left to reach the docks and Edgeworth House as soon as the horses could carry them. Liza estimated that Adam would probably be here in just over three hours, but the security personnel would probably not reach them for four hours. It was going to be a long day.

Liza turned and moved back into the house, putting her arm around April's shoulder as she went. Jamie came towards them and Liza told him that she was going up to the rooms that were theirs and taking April with her. "What is happening with Roberts?" she asked

"Absolutely nothing; in fact nobody else is being questioned and many of the guests are making their arrangements to leave. Lord Carlton and the Duke of Berkshire are remaining, and they have already expressed the opinion that the investigation is being handled incorrectly. Lady Redfern will have to leave shortly as she has to undertake her duties at the Palace," said Jamie.

"I'm sorry Jamie. I didn't want to embarrass you, but I couldn't let April take the blame for something she has not done. You know what the legal system is like; she would be tried, convicted and on her way to Van Diemen's Land or Tasmania as it's now called, before we could do anything to help. I had to stop what was happening immediately and if it means that I will be ostracised from gatherings, then sobeit," said a very unhappy Liza.

"I don't think you'll be ostracised from any gatherings Liza," said Lady Redfern. "You're only doing what should have been done in the first place."

Liza guided April up to their rooms and told her to rest on the bed and that she would stay with her until Adam arrived.

Lady Redfern with still talking to Jamie, "Edgar is reading the riot act to Isaac Flood who seems to have fixated on your maid. Is she the one getting married next week?"

"Yes, and Liza has sent for her fiancé and she's not letting her out of her sight until he arrives. Naturally April's very upset," said Jamie.

"I'm sorry that you've lost the Edgeworth emeralds Jamie," said Lady Redfern. "I remember you scrimping and scraping to make enough to get them back from the money lenders. Does your uncle still have the Edgeworth diamonds?"

"I have no idea," said Jamie and he smiled at Lady Redfern in such a way that told her to ask nothing further about the diamonds.

Liza and April had a stream of visitors over the following few hours. Jamie was there regularly as was Roberts. Lady Redfern came in to say that she had to leave but she and her staff would be available to help in any way they could. Lucille Fountain ensured that they had all that they needed, and Bella came to keep them company.

"I don't think that we will attend another function at the Fountains; their arrangements for security for their guests are woefully lacking. We always use your Company for our functions," said Bella.

"I would have thought that any professional security company would do an equally efficient job," said Liza.

"Lord Carlton used your Company, but Evelyn Edgeworth still got in," said Bella.

"Evelyn was partnering a bona fide guest at the time, so it would have been difficult to distinguish between who was welcome and who was not," said Liza.

"I find it difficult to understand how my jewellery was stolen as I didn't leave my room from the time I went to bed last night until after my breakfast this morning when I found that they were missing. I feel a little unnerved because I must have been asleep when the theft was perpetrated," said Bella.

"Did you tell the investigator that?" asked Liza.

"I haven't seen the investigator. He only spoke to the Duke and didn't seem interested in anything I had to say," said Bella.

"So what you are saying is that you were robbed whilst you slept. You are right, that is very unnerving," said Liza. "I wonder whether it was the same for us, but I would have thought that we would have heard something."

Bella smiled slyly, "Of course it's well known that you and Jamie sleep together; that's why you were given a suite of rooms. If somebody had come into your rooms at least one of you would have heard them."

April was still resting on the bed and she was trying to appear that she was not listening to the conversation.

"I think it's ridiculous that your girl, what's her name, is the only one that is being accused. Plenty of people saw a couple of strangers down in the kitchens but of course, as you mentioned earlier, how would any of us know who should be here and who should not. Even Edgar and Lucille would not know who any of the servants were who were accompanying their guests," said Bella.

"I'm glad that someone feels the same way that I do," said Liza.

"Plenty of people do Liza. I wonder if Lucille's jewels were also taken through the night whilst she was in her bed, or anyone else's bed for that matter," said Bella.

"Bella, you're spreading gossip and that could land you in a great deal of trouble if you say it to the wrong person," said Liza. "I suppose she knows when hers was taken."

"She hasn't said, but probably it would be best if she didn't comment on where she was at the time," laughed Bella.

Liza looked down and said nothing. "Ah, you're as discreet as always," said Bella once again laughing.

Roberts knocked and entered, "There's a Mr Andrews to see you your Ladyship."

"Thank you, Roberts," said Liza. "Can you stay here with April please? I promised that we would not leave her with anyone other than you, me or his Lordship."

"I could stay with her Liza," said Bella.

"Thank you, Bella, but she knows Roberts well and I'm sure she would feel more comfortable with him," said Liza, "but it is kind of you to offer."

Liza went over to April and put her arm around her, "Now that Mr Andrews is here it will all be sorted out properly. Adam will be here soon, that's something for you to be looking forward to," said Liza.

Liza and Bella walked out of the room together. "You're very caring of your staff Liza. I would have assumed that an investigator would have known what he was talking about, but I don't get to know my staff that well," said Bella.

"April has been with me since I returned from America after Patrick died. She looked after me, Matthew and John with so much care and in some ways, they also looked after her. She could hardly read and write then but she persevered, and the boys helped her. She is family now. She had no surname but felt that she needed one before she married Adam and after a great deal of thought she chose the name Kelly, because he had been her inspiration to get away from the life that she had and now she has a wonderful life ahead of her and I am not going to allow anything to get in the way of that life for her. She deserves a good life; she doesn't deserve the idiocy that is being thrown at her by that excuse for an investigator," said Liza.

"I knew that she had been abused," said Bella.

"I know you did Bella, otherwise I would not have told you anything about her," said Liza. "There is much more I could tell you, but she would not wish that. She is now embarking on a very normal, happy married life; one that at one time she never thought she would have."

"Do you get emotional about all your abused children Liza?" asked Bella.

"Yes, but I try not to show it to them. They don't want someone weeping all over them; they just want someone who can organise a better life for them," smiled Liza.

By that time they had both reached Edgar Fountain's study where Jamie and Edgar were talking to Cyril Andrews. Bella left her at the door and Liza entered. "It's good to see you again Mr Andrews. I presume you understand what has been happening here."

"Yes Lady Edgeworth," said Cyril and they both smiled as normally they were on first name terms. "I understand that young April is so far the only suspect in this sorry business. I'll see her in a minute if I may, but I would like you to be present when I do; she's been through enough in her life already, she doesn't need me to upset her further. I have four men arriving shortly and

166

they will have to talk to everyone here and I would also like to examine the rooms where the possessions went missing and I would like the owners to be with me when I do."

"What do you want me to do about Isaac Flood?" asked Edgar.

"I will interview him also and find out why he has a fixation on young April, but after that I would like to be left to my own devices to get on with the job," said Cyril.

"Just for your information Cyril, the Duchess of Berkshire did not leave her room from the time she went to bed and removed her jewellery to the time she discovered it missing. It is rather concerning to think that the thief or thieves entered her room whilst she was asleep. God knows what would have happened if she had woken up and confronted them," said Liza.

Both Jamie and Edgar were frowning at that piece of information. "Why didn't we know that before?" said Edgar.

"I'm afraid nobody thought of interviewing her, but I'll say no more on that subject," said Liza.

"Does that mean that somebody entered our room also whilst we slept?" said Jamie.

"Perhaps," was all Liza would say and she knew that Jamie was thinking as she was that they always slept naked and often the bedclothes were pushed to one side, especially if it was a warm night.

"If I may Lord Fountain, I'd like to see young April first and listen to what she has to say and then I'll talk to Isaac Flood and by that time my men should have arrived and when they have spoken to your guests and their servants, they can all get on their way to their various homes. It would be useful if we could know which servants are with which guests so that we can tidy everyone up together," said Cyril.

Edgar nodded and smiled, and Liza and Jamie could see that he was suitably impressed, and they doubted that Isaac Flood would have employment at any future functions in the Fountain household.

"I'll take you up to April and Roberts is with her so you may want to talk to him at the same time," said Liza.

It didn't take him long to establish the facts as April and Roberts knew them. He was interested in the two men that April had seen and who now seemed to have disappeared, but he did say that it could be a coincidence and he would find out more about them from the Fountain's butler and housekeeper. He smiled and said that they could go but he knew that Lord and Lady Edgeworth would be staying for a while longer.

"I understand you are getting married next week April," he said smiling. "I wish you well. I have met Adam Reece a few times and he is a wonderful match for you."

He turned to Liza and said that he would now like to meet Isaac Flood and if she could guide him in the right direction it would be better if she left him to meet up with the man on his own. Liza smiled and was under no illusions that Cyril would be putting Isaac Flood well and truly in his place.

When he had finished whatever he had to say to Isaac Flood the further security men had arrived and Cyril organised their interviewing guests along with their servants whilst he undertook seeing Bella personally as he knew the significance of what she had surmised and he went with her to the room where her possessions had been.

Liza rushed back up to April, who was looking so much better. Roberts was finalising packing and he was not allowing April to lift a finger. "You've had a shock April; you need to rest."

April was about to argue when the door burst open and there was Adam; he looked around and his eyes alighted on April and he dashed over to her and engulfed her in his arms. For them there was nobody else in the room. Liza indicated to Roberts to leave and they both moved out of the room and closed the door behind them.

"That's going to be one marriage made in heaven," said Roberts. "I think I'll go down to the kitchen and arrange a tray for them and after that I don't know what I'll do until it's time to leave."

"Oh, I'm sure you'll manage to amuse yourself Roberts," smiled Liza.

Jamie was with the Duke of Berkshire and Lord Carlton when Liza came to find him. "Excuse me gentlemen, I just wanted to let Jamie know that Adam has arrived and is with April now. I also believe that when Davis and Hendry have rested for a while, we will be able to leave. I'll go down to see how they are."

The men watched her leave. "Does she ever sit down Jamie?" asked the Duke. Jamie laughed. "Yes, she does, but her mind never switches off."

"I'm sorry about your emeralds Jamie," said Lord Carlton. "I know they meant a lot to you; I hope that you will eventually get them back. I'm glad it wasn't the diamonds that were taken, I suppose now that you are back with your uncle you have them in your possession again."

"I have no idea where they are; I don't own them; I don't even know that my uncle still does. They are not part of the reason why he is coming to live with us. He is coming to live with us because we want him and my cousin to be near us. He is proud enough not to live on our charity, they will therefore be occupying our gatehouse; the alternative was that he was insistent that he would rent a couple of rooms in the village and neither Liza nor I would tolerate that. The gatehouse is not prestigious, but it is being renovated and they assure me that they will be very happy there," said Jamie.

"You have all your family around you now Jamie; life has certainly changed for the better for you," said the Duke.

"Yes, life is very pleasant for me now," said Jamie.

Liza had missed lunch and Lucille insisted that she now had afternoon tea and by that time Liza had become a guest again rather than an organiser.

"You'll be leaving soon Liza, but you will still contact me regarding the opening of the Ffoulks Home. I do hope that what has happened will not make you change your mind over allowing me to help with the children," said Lucille.

"Of course she wouldn't do that Lucille," said a slightly irritated Bella. "Liza needs all the help she can get with those children and I just hope that we can do a good job for her because both you and I are not used to handling children and especially those who have been hurt. We have got to steel ourselves against what we are likely to see on that day. Personally I'm looking forward to it as it may well make us understand how and why Liza has championed the charity."

Liza was looking at Bella with her mouth slightly open, and Bella laughed. "Your face is a picture Liza. I have lived my life with what is termed a 'silver spoon' in my mouth; I have spent my time wining, dining, taking afternoon tea and generally being totally useless, apart of course from providing heirs for the Duke. This is the first time that I feel that I am going to be useful, and if I can cope with that one day, I would like to physically help at other times."

"That is extremely commendable Bella; let's see how you get on and we'll talk about it then," said Liza.

A short while later Jamie joined her and said that Davis and Hendry were now ready to leave and Roberts had gone to tell April and Adam. Bella walked with Liza towards their carriages. "You know Bella you don't have to feel responsible for the sins of your brother; much as I appreciate what you are doing to help, you must not take on any tasks because of any guilt that you may feel. You have done nothing wrong," said Liza.

"I have done wrong Liza," said Bella. "I knew that Binky had strange ways and I hid them from the outside world. If I had told my mother, then perhaps some children would not have had to suffer the way they did. My mother always thought that he liked men rather than women, but she never realised the depths that he had sunk to until you had problems with him. I owe a little of my time to the children, it's the least I can do."

"Whatever you are able to do will be appreciated but just do what you feel comfortable with," said Liza. "I'll let you know the exact date and time of the children's arrival."

Adam was guiding April towards the second carriage and Roberts was following them. Jamie called to Roberts, "you can travel with us Roberts; let's leave April and Adam to travel back alone."

Liza looked at Jamie and smiled, "I thought you said that I was the romantic in our family."

"They deserve to have time alone, it's been a very upsetting day for them both and it's going to take a while for them to settle down," smiled Jamie.

"I'll ride up with Davis," said Roberts.

"You'll need a coat for that Roberts; you know you can travel in with us," said Liza.

"No, it's quite a warm evening. I'll be perfectly alright, thank you," said Roberts.

"You'd better take one of His Lordships coats; there's one in the carriage, take that," said Liza and she handed it to Roberts.

Roberts took the coat and climbed up next to Davis; Jamie helped Liza into the carriage and climbed in beside her. "Thank you for giving my coat away Liza," said Jamie and he laughed.

"Do you think we will ever be invited to a function at the Fountain's home again; or to any of their other guests' events?" said Liza.

"I'm sure we will be, although I dare say that it wouldn't worry you if we weren't," said Jamie. "I know why you were so insistent that the Marchant & Fuller security chief came to investigate. Isaac Flood was too keen to find someone to blame and if he had chosen somebody other than April then we might not have taken so much notice. Because we know her so well, we knew that he was being totally absurd and he had to have a reason for getting the problem over quickly, presumably so that he could leave as soon as possible."

"It dawned on me when I saw the look of panic on his face when he realised which security company I wanted, and he then said that he knew who I was. It seemed very plain to me that he was too anxious to appear to do his job and go, presumably to join his two accomplices. He obviously chose the wrong person to blame, I would think that he could kick himself now," said Liza.

"I suppose you told Cyril Andrews of your suspicions," said Jamie.

"I didn't need to, he already knew. He didn't say so, but I know him well enough to know that he was taking on board what the situation was all about, and of course it was all about money. I wonder how many houses have been robbed whilst Isaac Flood has meant to be keeping them safe," said Liza.

"Poor April certainly went through a terrible time. I was pleasantly surprised at the number of people who dismissed out of hand any thoughts that she was guilty of anything," said Jamie.

"I'm sorry you've lost the Edgeworth emeralds Jamie," said Liza. "Emeralds have not been a very lucky stone for me and yet they are my birth stone."

"If we don't get them back, I'll buy you some more," said Jamie. "I was asked about the Edgeworth diamonds a couple of times. People seemed to think that because my uncle is now with us that we naturally have the diamonds."

"Your uncle bought those diamonds many years ago, so they are his to do as he wishes with them. He's probably sold them; he would have needed the money no doubt. I hope he doesn't think that we have organised a home for him so that we can have the diamonds," said a worried Liza.

"I know that he doesn't think that, Liza; he wanted us to take in Grace and I have a feeling that he was going to offer us the diamonds when she said that she couldn't live on our charity. Do you remember he said that he had a way of sorting it out?" said Jamie.

"I'm still surprised that he could afford to buy them back in the first place. I suppose we will never know how he managed that," said Liza. She put her head back against the seat and closed her eyes.

"You're very tired aren't you Liza," said Jamie and he put his arm around her and moved her head onto his shoulder. She smiled and slept for an hour.

Both carriages pulled up in front of the house and everyone wearily climbed out and made their way up the steps to be greeted by a chorus of shouts of pleasure from the boys. Miranda and Lucinda guided them into the drawing room together with Adam and April. Estelle came in with David and Grace, so it was a very noisy welcome home.

April seemed overwhelmed and then burst into tears; Liza jumped up to go to her, but Estelle got to her first and put her arms around her.

"It's alright April, you don't need to cry," said Matthew. "We know you didn't take anything. We'd have got you out of prison," which made April cry even harder. Adam stepped forward and suggested that April went to her room for a while.

"That's a good idea Adam," said Liza. "I'll arrange a tray to be taken up to her in a little while. It's been a very bad day for her, but she's home and safe now."

"We'll look after you April," said John.

"We'll bring your tray up to you," said James. "We'll have to look after you now instead of you looking after us."

"That's very kind of you all," said Adam. "Perhaps you can do that in a little while."

April, Estelle and Adam left the room and the boys went to the kitchen to see what Mrs Lambert could organise for April.

Jamie and Liza were asked exactly what had happened and it took a little while for the whole story to be told and in the end it was commented that it was a shame that the Edgeworth emeralds were now missing.

"Bella and Lucille also lost jewellery, but everyone seemed more concerned about our emeralds as we were reminded on many occasions that they were part of the Edgeworth history. The others' jewels were fairly new and apparently didn't mean so much to the owners," said Jamie.

"You must be upset by their loss Jamie as I know that you had to work very hard to get the money together to redeem them," said Miranda.

"Yes, it's a shame but they are possessions; people are more important," said Jamie.

"That's well said Jamie," said David, "but people should not take what does not belong to them, so I hope that your security man will be able to find them for the family."

Noises were coming from the hallway and up the stairs and when Liza went to investigate, she saw the three boys each precariously carrying a tray. Mrs Frances was watching over them and Liza asked her if April was hungry enough to have three trays of food.

"No, they decided that Mr Adam and Miss Estelle as well as April needed to eat and they would take no argument over it. I hope that it reaches them in the various dishes rather than in a mess on the trays or on the floor," laughed Mrs Frances. "Their hearts are in the right place but I'm not sure that anyone is very hungry after the day they have had."

"They think that they are helping to make them feel better and that's important to them. I know that Adam, Estelle and April will appreciate the sentiment," said Liza.

Back in the drawing room Liza explained the good intentions of the boys although it was doubtful that the food would arrive at its destination intact.

Jamie and Liza decided to freshen up before dinner, although they also didn't feel very hungry, but it was a gathering that was important to Miranda, Lucinda, David and Grace. Many thoughts and opinions were voiced over the Edgeworth dinner table and it was a time that everyone looked forward to.

Once around the table further questions were being asked. "Do you really think that the thieves came into your room whilst you were asleep?" said Lucinda.

"Well Bella certainly did not leave her room from the time she went to bed until she woke the following morning and found that her jewellery was missing," said Liza.

"That's very disturbing; what if she had woken up? She could have been killed in her bed," said Lucinda.

"Do you think that your possessions were taken whilst you slept?" asked David.

"All we know is that I breakfasted in our room and Jamie ate in the dining room with the other gentlemen. When I had finished, I made myself ready for the day and April started packing our clothes. Jamie gave Roberts the keys to the safety drawer which unfortunately was already unlocked and the jewel case open. We had only left our room empty for ten minutes and maybe that was when they took our jewels because the only alternative was when we were both sleeping. It is frightening to think that someone may have been prowling in our room whilst we were there and we prefer to think that it was whilst the room was empty," said Liza.

"Do you know when the Fountains first noticed their loss?" asked David.

"No, Lucille was very quiet about that," said Liza. "I suppose it was embarrassing enough for their guests to lose their possessions that they didn't feel that they could say too much about their own loss."

"I do hope you get them back," said Miranda. "The emeralds suited Liza so well and you wear them more than the rubies."

"Didn't you have a set of sapphires also?" asked David.

"Yes, we do," said Jamie. "But Liza rarely wears anything that they would go with, but my mother does, so she wears them on special occasions."

"You really did work hard to redeem them Jamie," said David. "I remember all the jewellery being in the money lenders' hands more than it was in the family's hands."

Jamie just smiled and nodded, and Liza engaged Lucinda and Miranda in conversation and Grace was also discussing decorations for her new home.

"I believe you know that I redeemed the Edgeworth diamonds," said David suddenly. All other conversations stopped, and Grace looked at her father in shock, making it obvious that this was news to her.

"Yes Uncle, I had heard that. In fact it was how we first knew of your existence. We were at the Duke of Berkshire's function and Liza was wearing some of the Edgeworth jewels. The Duke asked me if I had managed to redeem all the family jewels. I said that the only ones I could not redeem were the diamonds as they had already been sold to someone else. I think it was Lord Carlton who said that he could not believe that I did not know who had bought them and that was the first time that I knew that I had an uncle," said Jamie.

"Lady Redfern called me to one side when the ladies had retired to the drawing room and she told me what she knew of you, which was that you were a man of the cloth and informed me of the circumstances of your marriage to Holly," said Liza.

"The next day we firstly asked my mother if she was aware of you, but she had no knowledge and we then went to Bernard Collins and as you know he and young Derek searched the records and found you. Bernard also wrote to the Archbishop and he gave us your address," said Jamie. "So we would still have not known of your existence if the Edgeworth diamonds had not been mentioned that evening."

"You haven't asked if I still have them," said David.

"What you have done with them is your business. You bought them so it was up to you to do as you please with them; I'm just thankful that they were mentioned as we are now all sitting together around this table because of them," said Jamie.

Liza smiled happily at everyone. "I have to tell you that to come back home to you all after the very trying time we have had is so very comforting. We are so often on show nowadays that times like this mean that we can relax and be ourselves."

"I wonder how April got on with the meals that the boys took up to her?" said Miranda.

"I really should have rescued her from them, but they were so anxious to make her feel better that I didn't have the heart to take their pleasure away from them. Adam and Estelle were gently dealing with them and I know that April appreciated it," said Liza.

Grace was still staring at her father and she appeared to be holding her breath; Lucinda was looking at her with concern. "Grace," she said gently, "can I get you something to drink, you don't look too well."

"Thank you, Lucinda, I'm fine," said Grace. "I find that I am beginning to realise that there is a great deal about my father that I never knew. I wonder if my mother ever knew him at all."

David smiled at her, "your mother encouraged everything that I did in my life. She knew me better than I knew myself. It was at her instigation that I found a way to redeem the Edgeworth diamonds. In fact, it was mostly her money that I used for it, and she was very happy that they were safely in the care of an Edgeworth. We both knew that they really belonged here, but at the time Jamie's father was still around and Jamie was seriously playing the tables."

Grace was thoughtful and then said, "I had a very happy childhood; I had enough clothes to wear and adequate food on the table, but we didn't have a life that someone with that sort of money could have had. Please don't think that I am complaining; I am just puzzled."

"For many years Holly's father refused to have anything to do with us; he didn't even tell us when her mother died, which was really upsetting for her," said David.

"Uncle, perhaps this is something that you would prefer to speak to Grace about alone. We are very happy that you and Grace are going to remain here with us; we do not need to be privy to your personal life," said Jamie.

"Around this table are your close family, Jamie, and that includes you Lucinda," said David. "I think that the time has come for an explanation or two. A few years after Holly and I married and Grace was a toddler, Holly's father came to us. This may upset you Jamie, but the way your father was acting at that time made Holly's father realise that marriage to him would have been a disaster. He was so sorry for the way he had reacted and was delighted that she had a much better life with me than she ever would have had with him. I believe he also knew what an unhappy life you were having with him Miranda."

Miranda appeared very close to tears and Lucinda was patting her hand reassuringly.

David carried on, "Holly's father visited us on a few occasions, but he was getting older and as he lived in Hertfordshire, the trip to see us was quite strenuous for him but he told us that the Edgeworth jewellery was being used to finance your father's gambling addiction. However, your father was managing to redeem them with some winnings but carried on gambling, so it was beginning to appear that the jewels were with the money lender more than they were in the Edgeworth safe. We received a letter from Holly's father telling us that your father was in serious financial difficulties and the family was in danger of losing everything. He sent money for me to make a trip to London where he met me, and he paid for the Edgeworth diamonds to be redeemed. He said that as Holly would inherit whatever he had then she might as well have it then, although he felt a responsibility towards the Edgeworth family because of the circumstances of our marriage and wanted the diamonds to stay with a branch of that family."

"That was very generous of him," said Jamie.

"He was not a poor man, but his finances did not stretch to buying all the Edgeworth jewels. He did however realise that the diamonds were exquisite and needed to be kept within the family. He died a few months later and Holly and I did not attend functions where such pieces of jewellery would be worn so they have stayed safely packed away for all these years," said David.

"I followed what you were doing Jamie and for some time I wondered what I would do with the jewels as I knew that you were following in your father's footsteps but a few years ago I found that you were working well and slowly getting your estates back on their feet. I also knew that you were gradually buying back your items from the money lenders, so I made my Will and in it stipulated that the Edgeworth diamonds were to be returned to your safekeeping. This was something that Holly and I had discussed and we both felt that it was the right thing to do," said David.

"I really don't know what to say Uncle. All I can think of is to tell you again that they are yours and should eventually be Grace's not mine," said Jamie.

"No Jamie, you are wrong," said David. "I have never considered them mine; they are part of what should be within this household and handed down to young James and his offspring. They have no place in a vicarage and they would look beautiful on Liza; she should wear them as she would show them off to perfection."

"Are you saying that you are thinking of giving them to Jamie now because if you are then we cannot allow that," said Liza.

"Liza, you both have already said that they are mine to do with as I wish, and I wish to put them into the safekeeping of Jamie and this household," said David rather testily.

"I believe what Liza is trying to say Uncle, is that we will buy them from you, as we cannot allow you to give away Grace's inheritance. It is money that she will need in the future," said Jamie.

"I've told you that I am not in need of money. Our needs are not vast and now that you have so generously provided a home for us, our money will last us as long as necessary. We will of course pay a contribution towards renting the property," said David.

"Please Uncle, don't insult us. We are not in need of any rent for the gatehouse; it is our pleasure to do this for you and Grace. You know that if the circumstances of your marriage had been different and if my father and grandfather had not gambled away a great deal of money, you would have inherited at least enough to keep you with no monetary worries. Also Holly would have inherited from her father and part of that inheritance was spent on redeeming the diamonds, so therefore the jewels are yours and should in turn go to Grace. What you are suggesting is not right," said Jamie.

"I know that it really is none of my business," said Miranda, "but I believe that what Jamie and Liza are saying is right. It would be a different matter if they had very little funds, but you know that they have no concerns in that respect. Holly's father spent his hard-earned money on preserving the heritage of the Edgeworths and by rights that money, or the jewels, should eventually have gone to Grace."

"It is your business Mother," said Jamie, "after all you are an Edgeworth. I would like to suggest that we have the diamonds valued and we give you a fair price for them. If we hadn't managed to lose the emeralds, we would have had in our possession the complete Edgeworth jewels."

"That is a great shame," said Lucinda. "I wonder if they will ever be found. The man that you put in charge sounds very efficient."

"I am so shocked that we have had these items all these years and I had no knowledge of them," said Grace. "I believe that Jamie and Liza are being more than fair, and they should have them in their possession. We have always had to watch how we spend our money and now for once in our lives we are being offered the opportunity to have no worries. I would find it a great relief."

"Is that settled then?" asked Liza. "We will get a valuation when you return and see what amount we are talking about."

"I brought them with me," said David quietly.

All eyes turned to him. "You mean that we travelled all the way here with valuable jewellery in our possession," said a shocked Grace. David nodded.

"I think that perhaps the time has come to put them in my safe. They are still yours Uncle; would you like me to take charge of them now," asked Jamie.

"I presume you would like to see them Liza," said David.

"There is time enough for that," said Liza. "I will be delighted to see them when the time is right, and I shall be proud to wear them."

"You look very tired Liza," said Miranda. "It's been a very long day for you."

"It's also been a very unsettling day and I must go and make sure that April has recovered from her ordeal," said Liza.

Harper was called and he saw Miranda and Lucinda back to the Dower House; Jamie went with his uncle to collect the Edgeworth diamonds from his room and place them in the safe and Liza and Grace called in to see that April was now relaxing comfortably.

"You're very caring of your staff," said Grace as they left April's room.

"They are very caring of us," replied Liza. She said goodnight to Grace and made her way to the boys' room. They always made her feel happy as she watched them sleeping. Then she went to her room and got ready for bed having already told April not to worry about her. She finally heard Roberts leave Jamie's room and as she crossed the corridor Jamie opened his door for her.

"Mother was right, you do look tired Liza," said Jamie.

"It has been a very tiring and very long day, and I really feel unnerved by the fact that someone could have been in our bedroom last night. Taking our possessions was bad enough but our times in bed are very private and precious to us. I do not like the thought that someone was spying on us when we were at our most vulnerable," said Liza.

"I know exactly how you feel, as I feel the same. We have no inhibitions with one another, and I would hate to think that a thief could have seen you naked. I hope they were not hiding somewhere whilst we were making love; I'm sure we would have known if there was someone in our room whilst we were awake and of course we are not sure when the theft took place. It could well have been in the ten minutes that the room was unattended. Let's hope that it was the case," said Jamie. "I do hope that it hasn't put you off sleeping with me."

From the look on Liza's face Jamie realised that it would take a great deal to put her off sleeping with him and he laughed and engulfed her in his arms.

***

It was Saturday and neither Liza nor Jamie had any commitments that day although Liza had correspondence to catch up on. Grace came to help, and they worked together well through until lunchtime. The boys were being overly helpful to April as they felt that she needed their assistance especially as she had escaped 'a fate worse than death' as they called it. Adam could be seen on occasion smiling indulgently at the boys' efforts to make April feel better.

David and Jamie were closeted in the study reading newspapers as well as discussing the future and Estelle was once again working on the preparation for the lessons that she was intending to give to the children once they had settled into their new surroundings.

Miranda and Lucinda were going to enjoy a day in their own home as the next day they would be with their family for Sunday lunch followed by watching the cricket practice during the afternoon.

Just before dinner that evening a rider came to the house and was ushered into Jamie's study. It was Cyril Andrews and Jamie welcomed him. He was about to send someone to fetch Liza, but Cyril stopped him.

"Of course, I'm always pleased to see Lady Liza, but it is rather a delicate matter. I have your emeralds; we found the thieves and have managed to regain most of the stolen property; they did try to break up the tiara as they realised that it was a very noticeable piece, so there is some damage to it," said Cyril.

Jamie was looking at him intently, "I thank you for bringing them to us, but I am concerned that you feel that what you have discovered is rather delicate; although I have a feeling that I know what is making it so."

Cyril was looking decidedly embarrassed. "I'm afraid that the thieves gave themselves away by boasting about a particular incident."

"Liza and I have no secrets Mr Andrews, but I understand that you may find it easier to talk to me than to my wife. I presume that the thieves were in our room when we were also there," said Jamie.

"That's correct, I'm afraid and they were unable to refrain from boasting about what they saw and heard whilst they were there," said Cyril.

"So, the thieves not only stole our possessions, but they also stole our privacy. I suppose it has been shouted about to all and sundry. Liza will not be happy about that, although I don't think she will be surprised as she knows that the Duchess of Berkshire had her jewellery stolen whilst she was asleep in her room and Liza wondered whether the same had happened to us," said Jamie.

"When Isaac Flood left, I had him followed as I did not trust his honesty and I was right unfortunately," said Cyril. "He met up with two men who had been posing as those who were meant to protect the Fountain household. I had sent two of my men to see where he had gone, and they found him in an inn around ten miles away. One of my men came back to inform me of their whereabouts and I in turn sent for the authorities. Luckily Isaac Flood and his men were staying the night at the inn and we managed to get to them before they moved on. They were drinking a great deal and were unaware of my presence and of course they did not know who my men were. I'm afraid that the thieves had been in your room whilst you and her Ladyship were in an intimate situation and with their alcohol intake and presumable feelings of impending fortune, they were very vocal and animated over what they had witnessed. Unfortunately they were also telling all and sundry who you both were, which really led to their downfall."

"So many frequenters of a particular drinking establishment know how much Liza and I love one another," said Jamie. "It is not something that I would have wanted bandied about; however, I am upset that these rogues have seen my wife as only I wish to see her and how she wishes me only to see her. That is going to really sadden and embarrass Liza."

"Perhaps it would be best if she did not know," said Cyril.

Jamie looked at him and smiled, "I thought you knew Liza."

"Yes, I suppose that was a rather foolish comment," said Cyril.

Liza breezed into the study at that moment and greeted Cyril warmly. "Have you found what you were looking for Cyril?"

"Yes, I have, and the perpetrators are now under lock and key," said Cyril.

"I knew you'd be able to do it," said Liza. "As it's so late you'll stay for dinner and I can arrange a room for you for the night."

"A room would be wonderful, thank you, but I'll eat down in the kitchen if you don't mind. I'd be more comfortable doing that," said Cyril.

"Certainly, I'll tell Mrs Frances to expect you and when you make your way down to the kitchen no doubt Jamie will tell me what it is that you can't bring yourself to divulge to me," smiled Liza.

Jamie and Cyril looked at one another and nodded. "Yes, I'll tell you all about it when we're alone Liza," said Jamie. "At least we have our property returned, but unfortunately some of it has been damaged."

"I suppose it's nothing that can't be mended. Did you manage to get the Fountain's jewellery back and the Duchess's also?" asked Liza.

"Yes we found it all, they didn't have the time to sell it on, but they knew that yours was well known which was why they were breaking it up," said Cyril. "It wasn't very clever of them to steal the Edgeworth emeralds as they would be far more difficult to sell on to anyone."

"Perhaps they chose the wrong room to rob; maybe they thought somebody else would be sleeping there," said Liza.

"How is young April? Has she got over her ordeal?" asked Cyril.

"She was very shaken by it, but she has settled back quite well. Unfortunately for her our boys think they are helping her by being so attentive that she can't move without falling over one of them. They kindly said that they would have visited her in prison. They will be going to bed soon and I think she may well breathe a sigh of relief then," smiled Liza.

"They are very caring," said Cyril. "I'll leave you now and go and see my friends downstairs. I'll see you again before I leave tomorrow."

"There's a cricket practice here tomorrow afternoon if you would like to stay a little longer," said Jamie. "It will be a gathering of villagers as well as the rest of us and creates a great deal of pleasure for everyone."

"I may well do that; I've heard that your Edgeworth team is becoming quite proficient; I could stay another night if you have no objection. I'm not on duty again until Monday afternoon," said Cyril.

"Yes, I'm sure Mrs Frances will be pleased to help you get settled," smiled Liza knowingly.

"I gather that Cyril and Mrs Frances have an understanding," said Jamie when Cyril had left to make his way down to the kitchen.

"I'm not sure how serious it is, but they seem to enjoy one another's company. Are you going to tell me what has concerned you? Is it that we did have somebody watching us when we were at the Fountain's?" said Liza.

"I'm sorry Liza. I feel that I have failed in my duty towards you; I should have kept you safe and away from prying eyes. If I hadn't been so keen to bed you then I would have been aware that somebody was trying to steal from us and they would never have seen you as only I should," said Jamie.

"Jamie, you can't blame yourself. Blame the thieves, they were determined to get what they wanted and unfortunately, they got into our room when we were enjoying ourselves. You have to admit that I was just as keen to be bedded as you were to bed me," said Liza. "Do you know whether they saw everything?"

"I'm afraid they did and unfortunately they boasted about what they saw to whoever would listen. One of Cyril's men followed Isaac Flood when he left the Fountain's house and he met up with the two men in an Inn a few miles away. The more I think about it the more I want to get a gun and shoot them. I'm so annoyed that my beautiful Liza has been ogled by loud mouthed, uncouth villains. I should have protected you more," said Jamie.

"When we are in a bedroom and in a bed together, how could you possibly think that I needed protection; just by loving me makes me feel protected. They must have seen you also when you were naked. I don't like the thought that somebody has been looking at your body. I'm going to try to take a positive attitude and hope that we taught them how expert love making should be done," said Liza trying to make light of an embarrassing situation.

Jamie picked up the bag that the jewels were in and opened it up. "It seems that only the tiara has been damaged. No doubt all the rest would have been taken apart if the thieves had not been caught. Well Liza, we now have all the Edgeworth jewels back in our possession, but it seems a high price to pay for the emeralds."

"I think that eventually our annoyance will ease and we must be grateful that we were not hurt; it could have been a different story if we had disturbed them, they might have become aggressive if they were cornered; so we must look on the bright side. We must get ready for dinner and we will keep some of the indelicacies to ourselves. Everyone will be pleased that the Edgeworth emeralds are back with us," said Liza.

Liza was right that the family were pleased that the emeralds were back where they belonged but it was Miranda and David who realised that Liza and Jamie were keeping something to themselves and perhaps they would find out what it was in the fullness of time, but of course that was not going to happen as Liza and Jamie never talked about their private lives, and they were unaware that the problem was so intimate.

Jamie came to Liza's room that night. "I felt like being in your pretty surroundings tonight Liza."

"As long as we intend to sleep together, I don't care which room we are in. I need you very much tonight Jamie; I have been unnerved by having intruders when we should have only had one another and I know you are going to make me feel better tonight," said Liza.

"I believe that you will also make me feel better but I know that it is going to take me a long while to get over having been watched at such an intimate time," said Jamie and they just lay in each other's arms enjoying the feeling of security that they gave to one another.

***

Nobody would allow Adam to hold Derek in place at the cricket practice as they did not want him to be covered in cuts and bruises for his wedding day the following week. Cyril volunteered and Jamie and Mr Rogers were on picking up duty. John was to take his runs as usual.

Everyone was in even more high spirits than usual and it seemed that the only conversations were about April and Adam's wedding and Liza noticed that the happy couple were not looking as happy as they should have been.

"I think that all the villagers and farmers have decided that they will be attending your wedding," said Liza to them.

"We hadn't planned for that," said a worried looking April.

"No but Mrs Lambert and I had," laughed Liza. "So don't worry about it. We didn't want to take over your wedding arrangements, but we know what the village is like and they won't want to let a good wedding go to waste. They'll be celebrating into the early hours of the morning but you two will be well on your way to your honeymoon."

"We didn't want to take advantage of you," said April. "We thought that we would be able to arrange it all ourselves, but you are right, we did not take into account the fact that the village wanted to join in."

"Well, we normally provide for the cricket matches, so we'll just do the sameas usual. I presume that there will be enough room in the cricket pavilion as you had originally planned for your wedding breakfast," said Liza.

"If we pray for good weather, then there will be more than enough room," said Adam. "We have accounted for Hector by the way; he was going to accompany Estelle even though he wasn't invited, but we didn't mind. He's very caring of Estelle."

"Yes he seems very fond of her," said Liza in a very noncommittal way.

By that time Derek had been bowled out and Cyril was brushing himself down and laughing with both Jamie and Mr Rogers patting him on the back. Matthew and James ran across with Derek's crutches and John joined them and they all went off also laughing.

David was next in and he made a few runs before being bowled out and he went to sit with Grace, Miranda and Lucinda for the rest of the afternoon.

As all the villagers and farmers were leaving, they waved and shouted to Adam and April that they would see them at their wedding the following week. Adam and April waved back with resigned smiles on their faces which amused Liza.

Grace wanted to call in at the gatehouse on the way back to the main house and David said that he would go with her. Everyone let them be alone as they had a great deal of planning to do. They would be leaving for Truro in a couple of days and Grace wanted to make a list of what would be needed in their new home.

Miranda and Lucinda went on to the Dower House and Jamie, Liza and the boys carried onto the main house. It didn't take long for the boys to wash and change and make their way down to the kitchen for their supper. Once again Jamie marvelled at how they managed to eat throughout most of the afternoon and then be ready for supper.

Cyril Andrews left the following morning, having thanked Jamie and Liza for their hospitality. Jamie commented on how discreet he had been and Liza looked up at him questioningly.

"Come on Liza; you know what I'm talking about," said Jamie. "He said nothing about how the thieves had taken Lucille Fountain's jewels and she didn't know when they went missing. She was also unconcerned that her possessions may have been taken whilst she was asleep. She wasn't in her own room, was she? She was in someone else's room, wasn't she?"

"Jamie Edgeworth," exclaimed Liza. "You're gossiping!"

"I know, but only to you," he laughed. "Obviously Edgar condones whatever relationship she's having. I could never do that," suddenly Jamie was very serious.

"But you did when you were married to Evelyn," said Liza quietly.

Jamie was frowning, "That just proves how much I didn't love her. It also shows how the lives of people like Edgar and Lucille Fountain and Bella and the

Duke are complete shams, as are probably most of the landed gentry in this country. It would seem that we are unique Liza."

"Anthony and Diana are like us Jamie, so are Edward and Nicole as well as Joseph and Lily," said Liza and then she smiled, "and the greatest love of them all has to be Wendell and Amelia."

"I see that we are both romantics," laughed Jamie.

Grace knocked and entered, and Jamie retreated behind his newspaper and for the next hour Liza went through the list of items that were needed for the gatehouse.

"I feel guilty expecting you to do all this Liza," said Grace. "You have so much to do already and I won't be here to help you for the next couple of weeks or so, and you know we can afford to buy some of the furniture ourselves."

"Don't worry about that Grace; I have many people who can help me and if everything isn't in place by the time you return, we have plenty of room for you here. Hopefully you'll be back by the time we open the Ffoulks Home," said Liza.

"We will be, and I understand that the undertakers are already on their way to Truro, so we'll be able to re-bury my mother as soon as we return. That will be very comforting for my father, and for me also," said Grace.

"Are you organised for your trip?" asked Jamie from behind his newspaper.

Both Liza and Grace smiled being familiar with the Edgeworth newspaper routine.

"Yes, naturally we are not taking everything back with us, we will be travelling very lightly one way and rather heavily on our return," smiled Grace. "I'm really looking forward to at last having somewhere that I can call home. You and Jamie are so very kind to us. I was hoping that we would be able to settle somewhere nearby, but I never thought that we would be living so close, and in a house rather than in a couple of rented rooms."

"As we told you Grace, you were more than welcome to live under this roof," said Jamie, "but I can understand why you wanted your independence; I think I would have felt the same."

"I'm sorry that we won't be here for April and Adam's wedding. It's going to be a really happy occasion for not only them, but it seems that the whole of the village and farms have made it their day also. I could see that April was looking concerned when she realised just how many people had invited themselves to her special day," said Grace.

185

"It's something that Mrs Lambert and I had assumed and allowed for. I know that April and Adam wanted to organise everything themselves, but knowing the people around here, they were never going to achieve a quiet wedding," smiled Liza. "I believe that when they get over the shock, they will be delighted that people think so much of them."

Grace then went to finish her packing and Jamie retired once again behind his newspaper and Liza had many things to do to make sure everything was running smoothly for not only April's wedding, but also what was needed for the gatehouse and lastly she studied her list of all that would be needed for the opening of the Ffoulks Home.

Chapter 10

On the morning of the wedding the house seemed to be in uproar. The only calm places appeared to be Adam's room and surprisingly April's also. The boys kept calling into both rooms to make sure Adam and then April were not nervous; Liza finally told them to go to their own room and make sure their clothes were in order for the event and she would see them shortly to make sure they were properly dressed.

It had dawned a beautiful day so there would be no problem accommodating the number of guests in and around the cricket pavilion.

Liza and Estelle were helping April to dress and when they had finished, they stood back and told her how beautiful she looked. Estelle then dressed ready to be April's bridesmaid.

One of Adam's old school friends was his best man, and Mr Lambert was waiting to walk April down the aisle and give her away.

Hector had arrived the previous evening and when everyone seemed ready, he, Liza, Jamie and the boys left for the church and naturally Liza shed a tear as April walked down the aisle and shortly afterwards Miss April Kelly became Mrs Adam Reece.

Liza watched them walk happily back up the aisle, followed by Estelle and the best man and she thought how wonderful it was that she and Jamie had brought these two together. It did seem to be a marriage made in heaven, and then Liza laughed and thought it was really a marriage made in Edgeworth house. She experienced a very warm feeling about that.

All the villagers and people from the farms cheered as they came from the church and made their way to the cricket grounds and pavilion. It was going to be a very long and drawn-out affair, but April and Adam would be on their honeymoon by the time the celebrations ended.

Hector was a popular figure with all the guests, but he sought out Estelle at every opportunity and Estelle seemed quite happy with that situation.

Jamie, Liza and the boys were going to leave for home as soon as Adam and April started on the journey to their honeymoon. Lucinda and Miranda decided to leave at the same time and when that time came April threw her bouquet and Estelle caught it and a great cheer went up from the guests.

They watched the happy couple drive away and Liza had a small pang of loss which she pushed out of her mind because April was not her property, but she had been with them for so long that Liza almost felt like a mother to her; she had become so much part of the Edgeworth family that it was rather like losing one of her own.

Slowly they made their way back to the main house and it seemed very quiet as most of the staff were still enjoying the reception. The boys were tired and went to their room to rest before they had supper, which had been organised by Mrs Lambert and set out for them in the kitchen for when they were ready. Jamie and Liza could also have a cold meal if they so wanted, however they both felt rather full but knew that it would be otherwise with the boys.

"I wonder where Adam is taking her," said Liza.

"I would have thought that you would have known that," said Jamie.

"No, I have no idea; Adam was keeping that a secret from everyone. It's bound to be somewhere nice; Adam has good taste," said Liza.

"I suppose that we now have to concentrate on making sure the Ffoulks Home is ready to receive the first children and of course you will be getting the gatehouse ready for my uncle and Grace. Do we have any functions to attend before that?" asked Jamie.

"Yes, we have one next week, but it's at the Parker's and that's only five miles away, so we don't have to stay the night. It's a dinner and a musical recital after, it will be over by midnight so we will be home in an hour or so," said Liza.

"You're going to miss April; she's been with you for such a long time," said Jamie.

"She's only going to be away for a week or so, but I have to accept that her life will now change, and her first loyalties must be to Adam. Of course, in the fullness of time there will probably be children and that is when she will really leave us," said Liza sadly.

"Of course, our boys will be at Cambridge by then, so we will also lose Adam," said Jamie.

"It will all change, but I know that Adam is in line for the headmastership at our village school. He has already seen the current headmaster and it seems that when he retires Adam will have the opportunity to take over if that is what he wants," said Liza.

Jamie looked at Liza and said, "I suppose that is something that you have had a hand in."

"Well, I did know that the headmaster was due to retire in about a year and there would be a vacancy and you know that Estelle has been working there on occasion. It seemed a logical step but only if Adam wanted it. He may feel that his talents would be appreciated more elsewhere. I hope that he is going to take the position because it would mean that he and April would stay here and that would be good," said Liza.

"When you say 'here' do you mean in this house?" asked Jamie.

"No, there's a headmasters' cottage next to the school which I'm sure April and Adam would make into a very comfortable home. But as I said, Adam may wish for a different situation," said Liza.

"I doubt that he would. He and April have become very much a part of the village, but of course only time will tell," said Jamie.

The boys made their entrance saying that they thought that they should go for their supper now.

"Why don't we all go down and find what there is and bring it up to the dining room," said Liza.

"I'll get some wine for us Liza, and I presume there will be something for the boys to drink," said Jamie.

"Oh I think that a little white wine mixed with lemonade will do no harm, they can toast what a wonderful day April and Adam have given us," said Liza and she made her way down to the kitchen with the boys and they brought up cold cuts, pies and salads with plenty of bread.

It was a happy way to finish a memorable day with Jamie sitting at the head of his table with those around him that he loved above all else and talking comfortably as only family members can. It reminded him of the times that he had sat at Liza's table in Belfast with the boys around them and he had wished that he could be permanently in her life. He sighed whilst smiling because his wish had come true.

Chapter 11

The Parker's evening went off without a hitch. Bella and Lucille were there as were their husbands and final arrangements were made with them for the arrival of the children at the Ffoulks Home. Once again Edgar apologised for the problems experienced at their function and both Liza and Jamie brushed them aside as nothing, especially as now all the stolen items had been returned.

"I hear that the thieves had been spreading gossip about you and Jamie and that was how they were caught," said Bella with a sly smile.

"Jamie and I can rise above any unseemly gossip I'm pleased to say," said Liza.

"There was no gossip about Lucille as apparently they never saw her," laughed Bella. "They saw me, but I wasn't interesting enough for them to brag about, whereas you and Jamie, well .... "

"Well nothing Bella," said Liza "I have better things to think about than what two stupid men believe they saw in the middle of the night in a dark room."

"Of course Liza," smiled Bella and they carried on talking about the plans for the Home opening.

"Did Bella have anything interesting to tell you?" asked Jamie when they were on their way home.

"Nothing of any great interest," said Liza.

"Apart from our nocturnal activities at the Fountain house no doubt," said Jamie.

"Was it mentioned to you also?" asked Liza.

"It was hinted at," said Jamie.

"I told Bella that I had better things to think about, after all those men were in our room when it was dark so who knows what they believed they saw," said Liza.

"We did have some lamps alight," said Jamie.

"Yes, but Bella didn't know that," smiled Liza. "I suppose it will be talked about from time to time, but I don't care that people know that we make love to one another. I think I've got past the embarrassment."

"Are Lucille and Bella still planning to help with the children's arrival?" asked Jamie.

"Yes, and they seem to be looking forward to it, although I have a feeling that they are more excited about dressing in very casual clothes. Lady Redfern is also going to be there as apparently she has been asked to report back to the Palace," said Liza.

"Aren't they going to get in the way?" asked Jamie.

"I don't think so as I have arranged with the Major to give them specific duties which should keep them occupied. Your uncle and Grace should be back in a couple of days and tomorrow I must go to the undertakers as well as see Bernard because Holly's remains have arrived and I must make sure that everything is planned ready for her reburial," said Liza.

"I'll come with you for that if you would like," said Jamie.

"Thank you, Jamie, I would very much appreciate that. I'm hoping that we will be able to lay her to rest on Friday and we have to see that the coffin is in order and if it isn't, we must organise another one," said Liza.

"You always seem to end up with some difficult tasks, but as he is my uncle and she was my aunt I will do my best to help with that situation," said Jamie.

Estelle was still up when they arrived home. She had been completing some work for the new Home which she had not carried out through the day because she was undertaking Adam's duties with the boys. They had hoped that because Adam was away, they would not have to undergo lessons, but were disappointed when told that Estelle was taking his place as well as April's for when lessons were over.

Liza said that she needed no help that night and she made her way up to bed. Roberts helped Jamie out of his clothes and Liza waited for him to leave and when he had left Liza went into Jamie's room and asked for his assistance as she was having difficulty getting

out of her clothes at which Jamie laughed and proceeded to enjoy the task.

**

All was in order at the undertakers the next day. They had polished the coffin and it looked like new as did the headstone and Liza and Jamie thanked them for their thoughtfulness.

Their next call was at the church to see Bernard and they arranged the time for the reburial of Holly Edgeworth.

"Now I can concentrate on the opening next week," said Liza as they made their way home. "I'll go to the Ffoulks house tomorrow. Would you like to come with me?"

"Yes I would Liza," said Jamie. "I'll enjoy the trip and no doubt we'll see Anthony and Diana as well as the Major and Hector. I suppose Rose will also be around. When is Estelle moving there?"

"Adam and April will be back later tomorrow, so I think it will probably be at the weekend. I want to stop at the gatehouse to see that the beds and other furniture are properly in place but I'm doing no more than that as Grace wants to make the house her own and I know she's bringing some furnishings; we have just provided the bare essentials and we'll see what else is needed when she has sorted out what she already has," said Liza.

"I believe that this is the first time since her childhood that Grace will have a permanent home," said Jamie. "She naturally travelled a great deal with her husband; it's such a shame that he died but many did in that war. You are very wise letting her get it ready as she wishes after all it is going to be her home, and my uncle's of course, but it is more for her really. I think that my uncle will take a great deal of pleasure in seeing her making a home for them. I wonder if she looks like my Aunt Holly did and that we will never know."

"I think we would have liked your Aunt Holly; she sounds as if she was a very loving person and very brave," said Liza as they stopped at the gatehouse and went in to inspect that all was as it should be. Two of the bedrooms each had a bed, wardrobe and chest of drawers. Downstairs there was a dresser and a table and six chairs and the sitting room had a small couch and two armchairs. Liza would have liked to have furnished it completely but she knew how important it was for Grace and David to make the place their own and she didn't want to take away any of Grace's pleasure.

The next morning, before Liza and Jamie left for the Ffoulks house, the wagon carrying David and Grace's belongings arrived, it was well packed, and it was rolled into a storeroom and locked up. Liza and Jamie could visualise Grace's excitement when she unpacked it.

They set off early for the Home and firstly they called on Anthony and Diana. Thomas was sulky because Matthew wasn't with them and after making arrangements for the opening day, Jamie and Liza made their way to the Home and found the Major and Hector going through each room with the house mother, ticking off items on a list.

The Major left Hector to carry on and he went with Jamie and Liza firstly to the kitchens where the head cook was logging in various trays of dry goods and the vegetables and fruit were being placed in the cold room. All the equipment was in place and the kitchen would start making pies, bread and cakes nearer the time.

Next they went to the dining room and it was set out with various tables rather than one long impersonal one, and Liza nodded her approval. The large communal restroom had comfortable chairs and side tables and shelves for books and games.

"I think that when the children get used to the idea that they can relax safely, this room is going to be well used," said Liza. "We'll go to Estelle's domain next."

The schoolroom was set out casually with tables rather than formal desks. There was still a blackboard and slates for the children to write on. There were pretty pictures on the walls and the whole room looked inviting rather than intimidating.

"This has been set out very well," said Jamie. "The children should feel comfortable here which would make them enjoy learning. Estelle has a very nice nature which will come over to the children, although I suppose she is aware that they will probably try to take advantage of her."

"I believe she is well aware that they will probably test her at every opportunity," smiled the Major.

They then inspected the dormitories and washrooms. Each bed had a small wardrobe and set of drawers and a movable screen separated the sections to give privacy when needed. There were several smaller rooms which could be needed for special children.

Lastly, they looked briefly into the rooms set aside for the staff and they noticed that Estelle had already moved many of her possessions into place. The Major also had a bedroom set up for when he found it necessary to stay and they did not intrude on the head cook's room as she had already moved in, as had her assistants into their smaller rooms. There was a general room for the staff to relax in when off duty.

"You really wouldn't recognise it as the same house that Anthony and Diana lived in," said Jamie. "It does appear much lighter and far friendlier; have they seen it since it was altered?"

"No, but they tell me that they are looking forward to joining us at the opening," said the Major.

"I do hope that nobody really believes that we are having a grand opening; we are opening our doors to the first influx of children from Ireland and anyone who is coming especially for that day has been told that they will be helping in whatever way you think fit Major," said Liza.

"Our head cook is arranging food for everyone so there will be a little more available than will normally be the case, but I have some very important tasks ready for your three lady helpers," smiled the Major. "You are right because these children are not on display, they are here to make this their home and hopefully we will be able to help them eventually get over the traumas that they have experienced. All our workers understand their tasks will not be easy, and they are prepared for that."

"You really are now quite ready for the first twenty children," said Liza.

"Yes, I believe we are," said the Major. "You are meeting them at the docks, aren't you?"

"Liza and I will be there waiting for them," said Jamie. "It will take us under two hours to get from there. We've organised five coaches for them. I'll be in one, Liza in another and you know that Jennifer is travelling with them and two nurses from the Homes in Ireland, so we will have an adult in each coach."

"Have you sorted out where Jennifer will be staying," Liza asked the Major.

"Yes, she will be staying at my house. I will be living here for a while, so Jennifer will keep her respectability," laughed the Major.

"Major, you are a gentleman, and nobody would have any fear that you would act otherwise," smiled Liza with a twinkle in her eye. "I suppose Rose will also be looking forward to seeing her again."

Jamie and the Major looked at her with amused raised eyebrows.

"I'd like to see what is happening in the grounds," said Jamie and they made their way through the kitchen to the gardens where Hector joined them.

There was a semi-closed in kitchen garden and men were busy planting various vegetables and herbs, although it would be a while before they would be ready for use. Through the gate to the main grounds there was an orchard with a few mature fruit trees and others that had recently been planted. Further to the left were sectioned off areas for animals and those that were there were all young as it was thought that the children would enjoy seeing them grow. One section was wired off and had a chicken house and a few chickens roaming and the Major had arranged that in the days following the children's arrival, chicks would be brought for them to see, touch and feed. The area where they were going to play was set out to the right of the front of the house, where local workmen had given their time to make swings and roundabouts and there was a cricket pitch near the entrance gates.

"I see that the Edgeworth team is going to have its work cut out to keep ahead of your team Major," smiled Jamie. "We keep calling this the Ffoulks Home, but we really should find another name for it."

"Perhaps when the children have settled in a little, we should ask them what they think it should be called," said Liza.

"That could be rather dangerous," laughed Jamie.

"When is Estelle moving in?" asked Hector.

"Adam and April will be back later today, and I know that she wants to see Jamie's uncle and cousin who are returning tomorrow, so I suppose she'll take up her position sometime over the weekend," said Liza.

"I think I'll come and stay with you on Friday then," Hector told Liza and Jamie. "I'll bring Anthony's carriage to make it easy to bring Estelle and any luggage she may have back."

"She may have already made plans Hector," said the Major who was used to Hector's thoughtless words.

"Well that won't matter because I have a room at Jamie's and I'd like to spend some time with them anyway," said Hector.

Jamie and Liza just smiled at Hector who always assumed that he would be welcome.

"We have one or two duties to carry out on Friday," said Liza, "but you know that you can make yourself at home as always."

"I'd forgotten, you are laying your aunt properly to rest aren't you, Jamie?" said Hector.

"I didn't think that you would have known that, Hector," said Jamie.

"It was mentioned at Adam's wedding. Which was rather morbid at such a splendid affair," said Hector.

"It seems that you have everything ready Major; you have done an excellent job and so have you Hector," said Liza. "And I must also compliment all the workers; they have brought this place up to a wonderful standard. I know that they are well aware that they may not be thanked by the children; they will be frightened and nervous; they can also be sullen and will naturally have chips on their shoulders. It's going to take time to gain their confidence as well as make them feel totally safe. You have a very big task ahead of you."

"Have you thought about Langston House yet Liza?" asked Hector.

"Yes, I've thought about it and from what you have said it's a distinct possibility, but I want to inspect it closely and think about what a sensible price for it would be," said Liza. "I trust you and the Major will be with us when we look at the property. Also, as Peter Fuller will be arriving at the weekend, he should be able to inspect it with us."

"Yes, we'll make sure that we are free when you are ready to visit," said the Major. "It's a pity that Wendell and Amelia can't come for the opening."

"They may make a trip later in the summer, but Amelia feels that it would be too much for Wendell to be involved with the children's arrival, but Peter will represent them very well," said Liza although she was sad that she had to admit that her much loved friends were not getting any younger.

Liza and Jamie then made their way back to Anthony and Diana's house where they made the arrangements for their attendance on the day that the children arrived.

"We'll be there early on that day," said Diana, "and I know that my mother-in-law is coming with us. Are Miranda and Lucinda also coming then?"

"No, they will be looking after the boys for the whole of that day," said Jamie. "We don't know what time we will be returning and although the boys wanted to join us, we did not think it wise on that day. Peter Fuller will be with us and my uncle and cousin will be putting in an appearance, but they didn't want to crowd us, and we do have one or two jobs that they could carry out. As you know Liza didn't want the children to feel that they were on show."

"The Major has given us tasks to undertake," smiled Anthony. "Diana will be helping to show the children around and I am on food duty. I don't know what he has in mind for my mother, but no doubt she will make herself useful. Hector has told us how different the house now looks and what has been organised within the grounds; I shall be very interested to see it. We have kept out of the way whilst the alterations were going on."

"I can assure you that we will not be wearing 'posh' clothes," laughed Diana. "I do understand your reasoning behind that request. Bella and Lucille Fountain are also helping on the day, have you told them to dress in 'old' clothes?"

Jamie laughed, "Yes she did Diana, and she told Lady Redfern to do the same."

"How did they take that request?" asked Anthony.

"They understood completely," said Liza.

"I believe that Jennifer is travelling with the children," said Diana. "I'm sure that it will please the Major. Do you know where she will be staying?"

"I'm sure that the Major has it all in hand and he will not be putting her reputation at risk," said Jamie.

Soon after their conversations Liza and Jamie left for home and on the way, Liza commented that it appeared that Diana and Anthony wanted to gossip about Jennifer and the Major.

"I think we managed to diffuse the situation," said Jamie.

"Maybe," said Liza.

The boys were anxious to see them when they came home to tell them how their day had been. April and Adam had arrived back earlier that afternoon and had immediately set about their duties towards the family. Liza went to find them, and they were in the kitchen telling Mrs Lambert and Mrs Frances all about their honeymoon. Adam had taken April to an idyllic country cottage and had arranged for someone to come in every day to make meals and generally look after them. They both looked very happy and contented and Liza told them that they had no need to start work until after the weekend.

"We're going to have quite a full house this weekend," commented Jamie when Liza came back from seeing April and Adam.

"Your uncle and Grace will be with us tomorrow and it would appear that Hector is coming to stay on Friday, and of course Peter will be with us at the weekend," said Liza. "I will have to check the time of the burial on Friday; I believe that it is to be at eleven o'clock. David has said that he only wants to have a few prayers said when she is laid to rest as she had a full funeral service in Truro. He feels that she would approve of that."

"We'll give her the respect that she deserves," said Jamie. "I presume that the boys won't be present."

"No, they don't need to attend. It will just be David and Grace, you and me and Miranda and Lucinda. We are not to dress in black so David says, but obviously bright colours would not be appropriate," said Liza.

"Are we dining alone tonight Liza?" asked Jamie.

"Yes, it's just you and me tonight," smiled Liza.

"I like it when we dine alone; we aren't going to have many opportunities to do that for a while. It reminds me of how you used to invite me to join you when you returned to Belfast. I used to make sure I visited you near your mealtime because I knew you would ask me to stay," smiled Jamie.

"I knew that you used to do that on occasion and I always hoped that you would stay," said Liza. "I enjoyed your company and especially around the dinner table; I still do."

"We must make the most of this evening as we will have very little time to ourselves over the coming weeks," said Jamie. "I suppose that once those children are settled, we will be in demand again on the social scene."

"Yes, I have a whole list of engagements starting at the end of June, and quite a few will take us away from home," said Liza. "We'll have to be especially careful of where we keep our jewellery and also put barricades up against our doors."

"I have a feeling that what happened at the Fountain's will never be allowed to happen again. A very big lesson was learned over that particular occasion," said Jamie. "I believe that the Marchant & Fuller security division has become much more popular."

"You're right Jamie, we are creating many more jobs for people, but we have to be very careful over who we employ," smiled Liza.

"You thought of a security division in America, didn't you?" said Jamie.

"Yes, you were there at the time I think," said Liza. "It was at our first fund raiser in New York and we had our security breached."

"I seem to remember something about that. What was done about it?" asked Jamie.

Liza laughed, "I set a thief to catch a thief."

Jamie thought about that for a while. "Is that why Walter Anderson is so loyal to you? You gave him the chance to get out of a life of crime and onto the road to respectability. It worked for him; I wonder how many it would work for?"

"Many more than you would think, but there are those like Isaac Flood who have thrown away the opportunity of a lifetime," said Liza.

"What about the American you met up with in Liverpool a few years ago, was he also one of your reformed thieves?" asked Jamie.

"No," said Liza. "I just knew his family."

Jamie looked at her and realised that although she was not lying, she was definitely keeping most of the truth to herself.

"He may not have been a thief, but he certainly had something to hide and I think you helped him do that," said Jamie.

From the look on Liza's face Jamie realised that he had annoyed her. "You know nothing about him or about his circumstances," said Liza sharply and then she smiled at him and her annoyance had completely disappeared and he knew exactly why he had always loved her so much; her smile was something that he could never resist.

He decided that he would never ask her about the past as she would do anything for those she felt deserved it and she would keep their secrets possibly to her own detriment. He would know about the American in Liverpool when and if she was ready to tell him but it really did not matter if he never knew that secret, they had their own lives to get on with, the rest was unimportant.

***

Liza had forgotten her annoyance over Jamie's questioning the previous evening and she was sitting with him whilst he read his newspaper and she was going through her correspondence. A carriage could be heard coming up the drive and Mr Rogers could be seen helping David and Grace down together with their luggage.

Jamie and Liza made their way into the drawing room and waited for Harper to bring them in. They could hear Grace helping to organise which case went into which room and then finally they appeared, both with very wide grins on their faces.

"Welcome back," said Jamie and Liza nodded her approval at seeing them. "I trust you experienced no difficulties with your move," she said.

"It all went very smoothly," said Grace. "Some of my father's parishioners were sorry to see him leave, but it was time for us to go and leave the parish to the current vicar."

"All your household goods are stored safely in one of the dry outhouses. I promise I didn't unpack them although I was tempted to do so," smiled Liza. "I didn't want to take away any of your pleasure."

"Did the undertakers get back safely?" asked David.

"Yes Uncle. We have been to see them, and everything is comfortably in order. We have also arranged a time for the reburial tomorrow with the Reverend Collins," said Jamie.

"Thank you," said David. "It has all been handled very well."

"You must be tired; it's been a long journey for you. Your rooms are ready for you whenever you want to rest," said Liza.

Grace asked how April and Adam's wedding had fared and Liza explained that the whole village had turned out and those from the farms also and everyone had a wonderful time. "April will tell you herself all about where they went for the honeymoon. I had not realised just how romantic Adam could be, but it's their story, not mine."

The boys' morning lessons were over, and they appeared to greet David and Grace and then go on their way to the kitchen for their lunch.

"I think I would like to freshen up before lunch," said Grace and she and her father made their way up to their rooms and Liza said that she would have them called when lunch was ready.

Liza smiled at Jamie and said, "Well Jamie, you have all your family back together again. It must make you feel happy."

"Yes, I'm very happy about it, but I was happy once we got together. This is just the icing on the cake," said Jamie.

At lunch Grace was showing her keenness to visit the gatehouse and David was equally excited.

"I'll walk over with you after lunch," said Liza, "and when you are ready, I'll arrange for your goods wagon to be driven over. I promise you I have only had what was necessary put in place; you can have the pleasure of making the place your own."

"Do you think it would be possible to have the wagon brought over after lunch," asked Grace and everyone smiled at her.

"Of course it would be," said Liza and she rang the bell for Harper and when he arrived she asked him to make the necessary arrangements.

By the time lunch was over and they all walked over to the gatehouse the wagon was already there and two men were carrying the goods into the house. Grace rushed in and started organising where everything should be placed. David made his way up to what was to be his room carrying what he knew were his goods and to his credit he put them neatly away.

Jamie looked around and decided that he was in the way, so he left for home. Grace was carefully unpacking her clean household linen and placing it across a washing line in the garden to air in the sunlight. Liza smiled at the happy look on Grace's face and she had her own memory of setting up her home in Benson; she envied Grace.

David came down from his room and asked what he could do to help, and he was given the task of carefully unpacking cups and saucers and putting them on the dresser. Liza helped him with that and at that point Miranda and Lucinda arrived having brought cakes and lemonade with them.

"I think we'll be ready to move in tomorrow," said Grace.

"We have an appointment at eleven o'clock tomorrow at the church, but after that the choice is yours. If you would like I'll arrange for one of our maids to come over tomorrow to give you a hand with making up your beds but I don't want you to think that we are taking over your home," said Liza.

"I could do with a hand with that thank you Liza, and one or two other more difficult jobs. I also have to study how the cooking facilities work," said Grace.

"Well, don't ask me to help you with that as I'm afraid my lack of cooking skills is legendary. I can, however, boil a kettle," said Liza.

Liza left to let Grace and David sort out their home and she walked back with Miranda and Lucinda.

"We're a very big family now Liza," said Miranda, "and it's right that we all have our own homes. It makes us independent and gives you and Jamie your time alone with just your boys. I can see that Grace is very happy and excited at the prospect of at last having a home of her own, because it really is more hers than David's. You are really very kind Liza; I know that you sorted out my home and now you are doing the same for Grace."

"It's nothing special," said Liza, "and you have to admit that it's better to have houses lived in than going to rack and ruin."

Both Miranda and Lucinda smiled at Liza as they always knew that Liza pushed away compliments.

"You're with us for dinner tonight, aren't you?" said Liza and they nodded and said that they would see her later as they went into the Dower House and Liza carried on up to the main house. She called Mrs Frances when she arrived and arranged for someone to help at the gatehouse the next day.

She found Jamie in his study once again reading his newspaper and she smiled at him and then carried on reading her correspondence. It was as though the last few hours had not happened as they were in exactly the same situation as they had been in that morning.

"I shall be pleased when Grace has settled in and can return to helping me with my correspondence," said Liza. "I suppose Peter will have some more work for me when he arrives at the weekend. I'm still sad that Wendell and Amelia won't be coming with him."

"I think that they have got to the time in their lives when we will be travelling to see them rather than the other way around, but you have to admit that it has been like that for a while now," said Jamie.

"Perhaps we could take them on another trip some time," said Liza.

"Do you need to go on another trip?" asked Jamie.

"No, but I enjoy seeing how the farms have progressed," said Liza.

"Well, you can't now take them to your holdings in Wales," said Jamie. "You've given away your house there and I don't think they would appreciate coming face to face with Evelyn and they would only keep telling you how foolish you are to help her yet again."

"I wonder whether they could manage a trip to New York. I know that the sea journey is long, but they wouldn't have to exert themselves very much and the trip from the ship to the house is very short," said Liza.

"I suppose we could do as we did when we went to Italy and that is join them at the docks so that they didn't have to make the journey to us. When would you think of doing the trip?" asked Jamie. "Unfortunately we do seem to have many commitments at present."

"Yes it couldn't be until sometime next year; probably after Easter," said Liza. "Anyway, it would be something for us all to look forward to."

"That would be around the time that young Si would be coming to live with us, so it could work out quite well. Anyway it's a long time away yet," said Jamie.

"It will be nice to think about and plan for," said Liza.

A little while later it took all their powers of persuasion to stop the boys visiting Grace and David and when they succeeded the boys decided that their grandmother needed their company. Once again Liza and Jamie started to tell them that it was not a good idea but fortunately Mrs Frances sought them out to tell them that supper was ready, and they disappeared to the kitchen at the speed of light.

"Are you sure we are going to survive four boys when Si joins us?" asked Jamie.

"I'm beginning to wonder," laughed Liza.

Grace finally arrived back from the gatehouse and she and David joined them for dinner. The talk around the table was what was planned for their move. David and Jamie became a little bored with the conversation about fabrics and furnishings and they excused themselves and retreated to the study for a while.

"I suppose they were a little outnumbered," observed Liza and they carried on with their suggestions and thoughts until it was time for Miranda and Lucinda to leave for their home and both Jamie and David saw them to their door. By the time they returned Grace and Liza had made their way to their rooms.

"I hope that tomorrow won't be too upsetting for my uncle and Grace," said Jamie as he and Liza were in bed that night.

"It's bound to be a little as they will be going through their beloved Holly's burial for a second time, but once it's over I'm sure they will settle down well," said Liza. "Grace is so happy getting a home ready for them that she will soon get over it; I'm not sure that your uncle will ever get over losing his wife. Their love was obviously very strong, but at least now he can visit her whenever he wishes."

The reburial the next morning went as well as could be expected, Grace shed a tear as did Lucinda and soon after they went back to the house leaving the gravediggers to tidy up and put the headstone in place. David was going back later to sit with Holly for a while.

Grace headed off to the gatehouse with one of the housemaids and she was convinced that the house would be ready to move into that afternoon. Liza went to the kitchen and arranged with Mrs Lambert that baskets of essential food as well as various ingredients were taken to Grace. A pot of stew and ample bread was to be their meal that evening with a fruit pie for dessert. Jamie sorted out with Harper several bottles of wine for his uncle's cellar.

Two housemaids were busy packing up Grace's and David's belongings from their rooms and would shortly be taking them over to the gatehouse using the small carriage which would also have the food and wine on board.

Liza decided not to visit until later in the afternoon and she would take the boys with her. She had already elicited a promise from them that they would not get in the way. Each boy had made a card welcoming their great uncle and second cousin to their new home. James' and Matthew's were really well done, but John's was very artistic, and it was obvious that he had a very special talent in that respect.

After their lessons that afternoon Liza and the boys made their way over to the gatehouse. They found David with his sleeves rolled up and helping to carry linen up the stairs to a store cupboard. Grace was arranging crockery and cutlery and it was obvious that Miranda and Lucinda had already called as there were fresh cakes on the table. Grace greeted them warmly and accepted and admired the boys' cards which she placed in full view on the dresser. The boys were eyeing the cakes on the table and Grace smiled and handed around plates cutting each boy a slice of cake. They thanked her for it politely and sat at the table and thoroughly enjoyed eating the cake and luckily did not make too much of a mess.

"I think that we'll call on you regularly," said Matthew between mouthfuls and the other two nodded their agreement.

"That will be very kind of you all," said David who had just come into the room. "We'll have to make sure that we always have plenty of cake in the house."

"It's looking very homely in here Grace," said Liza. "What else are you thinking of having here now?"

"I have curtains for these rooms, they just need altering slightly. I would like a sideboard; the dresser carries a great deal, but a sideboard would take our table linen and cutlery. I presume you know of a good carpenter," said Grace.

"Yes, there is a good carpenter in the village, but we do have a sideboard stored in one of our outhouses. I don't want you to think that I am just making you have all our old furniture, but it is sitting there doing nothing," said Liza.

"Is it similar wood to the dresser?" asked Grace.

"Yes, it matches the dresser; it probably needs a clean and polish. You are welcome to it if you think it would suit you," said Liza.

"I know it would suit us as I know that you would not have offered it if it didn't," said Grace. "Do you think we could get it over here today?"

Liza smiled at Grace's keenness and called the housemaid, who was just about to leave, and asked her to get Mr Lambert to organise bringing the sideboard across.

"I think when you have that in place you will have earned a rest, but I have a feeling that you will be working all night. I trust that you have your bedrooms ready so that you can just fall into bed when you finally finish," said Liza.

"Yes, the beds are made and the curtains are in place; I'm sure we are going to sleep well tonight," said Grace.

David was now making efforts to light the stove. "Don't tell me that you haven't yet even had a cup of tea since you have been here?" said Liza.

"Your mother-in-law and Lucinda brought us lemonade and that's all we've had. Oh good, I think I've managed it," said David triumphantly as he mastered the cooker.

"Well done Father," said Grace as she placed the stew pot on the top and rummaged and found a kettle and filled it from the pump in the washroom.

Liza suggested that the boys take their leave and they thanked Grace for the cake and said that they would be back the next day to make sure that they were alright.

Both David and Grace took their concern seriously, thanking them and saying that they looked forward to seeing them the next day.

Liza was going to stay until the sideboard arrived and then she would leave them to their own devices. When it arrived Jamie was also with it.

"I thought I would come to see how you were settling in and I can see that this has truly become a home. It most certainly is different to the place we saw just a few weeks ago," said Jamie.

Mr Lambert and one of his men struggled in with the sideboard and Grace directed exactly where she wanted it.

"It's in need of some polish I'm afraid," said Liza.

"It's perfect Liza," said Grace, "but of course you knew it would be and I'm quite capable of polishing it."

"You know that you only have to ask if you need help with anything," said Jamie.

"We know that Jamie and I don't think that we need to tell you how happy and grateful we are to be here and for what you have done for us," said David.

"There's no need to thank us Uncle, you're family and we all look after one another," said Jamie and he immediately changed the subject. "Peter Fuller is arriving tomorrow, and I hope that you will be joining us for dinner in the evening."

"Yes, we'd be delighted," said Grace.

"Well you don't have to wait for the evening to visit; you know that you are welcome at any time. When do you think you will be able to resume helping me, Grace?" asked Liza.

"Probably as soon as Monday," said Grace.

"I think that would be wonderful. As you know the children will be arriving on Wednesday, so I am going to have a busy time from Monday onwards," said Liza.

"We'll leave you in peace now and look forward to seeing you tomorrow," said Jamie.

They left and slowly made their way back to the main house, enjoying the walk and their own company. They waved at Miranda and Lucinda who were taking the last of the sunshine in their garden.

Mr Rogers drove by taking Derek home and they could hear the boys who were practicing cricket before their supper.

Jamie was smiling and Liza asked him what was amusing him.

"Behind us we have an uncle and cousin, alongside us now we have a mother and close friend and in front of us we have our three boys. We are indeed a very large family now. When my father died there was just me living here, and then just James and me. It was a very cold and unfriendly place. It became friendlier when James and I used to get ready to travel to Belfast to see you and Matthew and eventually John also," said Jamie.

"Didn't you ever have any guests for dinner or other functions; surely Evelyn enjoyed entertaining," said Liza.

"Anthony used to visit on occasion, but when Diana came onto the scene, he was naturally very occupied with her and then of course she had her problems and I rarely saw him here. I saw him more when he and I were in Belfast. Evelyn didn't really like the house; she said that it needed gutting and that she would feel too embarrassed to bring anyone here. In some ways she was right as I really didn't have the funds to do much updating to the house at that time. It was the same with Belfast until you came to my rescue a few years ago. I renovated much of the Belfast property before I started doing the same to this place. It's all so very different now, I can look at the house and see and hear that life has been put into it," said Jamie.

Liza laughed, "Yes, you can certainly hear that there's life here now." A loud cheer had just gone up as obviously one of the boys had played a good shot. Suddenly there was silence which meant that the boys' supper was ready for them. Liza smiled up at Jamie and said, "With any luck we might be able to get an hour's peace before we get ready for dinner."

As Liza uttered those words a small carriage drew up beside them and Hector shouted a greeting and then told them that he had come to help Estelle with her move to the new Home.

Jamie smiled and nodded as he watched Hector take the carriage to the stables, "I think perhaps we will not be having any peace before dinner," and he sighed, and they made their way up the front steps. They carried on up to the drawing room and as they waited for Hector to arrive, they reflected on the events of the day.

***

John was very excited as he knew that his beloved Uncle Peter would be arriving that day. Matthew and James were also looking forward to seeing him, he was not such fun as their Uncle Edward and Uncle Joseph but they were busy with their wives now and couldn't spend as much time with them as they

206

had in the past. They loved him anyway and he always spent time with them and explained in detail whatever they asked him.

Jamie looked at Liza and told her that she looked as excited at the prospect of Peter arriving that day as John did.

"I know," said Liza. "He always puts everything into perspective. He probably would prefer to be behind his desk in Belfast, but he knows how important this first Home in England is and that the charity should have a Fullers' presence."

"It isn't really the first Home here; there's one in Liverpool and one near the London docks," said Jamie.

"They are only fairly small houses and they just take children who are on their way to a better life in America. They are never there long," said Liza.

Peter arrived just before lunch and John raced out to meet him before Liza and Jamie could reach him. Matthew and James were not far behind.

It didn't take long to get Peter settled into his room and in no time at all he was down and looking for Liza who he found in the library with Jamie.

"I have letters from my mother and father for you Liza, as well as documents for you to read. You must also give me the itinerary for when the children arrive. I've seen them and they were in a sorry state, but they have been cared for and look a lot better now. I worry about how they will get on sailing here, but we have two nurses and Jennifer with them. My mother wanted to come but my father needs her more," said Peter.

Liza looked worried, "He's not ill, is he Peter?"

"No, but he's not getting any younger and we don't want him to have another stroke. He gets a little annoyed at the way she fusses over him, but he really wouldn't have it any other way," said Peter.

"Fussing over him gives him something to grumble about," smiled Liza. "They really are devoted to one another. We were thinking that perhaps after Easter next year they may feel like a trip to New York. Perhaps our new steamship will be ready by then and we could go on the maiden voyage but if not we could go on one of the other ships and you know we would make it as easy for them as necessary."

"It's something that I'll mention to them when I return. I know you'll look after them and it's been a while since they have been to New York. They really enjoyed their trip with you to Italy; it did them both good and I'm sure if they are fit enough, they will want to be with you and the boys. Would your mother also go with you Jamie?"

"It's most likely that she and Lucinda would enjoy the trip; they did last time they were there," said Jamie.

"I believe lunch is ready and the boys will be joining us, perhaps we could go through our documents after that time," said Liza.

"I'll leave you two then as I can see that you have many to look through," said Jamie.

"You don't have to leave Jamie," said Peter. "We will be talking about your estates also."

The boys enjoyed their lunch with their Uncle Peter, and they spent a little time with him afterwards before Adam called them for cricket practice. Hector had been noticeable by his absence and Liza assumed that he was with Estelle. Liza, Jamie and Peter discussed business for the rest of the afternoon.

At dinner Miranda and Lucinda were delighted to see Peter again. Jamie introduced him to his uncle and Grace and for the first time in Liza's memory Peter showed a keen interest in a female and he attempted to include her in every conversation. Liza had asked Estelle to join them for dinner which overjoyed Hector. When the time came for everyone to leave Jamie said that he would see Miranda and Lucinda home and Peter said that he would join him, and he took Grace's arm and led her to the door.

Liza waited in the drawing room for Jamie and Peter to return and was surprised when it was only Jamie who came through the door.

"Has Peter gone straight up to bed?" asked Liza.

"No, he decided to walk with my uncle and Grace to their house. Did you notice that there appeared to be an attraction between Peter and Grace?" said Jamie.

"I think that everyone must have noticed. I have never seen Peter act that way before and Grace seemed to enjoy his company," said Liza.

"She's older than he is, isn't she?" said Jamie.

"She must be at least ten years older, but what does that matter. Age is nothing if they get on well together," said Liza.

They heard Peter returning and he came into the room smiling.

"Their cottage seems very nice," said Peter. "Grace seems to have made it very cosy and she tells me they only moved there yesterday. She also tells me that she is helping you with your work Liza and that she and her father are going to the Ffoulks Home to help when the children arrive."

"Yes, that's right Peter, she will be doing all of that I'm pleased to say," said Liza.

"Do you know how long she has been widowed?" asked Peter.

"Her husband was killed at the beginning of the Crimean war," answered Jamie. "You seemed to get on very well with her."

"I get on with her just as I get on with you Liza; I admire people who have a certain intelligence and she has a very nice nature," said Peter. "I'll say goodnight to you now and see you tomorrow morning."

Jamie and Liza smiled at him and wished him a peaceful night and when he had left the room, they both looked at one another and grinned.

***

Sunday was as usual. Church in the morning followed by family lunch and then cricket at the pitch. Adam was back on Derek holding duty and both David and Peter joined in, with cheers coming from everyone. Hector and Estelle left for the Home saying that they would see everyone again soon.

On Monday Liza and Peter visited the Ffoulks Home and met up with the Major and Hector, as well as the rest of the staff. They called on Anthony and Diana on their way home and arrived back late in the afternoon. As they drove past the gatehouse they saw Grace in the garden, and they stopped to see how she and David were getting on.

There was a delicious smell coming from the kitchen and Liza commented that she must have mastered the new kitchen stove and Grace said that she soon would be able to invite everyone to dinner. Peter hoped that he would be around when she did that and she promptly told him that he would be more than welcome and Liza could not quite understand how it happened but Peter had been invited to dinner that evening and he turned to Liza and hoped that it would not disrupt her too much if he accepted Grace's kind invitation.

Peter was going to come to the main house to change for dinner, but Grace told him that there was no need; he was perfectly acceptable as he was. He replied that he would however just like to wash his hands and face before sitting down to dinner.

Liza smiled at them both and said that she would see him later, but if she was already in bed when he arrived back, she would see him the next morning and she went on her way home. Naturally Jamie asked her where Peter had got to and he smiled when told that he was dining at the gatehouse.

"Do you think that the age gap would be so very significant?" asked Jamie.

"Peter has never shown very much interest in any lady until now and I would expect that such a gap in their ages would make absolutely no difference to him," said Liza. "Should it go further I believe everyone would be very happy for them both, especially his parents as they would like to see him settled. But it's very early days."

"You've just got my uncle and cousin happily ensconced in their own home and Peter could whisk her off to Belfast. What would you do with my uncle?" smiled Jamie.

"I'm sure if that were to be the case then Grace would make provision for him and we could always arrange for someone to keep house for him and he can eat with us. It wouldn't be a problem," said Liza.

Jamie laughed, "So you've solved a problem before there is one."

The boys were a little upset not to have seen their Uncle Peter before they went to bed, but they knew that he would be with them for a few days, so they were not too disappointed.

Liza and Jamie had already made their way to bed by the time Peter arrived home, so he had obviously had an entertaining evening.

The following morning he apologised for returning so late and Liza said there was no need and she hoped that he had had an enjoyable evening.

They went through all the arrangements for the following day and Peter spent some time with the boys. Their evening meal was to be with everyone and over dinner it was finally established what would be happening. Lucinda and Miranda would be remaining at home. They could not estimate how long everyone else would be needed at the Ffoulks Home. Jamie and Liza were going to the docks early in the morning to meet the children, Jennifer and the nurses. Peter, David and Grace would be going directly to the Home and waiting with the Major and Hector and the rest of the staff for their arrival. They were aware that Diana, Rose, Bella, Lucille Fountain and possibly Lady Redfern would be there, and they had been given specific duties to undertake.

"I'm surprised that Lady Redfern may be attending," said Lucinda.

"I believe that she has been commissioned to report back to her employer," smiled Liza and everyone understood what she was saying as they knew that Lady Redfern 'worked' at the Palace.

As they all had a great deal to do the next morning, they all decided to have an early night. Peter offered to show Miranda and Lucinda to their home, but David said that as it was on their way to the gatehouse, he was not to bother himself and should also get an early night.

Everyone was up early the next morning and Liza and Jamie were well on their way to the London docks by nine o'clock. Peter, David and Grace would be reaching the Ffoulks Home by lunchtime.

The ship carrying the children was docking as Liza and Jamie arrived. Davis drove their carriage over to where the other carriages were waiting.

Liza and Jamie watched as the gangway was put in place and a nurse appeared leading the children, some of whom were looking around dazed and others fearful. One of the offices in the Marchant & Fuller premises had been set aside so that the children could gain their land legs and settle their stomachs if necessary. A small snack was waiting for each of them and they would not be travelling onwards in the carriages for at least an hour.

Jamie was helping to usher the children into the room and Liza was watching them coming from the ship. Jennifer appeared holding the hand of a very small boy and guiding an older girl with him. He seemed to be around three or four years old and both he and the girl were in very ill-fitting clothes and the boy was holding onto a strange hand knitted toy as if his life depended on it. Liza had not been expecting these two and as Jennifer brought them over to her she explained that the two children had been in great danger and could not be left in Belfast.

"An immediate decision had to be made to bring them here," said Jennifer.

"Of course Jennifer, shall we take them over to the room and then you can tell me their background," said Liza and she smiled down at the children and started walking with them. Jamie saw her coming and he was smiling at her happily.

"Have you seen who's disembarking Liza," he said and she turned and was amazed to see Amelia being helped down the gangway by the first mate, followed by Wendell talking to the captain as he walked towards the dock.

Jennifer laughed and said that she thought that Liza would be surprised but did not want to take the pleasure away by telling her and said that she would take the children to the room herself leaving Liza to greet her special guests.

Liza was then making haste towards her dearest and oldest friends and was engulfed by Amelia and then kissed heartily on each cheek by Wendell.

"I hope you don't mind that we have imposed ourselves onto you, but it was a last-minute decision and Wendell is feeling remarkably fit considering," said Amelia.

"Mind!" exclaimed Liza. "Of course we don't mind. I cannot tell you how pleased I am to see you both."

By this time Jamie had joined them and was kissing Amelia and shaking Wendell's hand. "This is a wonderful surprise. I hope you are going to be able to stay with us for a long while."

"We can stay until you kick us out," smiled Wendell. "I know you have a great deal to do today; so we'll hire a cab and make our way to your house as I know that we'll be less than useless attempting to help with the children today."

"We have more than enough carriages to take us all to the Home, so you can take our carriage with Davis driving you. You do remember Davis don't you," said Jamie. "I'll go and find him for you."

"Are you sure that won't put you out?" Amelia asked Liza.

"Of course not; I'm just sorry that I can't be with you today to see you settled in your room. We always keep your room just for you. Oh I'm so pleased that you are here, but I must go and see to the children now and I'm not sure what time we'll be home tonight. Did Peter know that you were planning this trip?" asked Liza.

"No, he'll be just as surprised as you," said Wendell.

"I must tell you Liza that the two very young children are rather traumatised, and I think that they will need quite some help, but I know that you will sort that out. Here comes Jamie with Davis and you can leave us in his very capable hands, and we'll see you when you have everything sorted today. We want to visit the Home but know that the children need to settle first," said Amelia.

"The boys are going to be delighted to see you, as are Miranda and Lucinda. Jamie's uncle and cousin are with us today, so you won't meet them until tomorrow. We have a very happy extended household now and the two of you will just make it complete. Goodbye now and we'll see you hopefully later, but probably it will be tomorrow," said Liza.

Jamie had already given Davis instructions and when he had dealt with Wendell and Amelia, he was to go to the Ffoulks house to eventually bring Liza and Jamie back home.

Liza smiled happily at them and then made her way to the room where the children were relaxing after their long sea journey. She went round each child to make sure they were not feeling too scared and finally she reached the two little ones who were sitting quietly together, and they looked up at her with fear in their eyes. Liza crouched down to their level and asked them if they had been given anything to eat; the girl nodded and showed that she was holding the food and not eating it and Jennifer said that they were not used to being given good food and they were saving it just in case there was nothing else for a long while.

"If you are hungry you can eat now and I'll get you some more so that you can take it with you, do you understand?" said Liza and the girl nodded and they both started eating what they had hidden whilst Liza brought more for them.

Liza whispered to Jennifer, "What on earth has happened to them? I can see that all the children have that look of resignation in their eyes that all abused children have, but these two are different, they are traumatised."

Jennifer moved slightly away from them so that they could not hear what she was saying. "They were brought to your house by an older boy. Mrs Edwards answered the door to his loud and insistent banging and he pushed these two in but he was grabbed by a ruffian and all Mrs Edwards could do was bang the door closed unfortunately leaving the boy in the hands of the man. Luckily Mr Grouch was there and managed to wrestle with the man and the boy ran off. They hoped that he would make it back to them but sadly he was found dead the next day, he had been beaten badly and had obviously died of his injuries."

"Do these two know that he is dead?" asked Liza.

"The girl has said that he must be because he would have come to them if he was alive. The boy hasn't spoken to us, but he does communicate with the girl. The doctor was called to see them and was accosted as he tried to get into your house. Mr Grouch got a message to the authorities who did manage to guard your house along with security staff and it was decided that we had to get them away from Belfast as quickly as possible. If you hadn't already had children coming here today, we would have got them on the first available ship to somewhere in England," said Jennifer.

Jamie joined them and said, "I've seen Wendell and Amelia comfortably settled in the carriage and Davis knows what to do. Wendell has told me about the two young ones. I hope that Mrs Edwards and the Grouches are not in any danger, but I understand that they are being well guarded by the authorities and security staff. Wendell has told Mrs Edwards and Mrs Adams to go to their house if they feel threatened or unnerved in any way."

"I'll take them with me in my carriage," said Liza.

"I have a carriage full of boys," laughed Jamie.

"It is going to be rather cramped as we are one carriage less now," said Liza, "but we'll manage."

Jamie was to have five boys with him, a nurse had six girls with her, and the other nurse had a mixture of six girls and boys, Liza and Jennifer now had five children with them. Finally they were all settled and off they went in convoy for the hour and a half journey.

They started by asking the children their names which was successful until they got to the two that Liza had sitting next to her. "What's your name?" she asked the boy and the girl said quietly, "he hasn't got a name."

Liza looked at the boy and asked him if that was correct and he nodded. "Have you never had a name?" she asked, and he shook his head.

"Then we must think of a name for you. Is there a name that you would like?" asked Liza and he shrugged his shoulders and looked as if he was going to cry. He put out his hand to the girl and said, "Ber" and she took his hand and he held even more tightly to his knitted toy.

"What does he mean by 'Ber', is that your name?" Liza asked the girl.

"He calls me Ber because he can't say Amber," she said.

"Amber, that's a very pretty name," said Jennifer and the girl smiled for the first time.

Liza lifted the boy onto her lap and said, "Would you like us to give you a name?" and the boy nodded.

"Well little boy," said Liza. "You look very like my brother when he was a little boy; his name was William. Would you like to have the name William?"

He also smiled for the first time and nodded shyly. "Then William it is. What do you think Amber, does he look like a William?" asked Liza.

Amber smiled and nodded. "I think the name William suits him very well," said Jennifer. "Have you thought of a name for your toy William?"

He shook his head and Jennifer then asked all the children what they thought his toy should be called and some of the answers were a little coarse but finally William approved the name 'Softy' for his much loved unusual knitted toy.

"Do you know how old he is Amber?" asked Liza and Amber shook her head.

The other children were asking questions about where they were going, and Liza and Jennifer answered to the best of their ability. Amber was now leaning on Liza and William was on her lap and they both settled and slept for the rest of the journey. The others also slept on and off and when they arrived they were all helped down, and Liza still had a sleeping William in her arms and Amber clinging onto her skirt.

True to their word Bella, Lucille and Lady Redfern and Diana were dressed in very ordinary clothes and were helping to get all the children out of the various carriages. The Major, Estelle and Hector were smiling and making them all comfortable in their new surroundings. Peter, David and Grace were asking their names and leading them towards the house and when they reached it their noses were assailed with the smell of well-cooked food.

It was useless to tell the children to wash their hands as food was the main thing on their minds. They were settled at the various tables but Amber and William stayed closely to Liza and the Major came over to her and Liza introduced him to the pair. They looked up at him with frightened eyes but the smile on his face soon made them relax and they allowed him to lead them to a table and seated them as comfortably as possible as it was obvious that the little boy was in some discomfort.

"I think that the nurse will have to gently examine little William, he seems to be in difficulty. I dread to think what has happened to him and to Amber; they both seem traumatised," said Liza and she gave him a brief history of why they had to leave Belfast so suddenly.

It was noticeable that some table manners were urgently needed, and Estelle said that it would become part of her itinerary.

Peter came over and said that Jamie had told him that his parents had taken the sudden decision to make the trip. "I'm delighted that my father felt well enough to visit; he obviously twisted my mother around his little finger. They'll be able to meet Grace and her father."

Liza smiled at him thinking that he hadn't mentioned meeting anyone else but that did not surprise her.

The children's meal was over and they were now going to be shown to where their beds were, and it was astounding that there was hardly a sound coming from them. All the adults looked at one another in amazement and the Major stood and smiled as only he could, and he seemed to have the ability to calm the children.

He told them that they were then going to see where they would be sleeping and when they had found their beds, he was going to arrange that they be taken on a tour of the house and grounds and over the following days they would soon familiarise themselves with their new home. They all looked at him and followed him out of the room; it appeared that they were used to doing as they were told. Liza wondered how long that would last.

The only two not moving were Amber and William, they were clinging to one another again and Liza and Jennifer gently took their hands and led them up the stairs to a room with just two beds in it.

"This will be your room for the time being," said Liza and she showed them their wardrobes and chests of drawers and they stared at them with wonder in their eyes.

"In a little while one of our nurses will organise baths for you both and when you are clean and warm, we will put some soothing cream on where you are hurting," said Liza.

"His bottom hurts," said Amber. Her broad Irish accent was making it a little difficult for them to understand.

"Well, we have a doctor coming later and he can take a look and I know that we can make him more comfortable. Do you hurt anywhere Amber?" asked Liza gently and she nodded and pointed to her back.

"Can I have a look please?" asked Liza and once again Amber nodded and Liza and Jennifer were horrified to see the marks of a severe beating on her back.

"We'll get you into a nice warm bath and let the doctor look at you also. Is there anywhere else that you hurt?" asked Liza and Amber nodded again but wouldn't say where, so Liza and Jennifer drew their own conclusions.

The nurse arrived and said that two baths had been set up in the small washroom and were filled with nice warm water and Liza persuaded both children to go there with the nurse, but of course 'Softy' had to go also. Jennifer said that she would go to see how some of the other children were getting on and Liza said that she would join her shortly.

Slowly Liza made her way down the stairs and into one of the rooms and she leant against the wall and sobbed for the children and that was where Bella found her.

"I thought you said that the children don't need someone who just cries over them," said Bella. "But I know how you feel; I've just done the same in another room."

"You're right, I must stop; these children are starting out on a new life and they don't need tears, they need love and people who can help them get over what they have been through," said Liza.

"I am so disgusted that my brother took pleasure from hurting and degrading such youngsters. I feel quite sick at the thought that someone like that is in my family. I hope that he dies in excruciating pain in some dirty hovel in India. I'm going to have to watch my boys closely as I don't want them to show signs of any leanings in that direction," said Bella and Liza could tell that she was furious at what she had seen that day.

"Unfortunately none of us can completely govern another person's life or their strange tendencies. You can only show an example and hope that they follow you in that," said Liza who was now beginning to control herself and feeling that she was nearly ready to face the children again.

"I am going to suggest to the Duke that my boys spend some time with your boys; I think it would do them some good as I know that your boys have their feet firmly on the ground. I suppose they will soon be going to Cambridge. I must check with the Duke to see what he has arranged and see if it's possible for them to attend the same university," said Bella and she sounded very like Hector in her assuming nature.

Liza just smiled and nodded, knowing that no matter what Bella said the Duke had the last word on the subject of the education of his sons.

"Your sons will always be welcome at our house Bella and we have room for them to stay on occasion. You know that we have cricket practice every Sunday afternoon and everyone joins in from the farms and village, so it would be a good idea for you to plan a weekend for them," said Liza.

"You let them mix with farmers and villagers? Is that not a little dangerous?" said Bella.

"Why? What's wrong with that? They get a good sense of perspective and are able to communicate with everyone. The villagers and farmers love them; they know that they are from the 'big house' but our boys don't see any difference between themselves and the village and farm children. They run, laugh and play together, the only thing which is different is that they are educated at home instead of in the village school and sometimes they wish that they could join with the others, but they do every Sunday at church and then at the cricket practice. I know that the Major is keen to arrange a cricket side from the boys here, so that will be interesting," said Liza.

"Are you going to bring your boys to visit here?" asked Bella.

"Not for a while; it would be best if the children settle into their surroundings and get to know one another before my boys come to visit," said Liza but really her motive behind that was that she didn't want John to relive

217

his past and she could not explain to Bella that children, once abused, took that nightmare with them to the grave.

Bella looked at Liza and said, "It's because of your John, isn't it?"

Liza frowned and didn't know what to say.

"I know you keep that quiet, and I understand why, but my brother admitted his guilt in that respect and the Duke and my mother realised that all the hard work you had done to make him feel as normal could have been wiped out in just one minute when my brother attacked him and I am so sorry for that. I do hope that he is back to having a normal childhood," said Bella and she had tears in her eyes.

"Yes, he is back to normality Bella and I don't want to remind him of his past if it is not necessary to do so. It is amazing that an abused person recognises that in others when we would not see anything out of the ordinary," said Liza. "We must get back to our duties for today. We mustn't leave others to deal with everything without our help." And Liza laughed intimating that no one person was essential to the smooth running of that day; they all were.

Liza and Bella found that the children were now being shown around the kitchen garden and the animal pens and they could hear the cries of pleasure coming from them. The Major and Hector could be seen and heard explaining that they could help with the gardens and the animals and that they would be receiving more chicks in the next few days. They carried on walking around the side of the house and onto the playground and there were shrieks of delight from some of the children, others just stood and stared. The Major was then explaining that there was also a ground for playing cricket or any other sport that they would like.

Jamie and his Uncle David came to tell them that it was bath time to the moans of some but the pleasure of others and as they walked towards the house Lady Redfern and Diana were waiting for them to tell them to go to their sleeping area and collect their night clothes, dressing gowns and slippers and bring them down to the washrooms and once they were scrubbed and clean it would be time for supper.

"Are we going to have more food?" came one small voice.

"Yes, you will have three meals a day; breakfast, lunch and supper," said Lady Redfern.

There was a chorus of "Oooh" from the children and they happily made their way up to their rooms, followed by the sound of feet coming back down the stairs to the large ground floor washrooms.

"Boys to the left and girls to the right," shouted Lady Redfern.

There were six filled baths in each washroom with a small screen between each of them for privacy. Diana and Lady Redfern were on duty in the girl's washroom, whilst two of the nurses were supervising the boys. With the first bath time over, the baths were quickly emptied and refilled for the last ten children and those who had bathed were dressed comfortably in their night clothes and slippers and ushered into the recreation room to wait for everyone to be ready to take supper together.

Estelle was in the recreation room talking to each child and making a note of their name and Grace was helping her. Bella and Lucille were setting the tables. The Major and Hector were making sure that all the children were accounted for. Anthony had just arrived with Rose who was going to take over Lady Redfern's duties as she was due to leave shortly for the Palace. Jamie, Peter and David were making sure that all the security arrangements were in place.

Liza made her way up to Amber and William's room and they were both sitting on one bed looking very clean and comfortable in their night clothes. The doctor was also in the room as was Jennifer.

"Ah Lady Edgeworth," said the doctor as he ushered her out of the room. "I have examined these two little ones and they have both been appallingly misused, especially the little boy. He can only be three or four years old and the little girl is not much older, maybe six or seven. I despair over what they have been put through, but they are safe now and hopefully they will be young enough to get over the traumatic time that they have had. I have dealt with their bodily hurts as best I can, but God knows whether their minds will ever be healed. I'll return tomorrow and the next day until I finish making sure that all the children are as fit as they can be."

"Thank you, doctor; you know that what you are doing is very much appreciated. I believe the Major is in the recreation room, would you like me to show you the way?" asked Liza.

"No Lady Edgeworth," said the doctor, "Those two little ones need you more than I do. I'll find my own way."

Liza went into their room and they were still sitting side by side on one bed.

"Which bed are you going to have Amber?" asked Liza.

"Don't know," said Amber.

William was looking at the one that they were sitting on. "Is this bed yours William?" and he nodded. "So Amber will be in that one," smiled Liza. "Come with me now, we'll go down and see if supper is ready. I wonder what it's going to be."

Liza took one in each hand and helped them down the stairs. 'Softy' was also going down to supper and Liza made a mental note to find something for Amber to love and cherish. All the other children were quietly making their way into the dining room; it was noticeable that they were very quiet for children their age and Liza thought of how noisy her three were when they were making their way to the kitchen for supper.

She led Amber and William to seats at a table near the door where she could keep an eye on them. The Major stood and told them that all the adults would also be eating with them that evening and everyone took a place at each of the tables with the children. The meal was relatively light that evening of salad, ham, hard boiled eggs and cheese with bread. Once again table manners were noticeable by their absence.

Liza found that she was hungry as she hadn't eaten since breakfast. She found that some of the children on her table were copying the way she was eating. Amber and William used their fingers and she noticed that they were wrapping some of the food in a napkin.

"Amber you don't have to hide food away; there will always be plenty for you," said Liza and she carried on talking to the children and asking them their names and how they liked being there.

After supper the children went into the recreation room for a while to let their supper go down before they went to bed. Liza led Amber and William in and Grace came over and took their hands and sat with them. Liza said that she would see them when they were in bed and she would tuck them in.

She went to find Jamie; she was missing him, and she found him with the Major and Peter.

"I think that today has gone according to plan," said the Major. "All the children seem as contented as possible under the circumstances. The only ones that I am really worried about are the two little ones that you have been looking after Liza. I realise why they had to get away from Belfast and I hope that we are equipped to handle their traumas. I can see that all these children have been hurt and need special handling but to have hurt ones that are as young as those two is despicable. I understand that the lad who brought them to your house was murdered; it is so difficult to believe that there is so much wickedness in the world."

"I'm afraid that you have to believe it Major; you are now surrounded by proof of it," said Liza. "The little boy never had a name, so I named him William and the girl is Amber. William calls her Ber, he hasn't yet been able to call her by her full name. They may be brother and sister, but we will never know that as they have no memory of their past, perhaps that will come back in time. I'll see them settled before I leave tonight. Your people have shown that they are very caring. I presume you saw the doctor before he left; he'll be back to see all the children."

Grace was in the process of taking William and Amber up to bed. Several of the children were showing signs of tiredness and those that weren't were looking forward to being in their permanent beds. Liza walked up the stairs with several of the children and watched them go to their beds. Diana was already there with Bella and Lucille and they were talking to the children as they helped them into bed and hung up their dressing gowns and placed their slippers beside their beds. Liza smiled and then made her way to William and Amber's room.

Grace was looking after Amber and Liza helped William and 'Softy' into bed. Liza had found a soft toy for Amber and she had it lying beside her. Liza tucked them in as she had promised, and they looked like the babies that they were and she found it difficult not to shed a tear. Grace had a book with her and she started to read to them, but it wasn't long before they appeared to be sleeping peacefully. She and Grace left and placed a lamp on a table in the hall opposite their door as they both felt that it would be better if they woke up not to be completely in the dark.

They made their way to the dormitories and made sure that all the children were comfortable and happy. They seemed to be but who knew what was going on in their minds. Everyone seemed settled and the nurses were watching over them until they were asleep, and they also would have a lamp lighting their rooms from the hall.

Down in the dining room everyone was sitting having a cup of tea and discussing how the day had been. Diana, Anthony and Rose were the first to leave and Hector said that he would stay in one of the spare rooms just in case he was needed through the night. The Major looked at him and said that there was a room off his and it would be a good idea if he used that one. Lady Redfern had left earlier but Bella and Lucille were travelling home together, and the Major thanked them profusely for all they had done. Peter, David and Grace had a carriage and would be leaving shortly. Jennifer's bags had already been taken to the Major's house and Liza and Jamie would make sure she was safely ensconced on their way home.

"I must just check on the children before we leave," said Liza to Jamie, and Estelle said that she would go with her.

It was very quiet and peaceful in all the dormitories. Liza looked in on William and Amber and found them both sleeping in William's bed clasping their toys.

"There's no point in moving them," said Liza. "They would only get back into bed together; they need one another; that's the only comfort they have had for a very long time. They look very settled."

"I'll make sure that a special eye is kept on them through the night; they do seem the most vulnerable of all the children," said Estelle. "It is so appalling that places like this are needed and I think that no matter how much love and affection they are all now given will ever make them truly forget their pasts."

They walked down the stairs together and Jamie was waiting with Jennifer to go to the carriage and at last make their way home to their boys and Wendell and Amelia.

They arrived home just before eleven o'clock that night, having first taken Jennifer to the Major's house. They didn't expect anyone to still be up, but they were delighted to find that both Wendell and Amelia were waiting for them in the drawing room.

Of course Wendell and Amelia wanted to know how the day had gone and Jamie gave them a brief outline of all the events. Liza excused herself as she wanted to see the boys to make sure they were well and as she returned Peter came in through the front door.

"Your mother and father are in the drawing room Peter," said Liza and he bounded in to see them.

"I didn't expect you both to still be up," said Peter.

"We had a wonderful rest this afternoon and felt quite refreshed by dinner time," said Wendell.

They stayed talking for another hour but then tiredness overcame Liza, Jamie and Peter and they all made their way to bed feeling that the day had been as much of a success as it could have been under the circumstances.

Chapter 12

Amelia was enjoying the pampering she was being given in bed the next morning. She had relished her breakfast and was now relaxing whilst water was being brought up for her to soak in the luxury of a hot bath.

The journey from Belfast had not been too onerous but because they had made the sudden decision to visit Liza, packing what was needed had been quite traumatic and Amelia was still not sure that they had all they needed. Wendell had brushed aside her concerns by saying that if they needed anything, and Liza did not have it, then they would buy it. She thought that as far as he was concerned, he would have arrived in only what he was wearing. However, the thought of spending time with their beloved Liza pushed aside all the problems of speedy, last minute travel arrangements.

She finally lowered herself into the relaxing hot tub and smiled her delight. She knew that for the next few days Liza would be occupied helping to settle the children into the new Home, but she would have the pleasure of seeing the three boys who had welcomed them so noisily the day before. Edward's baby was not due for around six weeks and so Amelia knew that they could stay with Liza for at least four weeks, possibly five.

Peter would be returning to Belfast in the next day or two, so the company would be in safe hands, but Brendan was coming along in leaps and bounds and Peter's assistant was a very responsible overseer. Edward and Joseph were competent although Amelia had to admit that they did not have their father's business acumen.

As she soaked in her bath, she looked around the bedroom and noted all the improvements since she was last there and thought that some of them would work quite well at her home in Belfast. Wendell would not see the need, but she knew just how to put the idea in his mind and that was to get Liza to suggest them.

Jamie, Wendell and Peter had already breakfasted in the dining room and were now in the library going through the usual morning newspaper ritual when Liza entered. She was dressed ready to go to the Home but was not going to leave until Amelia had finally finished bathing.

"Good morning gentlemen," smiled Liza and true to form all three newspapers dropped slightly and three pairs of eyes looked at her and in unison three voices said, "Good morning Liza."

Liza laughed and she wondered whether to say something outrageous and make their newspapers drop completely but decided against it. "What are your plans for the day gentlemen?" asked Liza.

Wendell's paper dropped halfway, "I'm going to do nothing strenuous today Liza. I shall probably take a walk around the grounds and perhaps visit Miranda and Lucinda. I hope that you will introduce us to Jamie's uncle and cousin before you leave for the Home."

Peter's and Jamie's newspapers were now also halfway down. "If Liza and Jamie don't have the time Father, I will take you to their house and introduce you. Of course, if you have no objection to that Liza."

"That's very kind of you Peter, but I think we may well have the time to make the necessary introductions. However, if we do not have a chance to do so then I'm sure David and Grace would have no objections to you doing so," smiled Liza.

Jamie looked over the top of his paper and raised an eyebrow to her. Wendell and Peter's newspapers went back up again.

"And what will you be doing today Peter?" asked Liza.

Peter's newspaper dropped, whereas Jamie's stayed with his eyes just showing, he seemed to be waiting to see what was going to be said.

"I shall be going to the Home again today. Grace has said that she would like to go there and see what she can do to help so I have offered to take her. I presume I can borrow one of your small carriages," said Peter.

Now Wendell's newspaper was completely on his lap and a curious frown was on his face.

"Well, we could take her if you like Peter. It would save you a journey," smiled Liza. Jamie seemed to develop a coughing fit. "Would you like a glass of water Jamie?"

Wendell's frown had become even more intense.

"I don't want to bother you and Jamie, Liza, but thank you," said Peter. "I have one or two things that I want to check on at the Home today."

"Well, if you're sure Peter," said Liza innocently and Jamie looked at her and shook his head smiling before he raised his newspaper back up again.

224

Wendell was still staring at his son as he realised that he was sounding a little too keen to be the one to take Jamie's cousin to the Home and he also could see that Liza was playing a game with him and that Jamie knew that too. *So,* he thought, *my son is at last showing an interest in a lady.* He looked at Liza and could see the twinkle in her eye.

Peter stood up and said that he had now better get ready for the day and he hastily left the room and made his way to his room to change.

Wendell turned to Liza and asked if Peter was as keen on Jamie's cousin as he appeared.

"Well Wendell, they certainly seem to get on well together, but he only met her a few days ago, so I really think that it's too soon to make a judgement on the relationship. Grace is an intelligent lady and of course you know that Peter doesn't suffer fools gladly, so he would keep company with her more so than anyone else," said Liza.

Jamie kept his newspaper well over his face as he had decided not to enter into this conversation.

"I don't think I'll say anything to his mother as in her mind she will have him walking down the aisle in no time at all, which would probably mean the kiss of death to any blossoming relationship that he might have," said Wendell.

"I'll say nothing to her, but she's not stupid and a mother notices changes in her children, no matter how old they are," said Liza. "We'll have to leave soon Jamie. I'll see if Amelia is ready before we leave and of course I'll see the boys. I also want to call on your mother and Lucinda on our way. We won't be home as late as yesterday; we will be back well in time for dinner. I think the whole family will be with us for that, so if you haven't managed to meet Jamie's uncle and cousin before, then you will do at dinner."

Having spent a little while with the boys, Liza then went to find Amelia and after discussing the plans for the evening, she then found Jamie waiting for her in the study.

"You were a little wicked with Peter this morning Liza," said Jamie. "Do you think he noticed?"

"I'm sure he did, and he will seek me out at the Home to tell me so," laughed Liza.

They made their way to the carriage and today it was driven by Hendry and firstly they stopped at Miranda's and Lucinda's and spent a little while telling them how the previous day had gone and that they looked forward to seeing them for dinner that evening.

They drove on and stopped as David and Grace came from their front door and told them that they were going to the main house as Grace was once again going to the Home with Peter and David said that he would introduce himself and Grace to Mr and Mrs Fuller.

"Yes, Peter is there, and I know that we will see you both at the Home shortly," said Liza with a smile.

"I think that when I have seen them, I will spend a little time with Holly," said David quite happily. Liza and Jamie said goodbye and finally they were on their way to the Ffoulks Home and Liza was going to enjoy just having Jamie to herself for the next hour or so.

"What will you do when you get to the Home?" Jamie asked Liza.

"Naturally I want to find out how all the children enjoyed their first night in their new home and I want to see what the Major has on the agenda for today and the next few days. We were so busy settling them in yesterday that I had no chance to find out what the plans were for the immediate future apart, of course, from basically looking after the children," said Liza.

"What's Peter planning for today?" asked Jamie.

"I'm sure he will be looking at the costs of the overall running of the Home because that will be what each Home will therefore cost. We know how much the renovations have cost and the salaries of the staff, but there are unforeseen expenses that we will have to take into account for future ventures and naturally we have to show some accountability to those who generously sponsor us," said Liza.

"I suppose you are anxious to find out how the two small ones are," said Jamie.

"Yes, I am Jamie, but I know that I must not show favouritism towards any one child, or two in this case. It's difficult though as I feel so sorry for them. They seem so lost; at least they have one another however I hope that they soon integrate with the other children so that they can each learn to be a child," said Liza.

"There are very many there who need to learn that, Liza; just because those two appear more traumatised than the others doesn't mean that the others won't have to be shown how to have some fun," said Jamie.

"You're so very right Jamie," said Liza. "I can't wait for the day when their shouts of fun and laughter echo throughout the house. We have quite a few requests for adoptions and for some bond servants from America but it's a little soon to think about that for these children."

"Aren't you worried that some of the children have been abused for so long that it has become a way of life for them and they may have a detrimental influence on some of the others?" asked Jamie.

"That's always a possibility but we must remember that they have all risked their lives to get away from the things that were being done to them. There may be children who enjoy being in that life, but the ones that we have in our care did not, which is why they have made such efforts to find us and also bring vulnerable little ones to us for protection. If they were hardened in that trade, they would not have come to us," said Liza.

They arrived at the Home as the children were having lunch and a few were attempting to use cutlery with Estelle encouraging them to do so. Amber and William were sitting quietly together and still hiding food in their pockets. The Major was having his lunch with the children and surprisingly Hector was sitting at one table and attempting to show those around him how a knife and fork should be used.

They waved to the Major to stay seated and they went into the office and waited for lunch to finish and a short while later Peter and Grace arrived. "I introduced your uncle and Grace to my parents," Peter said to them. "I believe your uncle was going to spend a little while with them and then visit Grace's mother in the churchyard."

Both Liza and Jamie nodded at that information and by that time the Major had joined them and gave a detailed report of how the children had fared through the night. There had been a few wet beds, but that was to be expected. "The two very little ones slept quite well; the nurses and Estelle kept a particularly close eye on them and it would seem that for the time being they are going to stay sleeping together. They are giving one another a great deal of comfort; hopefully they will mix with some of the others in a while, but it is very early days for all the children here."

"Some of them have been a while in the Homes in Belfast but they were getting overcrowded and that's why they are here and because they are overcrowded they can't have the care and attention that we really would like to give them, hence why some of them don't know how to use their cutlery. It's only the two little ones who have spent really no time at all in any of our Homes," said Liza.

"Are there many children still to come here from Belfast?" asked Jamie.

"That depends on whether we have more children brought to us," said Liza. "There are one or two children waiting in the houses in London and Liverpool,

227

other than those who are waiting to go to America. I don't doubt that we will soon see them arriving from many places here in England. The authorities are closing in on the perpetrators of the trade and we will have to receive those who are left when their owners are imprisoned or transported to Tasmania."

"So you could have some hardened children brought to you under duress," said Jamie.

"I doubt it as those who want to carry on in the trade won't want to be with us and they'll probably have already found an alternative place to work from and we can only assume that they will be older than the children brought to us. The only older children that we have are those who have risked all to get to us and normally they have a young child or two in tow. But we must watch out for disruptive elements in all children; what we are now doing is not as easy as it was in the early days," said Liza.

"Was it easy in the early days then?" asked Hector.

"It was comparatively so; the children found us and we did our best to look after them and much as it seemed that children were coming from all over the place, really they were only from Belfast and we easily found them homes and jobs in America," said Liza. "Now we have the good fortune to have ample funds and with that comes expansion but not only do we have to answer to numerous sponsors, our expansion gives a vulnerability, as was seen with the murder of the lad who brought William and Amber to us."

"What is it that you're not saying Liza?" asked Hector.

"What Liza isn't yet saying Hector," said Peter, "is that it won't just be the children who are vulnerable; we all are. Liza was attacked in New York; Jamie was stabbed in Belfast. There have also been verbal slurs on Liza and Jamie. That is something that we must all expect and guard against. What also has to be appreciated is that Liza and Jamie are the faces of the charity and they are on show at various functions; unfortunately their everyday lives now are not as carefree as they should be."

"We have not experienced any problems currently but as children start coming from relatively close to us that may be the time that we have to watch out backs," said Jamie.

"As you say Peter, our faces are now becoming well known, but so are those of the Duke and Bella, the Dowager Lady Redfern and Lord Carlton and several others," said Liza who nearly said the Queen and Prince Albert but just stopped herself in time. Jamie and Peter realised who she was referring to.

"Ah you mean Prince Albert," said Hector. "I don't think anyone is going to attack him."

"Well, let's not worry too much about our safety, after all Marchant & Fuller have the best security personnel on their payroll," smiled Liza. "Shall we get on and see how the children are doing after their lunch. Are they eating well?"

"They most certainly are," said Estelle, "with the exception of Amber and William who eat a little and hoard the rest. Obviously they have hidden food for a while, or their friend who brought them to you did that for them to keep them alive and they think that is the way to survive."

"That's surprising because their 'owner' was so anxious to reclaim them that he or she must have thought them valuable and it wouldn't follow that they would be starved; they would want them in relatively good condition and they don't look starved," said Liza and then an idea struck her. "Of course, they saved food for the boy who helped them. He was obviously of no value to the 'owner' otherwise he would still be alive and working. I wonder what they are doing with the food."

"No doubt we will find that out eventually," said Estelle. "I was thinking that I will ease the children into lessons starting on Monday. I'm not going to push them into it but I'm hoping that it won't take long for them all to attend voluntarily."

"You've done a great deal of preparation Estelle, so I'm sure you are going to make the lessons entertaining enough for those who go willingly and they in turn will tell the others how much fun your teaching is," said Liza.

"My only problem is that some of the children will have to teach me to understand their broad Irish accents," said Estelle. "Did you find it very difficult to start with Liza?"

"I still do and I do guess what they are saying quite a lot of the time and luckily I believe I have guessed correctly so far, but the time will come when I say yes to something that I should have said no to," said Liza.

"You're right Liza, I have the same problem," smiled the Major and all else were nodding their agreement. "I wonder if Jennifer understands them more than we do; and you Peter, you're from Belfast, do you understand their accents?"

"I'm the same as Liza I'm afraid; I guess what they are saying mostly," said Peter.

They all left the room and found Jennifer talking to one of the nurses and watching the children attempting to understand the meaning of the word play.

Liza and Jamie moved over to talk to her; she said that she had had a restful night and had been visited by Rose, Diana and little Thomas that morning. Whilst they were talking Liza felt a tug on the back of her skirt but thought nothing of it until she felt a more urgent pull and when she turned she found Amber holding onto her skirt and William put his arms up for her to lift him up whilst he was still clasping 'Softy' and of course she couldn't resist such a request; she scooped him up and held him tightly. Amber pushed into her skirt and Jamie, seeing this, bent down and she put her arms out to him and he lifted her up whilst talking gently to her.

It was a beautifully sunny afternoon and they carried the children over to a nearby seat and sat with them for quite some time. Liza asked if they had slept well and they both nodded and then she asked if they had enjoyed their breakfast and lunch and once again they nodded.

"What are you going to call your lovely toy?" asked Liza of Amber.

"Softy," she said.

"That's William's toy's name," said Liza. "What do you think you should call yours?"

"Softy," she said again.

"So they're both going to be called 'Softy'; won't that be a little puzzling for you both?" asked Liza.

"No," said Amber.

"Well I suppose that makes them easy to remember," said Jamie.

The Major walked across to them with Jennifer and Estelle and the Major said that perhaps William and Amber would like to go with them to the playground and they could have a ride on the swings. They seemed to like that idea and Liza and Jamie lifted them to the ground and Jennifer and Estelle took their hands and led them away.

Liza turned to the Major and thanked him. "It was difficult not to pick them up and hold them; they put up their arms to us and it was right for us not to reject them. However, it cannot be seen that we show favouritism to any one child, but it was not easy today."

"I saw Amber pull at your skirt Liza and I saw William show that he wanted to be picked up and I know you had no choice but to lift him up and you Jamie had to make Amber feel just as wanted. Running a place like this is not easy, is it?" said the Major.

Liza stood up and brushed her skirt down. She felt something in her pocket and when she pulled it out she found that it was bread wrapped in a napkin.

The Major and Jamie stared at it as Liza said, "So we have found where they put their food."

The Major looked quite emotional which was matching how Liza felt. "They give it to people who have been kind and helpful to them," he said. "Food was their thanks and you must have been right Liza; they gave it to the boy who helped them and he probably really needed it. I suppose there may be many of us who will receive their 'food parcel' over the coming weeks. We'll have to make sure that they have extra food to compensate for their generosity. I'll warn whoever is on meal duty."

Hector passed them with a group of boys all carrying cricket bats; Liza and Jamie stared at him and he smiled back at them. "Are you going to show the boys your cricketing expertise Hector?" asked Liza.

Jamie and the Major laughed, knowing that Hector was not the best person to show anyone the finer points of cricket. "I'll come and give you a hand Hector," said Jamie.

"Thanks Jamie; hopefully I was going to show them how a ball should come In contact with a bat but I wasn't feeling very confident knowing my lack of abilities in that respect," said Hector and he and Jamie marched off towards the green followed by ten boys.

Liza and the Major made their way towards the playground and watched as Jennifer and Estelle placed Amber and William on the seats of the swings and gently started pushing them. A few of the slightly older girls were watching them and Liza and the Major walked to them and asked their names, one was called Hazel and she slowly went to the swings and helped to push both Amber and then William. Jennifer and Estelle stood back and let her take over from them. She smiled as she talked to the little ones and all the while they both held on to their 'Softies' and laughed with pleasure. When they had finished, she helped them down and walked with them towards Liza and the Major.

Their faces were glowing with happiness and William put his hand deep into his pocket and brought out a squashed piece of bread and handed it to Hazel. She frowned and was about to refuse the gift when Liza stepped in and said, "Take it Hazel; it's their way of saying 'thank you'." Hazel nodded, took the bread and muttered in her broad Irish accent that she would have needed it not so long ago.

She moved away and joined the girls that she had been with previously.

Estelle and Jennifer walked with William and Amber back towards the house, asking them if they had enjoyed the swings to which they nodded happily. Liza and the Major made their way towards where they knew Jamie and Hector would be with the boys.

"You were right about William and Amber's motives behind hiding food and I heard what Hazel said about her needing it at one time. What a sad life these children have had but that's all going to change now. Will you be with us again tomorrow Liza?" asked the Major.

"No Major, I shall leave you to your own devices. I know that the Home is in very capable hands and I must spend some time with my boys and with Wendell and Amelia; I've hardly seen them since they arrived. They would like to visit, but not until after the weekend. We'll leave you in peace until then," smiled Liza.

"I don't think that 'peace' is the right choice of word Liza," smiled the Major.

"How are you getting on with finding out their names?" asked Liza.

"They all have first names, although some of them ought to be changed for the sake of decorum, but not many have surnames and I think that we ought to do something about that and get them registered legally," said the Major.

"Yes, I was thinking along the same lines. Perhaps we should make a list of surnames and let them choose what they would like. I'll think of some over the weekend as no doubt you will also and perhaps we can discuss it when I bring Wendell and Amelia here on Monday," said Liza.

"Your previous name has been used before, hasn't it Liza?" said the Major. "Would it upset you if one or two of them want that name because it was the one person that they were aiming for?"

"It did shock me when I was asked if the name Kelly could be used; it did take my breath away but it was a wonderful compliment and he would have been so proud that he was giving an identity to someone who desperately needed it. Jamie also thought that it was the right thing for the person in question," said Liza.

"That was young April, wasn't it? I know you don't talk about anyone's past, but she is someone to admire and I believe that her choice of name was the correct one. Of course she now has a different name, so currently there is no one called Kelly. I wanted to have your opinion on the subject just in case someone wants to use it," said the Major.

They arrived at the green where an excuse for cricket was being played. "What are they doing?" asked the Major somewhat mystified.

"I don't think they are quite ready for a cricket match yet," said Liza laughing. The boys were taking it in turns to have Jamie bowl to them and they were holding their bats in many strange ways with Hector encouraging them to "hit it, just hit it."

Jamie was shouting that it just wasn't the way it was done, and Hector was brushing his concerns aside saying that it was just for fun.

"I think it will take a little while before your team is ready to compete," smiled Liza. They walked back to the house and found Peter pouring over the accounts and making notes of costs that would be useful information for any new properties that they acquire. Liza asked where Grace had gone and was told that she was reading to some of the children in their recreation room.

"Wonderful," said Liza. "Hopefully that will get them interested in learning to read."

"I'd like to visit the Langston House," said Peter. "I don't have to go back to Belfast until next week and I know you want to spend some time with the boys tomorrow and at the weekend, so perhaps we could make arrangements for early next week."

"Would you be able to join us also Major? I know that Hector would oversee much of the renovations, but you will be running it so it would be a good idea to see what you are letting yourself in for," said Liza.

It was decided that Tuesday would be a good day as Wendell and Amelia wanted to visit on Monday. Jamie and Hector could be heard arguing as they approached the office. "It was no way to show the boys how to play cricket," Jamie could be heard saying to Hector.

"They had fun Jamie and I thought that was what it was all about," said Hector defensively.

"Yes they should enjoy it, but they should be taught what cricket is really all about," Jamie told him.

"Well that will have to be down to you because I really have no idea of the rules of the game. As far as I'm concerned, a ball is bowled and someone hits it with a bat and makes some runs," said Hector.

"Hector, you're worse than Liza," said Jamie "at least she knows how a bat should be held."

Liza, the Major and Peter stood looking at the door waiting for them to come in and when they did they realised that everything they had said had been heard. "Ah, so you heard our little difference of opinion," said Jamie.

"At least Jamie was complimentary to you Liza," said Hector.

Liza laughed and said that they had to leave now as they were dining with the family that evening. Peter said that they would soon also be leaving, and they all wished the Major good luck and hoped he had a happy weekend. Hector was smiling happily and said that he felt he should stay for another night just in case there were any problems. Nobody liked to intimate that Estelle being there had anything to do with his decision.

Once again Liza enjoyed the journey home having Jamie to herself for the time.

"I gather you didn't enjoy the cricket session with Hector," smiled Liza.

"He really is a law unto himself, but I have to admit that the boys had quite some fun. I dread to think how the boys within his care are going to turn out. He has a very strange outlook on life, but the boys seem to have warmed to him. I think that they enjoyed our banter," said Jamie. "How did William and Amber get on after I left?"

Liza told him about their fun on the swings and how they gave Hazel some bread as a 'thank you'.

"They really are lovely looking children," said Jamie. "I suppose that is why their 'owner' wanted them so much. Good looking children like that must command a high price from their punters. They probably also paid a high price when buying them. I know that you have formed an attachment to them and I wondered whether you would like to take them into our care. We have the room for them and we can afford to look after them well."

"That is so tempting Jamie, but I believe that I am going to come across many children like William and Amber and I would want to take them all and you know that it wouldn't be fair on our boys. We will have Simon with us from next year and we have Derek with us every day," said Liza. "Also I really don't want John confronted by children who have been through what he went through all those years ago. Meeting up with them for a cricket match or just a visit is different to having them living with us."

"You took April on and she had the same background as John," said Jamie.

"She was older, and John was much younger and at that time he would not have recognised her unhappy background," said Liza. "No Jamie, much as I would love to have William and Amber as ours, I love our boys more and cannot introduce unsettled children into our household."

"You are very wise Liza; I have to admit that those two children pulled on my heart strings, but you are right and hard as it seems it would be better for them to go to someone else. Have you anyone in mind?" asked Jamie.

"There are some in America who are looking for a family and although there are suitable children in New York I think that Amber and William need to be settled very quickly and away from here. I have a bad feeling about who they came from; they seem extremely violent and I don't think that they are very short of funds, but they will see that what we are doing is limiting their income. I can see that children as pretty as Amber and William would command a very high price and it was deemed necessary to move them away from Belfast as soon as possible and I would like them away from these shores also as soon as possible," said Liza.

"That's a little unsettling, does the Major know that you are concerned?" asked Jamie.

"He is aware of the problems surrounding William and Amber and he is being extra vigilant, as is Hector. We all know that Hector wants to remain at the Home because of Estelle, but you know as well as I do that he is an ex-soldier and is therefore well aware of when there is an element of danger surrounding him or those around him," said Liza. "But I am more concerned for those in Belfast and I know that extra security has been arranged for all our people."

"This charity seems to be becoming more and more complicated and dangerous," said Jamie and then he smiled, "I'm going to have to look after you so much more than I thought, but I shall enjoy that."

"I like you looking after me Jamie," smiled Liza.

"I'm looking forward to our evening with our family and Amelia, Wendell and Peter," said Jamie.

"All the Fullers are our family Jamie; they have been close to me since I was just a girl, I can't think of them as anything other than family and the boys feel the same," said Liza.

"Of course, I feel the same because you know that I have known Wendell and Amelia longer than you have," said Jamie.

"Really, I hadn't realised that. You must have been at the same functions for some time before I came on the scene and you must have known James and Frederick well before I did," said Liza. "It's strange that I had never thought about that before. How conceited of me to think that all your lives started with I arrived."

"You're not conceited Liza and as far as I'm concerned my life did start when you arrived," smiled Jamie.

"That's a lovely thing to say, but totally untrue. You had a very good life before you knew me, and after. It was different, but quite full," said Liza.

"It was not very happy though Liza; I'm so pleased that our boys are having a better childhood than I had. I love watching them laughing and playing together and sleeping peacefully with not a care in the world. That's the life that children should have, and I hope that some of the ones who have ended up with the charity manage to have as good a life," said Jamie.

"It's what we are all working towards for them," said Liza.

As they arrived home Derek was leaving, and the boys were relaxing before their supper and they were happy to see their parents. A letter had been delivered for Jamie from his lawyer and it said that the boys' adoptions were going through court the following week.

"This time next week we'll all be Edgeworths," said Matthew happily. "Matthew James Edgeworth sounds good."

"So does John James Edgeworth," said John.

"Aren't we a family of James'?" said Jamie. "I hadn't really thought about that before, even though I knew your names it is strange how it's only really struck me now."

"When you get Matthew and John adopted, will you try to arrange for Mum to adopt me please," said James.

"Yes, of course I will James. It will be the first thing that I do once Matthew and John become Edgeworths," said Jamie. "My lawyer is already looking into it, but we do have one bridge to cross first."

James looked dejected, "She won't agree," he sulked.

"Yes she will agree James; it will just take a little while, but I can assure you that it will happen," said Jamie.

That seemed to settle James and the other two told him not to worry as their Dad had told him that it was going to be alright and he doesn't lie.

As Liza and Jamie walked towards their rooms to rest and change for dinner Liza said how wonderful it was that the boys had such faith in him, and she commented that she had exactly the same.

"I hope I can get it sorted without too much difficulty. Have you heard how Evelyn has settled into her surroundings? No, that was a silly question as I know you would have told me if there was any news about her," said Jamie.

"You're right I would have told you. All I have heard was from the Evans' that they had all in hand for her arrival and by the time I had their letter she would have been with them anyway. No doubt they will write in the not too distant future but at the moment I don't want to hear as there may be a problem that I have to deal with and I really don't have the time to do that," said Liza.

"I had better write to Evelyn as a letter from my lawyer would be too formal for what we want for James. It would probably annoy her and really I wouldn't blame her. I suppose we don't have the time to visit her directly. I can take the decision myself as I have complete custody of him but it would be another reason for her to show hatred towards our family, and it really would be courteous of us to discuss the situation with her," said Jamie.

"As I haven't heard of any problems with her at the moment, I can only assume that she is settling in well and it would be a pity to unnecessarily antagonise her, but it is a shame that you can't talk to her about it face to face. I'll have to look at the diary and see if we can make a visit to the Evans'. I think you would enjoy visiting them; they are good, honest farming folk with no airs and graces. They brought Evelyn down to earth and surprisingly she enjoyed their company. I think it was the first time that she had been treated with homely kindness. She has kept in touch with them you know," said Liza.

"I only realised that when I overheard your conversation with her when you organised her move. She has a caring side to her that comes to the fore on occasions, but it is on very few occasions. I have also seen how she loves her daughter, although some of her actions could have meant that her daughter be ostracised or even left without a mother," said Jamie. "The Evans' sound interesting and I think I would enjoy being at a true family farm. I daresay the food is good and wholesome."

"Yes, if you stayed with them too long you would certainly put on weight. Of course they don't because they work off their overeating. I'll see if we can take a few days away. I wouldn't go with you to see Evelyn, that could be a red rag to a bull, which is a shame because I would like to see how she has arranged the house," said Liza.

They heard Peter arrive and bound up the stairs to his room, presumably to get ready for dinner.

"I wonder if Amelia realises the situation between Peter and Grace," said Jamie.

"I would think that she does. Peter looks and acts differently to usual. Mothers would notice that," said Liza. "I won't say anything unless she does."

Jamie laughed, "That's going to be difficult for you. You and Amelia have been so close for so many years and I'm sure you normally have no secrets from one another."

"There have been times when I couldn't tell her what I was worrying about, but she knew I was in difficulty and helped me without asking questions. This is different because it involves her son and I know that she would love to see him happily settled," said Liza.

"Do you think that the situation between Grace and Peter is serious?" asked Jamie.

"It is the first time that he has taken more than a passing interest in a woman but much as he appears quite keen, Peter is a very cautious man and will take his time over any decisions that both he and Grace may feel they would like to make. He also is very business motivated and he will bear that in mind no matter how he feels about their relationship," said Liza.

Jamie then went to his room to get ready for dinner and a while later he and Liza joined everyone in the drawing room for drinks before dinner. The boys came in for a short while and they were full of the news that Matthew and John would become Edgeworths the following week. "Then I'm going to properly become our mother's son as soon as my father can arrange it," announced James to the whole room.

"That will be really nice for you James," said Amelia and Wendell agreed with her.

"It will tidy your family up nicely," said Peter.

"A few weeks ago I only had Grace as my family," said David. "Now I also have a nephew, his wife and their three sons, a sister-in-law and I know that Wendell and Amelia and all the Fullers are considered family just as Lucinda is. I feel that I have received a wonderful gift; I just wish my Holly was here to see it."

"But she is David; she can see everything that is happening to you and you must know that she is very happy about it," said Liza.

"Yes, she is, isn't she? I feel that she is," said David.

The boys had been chatting to Peter whilst Liza and David were talking, and the time had now come for them to leave and they made their way to bed and everyone else went into the dining room.

As always Jamie was at the head of the table and he watched as everyone was gently guided to their seats by Liza. *David was right*, he thought, *to have a family like mine is a wonderful gift*.

"You're very thoughtful Jamie," said Wendell.

"I'm just enjoying having you all here tonight. Not so very long ago my life was like my uncle's, I just had James as my family, now look at you all. It is indeed a gift."

By that time Liza had made her way to her seat next to him; she smiled up at him once again mesmerising him with the sparkle in her bright green eyes.

"Your boys are very happy about their adoption Liza; I hope that James will get what he wants," said Wendell. "He needs the same stability as Matthew and John. Do you think that Evelyn will agree?"

"I hope so Wendell, but even if she doesn't Jamie has total custody of James and he can make any decisions concerning him. It would be better if Evelyn is in agreement otherwise it's just another battle to be fought which she has no chance of winning. We really do not need any more unpleasantness with her," said Liza.

"I have heard that she made a very foolish decision and has ended up being ostracised. She really is her own worst enemy," said Wendell.

"Yes, she hasn't helped herself," said Liza and then she changed the subject to what they would be doing over the next few days.

Wendell looked at her and smiled, "Alright Liza, you can change the subject, but I know that you have put Evelyn and her daughter in a place where they will be safe and able to lick their wounds. I know that I have said it before, but I will say it again; you will never be thanked for what you do for her. However I will leave it at that for now."

The conversation over dinner was lively and they all were hoping that the weather stayed fine for the Sunday afternoon cricket event with the villagers. It was always the highlight of every weekend.

Liza noticed that Amelia was watching Peter and Grace closely and she knew that she was going to be quizzed by her on the relationship, if indeed there was one.

Lucinda was in one of her very happy moods which had come about when David had included her as one of the family and her glass of wine had released her inhibitions. Lucinda's answer to happiness was to cry and tell everyone how wonderful they were and then cry again. As always Miranda stepped in telling her to stop being silly as of course she was now family. "I suppose you would like me to adopt you; I wonder if that's possible," said Miranda who had also enjoyed one too many glasses of wine. "Would you do that Miranda?" said a tearful Lucinda. "Of course I would, if that is what you want," said Miranda. "Will you look into that for us please Jamie?"

All eyes were staring at the pair with amusement and Jamie said gently, "Yes Mother, I'll look into that for you."

"Thank you, Jamie; you really are very kind," said Lucinda whilst mopping her eyes.

They all dutifully kept straight faces as they could see the lunacy of the request, but Lucinda and Miranda didn't and talked animatedly about the possible process of adult adoption. "I suppose I would then be known as Mrs Edgeworth," mumbled Lucinda into her dessert, with Miranda nodding and the rest of the gathering having various amused looks on their faces.

Jamie's shoulders were shaking with concealed laughter and David had his hand over his mouth. Peter and Grace suddenly started an interesting conversation concerning the Ffoulks Home and Wendell and Amelia suddenly remembered an amusing story so that their laughter could be attributed to that and Liza just stared ahead with her eyes watering and the odd hiccup hiding her mirth.

Liza wondered how Miranda and Lucinda would feel the following morning when they realised what they had said and that combined with a possible hangover would be interesting to witness.

They moved into the drawing room for coffee and Miranda apologised saying that she was experiencing a sudden headache and felt that she should make her way home, Jamie said that he would see her back safely but David told him that it would be his pleasure to show both ladies to their home and Harper said that he would assist. David took each lady by the arm and led them out of the drawing room whilst Harper lit the lantern.

When they had left, the room descended into laughter. "Surely they didn't mean what they were asking," said Amelia.

"I would think that they were quite serious at that moment, but the morning will tell them a different tale. I do love them, they really do make our lives interesting," said Liza with amusement.

"I really find my mother and Lucinda wonderful company," said Jamie. "However, I have to say that they and alcohol make for some interesting dinners. Luckily it doesn't happen very often. Lucinda seems unable to be happy without crying; we have become used to her and my mother wouldn't be without her, and neither would we."

***

Liza had been right, both ladies did not appear the next day until well after lunch and then they looked slightly under the weather, much to the amusement of everyone they came into contact with.

Amelia sought Liza out and asked her opinion of Peter's association with Grace.

"They only met about a week ago Amelia, so I wouldn't read too much into it yet," said Liza. "You know that Peter shows an interest in anyone who has a certain amount of intelligence and you can see that Grace is not stupid."

"She's a little older than he is, isn't she?" said Amelia.

"Peter has no tolerance of those he sees as silly young girls, so he would possibly feel more comfortable with someone who is more mature," said Liza.

"I like Grace," said Amelia. "It would be nice if Peter could settle with someone."

"Well don't try to push the relationship Amelia; you know that any such association should not be rushed. If there is anything to their involvement then they will sort it out themselves," said Liza.

"Wendell has said the same. I really would like to see him happily married. His concentration has always been on business and I know that will never change but it would be nice if he had someone special to come home to at the end of a long day," said Amelia.

"Peter will be returning to Belfast next week so we will see if absence will make the heart grow fonder for them both. We have only just got to know Grace; I was looking forward to having her around for a while. I hope that what she sees as her duty towards her father doesn't get in the way of her own happiness. We would make sure that David is cared for should the need arise," said Liza.

"I know you would, and so does Peter if the situation ever comes about," said Amelia who then changed the subject. "I'm looking forward to the cricket match on Sunday, it will be just like when you and Jamie got married; that was such a happy time for everyone."

"What do you think of our suggestion that you and Wendell join us on a trip to New York next year?" asked Liza. "Wendell seems to be back to his old self and I'm sure you both would enjoy it."

"Since it was mentioned, we have given it some thought and feel that if we are both as fit as we are at the moment then we can seriously consider it," said Amelia. "The trip across should be quite relaxing for us as long as the weather doesn't make the sea too rough and once we're there, we can put our feet up and do nothing if that is what we want. You, Jamie and the boys will be entertainment enough for us, and if Miranda and Lucinda are also with us then we will indeed be kept amused."

"Good," said Liza. "We'll work towards that and make some plans for after Easter next year. The boys will be pleased, and it will be the time that Simon will be coming to live with us, so it could all work out rather well."

Liza spent the rest of the day with Wendell and Peter discussing various aspects of business and Amelia visited Miranda and Lucinda and then David. Jamie went with his overseer to inspect his lands.

After school the boys practiced cricket with Jamie and Peter until supper time and Liza thought what a lovely day it had been. Miranda and Lucinda had decided that they would not join them for dinner that evening much to the amusement of everyone, and Peter had been invited to dine with David and Grace, so dinner was a cosy time for Liza and Jamie with Wendell and Amelia and they made plans for the weekend.

Chapter 13

Saturday was overcast and threatened rain and they all hoped that Sunday's weather would improve. The boys were to lunch with the adults, and they were looking forward to that.

Jamie, Wendell and Peter were in the library going through the newspaper ritual and Liza and Amelia had been in to see them and watch the various stages of the newspaper movements.

Liza went down to the kitchen to let Mrs Lambert know that everyone would be dining with them that night and to finalise the menu. As she was walking back to join Amelia in the drawing room, she heard a carriage draw up.

"Are you expecting anyone Liza?" asked Amelia.

"No, not today," said Liza.

Harper knocked and entered and was about to make his announcement when he was brushed to one side and there was Bella, flanked by two very grumpy looking boys.

"Good morning Bella, this is a pleasant surprise," said Liza.

"I thought I would take you up on your kind offer to have my boys spend some time with your boys. When I mentioned it to the Duke, he thought that it was a wonderful idea, so here we are. I've brought their night clothes and extra clothes for tomorrow," said Bella.

Liza and Amelia sat blinking up at Bella as Jamie came into the room. "I thought I heard someone arriving. Good morning Bella, how are you?" he said.

"I'm very well, thank you Jamie," smiled Bella.

"Bella has brought her boys to stay with us Jamie," said Liza and Jamie turned and looked at her quizzically.

"That will be nice for our boys," said Jamie cautiously having seen the looks of displeasure on the faces of Bella's two boys.

"I thought that I would stay also and see what your cricket matches are all about," said Bella.

"Of course," said Jamie who was used to Bella's demanding ways from the time he had spent with her family in his youth.

Liza suddenly came to life and echoed Jamie's words and rang for Harper and when he arrived, he was given instructions for Mrs Frances to organise a room for the two boys and one for Bella, and then rearrange all their meals.

"Bella, this is Amelia Fuller and later you will meet Wendell. They are staying with us for a while; you haven't introduced us to your sons," said Liza.

"My apologies Liza; this is Nicholas and this is Richard," said Bella.

"Welcome Nicholas and Richard," smiled Liza. "I'll fetch our boys to meet you."

"That's alright Liza, I'll go and find them," said Jamie who seemed to want to remove himself from an awkward situation.

"Everyone, please do sit down," said Liza as she looked at the two increasingly unhappy boys who had obviously been taken out of their comfort zone.

"Nicholas will be going to Cambridge with your boys now Liza, and Richard will follow the next year," said Bella. "The Duke arranged all that for them."

"That will be good for them; you know that their long-time friend from America will also be with them. It will be very sensible for them to get to know one another beforehand," said Liza.

Jamie appeared with three cautious boys in tow and Liza then proceeded to introduce them to one another. All the boys were very polite, and Liza thought that this was not going very well. As always Matthew took the lead.

"So you're Nicholas and you're Richard. Your room is being arranged for you and it's right opposite ours so that will be useful," said Matthew. He continued, "How old are you?"

Nicholas grudgingly replied that he was fourteen and Richard nearly thirteen.

"That's very good," said Matthew. "James and John are your age and I'm Richard's age. We are going to get on well."

"We were just playing a board game before lunch, why don't you come up and join us," said James and he turned to Jamie and said, "If that is alright with you, Dad?"

"Of course," said Jamie. "Off you go."

"Lunch will be in about half an hour, boys," said Liza as two not so grumpy boys left the room and all the boys could be heard chatting as they made their way up to their room.

"Will the boys be eating with us then Liza?" asked Bella.

"Yes they will today at lunchtime and tomorrow before the cricket match. Their supper is always taken in the kitchen and they never know what they are having until they are served," said Liza.

"My boys are very fussy over their food," said Bella.

"Really," said Liza thinking that if that was the case then they would be very hungry by the end of their visit.

"Will the Duke be joining us this weekend?" asked Jamie.

"No, I believe he's otherwise occupied," smiled Bella leaving everyone to draw their own conclusions.

Wendell and Peter joined them. Peter already knew Bella and he introduced Wendell to her.

"I've heard a great deal about you Mr Fuller and I am so pleased to meet you at last," said Bella with rare charm.

Harper came in and whispered to Liza that both rooms were now ready and also rooms for the Duchess' maid and driver. Their nurses' room had yet to be organised and Her Ladyship was needed to decide on one or two things.

Liza excused herself and went with Harper to see Mrs Frances.

"I presume that it will be correct to give the nurse April's old room. It's near all the boys but it has been April's domain for so long that I am reluctant to make that decision. There are still some of her belongings there," said Mrs Frances.

"Have you spoken to April?" asked Liza.

"She has gone into the village with Mr Reece and won't be back for a couple of hours," said Mrs Frances.

"April won't mind if you move her belongings. All the things that she cherishes most are already with her; these are probably items that she has not yet found a home for. If you put them in one of the rooms in the east wing for now she can sort them at leisure," said Liza who was also feeling reluctant to disturb what she felt belonged to April, but they needed the room.

Liza turned and was about to return to the drawing room when she heard laughter coming from the boys' room and she heard John saying that they were not to worry as he would help them. "This is good," Nicholas was heard to say, "How are you doing Richard?" "James is helping him," said John, "Matthew, it's your turn."

Children always sort themselves out, thought Liza and then she called out telling them that they should get ready for lunch and show Nicholas and

Richard to the dining room. Amelia was showing Bella to her room to freshen up before lunch with Mrs Frances directing them.

Amelia then turned and came back down the stairs with Liza. They said nothing until they reached the drawing room and closed the door. Wendell, Jamie and Peter were chatting quietly and turned when they entered.

"Does she always act like that?" asked Amelia.

"Yes, she does Amelia," said Jamie. "She was just the same when I used to spend some of my holidays with the family. Her mother isn't so very different."

"So you have surprise house guests for the weekend. Most of your guests have been a surprise for you," smiled Wendell.

"You and Amelia were a wonderful surprise; I'm not so sure about our current guest, but I have a feeling that it's going to be interesting," said Liza. "The boys seem to have bonded I'm pleased to say."

"They didn't seem too pleased to be here," commented Peter. "How many staff has she brought?"

"A maid, a nurse and her driver," said Liza. "It's not a problem, Mrs Frances will soon have it all sorted. I hope Mrs Lambert won't feel too stretched. I'll see her later and make sure all is well in hand."

They could hear the boys heading towards the dining room, and Harper came to say that lunch was ready. Bella was making her way down the stairs and Jamie took her arm and led her into the dining room. Liza sat to the left of Jamie and Bella was placed to his right. John seated himself beside Peter with Amelia and Wendell opposite. Matthew took charge of Richard and Nicholas seemed happy to be with James and all the boys showed that they had impeccable table manners.

After lunch Matthew suggested that they introduce their new friends to their grandmother and then to their uncle and cousin and after that they would practice their cricket skills.

"I'll take you to them," said Jamie but Peter butted in and said that he would take them to see Jamie's mother and then on to his uncle.

"I believe that David was going to help the boys with their cricket practice," said Liza.

"Yes, that's right so we'll bring him back with us," said Peter.

Liza wondered how Miranda and Lucinda would cope with the influx of five boys, but they would probably rise to the occasion.

The weather was becoming heavy, but it wasn't raining so the boys would be able to get in some cricket practice. Jamie would be part of it and Liza hoped that Nicholas and Richard would feel able to join in, but she knew Matthew's powers of persuasion, so they would probably enjoy the afternoon. Whilst Amelia, Wendell and Jamie entertained Bella, Liza made her way to see Mrs Lambert in the kitchen and she assured Liza that there were ample provisions to cater for the surprise guests. Mrs Frances was there and she told Liza that April's old room was ready for the nurse who had commented that the accommodation was extremely comfortable.

Wendell, Amelia and Bella were taking a walk around the grounds but in the distance they could hear an approaching storm.

Jamie was waiting for Liza in his study. "So our sons are going to have the pleasure of the Berkshire boys for company when they go to Cambridge. They seem to enjoy one another's company so I suppose we will see a great deal more of them from now onwards."

"So it would seem," said Liza. "I presume they will only be staying one night; Bella hasn't said how long she is going to be here. I'm surprised that she didn't leave them with us. Still none of it is a problem and the boys seem to be accepting of one another. We had better try to catch them up in the grounds; I think we are in for a storm which is rather early in the year. I do hope that it clears before tomorrow afternoon; everyone does enjoy our Sunday afternoon gatherings."

In the distance could be seen the boys being ushered by Peter from Miranda and Lucinda's home and down the drive towards David and Grace's house.

"It's nice that your uncle has got used to our boys; I wonder how he is going to react to two more," commented Liza.

"I'm sure he'll cope with them; I know that Grace will, although Peter could be keeping her preoccupied," smiled Jamie.

They caught up with the others and Wendell said that the boys seemed to be getting on well together, "Do your boys play cricket Bella?" he asked.

"I have no idea what they do in their spare time; their tutor organises their leisure entertainment," said Bella.

Nobody passed a comment on the information. There was the sudden sound of enthusiastic boys nearing the house.

"I must leave you now," said Jamie. "I promised that I would help with the cricket practice. I don't think we will get much training in today; the storm seems to be getting nearer."

Wendell was going to watch for a while and Bella said that she was feeling a little tired and would rest, which left Liza and Amelia to their own devices and they went to the comfort of the drawing room and put their feet up as Mrs Frances brought them a pot of tea.

"I think you are going to have your hands full on many occasions now," said Amelia. "I'm sure that young Nicholas and Richard will be visiting quite often in the future and you are going to have Simon with you in the next year. You are going to be very much in a minority; this house will be male dominated."

"I'll have Grace, Miranda and Lucinda to protect me," smiled Liza. "However, you are probably right, at least I have Adam and April to help, as well as Mrs Frances and I dare say that their nurse will be with them also."

Wendell came in and said that the storm was getting nearer. Liza helped him to a cup of tea, and he sat and rested for a while. "I think it is going to be quite a noisy night tonight with the storm, so I will go to our room and try to get some sleep now. Will you come with me Amelia?"

"That would leave Liza by herself," said Amelia but Liza assured her that it would not be a problem and she knew that the cricket practice would not be going on long as the sky was now getting very dark.

Liza moved into the comfort of her study and flicked through some of her correspondence, she could hear the boys shouting their enjoyment. She could also hear Jamie calling out instructions, mainly to Nicholas and Richard. She presumed that David and Peter were also giving some helpful advice. There was a flash of lightning followed quickly by a crash of thunder and then the rain started, and the boys and men could be heard running quickly into the house through the nearest door which was into the kitchen.

Matthew was organising the boys, telling them that they could carry on with their board games in their bedroom until supper time.

Jamie put his head around her door and said that 'rain had stopped play'. David had rushed back to his home and Jamie hoped that he had made it there before the heavy rain had come. Peter had gone to the library and was going over some figures.

"That leaves just us Liza; what would you like to do as I don't think that we are going to get much peace for a day or so?" asked Jamie.

"I'm just happy sitting here, I think that it's going to get a little noisy; I hope that it clears in time for the match tomorrow," said Liza.

"I hope so too. Is Bella resting?" asked Jamie.

"Yes, so are Wendell and Amelia and I can hear that the boys are amusing themselves," said Liza.

Jamie got his newspaper, smiled at her and buried his head in the paper. They had the odd conversation and all the while the storm was drawing nearer. "If this rain carries on, we'll have to send the carriage for your mother and Lucinda and then it should go on to collect your uncle and Grace," commented Liza.

"I'd better see if the boys are alright," said Jamie. "I know that John is always a little on edge when there's a storm around."

"Yes, we've had one or two bad experiences during storms," said Liza.

They went up the stairs towards the boys' room and found Bella listening at their door as Matthew regaled the other boys of his and John's time on board ship in a storm on their way to New York and all the disasters that had befallen them on that journey. Jamie put a hand on her shoulder and Bella was watching her curiously but Liza was not aware of them, she had gone back into the past and was reliving the memory of that voyage with Patrick and how he had protected her from the superstitions of the sailors who had thought she was a Jonah.

"Liza," said Jamie gently. "Come on Liza; let's rest before dinner." He guided her towards her room and Bella was asking if she was well.

"Yes Bella, she's quite well," said Jamie and Liza came out of her reverie and turned to Bella, telling her that storms always gave her slight headaches.

"It must be the boys' supper time," said Liza and she called to them. Matthew, John and James guided Nicholas and Richard out of the room, and they all ran down the stairs to the kitchen much to Bella's surprise.

"That was quite a story that Matthew and John were telling my boys; is it true, did the sailor's try to kill you?" asked Bella.

"Yes, unfortunately it is true, but it was all a long time ago and much as Matthew now finds it exciting, at the time it was very frightening," said Liza and she changed the subject by asking Bella if she had everything that she needed for her comfort.

"You've made me very welcome, thank you Liza and yes, I have absolutely everything that I could possibly need. I'm looking forward to dinner tonight as I shall be amongst a family gathering and I have a feeling that it is going to be a much more relaxed time than most of the dinners that I attend," said Bella.

"Yes, we don't stand on too much ceremony when dinner is with family and close friends," said Jamie and he put his hand on Liza's shoulder again and led her towards their rooms and Bella went to hers.

"Are you really alright Liza," asked Jamie when he had her safely in her bedroom.

"Yes, I am Jamie, it was just that a vivid memory came to me and it was one that was not happy, but it's passed now and I'm safely with you. Thank you for looking after me," said Liza.

"It seemed to be a very strong memory but it's over now and you know I like looking after you," smiled Jamie. Liza laughed and put her arms around him and they both lay on her bed and rested together for a while before they had to dress for dinner.

Later Jamie came to see if she was nearly ready and to take her down to dinner; she was sitting looking into her mirror and he asked her what she was thinking about.

"I'm thinking that I seem to spend my time either getting ready to eat or eating. I really don't need all the food that I consume," said Liza.

"I know but our dinner table has become a very social occasion; we don't stand on ceremony when we are surrounded by our family," said Jamie.

"Has Bella now become part of our family?" asked Liza.

"In my youth I was considered part of her family. Anthony, Binky and I spent a great deal of family time together and of course Bella was there also, so I can understand why she felt she could just turn up here out of the blue," said Jamie.

"It's surprising that you never saw how Binky was turning out," said Liza.

"We always knew that he was very affected in his ways, but Anthony and I used to make fun of that, and Binky used to laugh and make himself even more affected. The three of us spent a great deal of time together, rather like our boys do; not that I am suggesting that there is anything wrong with any of them, but when you grow up close to somebody you just accept them as they are and never think that there is anything evil in them," said Jamie.

The storm seemed to be easing and the rain had stopped but it seemed very wet underfoot, so Jamie still organised Hendry to fetch his mother and Lucinda and then on to his uncle and Grace.

Liza wanted to make sure that all the boys were settled and so she made her way to their rooms and found all the boys dressed ready for bed sitting on the beds in her boys' room. They were talking about their plans for the

250

following day and telling Nicholas and Richard that they would meet all their friends from the village and especially Derek who came to their house every weekday for lessons with them.

The nurse came in to take the boys to their room. "They will be very comfortable in their room," she said to Liza. "It's nice that their rooms are opposite one another; I'll leave their door open so they won't feel cut off from the other boys."

There was a flash of lightning and an immediate clap of thunder and everyone jumped. "Will Nicholas and Richard be worried about the storm," whispered Liza to the nurse.

"I don't think so; I'll keep my eye on them, especially if it gets any worse. Will your boys be concerned at all?" asked the Nurse.

"Not really, I was just thinking that as Nicholas and Richard are not in their normal surroundings it may make them feel unsettled," said Liza.

April had finished in the boys' room, "I'll keep looking in on them also." April smiled said goodnight to all the boys and went on her way to her comfy rooms with Adam.

Liza and the nurse watched as she skipped away, and the nurse commented that she looked like a very happy lady.

"She is," said Liza. "She and Adam have only recently married. They are a lovely couple."

Nicholas and Richard were settling into their beds and Liza stood at their door and enjoyed watching them comfortably pulling their covers up around them. She said goodnight to them and they called goodnight back to her; she then went into her boys' room and made sure that they were settled. She thought that no matter how old they were getting they still looked like babies when they were lying in their beds. She received a chorus of 'goodnight Mum' from the three boys and she then finally made her way down to the drawing room and waited with Jamie for everyone else to join them.

Peter was the first to arrive followed shortly by Wendell and Amelia. They heard the carriage drive up and Miranda, Lucinda and Grace were escorted in by David. Lastly Bella joined them, apologising if she was late but she had looked in on her boys before coming down. "I must say they look extremely comfortable in their beds Liza, as did your boys as I couldn't resist peeping in on them also."

There was another flash of lightning once again followed by an immediate clap of thunder. "I think we're in for a bad night," said Jamie. "It will be a shame if it doesn't clear by tomorrow afternoon."

"Yes, Nicholas and Richard were looking forward to the cricket match," said Bella. "Still they seem to be having a nice time with your boys Liza. I'll have to bring them here regularly."

There were smiles all round at Bella's assumption that her sons would be welcome.

At the dinner table Bella sat next to Jamie with David on her other side, followed by Grace and then Peter. Liza was on the other side of Jamie with Amelia, Wendell, Miranda and Lucinda. "We need more men to even up our table tonight," smiled Liza.

The storm was easing again, and the conversation turned to previous storms that people had experienced and Amelia was telling everyone about the one when they were in Italy with Liza and Jamie and how Bibiana had lost her baby that night.

"I am always uneasy during a storm; so many times unsettling events happen then," said Liza.

"Your son was telling my boys of the time you experienced one on the high seas," said Bella. "Was it as exciting as he made out?"

"I told you that what he now thinks of as exciting was in fact extremely frightening at the time and I certainly would not want to live through that again and being a mother, your fears are not just for yourself but for the safety of your children also," said Liza.

Amelia and Wendell were quiet as they were remembering a night a long time ago when a storm raged and James and Frederick died on the high seas and another one a little while later when Liza lost James' baby. They both were thinking that Liza did indeed have reason to be uneasy when there were thunderstorms.

"We seem to have become a little thoughtful tonight," said Grace. "Were the storms in America fiercer than the ones we have here Liza?"

"They seem to reverberate longer and of course if you are travelling across the plains the lightning seems never ending. There were hills surrounding Benson and the thunder echoed for a long while. It was just the terrain that made them seem more noticeable," said Liza thoughtfully. Her mind went back to the day when she had assisted Mark Kendal to escape from prison helped by a storm and she pushed the memory from her mind.

Jamie had been watching her closely and knew that she was remembering yet another time which he knew nothing about. He thought that his Liza was full of secrets and then he was reminded of something that she had said in the past, that she only ever kept confidences, not secrets.

"Why did you choose Benson to settle in?" asked David.

"It was a town that was up and coming and the people were very welcoming," said Liza.

"Why didn't you go back to Belfast when you were set free?" asked Bella.

"I was determined to find my friend Kate and I was not going to leave until I had done that," said Liza.

"Ah yes, I had forgotten that she had also been captured," said Bella.

David and Grace were frowning as they had no knowledge of Liza's past and Miranda and Lucinda only had a vague idea of what had happened to Liza in America.

Peter chimed in changing the way the conversation was going, "Is there much difference between the way life is in America and here?"

Both Liza and Jamie smiled at him gratefully and Liza said that she could only say how it was different for her.

"Life in Benson was relatively carefree in comparison. I could get up in the morning, get the boys ready for their day and stand at my gate and watch them run up the road to school. I could then get dressed and go over to Kathy and Joe's general store and have coffee with them; pass Charlie Penn's carpentry shop, see Caroline at her dress shop, pass the bank, see Laurie and Greg at the print shop and after chatting to everyone go home for lunch. After lunch get out my pony and trap and ride to the fort, call in to see the Colonel for a while and then go on to see Ada and Bea before making my way home in time for the boys' return from school. All that was between giving English lessons to the Dornbergs and the Tolanys," said Liza.

"That sounds too busy for my liking," said Bella.

"I didn't tell you this to make myself out to be so busy; it was to show that I could go out of my house and visit my friends without having to make arrangements. My life now is very different, but I was happy in my life in America and I am equally happy with the life I have now. In fact I am more so. As I said, it is just different."

"I can understand the difference Liza," said Grace. "An army life creates its own close community and yours seems to have spanned both the army post and the town which grew up around it and that made them one and the same."

"Yes, but I'm very lucky because I have a close community here now; I have Miranda and Lucinda in their home and now I have you and your father. Most of all I have my Jamie and my lovely boys. I have all the people who work here and I can go into the village, pass the church and Bernard is always ready to have a chat and in the village there is Mrs Price with her two children, Mr and Mrs Rogers; I can't name them all, it would take too long. The difference here is that the villagers know me as the 'lady of the manor' so there are no first name terms; no calls of 'hello Liza, how's the family?' or 'what are you up to today?' That's the part that I miss but it most certainly is not a serious loss," said Liza.

"In a similar way, I felt that loss when I finally had to accept that my Geoff had died and I therefore had to move away from being amongst the close knit army community; I was lucky because I still had both my mother and father at that time and I moved back to my old family home, but I did miss just calling in for a cup of tea with people whose lives mirrored my own," said Grace. "I'm so very lucky to now have another community and one that is based around my own family."

"Sadly I never had the pleasure of such community associations, but I can imagine how comforting and friendly they would be. I actually look around this table and I can see that Liza is right as you have such a community here," said Bella. "I know that Wendell, Amelia, Peter and of course Lucinda are as close as family to you. You are all so lucky, I am very envious."

Jamie was sitting quietly and looking a little sad; Liza put out her hand and reached for his. She smiled at him and if he had been feeling unloved the look in her eyes took all such thoughts away from him.

The storm was still rumbling around, and the noise seemed to be strangely different. They were all now listening. "That's furniture being moved," said Liza and she made her excuses and quickly made her way up the stairs.

"I think your boys may be changing rooms," said Amelia to Jamie.

"Oh," said Jamie. "I suppose Matthew is behind it. I'll give Liza a little while and then, if necessary, I'll see what I can do."

Liza found the doorway to her boys' room blocked by a bed that had been turned on its side and Matthew giving instructions on how to move it into the place that he wanted. Before Liza could ask what they were doing April and

Adam appeared on the scene closely followed by Nicholas' and Richard's nurse.

"What on earth do you think you are doing?" demanded Liza.

The nurse was saying that she had only just gone down to the kitchen to get some supper and April said that they were all settled nicely when she had gone to her rooms just a short while before.

"Nicholas and Richard didn't want to be alone in this storm, so Nicholas is going to have Si's bed and Richard needed his bed brought in," said Matthew.

"Nicholas and Richard aren't alone, they have each other and you were only opposite. Their nurse was next door and April and Adam are only down the corridor, so what you are doing is ridiculous," said Liza.

"Oh, we didn't think you would mind," said Matthew who was always the spokesman for all the boys.

Nicholas and Richard were looking frightened, whereas Matthew, John and James were just pouting a little.

"Well you've got the bed this far; you might as well push it a little further and put it somewhere in your room. Where were you going to put it?" asked Liza.

"We were going to worry about that when we got it in the room," said Matthew.

"You'll have to move your table out to the bottom of your bed Matthew and push Si's bed nearer you so that we can get this one in. Oh boys, you do try my patience," said Liza.

Adam and the nurse pushed the bed further into the room so that Liza and April could get in and rearrange some of the furniture to accommodate the bed. All the boys were now sitting on the two beds on the opposite side of the room watching as the furniture was being put in place with Matthew giving what he thought were useful instructions.

Jamie appeared on the scene asking what was happening and when told he just nodded with a resigned look on his face. "I can hear that Matthew is telling you where everything should go. I'll go back to our guests and hopefully you will join us in a little while." Liza smiled and nodded.

With their room in some sort of order and the bed clothes put properly in place Liza turned and said, "Right boys, into bed and settle down and I don't want to hear any more from you tonight." She went around each one of them and made sure they were comfortable and kissed them, much to Nicholas and Richard's surprise.

"Thank you, Adam; I'm so sorry that your evening has been disturbed, and you Nurse, it wasn't your fault, you had every right to your supper," said Liza.

The storm was returning, and Liza thought that perhaps the boys were right and they needed one another's company that night.

"Your mother was really annoyed," whispered Nicholas. Liza and the nurse looked at one another.

"No, she wasn't annoyed. She doesn't get annoyed; she just tells us what we should have done and pretends to be annoyed," said Matthew.

"I just can't win, can I?" Liza said to the nurse.

"They all love and respect you, so I don't think you have too much to worry about," smiled the nurse. "I'll try to keep an eye on them, especially with this storm still around."

Liza made her way back to the dining room and found everyone smiling up at her.

"Are they all settled now?" asked Jamie and Liza nodded. "I seem to have heard that the leader of this exercise has very blond hair and green eyes."

"Yes, I'm afraid so; he does seem to get everyone doing his bidding, including me;" sighed Liza.

"So my boys are sleeping in with them now and I'm told that they are happy to do so. This is a far cry from what they would normally want to do," laughed Bella.

"They may not have had a choice, Matthew does seem to have the ability to tell people what they want whether they want it or not," said Liza. "But if Nicholas and Richard are nervous of the storm then it's just as well that they are all together."

"Nicholas and Richard have never been nervous of storms; they probably wanted to be in with the other boys just as much as they seemed to want them; yes, I'll definitely be bringing them here quite often," said Bella and she couldn't understand why everyone was laughing.

"Of course they are welcome Bella, as are you whenever you want to join us," said Jamie.

"Yes, you know that you are, but I'm not sure that the boys' room is capable of accommodating six beds," laughed Liza.

"Six? Why six?" asked Bella.

"Because we have Si coming from America to live with us for around a year before they all go to Cambridge together, and Si has been friends with Matthew for at least eleven years and John nearly the same. Tonight Nicholas is in Si's bed and that has been reserved for him by the boys since we all moved here. They also have his bed in their room in Belfast, so it seems that we are going to have a gang of six under our care in the future," said Liza.

"The one thing that you will find Bella," said Wendell, "is that as your boys have been accepted as friends of Matthew's, John's and James' they will never be put upon by anyone else as they will defend and protect them even if it is to their own detriment."

"That's very profound of you Wendell," said David. "I would have thought that the boys are still too young for any future reasoning to be determined."

"It's wonderful that you are here and are part of this very loving family, but I have known these boys since they were tiny, and the loyalty between them is something that we adults could learn from," said Wendell convincingly.

"Well, if you are right Wendell, then I really want my boys to be part of whatever it is that the Edgeworth boys possess," said Bella. "I also believe that this could be why the Duke seemed to be insistent that they meet up with them, apart of course because he would really like to get to know Liza a great deal better."

"Bella!!" exclaimed Liza.

Jamie seemed lost for words and everyone else seemed to be sitting with their mouths open.

Bella laughed, "Surely I haven't shocked you. I know that Jamie and Liza were well aware that my husband was really taken with Liza when he first met her, and Liza, to her credit, amused him greatly by refusing all his advances. He is still amused by her and respects both Liza and Jamie for their affection and loyalty to one another, but he is a little saddened that Liza's head will never be turned by compliments or flattery."

"Bella!!" exclaimed Liza again.

"I think you may be giving away too many secrets, Bella," said Jamie.

"If I am giving away secrets then I am only giving them away to people who keep secrets," said Bella. "I know that Liza keeps all secrets and probably has done herself damage by not divulging them. But I feel that I am sitting around a table with friends who, no matter what they hear, keep their own counsel. I feel the most confident and relaxed than I have ever felt here tonight; I am not on show and do not have to keep up appearances for the sake of my position, I feel that I am very much amongst friends and I hope that you all feel the same."

"You have not had a very happy life have you Bella?" asked David.

"I have been pampered and cosseted. I have never had to worry about money, whatever I needed was given to me and when I came of age, I was married to someone much older than myself. This I accepted as my role in life. The Duke is not a cruel man and with him I have continued to have everything that I could desire, and I have honoured my agreement to him, and they are sleeping upstairs at this moment. We now have our own lives to follow, but even though I have everything I could possibly want, when I heard what Liza was saying about her life in America and just being able to have coffee with friends at a moments' notice, I was so envious of such a life and I can understand why she misses that life, but I can also see the love and friendship around this table and I am also envious of that and I want my boys to experience what your boys have and I don't think that I or the Duke are capable of giving them that, which is why I want to impose them upon you on occasion," said Bella.

"They are welcome," said Liza.

There was another sudden flash of lightning and crack of thunder overhead which shook the whole house and made everyone jump and voices could be heard all around the house.

"I'll check on the boys," said Liza but Jamie stopped her and said that he would do it although he was sure they were alright as they had their nurse and April nearby.

There was another flash with an immediate clap of thunder as Jamie left the room.

"I seem to have put a dampener on this evenings' dinner," said Bella.

"No you haven't" said Peter. "You have made some very interesting observations and shown concern for your children. I think we all appreciate that you are not as demonstrative with your affections as Liza, but you want the same for your children as she does for hers."

Jamie returned saying that Matthew and Nicholas were still awake, but the others were sound asleep. He motioned to Harper to fill their wine glasses and Miranda mentioned that it was a good idea.

"You're not going to offer to adopt Lucinda again, are you Mother?" asked Jamie. "And before you ask, no I haven't yet had time to look into such a situation."

"I've never heard of anyone your age being adopted," said Bella.

"I know," said Miranda. "We had a little too much wine that night and it seemed like a very good idea at the time. I still think it a good idea but totally impractical."

"This time next week Matthew and John will be Edgeworths," said Jamie smiling. "They are looking forward to it and so are we."

"When does the adoption go through?" asked Lucinda.

"Next Wednesday," said Liza.

"Are you also going to adopt James?" Bella asked Liza.

"Eventually we are hoping that I will be able to do that," said Liza.

"Ah, of course, Evelyn won't want that," said Bella, who was not known for her tact.

"It will probably all be worked out properly," said Liza.

"I presume you have custody of James," Bella said to Jamie, who just nodded his agreement. "You don't have a problem then."

"Evelyn is his mother and she therefore has the right to be consulted," sighed Liza.

"I wonder where she is," said Bella almost to herself. "She seems to have disappeared from the face of the earth which is probably just as well considering the people she has been associating with. I know that she has been ostracised by those who were her friends, but somebody must have helped her."

Bella thought that she was talking to herself as everyone was deep in conversation with others around the table but then she realised that her conversation was being ignored for a reason and that reason was probably because they knew where Evelyn was and they had helped her out of her predicament. *Of course*, she thought *they were protecting young James and the Edgeworth name.*

Jamie looked at Bella and acknowledged that she had realised their involvement in Evelyn's disappearance and appreciated her approval and silence on the matter.

They enjoyed the rest of their time around the table and when they had finished, made their way into the drawing room. The storm was beginning to ease, and the rain had stopped. David and Grace said that it would probably be a good time for them to make their way home, and Miranda and Lucinda agreed that they should also leave just in case the storm and rain returned. They all hoped that the weather would clear in time for the afternoon cricket match the next day.

Liza and Jamie saw them into their carriage for the short journey to their homes and then returned to the drawing room where Wendell, Amelia, Peter and Bella were waiting for them and chatting about all the plans for the coming week.

"I might stay a little longer than just tonight," announced Bella and by that time they were all getting used to the way Bella assumed that she would be welcome.

"Won't your boys need to be back in time for their tuition?" asked Liza.

"They can always join your boys for their lessons," said Bella.

"I'll see if Adam is agreeable to including them on Monday," said Liza.

"You shouldn't have to ask him, after all he is employed by you," said Bella.

"He may be employed by us Bella, but he is employed to just teach our boys and Derek and no others, besides it would be courteous for us to ask him," said Liza.

"I don't think that there will be a problem," said Jamie, "but Liza is right; we must make sure that Adam is happy to undertake further students even if it is only for a day. We are taking Wendell and Amelia to the Home on Monday."

"I might come with you," said Bella and then she asked how Amber and William were getting on.

"I haven't seen them for a couple of days, but they were settling well," said Liza and then she went on to explain how Amber and William kept food so that they could give it to anyone who had been kind and had helped them.

"Surely it would have been better to keep food for themselves," said Bella.

"You probably noticed that they were thin but not really undernourished. They were more use to their owners if they looked well but no doubt others who were with them went hungry and Amber and William helped by bringing food for them. I am told that the boy who brought them to my house in Belfast was pathetically thin; he had grown out of his usefulness so they were not wasting food on him and I believe that the two little ones tried to help him as he was one person who tried to help them. Their way of saying thank you was to give him food and they are still doing that to anyone who helps them now," said Liza.

"They are very pretty children," said Bella.

"That is why they had to be quickly brought away from Belfast. The more attractive a child is, the more money they make for their owners. The boy who saved them was beaten to death and we are aware that the children are being hunted by these violent and unscrupulous people. We hope that they aren't

260

aware of where they are, although I don't think that they would come here to get them. I am however making arrangements for them to travel to America as soon as possible and we already have two families who are looking to adopt children. We don't want to separate them. They may, or may not, be brother and sister, but they consider themselves as such and they get such comfort from one another that it would be cruel to make them live apart," said Liza.

The storm seemed to have abated and it was now getting quite late, so they all made their way up to their various beds. April came to help Liza out of her clothes, and they talked about that evening's sleeping arrangements of the boys and the fact that Nicholas and Richard would probably be staying the following night also.

After April had left, Liza was about to make her way to Jamie's room, but he beat her to it and came to her instead.

"You want to be in my room tonight Jamie," stated Liza with a smile.

Jamie smiled back at her. "I did not realise just how much you missed your life in Benson. I believed that you had settled here with me to such an extent that you no longer thought about it."

"You look sad Jamie," said Liza. "There's no need for you to be sad. I'm not sad. I'm very happy. It's only natural that I would miss my friends. I miss all the Fullers when I'm away from them and I missed your mother and Lucinda when we were in Italy last year. It's true that I used to enjoy the freedom of visiting people at a moment's notice. You used to enjoy visiting me on a whim, didn't you? You and I had that sort of association before we were married."

"Yes, we did, didn't we? I used to think up reasons to call on you in the early days and then I just didn't bother to pretend that I had a reason. You didn't call on me unexpectedly though," said Jamie.

"When did I have the time to call on you; you were always at my house, but I did call on you unexpectedly on the one most important occasion, didn't I Jamie? Don't you remember?" said Liza.

Jamie frowned and then realisation set in. "Of course. Yes, I remember, of course I do. I was going to leave and go on the Grande Tour without telling you. I didn't think that you cared for me at all and I really needed someone to love me, and you came to me and asked me not to go because you loved me. You then started eating my dinner and got the most horrendous hiccups. You were also very naughty; you brought your overnight bag with you and you bedded me, didn't you Liza?"

"Yes, I did, and wonderful it was too. It is a night that I will never forget, and I had a feeling of excitement that night, just as I have now because of the way you are looking at me," said Liza.

"Ah my Liza, you always manage to take my concerns away and make me feel good," said Jamie. "Your bed looks very inviting tonight, as do you."

***

It was Sunday morning and the sun was shining brightly. All evidence of the previous night's storm had disappeared and Liza stretched lazily in bed. Jamie was already up and about, and he put his head around her door to tell her that he was on his way down to breakfast but he would be back shortly to wipe whatever she had dribbled off her chin. She laughed as April brought in her breakfast tray and set it down in front of her.

The sounds of the boys could be heard running down the stairs to the kitchen for their breakfast and Liza supposed that it was the first time that the Berkshire boys had breakfasted in a kitchen. Amelia and Bella were probably also taking their breakfast in bed, which left the men to their own devices.

True to his word Jamie appeared later and picking up her napkin wiped her face.

"I didn't think that I had dribbled," said Liza.

"You always dribble when you eat in bed," said Jamie casually.

Jamie helped her out of bed and April came in having organised hot water for a bath and eventually Liza was left to soak comfortably for a while. She could hear the boys making their way back up to their room to finalise getting ready to go to church. Bella had said that she had no objections to Nicholas and Richard going to church with Jamie's family, but she would take the opportunity to stay behind and relax. Wendell and Amelia would also be staying at home, but Peter would be joining them, and Liza thought that the reason behind that was probably another opportunity for him to spend time with Grace.

Although the weather had cleared and the sun was shining, it was still a little wet underfoot so they decided to take the carriage with all the boys and they would send a second carriage for Miranda and Lucinda and also pick up David and Grace. Peter said that he would go in the second carriage which was not a surprise to them.

After the service, as always, the boys met up with others from the village and Derek was included and although he could walk with his sticks he now always came with his wheelchair so that they could all go off and do whatever it was that the boys do after church. Nicholas and Richard were staring at Derek but whatever Matthew said to them made them shrug and go off with the rest.

Liza and Jamie were talking to most of the churchgoers and Bernard and the discussion turned to the afternoon's cricket match and some of the men, including Jamie, went off to examine the pitch and on their return their verdict was that it would be alright for play, but it would not be advisable for anyone to sit on the grass for the picnic so everyone would bring chairs with them.

They all began to make their way back home and David decided to stay and spend a little while with Holly, everyone else made their way directly back to the main house to relax before Sunday lunch. The boys decided to get in some cricket practice with Peter and Jamie helping them.

Wendell, Amelia and Bella were already in the drawing room when they arrived and once again there was a pleasant gathering of family and friends. David arrived about an hour later having spent some time with Holly and then walking back from the church.

Sunday lunch was its normal happy affair. Peter had John on one side and Grace on the other. Matthew and James took charge of Nicholas and Richard. Bella aligned herself with Wendell and Amelia and David had Miranda and Lucinda either side of him. Liza and Jamie sat back and looked around their table at everyone enjoying the company with nobody needing their attention.

"Do you normally have Sunday lunch like this?" Bella asked.

"Normally it is just family, but close friends are always welcome," said Jamie.

"When does the cricket match start?" asked Bella.

"Everyone will start gathering in a couple of hours and the match starts when we're all assembled," said Jamie. "There are no hard and fast rules regarding timing. Although it is considered a match, it really is practicing for the final Edgeworth team and it also gives some of the children a chance to join in. The women and girls enjoy the social side of the afternoon."

"I'm looking forward to the experience," said Bella.

"I think you will enjoy it," said Miranda. "It's also a chance for Liza and Jamie to meet with the villagers and the farmers on the estate. All the Edgeworth staff also join in."

"The boys also meet up with the other children from the farms and village and that is good. They play together well," said Lucinda.

After lunch everyone got ready for the afternoon and Liza organised that a dozen chairs be transported to the grounds along with their food contribution.

The boys were allowed their turn in the match and Nicholas and Richard did well and had been vocally encouraged by the crowd. Adam held Derek upright as usual and Jamie and Peter picked them both up as they fell, and John took his runs. Bella was fascinated by this spectacle and observed that she would never have thought that someone like Derek could do so well and be accepted and cheered on by all the people.

"There are a lot of lessons to be learned by this afternoon's event," said Bella. "The children just accept him as if he were normal."

"He is normal Bella; he just can't walk as well as others, but he is improving. Three years ago he couldn't leave his wheelchair and now he is walking, differently to others, but walking none the less. He's very bright but of course all he could do for many years was read. He'll probably never be able to run, but he can get around and is one of the boys," said Liza.

"You've done that for him, haven't you?" said Bella to Liza.

"He's done it for himself Bella, he just needed a little encouragement and other boys accepting him as he is helped him more than anything," said Liza.

"Oh Liza, you never take credit for anything that you do for others, but that's how you are. You put many of us to shame," said Bella.

"Don't say that, Bella. Most people pull themselves up on their own, they just need a little push now and again," said Liza and she smiled at Bella and moved away before anything else could be said.

Bella joined Wendell and Amelia sitting comfortably in the sunshine watching the afternoon's game and once again she felt envy as she watched Liza laughing and chatting in the centre of a crowd of villagers.

"Liza is at ease with people from all walks of life, isn't she," said Bella to Amelia.

"Yes, she can talk to anyone and they feel that they can talk to her, she has always had that ability and young Matthew is taking after her. Jamie also now enjoys afternoons such as this and you can see that he has become quite approachable," said Amelia.

"He has become more human," said Bella, "I remember when he was young he had his nose permanently in the air which was probably his defence for an unhappy childhood. He and Anthony Ffoulks spent a great deal of time with my family and although Anthony relaxed in our company, Jamie rarely dropped his guard."

"Well he's one happy man now," said Wendell.

"He was mesmerised by Liza from the day he first saw her and that was before James died. Jamie hardly ever talked about his private life, but the one person he mentioned frequently was Liza and when we all thought that she had died he went totally to pieces. I know my mother was very concerned about him and to help him she reintroduced Evelyn to him, which seems to have been the biggest mistake of her life but it was done with the best of intentions," said Bella.

"To her credit Evelyn did help him through a difficult period in his life," said Amelia. "But it was never going to be a marriage made in heaven. Anyway that's all over now and both he and Liza are very happy, as are their sons."

"Do you think that Evelyn will be happy with Liza adopting James?" asked Bella.

Wendell butted in before Amelia could enter into any more gossip about the Edgeworth family. "I'm sure it will all work out well," he said and then he clapped and shouted "Well played" at a particular moment in the cricket match.

Bella smiled and yet again experienced envy at the closeness that Wendell, Amelia and the whole Fuller family had with Liza. It then dawned on Bella why Evelyn hated Liza so much; she really envied her and that envy had turned to hatred, but she still turned to Liza when she was in trouble and that was pure selfishness.

"You're very thoughtful Bella," said David who had quietly moved next to her.

"Yes, I've just been watching Liza moving amongst everyone and appearing very comfortable in their company and they are in hers. I can see why some people love her and a few experience the opposite," said Bella thoughtfully.

"I think that you have realised that those who experience the opposite are really jealous of her," said David.

"I have realised that," said Bella.

"I do hope that your envy of her does not turn to hatred Bella," said David.

A look of shocked superiority crossed Bella's face for a moment and then it changed to a look of resignation. "You're very astute David. No, my envy will never become hatred; in fact I am determined to attempt to emulate her. I do not have the happy marriage that she has but I have a good life and I have a duty to get to know the people who look after us and work for the benefit of our estate. It has dawned on me that I would not have all that I could possibly want without those people. I also presume that my husband and his family before him have invested wisely over the years and that is something that I have never thought about previously."

David smiled down at her and said, "I hope that we see a great deal more of you Bella, and your boys. They do seem to be getting on well with the other children. They didn't look very happy when they arrived, but that soon passed."

Bella laughed, "No they were not looking forward to being forced to meet people that they did not know; they were determined to have a miserable weekend and create a miserable weekend for those they were visiting. They were prepared for any punishment that would be inflicted on them when we returned home."

"Luckily that won't be necessary," said David.

Everyone was now sitting around and eating their picnics as well as choosing what they wanted from the table with the food from the main house.

Liza came over and asked David if he would be playing that day.

"I think I'm getting a little old for that Liza," he smiled at her. "I felt every bone in my body last time I picked up a bat."

"I'm sure all the players appreciate you cheering them on," smiled Liza and she then moved on to someone else and talked to them before going on to another family.

Jamie was first in after refreshments and he made twenty runs before being bowled out and he was followed by John and then Peter. And so the afternoon continued until tiredness crept over many, especially the children and everything was packed up and taken back home.

Back at the house the boys made their way down to the kitchen for supper, even though they had not long eaten at the picnic. Liza and Jamie had spoken to Adam about the Berkshire boys joining the lessons the next day and he agreed that it would do no harm and that it would be interesting to find out the standard that they had achieved so far.

Supper for the adults was very light and soon after Miranda, Lucinda, David and Grace made their way home with Peter escorting them. Nobody waited up for him as it was realised that he would return in his own good time.

"That was a good day," said Liza to Jamie when they were finally in bed.

"Bella and her boys seemed to enjoy it, which means that we will probably see them on a regular basis," said Jamie.

"I'm surprised at how pleasant Bella has been this weekend; I thought that it would become quite awkward, but she has been no trouble at all and neither have her boys," said Liza.

Jamie grinned at Liza and said that they had to remember that they had an early start the next morning to go to the Ffoulks Home. She laughed and quickly moved closer to him and sighed contentedly.

Chapter 14

Grace arrived for work the next morning and when Liza had gone through various documents, letters and invitations which had accumulated, she was aware of what Liza required of her that day and she settled comfortably at the desk. Peter would probably offer to assist her and Liza smiled at the thought.

They left early for the Home and called in on Anthony and Diana on the way. Rose was also there and was pleased to see the Fullers and surprised to see Bella with them. They saw Thomas, whose speech was improving and he managed to ask where 'Maffew' was and when was he going to see him again.

At the Home the Major greeted them and welcomed Wendell and Amelia; he also showed surprise that Bella was visiting again but was none the less pleased to see her. Whilst the Major was showing Amelia and Wendell around, Liza, Jamie and Bella made their way to the recreation room as they could hear some noise coming from there. They found Hector loudly calling out names of boys to form two teams for what he called 'bat and ball' as he told the boys that it would take too long for him to explain the intricacies of cricket to them.

Bella noticed that Jamie was looking puzzled and Liza explained to her that Hector had no idea what the intricacies of cricket actually were, but he was managing to convince the boys that he was all knowledgeable on the subject. Jamie decided that he would go and watch how Hector was handling the boys.

It was approaching lunchtime for the smaller children and Estelle was guiding them into the dining room and she looked up and greeted Liza and Bella.

"There are the two little ones," whispered Bella to Liza and they watched as William and Amber walked into the room hand in hand and found their seats at the table. Amber said something to William and they both turned and smiled and waved at Liza, who waved back to them.

"They really are adorable," commented Bella.

Once the children were settled and being served their lunch, Estelle came over to Liza and said that this was the first day that she had given lessons and although the older children seemed not to feel the need to read and write, the younger ones were enjoying being read to and she felt that they would be quite receptive to learning.

"There are two things that we need to do," said Estelle "and the first is to give names to those children who have never been registered. They need to create their own identity."

"Yes, I have discussed that with the Major. We should make a list of likely names and let the children choose from that and then we can arrange to have them registered legally. You're right, it will give them an identity and I'm sure that it's important to them. What's the second thing that you think is needed?"

"I believe that one of your speeches about the importance of reading and writing would be of great help," said Estelle. "I know that you have persuaded people to learn by pointing out the various disasters that could befall them by not knowing what has been written."

"Yes I have, but mainly to adults and those whose first language was not English," said Liza.

"I can get the older children assembled once Hector has finished his cricket practice," said Estelle.

Liza and Bella smiled at Estelle's cricket practice comment. "Well if you think it will help, I will do my best," said Liza. They then went and joined the children for lunch.

When they had finished William and Amber came over to Liza and gave her a very squashed and cold potato, which Liza thanked them for, and they ran off hand in hand.

The Major came in with Wendell and Amelia and Estelle went over to them and Liza and Bella joined them.

"Estelle tells me that you are going to give a talk to some of the older children and try to persuade them that it's a good idea to learn how to read and write," said the Major.

"If anyone can persuade them then Liza can," said Wendell. "When are you going to speak to them?"

"I'll do it a little later this afternoon. Estelle says that she will get the children assembled after Hector finishes giving the boys instruction on the finer points of cricket," said Liza.

The Major raised an eyebrow at Liza's remark concerning Hector's cricket prowess but made no comment.

Jamie and Hector could be heard arguing as they walked into the room. "You will have to get someone to teach the boys cricket because what you tell them is just not as it should be," said Jamie to Hector.

"They're quite happy with what they do; it may not be cricket Jamie, but they enjoy it," said Hector.

The boys were washing their hands before having their lunch and the older girls joined them. Liza went up to the schoolroom with Estelle and said that perhaps it would be better if the meeting was held in the recreation room, even though the schoolroom was set out quite casually.

"I don't want them to think that it is a lesson, I want them to listen, ask questions and give their thoughts on the subject," said Liza. "The easiest way for them to want to learn is for them to answer their own questions. Have you got a small blackboard that I could use?"

Liza and Estelle moved the blackboard down into the recreation room and they looked around to make sure that the rest of the room looked more relaxed than a schoolroom.

"I'm not sure what you are going to do Lady Edgeworth," said Estelle.

"There are times when it's appropriate for you to use my title, but this is not one of them. My name is Liza and I would appreciate it if you used it," said Liza.

Estelle smiled, "I have to admit that it runs off the tongue much better than your title."

"Good, then we have an agreement," said Liza. "What I am going to do is tell them a story and then show them an example of why it is important for them to know how to read and write."

Hector and Jamie came into the room still arguing the merits of teaching cricket correctly as opposed to just enjoying what Hector thought was a fun game. They stood at the back of the room.

The Major arrived with Wendell, Amelia and Bella. Liza turned to them and said that she didn't think that they would be interested in what she was going to say to the children.

"We have had several opportunities to listen to your speeches and I would not want to miss yet another," smiled Wendell.

"Neither would I," smiled the Major.

Estelle left the room and waited for the children to finish their lunch and slowly they were ushered into the recreation room. Some of them were sullen, having caught sight of the blackboard; others just did as they were told as that was what they were used to doing.

Liza was sitting at one of the tables at the front of the room and she waited for Estelle to come in and intimate that all the children were there. She looked around and smiled. Jamie had to admit that her smile made each one of them feel that she was only smiling at them and the children responded well to her.

"Does anyone here know how to read or write?" asked Liza and nobody answered.

"Well, I'm not going to give you a lesson in either of those today. I thought that you might like to hear one of my stories instead," said Liza as she looked around the room and could see that the children were beginning to relax.

She smiled again, "A few years ago I and my family were sailing to America." A few voices said "Ooh". Liza carried on, "Already on board were two Irish families; we stopped to take on board a French family and a Spanish family. The French family were well prepared for the trip, they had been correctly told what they would need, but the Spanish family had incorrectly been told by an agent that they needed nothing and that all would be provided by the shipping company. I checked their papers and could see that what they had been told was different to what their papers said, but we managed to sort out what they would need, however they were very much out of pocket."

"There are rules on board ship and some of those rules showed times when passengers could come on deck, when they could organise their food, where they could hang their washing and many others. The times of such events could vary from day to day and therefore a list was posted each day on the entrance to where the passengers were living. Unfortunately the passengers seemed unable to stick to the rules and one day when I was passing I could hear the second mate telling them that they should not be where they were. I could understand why the French and Spanish passengers did not understand but it dawned on me that perhaps the Irish passengers were in difficulty, so I made it my business to see if there was anything I could do to help and was told by one of their number that there was no point in having lists posted on their entrance because they could not read."

"However that was the least of their problems; they had made their marks on bond servant documents which meant that the parents would work for their employer for seven years. This is not a vast amount of time, especially when the employer is also paying the passage for their children and housing them and also they would be earning a small wage. If it was just the parents,

271

their term of indenture would probably have been five years. They were very happy with their agreement and we were shown their documentation which unfortunately told a different story to what they believed to be the case. The papers said that not only were the parents indentured for seven years, so were their children from the age of seven and their children's children, and the parents were indentured until the last child or grandchild had worked their seven years. In fact they had enslaved their whole family."

"The fathers in the families were beside themselves and started yelling that it was not what they had made their mark on and the mothers were saying that they were prepared to kill their children rather than enslave them. When they had calmed down they mistakenly believed that as they had been told differently to what the documentation said, it could all be sorted out, but that was not the case and I gently had to tell them that their mark was legally binding; they had signed the documents in front of witnesses and no matter that it was morally wrong, legally it had been correctly undertaken and would be upheld in a court of law."

Liza paused for a while and then said, "Have you all understood what I have been saying?"

There were nods and many said "yes", and Liza said that was good.

"I know you are all young, but can anyone tell me what the moral to this story is? And how the situation could have been avoided?" said Liza.

"Always get somebody you trust to read the papers to you," somebody said.

"That could be one way, but who do you truly trust?" said Liza.

"That was a silly answer," said one girl. "What you were saying was that if the Irish families could read and write they wouldn't have signed themselves and their children away."

"Yes, you're right. They would never have committed their families to such an agreement if they had been able to read exactly what had been written," said Liza.

"What happened to them?" asked another boy.

"By the end of the voyage not only could the Irish families read and write, but the French and Spanish families could speak English," smiled Liza. "But what you are really asking is whether or not they had to keep to the bond servant agreements. Luckily, I knew someone who knew of the employer, and that employer did not want it known that he had engaged in such underhand arrangements. His standing in the society that he enjoyed would have been over, so he released them from the agreement and our own agent drew up the correct one which the Irish families were by then perfectly capable of reading and putting their names to."

"Would we have to sign papers like that if we become bond servants?" asked the first boy.

"Yes, you would, but hopefully you would understand what you were signing by that time," said Liza. "This is just one example of how unscrupulous people prey on the vulnerable and it's up to each one of you to make yourselves less vulnerable."

"I don't want to be a bond servant," said one boy.

"What do you want to do?" asked Liza.

"I would like a farm, I like animals," he replied.

"That's a good aim. You would need to enter into a legal agreement either to buy or rent a farm. Who can count?" said Liza suddenly changing the subject. Many hands went up.

"Good," said Liza and she picked up some chalk and moved towards the blackboard. "Shall we start with something easy? What does two and two add up to?"

She wrote two and two on the blackboard and waited for the children to answer. "Four" they were shouting, and Liza wrote an equals sign and put the number seven after it. She waited to see if anyone had noticed, but nothing was said.

"Let's go for another one, what are three and three?"

"Six" they shouted, and Liza wrote three plus three on the board with an equals sign and put the number eight against it. No child noticed it.

"Shall we do one more?" she asked smiling. "What are five and two?"

Many fingers were being used for this one until the answer of seven was finally settled upon. Liza wrote five plus two equals and the number nine after it.

"Shall we add all this up and pretend that it's for goods that we've bought. Seven plus eight is fifteen, fifteen plus nine is twenty-four. Are you all happy with that?" asked Liza.

"Yes," they chorused.

"Are you really sure?" laughed Liza.

"Yes," they shouted.

"Well you would have lost a lot of money if you had been buying goods at these prices, because the answer should have been seventeen and not twenty-four. You see, I didn't write your answers to the numbers; I wrote higher numbers and if I had been a storekeeper selling you goods I could have made another seven pence or pounds if that was the case, and that would have been because you were not able to read," said Liza.

"I believe that you all are really aware that there are people who would have no difficulty in taking from those who can ill afford to lose anything. You have come from places where there is very little loyalty and taking from others was a way of life. In my time I have seen those who cannot read pay far more for their goods than was necessary and dishonest people make fortunes out of those who are illiterate. I would hate that to happen to any of you and we will all do our best to help prepare each one of you for a good and happy life," said Liza.

There were thoughtful frowns on many of the children's faces and Liza thought that she had better lighten the atmosphere, so she smiled and said that not all people were dishonest and trying to take from others. There were many whose only aim in life was to deal correctly and help those who needed it and that all she had been trying to do was demonstrate that they all needed the ability to carefully choose between those who are honest and those who are not.

"But there is another wonderful side to reading and that is to be able to get lost in the world of books. To sit and relax with the words of a good author is one of the greatest pleasures imaginable. I know that Miss Reece is planning to spend time reading to you and when you hear the stories, I know that you will want to be able to sit and read such books for yourselves. Then there are newspapers where you can keep up with what is happening in our country and also in the world," said Liza.

"When you are older and you all go your separate ways, what could be better than to be able to write to one another telling of what you are doing and receiving letters from your friends with all their news. You would be able to keep a journal of all that you are doing, so that in years to come you will be able to look back and remember exactly what, when and where the good times in your life happened," said Liza.

"Many people want to see you all do well in life and here there are those whose only aim is to help you. They want to make your lives much easier than they have been in the past and prepare you for your future, but they can't help you unless you are willing to help yourselves. Nobody is going to force you to do anything that you do not want to, but nothing would give me, or anyone here, greater pleasure than to see some, if not all, of you stand up and entertain your fellow students by reading them the words from one of the popular novels of the day. You might even become capable of teaching or keeping company books. There is no end to what you can achieve with a little help from the Major, Miss Reece, Mr Ffoulks and all the others who are prepared to give up their time to encourage you to succeed."

"Does anyone have any questions?" asked Liza.

"Do you also teach?" Liza was asked.

"I have done, and I may well be able to do so on occasion, but Miss Reece is in charge of all teaching here, and she is preparing to read to you in a short while," answered Liza.

"Is it difficult to learn?" was another question.

"You may think so to start with, but I have taught many people to read from very many countries and it does not take long for it to become understandable and eventually easy," said Liza.

"When do you want us to start?" said one of the boys.

"When do you want to start?" answered Liza.

"I dunno."

"Well, Miss Reece is going to start this afternoon by reading to those who are interested and tomorrow she will continue reading to you but you will also have the same book which will start you recognising some of the words. After that she will show you how to write some of those words," said Liza.

"I don't want to do that," was the retort from one of the boys.

"I told you, nobody is going to force you to read," said Liza dismissively, which surprised the boy. "Now all those who want to stay and listen make yourselves comfortable because I know what the book is and it's really good and interesting."

Estelle stood and moved to a seat at the front of the room and opened her book. She looked around and saw that apart from the adults, nobody was leaving the room.

They went up to the Major's rooms where Jennifer was also visiting. "How did your talk go Liza?" she asked.

"I felt at one stage that I was patronising the children but found it difficult not to. I also felt that I was convincing them that everyone was out to defraud them and that there were very few people in the world that were honest," said Liza. "I was not satisfied that I got my message across satisfactorily."

"Those children are far older than their years," said the Major. "They have been out in the world long enough to know and understand what you were telling them. You didn't really turn it into a lesson; you told them some stories; the only item that could be considered a lesson was your supposed inability to add up. I was about to correct you, but Hector nudged me to stop me. I was watching the children and they were listening to you quite intently."

"I found your stories quite interesting. Were they true?" asked Hector.

"Yes, unfortunately they were," said Liza.

"The information about the bond servants was rather disquieting. How anyone would think that it was right to dupe families like that is beyond belief," said Hector. "At least you have an agent who handles the contracts correctly for our children."

Liza smiled and nodded but Jamie, Wendell and Amelia felt that they knew who had attempted to perpetrate the deception and realised that Liza had somehow blackmailed Charles Enderby into turning over a new leaf and working for the company in an exemplary manner.

"I thought that some of the children, especially the boys, were not going to stay to listen to Estelle," said Jamie. "You let them make their own decision and they decided to stay. It will be interesting to hear what Estelle has to say at the end of today."

On the way home Wendell turned to Liza and asked quietly if Charles had allowed his agent to create such inhuman terms for his bond servants because he hoped that he had not organised them himself.

"Charles used an unscrupulous agent in Ireland, who took a great deal of money from the families and when the situation was pointed out to him he immediately changed the terms of the contract to what everyone thought had been the correct details. He also now studies each and every bond servant document for us and allows nothing untoward to happen to our people. You have nothing to reproach Charles for," said Liza quietly but somewhat testily.

Wendell stared at her in surprise as she never spoke to him sharply and he realised that she was right in that Charles did handle all their bond servant cases impeccably and whatever had been in his past was no longer relevant. He was pleased that Bella had not heard their conversation.

Grace was still there when they arrived home and Peter was also in the study reading a newspaper. Liza wondered whether he had been there all day.

After asking how their day had been Grace told her that Adam wanted to see her and Bella when they were free. Liza hoped that he was not going to complain about Nicholas and Richard but wondered what else he would want if it wasn't for that reason. She sighed and said that she would see him shortly.

She had wanted to spend a few minutes quietly with Jamie before getting ready for dinner but instead she sent for Mrs Frances and asked her to let Adam know that she would see him in the library and asked her to send Bella's maid to ask her to join them. Jamie was in the library and she asked him to leave as she had a problem to sort out with Bella and Adam.

"Of course Liza; I've always said that you don't get the easy tasks. I suppose Grace is in your study, so I'll make myself scarce in the drawing room. We don't even have our own domains to ourselves any more, do we?" said Jamie.

"At least we get some privacy at night in our bedrooms," said Liza. "You are right, Grace is in my study and Peter is with her."

Jamie smiled and nodded. He kissed her on the head as he left the library and Adam knocked and entered. He was carrying papers that were obviously the work of the boys.

"Come in Adam and sit down. I've asked the Duchess to join us and she will be with us shortly," said Liza. Bella swept in with a look of superiority on her face and Liza thought that the meeting was not going to go well. Bella acknowledged Adam with just a nod and sat down staring into the distance.

"Well Adam, what is it that you feel you have to tell us," said Liza with what she hoped was a reassuring smile.

"I really wanted to discuss how Her Grace's sons had fared in their lessons with your sons today, your Ladyship," said Adam.

"I do not need to be told how disruptive they have been; they always are, especially Richard. No matter what threats and punishments their father inflicts on them does not alter their behaviour. I had hoped that a different environment would have made an improvement, but obviously not. There is therefore no need for you to tell me what I already know, but you do not have to worry as I shall be taking them away tomorrow," said Bella imperiously.

"My intention was not to complain about your sons Your Grace, but to give you my humble opinion on their intelligence which I would like to say is far higher than I had expected," said Adam.

Bella looked surprised and Liza smiled nodding for Adam to carry on.

"Your eldest son, Nicholas, is very bright and is quite capable of reaching the same level as James and John and much as I do not wish to criticise whoever you have tutoring him at present, but the standard he has currently reached is less than he should have achieved at his age," said Adam.

Bella was still looking surprised but was now slightly smiling. "You must also have an opinion on Richard," she said.

"Yes, I have," said Adam. "Richard is on the same level as Matthew."

Before he could say more Bella said, "Yes, well they are a year younger, so I wouldn't expect them to be as the others."

Liza was smiling as she had an idea what Adam was about to say.

"Your son, Richard, has not been stretched enough. I give Matthew special lessons which are normally for children who are even older than James and John and Richard coped with them easily. James and John know that Matthew has slightly different lessons to them, but I do not say that they are of a greater standard; I believe that they think that because he's younger his lessons would naturally be different. Your son and Matthew did an exercise together and they were as good as one another. Richard enjoyed the challenge and there was no disruption in my classes today," said Adam.

"So how would you summarise your opinion, Adam?" asked Liza.

"I believe that Nicholas is not receiving the correct education for his age, and I believe that Richard should be given special lessons which will stretch his mind as it should be. I also think that if both are given a challenge in that respect, they will become exemplary students and all thoughts of disruption will disappear." said Adam.

"What would you suggest Mr Reece?" asked Bella.

"I cannot tell you who to employ for your sons Your Grace and I feel very guilty criticising their current education, but my concern is always for students and it hurts me to see intelligence going to waste. They have become bored with their tuition and one of my suggestions would be that Richard goes to Cambridge at the same time as Nicholas and our Edgeworth boys; he may be a year younger but he will keep up with them if not go ahead," said Adam.

"Thank you, Mr Reece, you have given me a great deal to think about and you can be sure that I shall discuss your findings with the Duke. He will not want his sons to miss out on opportunities due to lack of the correct education. You are very caring of your charges and your thoughts are appreciated," said Bella.

Adam left and Liza turned to Bella and said, "I had not expected that we would be having such a conversation with Adam."

"You are right, my boys have always been so disruptive but perhaps we now have the answer as to why they act that way," said Bella. "Mr Reece is the young man who took a bat to my brother when he tried to hurt John, isn't he?"

"Yes, he would defend our boys with his life. I know that Binky threatened to have him arrested but Adam told him that he would be pleased to answer for his actions in a court of law," smiled Liza.

"What are you doing tomorrow Liza?" asked Bella.

"We are going to inspect the Langston House to see if it's suitable for our needs. Hector and the Major will also be with us as will Jennifer no doubt," said Liza.

"May I join you? It seems that my boys are quite happy in your schoolroom with Mr Reece. I do have an engagement on Wednesday, so I will have to leave then," said Bella.

"Of course Bella, although I do trust that you do not have a problem with Lord Randolph Langston, or more to the point, that he does not have a problem with you," said Liza.

"His problems were with Binky and his associates and he is well aware that I had no knowledge of his difficulties until a long while after the event, my mother made that quite clear to him fairly recently and I have nothing but admiration for him following his and Hector's altercation with the Honourable Archie Goodman at Lord Carlton's evening event."

"I'm pleased about that as there will therefore be no awkward situation tomorrow," said Liza. "On Wednesday Jamie and I must go to court for our boys' adoption, so we will not be able to see you off, but Wendell and Amelia will be around for you. I'm not sure when Peter will be returning to Belfast, he seems to have extended his stay quite considerably," said Liza.

"I think that your cousin Grace may have had something to do with that," smiled Bella.

They both left the library and went to change for dinner.

***

The Major, Jennifer and Hector arrived at Edgeworth House so that they all could travel on to Langston House together. Their carriages passed a relatively large house near the entrance of the driveway and they assumed that it was the house that Lord Randolph had suggested that he and his sister moved into.

Lord Randolph and Lady Penelope came down the steps to greet them and Jamie introduced Wendell, Amelia and Jennifer to them; they knew everyone else. They seemed a little surprised to see that Bella was with them, but no awkward situation arose.

279

A light lunch had been arranged for them and this created a very relaxed atmosphere. It was noticed that Lord Randolph referred to his sister regarding many of the questions which were being asked.

Hector had been right; the house was ideal for their purpose. With a few alterations and a great deal of decoration the house could be made extremely comfortable for the children. The grounds did not need to be sectioned as the Langston's no longer owned any of the farmland around them. They had sold it off many years before, but they still had substantial grounds around the house that could be used as had been organised at the Ffoulks house.

"You may or may not remember, Jamie, that your father and grandfather were friends of our father and grandfather. They spent a great deal of leisure time together," said Lady Penelope. She did not need to say anything further; Jamie nodded realising that the Langston family had lost most of their land and money to gambling and if Jamie's father had not died relatively young, then the Edgeworth family would have been in the same situation.

"I'm afraid I don't remember Penelope; I rarely saw my father's friends, in fact I rarely saw my father, but I believe I did not suffer too badly because of it," said Jamie.

"Then you are lucky Jamie; you can see the situation that we have been left in," said Lady Penelope. Lord Randolph was staying quiet on the subject.

"I see that you are in the process of packing," said Liza.

"Yes," said Penelope. "We are moving into the Dower House. We will not get in the way of what you would want to carry out here."

"I realise that, but we are very security conscious where our children are concerned and much as we would want to keep the property secure from anyone untoward entering, I'm sure you would not want to be restricted in your movements or those of any guests you may have," said Liza.

"Do you keep the children locked in?" asked a concerned Randolph.

Liza smiled, "No, we keep unwelcome guests locked out."

"Are you saying that it would not be ideal for us to move to the Dower House," asked a concerned Penelope.

"I would like to study the area to see if the Dower House can be permanently separated from the rest of Langston House. If it is easy and cost effective to make an alternative entrance then it would be possible," said Liza.

"The Dower House would be ideal for you both, but Liza is right, our priority must be the safety of the children and I'm sure you do not wish to be locked in, or any guests locked out. Also we would have to know the identity of your guests, also for the safety of the children," said Wendell.

"I understand that," said Randolph. "Nobody knows the leanings of some people."

Liza was convinced that she saw a slight look of embarrassment cross Bella's face, but it soon disappeared.

They made their way to the Dower House and several suggestions were made regarding how it could be permanently separated and it was decided that the Dower House could retain the current entrance and Langston House would create another entrance and driveway which would join the main driveway nearer the house. A large, tall, strong fence would have to be built between the Dower House and the main house, but it was not an insurmountable problem. Randolph and Penelope would have the freedom to come and go as they wished, and they would just have to get used to a large, but hopefully not too unsightly fence bordering their home.

"Well, we have discussed the feasibility of separating the two properties, we now have to discuss what price you think you are expecting for Langston House," said Peter. "Shall we go inside and talk about it?"

Amelia, Bella and Jennifer went for a walk around the grounds, whilst Hector and the Major decided to look around the house again. That left Liza, Wendell, Jamie and Peter to discuss terms with Randolph and Penelope.

They did not have to drive a very hard bargain with them as Randolph and Penelope asked what was reasonable for Langston House and by that afternoon the Marchant & Fuller charity owned yet another property. They would have vacant possession of the property before the month was out and Hector said that he would then take over and start organising builders and decorators.

"I think that the first step should be to bring an architect in to see just how some of the rooms should be safely altered," smiled the Major. He was amused by Hector's keenness and wondered whether he would be quite so happy when he realised that Estelle would be that much further away from him.

Wendell and Peter went off to look around again and find the Major and Hector, leaving Liza and Jamie with Randolph and Penelope.

"Will you not find it difficult to move to the Dower House being so near your family home?" asked Liza.

"If you think that leaving this house will upset me you are mistaken. This has been a place that I never expected or wanted to inherit and you must have realised that there is nothing that I can do to earn enough for its upkeep. I'm pleased that it is going to be used to help abused children, it has gratified me that it is for that charity," said Randolph.

"My brother is an artist; he is talented but unfortunately no matter how talented, he cannot bring in the funds that we need," said Penelope. "Randolph is right though, we have lost two brothers in recent years, neither of whom had the opportunity to marry and have a family, so we are the last to bear the Langston name, so a family home is unnecessary. We will be very happy in the Dower House; we will hear your children playing and we may find some way to help you with your enterprise."

"I must introduce you to our son John," said Liza. "He is also an artist and would much rather indulge in drawing than any other lesson."

"I have heard of your son John," said Randolph. "I believe that we have something in common. I'm pleased that he is having such a happy life. I would like to meet him and see his talent; in fact Penelope and I would like to meet all your sons."

"You will meet them as they are always interested in what we are doing," said Jamie.

"I'm sure that one or two of the children would be interested in art, so in the future you may find them knocking on your door," smiled Liza.

"I would be very happy to guide anyone with talent along the right road, although I know that a career in art is not very lucrative," said Randolph.

"That is something that we will bear in mind," said Liza.

As they arrived home, the boys could be heard going back up to their room having finished their supper. Liza followed them to make sure that they knew that they needed an early night as they had their important adoption appointment the next day.

"I know that we are leaving tomorrow, so we will also have to be up early," said Richard.

"Have you enjoyed your stay with us?" asked Liza.

"Yes, it's been very interesting, and we have had a great deal of fun also," said Nicholas.

Bella had quietly entered the room, which seemed to surprise Nicholas and Richard.

"We'll come again if we may," said Bella.

"Of course, you know that you are all more than welcome. We'll just have to check our diaries to make sure that we are all free," said Liza.

"I think that the Duke may wish to see you, as well as Mr Reece," said Bella. Liza turned and told the boys to get organised for the night and that she would be up to see them in a short while.

"Your boys are very excited about their adoption tomorrow. I understand that James wants you to adopt him; do you think that Evelyn will agree to that?" asked Bella.

"I hope that she does as I don't want any awkward situations for James," said Liza.

"If Jamie has custody then surely you don't need Evelyn's agreement," said Bella.

"You're right, but Evelyn can make life very difficult for us, and especially for James. He seems to desperately need Evelyn out of his life, and much as I believe that children should be with their parents, you don't need me to tell you how unsettling a fight between parents would be for someone like James. He loves his brothers and wants to be just like them," said Liza.

"He loves you Liza and he knows that you love him also. All children love being in your company, including my two," said Bella.

"Well, we'll have to make sure that they meet up regularly, especially as they will be going to Cambridge at the same time," said Liza.

Bella seemed genuinely sorry that she would be leaving the following day, but she informed everyone that she would be visiting again, much to everyone's amusement as by that time they had become used to Bella's direct ways.

Chapter 15

It was a very important day in the household; the boys were full of excitement and Liza and Jamie were surprised to see that they had had they breakfast, were washed, dressed and ready to leave by eight o'clock the next morning.

Bella and her boys managed to make their farewells and Miranda and Lucinda waved to them as they passed the Dower House. Both David and Grace called out to them from the gatehouse and then they were on their way to Jamie's London lawyer and would finally go to the courthouse to finalise Jamie's adoption of Matthew and John.

"I wish it was for me also," said James.

"It will be James," said Jamie. "That I promise you, but you know that we want to do it with as little difficulty as possible."

It did not take long for the process to be completed and afterwards they went to one of the Coffee Houses where Jamie was known and which he had organised lunch for them all. They walked in and were guided to a table on which were some place tags for Lord Jamie Edgeworth, Lady Liza Edgeworth, Master James Edgeworth, Master John Edgeworth and Master Matthew Edgeworth. This delighted all the boys and they said that they would keep them forever.

"Your adoptions will be announced in the Times shortly, but first we want to see if we can also get yours agreed shortly James, so that they can all be announced together," said Jamie.

"It's going to take a while for that to happen," said James sadly.

"Not necessarily James," said Liza. "Tomorrow we want you to get together what you may need for a few days holiday as we are going to visit one of our farms in Wales and that is very near where your mother is staying at the moment. You will have a good time on the farm whilst we visit her and sort everything out with her. We'll be taking Mr and Mrs Reece with us, so that you will be well looked after whilst we are busy."

"It sounds funny calling them Mr and Mrs Reece," laughed Matthew.

"I know, I find it difficult to remember that it's now April's name. I think they will enjoy seeing the farm and the people who run it. There's a nice village there with a rather large sweet shop which also sells cakes and lemonade," said Liza.

"Do they sell ice creams?" asked John.

"I don't know, but no doubt you will find out," said Liza. That seemed to cheer James up.

"What if she doesn't agree?" asked James.

"Then we'll have to do it the hard way, but the outcome will be the same. You will be mummy Liza's son; it will just take a little longer. However, I don't think that there will be a problem," said Jamie.

There were several people in the Coffee House that Jamie knew, and Liza had met one or two of them. Both Liza and Jamie were proud of the way that their boys behaved, their manners were impeccable.

At the end of their meal Jamie said, "come on Edgeworth boys, shall we take you home to the rest of the Edgeworths?"

Grins appeared on the three boys' faces. They also had a small holiday to look forward to, although James was a little apprehensive but both John and Matthew told him not to worry as they knew that it would all work out well.

"Our boys have a great deal of faith in us," whispered Liza and Jamie nodded and smiled.

Everyone was waiting for them when they arrived home. Bella and her boys had left but Peter had stayed another day just to greet the 'Edgeworth' boys, or that was his excuse, but nobody believed it.

"I have never known Peter be away from the office for so long," said Wendell. "I'm pleased for him. I just hope that he doesn't read more into it than there is."

"Peter will never let emotions get in the way of business, but it would be nice if he can combine the two," smiled Liza.

"You've managed to do that Liza," said Wendell.

"I've been very lucky; I've had a great deal of help," said Liza.

"Yes you have but there have also been very many times when you have had no help at all and you have still succeeded," said Wendell.

"You're just flattering me, Wendell. Our boys acted impeccably this morning," said Liza changing the subject much to Wendell's amusement.

"How long will you be away?" asked Wendell.

"Three or four days, and after that I will be all yours," said Liza.

"Amelia and I thought that we would visit the Ffoulks House again. We'll call in on Anthony and Diana and see Rose and Jennifer also," said Wendell.

"Davis will be free to take you wherever you want to go. We are taking Hendry and the young trainee lad, which will be good for him. We'll be leaving soon after dawn and no doubt the boys will sleep some of the time. We'll be stopping at one of the Marchant & Fuller Hotels which will give Hendry and his assistant a time to rest and we'll arrive at the farm late afternoon," said Liza.

"We know why you are going there now, and I doubt that you will get the outcome that you wish for, but I know that you have got to try," said Wendell. "She should thank you for all that you have done for her, and this could be one way of her doing that, but she won't and you, Jamie and young James will have to go through a difficult time trying to achieve what is right."

During part of their lessons that day Adam had the boys practicing writing their signatures and the following day they had very few lessons as they had to get ready for their long trip. They would be going to bed early, having already bathed so that they only had to dress for their journey. They were finding it all very exciting as it was the first time that they had set off at such an early hour. They would not be taking too much luggage with them and they were to organise with April clothes that would be useful around a farm, they would need very little in smart attire.

Liza could also see that April was getting excited and Adam was smiling indulgently at her and the boys. The piles of clothes that were appearing on the boys' beds were increasing alarmingly and April was asking Liza's advice on what she should take. Adam was quite calm and had already packed his case. He, Liza and April looked at what the boys wanted to take and soon they had their cases packed and ready. Adam said that April would shortly be with Liza to sort out her case, but first he would organise what April was taking.

Roberts had packed Jamie's bags and finally April appeared to finalise Liza's packing. The bags were taken to the carriage to join Hendry's and the trainee's cases.

The boys were in bed and asleep when Liza and Jamie came up to rest before their journey. They had left Wendell, Amelia and Peter in the drawing room, and Miranda, Lucinda, David and Grace had gone to their homes, but no doubt they would wake everyone when they left.

Liza and Jamie were resting comfortably in Liza's room and at one o'clock they quietly went to the boys' room and shook them awake. Liza then knocked on Adam and April's door and returned to help with getting the boy's ready, and they really didn't know what they were doing as they appeared to be still asleep.

They had mattresses placed on the floor of the carriage and when they were ready Jamie carried James and Adam carried Matthew down the stairs and placed them comfortably on the mattresses. Jamie returned and carried John and carefully placed him also on the mattresses, covering them all with blankets. It left enough room for the adults to place their feet on the floor, but only just.

Hendry and young Ernie were holding the horses ready for everyone to climb aboard. They had a breakfast picnic basket with them as they were sure that the boys would be hungry when they awoke. Finally they were settled, managing to place their feet in relatively comfortable positions around the boys and quietly Jamie knocked for Hendry to start on their journey. They were going to stop at one of the hotels at around midmorning to change the horses and take refreshments, with one more change of horses at around two o'clock in the afternoon.

Jamie and Adam wriggled themselves comfortably into the corner seats and Liza swung her legs up onto the seat and rested her head on Jamie's stomach. April watched and decided that it was a good idea as there was little room on the floor for their feet and they carried on in that way until around seven o'clock, which was when the boys started rousing.

"I didn't know that we'd started on our journey," said Matthew rubbing his eyes, and the other two looked just as surprised. Liza and April put their feet down making room for the boys to sit. Jamie and Adam stood and stretched.

"I think that we'll be at our first stop earlier than planned," said Liza. "It means that Hendry and Ernie will be able to rest for a little longer than we originally thought."

Adam looked quizzically at Liza. "They need their rest to get us there safely, Adam," smiled Liza.

"I really hadn't thought about that, but of course you're right," said Adam.

"Only you would have thought of that," said Jamie to Liza.

The boys were now sitting comfortably between the adults and gradually coming to their senses. Liza asked them if they wanted some breakfast and Adam proceeded to reach up for their picnic basket, and they were all grateful for something to eat.

"What about Hendry and Ernie?" asked April.

"They have their own picnic basket," said Liza and Jamie nodded realising that Liza had thought about that also.

"We'll be at our first stop in just over an hour, so we can make ourselves more comfortable and we can pack up the mattresses for the rest of the journey," said Liza as she yawned and stretched. The boys were asking questions about the farm and Liza tried to answer them as best she could.

"It's going to be rather like when we went to the Barrows' farm for Easter a few years ago. We had a good time then," said Matthew and James started asking Matthew and John questions about that time.

"Did you know that farm?" James asked Jamie.

"Yes, I met the family briefly," said Jamie.

"Was that when you were rescuing our mother from the Indians?" asked James.

"I believe it was around that time," smiled Jamie and he changed the subject by asking what the boys thought they would do at the Evan's farm.

"I want to see all the animals," said John. "I also want to see what they grow there. Will it be different to what you grow Dad?"

"It probably will be," said Jamie. "I shall find it very interesting also."

"I'm looking forward to seeing the village and going to the sweet and cake shop," said Matthew, who always put his stomach before all else.

"We'll have to behave ourselves, because we are all Edgeworths now," said John.

"You always behave yourselves," said Liza. "It wouldn't matter whether you were Edgeworths or not, you know exactly how to behave in company."

There were slight smiles on all the adult's faces and their thoughts must have been the same as Liza's. It was as if by becoming Edgeworths their lives as well as their manners had to alter for the better.

"There is nothing wrong with your manners," said Jamie. "You know exactly how to treat others, but I am very pleased that you are so proud of your name."

Liza had been right, in less than an hour they were pulling into the hotel for their first stop. Liza went with Hendry and Ernie to make sure that they were happy with the horses which had been organised for their onward trip and the stable workers knew what they had to do.

"I've organised a room for you both on the top floor within our suite, so when you are ready, I'll get someone to show you the way," said Liza and they bowed and thanked her.

In their suite food had been laid out for them and the boys did not have to be told twice to help themselves.

"Jamie, Adam, you both look very tired. Why don't you both take advantage of comfortable beds," said Liza and she indicated towards one of the doors. "Don't worry, you don't have to sleep in the same bed; there are two in there. I've kept one of the other rooms for the boys, and the last room is for Hendry and Ernie. I'll rest on the couch and there's another bed in the boy's room if April would like to take that."

Jamie frowned, wondering what her logic was and she laughed. "Neither you nor Adam slept on the coach ride whereas April and I did."

There was a knock on the door and a rather bemused Hendry asked if he was in the right place. "Come in Hendry and Ernie. There's some food for you here and your room is over there. I'll wake you if necessary, around half an hour before we have to leave." They were both looking at the food and Liza told them to take what they wanted and eat it in their room if they were happy to do so.

"You'll both be more comfortable taking your boots off and relaxing before the next stage of the journey," said Liza. She turned her back leaving them to pick what they wanted to eat and ushered Jamie and Adam into their room. Lastly the boys went into the final room and lay on their beds. When she came out from their room, Hendry and Ernie had disappeared and April intimated that they had taken advantage of the room to rest in.

"I said that there's a spare bed in the boy's room if you would like to use it," smiled Liza.

"What about you?" April asked.

"I'm going to put my feet up on the couch and I've arranged that somebody comes and knocks on the door in time for us to get ready to leave; so you use the spare bed and I hope the boys don't keep you awake," said Liza.

Liza could hear Hendry and Ernie muttering in their room, but everything soon went quiet, and Liza also nodded off for a while. She was woken by a kiss on the head and she smiled and sat up, making room for Jamie to sit with her. He informed her that they had all slept for about an hour and a half.

"Well we have five or ten minutes before we must wake the others," said Liza, but there was loud knocking on their door and Liza sighed and called out a thank you to whoever was knocking. The boys had heard it and April could be heard organising them. Hendry and Ernie made an appearance looking very refreshed and said that they would be on their way in no time at all.

Adam appeared looking his usual smart self and said that he would help April get the boys ready and Liza went into the room that Jamie and Adam had used and washed her hands and face and generally tidied herself.

It wasn't long before they were on their way again and Adam had brought a book with him that the boys had recently started reading and so they were taking it in turns to read to one another.

They just had one more stop to change the horses and stretch their legs before arriving at the Evans' farm just after four o'clock. Jamie helped Liza down and she was immediately engulfed in Taffy's arms and swung around with a resounding kiss finally landing on her forehead. Liza looked up at him and grinned, he had been scrubbed clean and no doubt threatened that he had to stay that way until their guests arrived.

Bronwen appeared at the kitchen door, shouting her greeting and she was followed by Carys and Dilys and Liza was once again engulfed by them all. She then started introducing everyone and Jamie was fascinated by these homely, loving people. There were lots of handshakes but when it came to the boys each one of the Evans' grinned and looked at them closely.

Liza had managed to master some of the Welsh language and Bronwen was saying that it was obvious who Liza's son was and she indicated his eyes and then she turned to James and said how like his father he was, but as John was really good looking it was understandable why he had been chosen and loved by them both. Liza smiled and kissed her again on the cheek and said that John was indeed loved and was now a very contented child.

Dilys was guiding them all into the house and the wonderful smell of cooking assailed their nostrils and took away any shyness that the boys were displaying. Plates were already on the table and teacups and saucers were at each place. Jamie smiled realising that this was exactly how farmers lived and he was looking forward to being treated as one of the family. Adam and April were looking very relaxed and were joining in with the great chatter around the table. Hendry and Ernie looked into the kitchen and were slightly mystified and then even more so when they were called to join everyone at the table and from the smile that Liza gave them, they realised that this was how the next few days were going to map out.

There were shouts from outside the kitchen door and two very large men appeared. Immediately Liza was whisked up and around with another kiss planted on her forehead. Liza turned and introduced Rhys and Owain to everyone there. Jamie looked mystified until Liza explained that they were

Taffy's and Bronwen's sons. They all sat down around their enormous table and everyone enjoyed the wonderful homemade cake. Jamie's and the boys' faces were pictures of contentment, as were April's and Adam's. Hendry and Ernie were attempting to talk to Owain, and Liza helped them out as it was difficult for them to understand the Welsh accent, but they were all getting on well. If they didn't have a difficult meeting the next day with Evelyn this would have been the perfect holiday for everyone.

Bronwen, Dilys and Carys cleared the table and started organising the main meal for the evening whilst they suggested that Liza and Jamie and April and Adam went to their rooms and unpacked their clothes as well as organise the boys' room. Rhys was going to show Hendry and Ernie their room and Owain and Taffy decided that the boys should go for a short walk with them so that they could see a small part of the farm. Liza wondered how they would get on as the boys would be unable to understand Taffy and Owain and they in turn would be unable to understand the boys.

Jamie was standing in their room watching Liza unpacking their cases and he decided to help her. "It's a long time since I unpacked a suitcase; that Is If I have ever done so."

It didn't take them long and they met with April and Adam who were on their way to sort out the boys' room.

"I'll help April with that," said Liza to Adam. "Why don't you and Jamie go down and join the boys on their walk. I'm sure you would find it very interesting."

Liza and April were talking about the farm as they unpacked and finally, they went down to the kitchen to see if they could help Bronwen to get their dinner ready. A shout went up and voices frantically yelling for 'mum' and 'dad' could be heard and a boy came into view covered from head to foot in mud. Liza couldn't tell who it was, and Jamie and Adam were rushing towards him.

"Who is it Jamie?" called Liza.

"Can't you tell that it's your son, Liza," said Jamie.

"They're all my sons, Jamie," said Liza. "Oh, it's Matthew. Of course it would be. Don't you come into the house in that state! Just stay there and April and I will get some hot water for you."

It was a hot afternoon and Taffy and Owain set up a bath outside the backdoor. Dilys and Carys rushed out with hot water and started filling the bath. Everyone was laughing and James and John appeared with Rhys and they were telling everyone how Matthew had fallen into a muddy pit.

"Take your clothes off Matthew," said Liza.

"I can't do that in front of everyone," exclaimed Matthew but one look from his mother told him that it was exactly what he was going to do. Huge aprons were handed to Liza and April as well as towels and Liza told James and John to go up and find Matthew's nightshirt, dressing gown and slippers.

"I'm sorry Mum, I didn't mean to be naughty; I just fell into a muddy pool. I was really looking forward to our supper as it smells so good," said Matthew.

"You haven't been naughty; you just had an accident and as for sending you off to bed without your supper, I have never done that and I don't intend to start now," said Liza. She looked at Matthew and smiled at him. "I couldn't tell who you were covered in mud like that."

"It reminds me of when we were at Uncle Michael's farm and you fell in a mud pit and couldn't get out," smiled Matthew.

"Yes, that was a fun day, and we'll remember this one in the same way," said Liza.

Matthew was nearly clean, but they had to fill another bath to finally make him look respectable. Liza then wrapped him in a large towel and held him to her. "You look and smell a lot better now Matthew."

"April, I would suggest that James and John also get ready for bed, they can come down and eat their supper in their dressing gowns and slippers."

Jamie stood back and watched Liza handling Matthew and soothing an awkward situation. He could see her holding Matthew and smelling him and he knew that she would soon be doing the same to James and John. She sat on a seat and finished drying off Matthew and Jamie came over and joined them.

"Well Matthew, you certainly seem to have made an impression since you arrived," smiled Jamie.

"I'm sorry Dad; I didn't mean to fall in the pit," pouted Matthew.

"You do some strange things at times Matthew but throwing yourself into a muddy pit for fun is just not one of them," said Jamie. "You're not in trouble Matthew. You must watch where you are going in the future; you could have been badly hurt and you know that the others do tend to follow you, so you have to be especially careful and watch out for your brothers."

Matthew was now in his nightshirt, dressing gown and slippers and Jamie then pulled him towards him and put his arms around him. By that time James and John had joined them and they all sat on the bench and Liza had her arms around them whilst Jamie still held Matthew.

"Matthew was lucky today, but it just goes to show you how dangerous a farm can be," said Jamie. "You all must look out for each other and watch where you are going."

"You're going to visit James' mother tomorrow, aren't you?" said John. "What will we be doing whilst you are there?"

"April and Adam will be taking you into the village and while you are there, I'm sure that you will be able to find some cake and sweets," said Liza. "You'll probably find that Hendry and Ernie have the same idea and you'll possibly see them there. Dilys and Carys have some shopping to do, but no doubt you'll meet up with them."

"She's not my mother," said a very sulky James. "I bet she won't agree to my adoption."

"She may well do so James and that will make life very easy for us, but if she doesn't then you know that we have tried our best but will have to do it a slightly longer and harder way. I already think of you as my son and Matthew and John treat you as a brother. But let's not worry about it until after tomorrow and let's enjoy our holiday," said Liza.

"Yes," said Matthew. "There's no point in worrying about it; besides it's all going to work out right in the end."

Matthew said that with a confidence that nobody else seemed to feel and the boys made their way into the kitchen, following the smell of roast lamb and potatoes with carrots and cabbage.

Hendry and Ernie were already there, and they were being regaled with the story of Matthew falling into a muddy pit to which they were adding that the same thing had happened to their mother a few years ago in Ireland. April was helping Bronwen, Dilys and Carys and Adam was organising where the boys would be sitting. Rhys and Owain were asking if Matthew had come out of the accident unscathed.

"Do you know that I didn't recognise him; I didn't know which boy he was. All I could see were ovals where he had obviously cleaned his eyes, everything else was black and he was unrecognisable. I knew that he was one of my boys, but I had no idea which one," said Liza.

"You really knew that it had to be Matthew," said Jamie. "You know that he leads the way in everything, including getting into trouble. I know he doesn't mean to; he's very like you Liza."

293

"Do I get into trouble? I didn't think that I did," said Liza.

Jamie and everyone around the table just looked at her, each one thinking of times when she needed help to get her out of a particular difficulty.

The boys were eagerly sniffing the air enjoying the aroma of roast lamb and Hendry and Ernie were fascinated that they were being served by the ladies including Lady Liza Edgeworth. April was helping the boys and when the meat was on the plates, bowls of vegetables were being passed around.

It was a lively talkative time and Jamie watched Liza enjoying the companionship of these people. He imagined that it was probably as her life had been in Benson and he at last realised why she missed that life. It was friendly and classless, but he knew that she also loved the life that she had with him and the boys and now their extended family.

The evening was warm and pleasant, and the boys' eyes were slowly closing so Liza and April guided them up to their beds and tucked them in. James was the only one who, although tired, was not asleep and Liza sat on his bed and put a reassuring arm around him.

"It will all turn out right James; I promise you that. Whether it's tomorrow or sometime soon after, you will definitely be my son in name as well as feelings," smiled Liza and she kissed him and smoothed his hair out of his eyes.

As she left the room Jamie was waiting for her at the doorway and he whispered to her that James was worried about the next day. She nodded and suggested that he go in and also reassure him, which he did.

Down in the kitchen the men were chatting, and the women were clearing up after the meal. Bronwen moved towards Liza and said, "I know that you have a difficult day tomorrow. Mrs Carson has settled in well and is accepted in the village. My Rhys is seeing young Melanie's nurse, so I understand that you are here to see James' mother, but I don't know the reason why, although I have a good idea from what your boys have been saying. I hope it all goes well for you; I know that she can be a difficult person, although as I say, she seems to enjoy being part of the village."

Liza smiled, "There never are secrets when you have children. We didn't tell them to keep quiet, why should they as it is part of all their lives, and it means so very much to James. It will be sorted one way or the other. I was also very anxious for Jamie and the boys to meet you and your very happy family and to see how this wonderful place is run."

"Your staff appear a little bemused by our way of living," said Bronwen.

"Yes, life is very different at our home, which is a shame as it's so wonderfully relaxed and friendly here, we could learn a great deal from you," said Liza.

Rhys and Owain left for their cottage and Hendry and Ernie made their way to their room. Finally Liza told April that she would not need her that night and she and Adam went to their room. Liza and Jamie stayed for a short while chatting to Taffy and Bronwen. Dilys and Carys said goodnight and they would see them in the morning.

"I know who Mrs Carson is, Liza," said Bronwen. "I also know that no matter how you get her out of trouble she dislikes you. I can also see that young James is her son; there is a likeness although he is more like his father."

Jamie was looking slightly uncomfortable. "Don't be embarrassed Jamie," said Taffy. "You have nothing to be embarrassed about. She has blended in well with the villagers but young Melanie's nurse asked Rhys to warn you that Mrs Carson has made it quite clear that she has no intention of agreeing to whatever it is that you want and if there is a way that she can hurt you she will do so."

"It's none of our business Taffy," said Bronwen.

"I know that, but Liza has done everything to help that woman and don't forget that she has also helped this family out of difficulties and on the road to success," said Taffy. "If we are to have loyalties then they are to Liza and not Mrs Carson. That's all I am going to say on the subject."

"I thought that after her last gross breach of decorum and our assistance to get her out of trouble that she would have at least had a small spark of decency towards you Liza," said Jamie.

"I think we may be imagining the worst, after all we are asking something for her son; she must have some feeling for him," said Liza.

Three pairs of eyes stared at her in disbelief. Jamie laughed and said, "We have many friends and those who know Liza well have always said that her naivety astounds them. I think that you have both just seen an example of why they are right."

"But you wouldn't change her, would you Jamie?" said Bronwen.

"Not in a million years," said Jamie.

***

295

The boys were up early the next morning and could be heard asking a great many questions of any member of the Evans family that they came in contact with and also making an attempt to feed the chickens.

Jamie turned over and looked at Liza who was stretching lazily in their bed.

"This is a very comfortable bed," he said. "I wish we could stay in it all day, but we have a very important mission to get through today and from what was being said last night, it is not going to be an easy task."

Jamie ran his hands up and down her body and she giggled with pleasure. "Unfortunately we have to get ready to try to get our son to be truly ours."

By the time they came downstairs the boys had already had their breakfast and April and Adam were just finishing theirs. Neither felt very hungry, so they just had some toast and tea.

Hendry came in and Liza motioned for him to sit at the table. She told him that they would be borrowing the small carriage and she was sure that Ernie was quite capable of driving that. Hendry was to take whoever wanted to go with the boys into the village and end up at the café for cakes and sweets, including himself and Ernie.

"Ernie can leave us where we are going and make his way also to the café; if we haven't joined everyone there by the time you have all finished, then he should come back and wait for us," said Liza.

The boys came rushing in each wanting to say what they had been doing to help on the farm that morning and Jamie patiently listened to them and then handed each some money for them to spend in the village and they went off to find April.

"James seems a little better this morning," said Liza. "You must have put his mind at rest last night Jamie."

"His mind won't truly be at rest until you are officially his mother, but we both made him feel better and Matthew and John are very supportive of him," said Jamie.

"I suppose that we had better get ourselves ready for our trip Jamie. The sooner we go the sooner we will know what our next move has to be," said Liza and they made their way up to their room. Adam was in the corridor and said that they were not to worry as he and April would make sure that the boys were happy and kept occupied.

"Thank you, Adam; you and April are so very thoughtful," smiled Liza.

It wasn't long before they were climbing into the carriage and Ernie started them on the short trip to see Evelyn. It was not a visit that they were looking forward to and it wasn't long before they pulled up outside her house. The door was opened to them by Melanie's nanny and she told them that Mrs Carson was in the sitting room.

"Good morning Liza, good morning Jamie. To what do I owe the pleasure of your company?" she asked without a smile.

"There is no point in beating about the bush," said Jamie. "I would like Liza to adopt James."

Liza closed her eyes and felt that perhaps Jamie could have been a little less abrupt.

"I see that Liza's influence has failed to smooth your rough edges Jamie," said Evelyn. "And the answer to that is no, James is my son and will always remain so."

"I do not know how you can lay claim to James being your son. You may have conceived him and given birth to him, but you have never treated him as your son, in fact you have gone out of your way to ignore him and alienate him," said Jamie. "You have admitted that he is more Liza's than yours."

"But he's not Liza's, he is mine and I will take you through every court in the land before I will relinquish him to you," said Evelyn.

"Yes, you can do that Evelyn but in the end I have custody of him and will win that battle. It will however put James through a great deal of heartache," said Jamie.

"Can we please calm down," said Liza. "We all should be putting James first in this and I have to say that it is something that was his request and much as I love him and truly want to be his mother, this is what he wants above all else. Fighting over him will only make him more unhappy about the situation than he is now."

"Give me one good reason why you wish to deny him what he wants most in the world?" asked Jamie.

"Children never know what's best for them and I know that it's best that he remains my son; in fact I think that he should move back with me," said Evelyn.

"That will never happen," shouted an increasingly angry Jamie. "If you want to play it the hard way then so be it. Do not forget all the difficulties that you have been in and how they have been hidden to keep your reputation intact. All that would be out in the open if we have to end up in a protracted court case."

"And I shall say how you are trying to blackmail me," said Evelyn. "I suppose you will now try to take your house back from me Liza. It won't look good if you try to put me and my daughter out on the streets."

"Stop being stupid Evelyn," said Liza. "This conversation is getting out of hand and unfortunately it is exactly as I predicted that it would be."

There sounded like a scuffle in the hall and the door burst open and James was in the doorway with Adam trying to restrain him.

"I'm sorry" said Adam, "I tried to stop him, but he was too fast for me."

"That's alright Adam," said Liza. "After all we are discussing his future and he has a right to know what is happening. I trust that you have no objections Evelyn."

Liza beckoned both James and Adam into the room.

"It has always been my opinion that children should be seen but not heard and why do you want a member of your staff in on this conversation as it is absolutely no business of his," said Evelyn.

It was then that Adam came to the fore. "With all due respect to you Lady Edgeworth, but I was the one who was constantly attempting to cheer James up when he was so unhappy because he felt lonely and unloved. I may not be able to influence the outcome of this meeting, but I have a duty and responsibility to see James through yet another difficult time."

"Oh," was all that Evelyn could add.

Both Liza and Jamie looked at Adam with admiration.

James was standing quietly looking very close to tears and Adam put a reassuring hand on his shoulder.

Liza looked at him and smiled saying that he obviously had something to tell them and not to be shy. "There is nothing that you can say that will upset us."

James looked up at Evelyn with contempt. "You never wanted me, you told me that many times. You told me that I wasn't yours. When I was little I didn't understand why; it's only since I got older that I think I know; it's because my father wanted me to be mummy Liza's because he has always loved her. But I was yours and you should have loved me, I couldn't help being born. You used to go away without telling me and you used to bring some very funny people to the house when my father wasn't there."

"Your father also used to go away on many occasions," said Evelyn defensively.

"He always told me when he was leaving and always said goodbye," said James. "When I was very small you and my father used to take me to Belfast for holidays and one time there I met mummy Liza and Matthew. I used to go to their house, and it was wonderful. Mummy Liza treated me the same as Matthew and I found out what it was like to be hugged and cuddled and there was a lot of fun and laughter. One day Uncle Patrick came and the house was even happier, although I know that my father didn't like him and there was some trouble between them but it was sorted out and my father had to return to England leaving me with you, although you did take me to mummy Liza's with Nanny Jem, you said just for a short while."

"I was so happy there, but I heard Nanny Jem talking to the housekeeper and I knew that you had gone away and locked our house and we didn't have enough clothes or money. You left us with nothing, and mummy Liza and Uncle Patrick looked after us and I had the best Christmas ever. We went to Uncle Wendell's and Aunt Amelia's and Uncle Edward and Uncle Joseph played with us all day. We had presents and new clothes and I didn't want you to ever come back. I used to dream that I would go with Matthew back to America and always be part of his family."

By now tears were flowing down Liza's cheeks and James was also beginning to sob a little.

"But you finally came back, and I know that you tried to take Uncle Patrick away from mummy Liza. He wouldn't go with you, he wouldn't hurt mummy Liza, he didn't want you; he wanted her, just as my father did. I heard the staff talking about it. You finally were persuaded to take me back home to my father and I was very unhappy leaving. I know that it had been a worrying time for everyone, but I had loved every minute of it."

Jamie was looking furiously at Evelyn, "I didn't know you had actually tried that with Patrick. You mentioned it to me once in passing Liza; perhaps you didn't realise that she was serious in her intent."

"Oh yes, I realised," was all that Liza said.

"My father took me to see everyone before they left for America and that was when I met John and he also became my closest friend and I missed them all so much, but I wrote to them every week, although when I think about what I had said it was really rubbish," said James.

"They used to look forward to your letters James; you may think it is rubbish now but you all were so very young that it was anything but rubbish for your age," said Liza.

"I was so sorry when I heard that Uncle Patrick had died because he was nice but my father said that he was going to America to bring mummy Liza,

Matthew and John back with him and that took away my sadness and I hoped that he and mummy Liza would then get married. I knew that he and my mother were divorced by that time so he would be free to marry again and I could have the mother who loved me, and I would gain two brothers."

"Eventually my father brought mummy Liza and the family back and I used to live with them whenever I was in Belfast and even though they were still sad about Uncle Patrick they all loved me as one of the family. I always looked forward to my holidays with them and I had a wonderful time when we went to Italy, although that silly Count kept pestering mummy Liza until finally he hit her and me, Matthew and John had to defend her."

"You were stupid with that Count," said James to Evelyn. "We knew that he was only after her money, but she knew that and didn't like him anyway."

"Finally my father and mummy Liza married, and Matthew and John became my brothers and we look after one another. We are all loved by my father and mummy Liza as if we were all her own. You turned up at the charity function with that stupid man and tried to make fun of it, and that man attacked John, but Matthew and I stopped him. You tried to steal me away when my father was helping Uncle Hector, but mummy Liza got to me before you could take me to France. You did something to try to hurt my father and I don't know what it was but I do know that it was very bad and then you brought someone silly to Lord Carlton's evening and tried to get them to say terrible things about my father and mummy Liza," said James.

"How do you know all this James," asked Jamie. "I know it was not from us."

"Most people stop talking when they see me and my brothers, but sometimes they don't see us in time," smiled James.

"I know that I have done some foolish things, but hasn't everyone at some time," said Evelyn, "but that does not mean that I want to relinquish my right to have a son."

"But I really don't want to have you as a mother. I want to be the same as Matthew and John, I want to be my father's son and have mummy Liza as my mother. I love her and she loves me just as much as she loves Matthew and John. We live together and look after each other; we are a proper family. I want the same parents as my brothers."

"Matthew and John don't have the same parents," said Evelyn.

"Yes they do," interjected Jamie, "Matthew and John are officially Liza's and they are now officially Edgeworths and I'm proud to have them as my sons."

"Everything that you have done to hurt mummy Liza and my father has only ever hurt me and if you don't agree to this adoption then you will be hurting my brothers also. You have always made it obvious to me that you don't want me, so why do you want me now?" asked James. "You have Melanie to love and I know that you don't love me, so you must let me become part of those who do."

Evelyn was very quiet, as were Jamie and Adam. James was standing waiting and now his tears were beginning to fall, and Liza went over to him and put her arms around him holding him closely to her. "I shouldn't be crying," he said sniffing.

"You can cry as much as you like James, you have been very brave and honest with how you feel and we love you very much," said Liza who was crying with him.

Jamie cleared his throat but before he could say anything Evelyn said, "He's right, sadly I truly feel nothing for him but it's obvious that you do. I'll sign your papers Jamie. I presume you have them with you. Let me do this before I change my mind."

"We'll need some witnesses," said Jamie.

"Melanie's nanny is here, and Mr Reece can be the other witness," said Evelyn and she rang the bell and the nurse appeared very quickly and Liza wondered whether she had been listening.

Jamie opened his bag and got the necessary documents out, Evelyn read them through; they were very simple. Both Jamie and Evelyn giving Liza permission to adopt James and once signed and witnessed they would be placed with the court for final official authorisation. It was all over in five minutes and James just stood looking on in disbelief.

Noises could be heard in the hallway and above all else Matthew could be heard working out which room to go into. A knock came on the sitting room door and Matthew's fair head appeared around it.

"Ah good, there you are," he said. "May we come in? We feel that our brother James needs our support."

Before anyone could answer Matthew and John fell into the room. April was in the doorway apologising that she could not stop them.

"So you feel that James needs your support," said Evelyn.

"Yes, he is our brother and as we are now Edgeworths, we Edgeworths must stick together," said Matthew with John nodding.

301

James turned to them smiling broadly, "It's all going to be fine; she has agreed that your mother can now be mine also."

"Yippee;" came the shout from both Matthew and John but all Liza could see was a very large pink stain on the front of Matthew's shirt.

"Matthew, John, James behave please," said Jamie.

"I see that your son has not changed in his enthusiasms," said Evelyn.

Liza smiled and felt that the pink mark was getting larger.

"You've been to the cake shop then Matthew. You had that lovely strawberry milk drink, did you?" said Evelyn.

"Yes, how did you know?" asked Matthew.

"Just a guess," said Evelyn with a rare smile.

"Come on boys, go out to the carriage, your mother and I will follow shortly," said Jamie.

Adam and April ushered the boys from Evelyn's house and into the carriage.

"I apologise for that intrusion," said Liza.

"Well Liza, I met your son many years ago and he amused me greatly then, he has not altered, and you must find that he brightens your life immensely. I envy your ability to love and be loved, in fact I envy a great deal about you, but I will say no more," said Evelyn.

"Thank you, Evelyn, you've made a child very happy today. We will not bother you again, I hope you have a good life," said Liza and she left the room.

What Jamie said to Evelyn, Liza never found out, but it was obviously not something that was going to upset the situation, and he shortly joined Liza in their carriage.

"We should not have let James plead like that," said Liza. "We should have stopped him."

"I think we were all surprised, but who better to say how he feels?" said Jamie.

It wasn't long before they reached the farm and the boys were already shouting their news to Bronwen and Taffy.

"I didn't think that you would achieve anything with Mrs Carson, but I'm delighted at the outcome. We'll have to have a small celebration this evening," said Bronwen.

Matthew and John came rushing into the kitchen and launched themselves at Liza. "Where's James?" she asked; and she looked towards the door and he was standing very still in the doorway. "Why are you standing there James, don't you want to come to your mother?" She laughed as he also launched himself at her nearly knocking her off her feet.

Matthew and John moved away leaving James in Liza's arms and he was now crying bitterly. She was trying to calm him but was finding it difficult as she was also weeping. Jamie came and put his arms around them both saying that there was nothing to cry about, it was really a very happy day. "I know," sniffed James. "I'm really very happy. I've never been so happy."

The boys laughed. "Come on brother James let's go for a walk around the farm," said Matthew. "We've got to go back to the cake shop this afternoon; they're making ice cream especially for us."

"Matthew, how did you manage to get them to do that for you?" asked Jamie.

"We told them how good the ice cream was in Italy and they said that they could do better, and we had to go back and try it this afternoon," said Matthew.

"I trust you will change your shirt before you go back to the village," said Jamie to Matthew.

Matthew frowned as Jamie pointed towards the front of his shirt. "Oh, that's how she knew. I thought that she had some mental powers."

"Mental could be right," muttered Jamie to himself. "Off you go and try not to fall into any mud holes."

Jamie came back into the kitchen and sat at the table with Liza joining Adam and April. "Adam, April," said Jamie. "You are both very exceptional people and you have shown such thoughtfulness and care for our children over many years. I'm sure that other families do not have such loyalty and friendship from members of their staff. I had no idea that James was so unhappy when he was younger, and I feel very guilty about that."

"When he met Lady Liza and Matthew the difference in him was remarkable and I think that you realise that he lived for his visits once they were permanently in Belfast. He was rather depressed when they returned to America, but he enjoyed writing to Matthew and John and he was always delighted to receive letters from them," said Adam. "I tried to gently steer him away from his dream of going to live in America with his friends and as he said, he was sad that Uncle Patrick had died but delighted that you were going to bring Lady Liza, Matthew and John home. He now has everything that he has ever wanted. I'm sure that he feels that he is a very lucky boy."

"Let's hope that we can live up to his expectations," smiled Liza.

303

Adam stared at Liza thoughtfully and said, "I believe you have already done that."

"Oh," said Liza and Jamie put his arm around her shoulder and confirmed Adam's words.

Later that afternoon Jamie and Liza took the boys back to the cake shop, hoping that they had been able to make enough ice cream to satisfy the boys' needs. They were greeted like old friends and dishes were placed in front of them each containing some white and pink ice cream. They complimented the shop owners and told them that the ice cream was delicious. It was quite different to Italian ice cream, but nobody drew a comparison in front of the shop keepers. This time nothing appeared on any shirt fronts and both Liza and Jamie felt very contented surrounded by their immediate family.

The evening meal turned into a wonderful celebration. Even their ice cream afternoon did not deter the boys from their supper, and they were allowed to have a very small amount of beer with their meal to toast James officially becoming Liza's son. From the looks on their faces Liza worked out that beer would not become one of their favourite drinks.

When Liza and Jamie went to their room that night, he asked her to tell him about Evelyn's attempt to seduce Patrick.

"Will it hurt you to tell me Liza?" Jamie asked gently.

"It seems important to you Jamie. It's a long time ago and probably best forgotten," said Liza.

"But James hasn't forgotten and perhaps Matthew and John also know the story. If James does then they probably do," said Jamie.

"It was when you had to return to England and finally Evelyn turned up on my doorstep saying that she had nowhere else to go and that I was her only friend," said Liza.

"You surely didn't believe her Liza, I know you are naïve but you're not that gullible," said Jamie.

"I knew that I was not her only friend, but I had no idea where she could stay. I knew that your house was closed with no staff. I had her son and nurse under my roof so I agreed that she could stay whilst she prepared to travel with James to Surrey. I put her in my adjoining room, and she promised that she would see James and sort out what was happening with Nanny Jem. Patrick and I were going to see if we could find his old family home but before that I was visiting Wendell and Amelia," said Liza.

"So that was when she made her move," said Jamie.

"Wendell warned me to get home as soon as possible and I walked in on her trying to persuade Patrick to make love to her. She was dressed in the most scantily of nightdresses and she had smothered herself in my perfume," said Liza.

"I know she could be quite seductive when she wanted to be," said Jamie.

"I heard Patrick tell her that he was not interested and that he would never do anything to hurt me," Liza said quietly.

"What did you do Liza?" asked Jamie.

"I walked into the room and suggested that she put something warm on before she caught her death of cold, and Patrick and I started discussing what we were going to do that day as if she wasn't there and when we turned around, she wasn't there. We went out and left her to pack her bags, which she did but I relented and let her stay on the understanding that she sorted out what was to happen to James and Nanny Jem. She did that and travelled with them to Surrey," said Liza.

"I'm sure you've made it sound simpler than it really was," said Jamie.

"It was simple Jamie," said Liza. "She tried to create trouble between Patrick and me and she couldn't do it."

Jamie was very quiet for a few minutes, "but she managed to do it between you and me."

"We have no problems Jamie, we are as close to one another as it is possible for any two people to be and we now are the proud parents of three very happy boys, so don't dwell on the past. It's gone and forgotten," said Liza.

"You're right Liza. If I dwell on what happened a long time ago then Evelyn is winning once again and we have had a very successful day and made three boys very happy," said Jamie.

"Hasn't it been a wonderful day," said Liza. "I never believed that we would achieve what we set out to do with so little difficulty."

She climbed into bed and stretched out comfortably, grinning up at Jamie. "You're taking a long time to come to bed," she said and when he did join her all thoughts of Evelyn and problems of the past were wiped out of his mind.

***

They were up early the next morning and while Jamie and Adam took the boys around the farm April and Liza packed ready for the return journey. They were leaving after lunch but would be stopping overnight at one of the hotels.

Although Liza had enjoyed her time with the Evans', she was anxious to get home knowing that everyone would be pleased with the outcome of their meeting with Evelyn. They would be surprised because nobody believed that Evelyn would agree to Liza's adoption of James.

They left the Evans' farm after lunch and changed their horses once before finally arriving at the hotel where they would be staying the night. After supper it didn't take long for the boys to settle for the night. Hendry and Ernie had a room on the floor below whilst Adam and April had a room within the suite and after some discussion regarding the events of the past few days, they went to their room leaving Jamie and Liza alone in the sitting room.

"We should be home just after lunchtime tomorrow," said Jamie, "and I would like to take our documents to my lawyer as soon as possible, so we may be able to visit him in the afternoon. I trust you'll be free also."

"I want to get it organised quickly; I still can't believe that we have Evelyn's agreement, so I want to lodge the papers immediately," said Liza.

Jamie had been right; they drove up to their house just after lunchtime the following day and it wasn't long before they were surrounded by family and friends all anxious to know what had happened with Evelyn and then they all showed their delight at the outcome as well as expressing surprise.

"You obviously have very good powers of persuasion Jamie," said David.

"James did that himself," said Jamie. "He was very precise over what he wanted and in the end Evelyn agreed. He should not have been there but he decided that he needed to tell Evelyn exactly why she should let Liza be his mother and from what he said it made her change her mind and relinquish all her rights over him."

"We had no idea that he was going to do that and really it was not the right way to handle the situation, but it worked, and James is now very happy, as are we," said Liza.

A fair head with green eyes peeped around the door. Jamie looked across and said, "Yes Matthew, what is it you want?"

"We just wondered whether it would be possible to go into the village to see Derek. He'll be very anxious to hear about our time away," said Matthew as always the mouthpiece for all the boys.

"Hendry and Ernie are very tired, and I believe Davis will be otherwise occupied taking your father and I to our lawyers," said Liza.

"I don't wish to interfere, but we now have a small horse and trap and I could take them if you have no objections to their going," said Grace.

"What do you think Jamie," said Liza referring purposely to Jamie for a decision regarding his sons.

"Well Matthew, your cousin Grace has solved a problem for you, so you may tell your brothers that you can visit Derek but you must do as cousin Grace tells you and you must not annoy Mrs Price, she has enough to contend with without three extra boys to look out for," said Jamie.

"Thank you, Father, I shall tell my brothers," said Matthew with his tongue in cheek.

Matthew always brought a smile to the faces of the adults and Grace left to organise the transport. Jamie and Liza also left to get ready for a visit to their lawyer; they would all be meeting up later for dinner.

"I love our family Jamie," said Liza when they were on their way to see the lawyer, "but the past few days with the Evans', the boys and April and Adam were quite refreshing. Hendry and Ernie seemed quite relaxed once they got used to the idea that we were quite human."

"The Evans' are a lovely family and I know that we would have enjoyed it more if we had not had to visit Evelyn but it's all over now and hopefully by next week the adoption will be registered with the court. I'm glad that Wendell and Amelia are with us to celebrate the occasion. Peter had to leave yesterday. I have a feeling that we will be seeing more of him than we have done in the past," said Jamie.

Their visit to the lawyer didn't take long and they arrived home at the same time as Grace and the boys who were delighted to be told that they would all be visiting the court yet again the following week. The boys disappeared down to the kitchen for their supper and Grace made her way to her home and would be returning for dinner later.

Chapter 16

The next few days passed very quickly. Derek joined the boys for their lessons and the usual cricket match took place on the Sunday. The boys were excited at the prospect of James' formal adoption with the court and as before they went to a coffee house to celebrate and then had an afternoon gathering with all the family and friends. Jamie organised the notification of all the boys' adoptions in the newspaper and finally the boys could say that they had a mother and father and the Edgeworth name.

Liza and Amelia went to the Ffoulks Home and the Major and Hector showed them a very smooth running and happy environment for the children. William and Amber were still keeping close to one another and one or two of the older children were watching over them. Liza told the Major that there were two couples in America who were very good contenders for their adoption. One was a lawyer and his wife living in New York and the other was a childless couple who ran a small farm a hundred miles or so outside the city.

"Who will make the final decision?" asked the Major.

"I'll put in my recommendation, but Myra will have the final say. She has met the couples and is in the best position to work out which option is right for them," said Liza.

"They both enjoy being in the garden and watching over some of the animals. They get a great deal of pleasure out of feeding the chickens and collecting the eggs. I haven't been able to assess their intelligence, although Estelle will know more about them in that respect," said the Major.

"We also have a request for a couple of boys who would be interested in farming and a girl to be trained in domestic duties, but I'll talk to you about that later," said Liza.

"Have we any more children coming in from Belfast?" asked the Major.

"We'll move another half a dozen when we have seen who wants to take up positions in America. Some just may not want that life," said Liza. "How's Jennifer?"

"She's enjoying her stay here; she'll return to Belfast when Wendell and Amelia leave. She's here helping our housemother at the moment. She spends a great deal of time with us," said the Major.

"I'll see her before we leave; I'm going to see Anthony and Diana and hopefully Rose later today," said Liza.

"Hmm," said the Major and both Liza and Amelia detected a slight reluctance in his voice at the mention of Rose's name, but they chose to ignore it.

Liza felt a tug on her skirt and when she looked around William and Amber were happily smiling up at her. They still had their 'Softy' toys as well as one another for company.

They went in to see Jennifer and the housemother and Amber and William trailed after them.

"Amber and William spend their time wandering around the place, but they are always on time for their meals and get ready for bed at the right time. They sleep in their own beds now most of the time, although they move in together on occasion, presumably when one of them is disturbed at night," said the housemother.

"Are they still giving food away?" asked Liza.

"Yes, they are still doing that, but the other children have got used to it and they thank them, which is very thoughtful of them," said the housemother.

They then went to visit Anthony and Diana. Little Thomas insisted on seeing 'Maffew's' mother; he was growing fast and his speech was improving. They agreed that they would visit at the weekend and probably Rose would be with them.

Hector had said that the Langston's had nearly finished moving into their Dower House and he had already organised the architect to plan the necessary renovations. Builders and decorators were on hand ready to start within the week.

The following weeks passed quickly. Liza and Jamie had a few functions to attend, and as always, they were expected to make small speeches. Diana and Anthony spent some days with them, and Amelia remarked at how well and happy Diana now looked. Cricket matches took place each Sunday, often attended by Hector, the Major and Jennifer. Bella and her boys spent another weekend with them but this time the boys stayed in their own room.

The time was approaching for Wendell and Amelia to return to Belfast and Liza was not happy with that prospect, and neither was the Major as Jennifer was planning to return at the same time.

Then one day Joseph and Lily turned up on their doorstep with four young children in tow and from the looks on all their faces Liza knew that something terrible had happened. She ushered the children down to the kitchen so that they could have something to eat.

"What's happened Joseph?" she asked when she returned to the drawing room.

"The Home on the outskirts of Belfast has been burned to the ground," said Joseph starkly.

Jamie entered asking the same question.

"Oh my God," said Liza. "Has anyone been hurt?"

"I'm afraid the housemother and one of the older boys were killed, and several people received burns, although only one seriously. We've put the children in the other Home, but it's now grossly overcrowded. We brought the most vulnerable children with us. It appears that it has been done by the people who killed the lad who protected the two very young ones we sent over to you. These four were also being used by them, so we thought it best to bring them with us," said Joseph.

"Yes, you've done the right thing. I'll get a room ready for you," said Liza. "I'll take them out to the Ffoulks Home. We have plenty of people there to help with them."

"I'm coming with you Liza," said Jamie.

Wendell, Amelia and Grace arrived following an afternoon walk and after their initial surprise they asked what they could do to help.

"Jamie and I will take the children to the Major," said Liza.

"I'll come with you to help," said Grace and she left to tell her father what was happening, and he appeared a little while later to see if there was anything that he could do.

"Just be around to take care of everything in our absence. Hopefully we will not be back too late," said Liza.

Jamie was organising Davis to get the carriage ready and Liza asked Lily and Joseph to see the children and tell them that they were going to a lovely home where they would be safe.

"I would think that they trust you as you have already spent some time with them," said Liza. "I take it that they no longer have any belongings."

"No, just what they stand up in," said Joseph.

"Well," said Liza. "I'll get some blankets and it's only an hours' journey to the Home."

Liza went running up the stairs and into the schoolroom, much to Adam's surprise, although he knew that she did not normally interrupt lessons unless it was absolutely necessary.

She briefly told him what had happened and that she and Jamie had to leave with the children. The boys were concerned and expressed their sorrow at what had happened in Belfast.

"Thank you, boys," said Liza. "I know you'll be good whilst your father and I are away. We'll come in and see you when we get back; hopefully we won't be too late."

It wasn't long before they were making their way to the carriage and Joseph and Lily were helping the children into the seats. Liza, Jamie and Grace climbed in beside them and they were then on their way to the Ffoulks house.

The children looked rather frightened, but Grace and Liza soon put them at ease telling them that they were going to a very happy place where there were many children like themselves, and they would be well looked after there and have no reason to fear anything.

"I suppose we will now have to make a journey to Belfast," said Jamie.

"Yes, I'm afraid so. Wendell, Amelia and Jennifer were leaving in a few days, it would be best if we go back with them. I suppose Joseph and Lily will also leave then," said Liza. "We have an important function that we should be attending next week, but I'll ask the Major to cover that for us. He's more than capable of doing that and those attending will understand the reasons why. It may well boost the funds, which is the only good thing that could come out of this."

The Major was very surprised to see them when they drew up an hour later, and even more surprised to see that they had four extremely pretty young children with them, two of whom were very fair-haired identical twin girls. He sent for the housemother and she and Grace ushered them out of the room whilst giving instructions for baths to be made ready and clean clothes for them.

"It would appear that the Home in Belfast was burnt by the people who had William and Amber, and these four were also from them, the decision was therefore made to immediately bring them here," said Liza.

"I presume that the security here will be more than adequate," said Jamie. "Although we are not expecting that these people will follow the children, but we can't be too careful."

"I will have a word with those at the gatehouse and make sure that we are even more vigilant, although as you say it would be unlikely that they would find them here," said the Major. "Jennifer is at home at the moment, I'll let her know that Lily and Joseph are here; she'll probably want to visit tomorrow."

"We could call in on her on our way back," said Liza and then she went on to say that they would be travelling to Belfast in the next few days so she asked the Major to cover one or two of the important functions that were taking place the following week.

"Certainly Liza, although I doubt that the guests would be interested in a speech of mine; they look forward to one of your talks," said the Major. "I wonder if Jennifer will stay a little longer and be my guest at the functions."

"She may if she has nothing special to travel back for. Of course you could always invite Rose," smiled Liza with a twinkle in her eye.

Hector appeared saying that he had heard the news from Grace. "What are you going to do Liza?"

"Jamie and I will be travelling to Belfast in the next couple of days and we'll see if there is anything to salvage from the Home, but from what I have heard it has all been destroyed. The other Home is now overcrowded so we may have to bring a few more children back with us," said Liza.

They spent the next hour discussing how many more children they could accommodate without making the place difficult to administer and Liza asked how the Langston House was coming along.

"It will be a good few weeks before it will be ready to house any children," said Hector. "We could sort something out in an emergency, but it wouldn't be very comfortable."

When they were ready to leave, the four children had been bathed, dressed, and fed and were happily looking around the two rooms that they had been allocated next to William and Amber.

They called on Jennifer on the way home and she said that she would visit the next day to see Lily and Joseph. They were just in time to join everyone for dinner, but they firstly spent a little while with the boys as they had promised.

"You'll stay with us," said Amelia over dinner. "Your household will not be expecting you. It will be good to see Jennifer tomorrow. Is she still thinking of returning with us?"

312

"I haven't heard of any change of plans, although I think that the Major would like her to stay longer," said Jamie.

"They do seem to get on well together," said Wendell.

"He seems a very kind man and I know that my mother is very fond of him. If their relationship becomes serious, I will miss her very much, but she deserves a happy life. She had a difficult time with my father and as you know she had to bring me up with very little support from him," said Lily.

"She did a very good job with you Lily," smiled Joseph.

Wendell and Amelia were leaving in three days and much as the reason that Liza and Jamie were going with them was because of the fire, their leaving was not as difficult as it would have been.

Jennifer visited the next day and informed them that she would be staying a little while longer, especially as the Major had to represent Liza and Jamie at some important functions and he needed someone to escort. She also told them that the new children were saving food and handing it to those they thought were kind to them.

"That just shows us that they definitely came from the same place as Amber and William," said Liza. "I wonder if the lawyer and his wife in New York would contemplate taking on twin girls. If they are interested, it will only leave the boys that we have to worry about. I'll write to Myra and ask her opinion."

Liza also wrote to those who were organising the functions informing them that the Major and Mrs Jennifer Armstrong would be attending in their absence and also the reason why they had to leave urgently for Belfast.

Over the course of the following days there was a great deal of rushing around and organising for their trip to Belfast. Amelia was looking forward to returning as Edward and Nicole's baby was due in the next two weeks, and she was also happy that Liza would be accompanying them, even though it was for a disturbing reason.

David said that he would watch over the household in their absence; they thanked him and said that Adam and April would be in charge of the boys but they relied on him to look after Miranda and Lucinda as they knew that they would be concerned by the events in Belfast. Grace was aware of how to deal with any correspondence, and of course the rest of the household would carry on as if they were there. Roberts would have preferred to travel with them, but it was pointed out to him that they were not going to the Edgeworth house in Belfast, but would be staying with Wendell and Amelia and there were already adequate servants to attend to all their needs.

313

They were travelling from London docks so most of their journey was on board ship, which was much easier on Wendell and Amelia.

"We'll have to inspect what is left of the Home as soon as possible," said Wendell.

"From what Joseph says, there's very little to salvage. We'll have to get some costs for a complete rebuild and see if it's possible financially," said Liza. "We do have insurance on the premises; hopefully it will be enough; although it would be a good opportunity to make the Home purpose built."

By the time they arrived in Belfast the perpetrators of the crime had been arrested and court procedures were taking place. There were three men and one woman on trial. One was the organiser of the trade and the other two men had been identified as those who had beaten to death the lad who had helped William and Amber and they had also been seen setting light to the children's home. The woman prepared the children for use by men and also was accused of assaulting some children to the extent that they eventually died.

After Liza and Jamie had settled into Amelia's, they made their way around to the court to observe the proceedings. Wendell and Peter joined them. Some members of their staff were giving evidence and it was all rather damning. There were many people in the court and the feeling amongst them was of horror that not only were children being treated appallingly but that the place where many had found sanctuary had been burned with the children sleeping inside. The fact that the housemother and one of the children had died compounded the crime and that some of the children had been hurt. They were all found guilty of murder and the judge donned his black cap and passed a sentence of death on them all and that would take place within the week.

They quietly made their way back to Amelia's, all deep in thought. Death sentences on four people were difficult to comprehend but the four had been instrumental in killing untold numbers of people, including children in the past, so the sentence was a fair one.

Amelia knew that the perpetrators of the crime were going to die that week, but she said nothing and around the dinner table that night the mood was sombre but still it was not mentioned.

The next morning they went with Wendell, Peter and Brendan to see what was left of the Home and apart from a few walls there was nothing else. The gardens that had been so lovingly tendered were trampled and there was little sign of any animals apart from a few chickens. It had been such a happy place and Liza wondered whether it would ever be the same again as it was the scene of where people had died violently.

Brendan was adept at drawing up plans, so he was set to work designing some of the ideas that Liza and others had in mind to completely renovate the children's home. Meanwhile they were trying to establish which children they could take back with them to England.

***

The Major was making various notes for his speech at the functions that he would be attending for Liza and Jamie. Jennifer was attempting to help him.

"I wish I had Liza's ability to talk to the people without having to make notes," he said to Jennifer the evening before the first function.

"Perhaps you can Wilfred," said Jennifer. "I believe she treats them as if she knows them all and just starts talking to friends. You don't have to make a very long speech; you just have to let them know the facts and a brief outline of what the charity is about for those who have not attended before. You know all about it from the way it started to the unfortunate reason why Liza and Jamie are unable to be with them."

"You make it sound very simple Jennifer, but I don't have Liza's captivating powers," said the Major.

"I think you do to an extent," said Jennifer. "You have a very friendly and kindly face and that always makes people interested in what you have to say. Also your voice is very soothing."

The Major looked at Jennifer and smiled. "You certainly know how to make me feel important."

"You are important Wilfred," said Jennifer. "You know that Liza would not have asked you to take on such a role if it was not an important one that she knew you could handle well."

"I'm glad you'll be with me Jennifer. You give me confidence," said the Major.

"You were in command of many more soldiers than the number of people you will be meeting tomorrow Wilfred," said Jennifer.

"They had to do as they were told; I didn't have to persuade them to do anything," said the Major.

"No, but you had to inspire them to carry out their duties. You will do very well tomorrow Wilfred," said Jennifer.

It was at that moment that the Major realised that he didn't want a life without this woman, but he was nervous of telling her so. He wished that Liza was around to confide in. He closed his eyes and decided to concentrate on what he had to say at the function the following evening. Jennifer was watching him closely and wondered what he was thinking as his attitude had just changed.

"What's the matter Wilfred? Have I said something to upset you?" asked Jennifer.

"Oh no Jennifer, quite the opposite," said the Major. "I had just made up my mind to say nothing, but you are here and I may never again have the courage to say what I feel. Jennifer, I must tell you that I would like to spend the rest of my life with you and would ask you to marry me."

"Oh," said Jennifer. "I had a feeling that you were thinking along those lines."

"From that, I gather that you would not be interested. I'm sorry that I broached the subject. Can we just forget that I said anything," said a very disappointed sounding Major.

"I don't want to forget what you just said Wilfred," said Jennifer. "I think that we understand and get on very well together and it's a very long while since I have felt this comfortable with anyone, in fact I don't believe I ever have done so before. I would like to be married to you Wilfred, but I have a great deal to sort out before we can do that. I have my daughter to think of and possible grandchildren in the future. I presume you are offering me a home here, which will be a very big wrench for me as I have spent my whole life in Belfast."

Wilfred was smiling at her. "I'm just going to hear the words that you would like to be married to me; everything else can be talked about and solved in the fullness of time. Nothing is insurmountable to two people who want to be together. May I announce our engagement as soon as Jamie and Liza arrive back home?"

"I would like to write to Lily first after all she is my only family. I know she will be pleased for us," said Jennifer.

"If necessary, Jennifer, I will give all this up and move to Belfast with you because if you are happy then I will be also," said the Major.

"I think that what you are doing here is wonderful and I would like to help you in your work but as I say, I will have a great deal to sort out before I can come here permanently. It does not mean that we cannot be married; it just

316

means that there will be times when I will have to spend a while in Belfast," said Jennifer.

"I wish I could tell everyone at the function tomorrow, but it will mean nothing to them," said the Major.

"We could do what Jamie did with Liza when she finally agreed to marry him and she was announced by her name, but he added 'the future Lady Edgeworth'. He did it so casually that some hardly noticed it, but those in the know laughed and said that it was about time," said Jennifer smiling at the memory.

"So what you are saying is that we will be announced as Major Wilfred Styles and the future Mrs Styles, Mrs Jennifer Armstrong," said the Major. "Yes I like that idea. We are telling everyone gently."

"Yes, it's a very gentle way of letting people know," smiled Jennifer.

The Major was now sitting and grinning up at Jennifer. "It's a long time since I felt this happy Jennifer. Before I met Liza I was just sitting at home, reading my newspaper and having my meals served to me. I no longer had a family and I had no ambition and then one day Liza burst into my life and everything changed. If she had not appeared that day I would not be sitting here with you and making plans for our future. It is amazing how just one surprising event brought us together."

"I suppose I had better leave you to get on with your speech," said Jennifer.

"You won't disturb me Jennifer; in fact you give me inspiration," smiled the Major.

Whilst the Major put the finishing touches to his speech, Jennifer wrote to Lily informing her of her engagement to the Major.

The next evening the Major and Jennifer had feelings of excitement as they made their way to their first function. They were introduced to the hosts and the Duke of Berkshire and Bella were there as well as the Dowager Lady Redfern. Lord Carlton left who he was talking to and moved across to join them. Lady Redfern was smiling broadly. "It appears that we must congratulate you Major Styles; have you named the day yet?" she asked.

"Thank you, Lady Redfern. We have only recently made this decision and it will be just a little while before we tie the knot. We have a few details to sort out first," said the Major. The way that the Duke of Berkshire and his guests had greeted the Major and Jennifer put them both very much at ease and they were relieved to see that they were also placed on the top table with them.

At the end of the meal and before the piano recital, the host called the room to order and introduced the Major who stood and calmly looked around the room before starting his speech.

"I know that you were all looking forward to listening to Lord and Lady Edgeworth but sadly they were urgently needed in Belfast. Some of you may already know why this was the case but for those who do not I'm sorry to have to say that one of our Homes was burned to the ground by a set of disgruntled child traders. Unfortunately there has been a loss of life and several injuries. Some of the most vulnerable children have already been brought here to England and the others are now living in grossly overcrowded conditions in our other Belfast Home. Lord and Lady Edgeworth will be returning shortly with a number of children and we will accommodate them to the best of our ability at our Ffoulks house."

"We are in the process of renovating another property which will alleviate our situation but we are some weeks away from it being completed and we were originally organising the premises for the children who are coming to us from this country but of course we will help all children no matter where they are from."

He was asked by the host to give a brief outline of how the charity began and he was able to tell them of Liza's first encounter with abused children and how the word had obviously spread amongst them and she had found that they were making their way to her door in large numbers to be helped. Marchant & Fuller then decided to sponsor the charity but it had now become too big for them to fund solely.

He told the story of the tall American soldier and how he had become a legend but even though he had died some years before, he was still someone that the children aimed for, so that even in death he was doing a very needy job.

He quoted what Liza always said which was that with the new laws and severe sentences which hopefully would be imposed on the perpetrators of the disgusting trade, it was believed that eventually the Homes would only be needed to house orphans and that the trade in abused children would be totally wiped out.

The Major then felt that he should lighten the proceedings a little, so he decided to tell the guests about Amber and William. "These two youngsters came into our care when we opened Ffoulks house a few weeks ago. The little boy had no name and he clung onto the young girl and onto the first ever toy

318

that he had owned. We noticed that although they ate their meals, they always put food into their pockets, and we assumed that it was in case they needed it later. It was only the next day that we realised that food was mysteriously appearing in our pockets and that their motivation was to thank us for being kind to them. We are trying to curb their enthusiasm in this respect as we are able to deal with bread, maybe a cold potato, but we are finding it difficult when, soup, stew followed by rice or jelly are on the menu."

There was laughter around the room and the Major continued, "I tell you this story because even in children this young they know how to appreciate anyone who treats them well and shows them affection. We now have many children who are putting their pasts behind them and are learning how to eventually become normal members of society. Everyone here is helping them to achieve that goal and on behalf of our charity I thank you."

Many questions were asked of him and he was able to answer them all; he had been a wonderful ambassador for the charity. He and Jennifer enjoyed the recital and he felt very relieved that he had managed to successfully promote the charity.

Just as the Major and Jennifer were leaving, the Duke stopped them. "Ah Major, Lord Carlton and I have been talking. We have a few days with no commitments, and we thought that we would like to visit Belfast to see the scene of the fire and ask if there is anything we can do financially to help with the children. I have a house there that I rarely visit and I wonder whether it could be temporarily used to make the living arrangements for the children less overcrowded. I have to say that it is somewhere that I have been thinking of renovating, so it is somewhat old fashioned, but it is warm and waterproof and I could draw up an agreement for say a couple of years at no cost."

"Well, I can't answer for Liza or Mr Fuller, but your offer sounds very generous," said the Major.

"I know that there is an adequate hotel that we could stay at. I believe it is a Marchant & Fuller premises," said the Duke.

"I'm sure that if Liza knew you were contemplating visiting Belfast she would arrange rooms for you both at the Edgeworth house," said the Major.

"I know that she would Major;" said the Duke. "But she and Jamie have enough to contend with without worrying about us and we are quite capable of looking after ourselves. If, of course, there is no room at the inn then we may well have to throw ourselves on their mercy."

Lord Carlton joined them. "I presume that we would be able to get passage easily to Belfast," he said.

"Well, I'm not part of Marchant & Fuller, but I know that ships travel daily to Liverpool from London docks, and then on to Belfast. Would you like me to see if Liza's assistant can organise something for you?" asked the Major.

"No Major, we will make our own arrangements, you and all else in your organisation have plenty to deal with at the moment," said Lord Carlton.

In the carriage on their way home Jennifer commented that it would appear that both the Duke of Berkshire and Lord Carlton were taking over the charity.

"It may appear so Jennifer but I know that neither Liza nor Wendell would allow that to happen and really I believe that although their approach sounds dogmatic, it is through genuine concern and a wish to see the child abuse trade wiped off the face of the earth. They will do everything they can to assist in achieving that goal," said the Major.

***

Liza and Jamie were in the Marchant & Fuller offices with Brendan who was drawing up some of the ideas that had been put forward for a purpose-built children's home.

"In the meantime we will probably have to try to find somewhere that we can use to take the overflow that we are experiencing now. I could use my house, but really it is not set out to be comfortable for children as well as the necessary staff, but in the absence of anything else we will have to do that," said Liza reluctantly.

"You have always kept that house for yourself and guests such as the Major," said Jamie. "It is what James Marchant gave you to ensure your future. I know that it holds a special place in your heart. Eventually it could be for Matthew or John. I think we should look around for something else."

He moved over to the window and stared out thoughtfully, absentmindedly watching a ship's gangway being put in place. He came out of his daydream as he recognised a man organising a couple of travelling cases.

"Liza," called Jamie, "I may be wrong, but it looks like the Duke of Berkshire's valet is coming ashore."

Liza moved to the window and as she did so the Duke and Lord Carlton each shook hands with the captain and began to make their way down the gangway. The valet was attempting to organise a carriage but with little success.

"What on earth are they doing here? We had better go down and greet them," said Liza.

They called out for Peter to join them and they made their way to where the Duke and Lord Carlton were looking around and watching their valet trying to organise a ride for them to the hotel.

Jamie went ahead and Liza waited for Peter so that she could tell him who had arrived at the docks.

"I wonder what they want," said a mystified Peter.

"Well, we'll find out any minute," said Liza and by this time Jamie had reached the men and was ushering them towards the offices and at the same time calling for the valet to join them.

Liza and Peter appeared through the main door and they both greeted the Duke and Lord Carlton and Peter arranged for one of the hands to bring their luggage inside. They went into the office that Liza used which had originally been James'.

"We're very surprised to see you both," smiled Liza. "I presume you have a reason for being here but most importantly of all, have you a place to stay?"

"We did not wish to bother you as we know how busy you are at the moment, so we were going to your hotel in the hope that they could accommodate us," said Lord Carlton.

"They will be able to accommodate you; you can have our suite there. You'll be very comfortable. I'll just write a note for your valet to take to the hotel; he'll get your rooms as you like them. I'm afraid we are not staying at our own house otherwise you would have been welcome to stay with us," said Liza.

"We tried so very hard not to take up your time and we have failed miserably," smiled Lord Carlton.

"It's no trouble," smiled Liza as she wrote a note to the proprietor of the hotel. She beckoned the valet over and handed it to him and then called for one of the assistants to bring a buggy around and take the valet and the luggage to the hotel. With this done she turned and looked at Lord Carlton and then the Duke of Berkshire.

"I suppose you are wondering why we are here Liza," said the Duke and Liza and Jamie nodded. "We felt the need to see the damage done to the Home and to make you an offer which could alleviate your present overcrowded situation."

321

The Duke explained about his property which he was willing to let the charity use free of charge for the next couple of years. "It is a little old fashioned, but it is a sound property with no leaking roof or draughty windows. I am sure with the love and care that everyone bestows on the children, the rather dated surroundings will pale into insignificance."

"This could resolve a very serious problem for us. We are gathering the costs of rebuilding but once we have all that in hand it is going to take at least a couple of years to complete. Until we have those figures, we do not know the practicalities of being able to carry out what would really make the place wonderful for its purpose. We are already putting ideas together for such a building," said Liza.

They talked for a short while and the Duke and Lord Carlton expressed a desire to see the burnt-out premises the following day and also they wanted to visit the overcrowded Home. They asked how those injured were faring and said that they would like to attend the funerals the next day of the two people killed in the attack.

"You must join us for dinner this evening," said Peter. "My mother and father would not forgive us if we left you to dine alone at the hotel. She is already catering for the whole of our family this evening so I am sure two extra people will not faze her."

Liza smiled sweetly at Peter wondering how he could think that Amelia would not panic at having such guests for dinner at short notice. "Of course," said Liza. "We'll send a carriage for you at say seven o'clock."

She called for an assistant to bring the carriage and take the Duke and Lord Carlton to the hotel and when they had left, she turned to Peter and said, "Your mother is going to panic Peter. She is not going to see the Duke and Lord Carlton as just two extra people for dinner. I'll go and break the news to her and help her organise the seating arrangements and hopefully calm her down."

"I'll come with you Liza and make sure that Wendell isn't put under too much pressure," said Jamie.

Liza was right. Amelia went into a panic when she heard who she would be entertaining that evening. Liza took her hands and said that they would go down to the kitchen and check on how they were getting on with the food for the evening and if necessary add to what was being served and discuss with their butler the wine which should be served. The cook also had a slight look of panic on her face and Liza told her that she should not worry as her cooking expertise was legendary. They sat down and went through the menu in detail and Liza said that it was perfect.

"We'll go and reorganise the seating arrangements for the evening and help your housekeeper set the table," said Liza.

Jamie was in the library talking to Wendell and discussing the offer that the Duke had made whilst Liza continued to help with the seating arrangements. Wendell and Amelia would be either end of the table. Liza would be one side of Wendell and Jamie opposite on the other side. Lord Carlton would be next to Liza and the Duke next to Jamie. It would then be Nicole next to the Duke with Edward beside her and Lily next to Lord Carlton with Joseph beside her. Finally Peter and Brendan would be either side of Amelia.

"That's going to work out well Amelia, even though we have so few ladies," said Liza.

Amelia started panicking again.

"You have given untold successful dinner parties Amelia and you have also helped me entertain the highest in the land giving me the confidence to make it succeed. You entertain Jamie and me frequently and we have titles, there is no difference between us and the Duke and Lord Carlton, so please stop worrying, it is all going to run very smoothly, I promise you," said Liza. "Now what are you going to wear?"

They spent the next half hour in Amelia's room sorting out her dress for the night. She finally joined Jamie and Wendell in the library. "Have you calmed her down?" asked Wendell.

"Yes, it will all work out well. You know that they are very normal people and they blend in with any situation," said Liza.

"It's very generous of the Duke to offer his house. I suppose we had better go and look at it tomorrow. I hope that it will be suitable as the other Home is unhealthily crowded," said Wendell.

"We'll take half a dozen with us when we return sometime next week which will help a little," said Liza.

Liza and Jamie dressed early for dinner realising that Amelia would need all the support she could get to make the evening run smoothly. The table looked superb and the smell coming from the kitchen was mouth-watering. Wendell walked in looking very handsome and his features belied his age and Liza felt that she had been transported back in time to the early days of her marriage to James.

"You look confused," said Jamie to Liza.

"I just caught sight of Wendell and I had a feeling of déjà vu," said Liza.

"He's looking particularly well tonight. Obviously his time away from here has done him some good," said Jamie.

Amelia had sent word to both Edward and Joseph to arrive early and dutifully they did just that. Nicole and Lily were chatting excitedly as they came in. Lily had received a letter from her mother that afternoon and she gave everyone the news that her mother and the Major had become engaged. That delighted them all and Amelia said that she would write the next day with her congratulations.

"My mother says that they have one or two things to sort out before they can marry. I suppose one is what my mother will do with her house," said Lily.

"That can be sorted all in good time and shouldn't hold up any arrangements," said Wendell.

Peter and Brendan joined them just as they heard the carriage with the Duke and Lord Carlton draw up outside. Liza looked around and saw Amelia's concerned face and she smiled at her and put an arm around her. She whispered, "Just remember Amelia, they all make waste just the same as everyone else." Amelia laughed and her confidence came to the fore in time for her to greet her guests.

"This is very kind of you Mrs Fuller. We had no wish to impose ourselves upon you but your son said that you would never forgive him if he allowed us to dine in isolation at the hotel and we would not want to be responsible for creating a family rift," said Lord Carlton.

"He was right Lord Carlton. The hotel is very good, but there is nothing better than to dine with family and friends," said Amelia.

Liza smiled recognising that Amelia's confidence had returned. Wendell introduced his family and Brendan to the Duke and Lord Carlton. When he reached Lily and Joseph Lord Carlton said that he knew that Lily was Mrs Armstrong's daughter who he had met the other evening.

"Yes my mother is remaining in England for a short while. I heard from her today with the good news that she has become engaged to Major Styles who I know you have also met," said Lily.

"We had the impression that an engagement was imminent, and they seem admirably suited," said the Duke.

The dinner went well and Wendell and Amelia were superb hosts and the Duke and Lord Carlton were very relaxed and showed every sign of being well entertained.

"I understand that the people who perpetrated the crimes against the children have received the ultimate sentence," said the Duke. "It's good that they found them as I know that you would all have been worried that they would try to hurt the children and your staff again, not to mention that you all could be vulnerable. But this is too happy an evening to dwell on the darker side of life."

"I'm surprised that you haven't pleaded for clemency for them Liza," said Edward whose comment was met with silence from most of them around the table. Wendell raised his eyes to heaven as he so often did with Edward.

Jamie looked across at Liza with concern, but she smiled at him and all she said was, "I made that mistake once before and I'm not about to do it a second time."

"Of course Liza," said Edward. "I'm sorry, I shouldn't have mentioned it. I didn't think."

No you didn't, thought Wendell.

Liza skillfully changed the subject, but the awkward situation was not lost on the Duke or Lord Carlton. *I'll ask Wendell about that later,* thought the Duke.

The ladies withdrew leaving the men to their port and cigars.

"Liza looked a little upset a while ago," said the Duke. "She hides her feelings well but it would seem that talking about capital punishment disturbed her. She has a very kind heart."

"That was my fault," said Edward. "I always seem to say the wrong thing to Liza and I really never mean to hurt her."

"She had a very bad experience in the past and normally manages to put it behind her," said Jamie hoping that would be an end to that particular conversation, but of course Edward had different ideas.

"She pleaded for the life of a man who had seriously hurt her and killed her unborn child. They did commute his sentence to hard labour. He broke out of prison some years later and headed straight for Liza's family. He killed her husband and was going after her family and friends before finally killing her, however a friendly Indian managed to get to him but unfortunately not before her husband died in her arms," said a very informative Edward.

Once again Wendell's eyes turned towards heaven and other eyes turned towards Jamie who was looking ahead with a stony expression on his face.

"Well, that cannot have been easy," said the Duke and he changed the subject to describing where the house was that could be used to comfortably take many children, and Lord Carlton took his lead and nothing more was mentioned about the punishment that was to be handed out to the villains. Edward was totally oblivious to the awkward situation that he had created, but they knew him, and it was not unexpected.

In the drawing room Amelia put an arm around Liza's shoulders. "I'm sorry Liza, but Edward always manages to say something out of place."

Liza smiled at her. "I've said it before Amelia; it's what makes Edward who he is. He never goes out of his way to hurt anyone, and especially not me."

Lily was still excited about her mother's situation. "The Major is such a nice man; I'm so pleased for my mother. She deserves a happy life."

"I don't think she has been particularly unhappy in recent years, but you're right she does deserve a happy relationship. I do remember your father Lily; he was a nice man but when the demon drink got to him there was no judging what he would say or do. Your mother did well by you, she concentrated solely on you for many years and she saw that you were headed in the right direction, she has been a very good mother, she still is and in the fullness of time she will also be an excellent grandmother and the Major will be an excellent grandfather," said Amelia.

"Hopefully one of these days that will be the case, but in the meantime we have Nicole and Edward's little one to look forward to," said Lily.

"It's so wonderful that this family is so close. You all look after one another so well," said Liza.

"Well, you're one of us Liza," said Nicole. "You've been part of the Fuller family much longer than we have."

"Yes I have, I have been part of them for over twenty years and I love each and every one of them," said Liza.

"Even Edward when he embarrasses you?" asked Nicole.

"Especially then," laughed Liza.

The men then joined the ladies and Jamie came straight over to Liza and put his arm around her shoulder; she smiled up at him and just from that look Lord Carlton and the Duke could see that whatever had happened in the past had been dealt with and Liza and Jamie had a relationship which would never be broken.

Plans were made for the next day when Liza and Jamie would call at the hotel for the Duke and Lord Carlton. They thanked Wendell and Amelia for a delightful evening and bade farewell to everyone before climbing into the carriage to take them back to the hotel.

Having seen their guests off, Wendell returned and was about to give Edward a piece of his mind when he saw how tired Nicole looked and instead he kindly told them to get on their way home and for Nicole to put her feet up the following day. He smiled indulgently at her and told her how much he was looking forward to meeting his grandchild. "You're very lucky Nicole as I have had a great deal of practice overindulging Liza and Jamie's boys, so I know what grandchildren enjoy."

"Of course," said Brendan. "I forgot to congratulate you both on becoming official parents to all your boys. They must be very happy at the situation, especially young James as I know he has wanted to be your son for a very long while Liza."

"It has made them all very happy Brendan," said Jamie. "We had not realised how much they needed to establish a true identity."

***

In their carriage on the way back to their hotel the Duke and Lord Carlton were discussing how enjoyable the evening had been.

"I have a feeling that Edward Fuller quite often says the wrong thing," said Lord Carlton. "It was an awkward moment when he referred to Liza not instigating clemency for those murderers. Jamie looked somewhat upset and you could tell that Liza didn't want to discuss it. I believe we learned tonight what happened to the tall American soldier in the legend. We knew that he had died, but not how and the reason for it. That must have been very difficult for Liza to recover from."

"You know that Jamie has loved her for very many years, but it still took her a while to agree to marry him," said the Duke. "They do seem good for one another and Bella tells me that their boys are very happy. My two really enjoy their time with them. I have also realised that their tutor is a fine young man who doesn't hold back in his opinions where the best interests of the children are concerned, and that includes mine. He has made some very relevant suggestions regarding Nicholas and especially Richard who he believes is very bright."

"Peter Fuller is very dedicated to the business. He takes after his father," said Lord Carlton. "The other two are very adequate, but it's Peter who carries that company, especially since his father's slight stroke last year. I do also believe that Liza puts a great deal of time into the business even though she is in Surrey."

"Of course, I suppose James Marchant's shares went to her when he and his son died all those years ago," said the Duke.

"She has had more than her fair share of sorrow in her life, but it was good to see how close she and Jamie are now," said Lord Carlton. "She is so much better for him than that witch of a first wife that he had. She seems to have disappeared from the face of the earth since turning up at the function with that reprobate. She certainly has ruined her reputation; it will take some time before she will be able to show her face again on the social scene."

"Bella believes that Liza whisked her away and has placed her safely somewhere out of sight. Liza is very insistent that children do not have to bear the sins of the parents and both she and Jamie want to keep the Edgeworth name free of any scandal," said the Duke.

Lord Carlton laughed, "Do you know we are gossiping just like two old women. It was a very pleasant evening; I really enjoyed the company around that table. They may not all be blood relatives, but they certainly act like close family. Yes, it was a very good evening and I'm looking forward to seeing everything tomorrow."

They pulled up outside the hotel and thanked the driver before making their way up to the family suite where their valet was in attendance and he commented to them that he must make sure that he thanked Lady Edgeworth for her thoughtfulness over arranging an evening meal for him. Both Lord Carlton and the Duke nodded, realising that Liza would of course make sure that staff were well looked after.

***

Liza, Jamie and Wendell went to the hotel the next morning to collect the Duke and Lord Carlton. Amelia had been a little concerned that the day could be too much for Wendell's health but Liza and Jamie promised her that they would keep a close eye on him and bring him home immediately if they thought that he was becoming too tired.

They firstly visited the scene of the fire and the Duke and Lord Carlton were shocked to see the devastation that had occurred.

"I can only think that it is a miracle that only two people died. How did they manage to get all the children away?" said the Duke.

"The housemother, the lad who died and the boy who is being treated for burns were the ones who achieved that, as well as some of the other staff and most of them sustained minor burns. They will appreciate your visit," said Liza.

They went next to the Home that was at one time Jamie's family house and as they entered mattresses were being removed from the floors of various rooms which would normally have been used as recreation areas.

Many of the children were in the schoolroom and two teachers were attempting to instruct older children as well as younger ones. The separate schoolroom had been turned into a dormitory. Some of the older children were feeding the animals and others were trying to tidy some of the overcrowded areas. The injured boy was sitting on his bed swathed in bandages, he had been treated at the local hospital, but he wanted to move back with his friends, and he was feeling much better. Some other children also had bandages, but they were not injured seriously and were carrying on as if nothing had happened.

Several of the members of staff were in the kitchen helping to organise two sittings for the meals and the laundry room was working at full capacity.

The housemother came to Liza, "We're running out of clothes and linen. Can we get more from somewhere?" she asked.

"Give me a list of what you desperately need and I'll see what I can do," said Liza. "I already have linen and clothes on order, but you know that we have already taken what they had in stock, but I'll have a word with them."

"Is there anything we can do to help?" asked Lord Carlton.

"I wish there was, but we need bedclothes and children's clothes which I have organised but have yet to receive," said Liza. "The local churches have been very good, as have many of the local people, although I am reluctant to put the children in worn clothing, but we have to do what's necessary."

They called into Amelia's for lunch and by that time Amelia was quite relaxed in their company. Peter and Brendan were going to join them that afternoon to inspect the property owned by the Duke.

"You'll join us again for dinner tonight I hope," Amelia asked the Duke and Lord Carlton. "It will just be you and six of us tonight. My two other sons and their wives will not be joining us this evening; it will just be an informal affair."

"If you are sure it will be no bother, then we would be delighted," said the Duke.

"It will be no trouble at all, and you can tell me how you all got on today," said Amelia.

They then made their way to the Duke's property which was quite large and had an impressive driveway. It also had a gatehouse which it was thought would be quite useful for security reasons. Brendan and Peter had already arrived and were talking to the housekeeper.

It took them some time to look around and although it would not have been a first choice for them to house children, it could be adapted. Some of the rooms were dark and Liza suggested that they did the same as with the Ffoulks house which was to put very light screens in place which would make the rooms less oppressive. It would be a case of making the premises as child friendly as possible and Liza was sure that it could be done even though they would have to make adjustments to the way that they normally operated with the children.

Peter was agreeing with Liza and Brendan was making quick sketches of how they could make the property comfortable. They walked into the laundry room and Liza's eyes lit up.

"Will you need all that bed linen?" asked a very innocent looking Liza.

The Duke laughed, "I'm sure my housekeeper was going to pack it up and send it to my house in England, but I have seen that you are in great need so I'll make sure that they reach you by tomorrow."

"Thank you," smiled Liza. "Also I believe that we will have to have another oven fitted into the kitchen and another sink put in place. Would you have any objections to that?"

"No you may adapt what is necessary; also apart from the two large beds in the main bedrooms, all the other beds are yours to use as well as the furniture, except of course the large family table which is an antique and I will have moved to some storage place which I have yet to establish," said the Duke.

"We have spare warehouses at the docks which we would happily let you use for the duration," said Wendell. "They are very secure. You could put whatever you wish to keep there."

"Well, that solves my only problem," said the Duke. "If you are quite happy with the premises, I will see my lawyer later and have a lease drawn up ready for signature by tomorrow. I'll also organise the removal of all that I wish to keep, and I would say that you could have vacant possession the day after tomorrow."

"You are so very kind," said Liza. "Would you have any objection to a few animals being kept in the grounds? The children like to look after them and they also like to grow fruit and vegetables."

"Liza, you can see that this place needs to be renovated, so whatever you want to do here doesn't matter. Just make it so that the children will be well looked after and happy," said the Duke and he went with the housekeeper to list the items that he wanted placed in storage.

They all looked around the house again and made notes of how it could be arranged. Lord Carlton already knew the property and he undertook to explain the many rooms to them.

Peter and Brendan were about to leave and Wendell decided to go with them. He had enjoyed looking around, but he was feeling a little tired and wanted to rest before dinner. Liza looked at him with concern and he smiled at her.

"I am perfectly alright Liza, I'm a little weary that's all. I'm looking forward to another dinner with our guests and I want to be at my best for the evening," he said.

"Of course Wendell; we'll see you later," said Liza. "Shall we take some of the bed linen to the Home on our way back?"

Liza's question was really an instruction and Lord Carlton smiled at her way of getting people to carry out her wishes. He nodded and went with them to the laundry room and carried as much as he could out to their carriage. The Duke appeared again with his housekeeper who seemed to be a kindly woman.

"I've been talking to Mrs Mulligan and she has offered to help with settling the children in and perhaps working with them over the next two years. She knows the place well and would be able to advise on many of the ideas that you may have," said the Duke.

"Thank you, perhaps you could let her know that I will contact her in the next day or so and see what arrangements would be suitable," said Liza who never liked to have workers foisted upon her, especially where children were concerned. She had been quite impressed by Mrs Mulligan, but she wanted to get to know her better.

They stopped at the hotel to drop off the Duke and Lord Carlton who had made arrangements for a lawyer to call to draw up the lease. They then went on to the Home and delivered some of the bed linen, much to the delight of the staff. It was not enough but it helped.

The Duke brought the lease with him that evening and Liza and Wendell would sign it the next day in their offices with their lawyer.

"It seems that you have had a successful day today," said Amelia. "It is wonderful that you will at least be able to deal with the overcrowding situation for the time being. I know that it has been a worry to us all and Liza tells me that there will also be some beds and furniture that can be used. It is a kindness that will not be forgotten."

"Well Mrs Fuller, until a year or so ago I had no idea that the trade in children was so prevalent but once I realised the full extent of the problem I could not in all conscience ignore the situation and you must realise that many people that I know felt the same way. It is sad that those who perpetrate these crimes against the youngsters feel that they have a right to take matters into their own hands and destroy all the good work that has been done in that respect and that extends to the taking of life," said the Duke.

"Prince Albert was very upset to hear what had happened over here and of course it will follow that the Queen will be aware of the difficulties. They both do keep a close eye on what is happening with your charity. The Queen is particularly upset that such a charity is necessary," said Lord Carlton.

"As we have said before," said Jamie. "We hope that one day our charity will be solely for providing for orphans. Unfortunately we feel that it could be a long way off."

"I see that you are soon to become grandparents," said the Duke to Wendell and Amelia. "I suppose you are looking forward to that event."

"We are very much," said Amelia. "Although it will be our first grandchild, both Wendell and I have been grandparents to Liza's and Jamie's boys for many years and they have kept us on our toes. They are just as much family as any of the Fullers."

"Yes, we can see that. It is a family gathering around this table which makes for a very relaxed atmosphere and we feel privileged to have been included," said Lord Carlton.

There was a knock on the door and the Butler entered with a note for Liza. She frowned as she took it as she didn't recognise the writing. She excused herself from the table and left the room as she felt that the note was not going to be good news. Jamie also excused himself and joined her in the library as she was staring at the letter.

"I have a bad feeling about this Jamie," she said.

"Yes, so do I," he replied.

"It's from the warden at the prison," said Liza who still had not opened the letter. "I don't want to get involved with what is going to happen to those villains. They have been tried and rightfully sentenced for their despicable crimes; I don't want to have anything to do with them."

"Aren't you going to open it?" asked Jamie.

"Perhaps I'll hold onto it until after the executions," said Liza.

Jamie put his arms around her and said, "I know you won't do that Liza. I know that somebody thinks that you can help them, and you'll never brush that aside no matter what they may have done."

"It's bringing back too many unhappy memories and I don't know these people and they don't know me, so why should they contact me?" said Liza.

"You said that it's from the warden, perhaps it's not from them at all," said Jamie.

"I don't think that there's much chance of that," said Liza. She smiled up at Jamie and then unsealed the note and read it slowly.

"It's to do with the woman; she's asking to see me. She can't write so the warden has done it on her behalf," said Liza. "There is nothing I can do to help her. We must go back to our guests."

Everyone looked up as they entered the dining room. Wendell and Amelia looked concerned whilst Brendan and Peter kept the Duke and Lord Carlton occupied with various questions.

"Not bad news, I hope," whispered Wendell.

"No," said Liza. "I'll tell you when our guests have left."

The Duke and Lord Carlton were leaving the next afternoon and arrangements were made to meet them at the offices in the morning when the lease could be signed by Liza and Wendell. They bade everyone goodnight and thanked Amelia once again for arranging such a perfect evening.

When they had gone Peter rounded on Liza and said, "Your letter was from one of the criminals, wasn't it? I believe that it was not lost on our guests that whatever you had received had disturbed you considerably. We are your family Liza and what concerns you also concerns us. We can also see that Jamie is worried for you."

"Peter, Liza will tell us what she wants us to know, so stop bullying her," said Wendell.

Liza explained that she had received a request from the prison warden for her to visit the woman. "I don't want to do it, but I know that I will forever feel guilty if I do not."

"You have no reason to visit her Liza. It won't do any good and it will only do harm to you," said Amelia.

"I doubt that it will harm me Amelia, but I have no influence over the sentences that were given to them, so I don't know why she wants to see me," said Liza.

"If you do decide to go then naturally I shall be with you," said Jamie.

"When are the sentences to be carried out?" asked Brendan.

"The day after tomorrow," said Liza.

"So you only have tomorrow to see her, if that is what you want to do," said Brendan.

"You must remember Liza that these people not only killed two of our people, they were quite willing to see all the children and staff killed that night. They also have been responsible for hurting and killing countless others. This woman cannot expect any clemency; they gave none to their victims," said Peter.

"You're trying to bully Liza again Peter," said Wendell. "She will make the right decision when the time comes."

"I'm just concerned for her, Father. These people are putting the responsibility of life or death on her shoulders and it is totally unfair of them to do that. Liza has no power to alter the outcome, all it will do is upset her because facing somebody who is about to die is not an easy task, so it is best not to put herself in that position," said Peter.

Liza smiled at Peter, "I understand what you are saying, and I truly appreciate your concern. I will think carefully on everything you have said. I have a busy day tomorrow and in the morning we must sign the lease for the Duke's house and get what is necessary to make it habitable as soon as possible. With any luck some of the children and staff can move in there after the weekend."

Jamie also smiled at Peter's brotherly attitude towards Liza and he knew that Peter realised that Liza had managed to change the subject and he was letting her get away with it.

"Yes, we must all be up early tomorrow," said Wendell which was the sign for them all to go to their rooms and leave the awkward situation alone until the next day.

When they were alone in their room Jamie said that his opinion was that it would be better if she did not get involved with the woman, but he knew that she was being asked for help and it would be difficult to refuse.

"Whatever you decide Liza, I will back you one hundred percent and you know that I will be with you if you do go to the prison," said Jamie. "It always annoys me that you are the one who gets the nasty jobs. Me, or any one of the Fullers could deal with this situation, but everyone wants you."

"It is worrying, but I suppose I was the one who was known for helping those to reach safety," said Liza.

"You're being very thoughtful of me Liza," said Jamie, "I am sure that it's because you were the wife of the tall American soldier who has become the legend for those who want a better life. It doesn't hurt me; I do understand the reasoning behind it."

"I think I'll go to the prison after we have signed the lease and seen the Duke and Lord Carlton onto their ship," said Liza. "You are all right, my conscience won't let me just leave somebody to die without a few words of comfort. Not that she really deserves sympathy but knowing that you are going to your death must be horrendous."

Jamie kissed her on the cheek. "I thought you would do that."

***

Everyone was up early the next morning, even Amelia who normally preferred to breakfast in bed. Peter and Brendan would be leaving together for the office and Wendell was already dressed ready to accompany Liza and Jamie to meet the Duke and Lord Carlton also at the office. Amelia was toying with her breakfast as were Liza and Jamie.

"You've made up your mind to go and see that woman, haven't you Liza?" said Peter. "I think that it is a grave mistake. I would have thought that you could have dissuaded her from this action Jamie."

"Jamie also thinks the way you do Peter," said Liza. "It struck me that someone who knows they will be dead tomorrow must be going through absolute hell and if I can ease that fear a little then that is what I must do, no matter what they have done."

"She's just using you Liza," said Peter. "She will try to persuade you to get the death penalty commuted. Never forget what happened last time you did that."

"Peter, you and I have never had reason to argue before but this is one time when I do not need you to tell me what happened in the past, I am very well aware of it," said Liza angrily.

"Both of you calm down," said Wendell. "You both must agree to disagree and I don't think that Liza has the power to get the sentence lowered, so it will all be a waste of time, but if Liza is prepared to waste her time then that is her decision."

Amelia was shedding a tear at the table, "I've never known you two argue before. You have always been the closest of friends. You have been more brother and sister than most brothers and sisters. I don't like to hear you arguing; it really upsets me."

"Please don't be upset Amelia, Peter and I think the world of one another, and I know that he is only trying to save me grief. I have always appreciated his concern for me; he is my brother and I love him dearly," said Liza.

"You know that I will look after her and shield her from as much unpleasantness as possible," said Jamie. "But I know that this is something that she feels she must do."

"Hmmm," said Peter and then he turned to Brendan and told him that they had better make their way to the office.

A short while later Wendell, Liza and Jamie climbed into their carriage and drove to the office where the Duke, Lord Carlton and the company lawyer were waiting for them.

With the documents signed, the Duke and Lord Carlton made their way from the offices and towards their ship. The Duke looked down on Liza as they walked along the dockside. "You are going to see the prisoners aren't you Liza?"

Liza frowned up at him, "How did you know that? Am I such an open book?"

"Yes, you are on occasion," he answered.

"That's unfortunate. No wonder I'm unable to keep a secret," she smiled at him.

"Be careful Liza; I am aware of your past experience when pleading for clemency. I would hate to see you hurt because you are putting others before yourself, but it is none of my business and I'm sure you will act in a responsible way. It is a very difficult task to visit those whose life is about to be cut short no matter what the reason. Take care Liza and we will see you when you are back in Surrey," said the Duke.

He and Lord Carlton climbed aboard their ship. The Duke sighed as he looked back at Liza, Jamie and Wendell waiting on the docks. "She's one very lovely and thoughtful lady; Jamie is a very lucky man. I wouldn't mind taking his place."

"She looks at nobody but Jamie and that must have disappointed you," smiled Lord Carlton knowing that the Duke liked the ladies and that Bella had her own agenda.

Chapter 17

Wendell decided to stay and carry out some work with Peter whilst Liza and Jamie called on the local builder to organise various alterations at the Duke's house. When they had finished, they climbed aboard their carriage and reluctantly made their way to the prison.

"Do you know what this woman wants to see me about?" Liza asked the warden when they had been ushered into his office.

"I don't know what she thinks you can do for her," said the warden. "Are you ready to see her now?"

Liza and Jamie nodded, and the warden sent for the woman. She came in with a woman warden on one side and a man on the other.

"I knew you'd come," she said to Liza and Liza frowned at her. A memory was stirring; she had seen her before. When she was in the court she was covered in dirt, now she had been cleaned up and looked quite respectable.

"Oh, you don't remember me," she said disappointedly.

"Refresh my memory," said Liza harshly.

"You interviewed me for a job looking after your children," said the woman.

"I interviewed three people for that job, all of whom were from our children's home. That was five years ago," said Liza.

"Yes, my friend April got the job," said the woman. "I carried on learning how to cook and keep house from your housekeeper Mrs Edwards."

"Did you not find suitable employment after that?" asked Liza.

"Yes I was a chamber maid for a while, but I was grabbed when I was out shopping one day and ended up back where I had begun," said the woman.

"What's your name," asked Liza.

"They called me Treasure, but my real name is Theresa," said the woman.

"How do you know the girl April?" asked Liza referring to April as if she no longer knew her.

"We were together in a house and we managed to get some young ones out and to the tall American soldier's home. We were very frightened, but we

338

knew where he lived because another girl, Ellen, had pointed it out to us. She managed to leave with twins that had just been brought in. I don't know if she got to safety, but we hoped that she had. We didn't see her or the twins again," said Theresa.

Liza was watching her intently. "You helped to hurt children where you were living. You got them ready to be used and abused by those who should know better. Some of those children died. You were aware of what those men were going to do to our children's home and you helped them; you knew that they were determined to take the lives of as many as possible and you did nothing to stop them. You could have gone to the authorities and that would have saved lives, but you decided to align yourself with them."

"I helped to get the twin girls and two boys to safety; I kept everyone occupied while they were taken out of the house to safety. I knew what was going to happen to them and I couldn't bear the thought of how they were going to be used. I did my best," said Theresa.

"Why didn't you tell that to the court?" asked Liza.

"I was told to keep my mouth shut," said Theresa.

"Surely you must have realised that it was stupid to do that," said Jamie sharply.

"They said that if I said nothing then I couldn't be convicted of anything," said Theresa. "Yes it was stupid and tomorrow I am going to die for murders which I haven't committed."

"You stood by and watched children being abused and killed, that's the same as murder," said Jamie.

"What is it that you think we can do for you?" asked Liza.

"I don't want to die. I have killed nobody. I know that there were times when I had to do things that were wrong, but I was frightened for my life and I lived that way for many years. You help many people who have done what I have done; it isn't a life that I wanted, and I did try to get away from it. I wanted what April had and that was a proper job and nobody to hurt me," Theresa was now crying bitterly.

"I think we've heard enough," said the warden. "Take her back to her cell."

Theresa was still crying and begging for help. She suddenly stopped, realising that she had done everything she could. She turned as they were taking her from the room and asked how the other three children were.

"Wait," called Liza. "What other three children?"

"There were three hidden in the house when we were taken," said Theresa.

"We'll have to get there and find them. How old are they?" asked Liza.

Theresa shook her head and gave an estimation of their ages as four, six and seven. She said that they were two girls and a boy. Liza closed her eyes imagining how frightened these children must be.

"Thank you for telling us, we'll try to find them, and I'll see if there is anything I can do for you," said Liza.

Theresa was taken back to her cell and Liza and Jamie thanked the warden for allowing them to see her.

"Is there any possibility that her sentence could be lessened?" asked Liza.

"Only the judge who passed sentence could do that and the only alternative would be transportation and that is not an easy journey. Many don't survive it," said the warden.

As they left, Jamie said that he would go to the offices and get some help to find the three children. Liza was going to the court to find the judge who had passed sentence on Theresa.

"Having heard what she has said, I know that she probably isn't deserving of a death sentence, but please don't blame yourself if you can do nothing to help," said Jamie. "My priority must be those children. I'll see you back at the offices later."

Liza was dropped off at the court and she was quickly ushered into the judge's chambers. He was preparing for the afternoon session, but he had met Liza before and was pleased to welcome her.

"I've come on a mercy mission, my Lord," said Liza. "I have no difficulty with the sentences you have imposed on those despicable men who have not only used and abused children, but also killed without a second thought. I am concerned about the woman. She is someone who I met some five years ago and interviewed for a job looking after my children. She had managed to get away from her difficult life and had in fact helped others get to safety. She was lucky enough to find domestic work but unfortunately was taken captive once again by those men."

"She said nothing in her defence when she was in court," said the judge.

"I know and I asked her about that and she said that she was told to say nothing as then nothing could be proved against her," said Liza.

"That sounds rather a silly excuse," said the judge.

"She has not had the advantage of education. I do know for a fact that five years ago she did help save several children and I also know that there are two girls and two boys who are now safely in our care because of her efforts," said Liza.

"You did not come forward to defend her Lady Edgeworth, why was that?" asked the judge.

"I was only a very short while in the court and I did not recognise her. I also was concentrating on the two men who I know killed a young lad who saved another two children," said Liza.

"What are you asking of me Lady Edgeworth? She has done some despicable things against children in her time and I am surprised that you are seeking some form of clemency for her," said the judge.

"I know that she is not a murderess and I know that she helped to groom children to be abused, but where possible, when she was not in fear of her own life, she helped to remove those who were vulnerable. She has also just informed us that there are three children still hidden in their premises and my husband is at this moment trying to find them," said Liza.

"She could have told us this before," said the judge.

"It would appear that she thought that they were now in our care," said Liza.

"There are many crimes that this woman has committed, and her punishment should fit her crimes. However you are saying that out of all her misdemeanours, murder was not one of them. She knew that murders took place but did nothing to inform the authorities," said the judge.

"I think that I find her case so difficult because the two girls who managed to get away from that life at around the same time that she first made her bid for freedom, are now beautifully settled, one happily married and the other working in medicine. If this woman had been able to stay away from those men she would have been as happy as her friends are now," said Liza. "Unfortunately we cannot keep a watch on those who pass through our system, we always have to assume that they have made their own decisions and sometimes that just isn't the case."

"So what you are saying is that given the same chance as the other girls this one would have probably been a useful member of society," said the judge. "I am leaning towards considering altering her sentence, but I cannot pardon her. She has committed serious crimes although I can see that fear had a great deal to do with it. But there had to be occasions when she could have reported what was happening to the authorities. I hate to think how many children's lives must be on her conscience."

341

"Well, I have said what I came here to say and know that the final decision is yours alone," said Liza. "Thank you for your time."

She was escorted to the front of the building and was surprised to see Jamie and Edward climbing the steps towards her.

"The three children will be in court this afternoon; they were caught stealing food from the bakers and the grocers. They'll probably be sent to some awful children's prison, if there is such a place," said Jamie.

Liza turned and they all went into the courthouse. Edward was asking which court the children were likely to be in and he was directed towards one of the smaller ones. The judge that Liza had just seen asked what was happening and when told said that there was a great deal of theft by children going on and it had to be stopped.

Liza, Jamie and Edward found seats in the appropriate courtroom; they looked at the dock and could see two small faces peering over the top of the wooden balustrade. Liza wondered where the third child was.

The magistrate was listening to the charges against the children. "I thought there were meant to be three in the dock," he said.

"Yes there are three Sir," was the response from the usher.

"I can only see two, where's the third?" he asked.

"She's next to them," said the usher.

Liza whispered to Jamie that the court proceedings were developing into a farce.

"Is she sitting down?" asked the magistrate.

"No Sir, she's too short to see over the railings," said the usher.

"Oh, well give her something to stand on," said the magistrate. "I can't conduct a case against someone that I can't see."

Liza, Jamie and Edward were staring at the magistrate in disbelief. Several people were in the court and amongst them there appeared to be the baker and the grocer.

There was a scraping noise in the dock and a very small curly head appeared over the balustrade. All three children had very dirty faces and scared looks in their eyes.

The children were asked their names, but they appeared not to know them. The magistrate was getting a little frustrated.

"Surely you know your names," he shouted at them and they all shook their heads.

342

"Oh for pity's sake," said Liza loudly drawing the attention of everyone in the court. "Can't you see that they are traumatised? They have been used, abused, and left caged and unable to fend for themselves. It's just by luck that they managed to escape and find food. And I'm sorry that the baker and grocer were robbed but the alternative would have been the deaths of these three little ones."

"Who might you be?" asked the disgruntled magistrate.

"I'm Lady Liza Edgeworth and I and my colleagues take in children such as these. They need understanding not being frightened by people such as you. Don't you think they have been scared enough already, but at least the ones who have already harmed them will be feeling the full force of the law tomorrow. These little ones are victims not criminals," said Liza.

"Are you suggesting that we set these three robbers free; what sort of example is that going to be to others?" said the magistrate.

"They are not robbers Sir; they were just hungry, and they saw food and needed it. I would hope that the baker and grocer will be withdrawing all charges and that you will release these children into my care. After all we were told about them this morning and we went to find them to take them to safety when we learned that they were here and facing ridiculous charges. If the baker and grocer want recompense then I will undertake that," said Liza.

"Thank you, your Ladyship," mumbled both the baker and the grocer.

"We'll take the children into our care," said Jamie and he told them not to be frightened as they were going to a happy and comfortable place.

"I haven't said they could go," said the magistrate.

"Haven't you?" asked Jamie. "There is no case to answer now that the baker and grocer are satisfied."

"Who are you Sir?" asked the magistrate.

"I'm Lord Jamie Edgeworth," said Jamie imperiously.

"Oh," said the magistrate, "and I know that you are Mr Edward Fuller. I do not appreciate having my proceedings disrupted, no matter how well intentioned. Go on, take them; get them out of my sight before I change my mind."

Jamie paid the baker and the grocer whilst Liza and Edward ushered the children out of the courtroom. Jamie caught up with them as they made their way down the steps. Liza's name was being called by a court employee. She stopped and the man asked her to go back to the judge for just a moment.

"I won't be long," she said to Jamie and Edward and she returned to the judge's chambers.

"Lady Edgeworth," said the judge. "I hear you have disrupted the case in the magistrate's court. I presume that the three children there were the ones you were looking for."

Liza nodded her assent, "They are safely in our care now."

"I've been thinking about what you said earlier, and I have decided to show some clemency towards the woman. I have sent word to the prison warden that she is to be spared the noose but will be transported to the other side of the world as soon as is practical. Whether that is clemency or not is debatable. I hope that she survives the journey and eventually makes a good life for herself. It will be a hard life but she's young and strong and I believe that she knows how to look after herself," said the judge.

"At least it's a chance at life not death. I think that she was under no illusions what clemency would mean. I want to thank you judge, I think you appreciate that there are paths that are imposed upon us which alter the whole way our lives map out," said Liza.

Liza then joined the others in the carriage with the children and they went directly to the Home which, although already overcrowded, would make room for the three frightened children.

They made their way wearily back to Amelia's where Wendell was reading his newspaper in his library. He called out to them.

"So you managed to create havoc in the magistrate's court," he said with a smile. "Are the three lost children now safe?"

"Yes, they are being cleaned and fed in the Home," said Liza. "They are so small; they were very frightened. One of them couldn't see over the dock. Anyway they are safe now."

"I also hear that you twisted the judge's arm over the woman prisoner. So she will now be transported," said Wendell.

"Yes, but whether that is more lenient I don't know," said Liza.

"You have saved her life Liza, and transportation has to be more lenient than death. She could eventually do very well there. The main problem will be the journey. It will be long and uncomfortable," said Wendell. "You did your best Liza. She will be grateful for that."

"I had the choice of employing her or April all those years ago. I know I made the right choice, but it could have been otherwise, and she would now have been as happy as April. It is all the luck of the draw, isn't it?" said Liza.

"We realise why you took special interest in this woman," said Edward. "At least she will be far enough away not to come back and haunt you."

Wendell looked at his son in desperation. "You always manage to say the wrong thing don't you Edward?"

Edward frowned not realising what his father meant. Liza smiled at him and said, "Don't worry Edward; you will never upset me, and I know you only ever try to be helpful." She stretched up and kissed him on the cheek before she left to rest before dinner. Jamie followed her out of the library, also smiling at Edward, who was still looking puzzled. No doubt his father would enlighten him.

Dinner was a very quiet affair that evening. Much as a great deal had been achieved that day, they were all aware that executions were to take place early the following morning and although they all knew that they were the correct sentences, it still put a cloud over the evening.

***

In the early hours of the morning noises could be heard in the front hallway and Edward's voice was loudly asking for both his mother and Liza.

"Edward, what are you doing here? Is it Nicole?" asked Amelia.

"Yes, she started having the baby and she wants you both there," said a panicking Edward.

"We'll be ready shortly, Edward," said Liza and then to Amelia. "It's probably Edward who really wants us there."

Amelia called down to Edward, "Surely you haven't left her alone."

"No Annalise is with her and I've also sent for the doctor," said Edward.

"Is Edward panicking?" asked Jamie.

"It would appear so, but that's only to be expected," said Liza.

"No doubt I'll see you sometime tomorrow," smiled Jamie. "I'll spend some time with Brendan and help get the new premises ready for next week."

"Thank you, Jamie, it's just a case of doing our best to relieve the pressure on the other Home. We need to know how many beds would be useful and tables and chairs for the dining area. At the moment we might have to go to a second-hand shop for those. But we must make do and mend under the circumstances," said Liza.

"We'll get together whatever we can, and I'll see you later," said Jamie. "I hope all goes well with Nicole; I'm sure it will; she's young and healthy."

They climbed into the carriage with Edward and made their way to his home and when they arrived everything was very calm. Annalise greeted them and said that Nicole was doing very well but she was sure that she would be pleased to see them.

"We were under the impression that she had asked for us," said a smiling Amelia.

"We know that it was Edward who assumed that she wanted us here and we know that he wanted us here," said Liza. "But we won't get in the way. I would like to see her though."

Edward was in the bedroom when they arrived to see Nicole. He was clasping her hand tightly and looking very worried.

"This is earlier than it should be," he said.

"Only by a few days Edward, which is nothing," said Liza. "How are you Nicole? We promise that we won't get in the way."

"I'm pleased that you're both here. I hope that I won't keep you hanging around for too long," said Nicole.

"Take as long as you need Nicole, we're here for you," said Liza.

The doctor arrived and said that he would be back later as Nicole still had a long way to go.

"Shouldn't the doctor stay with her?" asked a worried Edward.

"It's going to take a little while Edward, do you want to go to the office for a time?" asked Amelia.

Edward looked shocked. "Don't worry Edward, I'll keep you company for a while," smiled Liza.

"Thank you, Liza, I'd like that," said Edward and they went into the sitting room and Liza arranged for tea to be brought in.

"Calm down Edward, childbirth can take some time; it's perfectly normal," said Liza.

"You shouldn't be here Liza, it must bring back some unhappy memories for you," said Edward.

"And some very happy ones. I have my Matthew, and I had five wonderful months with little Meg. I have John and James. I'm surrounded by my family; I have no true sadness's regarding my children," said Liza.

"Do you think that Nicole will be alright? You had some very bad times having children," said Edward.

"I had been attacked and seriously damaged because of that Edward; that is the only reason why I had difficulties. Nicole has had no such problems; she will come through this with flying colours; it's just that it will take a little while," said Liza.

"You're right Liza," said Edward. "Just think, in a while I shall be the father of either a boy or girl, and I don't care which. Nicole has made me so very happy; she has taken away all my sadness of the past, in fact it's as if the past never happened."

The clock struck eight o'clock and Liza went silent. Edward watched her closely; he was well aware of what was happening at that moment at the prison.

"They deserve it Liza," said Edward. "They have killed, maimed and hurt so many people and they would have continued in their evil trade. I suppose that we must be thankful that they got caught after torching the Home because otherwise they would still be procuring children for abuse. I'm glad you managed to help the woman; she was not a killer, but she didn't attempt to stop them."

They sat quietly for a while and then Edward said, "It's all over now Liza. They are gone and will never hurt another child."

Liza kept Edward company for a couple of hours and Amelia came to relieve her.

"What's happening Mother," asked Edward.

"Everything's going very nicely Edward; I think you will be a father within the next two to three hours," said Amelia.

"That's a very long time," said a worried Edward.

"It isn't Edward," said Amelia. "It's very normal."

Amelia was right because in just a couple of hours Edward and Nicole became the proud parents of a healthy boy.

Jamie brought Wendell to visit his grandson. Arthur then turned up as he said that he couldn't wait to see his nephew. Annalise was going to stay the night and when Amelia was sure that everything was in order, finally Liza, Jamie, Amelia and Wendell made their way home.

"It's been a very long day," said Jamie and they all retired to bed early that night.

*** *

It took just four days for the new Home to be up and running. The house was not as they would have liked it to be, but the children seemed very happy

347

and the members of staff were quite content to have their own rooms, even though they were rather old fashioned.

Enough beds were found and there were diverse styles and shapes of tables and chairs for the dining room. The recreation room was furnished with comfortable but mismatched chairs.

Liza had seen Mrs Mulligan and she was employed as the housekeeper, but Liza promoted one of the nurses to be the housemother. The two ladies worked together very well.

The second oven was being put in place, although they were just about coping with the one that was already there. Screens were in the process of being made and painted to lighten the walls and gradually bedroom cupboards were made and put in place. It was not how they liked their Homes to be, but everyone was happy not to be living in overcrowded conditions.

The Duke's previous gardener was employed to get the grounds in order for growing fruit and vegetables and organise an area for animals. There was already plenty of room for the children to play.

It had been a very busy few days, but both Liza and Jamie felt that they could leave everything in capable hands and Liza was now in a position to visit Theresa in prison.

She was brought to the warden's room and he left Liza to visit alone. There were guards outside his door, but nobody thought that there was any possibility of escape.

"I've brought you some fresh clothes and some food Theresa; the warden said that there would be no problem with me doing that," said Liza.

"Thank you," said Theresa. "I really didn't think that you would be able to persuade the judge to change the sentence; I am so grateful for that."

"It's not going to be an easy journey or life for that matter," said Liza. "There will eventually be opportunities for you to further yourself. You were beginning to read and write when I knew you; have you managed to carry on with that?"

"No, but I haven't forgotten what I learnt; do you think it would help me if I could do that?" said Theresa.

"There won't be many people who can read and write where you are going, so anyone who can do that will be valued. I'll get some learning books to you before you leave, it will give you something to do on the journey," said Liza.

"I was very frightened of being executed, but now I am equally frightened of where I am going," said Theresa with a sob in her voice.

348

"I'm afraid that there is nothing that I can say or do that will ease your fears and my only advice to you is to try to align yourself with one of the crew, or a soldier, or even a strong prisoner and I don't mean a thug, but one who also has a brain. I'm sure that you will be able to use your talents and intelligence to sort out who would be useful in helping you through this ordeal," said Liza. "Do you know when you are leaving?"

"I haven't been told that yet," said Theresa.

Liza said that she would try to find out all that she could.

"Normally the prison ships leave from London docks and that is quite close to where I live, so I may be able to visit you before you leave and make sure you have all that you are allowed to take," said Liza.

"Thank you," said Theresa. "I've made such a mess of my life."

"There wasn't really very much that you could have done to make it any different," said Liza. "It's very easy for us to say why didn't you go to the authorities or why didn't you stop them abusing and killing; it's not so easy to carry out the right thing to do."

"Others got out of this life," said Theresa.

"Yes, others have, but some others have also been pulled back into it. It is all a matter of luck," said Liza.

"Did April manage to keep out of the hands of the rogues?" asked Theresa.

"Yes she did; she is now happily married to a very respectable young man, and she still looks after my boys," said Liza.

"I'm happy for her," said Theresa.

"You also mentioned Ellen and the twins," said Liza. "I hope you'll be pleased to hear that they are all living in America and are much loved members of a doctor's family. Ellen has a very keen gentleman friend but because of her past she finds it difficult to make that final commitment, which is a great shame. The twins are a wonderful handful, they create havoc wherever they go, but everyone thinks the world of them."

"I'm pleased that they are safe and happy," said Theresa with tears now flowing down her cheeks.

"You are asking why that couldn't be you and I understand that. What you must now do is look to the future, it may not be what you dreamed of but it is a life and it will eventually be rewarding; I think you are strong and sensible enough to treat it as a new beginning. I'll call again before I leave Belfast and I will come and see you when you reach London docks. Stay positive Theresa, there is plenty to look forward to," said Liza. "Learn to write properly and write to me regularly, I will write back to you, but all letters will take a very long time to arrive."

Theresa was taken back to her cell and the prison warden returned. Liza asked him if he knew when Theresa would be transferred to the prison ship in London.

"I have yet to be informed when the London ship will leave for Tasmania; it will be a while yet, but I will keep the woman here as long as possible. The ship sitting at the docks for months is no place for her to be or for anyone else. The journey is long so why make it even longer than necessary. When you are back in England you will probably be able to find out the sailing date easily enough," said the warden.

"I'd like to bring her a few items, I trust you would have no objections," said Liza. "She began reading and writing some years ago, it would be a good idea if she were to continue with that. It could be useful to her when she reaches her destination."

"Bring her what you think is best, I have no objections; just don't let it be something that she could use as a weapon," said the warden.

***

Liza made her way back to Amelia's when they both went to visit Edward, Nicole and their little son. Annalise was still with them and she said that they had all had a very peaceful night.

"Have you settled on names yet?" asked Liza.

"Yes we have Liza," said Edward. "We have decided that his first name will be Edward." Liza nodded. "Then we thought that we would like his next name to be James after two people who were and are very close to our family and finally we want to add another name and that is Patrick, and we hope that it won't upset you Liza. He was a good, kind and caring man and we felt that we wanted him remembered within our family."

"Both James and Patrick would be honoured, as will Jamie, and I thank you for your thoughtfulness," said Liza. "So are you going to let me hold young Edward James Patrick Fuller?" said Liza as she desperately tried to hide her emotions. She knew that Wendell would say that it was just one more tactless act by Edward, but she knew that he and Nicole had really put a great deal of thought into the decision.

Liza held the baby closely to her, loving the feel and smell of him. "He's a beautiful little boy," said Liza.

Edward carried on, "Liza we would like you to be his godmother. We have already asked Peter and he has agreed to be his godfather."

"I'd be delighted to have Edward as a godchild. When are you thinking of having him christened?" asked Liza.

"We have already baptised him so there is no hurry to have the official christening. I know that you have to return to England in a couple of days, so just let me know when you can return and we will arrange it for that time," said Edward.

"I believe that we will be free in six weeks, if that will be convenient for you," said Liza. "We'll bring the boys; they'll enjoy a short holiday with you all. I'll arrange for our house to be made ready for us and you must let me know what I can do to help."

***

With everything to do with the children in order Liza and Jamie made arrangements to leave for Surrey. Liza visited Theresa one more time and reiterated that she would attempt to see her when she reached London. As the Duke had given them a Home for the children there was no need for them to bring any of them to the Major.

They would make their priority getting William, Amber, the twins and the two boys on their way to America as soon as possible. Nobody could be sure that there were no others looking for them as there had been rumours that those executed were only part of a gang of child abusers.

"We'll have to find at least two people to travel with them and we'll have to be very careful who we choose," said Liza.

"I think that you will have to employ a couple of nurses for the journey," said Jamie. "They may want to settle in America."

"I doubt that we would be that lucky," said Liza. "I've yet to hear from Myra about the adoptions."

They settled back into a routine with cricket matches on Sundays, daily family dinners and Liza and Jamie attending charity functions. The boys were quite excited that they would be travelling to Belfast for little Edward's christening; it meant a few days away from the schoolroom.

Liza heard that the prison ship would be leaving for Tasmania during the month and the warden from Belfast prison wrote to say that Theresa was going to be transferred to it before that time. A couple of days before the prison ship set sail, Liza and Jamie made the journey to the docks.

It was not a Marchant & Fuller ship, but the captain knew them and invited them into his cabin.

"I would like to see one of the prisoners; a girl by the name of Theresa who was brought here from Belfast. Perhaps one of your crew knows of her," said Liza.

"We have many prisoners on board, and I have to admit that I am not aware of the names of each and every one of them, but I do remember that one girl was brought here from Belfast. I'm surprised that you are asking after her, Lady Edgeworth, I would not have thought that one of our prisoners moved in your circles," said the captain.

"She is someone that I met a few years ago and if the circumstances had been different she would now have been a very useful member of society, but events conspired against her and now here she is. She has done things that she has not been proud of in her life, but she has also risked everything to help children out of difficult situations," said Liza. "I would like to make sure that she is as prepared as it is possible to be for the long journey. I hope she arrives safely and is able to make something of her life."

"Well, I hope she is strong as it will be a very hard life," said the captain. "I'll send one of the crew to fetch her as I'm sure you would not wish to go where the prisoners are held. It would also not do her any good to show the other prisoners that she has such illustrious friends, they would not make her life easy."

They waited a while before Theresa was brought into them. She looked very frightened but when she saw Liza a look of relief crossed her face.

"You said that you would come," said Theresa. "Thank you."

"I've brought you some extra clothes and some paper, pens and ink for you to practice your writing. Also a couple of easy to read books, they will keep you occupied. There is also a little food, but I couldn't bring much as it would not survive a long journey. Within the clothes we have placed a little money which could help you through some difficult situations," said Liza quietly.

"I don't know what to say. I'll try to be brave, but I am very frightened. I just try to keep in my mind that once we reach Tasmania it will be a chance at another life," said Theresa. "Does April know what has happened to me?"

"No she doesn't," said Liza. "April is a very caring and sensitive person and knowing that you are in this situation would worry her considerably. She would know that she could have so easily been in the same position. When I begin to hear from you then I may tell her."

"What are your quarters like?" asked Jamie.

"There are four of us in one cell and it's very dark and stuffy, but I understand that other ships are worse," said Theresa.

"Do you get on with the other three?" asked Jamie.

"They seem alright, but I only met them yesterday and of course we are all wary of one another," said Theresa.

"We both wish you well Theresa," said Jamie. "We wish that circumstances had been different. Keep thinking positively and try to make a life for yourself when you reach Tasmania. Liza is right that if you can read and write you could become a very useful and much needed member of that society."

"I will always remember your kindness and perhaps one day you will know that I survived and did well," said Theresa.

The captain had her ushered away before too many tears could be shed.

The captain asked them why they had such an interest in this girl. "It's unusual for any of the prisoners to have visitors, and especially not ones as illustrious as you."

A young subordinate brought in a tea tray with biscuits. Liza and Jamie eyed them cautiously and the captain laughed. "Don't worry they are not ship's biscuits full of weevils. We do try to keep to a healthy diet for as long as possible. I cannot guarantee what the food will be like as we near our destination, but we do make every effort to keep everyone alive."

"Of course, I'm sorry if we looked skeptical," said Liza. "It's very kind of you and we would be delighted to take tea with you."

"If I am not prying too much, I would like to know why you are so concerned about this girl. I have heard that she was part of a group that burned one of your children's homes to the ground which also killed some of your people," said the captain.

The young subordinate was making himself busy pouring tea and handing around biscuits and hovered around tidying up.

"Around five years ago I interviewed three young women. All of them had been in an abusive situation but had managed to get away and each had also brought out young ones at great risk to themselves. Theresa was one of the girls but I did not choose her for the situation, however she did gain employment elsewhere as a maid in a large house, and all was going well until one day she was spotted by her abusers and forced back into their employ. I suppose you could say that the rest is history," said Liza, "but it isn't. The girl that I did employ has looked after our children wonderfully and she is now happily married to a very intelligent and understanding young man."

"So what you are saying is that this girl, Theresa, could have been in the same situation as your current employee given the chance. Don't tell me that you blame yourself for her misdeeds," said the captain.

"Not completely as we are each master of our own destiny. What I did not know was that she had disappeared from her employment and nobody seemed to worry that she was missing. Everyone assumed that she voluntarily had gone back to the way she had to live formerly. We should have realised that someone who had risked life and limb to leave that life and help others would not have willingly returned to that existence," said Liza.

"So you do blame yourself?" said the captain.

"I blame myself for not checking on her, and perhaps others, more diligently," said Liza.

"Liza, in the last seven or eight years how many girls have you seen placed in employment. A hundred, maybe more? You couldn't possibly watch over every one of them. You helped them out of a difficult situation and then had to concentrate on the new ones who needed your help," said Jamie.

"With someone like the girl Theresa, it really was the luck of the draw. It's a shame but there are always victims in this world. All I can say is that I keep watch on all the prisoners to the best of my ability, but I will attempt to try to keep Theresa as safe as possible," said the captain.

"Thank you, Captain," said Jamie. "I think that we have done all that we possibly can to help Theresa. We'll leave you now to get on with your duties. We wish you a safe journey."

Chapter 18

Liza finally received a letter from Myra and the good news was that the couple who owned the farm were looking forward to having William and Amber in their family, and the New York lawyer and his wife were delighted and excited to be offering a home to the twin girls. Both families understood the children had been harmed but were prepared to give the children any special attention that may be needed. As yet no homes had been found for the two boys, but Myra said that there was room in one of the Homes for them and hopefully they would soon be successfully placed with loving families.

The other excellent news was that Myra and Henry had decided to take a months' vacation in England and hopefully they would be able to spend that time with Liza's family and at the end of that time they would return taking the children with them.

"So you've had the problem of how to transport the children safely solved for you," smiled Jamie.

"It's going to be wonderful. We have several functions to attend and Myra and Henry can come with us. We have little Edward's christening and I know that they will enjoy visiting Belfast and there will still be some time for a couple of cricket matches which will be an experience for Henry, although I believe he did have some practice when they were here before," said Liza.

"I remember that Charles Enderby also visited at that time; I wonder whether he'll decide to accompany them again," said Jamie.

"Jamie Edgeworth," exclaimed Liza. "You're jealous."

"Have I a reason to be jealous?" asked Jamie smiling.

"Absolutely not, but it's nice that you are." laughed Liza.

The Major and Jennifer were to spend the weekend with them. Jennifer would be leaving the following week for Belfast and the Major deserved a couple of days break away from the Ffoulks house.

Over dinner that evening the Major announced that he and Jennifer had decided to marry in Belfast at around the same time as little Edward's christening.

"We felt that it would be convenient as you and the boys will already be in Belfast at that time and of course we want you to be our guests," said the

Major. "Jennifer will go with Joseph to post the bans for us. We have yet to organise the small reception venue, but I'm sure that we could cope in Jennifer's house."

"My house is very small Wilfred; Joseph's and Lily's house is a little larger and I'm sure they will be pleased to assist," said Jennifer.

"You know that you are more than welcome to use our house Jennifer," said Liza but both Jennifer and the Major refused to put them to that much trouble.

Everyone was thinking about the problem until Jamie said why didn't they use Liza's other house. "You would have no objection to that would you Liza?"

"I think that's a wonderful idea," said Liza and she turned to the Major. "You were very comfortable when you stayed there the other year, weren't you Major? You could stay there before your wedding, have the reception there and stay on afterwards, unless you have some very posh place to go for your honeymoon."

"Yes, I enjoyed my time there Liza and I will take you up on your offer, but I insist that we pay and organise everything for our reception, although I would like to make good use of your Mrs Edwards and perhaps your Mrs Adams would also be able help us with our special day," said the Major.

"I'll write to Mrs Edwards and you can take her the letter next week Jennifer. You'll have plenty of time to dress the place as you would like it," said Liza. "I like the thought that it is being used for a very happy event."

"I'll be in Belfast just a couple of days before the wedding, but I know that Jennifer will organise everything well for us and thank you so much for letting us use your house Liza," said the Major.

"There'll be a couple of extra guests Major, our friends from New York will be visiting. When they return they'll take the children back with them. They have homes for William and Amber and also for the twins. They are finding it a little more difficult to find places for the two boys, but they have plenty of room for them in one of our Homes, although they are confident that they will be adopted quickly," said Liza.

Although invited to both the christening and the wedding Miranda and Lucinda decided that they would not travel to Belfast. David also decided that he would prefer to stay at home, but he insisted that Grace made the journey. He said that Liza would need her. Liza and Jamie smiled as they knew that David was match making for his daughter.

"We'll arrange a little celebration for you when you return," said Miranda.

"That's a good idea. I'm sure people like Hector and Anthony and Diana would want to join in such an event," said Liza.

"Who will we need with us?" asked Jamie later that evening.

"We'll just take April and Adam. I haven't the heart to separate them. I dare say the boys won't be pleased that Adam is going; they'll think that they will have to suffer lessons. You will want Roberts with you." said Liza.

"Will Myra and Henry have staff?" asked Jamie.

"They don't normally travel with staff; they have been quite used to caring for themselves in the past and once they are with us we can sort out anyone that they may need," said Liza.

Jamie was mentally working out how many would be travelling to Belfast in a couple of weeks and he didn't feel that it was going to be too daunting.

***

The day arrived when they were to meet Myra and Henry at Southampton and they would all stay the night at the company hotel, taking April and Roberts with them.

They settled into their rooms. They had already seen Myra's and Henry's ship sitting out at sea waiting to come into the dock, which would take at least another couple of hours, so Liza and Jamie decided to go down to the Marchant & Fuller offices at the docks. They spent half an hour or so with the manager and then went back to the hotel.

Jamie made his way up to their suite while Liza went to the kitchen to make arrangements for their meal that evening. When she had finished, she walked through the lounge and caught sight of a face that she seemed to know. It took her a minute or two to realise who it was and when she did it stopped her in her tracks. It was the young subordinate from the prison ship, and he looked shocked and frightened; there was a young woman with him and although her face was almost completely covered by an overlarge hat Liza knew exactly who she was. She stopped and stared into the face of Theresa.

The young man approached Liza and all she said to him as she put up her hands to stop him coming any further, "I don't want to know, please don't tell me anything. Whatever you have done to get this far is none of my business, in fact I haven't even seen you." She took one last look at them both, nodded to them and then left for her rooms. She wondered how she was going to keep this information from Jamie and she decided that she couldn't and hoped that he would make the same choice that she had and that was to forget that she had ever seen them.

Jamie was standing with an annoyed look on his face when she entered their rooms. He took her arm and pulled her into their bedroom quickly closing the door after them.

"What did he say to you?" asked Jamie. "You must tell me."

"I didn't let him say anything," said Liza. "I didn't want to know anything."

"I was shocked to see him, but not as shocked as you looked when you caught sight of Theresa," said Jamie.

"I wondered if you had seen them. I decided that I was going to forget that they were here and ask you if you were going to do the same," said Liza.

"I didn't know whether to tell you that they were here, but we have no secrets and what we decide has to be what is wanted by both of us," said Jamie.

"I want to go in an hour and welcome Myra and Henry and forget about everything else," said Liza.

"You know what we really should do, don't you Liza?" said Jamie. "Also at some time we may be asked if we know where they are because the captain knew that we had an interest in the girl, as well as sympathy for her situation."

"We can always admit to seeing him because as far as we knew he was a free agent who was able to come and go as he pleased," said Liza.

"Well as long as they don't get caught and tell everyone that we saw them," said Jamie. "We had better get ready to meet Myra and Henry, and let's forget that we saw anyone known to us."

Liza smiled up at him and said, "Why do we always get faced with problems?"

"It does seem to happen that way," said Jamie as he started to pull on his jacket.

Liza donned her cloak and they called to April and Roberts to say that they were leaving to meet their guests. April put her head around the door and said that the room was ready for them and she would make sure that refreshments were waiting for them on their return.

They took their carriage to the docks and watched as luggage was being unloaded and finally Myra and Henry appeared with the captain who escorted them down the gangway. Jamie and Liza greeted them warmly and guided them towards their carriage, whilst their luggage was placed on top.

Liza had a quick word with the captain as Jamie helped Myra and Henry into the coach. She turned and caught sight of Theresa and the young man waiting on the dockside along with several other people. She totally ignored them, and the captain commented that his onward passengers seemed eager to get on board.

"As you know Lady Edgeworth, many of our passengers can only afford their fares, they have no extra for staying at guest houses until we sail. We allow them on board as soon as we have their living area cleared," said the captain.

"Are you turning around and going straight back to America?" asked Liza.

"Yes, we'll be leaving on tomorrow evening's tide; the weather seems quite stable at the moment, so we should make good time," said the captain.

"I wish you a safe and uneventful journey Captain," said Liza and she turned towards her carriage but was aware that she was being watched fearfully by two young people waiting on the dockside. Liza just looked around and her eyes fell on Theresa and her partner and all she did was nod imperceptibly in their direction and she hoped that it would give them both some peace of mind.

Jamie helped Liza into the carriage, and they were then on their way to the hotel and looking forward to a wonderful four weeks with Myra and Henry and the many functions that were in store for them.

***

Two weeks after Myra and Henry arrived they all travelled to Belfast for little Edward's christening and then Jennifer and the Major's wedding. It was exciting for everyone and Myra and Henry were delighted to be included in these functions.

Miranda and Lucinda were delighted that they would be looking after David in Grace's absence; whether David was as delighted was debatable, but Liza thought that he would survive the ordeal.

The Major had introduced them to all the staff at the Ffoulks Home and they had concentrated on the children who would be their charges on the return trip and one of the nurses had expressed a desire to travel to New York and perhaps find employment there, so the children were going to be well looked after on their journey.

The christening was to take place on the Sunday afternoon and the Major and Jennifer's wedding was arranged for the following Wednesday.

Amelia and Wendell were delighted to have all their family and friends with them, and several dinners were organised at their house. Amelia loved entertaining in her own home and Wendell liked to sit back and let everything happen around him.

Peter was notably in high spirits which could only be put down to the fact that Grace was with them. Of course John was very content in Peter's company and Peter did devote a great deal of time to him which Liza and Jamie were very grateful for.

The christening went off without a hitch, apart from a very tired looking Nicole and an over enthusiastic Edward. Peter and Liza made their commitments on behalf of the infant and everyone then returned to Edward's house for a small celebration. It was difficult to wrest little Edward from a doting Amelia and Wendell had a permanent grin on his face. Liza looked on the scene with great fondness but suddenly a great feeling of sadness engulfed her. She wished that she and Jamie could have had a child of their own and then her thoughts went even further and she regretted the loss of James' son and Patrick's daughter. Jennifer was looking at her strangely which brought her out of her depression. She pushed all unhappiness from her mind; this was a celebration of the life of a lovely little boy whom she would love as much as she did her own children. She smiled at Jennifer and made her way towards Jamie as she felt the need to be near him.

The boys handed over their christening presents, and it wasn't long before chaos erupted in the garden with Joseph leading the proceedings. Edward looked towards where the noise was emanating from with longing but thought better of leaving his guests to join in with what he obviously seemed to think was more entertaining.

Myra and Henry were thoroughly enjoying meeting up with everyone, especially those they had not seen in a long while. They were pleased to hear that Wendell and Amelia would be travelling to New York the following year with Jamie and Liza, which would be on the maiden voyage of the new passenger liner.

The Major was due to arrive the next day, so Liza went with Jennifer to her house to see that everything was in order for his arrival. Jennifer had organised the entertaining rooms and was going to decorate them with flowers on the Tuesday with Lily's help, ready for the reception on Wednesday.

It was arranged that the Major would have one of the smaller rooms when he arrived which left the larger and more attractive room for after their wedding. Mrs Edwards was enjoying all the activity and Mrs Adams was preparing for the wedding breakfast.

"This is a lovely and friendly house Liza," said Jennifer. "I can understand why you don't want to sell it. It has a great deal of your character in it."

"Do you think so Jennifer?" said Liza. "I always thought that it has much of my first husband's influence."

"I knew of your first husband; he was a very good-looking man. He had a very kind face. I don't really remember when you and he married but I know that he was very happy with you," said Jennifer. "I think this house really is yours and that's because he wanted you to be happy and therefore he let you organise it as you wished."

"Perhaps you're right. I'm really looking forward to seeing you and the Major married on Wednesday. I know you are going to be so happy," said Liza. "Have you decided what you are going to do with your own property?"

"I think that I'll keep it for a while. It will be useful when Wilfred and I want to come to Belfast. We won't have to impose on you for a roof over our heads," said Jennifer.

"You know that you are both always welcome, although I know that you both also value your independence," said Liza. "You look well prepared and very calm Jennifer. All seems to be coming together well."

"I'm not as calm as I look Liza; in fact I am quite nervous," said Jennifer.

"I'm sure you'll feel better on the day," said Liza.

"It's not the day I'm worrying about," said Jennifer. "It's a very long time since I was married, and I really no longer know how to react to living with a man. I want to be with Wilfred and I know that he will be very kind and understanding but I feel like a very nervous teenager going into marriage for the first time."

"I don't think that the Major will be too demanding of you; he will want you to be comfortable with all aspects of your life together, but I will tell you something that happened to me very many years ago, and I have quoted it to a few people who have been in your circumstances," said Liza. "When I was first married all those years ago, I was only just seventeen years old. James knew that I had little idea of what married life should be like and he was right. I was very frightened of what would be expected of me on my wedding night, my mother had told me nothing and I only had whispered gossip to go on. He told me that he expected nothing of me then and that we would know when the time was right."

Jennifer could see that Liza had gone back in time to some very happy memories and she waited for her to continue.

"Weeks went by and they turned into months and then on James' birthday I organised my first party in his honour and it was a wonderful evening. Finally that night he came to me and we both knew that the time was then right for us to be together and he told me that I had given him the best birthday present that he could ever have wished for and we had a wonderful married life from then onwards," said Liza and once again her face showed that she had gone back in time and there was a mixture of love and sadness in her eyes.

"He must have been a very caring and wise man Liza," said Jennifer gently.

"Yes he was because he knew that if he had forced himself onto me when I was not ready, I would have been put off that side of married life forever," said Liza and then she laughed. "The moral of the story is that two people who really love one another will know when the time is right. I'm sure the Major would understand that, and he has probably thought of it himself."

"I'm sorry Liza, I seem to have stirred up some memories which were probably best left alone," said Jennifer.

"I have been very lucky in many ways Jennifer although I have lost two husbands who I loved dearly. My life would have been different if James had survived and of course the same could be said if Patrick had not been killed, but all lives have their twists and turns and I have been so fortunate to have found love yet again in a very good and caring man like Jamie," said Liza.

Jennifer laughed, "You kept him waiting a long while Liza."

"It takes time to get over some losses and it sometimes takes time to realise what you really feel," said Liza.

"Life has not been easy for you Liza and I admire how you manage to show a happy face to the world, but you do not fool me. I know that there are times when sadness overcomes you; I saw it this afternoon when you were looking at little Edward," said Jennifer.

"We all wish for things that we cannot have, but I am very happy Jennifer," said Liza. "I have a very caring husband and three wonderful sons and an extended family and friends that many would be envious of. So don't let some of my thoughts worry you. I am very contented in all that I have and all that I do."

They took the carriage firstly to Jennifer's house and at last Liza made her way home where the boys were still in high spirits with April trying to calm them. Jamie appeared in the hallway and looks from both him and Liza quietened them immediately.

"Joseph has a very bad influence on our boys," smiled Jamie, "but they do enjoy his company, or perhaps it's the other way around."

Peter had returned with them; he was obviously spending as much time with Grace as possible and he was going to join them for dinner. Grace asked if everything was in order for the wedding.

"Jennifer is decorating the house beautifully and Mrs Edwards and Mrs Adams are determined that it is going to be the wedding reception of the year," said Liza. "They don't get much of a chance to show off their skills at entertaining. I'm looking forward to seeing the Major tomorrow. It's surprising that Hector hasn't invited himself to the wedding, but as Estelle won't be here there is no incentive for him."

"As the Major will be here, Hector is needed to keep Ffoulks house running smoothly," said Jamie.

The following morning Liza and Jamie went to the Marchant & Fuller offices to meet with Brendan and the architect who had drafted the plans for the children's home on the site of the one that had been destroyed. They had worked together well and had come up with some very innovative ideas which were quite impressive.

They could see the ship that the Major was travelling on in the distance and down on the docks they saw Jennifer waiting for him.

"I think we should let Jennifer see him from the ship and once they have greeted one another we can add to the greeting," said Jamie.

"You're getting more and more thoughtful as time goes on," smiled Liza. "You are right; it is a private time for Jennifer and the Major. We can then make sure that they know that they are invited to dinner this evening."

"They may want to have the evening to themselves," smiled Jamie. "I know I wanted every minute alone with you."

"You really are a romantic," said Liza.

They watched as the ship docked and finally a beaming Major disembarked and made his way towards Jennifer. Both Jamie and Liza left the window that they were looking out of as they felt that it would be an intrusion to watch the greeting between these two people. They slowly made their way down to Jennifer and the Major and welcomed him to Belfast. Having extended the invitation to dinner that evening and had it accepted they left them to their own devices.

The following two days passed very quickly, and the day of the wedding arrived. Jennifer looked beautiful and the Major was elegant and proud. Lily was her mother's bridesmaid; Wendell gave her away and Jamie undertook the duties of best man. The ceremony was not long and they all soon made their way back for the reception.

Mrs Edwards and Mrs Adams had excelled with the wedding breakfast and the cake was something to behold. Jamie made a very fine speech as best man and then the Major made his speech.

"Not so very long ago I was leading a very lonely life; I won't go into the reasons for that on this very happy day, but luckily my world was turned on its head with the arrival on my doorstep of a panic stricken stranger desperately searching for her son. That meeting has led me to where I am today. From a very disturbing situation has emerged a wonderfully new life for me. I now have a beautiful wife, a family, and friends that I think the world of. I also have a worthwhile job where I can see broken children slowly mend and I try to help them become confident and useful members of society."

"I truly never thought that I would find love again; I am such a lucky man as I have found someone who is my soul-mate and I am so proud that she became my wife today and I will be proud of her always and love her always."

"I also want to thank everyone here today for all that you have done for me and for Jennifer; I have said that you are friends, but really you are all now my family and I like being part of this extended family; it gives me such a warm and loving feeling towards you all and a contentment that I never experienced before."

"Thank you, Liza, for loaning us your house for this wonderful gathering and also allowing us to start our married life under its roof. It is a very friendly place and one that I will always remember with great fondness."

"I would like to propose a toast to my wife and then to all of you. Thank you."

With the toasts completed, the happy couple cut the wedding cake, much to the pleasure of the boys as they had been examining it closely for some time.

The Major came over to Liza and kissed her on the head. "Jennifer told me a story that you had told her," he whispered. "It was a very sensible tale and one that I see merit in. Thank you, Liza, you do seem to have an answer for most situations."

"Oh Major, I really don't have all the answers; it just sometimes seems that people think that I have. You look so happy and so does Jennifer; it just shows us that good does come out of evil. If your previous next-door neighbour had not acted in such a malicious way, we would not have met and you and Jennifer would not be celebrating your wedding today. It's all just a matter of providence," said Liza.

The rest of the reception went well, and later Liza and Jamie took three very tired and over fed boys home. April smiled and said that she remembered how they had always eaten too much right from when she first looked after them.

"At least they now manage to keep their food down, especially John, although he always seemed to be proud of being sick," said Liza. "We'll be leaving in a couple of days; I dare say you'll be pleased to get back to Adam. When we travel here at Christmas, he will be with us and I'll make sure that you get plenty of time to yourselves."

***

The trip back to Surrey was uneventful and once everything had been unpacked Liza gave April two days off and she also pleased the boys by saying that Adam would not be conducting lessons for a couple of days. They were a little disappointed to know that they would have some lessons prepared for them and that she was going to supervise their education.

David was pleased to see Grace home. Miranda and Lucinda had been very diligent in making sure that he was cared for, in fact they had been a little too diligent for his taste, but he had taken it all in his stride.

Bella turned up with her boys on the Friday evening; they were all now used to her appearance without warning and James, John and Matthew were always happy to see them. Bella was pleased to inform them that the Duke had arranged that Richard would join the others at university, so he and Matthew would be the youngest in their class.

"He's also told them that they are all to be in the same dormitory, they must not be split up in any way," said Bella triumphantly.

"Have they agreed to that?" asked Jamie.

"Of course, they wouldn't do otherwise," said Bella. "Why? Didn't you want them all to be together?"

"Yes we do Bella, but we do also like to make our own decisions regarding our sons," said Jamie with annoyance.

"You may not have been able to achieve what you wanted. Don't forget that the Duke carries more weight than you do Jamie," said an unconcerned Bella.

Myra and Henry were fascinated by Bella and the way she just assumed that she and her sons could come and go as they pleased, but they were also aware that her husband was the greatest contributor to their charity. She never overstayed her welcome and always blended in well with everyone. When Myra had asked Liza how the connection had occurred, she was told that Jamie had spent much time in her family home when he was a boy. Liza found it unnecessary to mention that Binky was her brother; she didn't want to remind anyone of Binky's terrible attack on young John which had happened when Myra and Henry were last visiting, although she believed that they probably knew.

Liza and Myra spent a great deal of time at the Ffoulks Home and Myra concentrated on the six children that she, Henry and the nurse would be escorting to New York. There was room for the nurse to be employed in one of the New York Homes and Myra was absolutely sure that the two boys would soon have homes to go to as they had several families who had shown an interest in adoption.

Amber and William always ran up to Liza when they saw her and now they held Myra's hand and frequently gave her their food. The twins were very happy that they would be travelling to another country; they were fortunate that they had one another as they appeared to have weathered their ordeal with no lasting effects. The two boys were still very wary of everyone, but they were slowly beginning to trust adults and the prospect of a new life away from all the reminders of their past was appealing to them. They appeared to relax a little more in Henry's company and he was determined to help them gain confidence.

The Major and Jennifer arrived back from Belfast. Hector had been very diligent in his duties in the Major's absence but now he needed to concentrate on the renovations to the Langston House.

The day finally arrived when Myra and Henry were to leave and Liza and Jamie were travelling with them to Southampton where they would stay overnight and the following morning the Major and the nurse would set off with the six children. Liza felt a little guilty that they would be travelling in comfort whereas the Major and the nurse would be squashed in a carriage with the children, but she wanted to be with Myra and Henry and spend the last evening with them.

"It's been a very busy month for you both," said Jamie.

"It's been wonderful," said Myra. "We've been to several charity evenings, experienced yet more cricket matches. Our trip to Belfast for little Edward's christening and the Major and Jennifer's wedding was a time that we will always remember. Don't worry; we also had plenty of time to relax."

They discussed plans for the visit to New York the following year and Myra started planning all the entertainments for that time, much to everyone's amusement.

Their ship had docked that evening and it was ready for them to board the next morning. The large cabin had been arranged so that the children and the nurse would sleep there. A smaller cabin was for Myra and Henry. Nobody would have to sleep in the hold as it was appreciated that the children could be frightened if they were below decks.

The captain and the first mate knew that these children had been hurt in the past and they were going out of their way to make the trip comfortable for them.

"I do hope that they stay well out of your way Captain," said Liza. "I know that it may not be an easy trip, but they do have a nurse with them, and Myra and Henry will be keeping a close watch over them."

Their luggage was on board and now all they had to do was await the arrival of the Major and his charges.

"I'm afraid your accommodation will not be quite as comfortable as on your outward journey," said Liza.

"It's comfortable enough Liza," said Henry. "Our bed looks soft and we don't need lots of room to move around in. The weather is still good so we can exercise on deck. We will be fine, please don't worry about us. We've had a wonderful time with you, and we are looking forward to seeing you and Amelia and Wendell next year."

"I believe we may well have all the Edgeworths with us then," said Jamie.

The Major arrived mid-afternoon and all the children had survived the journey without too much difficulty, although the Major and the nurse looked a little fraught.

After greeting them all they took them to their cabin and the nurse started arranging their clothes. Amber and William were holding their 'Softy' toys and they looked very happy. The twins also had toys and they were watching the nurse unpacking some of their dresses. The boys decided that it was time that they became boys and their excitement meant that they were getting under everyone's feet and shrieking at the tops of their voices.

Liza turned to the nurse and said, "Well, I don't envy you the journey with those two boys. No doubt they'll calm down. I hope that they are good sailors."

Finally it was time to say goodbye to everyone and Liza felt quite emotional and she could see that the Major was also holding back his feelings. All the children had been held in a special place in his heart, especially as they were the first to leave the Ffoulks Home.

The ship slowly left the dockside and all the children were on deck waving farewell to the Major, Liza, Jamie and also to England. They stayed on the dockside until they could no longer make out those on board and then they made their way back to the hotel where they would be staying the night.

"Well Major;" said Jamie when they arrived in their suite. "At least those children will have the chance of a better life and hopefully, with time, they will forget what has happened to them."

"Yes, it was right to send them to New York, especially those children. I still have my doubts that all the gang were caught, and those six children were exceptionally good looking," said the Major. "They will be safe there."

"I wish I could see them with their new families," said Liza.

"You will be able to when we go to New York next year, but I know what you are going to say," said Jamie. "It won't be wise to call in to see them as it would remind them of their past, and of course their new parents also may not wish to be reminded that they did not give birth to them."

"Yes, you're right, it's a shame but we have to do what's best for the children. Myra will check up on them for a while after they are placed, but she will also leave them alone unless they ask for help," said Liza.

"I suppose I will feel this way each time a child is placed with a family and leaves my Home," said the Major. "I felt quite sad to see them go."

"So did I," said Liza. "We are going to have to get used to it. At least I hope we are because I would like to see all our children happily placed with loving families."

"How's Jennifer settling in England?" asked Jamie.

"She's had plenty of visits, so she is quite familiar with it and she's having a wonderful time organising our house. She gets on well with my housekeeper, so there's no friction there," said the Major. "She's going to keep her home in Belfast which means that we never have to worry about where we will be staying when we visit, although I believe that Jennifer will travel there more than I will. She does have a daughter and son-in-law to see on occasion and many friends."

"Her friends are now your friends," said Liza. "Have you decided what you are doing for Christmas?"

"I don't want to leave the children. This is their first Christmas under our care," said the Major. "I believe that Lily and Joseph are thinking of joining us this year. I suppose it will be the first time for many years that the Fullers haven't spent Christmas together."

"Yes, but times often have to change," said Liza. "The boys will miss Joseph."

"Hmmm, they do seem to get on well. I have a feeling that our boys will grow up before Joseph does," smiled Jamie. "I believe that Edward is beginning to show more adult leanings since he became a father."

"Neither Edward nor Joseph act that way unless our boys are with them," said Liza.

Chapter 19

They arrived back in Surrey late in the afternoon the following day, and the carriage took the Major onto the Ffoulks house. The boys were pleased to see them as were the rest of the family.

"Hopefully we can now spend some time at home and enjoy our family," said Liza.

"No doubt you'll find something that we will have to do. We never seem to be able to have a few days to ourselves," said Jamie with slight annoyance. "I would enjoy a while to myself."

Liza frowned and looked at him quizzically. "I do try to arrange events so that we have some time together. I knew that it would be like this. You will remember that I told you so after the Duke's surprise function. I'll look at what has been arranged and see what I can reorganise."

"I wouldn't go to that bother Liza because no matter what you reorganise, something else will happen that needs your immediate attention and I will be expected to follow you around like a little lamb," said Jamie with a very sour look on his face.

It was just the two of them for dinner that night and Liza found it a little difficult to eat. Their conversation was stilted and when dinner was over Jamie decided to go to his study saying that he would see her later. Liza sat quietly at her desk for the rest of the evening, but she could not concentrate on any of her correspondence. As it neared time for her to retire, she went to find Jamie in his study, but he was not there. She slowly made her way up to her room where April was waiting for her; she quickly got ready for bed and told April that she could finish off herself.

She sat on her bed and waited, hoping that Jamie would come to her but after half an hour it seemed obvious that he would be staying in his own room. She made up her mind that she must talk to him and sort out whatever problem he seemed to have. He was probably feeling that she always expected him to agree with whatever she arranged and possibly she should have consulted him more on all that they undertook. She desperately wanted him to put his arms around her and accept her apology and they could carry on in their normal happy way.

Picking up her lamp she made her way to his room and when she opened his door, she was surprised to find that he was sitting in a chair rather than lying on his bed. He looked up as she came over to him and the expression on his face was not as welcoming as normal.

"What have I done, Jamie?" she asked. "Is it because I have made some arrangements and not consulted you beforehand? I thought that I had always discussed most events with you, but I suppose there were some that I forgot about and I am truly sorry for that. I will try to remember to ask you about everything in the future. Please forgive me Jamie; you know that I don't intentionally do anything to annoy you."

Jamie now had a slight smile on his face, but he said nothing.

"Please say something Jamie," said Liza quietly.

He took the lamp out of her hand and took both of her hands in his. "When we first married I knew that you had a great deal to occupy you with your businesses and the charity. I had this estate to administer and also spent time helping with the charity. We still had time to ourselves and the boys were all important to us. Now all I manage to do is exactly what you have organised for us and I am not enjoying being at your beck and call at all times. I enjoy being with you Liza, but not on duty every second of the day," said Jamie.

"Oh," was all Liza could say.

"I have decided that I am going to spend a little time away. I think it would do both of us some good," said Jamie.

As Liza stared at him her green eyes grew and the hurt that they displayed made him draw in his breath. He had seen that hurt before when he had been unfaithful to her and he remembered that he had promised never to hurt her again. He realised that this was another promise that he had broken, and he was sorry for it.

However Liza was remembering another time when Patrick had decided to leave her. How could she be unlucky enough to have had two husbands who didn't want to live with her? What was wrong with her that made them want to leave?

"Are you leaving me and the boys Jamie?" she asked as tears started running down her cheeks.

"Oh no Liza, I could never leave you. I just need a little time to myself," said Jamie.

Suddenly Liza became annoyed. "How very selfish of you Jamie. You have no idea of how many times I have felt the need for a little peace, but I must carry on so that everyone is happy and worry free. If you go away Jamie, then I will also go back to my home and lick my wounds. I will of course make sure that our boys and all of your family are unaware that you have deserted them. Good night Jamie. Please don't bother to disturb me when you leave."

She picked up her lamp and made her way back to her room. Jamie was surprised by her attitude; he had expected her to be upset but had not expected her to turn on him in such a way. He had thought that she would understand.

Her tears had stopped, and she climbed into bed, but before she could blow out her lamp, Jamie opened her door and entered her room.

"I'm not leaving you Liza; I'm just taking some time away. I'll go to my club for a while," said Jamie.

"You're not to be trusted away, look what happened last time you went to your club. You are leaving me Jamie; you want to be away from your family and that's just as good as leaving them. I shall take the boys home to Belfast with Adam and April. Everyone will be upset, but we've had to do it before so I'm sure we'll survive."

"This is your home Liza," said Jamie. "It will be too disrupting for the boys to move yet again to Belfast."

Liza stared at him in disbelief. "Your leaving will be the only disruptive element that the boys will experience, and this is not my home Jamie. It is your house and until now it was our home, but no longer; without you it is cold and unfriendly. You will have a great deal to do tomorrow so you had better go and get some sleep. Goodbye Jamie," Liza turned on her side with her back to him.

Jamie came over to her bed and lay down beside her; he attempted to put his arms around her, but she pushed him away.

He whispered to her, "I thought that I would be able to make you feel better tonight, because I can see that you need to be loved."

Liza turned to him with fury in her eyes. "Just leave me alone Jamie, it's something that I will have to get used to. There is only one way that would make me feel better and you know what that is. Just go Jamie; I do not want you near me."

It was the first time that she had ever refused him, but he could understand it, although he had always managed to arouse her in the past. He climbed off her bed and left her room, making his way back to his own room realising that it was going to be a very lonely night for him.

Liza cried herself to sleep that night and when she woke early the next morning, she wondered whether she had been unfair on Jamie. Would it be so wrong for him to take some time away from the family? A few days would not be too bad. Perhaps she had overreacted. She would go and see him and tell him that she would look after everyone in his absence. She put on her dressing gown and made her way to his room and was surprised to find that Roberts was already packing Jamie's cases and the amount he was organising was much more than he would have needed for a few days.

"His Lordship has already gone down to breakfast," said Roberts with a stony look on his face.

Liza nodded and went back to her room feeling very sick and as always when under stress she vomited luckily reaching a bowl in time. She then lay on the bed desperately trying to gain control of her stomach. There was a tap on her door and before she could answer Matthew entered.

"I heard you being sick. Is our father leaving us?" he asked.

"Just for a few days Matthew," smiled Liza hoping that she was allaying the fear that she saw in his bright green eyes.

Matthew nodded and she knew that he realised that she was bending the truth.

"The others haven't realised that something is wrong; but you know that I sense what you are feeling, and you are very unhappy at the moment," said Matthew. "I know it will pass because he really loves you. He just gets frustrated at times. It will be alright, but I'll say nothing to James and John."

"I really don't know what I would do without you Matthew," said Liza. "You have always been such a blessing to me."

"I'll see you later Mum," he said and left. What Liza didn't know was that he immediately made his way down to the dining room to find Jamie. He knocked on the door and entered.

"What is it Matthew?" asked Jamie who was surprised to see him.

"You know that you have made me and my brothers very happy; we are all very proud to be Edgeworths, but my brothers don't realise that you are leaving us and how unhappy our mother is because you are going. When you do go, they will also be very unhappy, as will I."

"I'm surprised that your mother has told you," said Jamie.

373

"She didn't but I know when she is unhappy; I sense her feelings just as she senses mine. She has said that you will be away for a few days, but I know that isn't true. You think that you will feel better by being away from all the functions that you have to go to, but you won't. You'll be miserable without my mother and she'll be miserable without you as will my brothers, and all the rest of the family," said Matthew.

"Your mother has accused me of being selfish and she is right but I want you to know that I do love her, I always have done, and I also love you, your brothers and the rest of the family and I will never hurt any of you," said Jamie.

"But you are and my mother will have to pretend that there is nothing wrong so that we all can be happy and she will smile and hide her tears and keep everything running smoothly and no matter how many people she meets she will be lonely. My daddy Patrick left her once, but he thought that he was holding her back making her live in a small town like Benson; he soon came back when he realised that he didn't want to live without her and at least he had thought of doing it because he was thinking of her and not himself," said Matthew much to Jamie's horror and realisation yet again that Matthew was much older than his years.

"You put me to shame Matthew," said Jamie.

"Don't worry Father, I'll look after our mother whilst you are gone. I know you will do what is right," said Matthew and he left to be with his brothers in the school room.

Jamie sat for a while poised over his breakfast which he did not want in the first place. Matthew had put into perspective what he was feeling, and he realised that Liza's accusation of selfishness was indeed accurate; he took a deep breath and slowly left the table and made his way up to Liza's room.

Liza was sitting at her dressing table when Jamie came in. Before he could say anything Liza started talking.

"I have decided that as you are so keen to have some time away from me, then instead of you having to leave then I will do so. The boys will be happy that you are here and so will your mother and Lucinda as well as your uncle and cousin. You will be able to handle the staff and you will also be capable of attending all the functions. Hector will be able to discuss the new Home with you and the Major can talk to you about all the possible adoptions and the new children who will need to be brought here. Grace is quite capable of dealing with the correspondence; she will just have to make sure that you are available when needed. It's near the end of the cricket season so for a short while you will only have to arrange what food is needed to supplement what the villagers bring. Bella and the boys' rooms are always available to them, so you will just have to make sure that there is enough food for everyone. Whilst I am away, I will still be able to deal with all the Marchant & Fuller and Bradley & Company business but of course you will still be looking after the estate. I shall miss you very much Jamie, especially our nights together, but as you need to be away from me then I respect that and will go and perhaps one day you will ask me to return, but until that time I will give you your freedom," said Liza as she began folding clothes ready for packing.

"Liza you know that you can't leave the boys and the rest of the family," said Jamie.

"Why not Jamie? It's exactly what you are thinking of, so why shouldn't I be able to do the same?" said Liza. "They are your boys and your family. You are just as capable as I of caring for all the Edgeworths and those surrounding them. Now if you'll excuse me, I have a lot to organise; you can tell Roberts to stop packing for you."

"I suppose you have in mind to go to Belfast," smiled Jamie as he did not believe that she would leave under any circumstances.

"No Jamie, I would not throw myself on the Fullers again. They have had to put up with my traumas on too many occasions. I will rent somewhere and when I am settled, I will let you know that I am safe," said Liza.

"Liza, I know that you won't leave; you wouldn't do that to your boys," smiled Jamie.

Liza turned on him with fury. "No, I wouldn't leave them if I thought that you wouldn't be here, but as you now have no reason to go then you can look after them and everything else. I'm tired and I am going to get some rest and if you think that I am not serious then you are very much mistaken. I am fed up with trying to juggle everything to keep everyone happy; I'm going to have some time to myself; I think I deserve it."

Jamie suddenly realised that Liza meant what she was saying and the pressure that he had placed on her the night before had made her decide that she needed a break away from everything. He had pushed her to the limit and for once she was not going to rise to the occasion.

"I came to tell you that I had changed my mind and I know that I had a moment of selfishness which was really very stupid of me," said Jamie. "I don't want to spend one minute away from you. I am not going to my club; you were right that it wasn't the place that I should be. I am going to be here and I hope that you will also, but if you decide that you need to get away then I will respect that but please go somewhere that you will be safe and near friends."

Liza carried on folding her clothes and trying to digest what Jamie was saying. She suddenly didn't feel well, and a bout of sickness overcame her once again and she rushed away managing to reach her wash area. She returned a short while later, but Jamie had never seen her look so ill. She looked up at him with panic in her bright green eyes and collapsed before he could reach her. He shouted for help but only Matthew heard him, and he rushed in to find Jamie trying to lift her onto the bed.

"What have you done?" he asked Jamie.

"Nothing Matthew; you know I would never hurt her. Can you get April?" said Jamie as he finally managed to place her on her bed. Her white face was frightening to look at. April ran in and looked accusingly at Jamie, but he was oblivious of what was being thought, he couldn't take his eyes off Liza's face. He was now panicking as she looked dead and he was desperately calling her name.

April took over the situation telling Matthew to find someone to fetch the doctor and all the while Jamie was trying to wake Liza, but she wasn't responding to his voice. In her mind she was tied down so that she couldn't move, she could smell smoke from several fires and the skins covering the tepee had their own aroma. Why had she told Jamie that he mustn't leave as it was essential that he did? She wanted to tell him that he must go because he would be killed if he didn't, but she couldn't open her mouth, she was gagged. Her punishment was going to be severe because they didn't normally tie and gag her, and she was becoming more and more frightened. She couldn't remember what she had done to deserve this; she had probably tried to escape yet again, why had she done that because she was always punished when they had caught her, but this time it was different and in her mind she knew with certainty that she was not going to survive.

Somebody was shaking her violently and calling her name, not her Indian name, but her real name. It was Jamie and she must tell him to stop yelling; he had to be quiet; he was in danger, but she still couldn't talk. She felt very ill and her world was going around; she couldn't work out what they were doing to her as she had never felt like this before.

Matthew came back into the room and he had brought Miranda with him. "The doctor will be here soon," he said.

"I can't get her to wake up," Jamie said to his mother.

"It looks like some sort of seizure," said a concerned Miranda.

"It's not a seizure," said Matthew and all eyes turned to him. "She's having a nightmare and she's so frightened that she can't move."

The doctor arrived and when Jamie told him what had happened all he could say was that as she had been under a great deal of stress her mind decided to rest. Jamie looked at him in disbelief and asked how that could account for the sickness.

"It can't, but could she be pregnant again?" he asked. Jamie frowned and looked around at Matthew who was standing watching what was going on, but it was too late to tell him to leave. "We must try to get a sleeping draught down her and that should relax her."

"With all due respect doctor, she's already asleep and I doubt that we would get anything down her without choking her," said Jamie.

"I know Your Lordship, but I don't know how else to relax her and the way she looks at the moment we have to try something to make her wake up," said the doctor. "She looks paralysed with fear."

"I can help her to wake up and so can you," said Matthew to Jamie.

"Matthew, I think you ought to leave and let the doctor do his job," said Jamie with some annoyance.

"No, I know what to do, he doesn't," said Matthew.

"What would you do Matthew?" asked Miranda.

"I'd get into bed with her and tell her that what she is having is a nightmare and that it was all a long time ago and she is quite safe now. And that she is never going to be hurt again," said Matthew staring defiantly at Jamie.

Jamie looked back at him and a memory stirred of a nightmare that Liza had experienced soon after they got together; it was not as violent as this one and he had coaxed her out of it by reassuring her that she was safe and that he would always be there for her. He had taken her feeling of safety away from her by telling her that he was going away.

Jamie turned and thanked the doctor for his help and that as soon as he could he would get Liza to take the sleeping draught, he then asked his mother to show the doctor out.

"Well Matthew, we had both better get your mother out of this nightmare. You take one side and I'll take the other," said Jamie. Matthew smiled and kicked off his shoes and climbed onto the bed and moved closely to his mother. Jamie did the same on the other side of her and he engulfed her in his arms and kept telling her that she was safe, and he and Matthew were going to help her through this nightmare.

After a while Liza started talking, "You know that you both must leave before he sees you here. You must take Matthew away quickly Jamie because he won't want him here and he won't want you here either. He'll kill you both and the chief will not be able to do anything about it."

"Nobody's going to hurt us, we're safely in England and you're just having a bad dream," said Matthew and he snuggled even more closely into her. "Do you remember that you used to let me get into bed with you when I had a nightmare and then James and I pretended that we'd had nightmares so that we could come into your bed? John and I also did it sometimes and we knew that you let us do it even though you really knew that we hadn't been frightened. All three of us did it once, but I think that was when you had been ill, and we wanted to make you feel better."

A slight smile was hovering on Liza's face, she still looked deathly pale, but she seemed to be listening to Matthew intently.

Jamie decided to join in the conversation. "Do you still have nightmares Matthew?" he asked.

"We never really did have them, Mum is the only one who has nightmares now, but she doesn't have them very often," said Matthew. "Her fears started before I was born, but her nightmares only started a few years later."

Jamie held her even closer to him. "Are you coming back to us Liza? Matthew and I are safely at home now and we have you with us, so all your fears are over. Thank you for worrying about us and telling us how we could save ourselves."

"I've had a dream," said Liza. "I don't feel well Jamie; I feel very ill. I'll get myself ready to leave as soon as I feel better."

"You're going nowhere Liza, and neither am I," said Jamie.

"That's good," said Matthew and he climbed off the bed, put his shoes on and told them that he was going back to the schoolroom and that his brothers would be worried so he can now tell them that their mother was feeling better and that their father was looking after her.

"Thank you, Matthew; you've been a very great help," said Jamie. "Tell your brothers that they can visit their mother later."

Liza was now shivering violently, and Jamie pulled the bedclothes over her and once again climbed in beside her.

"I promised that I would never hurt you Liza, and I have. I am so ashamed that I acted so selfishly. I came in to tell you that this morning, but you didn't give me the chance and I can understand why you felt the need to get away, but I don't really think that you would have left the boys. I think that if you had truly decided to leave you would have taken them with you," said Jamie.

"You and Matthew were in great danger Jamie. How did you get away? How did I manage to get away?" said Liza and Jamie realised that she was still not quite back with him and that her nightmare was still real to her.

"It was just a dream Liza; Matthew and I have never been in danger and you weren't either. You're not very well today and you need to rest, I'll stay with you until you go to sleep, I promise that I'll look after you," said Jamie and he put his arms around her and cradled her until she was sleeping peacefully.

Jamie lay there thinking. He still felt the need to get away from all the functions and events relating to the charity. He felt permanently on show and he was sure that Liza felt the same, in fact she had said that this was how it would be but they both had risen to the occasion but their smiles were wearing rather thin now. Was there a way out of it? Probably there was not. It was the price that they paid for the success of the charity and they were therefore giving a good life to children who otherwise would be used, abused and probably dead before they reached twenty years of age. However he did yearn for the time that he and Liza were first married and the freedom that they had. He suddenly realised that he had been blaming Liza for the situation, but it was not of her making, it was what was being demanded of them by those who wanted to help the children. He was now determined to make the most of the short amount of time that they managed to spend together.

He noticed that the colour was coming back into her cheeks and he breathed a sigh of relief. He made her as comfortable as possible and sat in a chair to watch over her. He decided that he would shortly find Grace and see Liza's diary as he felt that there had to be a few days when they could take some time away alone.

Liza's cheeks were looking quite pink now, but he noticed that she shivered every now and again. He looked more closely and could see that the colour creeping into her face was rather unnatural. He touched her forehead and realised that she was burning up and she was now trying to pull the bedclothes from her.

He went to the door and called for April who came almost immediately. "I don't like the look of her April; I think we ought to get the doctor again." She nodded and went to make the necessary arrangements. Miranda looked in saying that April had told her that Liza was very unwell.

"She looks very hot Jamie; that's so different to the way she was earlier. I'll get some water and a flannel and try to cool her down. This can't be anything to do with your disagreement or a nightmare. This is definitely a fever; do you feel alright Jamie?" said Miranda.

"I had better stop the boys from visiting her, just in case she has something contagious," said Jamie.

"Matthew spent a great deal of time with her this morning; I hope he stays fit," said Miranda.

Miranda was still mopping Liza's brow when the doctor arrived for the second time that day.

"We must get her fever down," which was an obvious remark by the doctor. He then went on to ask if they had an ice-house and made April start filling a bath with buckets of ice and when half full he covered it with an oil cloth and told Jamie to wrap Liza in a blanket and place her in the bath. The doctor then covered her with another oil cloth and continued to have ice put on top of her. Liza was no longer shivering; in fact she looked quite comfortable.

"She's cooling down now, but her breathing is rather laboured, we must pray that it doesn't turn to pneumonia. What is she saying?" asked the doctor.

Liza had started muttering in a strange language which Jamie could only assume was Cherokee.

"What are you saying Liza? I don't understand you," said Jamie.

"She's cool enough now; make sure she's dry and get her onto the bed," said the doctor as April and Miranda rubbed her with towels and Jamie covered her with another blanket.

"I need my son," Liza was muttering in Cherokee. "He knows what to do."

"She's talking rubbish," said Miranda, "she delirious."

"She's not;" came Matthew's voice from the doorway. "I know what she wants me to do."

"How can a child possibly know what to do?" said the doctor with some annoyance.

"Good my son," gasped Liza still talking in Cherokee. "You know where my bag is, don't you? Tell them to get you some hot water." Matthew nodded and pulled her bag from one of her dressing table drawers.

"I need some hot water April," said Matthew.

April looked at Jamie for guidance and he nodded for her to do what Matthew asked.

"What's he going to do?" asked the doctor with a certain amount of panic in his voice.

"I don't know," said Jamie as the drums started beating in his head.

The doctor frowned and asked where the noise was coming from. "There seems to be someone beating a drum somewhere."

Matthew and Liza smiled as they knew that the sound was really keeping Liza's heart beating regularly. Matthew was pulling certain dried herbs from Liza's bag and breaking them into a bowl ready for April's return with the hot water and when she did he poured some of it over the herbs and then strained some of the liquid into a cup.

"You're not going to like this," he said to her in Cherokee and she faintly nodded and turned up her nose at it.

"Are you going to let him give her that rubbish?" the doctor asked Jamie.

"I have seen her use similar on others and they have been helped. I have realised that Matthew has the same abilities as his mother and whatever he does it will do her no harm and hopefully some good," said Jamie.

"That noise is beginning to get on my nerves," said the doctor.

"Are you alright doctor, I can hear nothing," said Miranda and April was frowning with a look that seemed to show that she was wondering what the doctor was talking about.

Liza choked slightly on the drink and Jamie came over and helped Matthew give his mother the concoction. When she had finished Matthew pulled out a different herb and soaked that in more water until it softened.

He asked April for some cloth and they both wrapped the softened herbs in it and then wrapped it around Liza's chest and the aroma filled her nostrils and she started breathing more easily.

Matthew cleared away the unused herbs putting them carefully into the bag and placing that back in the drawer. He then sat on the edge of the bed and nodded in time to the drumbeats.

"She's alright now isn't she Matthew," said Jamie quietly and Matthew smiled and carried on nodding to the sound of the drum.

The doctor went over to Liza and took her pulse and felt her head. He also listened to her chest. "Well, I have to say that she's sleeping peacefully, and the fever seems to have passed and there is now no sign of anything wrong with her breathing. I think that I have something to learn from this, but I do wish that I could get this sound out of my head."

Matthew looked over to the doctor and muttered under his breath in Cherokee "Thank you for keeping her heart beating, but it is working well now so you may stop." The drums immediately stopped, and the doctor stared at Matthew wondering what he had done.

The doctor said that he would call again later, and Miranda showed him out. April was making Liza more comfortable while Matthew stood watching over her.

"You did a very important job today Matthew; you saved your mother a great deal of pain, if not worse. Thank you for that, you are very special," said Jamie.

"No need to thank me, it's what she would do for me or anyone else. I'm just pleased that I knew what to do and that's because she was able to tell me," said Matthew.

"I presume that you both were speaking in your Indian language. When did she teach you that? I had no idea that you knew it so well," said Jamie.

"She hasn't taught me. It's just something that I have always known, but we very rarely speak it. It's just at times like this that we use it. We did that when Aunt Diana needed to be purged and also when Zelma was hurt. We only use it when someone needs the help of the Cherokee medication," said Matthew. "When I have finished my education I shall become a doctor. I think my brothers would like to see our mother; shall I tell them to come in now?"

"Yes but warn them that she's asleep, so they will have to be quiet," said Jamie.

Miranda came back and she and April tidied the room whilst the boys quietly came into the room and stood looking down on Liza who suddenly smiled even though her eyes were closed. In unison the boys grinned, kicked off their shoes and climbed onto her bed, John on one side, James on the other and Matthew on the outside with John.

"What are you doing?" asked Jamie in surprise.

"Our mother knows that we're here and she knows what we are doing," said John smiling.

"We did this when we were little and she had been ill and it made her feel better then and we know that it will make her feel better now," said James and Jamie knew that Matthew had been the instigator of this and he couldn't help laughing.

Miranda was also laughing, "There's no arguing with what they are doing, and you can see that Liza is smiling. She's surrounded by her boys and she's always happy in their company. You boys are a tonic for anyone."

They stayed like that for a short while and then left but not before Matthew made sure that Jamie was going to stay and watch over her.

"I'm not going to leave her Matthew. I shall be here and make sure that she stays as well as you have made her, and I shall have my meals here with her and be with her all night. But you all can visit later if you like, I know that she would like that," said Jamie.

"Matthew is quite unique, isn't he?" said Miranda when they had left. "I think he'll make a very good doctor. He'll use ways which have been tried and tested as well as every modern method available. It will be a good combination and he'll save a great many lives."

When Liza finally awoke, she found Jamie sitting watching over her. It was very late in the afternoon and the sun was beginning to set leaving strange shadows dancing around the room.

"It's good to see your eyes looking bright Liza; they have been closed for a long while. The boys are having their supper now; they have been in several times to see you. So have my mother and Lucinda. Grace has been keeping the household running smoothly. I think that my uncle wanted to say a few prayers over you, but I managed to dissuade him by saying that you weren't awake so they would amount to nothing," said Jamie. "April has been looking after you as if she was your mother. I think she blames me for your illness, and she's probably right."

"What I had couldn't have been brought about by a disagreement; it's more likely that it was from a chill or something that one of the children gave me. I hope that the children on their way to America are fit, they all seemed so when they left," said Liza.

"I certainly added to how you were feeling and I'm sorry that I was so selfish," said Jamie. "I was going to leave you to deal with everything yet again. I did feel the need to get away and it hadn't occurred to me that you also felt the same. Grace is organising your diary so that we can have a few days away together with absolutely nothing to do but concentrate on each other. Would you like that Liza?"

"It sounds perfect, where shall we go. Don't tell me, you organise it and I'll just pack my case and go with you," said Liza. She lay back and smiled at him.

"It was unlike me to get so annoyed; I suppose I was beginning to suffer with my chill, or whatever it was."

"You were quite ill Liza; you were bordering on pneumonia. The doctor put you in a bath of ice to bring your fever down and Matthew worked wonders with your medication," said Jamie.

"Yes Matthew talked to me throughout; I knew what he was doing. It was exactly what I had done for others," said Liza and Jamie knew that she didn't want to talk about it any further.

"I shall be having my supper up here with you and I shall be sleeping in your bed tonight and every other night until you're fit," smiled Jamie.

"I'll be fit by tomorrow; we have the concert to attend tomorrow evening and it's an important one," said Liza.

"I don't think you realise just how ill you've been and still are. You will not be attending tomorrow's function; you'll just have to leave that to me. You must not worry about it," said Jamie.

"Oh," said Liza. "You'll have to get Grace to write to cancel for us," said Liza yawning.

"Liza, before we became engaged, I attended every function for many years on my own; I'm quite capable of representing us both or I might ask my mother to accompany me," smiled Jamie.

"She'll enjoy that," said Liza and within a minute she was asleep again. She woke and ate a little supper; the boys came to say goodnight and finally Jamie climbed into bed next to her and she was very contented sleeping in his arms. All their earlier arguments were completely forgotten.

She was pampered through the whole of the following day and late in the afternoon Jamie appeared handsomely dressed in his evening attire. Miranda came to show off her dress and she was also wearing the Edgeworth sapphires.

"You look so beautiful Miranda; blue suits you so well. I'm sure you'll have a wonderful evening," said Liza.

Jamie leaned over and kissed her. "You look really good tonight Jamie; I shall miss you. You must watch out for all those ladies, don't forget how many wanted you before I was with you and they probably still do."

"Don't worry Liza, I'll have my mother to make sure I keep them all at arm's length," said Jamie. "You rest and I'll see you later."

She was asleep when he arrived back and after Roberts had sorted out his clothes he came into her room and quietly climbed into bed with her. "Did you have a good evening?" she mumbled sleepily.

"Yes, we did, but everyone was disappointed that you weren't there, Mother did a very good job covering for you. I missed being with you," said Jamie.

"Are you going to love me tonight Jamie?" asked Liza.

Jamie turned on his side and looked at her smiling face. "Surely you're not fit enough for that yet," he said.

"Yes I am Jamie," said Liza. "Are you?"

"Well I've had a very tiring evening, but I think I may be able to manage," said Jamie.

***

It took a week for Liza to be completely fit and during that time Jamie organised a short holiday for them. He had heard from April about the cottage that Adam had rented for them after their marriage and it sounded idyllic. Jamie sought out Adam to find out if he thought it would be a suitable place to take Liza for a short break.

"It is a beautifully kept cottage. I could only afford a few days there but in that time we had a housekeeper who came in every day as well as a gardener who doubled as a stable hand. It was very clean and private. Obviously it doesn't have the facilities that you have here, but if you want to relax for a while it would be a place to take Her Ladyship. I'm sure she would recuperate well there, and you would be very comfortable," said Adam.

"Thank you, Adam. I could take her to one of the hotels, but that is nothing different for her. I could rent a huge house, but we have a huge house here. I'm sure she will enjoy the cosiness of a pretty cottage," said Jamie. "I'll write to the owners today."

Liza was quite excited when she learned that she and Jamie were going to a little cottage in the country.

"We have never had time away from everyone before. We always said that we would soon after we married, but we never managed it until now," said Liza. "I'm really looking forward to it."

April found it amusing that it was on her recommendation that the Lord and Lady of the Manor were going to a cottage in the country. "I had a wonderful time there. I had my meals cooked for me and the gardener brought me fresh flowers every day. I did nothing the whole time I was there."

"I wonder how Adam knew of the cottage," said Liza.

"I suppose one of his friends told him about it. I know you'll really enjoy it," smiled April.

I would enjoy anywhere that I was alone with Jamie, thought Liza as she smiled and nodded to April.

Jamie insisted that Liza was wrapped up warmly the morning they left for the cottage. He was to drive them in the small carriage and when it was packed and Liza was sitting in the passenger seat, Jamie climbed up beside her and they had every member of the family waving them off with the boys shouting to them at the tops of their voices.

It took just two hours to reach the cottage and Adam and April had been right, it was indeed idyllic and they were greeted by a very homely lady who welcomed them and guided them into a warm sitting room and immediately brought them tea and cakes. Whilst they sat there they could hear her upstairs unpacking their cases which had been carried up by the gardener who doubled as a handyman and was also her husband.

"There's salad, meat and bread in the larder for your lunch and all you have to do is warm the meat pie and vegetables for your evening meal," said the housekeeper when she had finished unpacking for them. "We'll leave you two love birds now and I'll be back first thing in the morning to get your breakfast."

They thanked her and she left. Jamie laughed, "I thought we were a little old to be called love birds."

"We're not old Jamie," smiled Liza. "We're just mature enough to know how to please one another. Many people never learn that."

They looked around the cottage and finally came to the bedroom, which was very prettily decorated, and the bed looked very inviting.

"It's strange to think that it's here that Adam and April probably consummated their marriage," said Jamie thoughtfully.

"I'd much rather think about how we are going to enjoy ourselves here, and how we are going to spend this week in this beautiful cottage," said Liza. "Adam certainly knew what he was doing when he chose this place; April must have been delighted to be here with him. I know I'm delighted to be here with you."

"I have my instructions from the family, especially young Matthew, and I have to look after you and make sure that you return fit and healthy; so I've got to pamper you a great deal," said Jamie.

They had a wonderful week; it was the honeymoon that they had both promised one another and when they returned home, they both felt refreshed and capable of handling all the pressures that were constantly being placed on them.

Chapter 20

The cricket season was nearly over, and the weather was growing colder but Bella still descended upon them on occasion without notice. The boys were beginning to make their plans for Christmas which seemed very early to Liza. The new Langston Home was going to be ready just after Christmas; Hector had been working diligently to get it organised.

Liza and Jamie were discussing just how many they would be taking to Belfast that year. "We might have to put some of them at my house," said Liza.

"Yes, we have to accommodate my mother and Lucinda and then my uncle and Grace. The boys obviously are no problem but then we have April and Adam as well as Roberts and Harper. Adam has asked if Estelle could come with us as this is the first Christmas without their mother. Do you think that Bella is going to turn up with her boys?" asked a concerned Jamie.

"It's a shame that we won't have the Major and Jennifer with us this year, or Joseph and Lily, but they now have become their own family. I think that the simplest thing to do is put your uncle and Grace in my house; I'm sure they will appreciate that we are getting overcrowded at your place. We could also put Estelle there; she will be more comfortable there than squashed in the tiny box room. It's not far away and Mrs Edwards will enjoy looking after them. If Bella and the boys turn up then they'll also have to be there," said Liza.

"So there will be fourteen of us altogether; that's a lot to be travelling with. I suppose your hotels can take fourteen of us on the way because it would be easier to travel from Liverpool," said Jamie.

"There might have to be a certain amount of room sharing, but it would only be for one night. Do you think that Harper and Roberts would survive sharing a room?" smiled Liza. "Of course we would also have to think about Davis and Hendry driving us all the way to Liverpool, but they've shared a room before."

"Mother and Lucinda have shared before; I suppose Grace and Estelle will manage together. My uncle will have the luxury of a single room, unless he has to go in with Harper and Roberts," laughed Jamie. "I'm sure they'll all survive one night."

"We'll have to decide on the day we will travel because I'll have to write to the hotel to organise it all," said Liza.

"We'll discuss it with the rest of the family over the weekend, that will give you plenty of time to arrange it all," said Jamie. "We will soon have to think about staying here for Christmas. Do you think that the Fullers would travel here?"

"They may do; as long as Edward and Nicole bring little Edward, I'm sure Wendell and Amelia would be happy to and if Peter is still keen on Grace then he would have no problem in coming here," said Liza. "That won't be until next year, so we'll worry about it some other time."

They heard a carriage draw up. "I suppose Bella has invited herself again for the weekend," said Jamie with a sigh.

Harper came into the room saying that two members of the Metropolitan Police force would like to see them both.

"Show them into the library please Harper and tell them that we will be with them shortly," said Jamie.

Liza and Jamie looked at each other as they knew that this day would come, and they calmly got up and went into the library with suitable questioning frowns on their faces.

"Gentlemen," said Jamie with a look that made them bow. "Who are you and what can we do for you?"

"I'm Inspector Wilkes and this is Sergeant Forbes," said the Inspector. "I understand that you know a Theresa and a Gareth Jones."

"I don't think so," said Jamie.

"I have one or two estates in Wales and I'm afraid that I don't know the names of all the workers and their wives or those in the villages," smiled Liza.

"They're not from Wales," said the Inspector.

"Oh, I assumed that they were as Jones is a Welsh name," said Liza and she looked at them and waited for them to explain further.

"I don't know the surname of Theresa; I don't believe she ever had one," said the Inspector. "I know that you both visited her on the prison ship."

"Ah yes, we visited the prison ship and saw a Theresa there," said Jamie. "I presume that's who you are talking about, but we don't know anyone called Jones. What has happened?"

"When the ship docked in Lisbon they found that Theresa wasn't on board, and it appears that she had not been on board since they left London docks," said the Inspector.

"I would have thought that all prisoners should have been checked before the ship left London," said Jamie.

"Yes, but the other women in her cell covered for her; they believed that one of the crew must have taken a fancy to her and they thought 'good for her'," said the Inspector.

Liza and Jamie created an awkward silence until the Inspector had to continue.

"Whilst the ship was in London a crew member jumped ship and it is now thought that he helped her to escape," said the Inspector.

"I presume that the crew member is called Jones," said Jamie. "I'm afraid that there is nothing that we can help you with Inspector. Theresa would not come here and if she did then we would have no option but to report it and we don't know the Jones person."

"Lady Edgeworth was seen talking to him at Southampton recently," said the Sergeant accusingly.

"I don't think so Sergeant," said Jamie haughtily.

"I am not familiar with the name Gareth Jones; I know a great many sailors Sergeant. I have travelled extensively and acknowledge those I recognise; I do not necessarily know their names. I own a shipping company and come across many faces that I could not put names to. I can only assume that Gareth Jones is one of those. So you know that he was in Southampton; I have been there twice recently and if I was being watched closely you would have seen me talking to a great many people," said Liza calmly.

"Are you saying that Theresa was with him?" asked Jamie.

"We believe so," said the Sergeant.

"We were in Southampton just over seven weeks ago and again around three weeks ago, so if they were there either of those times they will be well on their way abroad or have already arrived somewhere," said Liza. "So I don't see how we can help you."

"If she is on the run alone then she may well turn up here; you are the only ones to have shown kindness to her, which is what we don't understand since she helped to burn down your children's home where people were killed," said the Inspector.

"I'll tell you Inspector, it is no secret," said Liza. "Around seven years ago I interviewed three girls for a maids' position; all three were girls who had been abused and had escaped that life taking some of the little children with them. They put themselves in great danger to help those children. Each girl was being trained in domestic duties and I had difficulty choosing between them, but I did make a choice and it wasn't Theresa. The girl I took on is still with me, she taught herself to read and write and has been the most loyal of employees and is now happily married. If I had chosen Theresa perhaps the same would have happened to her, but I didn't, and she was taken on as a domestic servant in another household. Unfortunately she was found by her abusers and dragged back into that life. I know that her employer did look for her, but they assumed that the pull of her old life was too much for her."

"So what you are saying is that you feel guilty that you didn't employ her," said the Inspector.

"No Inspector, I don't feel guilty. I just recognise that people don't always have the same luck as others, and I know that she would have made something of herself if she had been given the opportunity. So my husband and I just tried to make her journey to Tasmania a little more comfortable, although a journey such as that would never be comfortable," said Liza.

"I have been told that you begged for her life," said the Inspector.

"When I realised who she was and how she had saved children in the past, and that her involvement in burning the Home was knowledge of it rather than any action in it, I did not feel that the ultimate sentence was fair and I talked to the judge about it. I naturally had to leave the decision to him, and I was surprised that he commuted it to transportation," said Liza.

"We gave her some money, extra clothes, books and paper and writing implements, because I know that my wife wanted her to carry on learning to write and eventually she hoped that she would write to let us know how she was getting on," said Jamie.

"It was also felt that anyone who could read and write would be found useful where she was going," said Liza.

"Young Gareth Jones was the captain's aide when you were there," said the Sergeant.

"There was a young aide there; I remember that, but I couldn't tell you what he looked like," said Jamie.

Liza just shook her head and made no comment.

"Well, if you see or hear anything to do with Theresa perhaps you would let us know," said the Inspector. "Thank you for your time."

"Do you have much of a journey back?" asked Liza.

"It's just over two hours back," said the Inspector.

"You must have something to eat and drink before you make that journey Inspector," said Liza. "It's a very cold evening."

"Please don't put yourself out your Ladyship," said the Inspector.

"It's not putting me out Inspector," said Liza as she rang the bell for Harper.

Harper appeared very quickly, and Liza wondered whether he had been listening outside the door.

"Ah Harper, perhaps you could show the Inspector and the Sergeant down to the kitchen and get Mrs Lambert to give them something to warm them up, they have a long journey back and it's turning very cold," said Liza.

"Thank you, Your Ladyship," said the Inspector and he and the Sergeant followed Harper out of the library and down to the kitchen.

"I think I'll go to my room and rest before dinner, would you like to join me?" said Liza and Jamie nodded.

Once in Liza's room with the door firmly shut. "Do you think they believed us?" asked Jamie.

"We told no lies Jamie," said Liza. "We just didn't add to what they already knew."

"It's seven weeks since they left, I doubt whether they will catch them now. I wonder where they were going," said Jamie.

"They were going to New York; they were booked on the ship that Myra and Henry came in on. I saw them waiting to board when I was talking to the captain and you were getting Myra and Henry into the carriage to go to the hotel," said Liza.

"Did they see you?" asked Jamie.

"Yes, but neither of us acknowledged the other," said Liza.

"Well, they'll be well and truly lost in New York by now; possibly even further into America. I know I shouldn't, but I wish them well," said Jamie.

"America is full of people who are running from something and many of them settle and make good lives for themselves. Their past is forgotten and they have a future to look forward to. I have met many like that," said Liza.

"I think I hear the carriage leaving; let's hope that it's the last we see of them," said Jamie. "I also think that we ought not to talk about it anymore. It would be best to forget all about it."

392

"No doubt we'll be asked by your mother and Lucinda, so we'll have to tell them as little as possible," said Liza. "Nobody's dining with us tonight, so that is useful. I suppose the boys will also be curious."

Liza was right, the boys were very curious, and they asked about the visit with expectation. They were disillusioned by the answer as both Liza and Jamie told them that the Police were looking for someone who had gone missing and that they had heard that they were known to them. "We could tell them very little, boys," said Jamie. "We had no idea where these people were and initially we didn't know who they were but found out that we had met them in passing a while ago. It seems exciting to you but really it's very mundane."

"Quite boring then," said James with disappointment.

"I'm afraid so James," said Liza.

Ten days later Inspector Wilkes and Sergeant Forbes called again. Jamie was inspecting the estate with his overseer and Liza had been going through correspondence with Grace when Harper came in to say that they would like to see her.

"Show them into the library please Harper and would you send somebody to find His Lordship," said Liza.

"They only want to see you, Your Ladyship," said Harper.

"That's what they may want, but I would like His Lordship to be here," said Liza.

Harper nodded and left to carry out her instructions.

"Would you like me to come in with you?" asked Grace.

"No thank you Grace, they can wait until Jamie gets back," said Liza.

Harper returned to say that a stable lad had been dispatched to find His Lordship and the two Policemen didn't look very happy.

"Can you arrange for Mrs Lambert to organise some suitable refreshments for them please Harper; that should keep them amused for a while," said Liza.

Liza carried on sorting her correspondence with Grace until she could see Jamie in the distance riding towards the house and she gauged that the time was right for her to greet her visitors alone knowing that Jamie would be arriving in less than five minutes.

"Good morning gentlemen," she said as she entered the library. "I'm surprised to see you back again. Have you managed to find the runaways?"

They both jumped up from their seats, with the Sergeant nearly dropping his teacup. Liza waved them to remain seated and she sat in a chair facing them.

393

"I'm afraid that all we have managed to do is definitely identify Gareth Jones at Southampton and we believe he boarded a ship to New York some nine weeks ago. It is believed that he had a young woman with him, although we cannot be sure who she was and she may have been no more than a passing acquaintance and not this Theresa person at all," said the Inspector.

Liza shrugged her shoulders and said nothing, waiting for them to continue without any help from her.

"You were talking to the captain of the ship when Gareth Jones was waiting to board and the passengers were very near you," said the Sergeant. "You must have seen him and seen if he was with somebody."

"Do you know how many people are on the dockside, especially when a ship has just come into port? Do you know how busy the sailors are unloading the cargo and getting the ship ready for its next voyage?" said Liza with some annoyance. "Of course I spoke to the captain; he had just delivered my very close friends safely from New York, I know that I also mentioned that he appeared to have a full passenger list for his return trip. But after such pleasantries I was more interested in getting my guests settled into the carriage which was to take us to my hotel for the night and making sure that their luggage was intact. I would not be aware of much else, nor am I capable of seeing through crowds of people to spy someone that I really don't know."

By this time Jamie had arrived and was just entering the library. He heard the latter part of what Liza was saying and recognised annoyance in her voice.

"You appear to be harassing my wife gentlemen," said Jamie curtly. "What is it that you want to know?"

"Nothing from you Sir; it's your wife that we want to question," said the Sergeant.

"Sergeant, will you please leave this to me," said an exasperated Inspector.

"I believe that we answered all your questions to the best of our ability last time you were here; I do not think that we need to answer anything further," said Jamie frowning.

"It would not be the first time that your wife helped somebody to break out of prison according to our information," said the Inspector with a little trepidation.

"Your information is incorrect Sir," said Liza. "I have never broken anyone out of prison although I know others have thought so, but it was a totally ridiculous suggestion. I did not do it then and I most certainly have not done it now. I have no idea where the girl would have been housed on the prison ship

394

and besides I have too much affection for my husband and family to jeopardise my life with them and especially not for someone that I hardly know."

"A murderer escaped when you were in America and according to our information you visited him every day," said the Inspector.

"My daughter's godfather was accused of murder and awaiting trial and I did visit him whenever I could. I took my daughter with me on occasion so that he could see her and hold her; it gave him a great deal of comfort," said Liza. "I don't want to be reminded of that time if you don't mind."

"I suppose your daughter is proud of the fact that her godfather is an escaped murderer," said the Sergeant nastily.

"She is no longer in a position to be proud or otherwise of him," said Liza quietly.

"I bet she isn't," said the Sergeant before the Inspector could stop him.

"I thought that you had done your homework Sergeant," said the Inspector between gritted teeth, "my apologies Lady Edgeworth."

"That's enough Inspector; I think you should leave now," said Jamie. "We have told you all that we can and whatever happened in the past in America has nothing to do with the current situation. Let me reiterate what we have told you before. We do not know where Theresa whatever her name is, nor do we have any idea how she is no longer on her way to Tasmania. You have managed to upset my wife by reminding her of a time that was deeply disturbing for her."

He rang for Harper and when he arrived Jamie asked him to show the gentlemen out, and they went without another word.

"I wonder how they knew about the soldier who escaped," said Jamie. "Still I suppose if you dig deep enough you can find out anything. Are you alright Liza, you look very upset?"

"Yes, I'm alright Jamie, but you were right that it was a time that I prefer to forget. I have lost two children and sometimes it hurts to think about them," said Liza.

"I know Liza, but it doesn't worry you thinking about other times in your past, does it?" said Jamie.

Liza was quiet for a long while and Jamie watched her carefully. "You want to know about the prison escape in Benson, don't you?" she said. "One day I will tell you."

"Today is a good day Liza," said Jamie.

"I thought that we had both put our pasts behind us. I don't ask you about what you have done so is it fair that you ask me?" said Liza.

"You have been accused of helping two people to escape their punishments and I would like to understand why you are being singled out as the main person they believe is behind these events," said Jamie. "I know that Matthew once said that you didn't think that you deserved the key to Benson, and it was because of his Uncle Mark."

"It really is a very simple story Jamie, but I want to assure you that I did not get Mark Kendal out of prison; it was more a series of errors on the part of the authorities at the fort. For a while Patrick thought that I had had a hand in it, but I did know that there were inefficiencies that could lead to someone escaping," said Liza.

"And you did nothing about them," said Jamie.

"The sergeant in charge of the prison knew about at least one of them; I didn't think that it needed to go further up the chain of command. When the key was turned in the lock of the prison cell it did not line up with the catch until the door was lifted slightly and then it would click closed. Sometimes Mark would lift it himself when we had finished our visit," said Liza.

"Did they let him out for your visits?" asked Jamie.

"The door was always opened, sometimes he would come out and sometimes I would go in," said Liza. "Quite often the sergeant would leave a private on duty, but he liked his drink and more often than not he would go to sleep on the desk and sometimes he would sit outside the block leaving us alone. It was all so very casual."

"The evening that Mark disappeared a storm was threatening so I left before it broke; I did not see what had happened as the thunder and lightning started to bother my pony and when I got to the gate all hell let loose and I fell from my trap luckily one of the soldiers caught me and we managed to calm the pony enough for me to get home, but the skies opened and it was an horrendous ten minute journey for me," said Liza.

"Many unfortunate events seem to happen when there is a storm," commented Jamie.

"Mark's escape was not noticed until early the next morning, the soldier on duty had been in a drunken stupor all night and somehow Mark had got out of the fort without being seen. It was then that Patrick thought that I had helped him and his reasoning was that I must have been in love with him or I would not have risked everything to do so," said Liza and Jamie could see the pain in her face at the memory.

"You don't need to tell me any more Liza; I can see that it is hurting you and you are right that we do not need to relive the past," said Jamie.

"I've got this far Jamie; you might as well hear the end of the story. Three senior army personnel arrived for Mark's court martial and as he wasn't there they assumed that I had been instrumental in his escape and they therefore decided that they would haul me up in front of them. I refused to go but they said that I was to be brought to them by force if necessary. I made them wait all day and then drove in and walked into the room with my head held high," said Liza.

"Didn't Patrick have something to say about that?" asked Jamie.

"Patrick did, but he was under orders and had to stand to attention and watch the proceedings," said Liza. "Although it didn't take him long to get me out of there."

"Liza you weren't in the army; you should never have been put in that position. That's scandalous and probably illegal," said Jamie.

"Yes, I told them that. I told them that they had no right to keep me there and interrogate me. I walked out much to their surprise," said Liza.

"Why didn't you tell them about the cell door?" asked Jamie.

"If I had mentioned the several breaches of security then it would have reflected badly on the Colonel and the Captain and they could have been demoted and transferred or they could have insisted that the Colonel take early retirement. I couldn't do that to them," said Liza. "The next day the three judges were due to leave and I went to the fort to visit Ada and Bea but I was marched unceremoniously back into the court situation but only one general was on duty, who you may remember from the past. He was General Maybury. Gabriel came rushing in to help and I was told by the General that if I co-operated I would only get a few years in prison. I told him that he had no right to even think that way and he told me that as there was a new President I was not to think that I would get any help there."

"You knew the President, I remember meeting him at one of your functions in New York before he was President," said Jamie.

Liza grinned, "I told him that I was well aware that there was a new President and that I did know him personally. I believe that it was at that time that I walked out of the court again, as did Patrick and Gabriel. Gabriel advised me to leave the fort as quickly as possible as I would be vulnerable on army ground. I didn't return to the fort for some time. I thought it best not to, but as it turned out little Meg took a turn for the worse and she died a couple of days later."

Liza's eyes filled with tears as she remembered that time and Jamie put his arms around her, and she let her emotions flow openly.

"The end of the story is that I wanted to see the Colonel to quietly tell him of the problems with the fort security, but because little Meg was so ill, I had to tell Patrick. He was horrified at how lax the prison was kept but even he hadn't thought about why many soldiers seemed to get into town without being seen and mostly get caught drunk on duty the next day. The Colonel and Captain were also horrified when Patrick told them and of course they took steps to rectify the situation," smiled Liza.

Jamie frowned and said that he didn't understand.

"Well, it was obvious that there was a way out of the fort that didn't take the men past the sentries on the main gate. Mark would have known about it as he used to visit Felicity when he really should have been on duty in the fort. It didn't take a genius to work that out. I didn't know where it was, but I knew that it had to be there, and it was," said Liza.

"So that's how he got out of prison and if you hadn't visited him so regularly you would not have been caught up in any of it, but of course that doesn't answer how he managed to disappear so completely in such a short space of time. Somebody with money and contacts must have helped him. I'm not a fool Liza and I know that I met him in Liverpool a few years ago. I also know that you will have had your reasons. Did Patrick know?" asked Jamie.

"He always suspected but chose not to question me. He and Sean realised that they were being led in many wrong directions when they were searching for him and they knew that Indians were masters of misdirection and that there was only one person who could arrange that," said Liza.

Jamie was now sitting and staring at her. "You risked everything for him Liza; the reason for that must have been important."

"Yes it was, and it still is," said Liza. "What are you going to do Jamie?"

"Well I'm certainly not going to inform anyone in authority," he smiled. "Thank you for telling me Liza. I always knew that there was an exciting side to you. I would have loved to have been there to help you organise it all, it must have taken a great deal of thought and planning. Are you sure you didn't arrange Theresa's bid for freedom?"

"No Jamie I didn't, you know that I didn't. I was so surprised when I saw them in Southampton and I really didn't want to know anything about what they were doing," said Liza.

"The more I learn about you the more I love you Liza. You really have done some amazing things. I wish I could say that I have had such a thrilling life," smiled Jamie.

"I thought that you would be annoyed with me," said Liza.

"Good heavens no! You must remember that I was instrumental in getting Hector out of prison, but I have to say that you really do need someone like me to protect you and make sure you don't get into any more trouble. I told you once that you weren't safe on your own, and I was right," Jamie laughed.

Liza couldn't understand why Jamie was so happy to have learned how she had helped Mark but she wasn't going to argue with him and when he put his arms around her she thought that he was never going to let her go. Suddenly she no longer felt sad or troubled and she presumed that it was because she realised that she would never again have to keep a secret from Jamie and that was a great relief.

"Now all we have to worry about is how we get fourteen people over to Belfast for Christmas," smiled Jamie.

Chapter 21

Bella and her boys came for the last cricket game of the season and at that time she announced that she would like to spend Christmas with them.

"Our house will be full Bella; but I can accommodate you in my other property which is only a small distance away from us. Will the Duke be with you?" asked Liza.

"Ah yes, the Duke said that he had seen your house and it looked very comfortable. No the Duke has a previous engagement," said Bella quite casually. "The Duke is organising our travel arrangements, so you won't have to worry about that."

"Just let me know when you'll be arriving and I'll make sure everything is ready for you," said Liza.

When Bella and the boys had left, Jamie looked up from his newspaper and sighed. "I had a feeling that Bella would invite herself to Belfast for Christmas."

"The boys will enjoy Nicholas and Richard's company and Bella does fit in well with everyone; she doesn't have too many airs and graces. I'll have to reorganise the sleeping arrangements. It would be better if Estelle has the box room at our place otherwise she might feel obliged to wait on everyone. I think that your uncle could have your room and Grace mine, that will leave the rest of the bedrooms for Bella, the boys and her maid and nurse," said Liza thoughtfully.

Jamie was laughing at her. "It's just another little thing for you to plan. Do we have to add her to our travelling arrangements?"

"No, apparently the Duke is undertaking that; all I need to know is exactly when they will be arriving," said Liza.

"Thank goodness for that," said Jamie. "We will definitely have to stay here for Christmas next year; it's just getting too complicated. I really enjoyed the Christmases that we had before we were married. I used to bring James to you and we then would go to Wendell and Amelia's for lunch. It was all so very simple then."

"Are you telling me that you are wishing that we weren't married?" asked Liza with a smile.

Jamie just laughed and Liza left for her study where she had correspondence to go through with Grace. She picked up several unopened letters and flipped through them; one she didn't recognise, and she opened it and read its message.

'Dear Lady Edgeworth,

Thank you.'

It was unsigned but Liza knew who it was from as she recognised the paper that she had given to Theresa. She looked at the outside and it appeared to have travelled some distance and studying it closely she recognised notations from New York.

"Is that something that you need me to deal with Liza?" asked Grace.

"No it's just a note from a friend," said Liza and she left the room and went back to Jamie to show it to him.

Jamie dropped his paper down slightly as she came into the library again. "What is it Liza, you look concerned?"

She handed him the note which he quickly read. "That must be from Theresa, mustn't it?"

"Yes and it appears to have come from New York. If she has any sense she will have left there by now and headed to some obscure border town. It's good to know that she got to New York safely," said Liza.

Jamie stood up and went towards the fireplace and threw the note into the fire. "That's the best place for it, Liza. We know that she arrived safely and that's more than we needed to know."

Liza nodded. "The Police seem to have decided to leave us alone. I hope that it stays that way. I'm pleased that she has learned how to write."

"It may be from the Jones man; perhaps he was educated enough to write. Hopefully we will never know," said Jamie.

He went back to his chair and picked up his newspaper. He looked at Liza over the top of it and said, "you had better carry on organising our Christmas break. Not that it is a break for you as you spend your time making sure that we all enjoy ourselves." His smile told her that he appreciated everything that she did.

***

It was very busy in the Edgeworth household in the lead up to Christmas. The boys were looking forward to having Nicholas and Richard with them that year. Jamie had to defuse a dispute between Harper and Roberts who were objecting to sharing a room on the journey to Belfast. Jamie told them that it was either that or one of them would have to sit up all night in the public drinking room; another alternative was that one of them could be left behind and Jamie would employ somebody local to carry out the duties, which quietened them quite considerably.

Bella would be arriving with her boys and staff the day after the Edgeworth arrival, so Liza had it all in hand until Hector announced that he would be travelling with them.

"When are Anthony and Diana arriving?" asked Liza.

"Oh I've decided to stay with you," said Hector.

"I don't think that I have room for you Hector. You would be far more comfortable with Anthony and Diana," said Liza in panic.

"No I wouldn't; I'd have to put up with my mother's nagging and little Thomas seems to like me so much that he never leaves me alone. No, I'll stay with you; I'm sure you could find some room for me," said Hector.

It was another occasion when Jamie's newspaper dropped down and he said, "Hector, are you sure you are not related to Bella?" That brought a smile to Liza's face before her frown reappeared and her problem of how she was going to house everyone loomed large again in her mind.

"When will you be arriving?" asked Liza.

"I'll travel with you," said Hector. "I presume we'll be staying somewhere overnight on the journey."

Jamie's newspaper now dropped to his lap. "Hector, do you realise how many people are in our party? We are already overcrowded in our carriages and the sleeping arrangements in the hotel means that people are doubling up in rooms. You are putting extra pressure on Liza to organise our trip."

"Oh, Liza will manage; she's good at organising things. I'll see you later," said Hector as he walked out of the room on some mission that seemed important to him.

"Are you going to be able to accommodate him? He's asking a great deal," said Jamie. "He does a good job with the Major, but he has no appreciation of the problems that he creates."

"He'll have to sleep in with your uncle at the hotel. I'll write and tell them to expect another guest. Now I must think about where I put him in Belfast," said Liza as she sat down and started visualising both houses in Belfast.

Jamie smiled at her, "I can tell him that we can't have him with us Liza. He does have a perfectly good home to go to."

"I'll see what I can come up with before we tell him that he's not wanted," smiled Liza.

"What about my old study room?" asked Jamie.

"That's in the worst part of the house and it's full of junk. I will never understand why you used that room as a study," said Liza.

"It wasn't my choice," said Jamie. "My father didn't want me to use any other room to work in. He didn't like to see me studying, it made him feel inadequate because he never used the brains that he was given and he didn't see the point of studying as we were the ones giving orders and everyone else had to do as we said."

"Did you enjoy studying?" asked Liza.

"I didn't mind. I enjoyed the challenge of attempting to come first in class on certain subjects and the only way to do that was to study," said Jamie.

"You did very well under difficult circumstances; aren't our boys lucky? They don't have to fight awkward parents," said Liza. "I'll have to write to Mrs Trent to arrange clearing your old study and making it look respectable. I suppose we'll find a bed from somewhere."

***

Their time for travelling was approaching fast and the boys seemed to be more excited than usual and Liza and Jamie put that down to the fact that Nicholas and Richard would be with them. Liza had written all her letters to organise the various sleeping arrangements. All the Fullers would be lunching with them on Christmas Day and Liza had given instruction that all the Edgeworth, Fuller and her own staff would have their Christmas dinner at her house three hours later. Mrs Edwards had written back that she would have all the rooms ready and everyone was looking forward to the staff dinner, including Mr and Mrs Grouch who were joining them.

"We will have to take three carriages," Liza said to Jamie. "Do you think that our smaller carriage will keep up with the other two?"

"I suppose Ernie has learned enough to drive it safely. It will take three as well as Ernie and it isn't as heavy, so I suppose it won't get too far behind. It may possibly keep up with the rest of us. Who will you let travel in that?" asked Jamie.

"I know the three boys would like to travel in it without an adult to supervise them, but I think that Hector should be next to Ernie as I know that Hector is quite experienced at driving carriages and I suppose Grace and Estelle could be the rear seat passengers. I'll make sure that they have plenty of rugs to keep them warm because even when it is covered over it is more open than the larger ones. I've already warned the hotel that the driver's room should be arranged for three of them to sleep," said Liza. "Mrs Frances is arranging a Christmas lunch here for all the staff and I think Mrs Price and Derek and his sister are also invited and one or two others."

Jamie looked at Liza and smiled, "I wonder who put that idea in her mind?"

"I just put into words what she was thinking," said Liza.

Two days before they were due to leave Liza, Jamie and the boys went to the Ffoulks Home to wish everyone a happy Christmas and they went armed with small presents for all the children, which they placed around the Christmas tree in the main lounge area. Liza thought that it was such a nice idea and one that Prince Albert had introduced to the country. The Major and Jennifer were going to have the pleasure of seeing the faces of all the children when they opened their presents. One or two of the children were still a little sullen but the Major was beginning to win them over.

On the way back from the Home they called in on Anthony and Diana and they apologised for Hector imposing himself on Liza and Jamie for Christmas.

"He should be staying with us, but he seemed determined to stay with you. I suppose Estelle has something to do with that," said Diana. "Although I believe my mother-in-law also seems to annoy him."

Little Thomas was ecstatic seeing Matthew, who took him in hand and told him all the good things that they would be doing at Christmas, and little Thomas sat on his knee happily looking up at him. John and James looked on indulgently and confirmed what Matthew was saying.

"I wonder how little Thomas will get on with Nicholas and Richard. I hope that they are kind to him," said Liza.

They left and made their way to the Major's house where Lily and Joseph were staying having arrived from Belfast the previous day. It was the excuse that Joseph needed to act like a child with the boys.

"We'll miss you at Christmas but it's nice that you will be spending it with your mother and the Major," said Liza.

"We'll also be spending it with many children and I'm looking forward to that," said Lily. "The Major is doing such a good job with them all and he's determined that they are going to have a wonderful time."

"I understand that many of the local people are sending food and other goods for the children. People are so very kind," said Liza. "I'm sure it's going to be a day that you'll never forget. I'm sorry that I'll miss it."

They had arranged with Hector that he and Estelle join them at the Major's house with their luggage for the trip to Belfast, as they would be staying at Edgeworth House ready for the journey. It meant that their carriage was a little crowded, but it did not take them too long to reach home and they were well in time to rest and change for dinner.

In the drawing room prior to dinner, Liza was saying to Miranda, Lucinda, David and Grace that they should rest the next day as they had an early start the following morning.

"Our luggage will be ready tomorrow," said Lucinda and Grace agreed that she and her father would be packed ready for the following day.

Hector burst into the drawing room, "Estelle won't dine with us tonight; she wants to be down in the kitchen with the staff. Can you make her change her mind Liza?"

"Hector, Estelle hasn't seen her brother for some time. Naturally she wants to be with him and April for dinner tonight. She will make up her own mind what she wants to do. No doubt you'll be able to see her after dinner if she's free and you'll be spending time with her when we're in Belfast," said Liza.

Harper poured a drink for him and he seemed to settle and accept the situation. Everyone except Hector saw the difficult position that Estelle was in as she was not a member of staff, but she was related to Adam, so where did she fit into the household.

That night when Liza went into Jamie's room, he pulled her over to him and said, "Estelle and Hector are quite a problem."

"Really it's Hector who has created the problem. Adam asked if Estelle could join us for Christmas as it is the first year without their mother and much as I have no objection to Estelle being with us, she is joining us because she wanted to be with Adam and April. Hector inviting himself has made it very awkward for everyone and especially for Estelle, Adam and April," said Liza.

"I'll have a calm word with Hector. I'm sure he'll see that he's putting Estelle in an awkward situation as she's welcome by us and also by Adam and April," said Jamie.

Liza smiled and said, "Has Hector ever seen anything logical as far as Estelle is concerned. I like her and I think she would be an asset to him. I've also seen her getting on well with Rose, which is no mean feat knowing how Rose is a little snobby where what she considers class is concerned. Anyway, I appreciate that you will have a word with him."

"I suppose we ought to get some sleep as we have a very busy day tomorrow," said Jamie. "Unless you need something, or someone to help you sleep."

"I always need you Jamie," said Liza.

***

Jamie was right; the following day was very busy. Everyone had their bags packed and David, Grace and Hector were the only ones dining with them that night. Miranda and Lucinda were dining at the Dower House and making sure that their members of staff were happy with the arrangements that Liza had made for them for Christmas. Jamie did talk to Hector and he did see the difficulty that he had created for Estelle and he promised to be more thoughtful. Liza doubted that he really saw the problem, but she would worry about it when they arrived in Belfast.

Finally they were on their way with Jamie, Liza, the boys and Roberts in one carriage and David, Miranda, Lucinda, Adam, April and Harper in the other large carriage. Hector was very happy to have Estelle and Grace in the smaller carriage with him and he understood Ernie was not as experienced as Davis and Hendry, so he felt that he was responsible for the safety of the two ladies.

They stopped for light refreshments at lunchtime and were back on their way within the hour. They reached the hotel where they would stay the night at six o'clock and they were all pleased to get into the warmth of the dining area, especially Estelle and Grace as their carriage was a little cold but the extra rugs had made them quite comfortable. Their bags were taken to the various rooms, but Liza insisted that they all sat down to dinner together before any attempts were made to unpack what was necessary for their night's stay.

Everyone then congregated in the sitting room in the family suite and Liza instructed where everyone would be sleeping and advised that they found their rooms before coming back to the suite to relax before bedtime.

By that time the boys were becoming tired, so she and April got them ready for bed and they were asleep as soon as their heads touched the pillows.

April and Adam were in the third room in the suite and all others were housed on the floor below. It became very cosy in the sitting room in the suite when they all came back from finding their rooms. Harper and Roberts seemed to have settled their differences over their sleeping arrangements and everyone accepted a nightcap, including the drivers. Gradually tiredness overcame them all and they slowly went to their rooms. April helped Miranda and Lucinda but everyone else coped by themselves. Liza and Jamie were last to leave the sitting room and they tiredly made their way to their bedroom which was the most comfortable room in the hotel. Once again Liza commented that there were perks to owning a hotel.

They left early the following morning and arrived at the hotel in Liverpool just before lunchtime and once again rooms were ready for them all. The drivers were also staying the night and arrangements had been made for them to stay at the previous hotel on their return journey.

Miranda, Lucinda and Grace decided that they would spend the afternoon looking around Liverpool and David said that he would accompany them. Adam, April and Estelle thought that it would be a good idea if they did the same and Hector insisted on being with them. The boys were very tired and went to their room to rest, whilst Harper and Roberts were busy making sure that all bags and cases were accounted for. What Davis, Hendry and Ernie were doing Liza had no idea, but they were now off duty so as long as the horses had been taken care of their time was their own.

Liza and Jamie sat in the sitting room of their suite enjoying the rare moment of peace and quiet.

"You are right Jamie," said Liza, "we can't go through all this again next year. It's just getting too much for us. The boys will be disappointed, but we can make Christmas in Surrey just as enjoyable."

"I hope that Wendell and Amelia can join us as Christmas wouldn't be the same without them," said Jamie.

Liza was very quiet at that thought because she realised that Wendell and Amelia weren't getting any younger and one day there would be Christmas without them. She brushed the thought to one side as this was not the time to have depressing feelings.

Dinner that evening was a free for all in the downstairs dining room. They had all had interesting afternoons but were ready for bed early, which was wise as they had an early start the next day.

They were at the docks by nine o'clock the next morning and boarding their ship. The luggage was aboard, and they were all sitting comfortably in captain's ready room, listening to the sailors casting off and weighing anchor.

The wind was favourable, and they made good time, arriving in Belfast as it was beginning to get dark. Wendell and Amelia had come to greet them, and Peter appeared from his office followed by Brendan who had become very smart and handsome. Carriages were brought over, and they climbed aboard with their luggage following on.

When they arrived at the house the boys raced up to their room to ensure that it was as they wanted it. Liza made sure that all those staying at the house were settled and she then went with Amelia and Peter to her house with David and Grace.

Mrs Edwards and Mr Grouch were there to greet them, and they were so pleased to have somebody in the house to look after.

"I hope you don't feel pushed out by staying here," Liza said to David and Grace.

"No, we can see that you are overcrowded at your other house, we will be more comfortable here," said David.

Grace had gone up to the room that she would be using and when she returned, she was in raptures over how lovely it was.

"Was that your room Liza?" she asked and when Liza nodded, she said, "I thought it had to be. I've looked into my father's room and it's also very nice, but masculine; you'll be very comfortable there, Father."

Mrs Edwards had arranged hot water for them and they were going to wash and change ready for dinner.

"We'll unpack properly later," said Grace.

Mrs Edwards told them just to see what they wanted for the evening and that she would unpack for them whilst they were out. Liza said that she would leave them to get organised and that Mr Grouch would bring them over to dinner later.

"There's no need for him to worry about them," said Peter. "I'll call for you later."

"That's kind of you Peter," said Liza with a smile and she left with Peter and Amelia to go back to the house to see that everyone was settling in well.

The boys had made their way down to the kitchen for their supper and April was unpacking their clothes. Liza went to inspect Hector's room and she was suitably impressed with how Mrs Trent had made it habitable.

"You certainly have a house full," said Wendell. "I understand from Jamie that Bella has invited herself for Christmas."

"Yes, Jamie did wonder whether she and Hector are related as they both have the same attitude towards visiting," laughed Liza. "She and her boys will be staying at my house; she also will have a nurse and maid with her."

"You and Jamie are too easy going for your own good," said Wendell. "Still I suppose you know what you are doing. When are they arriving?"

"Tomorrow. They're travelling on the ship overnight and they will be arriving around lunchtime," said Liza. "Where is Brendan? He's has certainly matured since I last saw him. I dare say that all the young ladies are looking at him favourably."

"He's gone home to change for dinner; he'll be back shortly," said Wendell. "There are one or two young ladies that seem to be taking notice of him; he is charming to them all but there is no one yet who he is interested in."

It was a crowded but happy dinner time; the only person who was dissatisfied was Hector as Estelle was spending her time with Adam and April.

Wendell, Amelia and Brendan left early, and Peter took David and Grace back to where they were staying. Miranda and Lucinda were tired and it wasn't long before they made their way to bed. Hector made his disgruntled way to his room and Liza and Jamie sat for a while with a nightcap before finally heading for their rooms.

Edward called in the following morning to welcome them back to Belfast and make arrangements for them to visit him as soon as practical. Peter arrived with David and Grace as he had planned the previous evening to bring them around. The boys were going shopping with Adam and April and Miranda and Lucinda said that they would like to join them. Hector was at last going to spend some time with Estelle.

Amelia arrived as she was going to the docks with them to welcome Bella and her boys. They sat and had morning coffee before leaving and Liza put the

409

suggestion to her that next year perhaps she and Wendell could come to Surrey for Christmas.

"That's a lovely idea Liza and I can see that your guest list is growing alarmingly. It must have been quite an effort to get everyone here in one piece. My only reservation is being with my grandson at this time of year," said Amelia.

"Well we would have plenty of room for Edward, Nicole and little Edward; also for Annalise and Arthur if they would like to spend the time with us. As you know Lily and Joseph will probably be with the Major and Jennifer, so really you would all be together again. I have a feeling that Peter would be quite willing to travel also and I know that Brendan wouldn't want to miss the opportunity to spend Christmas with us," said Liza.

"I'll discuss it with Wendell but I'm sure he would be happy to do so," said Amelia.

They arrived at the dockyard just as Bella's ship was coming into port, so they spent a little time with Wendell, Peter and Brendan in the Marchant & Fuller offices. They could see that the ship was beginning to put the gangways down, so they went to greet their guests.

Nicholas and Richard were the first down and they were followed by their nurse who was helping along a very white-faced Bella.

"I have a feeling that Bella has not been a very good sailor," commented Jamie.

Liza was so busy greeting the boys and asking if they'd had a good trip that she did not notice that the Duke was also with the party, as well as his valet. Jamie was staring with dismay and when Liza looked up, she was horrified to realise that she had two extra people that she had not catered for.

Amelia was very calm and smiling sweetly and between her teeth she said to Liza. "I see that Bella gets her assuming attitude from her husband."

Jamie turned to Liza and said, "Well Liza, how are we going to cope with this situation?"

"I'm glad you said 'we'. I think I would have hit you if you had said 'you'," said Liza and she put on her most disarming smile, took a deep breath and walked towards Bella and the Duke.

"This is a pleasant surprise," she said. "Welcome back to Belfast Sir."

"Liza; it's wonderful to see you and Jamie again. I trust my unexpected arrival will not put you to too much trouble. Bella told me that she and the boys would be staying at your house and she assured me that it is big enough to accommodate me and my valet also," said the Duke. "I am really looking forward to experiencing a true family Christmas."

"It's no trouble; it will just take a small amount of reorganisation," she said with a smile that did not reach her eyes.

Jamie decided to look after Bella, "I do not think that you have had a very good trip Bella. I take it that sailing is not one of your favourite pastimes."

"Everyone else seemed alright, obviously I am not a good sailor, but I am beginning to settle now," said Bella.

Wendell sidled over to Liza, "I suppose you already have got it all worked out in your mind."

"I think so, at least I hope so," said Liza and she ushered everyone towards the carriages leaving the maid and valet to come in the last carriage with the luggage, and there did seem to be an enormous number of cases and trunks.

When they arrived at the house, Mrs Edwards and a maid brought in refreshments. Liza thanked her and made sure everyone was served before she left Jamie and Amelia to entertain her guests.

Down in the kitchen she found Mrs Edwards looking rather puzzled. "Yes, Mrs Edwards, I had no idea that the Duke and his valet were also visiting. The room opposite the Duchess' will now have to be the Duke's room instead of a dressing room. I know there is still a bed in there and the small room next to that will have to be for the valet. Everything else will stay the same. I'm sorry to put you to this trouble. I trust you'll have enough food for breakfast for everyone. As you know all their other meals will be with me," said Liza.

Mrs Edwards rose to the occasion and in a very short while the Duke's room was organised for him and his valet was unpacking his trunks whilst the small room next door was being made ready for him.

Liza went in to join her guests in the drawing room and she nodded imperceptibly at Jamie telling him that all was in hand. She looked at Bella and realised that she still looked slightly unwell.

"Your maid is unpacking your things Bella, but would you like to go to your room and rest for a while, you are looking decidedly peaky and putting your feet up would probably do you good," said Liza.

"Yes, she can finish later," said Bella.

"I'll show you the way," said Liza. "Boys would you like to see where you will be sleeping. It's the room that my boys had when we lived here. When everyone has settled here, I'll take you to our place, the boys should be back from shopping soon; they've been looking forward to your visit."

Liza showed Bella to her room and when she opened the door, she said that the bed looked comfortable and she couldn't wait to put her feet up. The maid said she would come back later, and Liza showed her in turn to her room, which she seemed pleased with.

Nicholas and Richard were happy with their room and asked about the third bed because they knew that only Matthew and John had been there before Liza and Jamie were married.

"James always came to stay with us at Christmas, Easter and during the summer, so this is where he also slept, I think there may be some of their toys still here, but of course they were much younger the last time they were here so you may find them a little young for you. You'll be spending your days at our place so you will see what they now use. Come back down to the drawing room when you are ready," said Liza.

She saw the valet coming out of the Duke's room and she asked him if all was satisfactory.

"It's all very good Your Ladyship and I'm very happy with my room, I know I shall be very comfortable there," said the valet.

The nurse started organising the boy's clothes, so Nicholas and Richard went down to the drawing room followed by Liza.

David and Grace arrived back from shopping with the boys who greeted Nicholas and Richard as if they hadn't seen them for years. Jamie introduced the Duke to David and Grace and to their credit they said nothing about the fact that he had not been expected.

"We'll take all the boys with us for the afternoon, which will give you some peace. We'll send a carriage for you for dinner and send your boys back at that time. It will give your nurse and Bella's maid free time to organise for your stay," said Liza.

Liza ushered all the boys into the carriage. Jamie and Amelia were going to stroll back a little later.

Wendell was sitting in the library reading a newspaper when Liza arrived home. "No doubt you have got everyone housed comfortably. Are you alright Liza, you look a little tired," he said.

"Well it was an unexpected occurrence, but Mrs Edwards rose to the occasion and everyone will sleep well and warmly tonight," said Liza. "I must tell Mrs Trent that we have an extra guest for dinner."

"Would it be easier for you if Amelia and I dined at home tonight?" asked Wendell.

"Certainly not, you are my family. I miss you when I'm in England and want to spend every moment I can with you when we are here," said Liza.

"I know you've been unwell recently and you know that Amelia and I will do all we can to ease the pressure on you over this Christmas period, although knowing you everything will be organised and well in hand, but the offer is there," said Wendell.

Liza went over to him and put her arms around him, kissing him firmly on the head. "Thank you, Wendell, your offer is appreciated."

"Liza, you know that you have always been a daughter to Amelia and me; we love you very much and don't like to see you taken advantage of by anyone," said Wendell.

"I don't think of you as parents; I think of you as the greatest friends that anyone could have, and I have always considered you as family. You treated me with love and compassion when I was a very frightened child and have helped me to mature enough to deal with the world that we live in," said Liza.

Wendell held her hand for a moment, which told her exactly how he felt. She patted his hand and said that she must go to see Mrs Trent now.

As she left the room Jamie and Amelia came in the front door and said that all the guests at the other house were settling in as if they owned the place.

"I hope that David and Grace don't feel intimidated," said Liza.

"No Liza, David is quite capable of standing up for both himself and Grace; he won't let the Duke rule the roost, after all he is family and he will feel that it is his duty to make sure that all is fair in the family property," said Jamie.

"Wendell is in the library, Amelia, and he's already dressed for dinner; I've put your evening dress in my room so we can change together in comfort. I must see Mrs Trent," said Liza and she went off to the kitchen. Whilst she was there the boys arrived ready for their supper with Nicholas and Richard joining in with the intrigue over what they would be eating that evening.

"Nicholas and Richard have never spent Christmas with their father before. They normally see their mother on the day, but this is the first time that they have spent Christmas away from their home," said Matthew who was always the one to say what was happening in everyone's life.

"Well, it's going to be nice that they'll be having a family Christmas," said Liza. "We have the big tree arriving tomorrow and I'm sure you'll all enjoy helping to decorate it. It's going to be fun; we haven't had one before."

She left the boys to have their mystery supper, but from the sounds of approval that she heard after she had left, obviously it was to all their tastes.

Liza decided that she would like to take a short rest before dinner, so she quietly went to her room and put her feet up. She was surprised when Amelia gently tapped her on the shoulder telling her that the time had come for her to dress for dinner.

April came in with hot water for them and when they had washed, she helped them both into their dresses for the evening. Jamie tapped on her door to say that he was ready to escort them both down. Peter and Brendan had arrived, and Hector was already in the drawing room. They could hear Miranda and Lucinda making their way down the stairs. It was going to be quite a gathering for dinner.

Nicholas and Richard were getting their coats on with Matthew, John and James still talking and making arrangements for what they would be doing the following day. April saw them into the carriage, and they were on their way to the shouts of goodbye from their boys who then made their way to their room to get ready for bed.

It wasn't long before the carriage returned with David, Grace, Bella and the Duke. It was a lively dinner and the only one who was not as happy as normal was Hector, but he joined in well and his slight depression was only obvious to those who knew that he wanted to be with Estelle.

They made their plans for the next day. Brendan would be working. David was going to see some of the sights of Belfast with the Duke; Grace would be visiting the Marchant & Fuller offices with Peter. Miranda and Lucinda still had some shopping to undertake and Amelia said that she would accompany them. Hector muttered that he was going to persuade Estelle to visit the local children's home with him. Bella said that she would stay there and help Liza and the boys decorate the Christmas tree.

"What are you going to do tomorrow Jamie?" asked David.

"I think I would like to watch the boys and Liza enjoy decorating the Christmas tree and they may need my assistance with some of the high branches," said Jamie much to Liza's delight.

The house seemed very quiet when everyone had left for their various sleeping places. Liza checked on the boys before making her way to her room where April was waiting for her.

"Did you have a good evening April?" asked Liza. "When Christmas Day is over, I'll be able to look after the boys so you and Adam can have some time off."

"Thank you," said April and Liza could see that she was trying to say something but didn't seem to know how to start.

"What is it April?" asked Liza. "Is it to do with Estelle?"

"Yes, it is," said April. "She is concerned and is saying that she should never have come on this trip. It has become very awkward for her."

"I understand and I know that it is Mr Ffoulks who has made it awkward for her. There is no question that she should be here; she wanted to spend Christmas with you and her brother and rightly so," said Liza.

Liza waited for April to carry on and it took her a while to formulate what she was thinking. "Mr Ffoulks wants her to join with your family and friends especially at mealtimes and she feels that she should be with us. It's really embarrassing for her and also for Adam as he arranged that she spend the time with us."

"I suppose it is difficult for her being pulled in two directions," said Liza.

"She says that she feels happier being with us and the rest of the staff, but of course she does spend a great deal of time with Mr Ffoulks when she is teaching at the Home and there is no distinction between anyone there," said April.

"The only distinction here is that your employment is looking after the Edgeworth household and my employment is working for the shipping and property companies. His Lordship's business is running the Edgeworth estate; therefore we are all employed; therefore we are all equal," said Liza.

April laughed, "I think that we are hardly equal, but you are right, we are all in some form of employment. I don't understand what you are trying to say."

"I'm trying to say that the choice is Estelle's; she would be just as welcome at our table as she should be at yours. What she must work out is, does she want to spend the time with her family and where will she feel the most comfortable? I'm not going to make the choice for her, but whichever way she wants to go she must make her reasoning very clear to Mr Ffoulks," said Liza.

"I believe that she is more comfortable with us; she joins in well with everyone and Adam enjoys having her with him, especially at this time of year and it isn't long since their mother died and until then she had always spent the time with her," said April.

"If that is the case then Mr Ffoulks will have to be content with daytime meetings. I hope that he doesn't impose himself on your mealtimes; that could become awkward for all the staff," said Liza.

"Mr Ffoulks does fit in quite well when he visits the kitchens," said April.

"I see," was all Liza said.

April finished and left. Liza sat thinking for a moment and then got up and made her way into Jamie's bedroom. He commented that he thought that April had spent a long while helping that night.

"Estelle has a problem with Hector," said Liza. "He wants her to join us at mealtimes, whereas she appears to be more comfortable being with the staff. Apparently he does visit the kitchen and in April's words 'he does fit in quite well'."

"How is Adam coping with the situation?" asked Jamie.

"Adam's embarrassed as he asked that Estelle join us for Christmas," said Liza.

"What did you tell April?" asked Jamie.

"I told her that we are all the same as we all work in our different ways. I said that Estelle would be just as welcome at our table as at theirs and she should do what she is most comfortable with, but whatever she chooses she must tell Hector her reasons why," said Liza.

"Would she be just as acceptable at our table? I wouldn't want her to be embarrassed. It's very unfair of Hector to create this situation. I'll have a word with him tomorrow and point out to him that the reason she is here is to be with Adam and April, not with him. He can see her any time when they are both back at the Home," said Jamie. "I'll sort it out Liza; you have had enough to contend with organising for the Duke's unexpected visit."

***

The Christmas tree arrived the next morning and all the groundsmen and Mr Grouch came to help to raise it in the right place in the stairwell and put it in a huge barrel of earth, securing it carefully to the banisters. There was a wonderful smell of pine throughout the house. Everyone had been making decorations for it and John had made a most magnificent silver star for its top. Candles had been placed in protective containers and they would be put in places which could be easily reached. Red and gold bows were to be set on the branches. The boys were still making all sorts of shapes out of thick paper which they were colouring red, gold or silver. Liza had bought many different coloured beads from several local dressmakers and they were being strung together to be hung around the branches of the tree. Everyone had painted silver and gold both sides of many sheets of paper and cut them into thin

416

strips so that they shimmered with the movement of air. It seemed that guests and staff were finding odd decorative pieces to be placed on the tree and the number of items was growing by the minute.

The decorations for the top of the tree could be put in place by leaning over or through the banisters, but for some items Mr Grouch brought in his large stepladder.

Liza noticed that Nicholas and Richard's nurse was accompanying them that day and she also had a few baubles for the tree. Bella was fascinated by what was happening, but she was quite content to watch and shout instructions to her maid who was joining in with all the fun. April was busy stringing beads together and Adam was helping the boys to cut their coloured paper into strips. Jamie was leaning over the banisters attempting to put the star squarely in place with Roberts shouting 'left, no right' at the top of his voice.

Amelia appeared with her maid carrying boxes of pieces of material which she promptly started sewing into bows with long trailers. Mrs Trent and Mrs Edwards bustled in together with refreshments for everyone and Harper kept his dignity by dispensing the drinks and cakes to them all on plates, but he did have a slight smile on his face.

A red cloth covered the barrel that the tree was in and it was tied in place with a silver and gold ribbon. All the presents were to be placed around the foot of the tree.

Nicole and Annalise arrived with little Edward and all work stopped on the tree so that all the ladies could take a turn at holding the baby. Of course the boys and men didn't show the same interest and they carried on placing the decorations after a cursory nodding glance at little Edward.

Soon it was lunchtime and Mrs Adams and the kitchen staff had excelled in arranging food for everyone, including the workers. Bella looked on this in surprise but then realised that it was as the cricket matches at Edgeworth House were organised.

It did not take them long to finish the tree after lunch, although the boys were still making paper decorations and Liza told them that they could always find more room for them.

During the afternoon Miranda and Lucinda arrived home and said that they would be able to find one or two decorations for the wonderful tree. David and the Duke were also suitably impressed and when Peter escorted Grace back, they were fascinated by how lovely the room looked. Hector came in quietly with Estelle and was surprised to see everyone gathering in front of an enormous prettily decorated tree.

"Liza, that is a wonderful idea," said Hector. "How did you manage to think of that?"

"Oh Hector, it wasn't my idea. Prince Albert adopted it from his homeland some years ago; it's only now beginning to become popular. I must admit that it does look lovely," said Liza. "You obviously didn't see the one that the Major organised at the Ffoulks House."

"No, I must have been busy elsewhere when they were doing that," said Hector.

Mr Grouch was organising some of the groundsmen to collect holly and ivy so that the rest of the house could be suitably decorated and enough with red berries for table decorations.

Gradually the house was clearing; the Duke told Bella to join him on his trip back to Liza's house; he offered to take his boys with them but they were having such a good time that Liza suggested that they stay a while longer and their nurse said she would take them home later. Peter had already gone back to the office so David and Grace went with the Duke and Bella. They would be returning later for dinner. Nicole, Annalise and little Edward left with Amelia and Miranda and Lucinda went to their rooms for a rest.

Estelle seemed to have disappeared to her room and Hector said that he would go to the library to read for a while. Adam was still helping the boys with the last of their decorations and April was tidying up some of the bits and pieces that had landed on the floor. One or two of the maids were also picking up debris.

Finally Liza sat down and stared at the tree with satisfaction and Jamie joined her.

"This has been a very tiring but happy day Liza," said Jamie. "Who would have thought that everyone wanted to join in decorating the tree? I thought it was only going to be us and the boys and of course Bella said that she would help us. I didn't see her do anything to help, but that's Bella."

"The day has gone very quickly; the boys will soon be going down for their supper," said Liza.

"Why don't you go and lie down for a while Liza, you look very tired. What are your plans for tomorrow?" asked Jamie.

"Personally I have no plans apart from making sure that everyone is well fed. Anthony and Diana are arriving and I know that Amelia has made sure that all is in order at their house. It's the twenty-second tomorrow so we have a few days to relax before the big day," said Liza. "I think I will go and put my feet up for a while."

"I'll go and see Hector and have a quiet talk to him," said Jamie. "By the way, who are we expecting for dinner tonight?"

"Just the Duke, Bella, David, Grace, your mother and Lucinda. We're catering for Hector so I presume he will be with us. What's the Duke's first name?" asked Liza.

"Grenville," said Jamie.

Liza just made it to the top of the stairs when the boys emerged from their room to make their way to the kitchen for supper. They said hello and carried on down the stairs obviously looking forward to filling their stomachs yet again.

She lay on her bed planning in her mind yet again what was to happen on Christmas Day. *Twenty-two for lunch at midday*, she thought, *and Anthony, Diana and Rose joining us after lunch. The staff from all houses having their lunch at around three o'clock at my house and we have cold meat and pies, salad and bread for our supper with Christmas cake and cheese. We've done it before; it's just bigger this year.* With those thoughts she nodded off until April came in to help her get ready for dinner.

* * *

Jamie and Liza went to the docks the next day to meet Anthony, Diana, Rose and little Thomas. Their ship was due to dock early that afternoon and Liza was sure that they would be pleased to get to their home as it was quite cold and it had been raining since early morning.

Liza, Diana, Rose and little Thomas rushed into the first carriage out of the rain, whilst Jamie ushered Anthony, the nurse and valet into the second carriage. Their bags had already been placed onto both carriages. It took just fifteen minutes to reach Anthony's house and it was wonderful to get out of the rain and into the warmth.

Their housekeeper brought in tea and cakes and Liza and Jamie just spent a short while with them before leaving them to settle in. They arranged to have dinner with them the following evening, which meant that they would then leave their guests to their own devices.

"I don't think that we should do that Jamie, after all they are our guests," said Liza.

"Liza, our only guests are Bella, the Duke and their sons; all the others are our family and we often leave them at dinner time," said Jamie.

"There's also Hector," said Liza quietly.

"Did you say the Duke," said Anthony. "I thought he had other arrangements at Christmas, well that's what Bella said."

"Yes," said Jamie. "He turned up unannounced having been assured by Bella that he would be welcome and that there was plenty of room for him. It created quite a headache for Liza."

"Where on earth is everyone staying," demanded Rose.

"Across both the houses; I have David and Grace in our rooms at my house, and now I also have Bella's two boys, Bella, the Duke, his valet, their nurse and Bella's maid there also," smiled Liza. "Everyone else is at our house."

"Well at least Hector should come here; you've both been put upon enough," said Rose.

"He's quite settled Rose, so don't worry about him," said Liza.

"I suppose it's because Estelle is with you," said Rose. "I think that she's a very nice person and she seems to be good for Hector, but I don't know whether both worlds can meet."

Both Liza and Jamie thought it prudent not to comment.

"I see that little Thomas is growing rapidly," said Liza.

"He's so excited that he will be spending time with Matthew; I do hope that he doesn't bother him too much. We'll see Edward's little boy, he and Nicole must be over the moon," said Diana.

"So is Amelia, after all he is her first grandson," said Liza.

"That's not strictly true Liza, you know that Amelia considers and treats your sons as her grandsons. She loves them all dearly and boasts about their exploits to anyone who will listen," said Anthony.

"We'll leave you to settle in now, and look forward to seeing you tomorrow night," said Jamie. They left and climbed into their carriage and Jamie gave the driver instructions to drive around for a while.

"I thought it would be nice for us to have a little time to ourselves. I know that it's cold and wet, but we are dry enough in here and our house seems to be in permanent uproar. Just to get a short time together in peace is a bonus," said Jamie.

"You know that there have been a couple of times in my life when I have found it difficult to cope with what is thrown at me and I'm afraid a third is looming," said Liza tiredly. "I must be getting old, after all what is so difficult about organising Christmas for a number of people. I don't have to cook for them, I don't have to tidy their rooms or make their beds. I don't have to dust and polish or go shopping for food, so why do I feel this weight on my shoulders. You have been so good in helping wherever possible and indeed doing some of the organising yourself. I normally thrive on entertaining on this scale."

"I don't think that you are really completely over that bout of illness that you had a little while ago. You were very sick then and the doctor did say that it would take time to build up your strength and you know that people do expect you to know the answer to everything. Perhaps I haven't kissed you and cuddled you enough to make you feel better," smiled Jamie.

Liza laughed, "You've kissed me and cuddled me a great deal Jamie, but I'm happy to have lots more if you have the time."

They finally arrived back at the house and found that even more decorations had been placed on the tree and all wrapped presents had been put around the base. Liza and Jamie stood looking at it and Liza commented that the Christmas spirit had indeed entered their home.

Matthew asked after little Thomas and did not look very happy when told that he was in high spirits. The other boys laughed, and Liza did tell him that the little boy had grown quite considerably and she felt that his fixation on Matthew was easing although he did say that he was looking forward to seeing him.

"I didn't think that he could speak that well," said Matthew.

"He has improved but he still admires you Matthew, so there will be times when he would like to be with you," said Liza. "I know you will be kind to him."

The other boys were grinning, but John said that they would all help Matthew look after him, which Liza thought was very kind of them.

The evening with Anthony and Diana was very enjoyable and their guests and family managed to successfully survive an evening without them.

Christmas morning arrived and Liza and Jamie could hear the boys up and around before anyone else. Liza was aware of Nicholas and Richard arriving before she was out of bed and she hoped that their nurse was with them. She donned her dressing gown and went to their room to be greeted by five boys shouting happy Christmas to her. The Berkshires nurse looked tired and Liza asked her if the boys had been fed.

"No, they couldn't wait to get here so their mother told them to quickly dress and go. I'm hardly ready," said the nurse.

Liza laughed and told all the boys to go down to the kitchen for breakfast and that her three could wash and dress after breakfast. She told the nurse to have a word with Mrs Trent who would arrange for her to complete getting ready for the day. The nurse laughed and thanked her. Liza made her way back to Jamie's room and he asked what the time was.

"It's just turning seven o'clock. Our boys may look older, but they really haven't grown up, especially where Christmas is concerned," said Liza.

"Come back to bed Liza," said Jamie.

"I'll just relax for a minute or two, but then I have to make sure that everyone has an extremely happy day," said Liza and then she wished Jamie a happy Christmas. He put his arms around her and held her closely which made her feel that she would be well able to cope with all that had to be done that day.

Gradually everyone emerged for the day and by nine o'clock all had arrived apart from Bella who was not known for arising early. David held a short service in the library for all who wanted to participate. Some presents were handed out to the boys, but the main present giving would take place after lunch and when Anthony and his family had arrived.

Liza and Grace helped Mrs Trent to lay and decorate the table and they had organised place names for everyone. It was arranged that the boys would be interspersed with the adults, but Liza had arranged that Matthew and Richard were opposite one another and James and Nicholas also were opposite each other, John would be sitting next to Peter and that would please him immensely.

The seating arrangements were designed to please everyone but of course Hector would be the only one to not have who he wanted with him but Estelle had told him that she would be happier dining with her brother and the rest of the staff.

Liza ensured that all the staff knew what was happening with their own afternoon dinner. Amelia's cook and Mrs Grouch were in charge of the kitchen at Liza's house with all but the kitchen and serving staff at the main house helping them with all the arrangements. Adam, April, Estelle and the Berkshire nurse had made their way to the other house well before midday and Liza assumed that all Amelia's staff had also gone as soon as Amelia, Wendell, Peter and Brendan no longer needed their services. Liza and Jamie's staff would leave when the family had finished their lunch and all they would have to do is go to the other house and be served in turn; they would have already worked hard that day and deserved to be waited upon.

Bella managed to arrive just before lunch was served at twelve o'clock and as they all had just had a light breakfast, lunch was enthusiastically appreciated. Naturally Jamie was at the head of the table and Liza at the opposite end with Wendell to her left and Arthur to her right. Jamie had Bella to his right and his mother to his left. The Duke was next to Bella, Nicholas and James were opposite one another, John was next to Peter who in turn was next to Grace; in fact Liza had tried to arrange that everyone was where she thought they would like to be. Hector had Miranda on one side and Edward and James on the other and they managed to keep him well entertained throughout the meal and take his mind off the fact that Estelle was not there. Of course Amelia was next to Wendell and Brendan was between Nicole and Lucinda and Liza noticed that his art of conversation had improved greatly.

Just before three o'clock all was cleared away and Liza went to see Mrs Trent and Harper who had everything organised for supper. All that had to be done was for the prepared food to be brought up from the kitchen. The plates and cutlery were already on the sideboard in the dining room, along with wine glasses and all else that was needed. It was the same procedure the previous year when their gathering was at Amelia's house and the staff had arranged their Christmas lunch at Jamie's house.

Mrs Trent and Harper then left to join their friends at Liza's house. It seemed strange that no members of staff were around the house and Bella did wonder how they were going to cope by themselves.

Anthony's family arrived and soon the grand present opening took place and later the game that was always played by the boys at Christmas started. Initially it was just the five boys, with Nicholas and Richard being shown the rules, but then Edward found it difficult not to join in, after all it had originated when he was a child. Liza looked on but soon she was on the floor playing and finally Peter told them that they were playing it the wrong way and somehow he also ended up on the floor shouting what he considered the correct instructions to all the players. Hector was looking on and was of the opinion that they were all wrong in the way they were playing, and he too got onto his knees and tried to reorganise everyone. Arthur said that the boys had got it right all along and he said he would support them in the way they were playing. Brendan said that he had played something similar when he was a boy and it wasn't long before he was also on the floor. The Duke said, "No, no, no, you've all got it wrong, this is how it should be." They were all surprised to see him get on his knees between his two boys and start yelling as loudly as everyone else.

As always there was a great deal of laughter; Liza pushed Peter telling him that he was wrong and Edward did the same to her and she was pushed off her knees and landed on her side, much to the amusement of all those watching. She found it difficult to stop laughing especially with Peter telling her to be sensible.

She looked up, still laughing, and immediately found Jamie and once again he saw the seventeen-year-old who had fascinated him all those years ago. He was standing next to Wendell just as he had before, and Wendell voiced what he was thinking. "She hasn't changed in all the years that I have known her. Take care of her Jamie; she is far more vulnerable than you think. She says that she doesn't think of Amelia and I as parents, she thinks of us as her greatest friends, but we think of her as our daughter. We have done our best to look after her but unfortunately have not always succeeded."

"I will always take care of her Wendell and I do know just how vulnerable she is," said Jamie.

It was supper time and there were many helpers bringing the food up from the kitchen. Jamie was given the job of carefully carrying the Christmas cake up to the dining room, and even the Duke joined in much to everyone's surprise, especially Bella's. It was the usual free for all with them all choosing where they wanted to sit and of course Matthew decided that the Duke needed his company. Liza did not worry about what he would say as she knew that the Duke had researched the family very carefully before he had committed himself and his friends to supporting the charity.

Jamie and Brendan stoked all the fires making the rooms cosy; it was turning very cold out. Hector and Bella looked on in surprise and Jamie turned and said that he had put wood on fires before and he definitely wanted everyone to feel comfortable.

Liza cut the Christmas cake and Miranda and Lucinda handed it around. Liza's favourite way of eating it was with cheese and Grace offered it to everyone and those who hadn't eaten it that way before were suitably impressed.

Noises could be heard from the kitchen which told them that some members of the staff were beginning to return. Harper knocked and entered the dining room. "We are all now on duty Sir," he uttered. All eyes were on his bright red rosy cheeks which told them that he had enjoyed his Christmas meal and the wine that went with it.

"I trust it all went well Harper," said Liza.

"Oh yes, your Ladyship, we all had a most enjoyable time thank you," said Harper with slight slurring to his voice.

"That's good," said Liza smiling sweetly at him.

When he had left the dining room Jamie said, "I wonder if they are all in that condition." Every person in the room was polite enough not to laugh out loud but they were all sporting amused smiles; even the boys realised that Harper had over imbibed.

The boys had been given several games as presents and they congregated at one end of the table and were playing nicely together.

"I wonder what your house looks like after their party," said Bella.

"Oh, you'll never know that anything had taken place there, I can assure you of that," said Liza. "It's a matter of pride with them because they appreciate being able to let their hair down without us watching them. You will be returning to a pristine house Bella."

"I suppose our nurse will be here shortly to take the boys back," said Bella

"No my dear," said the Duke. "We'll take the boys back and she'll take over when we get there. The boys are still enjoying themselves; they are no trouble so they will go with us. The nurse knows that she will be on duty when we return and not before."

All eyes looked from the Duke to Bella, expecting a slight argument, but none came. She just nodded in agreement.

It was nearly eleven o'clock by the time the guests were ready to leave. Nicholas and Richard were very tired. They agreed that it would be a good idea to leave most of their presents there as they would be returning the next day. The Duke and David helped them into the carriage along with Grace and Bella and they made their way back to Liza's house.

Wendell had nodded off in a comfortable armchair and had to be woken when his carriage arrived. They were going to drop Edward and Nicole off on the way, little Edward had slept peacefully through most of the proceedings. They also managed to take Annalise and Arthur with them. Brendan and Peter wanted to walk back as they felt the need for some fresh air.

Another carriage took Anthony, Diana, Rose and a sleeping Thomas home. They would be returning the following day for a Boxing Day lunchtime cold cuts gathering. Hector had disappeared; presumably to find Estelle.

Liza gathered up the boys and went with them to their room and was surprised to find April on duty. "I thought you had gone to bed April, everyone else seems to have disappeared," smiled Liza.

"I don't drink alcohol, so I don't get as tired as some of the others," she said but without criticism. "You've had a busy day; I'll see to the boys."

"Thank you, April; there's no need to worry about me, I can see to myself later," smiled Liza.

As Liza was returning to the drawing room, Miranda and Lucinda were making their way to their rooms. "We've had a wonderful day Liza," said Miranda. "Thank you, we know that it has taken a great deal of organisation on your part to give us all a lovely Christmas. We are not going to let you do anything tomorrow, we have it all arranged with Harper and Mrs Trent and of course Jamie is in on it."

"Oh, that's kind of you; I shall have a good day, thank you. I have enjoyed today but it was rather a large gathering, wasn't it?" said Liza.

"And it will be tomorrow, but we are going to entertain you this time," smiled Lucinda.

Liza joined Jamie in the drawing room; he was having a nightcap and offered Liza one which she accepted.

"I think today went very well," said Jamie. "They all seemed to enjoy themselves. You know that my mother and Lucinda are hosting tomorrow's gathering. I think Amelia and Grace are assisting. They were talking to Harper and Mrs Trent whilst you were upstairs. I don't think that they have realised that you have already organised everything for tomorrow."

"I can stand back and let them work with Harper and Mrs Trent. They can greet everyone and I'm sure they are more than capable of making sure that everyone is happy and well fed," said Liza. "Your mother and Lucinda are very kind; they'll never know that it all wasn't their idea."

"I think that you are very kind in letting them believe that they have organised it all," said Jamie. "Don't worry, I won't tell them."

"I'm tired Jamie; I think I'll go up to bed now. Are you coming up because I've told April not to worry about me, so I need someone to help me out of my clothes," smiled Liza and she stood up, stretched and yawned.

"I do also Liza as I told Roberts not to worry about me," smiled Jamie. "Are we going to end the day in a very happy way?"

"As long we're not too tired. I'll just check on the boys and then I'll be in to help you," smiled Liza cheekily.

***

Liza heard noises coming up the stairs at seven o'clock on Boxing Day morning, followed by sleepy calls of welcome coming from Matthew, John and James.

"What's that?" asked Jamie.

"I believe Nicholas and Richard have arrived," said Liza. She donned her nightdress and dressing gown and left Jamie's room to find out what was happening and at the top of the stairs she came face to face with the Berkshire's nurse, who did not look her usual pristine self.

Liza looked at her and said, "I take it that your boys will need washing and dressing at the same time as ours."

"And so do I, Your Ladyship. They are still in their nightclothes, but I've brought all their day clothes, as well as mine. The Duchess told them to leave her alone and come here and they took her literally at her word," said the nurse.

"What is your name Nurse?" asked Liza. "We spend a great deal of time talking to one another and I don't know your name."

"It's Nurse Dawkins, Ruby Dawkins," she said.

"Good, now I know who I'm talking to," said Liza. "We had better go down to the kitchen to see what is happening and Mrs Trent will organise facilities for you to make yourself respectable. The boys can wait a while and have their breakfast in their nightclothes and when they have finished, they can get ready for the day. Apparently I'm not meant to be doing anything today." She laughed as the day had not started that way.

"So I have heard Your Ladyship," said Nurse Dawkins with a smile.

Mrs Trent organised a room for Nurse Dawkins to wash and change in and Mrs Adams said that the boys could come down for breakfast as soon as they liked. Liza thanked them and made her way up to the boys to tell them to go to breakfast and get ready later. They didn't need telling twice.

She went back to Jamie's room and he was sitting waiting for her wearing his dressing gown. "You weren't meant to be doing anything today," he said smiling. "The day hasn't started well. You had better go to your room and get into bed because I know that in a little while my mother is going to bring your breakfast in to you and I shall also be eating in your room."

Liza grinned, kissed him on the head and left his room. She climbed into her bed and made herself comfortable whilst waiting for her surprise breakfast.

She heard noises in the corridor outside her room and Jamie's voice saying that he would open the door. Miranda came in carrying a tray which she placed in front of Liza and Lucinda followed her with another one which she placed on a table for Jamie.

"Good morning Liza," they both said in unison.

"We have organised everything for today, Liza," said Lucinda. "You don't have to lift a finger. Amelia and Grace are coming to help us later. April and Nurse Dawkins are looking after the boys and we will be looking after everyone else."

Jamie was moving towards his breakfast which was the signal for Miranda and Lucinda to leave them in peace. When they had left Jamie looked over to Liza and smiled, "they really are wonderful; I'm so pleased that they are part of our family. I do love them both dearly."

"Bacon and egg, followed by toast and marmalade with coffee; lovely," said Liza.

"I'm ready with my napkin," said Jamie. "Do try not to get it on the sheets."

Liza grinned at him and then looked down at her breakfast, when she looked up there was a drip of egg on her chin. Jamie walked over to her with his napkin and wiped it away; he could not be sure that she had not done it on purpose, but he didn't care as it had become part of a breakfast in bed ritual that he enjoyed.

By the time that Liza had bathed and dressed, Amelia and Grace had arrived. Nurse Dawkins and April had the boys organised and they were going through their presents and playing together nicely in their room. Liza was ushered into the drawing room and told to sit and let the day happen around her.

Liza smiled sweetly at everyone throughout the day and apart from Jamie, it was only Wendell, Peter and the Duke who realised that she was going through one of the most frustrating times of her life. Every time she stood up; she was asked what she wanted. If her plate appeared empty, several people offered her food. Her glass was always full as was her coffee cup. Every move

428

she made was questioned. She knew that their hearts were in the right place and she wasn't going to let them know how she was feeling.

With the day finally over and as Wendell was leaving, he said, "Well Liza, you seem to have survived the day. Tomorrow you'll be able to get back to your normal busy self. You know that the ladies have loved thinking that they have given you a day of rest and you have been generous enough to let them believe it." He kissed her on the head and called Amelia to say goodbye.

As they were leaving Liza thanked everyone for giving her such a relaxing day and she hoped that they didn't feel that they had worked too hard.

"What will be happening tomorrow?" asked Jamie.

"I thought that I would go to the Home to see how they all enjoyed their Christmas," said Liza.

"I think I'll come with you if I may. It will give us a little time to ourselves," said Jamie.

"Yes it will," laughed Liza; "along with around fifty children."

"I understand that Edward and Nicole have been brave enough to invite the boys to their house for the day and also Annalise is to help with them," said Jamie.

"Yes, Arthur is back to work tomorrow but no doubt he will take a little time off as he loves being with children, as does Edward," said Liza.

"Mother and Lucinda have decided to do nothing," said Jamie. "Do you know what the Duke and Bella will be doing?"

"No, but I believe that Amelia and Wendell extended an invitation for them to visit but I don't know if that is for tomorrow," said Liza. "Peter, Grace and David will also be visiting the Home, but they are not going until the afternoon."

"I daren't ask what Hector will be doing," commented Jamie.

"I suppose his mother would like to see him, but no doubt Hector has other ideas and Estelle will be upper most in his mind. Anyway he and Estelle will have to sort out their lives without our interference," said Liza.

"It's just about a year since Diana had her drinking relapse," said Jamie. "She's done very well since then; I didn't think that she would get through that. She tells me that she can't stand even the smell of alcohol."

"Yes, the year has gone very quickly," was all Liza would say on the subject.

Jamie laughed, "I'm sure you hypnotised her, but I'll say no more. Have we many functions to attend whilst we're here."

"Quite a few, but the Duke and Bella have usurped our position on the social list, we are no longer on the top of it," laughed Liza.

"Good, that takes the pressure off us a little," smiled Jamie. "When are the Duke and Bella leaving?"

"I have no idea; that seems to be a detail that even they haven't decided on," said Liza.

"Do you need some help tonight Liza as you've given April time off to be with Adam over the next few days," said Jamie.

"Yes please Jamie," she answered as they made their way up to bed.

***

They attended several functions over the following days but as always Liza found it difficult to decide what to do on New Year's Eve and New Year's Day. Bella asked her several times, but she said that she would make up her mind nearer the time.

"I can't understand why Liza won't say what she has planned for the New Year," said Bella to Amelia and Wendell one day. "She's normally so organised over the functions that she attends."

"She has her reasons," said Wendell and he went into his study and retreated behind his newspaper which Bella recognised as his way of not wanting to engage in gossip.

Bella was having afternoon tea with Amelia, Annalise and Nicole two days before New Year.

"What will you do?" she asked them.

"We've been invited to several gatherings on that night, but we also wait to see what Liza feels able to do," said Amelia.

"There is obviously something quite significant about the New Year that I don't know about," said Bella.

"There is Bella; her last husband was killed early on New Year's Day. He was shot and died in her arms and much as she and Jamie have a very happy marriage, it is one time of year that has very sad memories for her and Matthew and John. They also saw it happen unfortunately, and it is something that none of them will ever forget," said Amelia.

"She and Jamie do now normally choose to go to one of the smaller parties," said Annalise. "I think that Liza would prefer to ignore New Year. To

430

others it is a time for celebration, to Liza and the boys it is a day that they are unable to forget the horror of it all."

When Bella arrived back that day Liza was waiting for her. "I wanted to know which New Year party you would like to attend," Liza asked.

"I didn't think that you wanted to go to any of them Liza, and I realise why," said Bella with rare understanding.

"I do try to put the past behind me Bella; so show me your invitations and I'll see if I have the same ones and we'll choose which one to accept," said Liza.

They looked through the invitations and Liza described to Bella who each person was, and they made a decision regarding which function to attend.

"What about Amelia and the others, will they have received invitations from these people?" asked Bella.

"If I have received them then they will have also received the same ones. I'll call into Amelia's on my way home and let her know what we have decided, and she will tell the others also," said Liza.

"It must have been a terrible time for you Liza," said Bella but Liza was very tight lipped and took her time to answer.

"Yes, but it will be six years, although it seems so much less. Anyway, let's sort out what we will be wearing and then I must see Amelia and tell her what we are doing," said Liza making it obvious that she didn't want to continue on the subject of Patrick's death.

New Year's Eve came and they all attended a lavish function. Jamie stayed very close to Liza as did Wendell and Amelia. Nobody at the event would have known that the last thing that Liza wanted to do was attend such an evening. She and Jamie left soon after midnight and she apologised to him for once again spoiling New Year's Eve for him.

"You haven't spoilt it for me Liza; you know that I can take or leave functions these days. We turn up to most of them because we have to. I would much rather have spent the evening at home. What are your plans for tomorrow?" he asked.

"I'm not going to make it a miserable day; I would like to do what we have done before and have time with the boys and remember all the fun times that we have had in our lives, including you Jamie," smiled Liza.

"I believe Edward and Nicole will be entertaining Nicholas and Richard tomorrow and I think that Amelia will be joining them, so it will give us some family time to ourselves," said Jamie.

"Everyone is so thoughtful," said Liza.

"Well you know that everyone appreciates how thoughtful you are, so they are just repaying the compliment," said Jamie.

The next morning Miranda and Lucinda made themselves scarce and went to see David and Grace at Liza's house. Hector had been told by Estelle not to interrupt Liza and Jamie that day and they made the journey to the Home again.

The boys came into the drawing room soon after breakfast; this year they did not bring Patrick's photograph with them and Liza did not know whether to be pleased or sorry. They then started talking about times past which now included their time with Jamie. Matthew's fall into the muddy pit at the Evans' farm was talked about and they all said how similar it was to Liza's fall into the mud at Michael's farm. So many happy memories came to the fore that it was impossible not to enjoy them and by lunchtime they had pushed the sadness of New Year's Day six years ago to the back of their minds once again.

At lunch Liza looked around the table and all that she saw was a very happy close family gathering; they all had their memories, but they were at last being replaced by happy ones, not sad ones.

By the time that Nicholas and Richard had returned from Edward's house the boys were ready to enjoy what was left of the day with their friends and it wasn't long before it was their supper time.

Around the dinner table that night everyone knew what New Year's Day had meant to Liza, but nothing was mentioned and from Liza's look nobody would have known that she had experienced any sadness. It was a lively and fun evening meal.

"I shall miss these family gatherings," said the Duke. "They are very different to what I am used to. I believe I shall try to make my mealtimes more convivial. I think that sometimes we should have our boys eating with us; what do you think Bella?"

The shocked look on Bella's face gave everyone the answer to what she thought about the idea and they all tried not to laugh.

"I see that you don't approve Bella," smiled the Duke. "Well, we'll see what we can come up with."

Chapter 22

Jamie and Liza would be visiting the Edgeworth and Bradley farmlands the next day. They were going to take David with them, and the Duke asked if they would mind if he went too and they set off early in the morning.

The crop farms obviously lay fallow but their barns were well stocked with produce to feed the animals on other farms at that time of year. They also stored non-perishables for the local population. At other times they grew to trade to many people in diverse areas.

The word amongst the farmers was that it was going to be a hard winter and although the snow had yet to arrive it was going to be severe when it did. One or two said that it wasn't far away. When they drove into the farm that had been Patrick's step-father's, the overseer came out to greet them and they were ushered into the farmhouse that had been Michael and Sally's home; it brought back strange memories for Liza.

"Is this where you fell into the mud pit that the boys are always talking about?" asked Jamie.

Liza nodded and the overseer said, "Oh you've done that too then." He laughed as did David and the Duke.

"That must have dented your dignity," smiled the Duke.

"You have no idea just how much it did dent my dignity," smiled Liza and once again Jamie noticed that the smile did not reach her eyes.

The overseer's wife had soup and freshly baked bread for them which was very welcome as the day was quite cold.

"We're bringing the animals down from the high ground; we want to be able to get to them to feed them when the bad weather arrives, and it will do in the next few days. It's going to be a harsh winter. We've already had a light covering of snow, but the signs are that we would not be able to reach them when it finally arrives, so we've got to them now.

"When do you think it's going to start?" asked Liza.

"Four to five days from now; the signs are all there. It will hit us first and then go on to where you come from," said the overseer.

"Last time we had a forecast like this we were snowed in until February," said the overseer's wife.

They thanked the overseer and his wife and Liza said that she would be able to give a very favourable report to Michael when she next wrote to him. In the carriage on the way back Jamie said that they had better consider cutting their stay in Belfast short.

"We normally stay until half way through January, but it may well be prudent to leave in a couple of days, which should mean that we will miss the worst of it here and hopefully get home by the time it arrives in England," said Liza.

"I was wondering when we should leave and it seems that the decision has been taken out of our hands," said the Duke. "I do have a couple of engagements that I should attend in just over a weeks' time."

"We won't have time to get a message to Surrey to get our carriages to us, so we will have to hire some," said Jamie.

"That won't be a problem, the only problem could be whether we can get some drivers who won't mind staying with us until the weather clears," said Liza. "We'll have to hope that the hotels can cater for us all."

"I thought you had suites in most hotels," said the Duke.

Liza laughed, "Yes, we do, but you don't. We'll be alright" she said to Jamie and then found it very amusing, especially the look on the Duke's face.

"She's playing with you Grenville," said Jamie.

"Well, it may not be what you are used to but I'll be able to find beds for you all but I'm hoping that we will only have a one night stop on the way," said Liza.

Peter was waiting for them when they arrived home. "I've heard that the weather is closing in quite rapidly and unless you leave soon you will be here for quite some time. Personally I would be happy if you were to stay until the weather clears but I hear that it could go on until at least February."

"I think we should leave the day after tomorrow. It will take us until then to organise our packing," said Liza. "Is there a ship leaving for Liverpool tonight Peter?"

"Yes one is leaving at around ten o'clock tonight, why, do you want to send some instructions with them?" asked Peter.

"I had better write to the carriage company. If we leave on or around ten o'clock at night, then we can sleep on board and make good time through the next day to our hotel en route. Hopefully they will be able to accommodate us all; well they will have to even if we are sleeping on the floor," said Liza. "I'll also write to the hotel in Liverpool so that we can all freshen up when we dock before we have to take the long carriage ride."

Jamie, Grenville and David were watching her. "So you have it all organised then Liza," said Jamie.

"Hopefully, the only thing not organised yet is telling everyone that they are leaving at ten o'clock at night the day after tomorrow. This is going to become a mad house soon," smiled Liza. She rang the bell for Mrs Trent and gave instructions to start the packing and to send word to Mrs Edwards regarding the same.

Liza went into her study and wrote her letters of instruction to the carriage company and the Liverpool hotel. Peter waited for her to finish so that he could take them to the ship leaving that night. He would be returning later with Wendell and Amelia for dinner.

Liza was right, the place did become like a mad house but between Mrs Trent, April, Roberts and Harper miracles were achieved. The same was happening at Liza's house; Mrs Edwards worked well with the maid, Nurse Dawkins and the Duke's valet.

The day before they left, Edward and Nicole visited with little Edward. They were sorry to see them go but realised that it was necessary. Annalise and Arthur called later in the day as did Anthony, Diana, Rose and little Thomas. They had no particular commitments in England so they decided that they would stay until the weather cleared.

There were flurries of snow as they made their way to the docks the night they were leaving. Peter, Edward and Anthony came to see them off. It was too cold for Amelia and Wendell to make the trip and then twenty-two people boarded the ship and attempted to become comfortable in diverse places. All the boys were bedded down on mattresses in one large cabin with Nurse Dawkins squashed in a corner. She said that she would be able to sleep especially as she was a very good sailor.

Lucinda, Miranda and Grace had one of the small areas below decks, as did Hector, David and Adam. Liza was with Bella, Estelle, April and Bella's maid in the cabin that she and Jamie had used on the trip over. Jamie, the Duke, Harper, Roberts and the Duke's valet were as comfortable as possible in the captain's ready room.

435

It was not going to be a very comfortable night, but at least they all had somewhere to rest their heads. Their luggage was stowed successfully below decks alongside the cargo that was being carried.

The trip was a little choppy and once again Bella proved that sailing was not ever going to be one of her favourite pastimes, although she managed not to be sick, but she felt extremely unwell and Liza felt very sorry for her. She remembered how she had felt all those years ago when James Marchant had brought her to Belfast when they married, and she thought that she was going to die on the trip across.

They all managed to get some sleep that night and there were three carriages and one cart waiting for them at Liverpool docks. They made their way to the hotel whilst the cart was loaded with their luggage and was going to follow on.

Breakfast was waiting for them in the dining room. Bella declined any food and was shown to a room where she lay down. Everyone else had something to eat and when they had finished, hot water was taken up to their suite and to several rooms on the floor below. Liza and Jamie had the luxury of their usual room and they washed and changed ready for the next leg of the journey. In the next bedroom all the boys were washing and getting dressed. The third room Liza had given to Bella and her maid was gently organising her.

Miranda, Lucinda and Grace were using a room on the floor below, as was April, Estelle, Nurse Dawkins and finally Bella's maid joined them. The Duke joined Bella in the suite and all the rest of the men went wherever there was space for them.

Their luggage was being carefully placed on the top of the carriages and all they had were small overnight bags on the racks above the seats. It was beginning to snow, but it was very light. The three carriages were lined up. Liza had hoped that there would have been four of them but only three were available. The drivers were aware that they may be away from home for some time.

Liza and Jamie were standing in the doorway waiting for the passengers to get to the carriages and Liza commented to Jamie that Mrs Frances and all the staff at Edgeworth House were going to be surprised to see them and that they may have to accommodate the Duke and his family and staff as well as David and Grace as their house did not have the benefit of staff to keep it warm in their absence.

436

"I hope we have enough food to feed everyone. We may not be able to get to the village for extra supplies," said Liza as the passengers started to move towards the carriages.

"These carriages should only carry six passengers inside, but we will have to accommodate seven in each of them. Liza has worked out the best way to make everyone as comfortable as possible," said Jamie.

"Right everyone I would like the Duke, your valet, the Duchess, David, Grace, Roberts and Harper in one carriage," said Liza and they dutifully moved towards the first carriage.

"The next carriage is to take the five boys, Nurse Dawkins, the Duchess' maid and myself," said Liza and the boys went excitedly to the next one.

"The next one will take, his Lordship, Hector, Miranda, Lucinda, Adam, April and Estelle," said Liza and they went to their carriage.

Jamie helped Liza into her place with the boys and he went off to join his carriage.

It was made clear that if it was too uncomfortable, one of the men could ride next to the driver and rugs were available should they be needed. They had refreshments with them, but they would be stopping on occasion to give the horses a rest.

They finally set off with Jamie's carriage leading the way, followed by Liza's and the Duke's bringing up the rear and it was cold but only snowing slightly. Liza wondered whether they had panicked unnecessarily. They stopped twice on the way to the hotel where they would be staying the night and Liza hoped desperately that they could accommodate them all.

Snow was falling as they pulled into the hotel, but it was not settling, and they all hoped that it would stay that way over night. They all said that the journey had not been too uncomfortable for them, but they were pleased to get to solid ground. The innkeeper and his wife were surprised to see so many guests, but they rose to the occasion and organised beds for twenty-five people. Of course the boys would be sleeping in one room in Liza's suite, and the other room would be for the Duke and Bella. The sitting room would have to be used as a bedroom and that was allocated to Miranda, Lucinda and Grace. Everyone else was sharing in various rooms on the floor below, but Liza made sure that April and Adam had their own room.

They had all slept relatively well that night and it was noticed that the Duke was in particularly good spirits. At the breakfast table he explained why to Jamie; "I have never before been in a situation where everyone has had to 'muck in' together. I have always been waited on hand and foot and I can now appreciate how others put themselves out to look after me. I am seeing another side to life and I am enjoying it. In fact since I arrived in Belfast, I have experienced a different life, one which I shall miss considerably. I can see why Bella likes to spend time with you and I truly see why my boys are happy in your company, and I mean everyone's company, staff included."

Liza came to join them, "I think we should set off as soon as possible, the snow is beginning to settle and there is a blizzard feel to the air."

"How do you mean 'blizzard feel' Liza? There's a slight wind and the snow is still quite light," said Jamie.

"I've seen and felt this in America. I hope that it doesn't get as fierce as I've experienced before," said a concerned Liza.

The luggage was loaded once more onto the carriages and everyone took their places. The drivers were given extra rugs and some hot bricks to keep their feet warm as long as possible. There was also bread, cheese and ham to keep them all well fed and beer, wine and lemonade to drink. They were hoping to reach Edgeworth House well before nightfall.

They stopped at a small inn to rest the horses and stretch their own legs and when they set off again the snow was getting heavier and settling but it was not icy underfoot for the horses. The blizzard struck when they were just under the hour away from home and the drivers were having difficulty controlling the horses. Jamie called for them to stop and he, Hector and the Duke climbed up beside each driver and helped to guide the horses on their way. They covered their faces with scarves so that all that could be seen were their eyes. The drivers were grateful for the company and the horses were easier to control with two pairs of hands.

The last fifteen minutes of the journey were a nightmare and they all breathed a sigh of relief as they turned into the driveway, although that was a hard task as the blizzard had blown the snow in that direction but they finally managed to draw up in front of the house much to the surprise of all the staff.

Mrs Frances, Mr and Mrs Lambert helped them all into the drawing room and took their outdoor clothes.

"We have some extra guests for the night Mrs Frances, and maybe even longer," said Liza.

"We kept the fires going in the gatehouse and the Dower House, but we moved the staff in here with us when the blizzard started and it's becoming difficult to leave here now," said Mrs Frances.

"His Lordship's mother and Mrs Peabody will be with us tonight, as will the Duke and Duchess and their boys. Along with our own staff we have the Duke's valet and Nurse Dawkins and the Duchess's maid. Of course the three drivers will have to be accommodated. I presume that Davis and Hendry are dealing with the horses and carriages," said Liza.

"I'll get fires started in the rooms that will now have to be used. I'll put the Duke and Duchess in the room that is normally used by Mr and Mrs Fuller. Their boys already have their room. Lady Miranda can have her old room and the one next to it can be for Mrs Peabody. Estelle can be in the room next to April and Adam," said Mrs Frances.

"I'm afraid His Lordship's uncle will have to be in the east wing as will his cousin, but that's quite nice now that we have renovated it. It just seems a little cold being in the east. Mr Ffoulks has his own room. I suppose you have no room in the staff wing now," said Liza.

"No, I'm afraid even Mr and Mrs Lambert have moved in for the duration, but there are still rooms in the east wing, and Nurse Dawkins can use April's old room which is near the boys," said Mrs Frances.

"Have we enough food for everyone Mrs Frances? I'll come down to the kitchen to see Mrs Lambert," said Liza.

"We do have stocks," said Mrs Frances, "but as you say it would be best if you see Mrs Lambert yourself."

"I'll be down presently, I'll just make sure that my guests are happy," said Liza and she made her way into the drawing room where everyone was warming themselves and drinking the tea that the maids had brought in for them.

"I suppose you have it all arranged Liza," said Jamie with a smile.

"Yes, everyone will be sleeping here; all your rooms will be ready shortly. Mother, all your staff moved here as the blizzard hit, although they did keep fires going in both houses so they won't be dreadfully cold, but it's now almost impossible to get to either house so your rooms have been organised for you. We are going to have an extremely friendly household over the next few days. As your rooms are made ready, Mrs Frances and Roberts will show you to them. You boys know where you are, and you can go and play whenever you want to. I think you will be eating with us tonight as Mrs Lambert didn't know that we were arriving," said Liza. "I must now go and organise supper for us all, that is if we have any food in the house."

She laughed and disappeared from the room and made her way to the kitchen.

"Is there nothing that she can't organise?" asked the Duke.

"Very little," smiled Jamie.

"I must help her," said Miranda and she got up and went down to the kitchen where Liza was seeing what could be sorted out for a quick meal for everyone.

"I have a large vegetable soup ready for everyone," said Mrs Frances. "I have three meat pies in the larder which I can warm up and a beef joint that I put on immediately I saw that you all were here. I'm having potatoes peeled which I'm afraid will only be boiled and a cabbage or two for vegetables and gravy to go with it all."

"That's wonderful Mrs Lambert, I hope we are not depriving you of your dinner because I know you weren't expecting us and I would hate to think that we are taking the food from you," said Liza.

"No, Your Ladyship, we always keep plenty of food here. We won't starve," said Mrs Lambert.

By this time Miranda had joined them. "Are we well stocked Mrs Lambert?" she asked.

"Yes we are, but I hope this weather doesn't continue too long, otherwise we could be in trouble," said Mrs Lambert.

"The boys will be eating with us tonight so there's no need to worry about them Mrs Lambert," said Liza.

Later Bella looked shocked when all the boys joined them for dinner dressed ready for bed. The Duke laughed. "Bella, haven't the last two days taught you anything? We have all had to abandon all the rules of etiquette just to get here and the boys eating with us in their night attire should by now appear quite normal to you."

"Of course you are right Grenville; I have always known that this very unusual household is regarded as quite usual to all who know it," said Bella.

"Exactly," said Grenville and then he added, "At least I think I know what you mean."

***

An unusual warm air flow drifted in overnight and the blizzard had stopped leaving just a thick slush underfoot, but Liza had seen this before when in

America and it meant that it was literally the 'lull before the storm', but it did give them the opportunity to prepare even more so for what was to come.

Liza was discussing this with Mr Lambert, and he was agreeing with her that they ought to get more supplies in and make sure that the farm animals were rounded up and moved nearer the farmhouses and had adequate feed. She was surprised to see Jamie dressed and appearing in the kitchen.

"I was just looking for you Mr Lambert. I haven't experienced a winter like this before and my wife has convinced me that we have a small window of opportunity to organise the household and the farmers before an even worse blizzard hits us," he said.

"You may not remember it Sir, but when you were away from here some twenty-five years ago we had a winter like this. We had a harsh but short blizzard and a day later we were hit with the worst winter storm in history. We lost all the animals and much of our produce. The house also did not come out of it intact. Many villagers suffered starvation and one or two died from cold. I am concerned that we are going to experience the same this year. We are already better prepared but I'm not so sure that it will be enough," said Mr Lambert.

"I'm going out to the farms Liza," said Jamie. "I'll set off immediately and take Hendry with me. Mrs Lambert, have you something warm for me to have before I leave? Ah there's Hendry, have you eaten?"

He hadn't so he and Jamie sat down together in the kitchen and enjoyed a bowl of porridge each.

"I'll go into the village and make sure everyone is provided for," said Liza. "I'll take Davis and see if I can get more supplies for us. Mr Lambert we are going to need plenty of firewood, so I suggest that everyone available starts chopping."

"Be careful Liza and make sure you are back well before the storm starts," said Jamie.

"I'll find the Duke and see what he wants to do and I'll tell your uncle and Grace and Miranda and Lucinda to go to their homes and bring back all that they may need over the next week or so. I'm worried about Mrs Price and her family; she doesn't have a great deal to keep them all warm and fed. She has enough but if we are snowed in, she will not be earning and she will find it difficult. I will have to be very tactful as she is a proud woman," said Liza.

"I'm sure you'll handle it beautifully," said Jamie.

Liza left the kitchen and went to find the Duke. She found him in the dining room talking to Hector and David. She told them what was being forecast for the next week or so and the Duke made the decision to leave as soon as possible. His home was less than two hours away and he felt that if they left within the hour the drivers could be there and back before the blizzard came.

Liza smiled at him and told him that she would leave it to him to tell Bella that she had an hour to get ready to leave. He left the room saying that they had better close their ears to the noise which could emanate from his wife.

Liza rang the bell for Harper or Mrs Frances and they both appeared. She told them what was planned and that they were to advise the drivers from Liverpool to get the carriages ready for the journey, but they were to emphasise that they were to return here as they would not be able to reach their homes and she would not like to have their deaths on her conscience.

"They are quite comfortably housed aren't they Harper?" asked Liza.

"Yes my lady, the coach house is large, and they were very warm and comfortable in the room that Davis arranged for them," said Harper. "Their horses are also well catered for; the stable is a little crowded, but it will keep all the animals warm."

Harper went to give the necessary instructions and Mrs Frances said that she would organise what was needed from the Dower House and the gatehouse.

"I'll help with that," said David, "and I'll find Grace and see what she is doing now."

"Liza, I think that I ought to get back to the Ffoulks Home. I'll make sure that they are well prepared," said Hector. He was looking worried.

"I'll find Estelle and see if she would also like to return with you," smiled Liza. "You left your own carriage here didn't you?"

Hector nodded.

"What's the matter Hector? Are you worried that there aren't enough provisions for everyone there? I know that they were well stocked when we left. Perhaps you could organise more flour, vegetables and meat. The older boys could be put to chopping as much wood as possible, but they would have to be well supervised because you know what boys are like. I'll go and see Estelle now," said Liza.

"Thank you, Liza, I would be happy knowing that they will all be safe at the Home," said Hector.

"I know you would," said Liza. She then went to find Estelle who said that she felt that she should also return to Ffoulks House to help with whatever was necessary.

Matthew came to find her. "What's happening, everyone is rushing around and packing. I thought that they would be staying longer."

Liza explained the situation to him, and his only comment was that it was just like when they were in Benson and he would tell his brothers what was happening.

The Duke came out of his room with a worried look on his face. "Liza," he said, "I know that it is a great imposition on you but Bella and I would be happier if our boys were safely here with you and Nurse Dawkins has said that if you are in agreement, she would stay to help look after them."

"Oh, I hadn't thought that either of you would want to be parted from them, but I suppose with all your commitments it is often difficult for both of you to spend the time that you would like with them. Of course they are welcome to stay and Nurse Dawkins also," said Liza.

"Would Mr Reece be quite agreeable to instruct them again, do you think? I had a long talk with him when we were in Belfast and I am so impressed with his approach to teaching. He has turned two very disruptive boys into ones who are now very willing to learn. I wish that I had found someone like him years ago. I suppose he was originally employed by you Liza," said the Duke.

"I'm sure he would be happy to have them in his schoolroom again and no, he was originally employed by Jamie. Many people don't realise the importance that Jamie puts on education. From what I have been told, his father only believed that all that was needed was the minimum as everyone had to do his bidding so it was totally unnecessary to learn very much, but Jamie knew differently and spent time studying with little encouragement from his father," said Liza.

Nicholas and Richard were pleased to hear that they would be staying for a while longer and they were in with the other boys being regaled with the stories of the snowstorms that had been experienced in America.

Hector and Estelle were the first to leave. They were wrapped up warmly although it had been colder the previous day. Liza told them that Jamie had already left for the farms, so he was unable to wish them farewell.

Only two of the three carriages were outside the front of the house and Bella and the Duke's luggage was being loaded inside each one. Liza was telling the drivers to make sure they returned here as they would be unable to reach

443

their homes and that she would have food and warm beds waiting for them. The third driver was going with them and they were smiling and thanking her and assuring her that they would not be foolish and would return.

Bella looked half asleep as she came down the stairs and Liza made sure that she had eaten, which she had, as had the Duke. Once again Liza apologised for Jamie being unable to bid them farewell and she assured them that she would look after Nicholas and Richard as if they were her own.

"I have every confidence that you will Liza," said the Duke. "As soon as we are able, we will return to bring our boys home. Thank you for everything that you have done and thank you for the wonderful time that we had at Christmas. My mother-in-law will be anxious to hear all that we have done."

Bella came over to Liza and kissed her on the cheek. "You are very kind Liza and I do appreciate all that you have done for us and the fact that you will be looking after our sons. They will be happy and very much warmer here than at our home. It is very draughty you know; I'm not looking forward to being there in this weather."

"Oh," was all that Liza could think of saying and she could imagine that Bella would have preferred to stay but they did have commitments, although if the weather was as bad as they were being told they would be going nowhere.

David joined Liza on the steps to wave them off as Bella and the Duke climbed into the first carriage and the valet and maid got into the second one and both carriages then moved off down the very slushy driveway.

"If it turns cold on top of this slush it's going to be lethal underfoot," said David. "Grace and I will go to our house now and see what we can bring back. Originally I thought that there would be no need to move in with you, but I also remember a similar winter in Truro, and it was indeed horrendous. We'll sort out what we can and perhaps one of the carriages could bring it up to the house. We have plenty of wood at the back of the house and it would be useful to move it up."

"Whatever you can do would be useful," said Liza.

"We'll also help Miranda and Lucinda, although they have their butler and maid, but I believe they also have stockpiles of wood and flour and all sorts of other things," said David.

Liza went up to see the boys who were still in their room and still in their nightclothes.

"We thought it best to keep out of the way," said Matthew. "But we are a little hungry now."

"That was very thoughtful of you all. You can go down to the kitchen for breakfast now; you can get washed and dressed when you have eaten," said Liza. "I'm going into the village and I'll call on Mrs Price to see that they will be alright."

April and Nurse Dawkins were sorting out the boys' clothes ready for when they returned.

Finally she was ready to leave for the village; Davis was waiting for her in the hallway and she told him that she would like to stop off at the vicarage firstly to make sure that the Reverend Collins was well prepared. Davis nodded and smiled as he knew that she would probably do that.

Bernard came to the vicarage door when she knocked. He had a shabby coat on and looked rather cold. He showed her into his living room where he had a small fire burning which was making very little difference to the temperature of the room. His bed was in the corner and when Liza frowned, he told her that he had moved his bed down as there was no fire in his bedroom.

"What food do you have in stock Bernard?" she asked.

"I'll be alright Liza. My parishioners look after me and so does your kitchen," he said.

"I'll just check to see what you need and send it down to you," said Liza and she moved quickly towards the cupboard where he kept his food and opened the door before he could stop her. She rounded on him and said that she thought that men of religion should not lie. "You have virtually nothing in and you look pinched with the cold. Bernard, the forecast for the next week to ten days is a blizzard unlike anything that has been seen in many years. Even if your parishioners wanted to give you food they won't be able to reach you. The Edgeworths are also your parishioners and we would like you to come and stay with us for a few days until the worst of the weather is over. You can put a note on the church saying where you are if anyone needs you urgently."

"I can't put on your kindness like that Liza. I'll be alright," said Bernard.

"But you won't be alright Bernard; you could die of cold here and that would be on my conscience for the rest of my life; you can't do that to me, Jamie or the rest of my family. Please pack what you need, and I'll pick you up on my way back from the village," said Liza.

"Thank you, Liza," said Bernard. "I will now admit that I was concerned about how I was going to cope if we do have the weather that has been predicted."

"I must rush now as I don't want to get caught out if the blizzard hits earlier than thought. It was a nightmare getting home in it yesterday," said Liza and she left him to pack up what he needed to bring with him.

Liza's first stop in the village was at the general store where she ordered extra dry goods and whatever vegetables that could be spared. Although they had farm animals Liza thought it prudent to arrange for various cuts of meat to be organised as well as several chickens. Jamie would say that they had such animals, but she wanted to be well covered. The bakers were the next stop and she hoped that Mrs Lambert would not be upset that she was bringing home bread and cakes that she was quite capable of making, but she felt that Mrs Lambert was going to be overworked with all the extra mouths that she had to feed.

Whilst it was all being packed for her she went to see Mrs Price and she was shocked to find that part of her house had collapsed under the weight of the snow the day before. Mr Rogers and a couple of other villagers were trying to shore up where it was damaged.

"We hadn't realised that you were back," said Mr Rogers.

"We managed to return just as the blizzard struck yesterday. I suppose that is when this happened," said Liza. "Was anybody hurt?"

"Just a few cuts and bruises," said Mrs Price.

Mrs Price's kitchen could not be used as part of the ceiling was resting on her table and chairs and her stove was out of action. Derek's chair had been damaged, but it could be mended. Only one bedroom could be used, and Liza doubted that it was safe.

"Mr Rogers can you protect Mrs Price's undamaged possessions?" asked Liza and he agreed that he could do that. She turned to Mrs Price and said, "This is a property that is owned by Lord Edgeworth and it is therefore up to him to make it safe and sound for you. That can't be done until the storm has passed but in the meantime I have room for you all at Edgeworth House. Derek can sleep in with my boys and you and Susan can have a room on the same floor."

"Your Ladyship, I can't do that; we'll manage here. Mr Rogers is making it weatherproof for us," said Mrs Price.

Liza sighed, "You are the second person who wants me to have your deaths on my conscience and that's very unfair of you. You know that my boys would enjoy having Derek with them and I know that my whole household would be delighted to have you and Susan under our roof and besides you know that it is our responsibility to house you and we are unable to do it here now."

Mr Rogers was smiling at the way that Liza had turned the tables on Mrs Price, and he said how sensible it was that they go with Lady Edgeworth until their home could be put right again. Derek was also smiling.

"Right," said Liza. "Can you collect up all your clothes and whatever else you think that you should bring with you and I just have to pick up my shopping and I'll be back for you shortly. Bring Derek's chair and we'll get it mended for him. If you have any food in the house, bring that also, as well as extra blankets which are always useful."

Liza moved out of the house and Mr Rogers followed her. "You're very kind. You know that we do our best to look after Mrs Price, but this was becoming an impossible task, especially as we know that the weather is closing in again."

"It's the least we can do," said Liza. "Will you make sure that she brings anything that is sentimental or valuable to the family with her? We must leave quite quickly as I can see that the snow clouds are gathering and I want to get back before the blizzard starts again and we must pick up the Reverend Collins on the way. Thank you for all your help Mr Rogers; it's you who are kind."

Davis had already organised the goods that Liza had purchased, and he was bringing the carriage back over to Mrs Price's house. He helped Mr Rogers strap Derek's chair onto the back of the carriage, and then steadied Derek as he climbed into it. Mrs Price and Susan carried bundles of clothes and blankets, as well as any food that they could salvage from the kitchen, and they climbed aboard. Mr Rogers told Mrs Price not to worry as he would make sure that her possessions were protected.

Liza turned to him and said, "Mr Rogers, when I was in America we had terrible winter storms but the whole of our town pulled together. We abandoned some homes and those families moved in with others and pooled their resources. Nobody was left alone to starve in a cold and lonely house. I am concerned that there may be some villagers who are not as well off as others and who may suffer greatly through this bad winter. I know that you and your wife are very caring people, but it would set my mind at rest if I could rely on you to see that nobody is without. Whatever is needed would you please see that it is supplied, and I will reimburse you and anyone else when the weather clears."

"Of course we would do that anyway, but thank you for caring," said Mr Rogers.

447

It was beginning to snow when they finally set off for Edgeworth House and it was getting quite heavy when they stopped at the church for Bernard, who was ready and waiting for them. He had very little with him and he climbed into the carriage and was surprised to see Mrs Price and her family also there.

As they arrived at the house it was now becoming quite slippery underfoot and Davis and Bernard helped them all up the steps and into the hallway. Mr Lambert appeared and lifted in Derek's wheelchair, commenting that it would need a little attention.

The goods were taken down to the kitchen and Mrs Frances came to see what was happening. Liza smiled at her and explained that Mrs Price's roof had fallen in and that she and her family would be staying for a while.

"Derek can go in the spare bed with my boys and Mrs Price and Susan can use the room that Miss Reece had as there are already two beds there. Reverend Collins can have the room next to Mr David Edgeworth," said Liza. "Has his Lordship arrived back yet?"

"I'm afraid not yet, and the drivers are yet to return from taking the Duke and Duchess home," said Mrs Frances.

"Well, I hope they all return soon as it's getting quite nasty out there," said Liza.

Mrs Price insisted on helping Mrs Frances to organise their rooms and the boys heard the commotion in the hall and came to see what was going on; they were delighted to learn that Derek would be staying with them for a while and helped him up the stairs to their room. Nicholas and Richard were just as pleased to see him, but all the boys ignored Susan. Their interest in girls had obviously yet to develop.

Bernard was already in the drawing room with Miranda, Lucinda, David and Grace and Liza could hear David saying that it was a very wise decision that he had agreed to stay with them for a while. Liza finally joined them.

"I see you have a few more visitors," said David tactfully.

"Yes, Mrs Price's roof fell in yesterday in the blizzard and we couldn't leave the family there. It is an Edgeworth property which we will have to put right when the weather clears. As you know Derek is already one of the boys and he is used to being in their company," said Liza.

The sound of carriages arriving was a relief to them all, but Liza was still concerned as Jamie had yet to arrive home.

Liza looked through the window and the forecast had been correct; the blizzard was starting quite fiercely and it was with relief that she could see

Jamie's carriage slowly making its way up the drive. She wasn't sure but she thought she could see two cows tied behind it. It stopped and Jamie alighted battling the wind and snow whilst climbing the steps to the front door. Harper helped him in, taking his hat, coat and gloves and Liza greeted him with such a relieved smile on her face that Jamie thought it was worth the cold that he had endured.

She ushered him into the warmth of the drawing room, and he smiled at everyone and then realised that Bernard was there.

"Bernard will be staying with us until the weather clears," said Liza.

"Yes, that's very wise," said Jamie holding out his hands in front of the fire. "It must be very cold in the vicarage and if this blizzard goes on too long God knows what would happen to you."

"Mrs Price, Derek and Susan are also with us Jamie," said Liza and Jamie raised an eyebrow waiting for an explanation. "Her roof fell in yesterday in the blizzard so she and her family will be with us until we can get it put right for her."

"Of course she should be here," said Jamie. "The boys will enjoy Derek's company."

"Also," said Liza and Jamie waited patiently for her to tell him who else was under his roof. "Bella and the Duke left this morning, but Nicholas, Richard and Nurse Dawkins are still with us."

"Why?" he asked.

"Because their house is cold and draughty and they are happy here," said Liza realising that it was really rather a lame reason for their still being with them.

Jamie just looked at her and shook his head. "I suppose it sounded quite logical when they asked you."

"Yes it did, but it doesn't now," admitted Liza.

"Looking after other people's children is quite a responsibility Liza," said Jamie.

"Yes I do know that Jamie," said Liza quietly and Jamie realised that he had made a rather stupid comment since Liza had been looking after other people's children for many years.

"My apologies Liza, of course you know that," said Jamie. "If you'll all excuse me I must get out of these clothes and into something warm and dry."

"I'll help you," said Liza and as they were about to leave the drawing room there was a commotion in the hallway. They looked out only to find John

449

running down the stairs with Derek's walking sticks and James closely following him. Nicholas and Richard were positioned halfway down the stairs and Matthew was holding onto Derek who was lying on his stomach with a leg either side of the banisters. Matthew let go and pushed him and he was off sliding down the banisters, reaching the bottom at the same time as his friends. John and James caught him safely, stood him up and handed him his walking sticks and without another thought they were all making their way down to the kitchen for their supper.

Liza and Jamie just stood there each wondering if they had really seen Derek fearlessly hurtling down the banisters.

"Wasn't that rather dangerous," said Liza.

"I never found it so when I was a boy," said Jamie, "but I will have a serious word with the boys. I can see why they encouraged Derek to do it. They wanted him to get down the stairs as quickly as they do, and he probably wanted the same."

"I wonder whose idea it was," commented Liza.

"Do you really have to ask?" said Jamie. "It has to have been Matthews'." Liza just nodded in agreement.

It was cosy and warm in Jamie's room and Liza sat with him whilst he removed his outer clothes and donned his dressing gown.

"Did you really slide down the banisters when you were a boy? I didn't think that you ever did anything that undignified," said Liza.

"I did it many times, but only when my father wasn't around. He never allowed me to do anything frivolous, although his life was full of frivolities," said Jamie.

"I'm glad that you did manage to have some fun when you were a boy, even if you did have to go behind your father's back," said Liza.

Roberts knocked and entered. He had organised a hot bath for Jamie and the water was now being brought in. "I'll leave you now Jamie; you'll enjoy soaking in hot water," said Liza.

"Keep me company while I'm in my bath," said Jamie. "You can tell me what you have been getting up to today; apart from rescuing people and bringing all of them home with you."

Roberts laid Jamie's clothes out for him and then left them alone.

"Does it worry you that we have Nicholas and Richard here without Bella or the Duke?" asked Liza.

"No, I'm just surprised that they left. They seemed quite comfortable here and I'm sure that most of their commitments will be cancelled because of the weather," said Jamie.

"I was also quite surprised, and I did question whether they would be happy being parted from them, but they did have commitments which meant that they wouldn't see them very much anyway," said Liza.

"The Duke was keen to talk to Adam which I believe he did when we were in Belfast. He probably would have liked to have enticed him away from us and into his household," said Jamie.

"Adam would never do that to us," smiled Liza with confidence. "Did I see you bring some cattle home with you?"

"Yes, I thought it prudent to have a means of fresh milk through this time and Mr Lambert is housing them in one of the nearest barns. I hope somebody is capable of milking them otherwise I have wasted my energies," said Jamie and he eyed Liza closely. "I suppose that is another little task that you have done in the past."

"You would be wrong Jamie, but I dare say that I would cope if we were desperate. Were all the farms prepared?" Liza asked.

"Our overseer was doing a good job; however he hasn't experienced a winter like this before, but many of the farmers have and as far as possible they have the animals under control and hopefully enough feed for them for the foreseeable future. Farmers and their wives are used to planning ahead so they won't starve, but whether all the animals will survive is another matter," said Jamie.

Whilst Jamie was drying off and dressing for dinner, Liza went to her room and also changed, they both emerged at the same time and were making their way down when the boys appeared fresh from their supper. Jamie said to them that he hoped that Derek had survived his banister experience intact and Matthew said that it was perfectly safe as they had positioned themselves all the way down to help him. "Besides," he added. "I showed him how to do it and he could see that it was easy."

Jamie looked at Liza, "What did I tell you. It had to be Matthew."

"We haven't yet thought of a way to get him up the stairs quickly, but we're working on that," said Matthew.

"I'm sure you are," said a resigned Jamie.

"Did Susan join you for supper?" asked Liza.

"Well, she sat at the table, but didn't say much," said James.

"I suppose she was shy with so many boys around her," said Liza.

"Yes, well that's girls for you," said a very dismissive Nicholas as they all went slowly up the stairs discussing methods that could be used to get Derek up the stairs quickly, some of which sounded rather dangerous.

"They'll soon think differently about girls," commented Jamie.

"When did you start thinking about girls?" asked Liza.

"When I was their age, of course I wasn't surrounded by friends then, although I did see Anthony and Binky quite regularly. University was when we all took a great interest in the opposite sex but when I think about what was discussed I now know that we knew absolutely nothing of great value in that regard," said Jamie.

Liza was grinning at him. "You have obviously learned a great deal since those days."

He also grinned, "I have indeed," he said.

Bernard was the only one in the drawing room when they entered, and he said that everyone had gone to change for dinner. "I'm sorry but I don't really have clothes which are suitable for dinner, would you like me to go to the kitchen for my meal?"

"You look perfectly respectable to me," said Jamie politely.

"And to me also," said Liza. "I suppose I did give you very little time to pack and really evening dress was the last thing on our minds. You'll do nicely, but if you do need to change whilst you are here, I know that Jamie has more than enough clothes and I'm sure he would be happy to lend you some, although I think he would struggle with your collar, but David would have that covered being a man of the cloth."

"Of course I would, but quite often we don't change for dinner and sometimes our boys have been known to join us in their nightclothes. We don't stand on ceremony too much in this household, only when it's necessary," said Jamie hoping that he hadn't said too much and undone all the good that they had achieved in making Bernard feel comfortable.

"That's very kind of you and I may have to take you up on that offer if I am unable to return to the vicarage for some time," said Bernard.

Over dinner Liza was asked about the winters in America and how she had coped, and she told them that all the winters in Benson had been severe, some more so than others but that everyone in the town planned for it. She told them how Gabriel and Simon moved in with her as did Zelma and that George either came to her or to Kathy and Joe. Ambrose was also with them

452

the year that Kate had returned, and that was when the scout Bandor had collapsed outside but they managed to bring him in, so her house was overflowing.

"Remind me who George is," said Jamie.

"He is the clergyman for the town. One year everyone thought that he was with somebody else and he nearly died. He managed to stumble from his house but couldn't get to any of the houses on the way down as the snow had reached all the upstairs windows, but we had an alleyway between us and Charlie Penn, the carpenter, and the snow had not piled so much there. We heard banging on our back door and when we opened it, he fell in and really it was a miracle that he survived. During the course of the next few hours people were putting messages in their windows and eventually they reached us. It was as if everyone had thought about him and they were asking where he was and of course we were able to say that he was with us," said Liza.

"I see why you are so anxious to have everyone safely under your roof Liza," said David. "It was obviously something that was truly necessary when you were in America. You mentioned a scout, was he Indian?"

"He was what is termed a 'half breed' which is now used as a derogatory term for someone who has one white parent and one Indian one. He is someone that I would trust with my life and the lives of my children, and indeed I have done so," said Liza quietly.

"I have met him, haven't I Liza?" said Jamie and Liza nodded.

"You said that he collapsed, and you took him in. You must have had a very large house in Benson," commented Lucinda.

"No, it was exactly the opposite, although compared to some places there it could be considered large," said Liza.

"I would have thought that someone with Indian blood would have known not to be out in such weather," said David dismissively which annoyed Liza.

"He was trying to get to the fort to warn them of something," said Liza and Jamie realised that it was a time that Liza wanted to forget but those around the table were intrigued and wanted to know more.

"There was a band of deserters who had killed many people and unfortunately they knew who I was and that I had no money problems. They had been captured, tried, and condemned to death but on the way to the prison where the sentence was to be carried out three of them escaped and were nearing Benson. Bandor had seen them near one of the outlying farms. He had been injured slightly but he still attempted to get to us and also warn

453

the fort that farmers were in danger. He got as far as the town but luckily we saw him as he fell and carried him in with great difficulty," said Liza. "We treated his wound and warmed him up and the next morning he managed to reach the fort with his information."

Jamie realised that she was not telling the whole story and that somewhere within the tale Patrick figured largely.

"Were the deserters coming to get you Liza," asked Lucinda with bright excited eyes.

"Apparently. They were going to hold me to ransom, but they didn't get the chance. The cold killed two and the ringleader suffered frostbite so badly that his fingers and toes needed to be amputated. So much as Bandor risked his life for us, the outcome was that he did not need to do so," said Liza.

"What an exciting life you have led Liza," said Grace. "You should write a book about your experiences."

"I have always kept a journal, perhaps one day someone will find it interesting, but by that time I will be long gone," said Liza with one of her moments of foresight.

Jamie looked at Liza and thought *Yes there is so much more to this story than you are saying Liza* but he decided to change the subject to his day and the two cows that he had brought back with him which started the discussion on whether or not someone would be able to milk them.

The snow had been falling steadily since Jamie had returned and every now and again the wind would increase and create harsher conditions, but as they were finishing their meal the blizzard started with a vengeance battering the house ferociously. It sounded like thousands of stones being hurled at every window and Liza and Jamie jumped up, both of them making their way up to the boys' rooms. Nicholas and Richard had been disturbed and were going into the other boys' bedroom where James, John and Matthew were looking out of the windows. Derek was attempting to also reach the windows. Nurse Dawkins was moving into their room and Liza could see Mrs Price making her way up the stairs to check on her children.

"Derek seems alright Mrs Price, I hope Susan isn't frightened," said Liza and Mrs Price went to see how her daughter was faring.

Jamie told the boys to get back into their beds as it was impossible to see anything from the windows. April was helping to tuck the boys in their beds and Nurse Dawkins was doing the same with Nicholas and Richard in their room. Liza was tucking Derek in and he was smiling excitedly. "It's very cold out there but we are warm and safe in here. Is my sister frightened?"

"I don't know Derek, but your mother has just gone in to see her so if she is, she will be alright now," said Liza. "I'm glad you are all here, I would have been very worried about you."

Jamie was going around to each boy making sure that they were settling back comfortably again, and he did the same with Nicholas and Richard. Liza knocked on Mrs Price's door and asked if Susan was alright.

"She is fine now thank you, but it has frightened her. She woke suddenly with the noise and of course she was in strange surroundings. She's settled back, but I think that I will stay with her now. Is Derek alright?" asked Mrs Price.

"Yes, he's happy being in with the other boys; the noise disturbed them all, but they are all back under their covers. You can go in and see him if you like," said Liza and she led Mrs Price into the boys' room and they all smiled up at her, Derek looking the most comfortable of them all.

"I don't think that my house would have withstood tonight even if the roof had still been in place," said Mrs Price.

"I know; I'm quite concerned for some of the other people in the village. I know that Mr Rogers is looking out for everyone, but there is only so much he can do and in these conditions he won't be able to get to anyone and nobody will be able to get to him. I hope it eases a little by tomorrow so that we can see that everyone is alright," said a concerned Liza.

Mrs Price said goodnight and returned to her room to be with Susan, and Liza went back down to the drawing room where Bernard was pacing up and down.

"I know what you are thinking Bernard; they are your parishioners and you feel that you should make sure that they are all safe and well; I feel the same way but I doubt that we will be able to reach the village tomorrow," said Liza.

"It was selfish of me to have left them," said Bernard.

Jamie came into the drawing room having been around the house with Harper and Mr Lambert making sure that all was safe and secure.

"Bernard," said Jamie. "If you had stayed at your place you would have been frozen to death by now, and even if you weren't you would not have been able to get out of your house to the village. The blizzard has already cut this house off from our stables, the Dower House and the gatehouse. You would have been stuck in your house with no means of helping anyone, so stop feeling selfish and just be thankful that you will be alive to comfort those who need it."

Liza looked at Jamie with admiration and it was obvious that everyone else agreed with him.

"Mr Rogers has said that he would look out for the villagers," said Liza not adding that he would only be able to do that if he could get out of his own premises and if the villagers could leave theirs. She hoped that some of them had moved in together and pooled their resources as she had suggested.

Liza and Jamie went down to the kitchens when all the others had made their way to their various rooms. Mrs Frances and Mrs Lambert were still on duty; Harper was tidying up the wine bottles in the small scullery and Mr Lambert appeared carrying wood, which he placed next to several buckets of coal.

"Are all the staff rooms warm Mrs Frances?" asked Liza.

"Those with fires have been lit; those without have been supplied with hot bricks or warming pans. Nobody will sleep cold tonight," said Mrs Frances.

"Good" said Liza, "because to be able to look after us, you must firstly look after yourselves. Have we found someone who knows how to milk cows?"

"I know how to do that," said Mr Lambert, "and so does young Ernie."

"Are all the men comfortable in the stable house?" asked Jamie.

"Yes they are warm enough and they have their own kitchen, although they normally eat here, but under the circumstances they have been supplied with plenty of stocks should they have to feed themselves," said Mr Lambert. "All the horses are well fed and as we have so many in the stables at the moment they are out of the weather and keep one another warm."

Harper emerged from the small scullery having counted the wine bottles.

"Good evening my Lord and Lady Edgeworth," said Harper. "As you can see everything is under control for the moment, but I have to say that if we are all unable to leave by possibly this time next week then we will have difficulty keeping the house warm."

"We'll see how things are at the weekend and make some further decisions," said Jamie.

"If it is still impossible to leave the house then we will have to close down some rooms and double up in some bedrooms. I'll arrange that we shut down the east wing; we'll save fuel wherever we can but still manage to keep ourselves warm," said Liza.

The blizzard was still battering the house when Liza and Jamie made their way to bed. It didn't take April long to help Liza out of her clothes and into her nightdress. Liza stood by the fire making plans in her mind should they have to take further steps to economise on fuel and food. She heard Roberts leave Jamie's room and she quickly went into him.

"I think I'll move in with you tomorrow Liza," said Jamie. "I'll get Roberts to move what I will need, I'm sure you have room for some of my clothes. Your bedroom is brighter than mine and on the warmer side of the house."

"That's a lovely idea; I'll get April to move all my summer clothes into your room and that will leave lots of space for you. I do love your room though Jamie, it has very happy memories for me," said Liza.

"I know," said Jamie, "but by doing this we will save enough fuel to keep someone else warm and it is certainly no sacrifice for either of us. We sleep together every night so it would be very wasteful of us to keep two fires going. You were a little reluctant to tell the whole story of your experience with the deserters tonight. I could see that it was upsetting you; I don't think anyone else noticed."

Liza gave him a smile, "Lucinda seemed quite excited by it all. I suppose that's because before being with us she had never travelled or thought about how difficult life could be elsewhere."

"Was it very difficult Liza?" asked Jamie.

"Sometimes it was, and sometimes it was very frightening, but that is all in the past and now nothing is difficult and I am no longer frightened," said Liza hoping that it would be the end to that conversation.

"One day I'm sure that you will tell me about that particular adventure, but I can see that my asking you has disturbed you and I don't want you to be disturbed. I want you to be happy, warm and comfortable and I shall keep you that way tonight while we listen to the blizzard raging outside," said Jamie.

"There are many things that I will tell you someday Jamie, but tonight I just want to think about you, me and our family. When the time is right you will enjoy some of my adventures, as Lucinda calls them, and I'm sure I'll enjoy some of yours," said a rather sleepy Liza.

Jamie kissed her and said, "You know that if you mention Patrick it would not hurt me."

"Yes, I know Jamie," said Liza but she added to herself, *but it would hurt me.*

***

457

The blizzard continued throughout the night and it appeared that there would be no let up through the following day but towards lunchtime it eased a little giving time to clear a little snow away from the livestock barn towards the kitchen door.

The drivers' house had a small door through to where all the horses were kept and by removing a couple of wall planks they could go on and get through to where the cows were being housed. The problem was from that barn to the kitchen as the land between was at least eight feet deep in snow and it was increasing by the minute. The only solution to the situation was to remove another couple of planks to the side of the barn which would be opposite the kitchen door. The snow had blown through the gap but because of how it was placed they only had to attempt to clear around a height of five feet of snow over a distance of around twelve feet, but everyone knew that in a short while no matter how much was removed it would be just as impassable.

One of the Liverpool coach drivers came up with a novel solution. His suggestion was to place two coaches side by side so that their doorways married up, having first removed the doors, and that would almost butt them up to the kitchen door. That way they could walk through from the stable house, through where the horses were housed, carry on through to where the cows were, climb up into the first coach, through the second coach and step down into the kitchen. They would have to cover some of the gaps, possibly with oil cloth, but they would not be cut off from the main household and Jamie's efforts in bringing the cattle home with him would mean that, if nothing else, they could all have fresh milk.

Jamie, David, Bernard and Adam had wrapped themselves up well and joined all the other men clearing snow and organising moving the coaches as well as taking the doors off. It was beginning to snow heavily again and everyone was rushing to get finished before the blizzard hit. Roberts looked out to see what was happening and he immediately grabbed his coat and hat and went outside to help. Miranda's butler, Stewart, was already pulling his weight.

Harper came to find Liza who was helping April reorganise her room to accommodate Jamie and said that if she did not need him at that moment, he would like to attempt to help with what was happening outside.

"Of course Harper, but please be careful as you are not used to manual labour. I know you work hard for us but what is happening outside is totally different to your normal tasks," said Liza.

"I will be careful, but thank you for your concern," said Harper and he left with a spring in his step.

"Can we go and help them please?" asked Matthew.

"I wish that we all could Matthew, but we would only get in their way at the moment," said Liza. "When they have everything in place there may be something that you can do to help."

There were looks of disappointment on all the faces that had appeared around the door into Liza's bedroom.

"When the men have finished they are going to need hot drinks and food, so it might be an idea if you went down to the kitchen for your lunch and bring it to the dining room so that there is plenty of room for them in the kitchen," said Liza. "I wish I could give you something important to do, but we must all stay out of the way of the men as when they have finished they are going to be cold, wet, hungry and exhausted."

Liza smiled as they went towards the stairs and positioned Derek on the banisters with John making his way down with the walking sticks and the others at various places to make sure he was safe.

When Mrs Frances heard that the boys would be eating in the dining room, she quickly threw a protective cover over the table, but left the boys to sort out themselves. Mrs Price helped to dish up their lunch and each carried their food up into the dining room with Susan carrying Derek's. They settled around the table and as Susan was leaving James said, "Why don't you join us for lunch Susan?" She turned and gave them all a beautiful smile and dashed off to fetch her own lunch.

Liza came down to check that the boys were behaving, and she was delighted to see Susan sitting with them and they were including her in their conversation. She carried on down to the kitchen and could see that it would not be long before the route from the drivers' house would be completed.

All the coach drivers were attempting to throw large oil skins over the various openings between the coaches and the buildings. They would have to be tied down well as the wind that came with the blizzard could easily damage them if they were not adequately secured. Others were piling snow up around the wheels of the coaches and tamping it down and by the time they had finished the coaches would not be moving no matter how strong the wind blew, also the blizzard would help to make them even more secure.

Finally it was done, and they all had to go into the stable house to work their way through to the kitchen as naturally the doorway to the kitchen had a coach blocking the way. It was successful and one by one they walked and climbed through the various barns and coaches into the warmth of the kitchen.

Mrs Lambert had made an enormous meat stew which was very gratefully received. They had finished just in time as the weather closed in and the noise against the house was once again horrendous.

"Well Ernie," said Mr Lambert. "We have one more task to carry out."

Ernie looked up frowning. "What's that Mr Lambert?" he asked.

"We've got to milk those cows," he said.

"That will be good," said Mrs Lambert. "I'll be able to make a large milk pudding with the stale bread and dried fruit that we have. It will be tasty, filling and warming for everyone."

Jamie was discussing what they had achieved that day with all those milling around the kitchen and gradually they all went their various ways. Liza asked those staying in the stable house if they had adequate food and fuel and Davis assured her that they were quite well provisioned, but they were all relieved that they could get to the main house.

When everyone had eaten, Jamie, David and Bernard went up to the drawing room and found that the boys had made themselves comfortable there. They were full of questions which Jamie answered and then the boys asked if the kitchen had cleared and when told that it had they went into the dining room and collected their dirty dishes and carried them down to the kitchen with Derek trailing behind them.

"Did I see Derek's sister with them?" asked a surprised Jamie.

"Yes, they seem to have accepted that she is now part of the household and they invited her to lunch with them," said Liza.

Miranda and Lucinda joined them. "We've moved into the same room. April and Mrs Frances helped us move the bed and that will save fuel. There is plenty of room for us and we have shared a room before."

"That's very thoughtful of you both. It will indeed help," smiled Liza at the two of them. They really were lovely ladies.

"That's a very good idea; perhaps Bernard and I could move in together. Would you have any objection to that Bernard?" asked David.

"I would enjoy the company, David," said Bernard.

Liza smiled and Jamie also grinned as he knew that Liza was going to suggest it, and Bernard and David had made their own choice.

"If we think about this," said Liza. "We could move you both into the room that Lucinda had and move Grace into Hector's room and we will then be able to close up the east wing, which is a cold part of the house."

"Won't Hector need his room?" said Grace.

"I don't think that Hector will be travelling to us until this weather clears and by that time you will be back in your home," said Liza. "I did think that we may have to double up, but I would not have been looking at that until after the weekend but doing it now will put our minds at rest and save a great deal of fuel. I believe that there are other rooms that we can close but I'll worry about that when we have organised your rooms."

"We'll help you move the beds; we can't ask the staff as they have been working so hard today already," said Jamie.

"Don't worry about that," said Liza. "The boys have been itching to help in some way today. They even took their own dirty dishes down to the kitchen. I'm sure that between them they can move the beds but don't worry I won't let them move your belongings and clothes."

"Do you think they will be strong enough?" said Jamie with a frown.

"Five able bodied thirteen and fourteen-year-old boys with Derek giving instructions should be more than capable of moving two beds. Let them feel that they are doing something to help," said Liza. "I'll obviously keep an eye on them."

"So will I," said Grace. "But we'll let the boys take all the credit for the move."

Liza went down to the kitchen and told Mrs Frances what they were planning, and she thought that it was good to let the boys help, especially as all the men in the household had been working so hard that day.

"When the beds have been moved, I'll come and make them up," said Mrs Frances.

"I'll do that," said Mrs Price "and Susan will help me."

Mrs Frances and Liza nodded their agreement as they knew that Mrs Price needed to feel that she was doing something to help.

There was the sound of furniture being moved and Liza found Adam and April taking their armchairs from their sitting room and putting them either side of their fireplace in their bedroom. They fitted in but only just.

461

"We're closing our sitting room down until the weather clears, it will help a little with the fuel situation," said Adam.

"That's very good of you. Hopefully you'll be able to move everything back in a few days," said Liza.

She then went in to see the boys and told them that they were needed to move two beds from the east wing into the room that Aunt Lucinda had used. Derek looked disappointed until Liza told him that it would be helpful if he could arrange the best way that the beds should be placed, and he made his way to the room and stood there studying it. Grace had already gone to the east wing and stripped the clothes from the beds.

With a great deal of noise the boys successfully moved the beds into the places that Derek had chosen. Mrs Price and Susan arrived and made the beds up and Mrs Frances moved the men's clothes into the wardrobe. It was warm and comfortable in the room and Liza was sure that the two men would be quite contented there.

Next Grace brought her bedclothes down to Hector's room and once again Mrs Price and Susan got the room ready whilst Grace concentrated on her clothes.

Liza and Mrs Frances looked around the east wing to make sure that nothing had been left behind and then the heavy door was closed, cutting it off from the rest of the house.

They all had been so busy that they had not noticed how fierce the blizzard had become. Jamie and David were watching through the window and it seemed that the work that they had carried out that morning was paying off. The two coaches were hardly moving in the ferocious wind and the oil skins were flapping a little, but the snow was beginning to hold them down.

Bernard had gone up to the bedroom and there was just enough room for a bath to be placed there and he was relaxing in its warmth. David would be doing the same in a short while.

"There are just a couple more changes that we can make," said Liza. "We can bring the dining table into the drawing room and close the dining room and close either your study or mine, but we can think about that tomorrow."

"Hmm," said Jamie. "You're right; we can take a couple of leaves out of the table and bring it in here. I can't think that there are going to be more than the seven of us for quite some time. The dining room is already nice and warm so tomorrow will be soon enough. As far as the study is concerned, I'll join you in yours if I may."

"We are all going to be warm and cosy here, including all the staff members. With the noise outside, it's nice that we are all together. I am worried about some of the villagers though and I'm also worried about how everyone is in Belfast. This weather has come from the Arctic and it will be even fiercer there than here. I do hope that they have all got together as we have, there's always safety in numbers although I know that the saying refers to something other than bad weather," said Liza.

"I haven't experienced weather like this before, but I know that you have and I can see why you have been so anxious to keep everyone under one roof," said Jamie. "It's how you had to react in America because without one another it could have meant death to many. I hope that we have been panicking unnecessarily; nothing would please me more than if we woke up tomorrow to find that the blizzard had ended and a thaw had set in, but what we have done is to prepare for the worst and you are right, we will all be warm, cosy and well fed. Most important of all, you will feel happy that we have done our best to protect everyone within this household. You can rest assured that I will go with Bernard into the village as soon as it is possible for us to do so."

Matthew's head appeared around the drawing room door, and he asked if they should go to the kitchen for their supper or use the dining room. Liza said that it would be better if he asked Mrs Lambert what should be done as she was not sure who was still in the kitchen and off he went on his important 'supper' mission.

"Nothing stops the boys' appetites. It seems that eating is always uppermost in their minds," said Jamie. "It is well that Matthew has a kind heart and easy nature because if it were otherwise, he would lead the others into all sorts of trouble. I wish James was a little more assertive."

"James is fine," said Liza. "If he doesn't want to do what Matthew or anyone else suggests, then he just doesn't do it. I believe also that he thinks of some of the more outrageous games that they like to play on us and one another, he just lets Matthew go in first and take the blame; that is if there is any blame to take. He has a very loving nature and I don't think that you need to worry about him."

"I worry about him because there has to be part of Evelyn in him. I know that he disowns her, but she is his mother and you can't take that away from him, although I don't see any of her nature in him. Let's hope that he is just influenced by you, which is how he seems to be at present," said Jamie.

"Jamie, your influence is just as important, and I see a great deal in him that is you. He is fine as he is and I'm sure he won't change his character drastically as he grows," said Liza.

***

The final rearrangements took place the next day and Liza had to admit that the drawing room had become very friendly with the dining room combined. Jamie moved his necessary paperwork into Liza's study and firmly closed his own room.

The staff had reorganised their own sleeping arrangements so that they all were comfortably warm at night. Mrs Lambert decided that the staff should have their main meal at lunchtime which meant that the boys ate in the drawing room at that time and that included Susan. Their supper was in the kitchen and nobody thought it unusual to see Derek sliding down the banisters accompanied by the other boys.

With the boys comfortably in bed and Susan also in her bed but no longer fearful of the storm, dinner was being served in the drawing room. They decided not to change into evening clothes for dinner, so everyone was sitting warmly around the smaller table.

Liza looked up from her plate and realised that everyone was smiling at her.

"Well Liza," said Miranda, "you have us all safely under one roof. It has been so important for you to have us all together; your time in America taught you that. Perhaps you could tell us a little more about your winters there."

"Please do Liza," said Lucinda, "especially about why your Indian scout risked his life for you."

"It's a long time ago and it's difficult to remember the details and I can only tell you what I told you the other day and that was that the deserters wanted to make some money out of me but they chose a terrible time to try it. They killed themselves trying, so really they died a little earlier than when their sentence would have been carried out. It's what is called poetic justice," said Liza.

"I thought that you said one of them had his fingers and toes amputated," said Grace.

"I said that he needed them amputated, he refused to have the operation unless I spoke to him and I wasn't going to do that," said Liza. "I wasn't going to be stupid enough to put myself in danger and I couldn't see the point in putting him through such an operation when he was scheduled for the firing squad, but of course our doctor thought differently."

"He must have really upset you Liza as I know your feelings on the death penalty," said Miranda.

"Yes, he had hurt Patrick very badly and he was going to kill him once he had his hands on the money he was demanding," said Liza. "I could feel no sympathy for him; he had killed many innocent people."

Jamie was frowning and Liza thought that he was unhappy at the mention of Patrick but she was wrong when he said, "I'm confused Liza; I thought that he was trying to hold you to ransom, not Patrick."

"Initially Patrick caught the deserters when he was on patrol but he was only with a lieutenant and four privates and unfortunately the lieutenant fell asleep when he was on guard duty and two of the privates joined the deserters therefore turning the tables on Patrick," said Liza. "One of the privates told them who I was, and the ringleader decided to hold Patrick to ransom. He sent a message back with the lieutenant and one of the loyal privates demanding money."

Miranda and Lucinda were listening intently and excitedly, and Jamie questioned Liza again, "You're saying that they didn't demand money for you at all."

"No, they never got the chance and it was only later that they thought of doing that," smiled Liza.

"I think that we could be upsetting Liza as it was obviously a time that was very concerning for her," said Grace.

"Oh yes, we're sorry, of course you would probably prefer to forget all about it," said Miranda.

"Mother, Liza can hardly forget about it when you have managed to bring it to the fore in her mind now," said Jamie testily.

Liza put her hand on Jamie's arm as she knew that he was concerned for her rather than himself and by doing that he knew that she was going to finish the story as quickly as possible so that she could satisfy all their curiosity.

"That was where Bandor came to the fore. He came back with his friends, surrounded the deserters, and held them until the army turned up and took them back to the fort. They stood trial and were convicted," said Liza.

"Of course, you already said that they escaped during a snowstorm and it seems the only one to survive for a while was the ringleader," said David. "I suppose he died because he refused the operation, which can't have been an easy way to die."

Liza toyed with the thought that she should leave them thinking that, but by staying silent it was obvious that she was keeping something back, so she decided to finish the story once and for all.

"No, he didn't die that way, Patrick shot him," said Liza starkly and they all looked shocked, including Jamie.

Liza carried on. "I told you that Patrick had been badly hurt and of course once he was a little better the Colonel still would not let him go out on patrol, so he was given office duties much to his dismay. I had been visiting the Colonel, where Patrick was based, and that was when I was asked to see the prisoner and as you know I refused. I left his office to visit the Colonel's wife, Ada, and Bea, the Captain's wife and I was totally unaware that the deserter had slit the throat of a young hospital orderly and was attempting to run towards me brandishing a cutthroat razor. I did not see him; he was behind me to my right. Somehow Patrick knew this and the first that I knew that I was in danger was when I heard a shot and was surprised to see the deserter lying dead close to me."

"My God Liza, you must have been frightened out of your mind," said Jamie.

"Well I would have been if I had been aware of what was happening, but I didn't until all the drama was over. We can all think of what might have been and that can be a little frightening. However, I was not hurt, just shocked," said Liza.

"Why was he going to kill you? Surely you would have been more use to him alive," said Bernard.

"I don't think he was going to kill me; at least not then. I think he was going to use me to escape and demand money for my release, but if anyone had been stupid enough to give him money he would have killed me then," said Liza. "However it didn't happen, Patrick saw to that."

"I said that you must have led an exciting life, but I hadn't realised just how dangerous it had been," said Lucinda whose cheeks were rosy with excitement. "You must have many interesting stories to tell. America seems a thrilling place to be."

"You've been there haven't you Lucinda," said David.

"Yes, and when we were there Liza was attacked by a demented woman. And our friend Zelma was stabbed when she got between Liza and the woman," said Lucinda. "Your security man was also stabbed, wasn't he Liza?"

"Good heavens Liza does danger follow you everywhere?" said David.

"That's hardly fair uncle," said Jamie. "Have you seen anything dangerous happen to Liza since you've been here? In fact nothing dangerous is going to happen to her ever again. I will see to that."

Jamie looked at Liza and smiled and she returned that smile leaving him in no doubt that as far as she was concerned the past was the past and that she loved him dearly. That evening Liza realised that she could talk about Patrick without the hurt that she had felt until that time, and she mentally thanked Lucinda for being inquisitive enough to make her recognise that.

"You must tell us more about your exploits in America Liza," said Lucinda. "I envy you your exciting life there."

"Lucinda, I lived in a very ordinary small town and just because it was in America people seem to think that it was exciting. Most of the time it was the same as any town in England," said Liza.

Lucinda looked disappointed and Liza felt sorry for her. "If I think of anything that might interest you, I will certainly tell you," smiled Liza.

The blizzard had ceased as they all made their way to bed, but it was now snowing steadily, and it was not thought that a thaw would be any time in the next few days.

Liza checked on the boys whilst Roberts was tut-tutting over Jamie's lack of use of evening clothes and when April appeared Liza told her to go back to the warmth of her room as she would manage that night.

Roberts came out of her room as she was heading towards it. "Are you warm enough at night Roberts?" she asked.

"Yes, thank you, Your Ladyship," he said. "Harper and I are sharing for the duration and we have a lovely fire going."

"That's good Roberts. I hope everyone is keeping warm," said Liza.

"We are arranged very well; nobody is without a fire in their room; we're all very warm and cosy. I do hope that this weather doesn't go on too long because many people could be in serious trouble if it does," said Roberts.

"I know Roberts, it is a worry. Good night," said Liza as she went into the bedroom.

Jamie was sitting in front of the fire in his nightclothes when she entered and queried that April was not with her.

"I told her to go back to her room. You can help me get undressed," smiled Liza

He sat her on his knee in front of the fire.

"You didn't tell the whole story tonight, did you Liza?" he said but he was smiling.

"I did Jamie," said Liza with a slight frown. "I didn't say how badly Patrick was hurt, or details of his captivity. I didn't mention that Bandor's friends were all Cherokee, or that I had the money together for his ransom. That would have added nothing to the story."

"You're right, it wouldn't as far as Lucinda and the others are concerned, but you know that I am always interested in everything to do with you," said Jamie. "Would you mind telling me why Bandor and his 'friends' went to the bother of rescuing a couple of American soldiers as the army could only be considered an enemy to the Indians."

Liza smiled at him, "I don't mind you knowing that Jamie. Patrick was classed as my protector and Matthews' also. It was their duty to protect my protector, therefore they felt that they were protecting me and Matthew. Now that Patrick is gone, they will know that you are my protector and they will always keep you safe."

"They must have felt that they had failed when Patrick was killed," said Jamie.

"Bandor was a second too late to save him. Frank Wyley pulled the trigger virtually at the same time that Bandor threw his knife and killed him. Yes, you are right that they felt they had failed and that was why they took me and wanted Matthew and John," said Liza.

"So they took you to protect you and they wanted to do the same for Matthew and John. I presume that they considered John your child as I know how Indians take children and make them their own, which is why Matthew is classed as the chief's grandson, isn't he?" said Jamie. "By the same logic, John is also thought of as his grandson. And you said that you led a very ordinary life in America."

Jamie laughed and held her even closer to him.

"You do realise that you are now the father of Matthew and John, so therefore you could be considered the son of the chief and James will also be thought of as the chief's grandson. It's all very simple really," laughed Liza. Jamie was now frowning and trying to work out what Liza had said and his relationship to the chief of the Cherokee nation.

"So wherever I go in America I will be safe. That's comforting to know," smiled Jamie.

"Don't forget that the Cherokees are only one Indian nation. You will still have to dodge arrows from every other tribe in the country," laughed Liza.

Jamie started to help Liza out of her clothes and he became very thoughtful until finally he said how frightened he had been for her when he knew that she had been taken again and how he thought she could be dead when he had seen her carried from a tepee by Zelma and her friend; he did not know for hours if she was dead or alive but the relief he felt when told that she had survived was indescribable.

"I didn't know that you had seen that Jamie. If I had seen you like that I would have been devastated," said Liza.

"It's nice to know that you cared, even then," smiled Jamie.

"I've always cared for you Jamie," said Liza. "It was in a different way to the way I care now, but I have always thought of you as one of my greatest friends. The difference now is that I love my greatest friend and am very content in his company."

"You say the nicest of things my Liza," smiled Jamie as he helped her into bed. "But you really didn't always think of me as your greatest friend; I do remember upsetting you so much that you ran away to America to rid yourself of me."

"And you followed me and by the time Kate and I had made our plans to go to visit Senor Valdez and his son, you had grown on me and I didn't find your company as distasteful as I had previously, but we had in hand what we were doing and it was going to be an adventure for us. Little did we know the disaster that it was to become," said Liza thoughtfully. "But I don't want to think about that time, I just want you to love me tonight and I'll love you in return."

***

"Is it still snowing?" asked Liza of Jamie as she had done every morning for the past six days.

"Yes, it is Liza, but I do believe that it is not quite so heavy. Perhaps we're reaching the end of this bad weather," said Jamie.

"It will still be a while before we can reach the village. Bernard is very concerned, as am I," said Liza.

It took another four days before enough snow could be cleared for them to attempt to make their way towards the village. Mr Lambert and the men spent all their time digging, sweeping and attempting to make a path down the driveway, past the Dower House and then onto the gatehouse, although Miranda, Lucinda, David and Grace were not going to even try to go to their homes as yet. On the fourth day they had reached the churchyard. Mr Lambert came to the house with the news that part of the roof of the church had fallen onto the vicarage, there was going to be a great deal of work to be carried out before any services could be held.

Bernard and Jamie donned heavy coats and went to inspect the church and whilst they were there, they could hear others clearing the snow in the village and they called out to find out if they had all survived. Sadly old man Jacobs had died but all else were fit and well.

Mr Rogers managed to shout across that they had all got together as Lady Edgeworth had suggested, but old man Jacobs had refused to leave his home and it had been impossible for anyone to reach him until a couple of days ago when they had found him dead. Everyone else had pooled their resources, closing some homes, and moving in with others. "Tell her Ladyship that it had saved many lives, especially the elderly."

"I'll tell her," shouted Jamie. "She'll be pleased that it all worked out well, but I know she'll be sorry about Mr Jacobs."

"I'm afraid that he was too stubborn for his own good. I don't know when we'll be able to bury him as the ground is so hard, and we no longer appear to have much of a church," shouted Mr Rogers.

"I'll have to see what I can come up with Mr Rogers," shouted Bernard. "We'll manage somehow. I'll try to reach you either later today or tomorrow. I know Lady Edgeworth is anxious to see you too, as is his Lordship."

Jamie and Bernard then returned to the house and updated everyone on the situation, and they were sorry to hear that Mr Jacobs had died.

"What a pity that he didn't move in with somebody," said Liza.

"To be honest Liza," said Bernard. "He really was a very difficult person and he always imagined that people were going to steal from him, not that he had very much to steal. Many people offered him food, but he said that he didn't need charity. Since I have known him he has always been his own worst enemy."

Mrs Price asked to see Liza. She wanted to see how her home had fared through the blizzard. Liza told her that they would be attempting to get to the village either later that day or early the next and she was welcome to join them but as her home was not habitable before the blizzard struck, it was unlikely that there was much to salvage now.

"I can't keep staying here on your charity," said a concerned Mrs Price. "I have jobs that I must continue with otherwise my family will not eat."

"Mrs Price this is your home and that of your family until such time as your house has been repaired satisfactorily. I do not know what work you undertake normally, but when you are under this roof you do not need to worry about feeding your family. Mrs Frances tells me that you and Susan carry out many tasks in this household so you do not stay here on our charity, and you and your family are welcome to stay with us for as long as you need to," said Liza.

"You're very kind My Lady," said Mrs Price. "I know that my Derek would not be walking as well as he does if it was not for you, and my Susan has more time to study now that she does not have to look after Derek while I work. They will both now be able to make something of their lives."

"I'm pleased Mrs Price, you know that I feel education is so important for both girls and boys and I'm glad that they are both taking advantage of the opportunity," said Liza and she told Mrs Price that she would let her know when they would be able to go to the village.

Bernard was concerned that the church was in such a bad condition, but he was more upset that he had not been able to give some comfort to the villagers. Jamie told him that he would have been no good to the villagers' dead, and that was probably what he would have been if he had stayed in the vicarage.

"At least you can give some comfort to them as you are alive and don't start moaning that you should have been suffering the cold with them as it seems to me that old man Jacobs is the only one who actually suffered the cold," said Jamie sharply. "They all got together and kept one another warm and in food and you did exactly the same by being with us. Do you know how many people stayed warm in this house by doing what the villagers did? Nearly forty people stayed under this roof for safety and they were just as much your parishioners as those who stayed safely in the village, so stop feeling guilty as you have absolutely nothing to feel guilty about."

It snowed a little over night but not enough to undo all the good work that had been done clearing the roads. The boys wanted to play outside and as long as they wrapped up well, Liza could see no problem with them doing so. They organised Derek's wheelchair so that he could join in with both making snowmen and playing snowballs. Liza was pleased that she would be going into the village as she was in no doubt that she would have been the main target in any snowball fight.

Jamie looked longingly at where the boys were organising their games as he climbed into the carriage that would take him to the village along with Liza, Bernard, David and Mrs Price. They were all shocked to see the damage that the church had sustained.

"That's going to take a great deal of money to repair," said a very despondent Bernard.

"We'll have to set up a fund for it," said Jamie and they carried on their way to the village. Most of the houses had sustained some damage but it was only Mrs Price's and Mr Jacobs' that were in a pitiful condition.

"I wonder why those two houses bore the brunt of the blizzard," said Jamie as they let Mrs Price down outside what was left of her home. David and Bernard started looking at the other houses and they made their way to one where they could see people. Jamie and Liza went directly to see Mr and Mrs Rogers at the Inn who updated them on how everyone had coped and discussed with them what was needed to get the village up and running again.

"The smaller repairs we are quite capable of doing ourselves, but houses like Mrs Price's and old man Jacobs' will need more than we can cope with, and of course there is the church; that is going to be an enormous task," said Mr Rogers.

"We don't own Mr Jacobs' house but even if we did our priority would have to be Mrs Price's as she has children to look after," said Jamie. "Sadly Mr Jacobs no longer needs a roof over his head."

The doctor had taken in a family of six and the good news was that it was now a family of seven. A baby boy had been born to them and the doctor had chosen that family to house knowing the condition of the mother.

The school only had minor damage as had the headmaster's house next to it. The headmaster had taken in a couple of families and they had survived comfortably. Overall the village and the villagers had come through the experience relatively unscathed.

Next Jamie wanted to visit the outlying farms but there still was no means of his reaching them and unfortunately it had started snowing again. He consoled himself with the thought that farmers prepared for harsh conditions and had the means for fuel and food surrounding them, but he was concerned that they would be unable to reach safety if they had an unforeseen problem.

Mrs Price had picked up a few possessions, but she had to admit that there was very little left that was not damaged beyond repair.

"Don't worry Mrs Price, we'll make sure that you are settled back comfortably once your house has been repaired, won't we Liza?" said Jamie.

"I can't take things from you. I'll be alright, I can borrow a few things from people in the village until I'm back on my feet," said Mrs Price.

"For heaven's sake Mrs Price! You have two children to care for, they need beds and furniture and many things that have been destroyed and both Liza and I cannot have your family's discomfort on our consciences whilst we live in warmth and comfort," said Jamie sharply. "So just accept that we will make sure that you have what you need. We would do that for anyone in your situation, we are not singling you out for special treatment."

Mrs Price looked shocked at Jamie's stern words, as did Liza and the others in the carriage.

Bernard was the first to speak, "He's right Mrs Price; you need help at the moment. You've worked hard all your life and made a home for your children under difficult circumstances and that has been destroyed. If you don't want it for yourself then you must accept it for your children. I am in the same situation; I have nothing to go back to; my children are my parishioners and I must concentrate on them and therefore I have to accept whatever I am offered to get my church up and running again, and a roof over my head because there is no use of a priest who cannot be reached at any time, day and night."

"Exactly," said Jamie with a decisiveness that made his word final. Liza and David nodded in agreement.

The carriage drew up in front of the house and Bernard and David helped Mrs Price and her packages down and up the steps into the house. Jamie helped Liza down and as she turned she was hit squarely in the face with a snowball. She had forgotten that the boys were probably still enjoying building snowmen in the grounds. Jamie turned and he also was hit in the face, he frowned as he cleared the snow from his eyes but by that time Liza was returning fire, but not very successfully. She was muttering under her breath "why am I always the target?" as she launched another badly made snowball in the direction of the laughing boys. Harper was waiting at the top of the steps holding open the door for them and he was surprised to see Lord and Lady Edgeworth running and hurling snow in the direction of six boys, one of whom was more accurate than the others and that was Derek from his

473

wheelchair. Neither Liza nor Jamie gave him any quarter and they pounded him mercilessly but the others came to his defence and Liza and Jamie could be seen ducking and diving until Liza was flat on her face in the snow with Jamie trying to pick her up. They were laughing so much that they couldn't fight back, and all they could do was stagger towards the house being bombarded from behind by six over exuberant boys.

They fell in through the front door covered in snow; Jamie had lost his hat and his hair was dripping; Liza still had her hat, but it was at a peculiar angle and her hair was plastered to her face. They both stood in the hallway looking at each other and laughing. Miranda and Lucinda looked out from the drawing room and Miranda remarked that obviously the boys had won the fight. Harper took their wet outdoor clothing; he pursed his lips but had a twinkle in his eyes and Liza and Jamie went into the drawing room to warm up.

David and Bernard were already there, and they smiled at them. "It's nice not to grow up," said David. "Holly and I used to play snowballs with Grace, it was always fun."

They could hear shouts from outside and they knew that somebody else was now on the receiving end of the boys' game. Jamie went to the window and looked out. "It's Adam and Mr Lambert, and I think that they have encouraged the boys and they are giving them a good run for their money."

"I don't suppose they allowed Susan to join them, after all she's only a girl," said Liza sarcastically.

"She's been with them most of the time, but I think her snowballs weren't finding their mark whereas the boys were quite expert. She started by helping Derek, but he was managing quite well by himself; she only came indoors just before you arrived home," said Lucinda, who had obviously spent a great deal of time watching the children enjoying their game.

It began snowing heavily and after a short while the boys, Adam and Mr Lambert made their way into the house through the kitchen entrance and Liza went down to see them and was assailed by the smell of wet clothes steaming near the fire. April and Mrs Price were helping to dry the boys off and with Adam and Mr Lambert telling of their prowess with a snowball, the kitchen was in utter chaos.

"I'm getting hot water upstairs for baths for the boys and when they've had them, their supper will be ready," said Mrs Frances.

"They can come down wrapped up in their dressing gowns for their supper; it's nice and warm down here for them," said Liza and she turned and looked at Adam and Mr Lambert. "You did better than I did out there;" and she laughed "I always get caught by them and I always come off worse."

Mrs Frances, Mrs Price and April went up the stairs with the boys; Derek trailed behind with John, but Liza noticed that he was getting faster each day.

Liza and Jamie went up to get changed out of their damp clothes and to have a little time on their own. They both got into their dressing gowns and relaxed before dressing for dinner. They discussed how they were going to rebuild the church and vicarage as well as Mrs Price's house and decided that, unfortunately, they would have to hire builders from outside the village although many villagers would be unhappy that they could not help, but they needed to get the work carried out as soon as possible.

"Many of the houses in the village need repairs and I'm sure that the villagers will be capable of doing those. They will realise that the church and vicarage, as well as Mrs Price's house, are far too big for them to undertake," said Liza. "You've yet to find out how the farmers have got on. They may need some help with their homes."

It snowed quite heavily for the next two days but after that a thaw set in, although Jamie was still unable to reach any of the farms until three days after that and he found that they all had slight damage but unfortunately they had lost a number of animals.

The three coach drivers from Liverpool were getting ready to leave. They had helped to clear their coaches from the barn to the kitchen door, reattaching their doors and cleaning them out. They had served a very unusual purpose but had kept the household in milk and it meant that all the drivers could have their hot meals in the kitchen each day. They would not leave for Liverpool for a couple of days at which time they hoped that the weather would have settled enough for them to make the journey.

Fires had been burning in the Dower House and the gatehouse for a couple of days, but both houses were still very cold, and nobody was going to move back until they could feel comfortably warm.

Mrs Price, Susan and Derek would be staying until their house was rebuilt as would Bernard and both Liza and Jamie realised that they could be with them for some time, possibly until the summer but that was not going to be a problem for them.

Chapter 23

The thaw was setting in and during the following week Miranda and Lucinda moved back into the Dower House with their staff and then David and Grace packed their bags and took them back to their home. Bernard seemed a little lost without them, but he saw them each day as he walked past them on his way to the church. He held an outdoor service for Mr Jacobs, and they did manage to dig a grave for him.

The weekend arrived and so did Bella and she made it quite clear that her boys had been better off staying with Liza as their house had been so cold. She was determined that she was going to persuade the Duke to buy a better home for them all, especially during the winter months. She also decried the fact that they had been unable to attend any functions; in fact she had been cold and bored to tears and they ended up having vegetable soup two days in a row.

Bella informed them that she would be staying for the weekend and Liza enquired whether she would be taking Nicholas and Richard with her when she left.

"I suppose I had better, although they seem very settled here," said Bella.

"I'm sure they will be just as settled in their own home," smiled Liza.

When Monday came Nicholas and Richard seemed reluctant to leave and Liza's boys and Derek were equally reluctant to see them go. They all felt that it had been an exciting time and from now onwards life was going to be boring. Nurse Dawkins had their clothes packed and she also seemed sad to leave.

Jamie was still using Liza's study and when Liza had waved goodbye to Bella and her family, she joined Jamie to discuss how to organise the rebuilding of the church and Mrs Price's house.

"Do you have builders that you have used in the past?" Liza asked Jamie.

"No Liza, we have only altered small parts of the house and decorated rooms. Mr Lambert has managed with a couple of helpers all that has been necessary here," said Jamie. "You know people who have carried out much more work with the Ffoulks house and those who are currently working on the Langston place."

"Yes, I'll write to the Major and see what he can come up with. I would much rather use somebody that we knew was reliable than just finding anyone that we don't know," said Liza. "I've also got to start planning for our trip at Easter. I'm really looking forward to the voyage in the new ship. You and I must go to Belfast to pick it up with Wendell and Amelia and all else can join it at Southampton docks," said Liza.

"Why are we going to Belfast?" asked Jamie.

"Because we have to be at its launch and Wendell has to break the champagne against it and name it, although he may be letting Amelia do that," said Liza.

"Of course; it's going to be exciting being on the maiden voyage. What is it to be called?" asked Jamie.

"It's a secret, but you can know. It's going to be called the SS Amelia, but Amelia doesn't know that yet. It will be a surprise for her on the day," said Liza.

"I would have thought that it could be called the 'Liza' as you instigated the building and design of it," said Jamie.

"Oh no Jamie, don't forget that Wendell started the business with James long before I came on the scene. It's only right that the founder's wife should have that honour," said Liza.

"You are one of the founders' wives, or you were," said Jamie.

"I think that you have hit the nail on the head, the operative word is 'were', not 'are'," said Liza.

"Who's coming with us this time?" asked Jamie and Liza went through the list telling him that many of their household would be travelling with them which included Miranda, Lucinda, David and Grace and their three boys.

"I can't take April without Adam, and then there's Roberts. I could do with another helper like April. I think that Amelia will be bringing her maid, but I know that Roberts can cope with Wendell as well as you. So there will be fifteen or sixteen of us. I don't know if any of the Fullers will be joining us; I'm sure they would like to, but they do have a business to look after," said Liza.

"Do you suppose Bella and Hector will invite themselves?" laughed Jamie.

"Surely not," said Liza with a worried look on her face.

"I was joking," said Jamie. "But really as far as those two are concerned you never know."

"We'll be bringing Simon back with us; the boys are looking forward to that and so am I," said Liza. "That is going to be quite a wrench for Gabriel and Kate and of course Zelma as she has looked after him since he first came to Benson."

"I know it will," said Jamie. "Our boys will be going to university next year and I'm not looking forward to that. The house will be so quiet without them."

Liza looked sad as she did not like the thought of not having her boys around her; they had been with her through so many different and difficult times and on some occasions if it hadn't been for them she would have had no reason to go on.

"Cheer up Liza, we have a wonderful trip to look forward to and you know that you like planning these things," said Jamie.

***

Once the roads were passable Liza and Jamie resumed their commitments to the charity functions and as the weeks passed Liza found that her smile was beginning to fade, and Easter couldn't come soon enough.

Bella seemed to think that it was her right to descend upon them with her boys, Nurse Dawkins and her maid every weekend, although she was also invited to most of the functions that they attended on those weekends.

"I don't know what I am going to do without you when you are in America. I wish I could reorganise my commitments so that I could join you, but unfortunately that would be impossible," she said to which both Liza and Jamie breathed a sigh of relief.

"I believe that the voyage is fully booked," said Jamie and Liza kept a straight face as she knew that he had no idea whether it was sold out.

The Langston House would shortly be completed and would be opened when Liza and Jamie were back from their visit to New York.

Three weeks before they were due to leave a very despondent Hector arrived at their door and he came and sat with Liza in her study saying nothing.

"You've obviously got something on your mind Hector, and you know that I will always listen and try to help if I can," said Liza kindly.

"I've asked Estelle to marry me and she has refused saying that it would never work as we are both from totally different backgrounds. I really can't see that it would be a problem. Well I suppose my mother would be a problem, but in matters of the heart you have to be your own person and not worry

478

about what others think," said Hector. "I know that you really can't help but I know that I can always talk to you and you do sometimes come up with suggestions for a solution to a problem."

"Do you know whether or not she loves you Hector? Or is it something that you want and you are riding roughshod over her feelings?" asked Liza.

"I know that I am quite blunt and brash but I do believe that I see a great deal of affection in her eyes and sometimes when she thinks I am not looking she shows a concern for me," said Hector. "I do believe that she loves me, and I know that I truly love her."

"You know that I have no prejudices where class is concerned, and Estelle has been very well educated and given time would definitely merge well into all societies. She has already, as you know," said Liza.

"My mother likes her, but she would not welcome her into our family and Estelle knows that, which is why she is refusing me, but I have told her that it is immaterial to me whether she is accepted or not, as long as we are happy together it doesn't matter what anyone else thinks," said Hector.

"Could you be deluding yourself over thinking that she loves you Hector?" asked Liza.

"I suppose I could be, but I don't think so," said Hector.

"Are you still not allowing her the freedom to not feel pressurised into making a decision?" asked Liza.

Hector thought about what Liza had said and finally answered, "I keep thinking that if I ask her again she will change her mind and accept my proposal. I just can't stop asking her and I call in to see her at every opportunity."

"Many years ago Jamie did exactly the same as you are now doing. I went to America to get away from him, but he followed me there and I went even further to be free of him. I know that it was a disaster, but the outcome for Jamie was much worse than for me because I fell in love with Patrick and when he died Jamie came to find me but it still took me a long while to realise that I didn't want a life without him. The moral of the story is that if Jamie had not crowded me so much I would have realised that I loved him a long time ago. I know that we would not have had James or Matthew, but we would have had children and both of us would not have gone through the heartaches that we each experienced in the subsequent years," said Liza.

"Do you really think that you and Jamie would have married years earlier than you did if he had given you the time to think about him properly and not constantly dogged your footsteps?" said Hector.

"Yes I do think that. I do not regret being with Patrick, I loved him dearly, but I would not have known that and I would have loved Jamie as much then as I do now, and neither of us would have gone through the traumas of the intervening years. I needed space and Jamie would not give me that and I know that he regrets that now. Please learn from our mistakes and be Estelle's friend first and hopefully you will be able to be her husband eventually," said Liza.

"You advised me to do that once before, and it worked," said Hector. "But I know that I will find it almost impossible to leave her alone."

"Well I may have a solution to that," said Liza. "You need to calm down and she needs to have room to breathe and think seriously about whether she loves you or not and how she sees her future."

"I don't think that I am going to enjoy your solution," said Hector.

"No you probably won't, but at the end of it you will know if you are going to have the wife that you want," said Liza.

"I think I'll stay here the night," announced Hector.

"Is that how you talk to Estelle?" asked Liza.

Hector looked puzzled and asked her what she meant by that.

"Telling her rather than asking her," said Liza.

"Do I do that?" he asked.

"Always; perhaps you should think about asking your questions rather than demanding and assuming," said Liza. "It's just a suggestion."

"Perhaps you're right," said a thoughtful Hector.

That night when Liza and Jamie were alone, she told him what Hector had said.

"If he loves her and she loves him, then there is no problem because they will make a happy life together and Hector will not worry about what anyone else thinks. Personally I think that they are well matched and she is really good for him," said Jamie.

"He's got to give her the breathing space that she needs to make up her mind whether or not she is prepared to withstand the wrath of Rose and possibly others in Hector's family," said Liza.

"I'm sure Anthony and Diana would be happy for him to have at last found someone to love and who loves him," said Jamie.

"Yes, I'm sure they would, but would she be invited to family gatherings and other events that Hector would normally be expected to attend?" wondered Liza.

"I see what you mean," said Jamie. "What are you thinking of doing Liza? I know that he must give her time to sort out whether she wants a life with him, and I know what happened when I didn't give you the time that you needed."

"I'm going to ask Adam if he thinks it would be a good idea if Estelle accompanied us to New York at Easter. I would like to have someone to help April with her duties and I hope that Estelle would not feel that such duties are demeaning, especially as she is really a teacher," said Liza.

"I think that she would jump at the chance to see New York, but certainly it would be a good idea to see what Adam thinks before you approach her and of course you will have to make sure that the Major can spare her, although it will be the Easter holidays," said Jamie.

"The Major probably knows what is happening with Hector and Estelle and no doubt he will encourage that they take a short time away from one another; he will see the merit in that, as will Jennifer," said Liza.

Adam thought that Estelle would find travelling to New York a wonderful experience and he did not think that she would find any of the tasks asked of her demeaning. "The opportunity for her to see a place such as New York outweighs any duties that you would need carried out, as do I," said a smiling Adam when Liza approached him the following morning.

"I'm planning to visit the Home today so I will ask her whilst I'm there," said Liza.

"I presume that this has something to do with Mr Hector Ffoulks. Has he decided to go to New York with us?" asked Adam.

"No, he will not be with us. Your sister needs some time to think and I do need someone to help with the boys, my mother-in-law and Mrs Peabody, especially on the voyage as we do have staff at the house in New York, so you, April and Estelle will have plenty of time to explore the city," said Liza.

"It's the maiden voyage of the new steam ship, that is going to be very exciting, I am really looking forward to it," said Adam and it was the first time that Liza had seen him acting like a young boy and she supposed that it was going to be quite an experience for him and one that he had never thought would happen to him.

Davis took Liza and Jamie to the Ffoulks Home later that morning and firstly they suggested to the Major that Estelle accompany them to New York and he could see no problem with that and Jennifer said that she could take any classes for the children, all she needed to do was liaise with Estelle to see what she had in mind for the children.

"I suppose that it is because Hector has been making a nuisance of himself with Estelle," said the Major.

"I think it's a little more serious than that and I believe that she needs time to get her feelings together and I do need another person to help on the voyage, so it could be considered killing two birds with one stone," said Liza. "I have yet to ask her, when will she be free?"

"In about an hour or so," said the Major. "I believe Hector is at the Langston House today."

"Yes, he stayed with us last night and of course you realise that he is very smitten with Estelle but it appears to be an awkward situation," said Liza and commented no further on the problem as the Major and Jennifer were well aware of the difficulty.

Jamie had been right; Estelle did jump at the chance of the trip to New York. At first she was concerned about her teaching duties at the Home, but Jennifer assured her that she could step in for a while, and besides it was during the Easter holidays so there were few lessons at that time.

They called on Anthony and Diana on their way home and Rose was also with them. They discussed how they had survived the blizzards in Belfast and they admitted that it was so severe that they had to close some rooms to keep warm and for the last few days they lived on weak soup and stale bread. It made Liza and Jamie realise that they had made the right choice in returning to Surrey when they had.

Liza said that she had yet to hear from any of the Fullers and Diana told her that she had called on Amelia and Wendell just before their return and Edward and Nicole and their baby had moved in with them during the storm as had Annalise and Arthur and they had stocked up on food and fuel before the worst weather had started.

Apparently Mrs Edwards, Mrs Adams, Mrs Trent and other members of the staff had closed both houses and collected up whatever they needed and moved into Mr and Mrs Grouch's boarding house. Liza presumed that their paying guests enjoyed the company.

"They took a leaf out of your book Liza and pooled their resources and stayed warm and well fed; we should have returned when you did," said

Anthony. "I was becoming quite concerned about how we were going to survive if it had gone on much longer."

"Have you seen Hector recently?" asked Rose.

"Yes, he was with us last night; he is working at the Langston House today and he will probably be back with us tonight," said Jamie.

"I'm very displeased with Hector; he is trying to get that woman, Estelle, to consider marrying him. She is a nice enough person, but not one who can be accepted into this family, or on the social scene. She will ruin Hector's reputation," said Rose.

Liza didn't comment, she did not want to get into an argument with Rose or anyone else in that household. Jamie was also quiet.

"I can see from your face Liza that you do not agree with me," said Rose.

"I do find it difficult to agree with you Rose as Estelle and I come from very similar backgrounds," said Liza sweetly as Anthony choked on his cup of tea and Jamie and Diana just stared in front of them.

"Oh," said a slightly embarrassed Rose.

"She will be coming with us to New York which will give them both time to think about what they want," smiled Liza.

"I think you surprised Rose," said Jamie to Liza when they were in their carriage on their way home.

"It's true, there is very little difference between how Estelle was brought up and educated and how I was, and I don't think that I have ruined your reputation," said Liza.

"No you certainly haven't; you have in fact enhanced it," said Jamie.

"That's very nice of you to say so Jamie," said Liza happily.

Hector was waiting for them when they arrived home. He had been supervising some of the finer details at the Langston House and although he had time to return to Ffoulks House he wanted to find out what Liza had in mind that would ease the situation with Estelle.

"Are you dining with us Hector?" asked Liza. "If you are will you be staying the night?"

"If it's no trouble to you, I would like to dine and stay the night," said a very humble sounding Hector.

Both Liza and Jamie stared at him as it was so unlike his normal demanding ways and Liza wondered whether her talk with him concerning his attitude could have had the desired effect.

"It's no trouble Hector, you always have a room here and you are welcome at our table," said Jamie.

"Did you see Estelle today?" asked Hector.

"Yes, and we saw the Major and Jennifer and then we visited Anthony and Diana. Your mother was also there," said Jamie trying to avoid the one question that he knew Hector wanted to ask.

"I must go up and change," said Liza also wanting to avoid the same question.

"Please Liza, I want to talk to you and to Jamie," said Hector.

"Yes, I'm sure you do, but I want to change and you're lucky tonight because it is only the three of us at dinner and we can have a long and comfortable discussion then," said Liza.

Hector nodded as Liza disappeared up the stairs to her room.

"We will try to help you sort out your problem Hector, but we can talk about it at dinner," said Jamie and he also went to his room to change.

When they were ready, they went to see the boys and then to find Adam and told him that Estelle would be accompanying them on the trip to New York. Finally they made their way down to the dining room where Hector was waiting for them.

Jamie decided to take the lead in the conversation. "I know that for some time you have wanted to get close to Estelle and I know that she and others have felt that the differences between you were too great for the relationship to become permanent. Neither Liza nor I feel that those differences are insurmountable but the only people who can decide that are you and Estelle, nobody else."

"I'm pleased that you feel that, Jamie. I know that Liza has no class prejudices and I wasn't sure of how you felt on the subject," said Hector.

"What you are asking of Estelle is a very difficult decision for her," said Jamie. "She will fit into neither world. I doubt whether she will be invited to any functions and when she is here or elsewhere, where does she eat? We would be happy with her at our table, but would she be comfortable there. Her brother would be eating in the kitchen whilst she was with us. Adam could have eaten with us at any time, but he made his choice."

"There's more to life than whether one dines up or downstairs," said Hector.

"Hector, you are well aware that Jamie is pointing out just one example of the perceived differences, and there are many others," said Liza. "You know that your mother is totally against your proposal to Estelle, I know that you can tolerate that, but can Estelle? She would feel that she has been the reason that there is a rift between you and your mother. How would Anthony and Diana feel because they are going to have to take sides in such a conflict?"

Hector was thoughtful for a moment and then said, "I hadn't thought that Anthony and Diana would be in an awkward position. I know that my mother would not approve but I was prepared to accept that. If I must lose the love and friendship of my brother, I would be sad about that, but I love Estelle and I would sacrifice my family for her."

"You may no longer be invited to functions and if we were to hold a function we would want to invite you both but there may be guests there who would feel that they should snub you, wrong as that may be. That would be very embarrassing for Estelle and as we wouldn't want Estelle embarrassed, we probably wouldn't invite you. The social scene can be very fickle," said Liza.

"I wouldn't want to attend anything like that and besides you could be wrong about that," said Hector.

"I hope that I am, but Estelle will think of it and feel that because of her you would not be accepted amongst those who were once your friends;" said Liza.

"I know that it seems that we are pointing out to you the reasons why you should not marry Estelle, but you would be wrong because if you and she can think of all these things and you both still want to be together, then you definitely have a match made in heaven and good luck to you. We will be the first to congratulate you on your marriage," smiled Jamie.

"Having said all that," said Liza. "What you must do is allow Estelle the time to sort out if she is prepared to put up with all the negative aspects of the situation and hopefully come to realise that all she truly wants is you no matter what you both have to endure. She needs that time Hector, and to be honest so do you. It will be a complete change of life for you both."

"Does that mean that I will no longer have a job Liza?" asked Hector.

"Of course you will still have a job; how could you think otherwise?" said Liza. "The Major and Jennifer will be very supportive of you both and they will also see the merit in you both having the time to think seriously about what you really want and what you feel."

"I believe that you were trying to persuade her to go to New York with you," said Hector.

"Yes, and she has agreed and is looking forward to it immensely and when she returns you will have your answer. By the same token you will have had

485

that time to make sure that marriage to Estelle is exactly what you want," said Jamie.

"I know you are both right, but I am going to find it so hard being away from her for so long," said Hector. "I will be patient and pray that she comes back with the answer I want."

"Just bear in mind what I did wrong all those years ago. I hounded Liza until she had to get away from me and it took me many years to win her back and when I stopped bothering her, she came to me and the rest is history. If I had given her the time that she craved we would have been together years ago," said Jamie.

They finished their meal and Liza left them to talk as she realised that Jamie wanted to spend some time with Hector alone.

"Liza says that she and Estelle are from similar backgrounds, but Liza was accepted into society before she married you. She was always high on the lists for functions so I don't understand why Estelle would not be," said Hector.

Jamie smiled at him and shook his head. "Hector, Liza started her social standing in Belfast; now tell me who would have ostracised the wife of James Marchant and would they dare upset any of the Fuller family. I know that those in trade can be looked down on by the landed gentry, but we all needed Marchant & Fuller to keep our estates running. They may have felt they should not associate with Liza, but they dare not snub her."

"On the few occasions that I attended the Belfast functions I would not have known that there was a problem; everyone seemed to like Liza and wanted to be with her. I'm surprised that she was really not accepted," said Hector.

"Everyone did like Liza, she had such an air of innocence about her that she never realised that there were those who were just paying lip service to her and to be honest it took very little time for those who thought they should not associate with her to change their minds and want to be with her and that included me," said Jamie.

"You are saying that if Estelle had money and influential friends in business she would be accepted in society," said Hector.

"I hate to say this, but Liza spent most of her time either in Belfast or in America, both places which are far more acceptable to those who are not amongst the landed gentry. Liza moved to England when she became Lady Edgeworth and people also knew that she was very rich and accomplished and the charity that she formed was drawing the attention of some very influential people. It is a very fickle society; it bends its rules when it suits," said Jamie.

486

"If you and Liza showed that you accepted Estelle then eventually the rest of society would. I am not concerned if I never receive another invitation to an event, but I know how it would affect Estelle. You and Liza could show that she is someone that you find acceptable and others will follow suit. You did that for Diana when she acted disgracefully; could you not do it for us?" said Hector.

"Yes, of course we could and nothing would give us greater pleasure than to be the means to make you both happy, but unfortunately for you we would never do anything that would jeopardise the charity that brings in so much money for all the children who sadly need us more than you do," said Jamie.

"Personally I would be quite happy not to have to attend all the pompous functions or associate with all those who think themselves so high and mighty that they are above everyone, but I know what Estelle will think. She will think that she has ruined my life and really she will have enhanced it," said Hector.

"Then it is up to you to convince her of that and when you have done that you must leave her in peace to make up her own mind about what she would really like in life, which you hope would be you," said Jamie.

"I'll see her tomorrow and hopefully she will believe me when I tell her how much I love her and that society means nothing to me. Once I have done that, I will allow her the time to make up her own mind but I hope that I will have made such an impression that she will only be able to give me one answer. I know that I can make her happy, I am sure of it. Thank you for your advice Jamie, I know that she will need time as it is a very important decision for her. I have already made my decision and I just hope that hers will be the same as mine," said Hector.

"I would suggest that when you plead your case tomorrow you stay calm and do not become impassioned, just state what you would like and that any adverse effects to that association mean nothing to you. You must keep a very cool head Hector because otherwise it will look as if you are trying to force your will on her," said Jamie. "You may also tell her that she will always be treated with respect in this house as the wife of Hector Ffoulks should be."

Hector smiled saying that Liza and Jamie treated everyone with respect, and he made his way to his room saying that he wanted to have an early start the next morning.

Jamie found Liza in her study going through her correspondence. She looked up expectantly and Jamie told her of his conversation with Hector.

"I think you have handled it very well Jamie," she said. "Now Hector has to handle it just as well. I have always said that Estelle is good for Hector and I do hope that they find a way of working out the difficulties. If it was a case of true love, then I would let nothing get in its way."

"Not so long ago you heard Rose and Hector say that you could be holding me back, and I remember how upset you were when you thought that it was true, so you must have an inkling of how Estelle must feel. In your case it was just a stupid comment that was totally untrue; in Estelle's case, unfortunately, it would be true, and she knows it," said Jamie.

"If Hector can really feel that it would not bother him, then there is no problem. He just has to convince Estelle that he feels that way," said Liza. "Well Jamie, it's his problem, not ours; all we can do is support him no matter which way Estelle's decision goes," said Liza.

Hector left early the next morning and both Liza and Jamie wished him luck with his mission. He promised that he would be very calm, state his reasons clearly and then he would ask her to think about all he had said when she was on her New York trip and that he would be looking for her answer on her return.

Chapter 24

Over the course of the following weeks a great deal of noise could be heard coming from both the village and the church. The builders had moved in and they were working hard to get both buildings completed as soon as possible. Both Mrs Price and Bernard went to inspect the work being carried out on a daily basis. Liza and Jamie also were interested in how the work was progressing, but they had been right that it was going to take until the summer before all would be completed. Mrs Price's house would finish first, but the church and the vicarage were in a very poor state and in many places walls had to be demolished. In the meantime church services were being held in the cricket pavilion.

The village builder and carpenter were busy as most houses in the village had been damaged and they understood why outside builders had been brought in for the church and Mrs Price's house as they could not possibly have handled all the repairs but they liaised with the other builders and worked well together.

Mrs Price had very little furniture left, and Liza told her to go to their storage area and see if there was anything that she would find useful. Mr Lambert was helping her, and Liza had told him that he was to persuade her to take what she wanted because she knew that Mrs Price would be reluctant to take anything.

"You've already done enough for us," Mrs Price had said. "We'll manage with what we can salvage, thank you."

"Mrs Price, there's very little to salvage and we have spare furniture stored in one of the outhouses. It's old but should help until you can find exactly what you would like. There are some beds there also, but they obviously will need mattresses. Is there somebody in the village who makes them?" asked Liza.

"I can do that; I'll be able to get feathers from the farms and the material is cheap enough," said Mrs Price.

"Well, if you can then that would be useful," said Liza but she made sure that Mrs Frances surreptitiously made everything available to her.

Liza was anxious that Derek didn't feel pushed out when they returned from New York with Simon and she told Mrs Frances to move another bed into the boys' room should Mrs Price and her family not have moved back into their own home.

"It will be quite crowded in that room," said Mrs Frances.

"I know but I don't want Derek upset in any way. He may think of moving into one of the smaller rooms which would be more comfortable for him when the other boys won't be there, but I'd like him to think of that himself," smiled Liza knowing that Mrs Frances could act tactfully enough to make Derek think it was his idea.

Hector turned up one day. He looked relatively contented and he told them that he had talked to Estelle at great length. He had told her that she would not make his life difficult, it would be the opposite, she would make his life complete but he had stated his case; he loved her and wanted to spend the rest of his life with her but he was not going to bother her again, he was going to let her think about what he had said and he had asked her to let him know her decision when she returned from New York. All she had to do was make up her mind whether she loved him as much as he loved her, nobody else mattered.

Liza went to him and kissed him on the cheek, "I'm very proud of you Hector. I know it's not an easy position that you are in and I do hope that it all works out well for you."

"May I stay with you until you leave for New York?" he asked.

"Of course, but I'll just tell you what our plans are. Jamie and I will be travelling to Belfast for the launch of the ship and we will be sailing down to Southampton with Wendell and Amelia where everyone else will be joining us. Estelle will be here for a few days before the trip, so if you don't want to see her then perhaps you could arrange to be somewhere else," said Liza. "You know that you have a room here whenever you want it Hector, so even when we are away you are welcome to call this your home."

"You are always so kind Liza," said Hector, "and I have never told you how much I appreciate all that you did for me in the past and all your support now."

"When you came back from Portugal, I remember you saying that friends do not need to be thanked; you were right and you are our friend," said Liza.

Hector looked down and seemed to be battling with his emotions; when he finally looked up he said, "I know exactly why Jamie wanted you Liza, you are the nicest person that I have ever known."

Liza puffed out her cheeks and brushed off Hector's compliment. She kissed him on the cheek and left to finalise what she needed for her short trip to Belfast. Her trunks were all ready for transport to Southampton later.

Whilst she was in her room she had a visitation from all the boys including Derek and of course Matthew was the spokesman.

"Derek's house won't be ready for some time yet," said Matthew. "We thought that he would probably be lonelier in our room when we aren't there so we thought that he would be better in a much smaller room. He would probably feel more comfortable whilst we are away."

"Hmmm," said Liza, "that's a good idea. I wish I had thought of that. Perhaps you should find Mrs Frances and get her to suggest the rooms that are available and let Derek choose one of them."

They found Mrs Frances quite easily as she seemed to be hovering in the hall outside Liza's room and off they went with her discussing the merits of some of the rooms. Later she came to find Liza and smiling she said that the boys had chosen a very suitable room for Derek which would also accommodate a desk and comfortable chair for him.

"He won't be moving in there until the boys leave and I know that Mr Reece has set him some studies and also he has given young Susan some work that he feels she is capable of undertaking," said Mrs Frances.

"Yes, I'm pleased that he doesn't feel that girls are precluded from furthering their education," smiled Liza.

**

Liza and Jamie would be away for ten days before everyone else left for Southampton. They were going to take an easy drive to Liverpool, stopping overnight on the way, and then arrive in Belfast two days before the launch of the new steamship and four days later they would be on board for its maiden voyage and picking up the rest of the passengers at Southampton.

All the Belfast dignitaries attended the launch of the SS Amelia, as well as hundreds of onlookers and once Amelia had smashed the champagne bottle, guided tours were given around the ship. The Fuller family were out in force and several people asked who was representing the Marchant side of the business and those who did not know were introduced to Liza as the widow of James Marchant. This had been discussed prior to the launch and Jamie felt that it was the right way to handle the situation, after all Liza was James Marchant's widow.

Many people had booked just to travel to Southampton and one or two were going on to New York, but most New York passengers were picking up the ship in Southampton. The cargo that they would be carrying was vast in comparison to previous ships' cargoes; it was going to be a very lucrative voyage and even more so as there were no available cabins and there was no more room even in the third class area below decks.

The maximum time it was estimated to take to New York was two weeks and they were all aware that the captain was going to attempt to make it under that time.

Amelia was so excited about the trip to New York and especially as she was travelling on a ship that bore her name. She had chosen her dresses and had many new ones made and she then decided that Liza must see what she was taking with her and her maid, Freda, was instructed to unpack her trunks and hold up each item so that Liza could pass her opinion on them all.

Peter had decided that he would also like to take the trip and luckily he could rely on both Brendan and Samuel Nedbury to take charge in his absence. It had been sad that Samuel had lost his ships and the small company that he had started three years before but it had been a blessing for Marchant & Fuller as he could take over efficiently much of what Peter undertook. Edward and Joseph were towers of strength in their fields and Brendan was an all-round asset. It would be the first time that Peter had taken so much time away from the company, but as Liza pointed out to him, she had dealt with many aspects of the company from afar. She did also wonder whether the fact that Grace would also be on the trip had made Peter make his decision.

The day arrived for them to board and Wendell and Amelia had the luxury of being ensconced in the owner's cabin; Liza and Jamie had the next best cabin. Peter's was slightly smaller but still luxurious.

The ship was virtually full on its journey to Southampton and there were cheers as they left Belfast and when they arrived in Southampton. As Liza came on deck when they approached the dock, she could see all her family and friends waving and cheering at them with the loudest noise coming from the boys.

Liza, Jamie and Peter disembarked to be with their travellers and make sure that everything was in order, although with David, Adam and Roberts having been in charge of organising getting everyone to Southampton on time, there was very little for them to do. They watched as their luggage was taken aboard and when that was completed everyone was escorted to their various cabins. It was all a very far cry from how Liza had first travelled to America.

The boys found their cabin and once they had approved it, they immediately went to find Wendell and Amelia who were delighted to see them. Peter went to make sure that Grace was happy with her accommodation, which she was. Adam and April had a very comfortable cabin and Estelle was next to them. Miranda and Lucinda were sharing one of the larger cabins. David's cabin was next to Peter's and he was overawed by its luxury. Roberts was smiling happily as was Freda. In fact everyone had found their quarters much better than they had expected.

They weren't sailing until the next day and they all spent a great deal of time exploring the ship and that evening in the dining room they all sat together and raised their glasses to the two Amelia's.

They had been pleased and surprised to see the name as it docked as Liza and Jamie had kept it a secret from them.

The following morning they sailed from port to the cheers of many well-wishers and they were on their way to New York. It was a pleasant voyage, and nobody appeared to suffer sea sickness, Roberts seemed to have been cured of that ailment, and after an extremely enjoyable journey the skyline of New York came into view.

Myra and Henry were waiting for them as they came into port and they had a variety of carriages waiting to take them to Liza's house. As they disembarked Walter came to greet them.

"You have a large number of people with you this time Liza," he said, and it surprised one or two in the party that he used her first name. Jamie smiled as he knew that Walter's familiarity was really a compliment to Liza.

"Yes I have Walter and I hope we won't cause you any of the problems that we did last time we were here," said Liza.

"If you do, I'm sure I'll be able to handle it with discretion," he laughed.

As always those who had not previously seen Liza's house were in awe of it. David's mouth was open, and Grace seemed to be asking Peter if they were really going to stay at such a place. Adam and Estelle were not totally surprised as April had obviously described the house to them in detail.

Bridget was now housekeeper and she appeared at the top of the steps as the carriages drew up and many were surprised to see her clasp Liza close to her whilst shedding a tear and mumbling something indistinguishable in her broad Irish accent. Mary was ushering the boys inside and shouting a greeting to April who was attempting to introduce Adam and Estelle to her. Freda and Roberts were helping Wendell and Amelia up the steps and Walter and Henry guided Miranda and Lucinda into the house. David was standing looking up and his mouth was still open, but Peter came to the rescue by taking his arm and guiding him up the steps having first seen Grace into the house.

As if by magic all their trunks and cases had disappeared into their various bedrooms and Liza was confident that by the time they went to their rooms they would have been unpacked and neatly put in place. She had already sent word about who would be sleeping where.

Refreshments were brought into the sitting room and Bridget brought word that Stephen, the chef, would like to see her Ladyship concerning that night's menu and he had been unsure of exactly the number dining. He also wanted to know whether the boys still dined in the kitchen, so Liza excused herself and sorted out all the details with Stephen.

When she returned Wendell and Amelia had already gone to their room to rest and the boys were settling into their room with the assistance of both April and Mary. Adam, David and Henry were looking around the grounds and Miranda and Lucinda were sitting comfortably with their feet up. Myra took the opportunity to inform Liza and Jamie of the functions that they would be attending, and she was assuming that they would also be holding one themselves, which they knew would be expected of them. Estelle and Grace decided that they would see where their rooms were and Peter said that he would show them the way, which was unnecessary as a footman was on duty to assist in that respect.

Gabriel, Kate, Simon and little Liza were due to arrive the following day and Liza hoped that Zelma would be with them as according to Kate's last letter Zelma had yet to make up her mind to travel that far again.

Estelle, Adam and April were invited to join everyone for dinner that night, along with Roberts and Freda, but all declined saying that they had already organised their evening meal with the rest of the staff, but they would be happy to join them on another occasion.

Jamie asked why she had done that, and she replied that America was totally different to England. There was a perceived class structure on official

494

functions, but all else was classless. "You could see that," she added, "by the greeting that Bridget gave me on my arrival, and it is only those who are trying to be above everyone else who need such a structure. Those who must earn money let them get away with it, but everyone earns money here in one way or another. Myra suffered her family's pomposity when she married who they thought was beneath her, but she is accepted now more than her over righteous family ever had been."

Over dinner they all planned what they would be doing the following day. Amelia, Miranda and Lucinda were going shopping as they all knew their way around New York. David was going with Grace and Peter to explore the city.

"What will you and Jamie do?" Wendell asked Liza.

"As you know Gabriel and Kate will be arriving tomorrow with Simon, and hopefully Zelma, so we will be spending our time with Myra whilst we wait for them. I know that Myra has a number of functions that we all will be invited to, isn't that right?" said Liza to Myra.

"Yes, it was known that you would be arriving and several hostesses expressed a desire to hold a function in your honour and I presume that you will be holding one yourself so we can go through the calendar and find a suitable date," said Myra, Henry just raised his eyebrows knowing how Myra relished organising such events.

"I think I would like to rest tomorrow, and it would be nice to be here to greet Gabriel and it will be wonderful to see Kate after all these years," said Wendell.

"When you have settled in, I would like to discuss one or two thoughts that I have had," smiled Henry and Liza, Wendell and Peter nodded their agreement and Peter said that the day after next would probably be a good time.

"Do you know what Adam and Estelle are doing tomorrow?" asked Miranda.

"I believe they have arranged to explore New York with Roberts and Freda. April and Mary will be also with them once their duties are finished," said Liza.

"I suppose the boys will want to go with them," said Amelia.

"No, they have decided that they want to wait here until Simon arrives. They are all excited about seeing him again. I have no idea what time Gabriel and his family are expected but I know that they will find enough to amuse themselves whilst waiting for them," said Liza.

"I think that I am going to put my feet up and help Liza sort out the functions that we are all expected to attend. It's going to be just like the old days when I was invited to so many events that I found it difficult to choose

495

which to go to," said Jamie and then he added, "that was when you weren't talking to me Liza."

"That was a very long time ago Jamie," smiled Liza. "I talk to you a great deal now, probably more than you would like."

"It has to be seventeen years since we saw Kate," said Amelia thoughtfully, "and for ten of those she went through hell. I don't know Gabriel well, but I believe that he has been good for her, I'm pleased that she has found happiness, she deserves it."

"Yes, it's a number of years since I saw her and I'm looking forward to meeting their daughter," said Liza.

"What's her daughter's name?" asked Lucinda.

"Liza," Jamie answered. "Her name is Liza."

"That is a lovely compliment for you Liza," said Lucinda. "I remember Gabriel; he is a very good-looking man and his son takes after him."

"You're going to have quite a house full here Liza," said David.

"Yes we are David, but each person is a very good friend and that makes Jamie and I very happy," said Liza.

Tiredness gradually overtook them and firstly Henry and Myra left for their home and then one by one they made their way to bed leaving Liza and Jamie alone in the sitting room.

"Are you happy Jamie; you've been a little quiet this evening, in fact you have been quiet all day," asked Liza.

"Yes Liza, I'm quite happy. Please don't worry about me; we are going to have a wonderful time here, as are our boys and when we return, we will have four instead of three boys to look after. I'm looking forward to meeting Gabriel again, I remember him as a stable person, and very caring of you and Matthew and John. He made sure that they were safe, and I know that he would have died rather than leave the boys unprotected," said Jamie.

"Kate was the same," said Liza. "I always felt guilty about what happened to her. I used to go headlong into plans without thinking that there might be adverse consequences for those other than myself."

"You can't blame yourself for what happened to Kate, if anyone is to blame it's me. If I hadn't been so annoying by following you everywhere, you would not have gone to visit Senor Valdez and you both would not have had to endure such terrible times," said Jamie.

"Let's not think about the bad times, we are surrounded by happy people and we are going to enjoy watching them having a wonderful time and seeing our boys having fun with Simon, and Wendell and Amelia being the centre of attention. I wonder what David is going to think of New York; he seemed a little awestruck when he arrived today," said Liza.

"Yes he did but I suppose it is a far cry from Truro," said Jamie.

Jamie put his arm around Liza, and he guided her up to their room where Roberts was waiting. Liza went to see the boys who were sound asleep and although they were now teenagers, they still were her little boys and she tried not to think about the day that they would leave to further their education.

She slowly made her way to their room and April appeared. Jamie was in the sitting area whilst April helped Liza out of her clothes and into her nightgown.

"I'd forgotten how comfortable this bed is," said Jamie later that night. "You must not worry about me Liza; I am very happy being here with you. I'd be happy no matter where we were."

***

Liza was up early the next morning. She wanted to be sure to be ready no matter what time Gabriel, Kate and their family arrived. The boys also had gone down to the kitchen for their breakfast early as they too wanted to be ready for Simon's arrival.

Within the hour the household seemed to come alive. David and Grace made their way to the breakfast table with Peter not too far behind them. Wendell and Amelia were going to breakfast in their room, as were Miranda and Lucinda. Jamie appeared looking as handsome as always and he sat in the seat to the left of the head of the table as he appreciated that it was Liza's house and therefore Liza's table and she appreciated his thoughtfulness.

She could hear movement in the hallway and decided to see what was happening. Adam and Estelle were getting ready to leave and Liza asked where April was, and Adam told her that she was finishing her duties and would join them later.

"She can have a day off today; do you want to go and tell her, I believe she's in my bedroom, tell Mary that she also can leave now so that she can show you around. I have no idea what Roberts and Freda have to do, but no doubt they can catch you up. I'm sure somebody will point them in the right direction," said Liza.

Estelle left to find April and Adam smiled at Liza. "You're very thoughtful," he said.

"How is Estelle," asked Liza quietly. "I know that she has a major decision to make. All I would say is that Hector seems to be a far more considerate person than he has been previously and I'm sure it has a great deal to do with Estelle. You know that his Lordship and I will accept her if she decides to marry Hector, but it is something that only she can come to terms with."

"I know that it would put you in an awkward position," said Adam, "and I have pointed out to her the good and the bad points of the situation but I do feel that she is more enamoured of him than she likes to admit. I just want her to be happy. I know that she is my sister and I am bound to support her, but she is a genuinely nice person who deserves a good life."

"Yes, she does deserve that. I hope that this time with you will help her to come to a decision that will be right for her," said Liza.

April, Mary and Estelle came down the stairs ready for their day in New York and they all thanked Liza for allowing them the time to explore. She waved them on their way.

Eventually the house quietened and Jamie, Wendell and Liza were left waiting for Gabriel and Kate along with the boys who were spending their time being amused with a particularly engrossing board game, although every now and again they would look out of the window hoping to see a carriage arriving.

Lunchtime came and the boys made their way down to the kitchen and a light snack was served to the adults in the dining room. After lunch Jamie and Wendell went into the library and disappeared behind their newspapers and much as Liza normally enjoyed watching them and making them drop their newspapers to look at her, today she found it slightly annoying and she knew that it was because she was getting excited at the prospect of seeing Kate and hopefully Zelma.

She sat at her desk and attempted to concentrate on some of her correspondence, but she was unsuccessful and ended up just sitting and staring into space, which made the time go even more slowly.

At last a carriage came up the drive and Liza jumped up and called for the boys to come down. Jamie and Wendell had also heard the carriage and they were also making their way to the front door.

Gabriel was the first out and he turned and helped Kate and little Liza down. Simon was next and Liza held her breath and was rewarded with the sight of Zelma's face appearing in the doorway. The boys reached them before Liza was halfway down the steps and they threw themselves at Zelma almost knocking her off her feet and then they turned to Simon and dragged him towards the house. They had totally ignored Gabriel, Kate and little Liza. Whilst Jamie was shaking Gabriel's hand and introducing him to Wendell, Liza had her arms around both Kate and Zelma as she shed tears over them. Little Liza looked rather bemused and then it was Wendell's turn to shed tears as he pulled Kate towards him and she also sobbed on his shoulder.

Jamie and Gabriel had to take charge and they guided everyone up the steps and into the house as servants appeared and unloaded the luggage which miraculously disappeared from sight.

Wendell was still holding Kate's hand as they moved into the sitting room where the boys had already made themselves comfortable. Refreshments were ordered and then Liza just sat down and stared at them all.

Gabriel had hardly changed; he was just a little grey at the temples, but it suited him. Kate looked years younger than the last time that Liza had seen her, which was of course a very stressful time. Zelma was as she always had been, very pretty but as usual a little shy; that would alter as time went by. Simon was tall for his years and he was becoming quite handsome just like his father. Little Liza looked a lot like Kate although her complexion was more like her father's.

Jamie was explaining to them that as they had only arrived the day before, those who had not been to New York previously were in the city with those who knew their way around, but they would all be back in time for afternoon tea.

There were the usual questions about how their journey had been and it was not surprising to learn that the meat stews had not changed since they had last taken that drive, although the train ride was making the trip far more enjoyable.

There was a slight commotion in the hallway and in burst Amelia who stopped in the doorway as she looked around the room and then her eyes alighted on Kate who slowly stood up. Amelia rushed to her and clasped her in her arms, and she could not stop her tears from flowing, which in turn started Wendell off again and Liza followed suit.

Jamie went to Liza and put his arm around her as Miranda and Lucinda came into the sitting room. Miranda smiled at everyone and said, "This is meant to be a happy time and not a sad one; when you have all dried your tears I would be pleased to meet Kate who I have heard many stories about since I moved back into the Edgeworth family. I will just say, welcome Kate, I am Jamie's mother, Miranda and this is Lucinda who is now a very much-loved member of our family."

Miranda had calmed down the situation and Jamie looked at her with appreciation. "You are right Mother," said Jamie, "this really is a very happy gathering, and when everyone else arrives back it will be even more so. We shouldn't really welcome Kate and Gabriel with tears, but they are tears of happiness, not sadness. We are going to have a wonderful few weeks together, I am really looking forward to that time with each other."

Bridget entered the room and looked towards Kate and in one bound she had her in her arms, sobbing pitifully and uttering unintelligible words which were probably of welcome. Jamie looked surprised but he saw that Liza was smiling and realised that the bond with Bridget went back a long way.

Zelma was sitting holding little Liza and watching intently all that was going on. Liza came and sat next to her and they didn't need words to tell each other how they felt, they never had. "You look well," said Zelma in Cherokee and Liza answered also in that language. "You do not age Little Dove; you are as I first saw you. I am so pleased that you decided to journey to be with us."

"I am going to enjoy this time with you, Green Eyes," said Zelma.

"And I you, Little Dove," said Liza.

Jamie was watching them both curiously and Liza smiled up at him and her eyes told him how happy she was.

Peter arrived back with Grace and David and he too bounded over to Kate and engulfed her in an enormous hug, which was most unlike his normal character.

"Peter," exclaimed Kate, "You were just a teenager the last time I saw you. I would have recognised you anywhere. I can see your father's likeness in you and I understand that you run all the businesses excellently, which does not surprise me as I remember how intelligent you were when you were so young." She went on to introduce Gabriel to him and little Liza and then said that Simon had obviously been taken under the care of Matthew, John and James and she hoped to introduce him when the boys would allow him a little time away from them.

Jamie introduced David and Grace to them, and Gabriel commented that he knew how large the house was and he was sure that it was now going to be filled to capacity with family and close friends. "But I know that it is how Liza likes it."

500

"You're right Gabriel, she's never happier than when she is surrounded by those that she loves," said Jamie as he looked toward Liza who was now sitting with little Liza on her lap and once again he thought that it was such a shame that she didn't have a daughter to love.

Afternoon tea was brought in and Liza apologised for not having given them the chance to wash away the dust of their journey.

"We'll survive a little dust and dirt Liza," smiled Kate.

The boys came to join them, and Simon was introduced to those who had not known him previously.

After tea Kate, Gabriel and Zelma were shown to their rooms where there was hot water for them. A bed had been placed in the sitting section of Gabriel and Kate's room for little Liza and of course Simon was in with the boys, where Adam had found them, and Matthew introduced him to Simon.

Estelle was making her way to her room and April was with her. Liza informed April that Zelma was with them and she turned to Estelle and asked how she had enjoyed the day.

"It's been so interesting so far, and it's so big," said Estelle.

"You know that we are quite happy for you to join us for dinner, also Adam and April," said Liza.

"I know you are, but we are very comfortable eating with the staff in the kitchen. In fact we enjoy eating with the boys, they make our mealtimes quite entertaining," said Estelle smiling.

"As you wish," said Liza and she made her way to her room to rest before dinner, and she hoped that Jamie was already there.

Roberts was coming out of their room and he was smiling happily. Liza asked him if his time in New York had been entertaining and he said that he had found it most interesting. Jamie was sitting and reading when she went in and he looked up from his book.

"You look very happy Liza," he said. "I have to say that Kate looks very well. Gabriel hasn't changed much, but it is only a few years since we have seen him. Simon has grown; he's going to be tall like his father. He's fitted back with the boys as if they had never been parted."

Jamie stood up and helped her out of her day dress and she kicked off her shoes and stretched out on the bed with a contented smile on her face.

"I think I'll join you, we have an hour to go before we have to get ready for dinner," said Jamie and he too stretched out and they were both surprised when both April and Roberts knocked on their door an hour later to help them dress.

Liza went into the boy's room. They were ready for bed but not ready for sleep. Liza sat on one of the beds and asked them what they would like to do the next day. They had many suggestions but the main one was to find an ice cream parlour, especially as Simon had never been to one before.

"Yes, there is one here. I'll take you there tomorrow," said Liza.

"Won't you be too busy to do that?" said John.

"I'll never be too busy to take my boys somewhere that they want to go. I'll see if your father could be free also," said Liza.

"My mum and dad might also be free, and I'm sure my sister would like it," said Simon.

"It's nice to see you all here together," said Liza and she went round each one and kissed them goodnight, leaving Simon until last and she put her arms around him and held him closely to her.

"You always used to do that mummy Liza," said Simon. "You used to do it every day until you had to leave. My new mother holds me the same way and it helped me to get over you and Matthew and John having to go away when you did. I'll miss her and my dad when I go to England with you, but I'll have you and Matthew, John and now James to keep me company. Mr Reece seems very nice."

"Yes, I'll be able to cuddle you every night," said Liza. "Mr Reece is very nice; you'll get on very well with him. Good night boys, I'll see you tomorrow."

She made her way down to the sitting room where Jamie was waiting for her with David and Grace, but it wasn't long before Peter arrived followed closely by Miranda and Lucinda. Gabriel, Kate and Zelma came in at the same time as Wendell and Amelia.

Liza asked Kate if little Liza had settled.

"Yes, she has, and young Mary is watching over her whilst we are here. I didn't think she would settle in a strange place, but she was tired and went down straight away," said Kate.

Liza announced that she was going to take the boys to find the Ice cream parlour the next day. Amelia's face brightened up and she said that she would like to go with them. Liza looked at Jamie and said that they had hoped that he would be able to join them and he smiled and nodded.

"I'd like to go with you," said Kate. "I've never been to one of those."

"Am I going to be the only man on this trip?" asked Jamie.

"I'll come with you, Jamie," said Gabriel.

"We have some plans for tomorrow morning," said David. "Grace and I are going to see one of the churches."

"You haven't forgotten that Henry wanted to see us Liza, have you?" said Peter.

"I thought that we could see him later tomorrow afternoon. Do you want to see him at the office?" said Liza.

"That depends on whether father feels able to go to him or not," said Peter.

"I think that I could manage a carriage ride to the offices at the docks Peter. I am not entirely decrepit," said Wendell.

"I know you're not Father, but I thought it may be better for your health to have a morning meeting," said Peter which created a slight awkwardness around the table.

"Well you thought wrong Peter because I'm going to the ice cream parlour with everyone else tomorrow morning. I haven't had much ice cream since we were in Italy, so I'd like to see if it's better or worse," said Wendell.

"Oh," said Peter. "Well, I'll probably go to the offices early as I have some work that I could do."

"Alright Peter, your father and I will join you as soon as we can," smiled Liza.

The rest of the time over dinner went smoothly and when Liza and Jamie were finally alone in their room, Jamie said that it seemed that Wendell had put Peter in his place. He added "I think that Peter forgets that you have a family to care for and I know that you do have some business commitments, you have come here to meet up with old friends and enjoy some time with our boys in a wonderful place like New York. It is also forgotten that you undertake all the costs for everyone on a trip like this and you are entitled to have some time to relax."

"I know that you will never say anything like that to anyone else. I would hate them to feel beholden to me," said a concerned Liza.

"So we are all off to an ice cream parlour tomorrow morning," said Jamie.

"It started out with the boys suggesting it as Simon has never been to one, so I said that I would take them and they wanted you to go also, but it seems that the number of those wanting to go has increased alarmingly. I suppose that Zelma, April, Adam and Estelle would also like to join us, and I would think that Mary could be interested," said Liza.

"My mother and Lucinda didn't say that they would like to go, but I suppose they won't miss out on the opportunity. We will probably have to go in two sittings. We'll take the boys with Wendell and Amelia, and Gabriel and Kate and the others can follow on at leisure," said Jamie.

***

The boys were up early and made their way down to the kitchen for their breakfast before dressing for the day.

Liza and Jamie woke with their excited chatter, as most probably did others in the household. "I suppose we had better get ready for the day," said Liza. "I wonder what Henry wants to talk to us about; he seemed quite keen on a meeting so it must be something other than the day to day running of the business."

The ice cream parlour was owned by an Italian family and they had a very large ice cellar, so there was no chance that they would run out easily. They were delighted to see so many people arriving and ordering diverse flavours. Simon was mesmerised by how it was made, as was Kate. Gabriel had seen the parlour before but had never visited it. Wendell and Amelia sat at one of the tables and waited patiently for what they had ordered. Liza wondered whether they would all come out with various colours of ice cream dripped on the front of their clothes; after all it had always happened before.

As they were being served, the next contingent of customers arrived, and the owner and his wife were surprised but rose to the occasion. The parlour was now crowded with standing room only and the owner called out for help from the rest of his family and a young boy and girl appeared and immediately assisted knowing exactly what to do.

It had become very noisy in the parlour and Liza hoped that they were not making too much of a disturbance, but the owners did not seem worried.

Liza asked Jamie if he wanted to join the meeting that she was to have with Henry and Jamie smiled saying that it was kind of her to ask but it was her business and she could tell him all about it later.

Wendell and Liza left everyone enjoying their time in the parlour and made their way by carriage to the offices at the docks. Henry greeted them and ushered them into the board room, and he sent for Peter. On the table were various maps and figures.

"You look very serious Henry," said Wendell. "Do we have a problem?"

"No Wendell, we have no real problems, but we do have an enormous opportunity that I would like you to seriously think about," said Henry.

504

He went on to explain that Myra had found two families to take the two boys that they had brought back to America with them. "They live in a small town about a hundred miles from here and we both went to visit them before we would allow the children to be adopted by them, just in case there was something untoward about them, but they were perfectly respectable, not uneducated but do believe in better for the children under their care."

"The town could do with some investment and normally I would not recommend buying somewhere that is relatively rundown but I have discovered that the rail line is to be laid just a mile away from the town and it will join with the direct line from New York and eventually head all the way to the west. It is going to put the town on the map and bring a great deal of business to and from the area. It is not common knowledge what is being planned but I happen to know the owner of the company hired to lay the tracks," said Henry.

"What are the likely businesses that could come to that area?" asked Liza.

"There is a very strong flowing river running past the town, which was of course why the town was originally put there, and I believe that many types of manufacturing could be undertaken. It may be taking some business away from our shipping line, but somebody will set up cotton mills, cigar manufacturing, and so many other factories and it might as well be Marchant & Fuller or Bradley & Company, or both. The town needs a bank, various stores, certainly a decent hotel. There is a church but there is no school. The general store is in need of renovation; in fact that is where one of our boys now lives. There is a carpenter and an adequate dressmaker. Other businesses have closed over the years but that town is going to become so important in the years to come and I will say it again, somebody is going to come in and probably not make a very efficient job of it and fleece those who have stayed and tried to make an honest living," said Henry quite passionately.

"It sounds rather like Benson was when I first saw it, and certainly Harris Town was in a worse state," said Liza. "Of course getting into manufacturing is a new area for us but not altogether an unattractive prospect."

"If we do seriously think about this, naturally we need to look at certain costs," said Wendell. "Of course having Peter here with you, Henry, will be an asset in that respect. I'm afraid that all I could do is say 'yes' or 'no' to the project as I no longer am able to run the company, but Peter and Liza have my full authority to undertake whatever is necessary."

505

"When will it be common knowledge that the rail line will be running there?" asked Peter.

"Not for at least three months, so if you want to invest now is the time to do so," said Henry.

"You are sure that it is going to happen," said Liza.

"Yes, Liza I am. If you would care to look at the documents on the table you will see that I have been given a letter which confirms that I have had sight of the contract for the go ahead and that letter is signed by the owner of the company, and the government official dealing with it," said Henry.

"I presume that there is nothing underhand in you having this confirmation as it does sound a little like insider dealing," said a concerned Liza.

"Absolutely not; the people concerned would be much happier that your companies became involved rather than some underfunded dreamers or worse, those who say what they will do and have no intention of carrying it out. I would also add that as far as the manufacturing side is concerned the government are prepared to invest some money in the venture and your reputation gives them the confidence that they would be using tax payers' money correctly," said Henry.

"Our investment would have to be quite vast," said Peter, "but I do believe that the rewards could be even greater."

"I do have one large reservation," said Liza. "Sadly I believe that this country will go to war. I hope that I am wrong, but if they do then the affect could be devastating on all our investments in this country, not just a new one such as this."

"I understand what you are saying Liza, and I too have a sinking feeling that the south of this country will do something silly and also those in the north who are shouting the loudest about slavery have never seen a black man or an estate worked by them. Everybody needs to calm down and think about what they would be fighting for. Feelings do run high every now and again and then ease before anything stupid happens," said Henry. "Even if we do go to war, I'm not sure that it would affect what we are talking about now, as a cotton mill would be needed for uniforms, whether tobacco would be in demand I don't know, but guns, ammunition, saddles, carriages and many other tools of war would be needed. I would think that the north would confiscate any goods coming from the south so we would have the means to supply the end product."

"That sounds very mercenary Henry," said Liza.

Wendell butted in saying, "If we don't do it, somebody will and probably rip off the government in doing so. We will suffer in England as much of the produce from the south is shipped by us and as we would not wish to lose our ships, we would have to cease sailing there. However, we are talking as if war is going to be definite and I truly pray that it is not. What we really must do is look at the opportunity as it is now and put to the back of our minds the prospect that there will be a war."

"Yes, of course you are right Wendell," said Liza. "I can see that what is proposed will bring a great deal of employment to the area, firstly in construction and then secondly by factory workers, as well as ancillary tradesmen. There are many in New York without work and this could be a means of helping them out of the depressing situation that they are in. Houses would also have to be built in the area, which is another good side to this."

"I really must look at how much all this is going to cost us and how much the government are prepared to invest also as we don't want to pauper ourselves over one project. I also think that we should visit the area; we have the time to do that on this trip," said Peter.

"I would not want to make such a trip," said Wendell. "I know that I can trust your judgement Peter, and Liza if you were to go also, I would be happy with that."

"You say that the hotel is not quite what we are used to," smiled Liza.

"No, it certainly isn't, but I know that the general store has a few rooms that they sometimes rent out and we could go under the guise of looking into how the children are and if there is a possibility of further adoptions," said Henry.

"What's the town called?" asked Liza.

"Daltons," said Henry with a smile.

"Presumably named after an original inhabitant," said Liza.

"Yes, I presume so, but no doubt we will find that out when we visit," said Henry.

They spent the next few hours discussing the pros and cons of such a venture and then Liza noticed that Wendell was looking very tired and she left Peter and Henry still discussing details and went home with Wendell.

Jamie, David, Gabriel and Adam were in the grounds enjoying cricket practice with the boys, and Amelia and Kate were reminiscing on old times in the sitting room having taken advantage of a quiet hour when little Liza was having an afternoon rest. Grace, Estelle, Zelma and April were shopping, and Liza found the house very quiet. Amelia jumped up when Wendell came in as

507

she noticed how tired he looked and she immediately ushered him up to their room for a rest, leaving Kate and Liza alone for the first time. They just sat quietly, and the years fell away. They had sat that way many times so long ago, but it felt like yesterday, somehow words were not necessary.

They smiled at one another and Kate said, "You haven't changed Liza, you still have that childish excitement which shows in your eyes. You and Wendell are planning something, aren't you?"

"Our companies are a little larger than Wendell and I now; but you're right, we are being offered an opportunity which seems too good to miss, but Peter is ever cautious and will point us in the right direction," said Liza.

"You can't pull the wool over my eyes Liza. I know that you will be the one to make the final decision on whatever it is that you are planning and then you'll let everyone else think that it was their decision," said Kate.

"You've always known me so well Kate," said Liza. "Life wasn't kind to either of us, but we have come out happily on the other side. It took a long while though. Do you ever think of our lives in Belfast?"

"Not anymore; my life is in Benson now. I have everything that I could possibly want there and because of the shares that you gave me we can have the little extras that most people only dream of. I shall be very sorry to say goodbye to Simon, but Gabriel and I know that he will be loved in your home, and we recognise the importance of his further education. We know that with his background he couldn't be accepted quite so readily here, which is a great shame;" said Kate.

"Yes, it is a shame and is totally wrong, but it is the way that it is and we are therefore giving him the best chance in life, probably better than those prejudiced toffee nosed individuals can offer their own offspring," said Liza.

"I suppose they will think that he is part Spanish, or Italian," said Kate.

"I would think that they would assume that he is from Mexican aristocracy as he comes from America. We won't lie but we won't disillusion them. They can think what they like but I know that when he is older, he will be very proud of his true ancestry; I don't think that his heritage has any bearing on his thoughts at the moment. He is our Simon and we love him dearly," said Liza.

"You've known him a long time," said Kate, "and I know that he still calls you 'mummy Liza'. You helped Gabriel bring him up and made sure he was educated well. He has a lot to thank you for."

"I don't expect my boys to thank me for that Kate, and I wouldn't expect Simon to either. I have known him since he was nearly three years old and

508

Matthew was not even two; they became firm friends then and nothing has changed since that time. When John came to us, they became an inseparable 'gang of three' and you know how difficult it was for us to leave him, but we had no choice and I believe that he understands that," said Liza. "How is Rachel taking his leaving Benson?"

"She wanted to come with him, but of course she could not," said Kate. "They will write to one another I have no doubt."

"Your little girl is beautiful; she looks very like you Kate and she seems to have a nice nature," said Liza.

"I hope you don't mind that we named her after you," said Kate. "You have been such an influence on all our lives that we wanted you to be remembered through her."

"I'm very humbled by that but I hope that she will be happy about it later in life," smiled Liza. "How is everyone in Benson, I do miss them all."

"Well, I don't suppose you have had time to read all the letters that we brought with us for you and when you have I will tell you how everyone really is and what's happening there now," said Kate.

It was time for the boys to come in for their supper and they washed their hands and disappeared down to the kitchen whilst Jamie and Gabriel came into the sitting room; David had gone to his room and Adam presumably to his.

"Was your meeting good Liza?" asked Jamie.

"Very interesting; I have a great deal to think about, but I'm not going to let it interfere with this evening," smiled Liza.

Kate decided to check on little Liza before dinner and Gabriel said that he could do with a rest after the strenuous afternoon he had spent with the boys.

"It was a very long meeting, is there anything that you would like to tell me?" asked Jamie.

"Yes there's a great deal that I want to tell you and I had better warn you that I may have to go away for a couple of days and I would like you to come with me," said Liza and she then told him briefly about the opportunity that the companies were being given and the outcome could be very lucrative.

"Liza they are your companies and I have no voice in whatever they undertake but thank you for asking me to go with you," said Jamie.

"Jamie I really would like you to come with us; you know that I value your thoughts, in fact we all do. You often see what we don't as we are so involved with what we are doing. Please will you join us; there are enough people here to make sure that the boys are well entertained, and Wendell doesn't feel up to going himself, so it will be just Peter, Henry and us. We will be going under the guise of seeing the adopted boys and wondering if there is room for any more," said Liza.

"From the little you have told me it does seem like a golden opportunity for both Marchant & Fuller and Bradley & Company. So you want me to go to a rundown town with very little of the comforts that we have become used to, wonderful!" laughed Jamie. "Thank you for wanting me with you Liza."

"I always want you with me Jamie," said Liza. "We will only be there for a couple of days; I don't want to be away from everyone for very long. It is fortunate that we are here at the same time as this opportunity has arisen. Once we have seen the area I do know that I will have to spend some time helping to plan it all if we decide to take up the option, but I am not going to let it spoil my time with you, our family and friends. If I must work through the night, then that is what I shall do."

"Your eyes are sparkling Liza. You love a new challenge in business, don't you?" smiled Jamie.

"I do, but not to the detriment of all else," said Liza.

It was Wendell who announced at dinner that Liza and Peter would be away for a couple of days on business.

"I've managed to persuade Jamie to accompany us," said Liza. "I value his opinion."

"That's a very good idea Liza; Jamie is very good at seeing what we don't because we are so involved," said Wendell and Peter agreed with him.

"I'm sorry to leave you all, but I am determined to not be away for long as I want to spend much more time with you all. Myra is organising a function for us here at the end of next week, so that should be something to look forward to," said Liza and from the look on Peter's face it was not something that he was looking forward to.

"I haven't brought any evening dresses with me Liza," said a frowning Kate.

"Neither have I," said Zelma.

"How many dresses do you think I have?" asked Liza. "I have plenty with me and you are both not so very different in size to me. I'll choose what I shall be wearing and then April and Mary can alter anything else that I have if necessary."

"I can confirm that she does have a lot of dresses," said Jamie.

"Well I didn't know how many functions Myra had organised for us and as it happens there aren't as many as I would have thought, thank goodness," said Liza.

"That will be fun, won't it, Zelma?" said Kate.

"We'll all help you, won't we Miranda?" said Lucinda. "I'm sure Amelia will also want to see what can be done. Grace what will you wear, I know you have brought a couple of evening dresses with you. Will you show us when you have a minute?"

"Yes, perhaps you will help me decide which one to wear for the event," said Grace.

The men around the table had resigned looks on their faces and they supposed that the conversation over the next few days would be all about dresses. Peter's face showed that he was pleased that he would be away.

***

Having packed their bags Liza, Jamie, Peter and Henry caught the train to the nearest point to Daltons after which they had a long carriage ride into the town. It was late afternoon when they arrived and having taken one look at the hotel, they decided to throw themselves on the mercy of the owners of the general store.

When Mrs Grant, the general store owner, recognised Henry and realised that these people headed the children's charity, beds were hastily made available to them. Henry and Peter had to share, but at least they felt that they were sleeping in clean beds, which is more than could be said for what they felt the hotel would have.

They were introduced to Mr Grant and Keith, their adopted son. He recognised Liza and Jamie and smiled, looking so much happier than when they had last seen him.

"Young Philip is happy with Mr Newley; he's the carpenter in town. He and Keith are inseparable. It's nice that you are thinking of more children being brought here. This town could do with some more life in it," said Mr Grant.

"I notice that you don't have a school here," said Liza. "How are the children educated?"

"We teach them ourselves," said Mrs Grant. "I'm good at arithmetic and Mrs Newley is good at reading and writing. I hope that not having a school won't put you off our town."

"How are the other children educated?" asked Liza.

"By their parents when they have the time," said Mrs Grant.

Liza made a mental note that the first place to be built would be the schoolhouse.

They asked about the hotel and were told that the owner was closing and leaving.

"Your company owns hotels, so I've heard," said Mr Grant.

"Yes, we do," said Peter. "But there obviously is not much trade for one here."

"You're probably right, but if it had been kept clean then it could have had more patrons," said Mrs Grant. "Anybody who comes to town only stays one night, and I realise that you had heard that before, which is why you are here staying with us."

Mrs Newley and Philip came to visit, and the boys looked very happy and after an initial greeting the boys went off to play.

Henry asked if there were any problems with the boys and the answers were that there were times when they cowered away from them as they obviously thought that they were going to be chastised; it was when they had played and broken something, but as Mrs Newley said, they would be told that they should be careful and try not to do it again, but they would not smack them as they felt that they had had too much of that in the past. It was obvious to them all that the boys loved their new parents.

The next day they took a carriage ride around the area and took their maps with them. They could see what Henry had meant when he told them that with investment the town of Daltons could well be a very good prospect for them. There was plenty of room for a large manufacturing area. Trees needed to be felled so a sawmill could be first to be established. The river would play a very big part in their decision and of course a rail link to New York would be an asset.

Next, they walked from one end of the town to the other making notes on what was urgently needed, and this was where Liza was in her element. She could visualise how a town should look and what businesses and houses were needed. She would work on it at leisure. Henry had the contacts for a workforce and Peter would make sure that the venture was within their means. Jamie had never been in a situation where he could see how the beginnings of a completely new town built around a manufacturing area was about to take place. He enjoyed helping to piece it all together.

On their last night there Jamie said that he knew that they had to watch that they did not go over the economical budget for the project, but it was wonderful to watch people talking and planning with no real financial restrictions.

"I know that you are quite capable of overseeing this Henry, but you do need some reliable staff to be here on site," said Liza. "Also we are firstly going to have to organise some temporary accommodation for the workers that we will need to bring in. We can't expect them to live under canvas, especially when winter comes. I'm sure we can build some one roomed cabins which can be removed when the work is over."

"What if they want to bring their families?" asked Jamie.

"Their families will not be our problem, but I'm sure we will come up with a solution," said Liza.

"Yes, I'll have to find a few reliable overseers," said Henry.

Liza was smiling and said, "I think that we are leaning towards taking on this project."

"I still have to study the figures closely, but it is a good area and will definitely be on the map once the rail link is here, but first we will probably have to bring what we need by wagon, however that is not a problem as we do have wagons at our disposal," said Peter.

"Do you think that Wendell will be in agreement with all this?" asked Jamie.

"Of course we will have to consult with him, but he was keen when Henry told us about it, and as long as we don't over-reach ourselves, I'm sure he will be quite happy. He has already seen the merit in the venture," said Peter.

They set off for home early the next morning and arrived back tired and hungry very late that night. Everyone was already in bed when they came in. Bridget got up and she quickly brought some food into the dining room for them.

Wendell had obviously heard their arrival and they were surprised to see him come into the dining room. He could not wait to hear whether or not they thought that it would be a worthwhile project and when they told him that it had seriously good possibilities he smiled happily and went straight back to bed saying that he would discuss it with them in depth the next day.

Roberts and April had not heard them arrive home, so Jamie and Liza helped one another to get ready for bed.

"I truly found our time at Daltons interesting Liza. I can see such prosperity in it, not only for your companies but for many others. It really could be enormously profitable, so let's hope that war is a long way off and that any talk about it is only talk," said Jamie.

Liza was stretching out in bed. "I really appreciate our bed tonight. I know it was very clean at Mrs Grants, but it wasn't very comfortable. This is absolute luxury."

Jamie watched her and thought how inviting she looked. She was many different people; she was an astute businesswoman, an excellent mother, a wife who made him very happy and a wonderful lover. How lucky he now was. He frowned for an instant and remembered that he had nearly thrown it all away with one stupid action. He shook his head to rid himself of the memory and realised that Liza was watching him through half-closed eyes.

"What's the matter Jamie; you look concerned," asked Liza.

"No Liza, I'm not concerned. I was just remembering one of those bad moments in my life, but it's gone now and I have no idea why it just came into my mind because looking at you I know that I have no worries," said Jamie. "I love you Liza Edgeworth and I am going to show you just how much."

Liza giggled and knew that she was going to enjoy whatever it was that Jamie had in mind.

Chapter 25

Whilst Liza was enjoying spending time with family and friends, as well as planning their new venture and getting ready for their grand function, Hector was going through every kind of mental torture imaginable.

He carried out what had to be done at Langston House efficiently, helped the Major interview staff, and contacted those who had children waiting for places. He was so busy that he hoped that he could put Estelle and the decision that she would be making out of his mind, but it was impossible, especially in the quiet hours of the night.

Sometimes he stayed at Jamie's house, sometimes with the Major at Ffoulks House, and sometimes with Anthony, and they all noticed that he was unusually quiet.

He imagined that Estelle would rush off the ship into his arms telling him that no matter what the outcome she wanted to be with him, but in his heart he knew that she would not. Jamie had been right; she would not want him ostracised from those he had known and she would not want the indignity of being snubbed by those same people. The only places that they would be accepted would be with the Major and with Liza and Jamie, and Jamie had said that he doubted that they would be invited to any functions as they would not wish embarrassment for them, wrong as that may be. Also they would be putting her brother, Adam, in an awkward position and she would never do that.

As the weeks passed he became more and more depressed. The Major and Jennifer tried to cheer him up, but to no avail. His mother was delighted that Estelle was not around, and she was attempting to introduce him to a few eligible ladies but to him they were all insipid and most certainly not like his Estelle.

Anthony spent as much time as he could with him, but no matter how much he tried to occupy him, the conversation always returned to Estelle. It was reminiscent of Jamie going through the same trauma over Liza.

On one of his quiet moments whilst staying at Jamie's house, Mrs Frances came into the drawing room with tea and one of the cakes that she knew was a favourite of Hector's. Hector looked up and told her that she was very kind, but it would take more than a cake, lovely as it was, to put him in good spirits.

"Have you heard from them Mrs Frances?" asked Hector.

"No, not yet and I'm sure they are too busy enjoying themselves to think of writing to me. I would think that they are going here, there and everywhere and having their own parties that everyone attends. It's not like here where there is a strict guest list. I know that they have entertained from the highest of the high to the lowest of the low. It's a much freer life in America, which was why Lady Edgeworth enjoyed her time there. Of course it wasn't the same for her for some time after her lieutenant husband was killed, but I think she is happy in both places now," said Mrs Frances who suddenly felt that she had said too much.

"Yes, you are probably right, America seems to have a very different society," said Hector as he eyed his favourite cake with a sudden hunger.

"A very different society," he mumbled to himself between bites of cake. "I know what I can do," he said, and Mrs Frances put her head around the door and asked if he had called her.

"I'm sorry Mrs Frances, I was muttering to myself," said an increasingly excited Hector. He knew that he had to sort out carefully in his mind his life changing idea, and when he had he was going to see the Major to ask his opinion. There was no point in talking to Anthony as he knew that he would be totally against his plan, but the Major and Jennifer were very down to earth and would give him sound advice.

He spent a very thoughtful afternoon and that evening for the first time in a number of weeks he enjoyed the meal that Mrs Lambert had made for him with such care. He drank no alcohol that evening as he wanted to keep his mind clear for the plans that he was making for his and Estelle's future.

The next morning as he left, he waved cheerily to Harper and Mrs Frances, both of whom were pleased to see a smile on his face for the first time in many weeks. "He's thought of a plan," said Mrs Frances to Harper. "I hope it works out for him," Harper replied.

The Major wasn't surprised to see him as he always turned up without notice but what did surprise him was the look of contentment on his face.

"What is it Hector, have you had good news?" said the Major.

"No, not really, but I have an idea that I would like to discuss with you and Jennifer when you are free," said Hector.

"Jennifer is with the smaller children, helping them to read, but we will be free after lunch," said the Major.

"I think I'll find some of the older boys and see if they want a lesson in cricket," smiled Hector whose lessons in cricket were anything but how cricket should be played, but the boys enjoyed it.

Hector made his way to the Major's office when lunch was over, and he paced up and down whilst he waited for the Major and Jennifer.

"Sit down Hector," said the Major when he and Jennifer arrived. "You look as though you need to calm down."

"I've made a decision Major," said Hector. "I'm going to move to America."

Both the Major and Jennifer looked at him in shock. "That is a very big decision Hector, would you mind telling us your reasons why."

"It's really very simple Major; in America the society accepts people from all walks of life. In some areas there is a form of class society but in the main you are what you make of yourself. Most people marry because of love and that is what I would like to do," said Hector.

"You obviously have only recently thought of this Hector; do you have any idea that Estelle would want to live with you there," asked the Major.

"I have no idea if she would agree to this, but my reasons are very sound. We can start a new life together without the disapproval of anyone. We would not be moving in the circles that are so stupidly adhered to over here and therefore neither of us would be snubbed or ostracised, although as you know that would not worry me, but it would worry Estelle on my behalf. We would not create an awkward situation for her brother, or for Jamie and Liza, who are the most supportive of people. We would not have to worry about anyone but ourselves," said Hector.

"But what would you do over there, Hector; you would have to be able to earn money," asked Jennifer.

"I've thought about that and I would not throw myself on Liza or the Fullers; I would go into the army. I know that the army would not be my first choice of employment but they would probably be happy to have me as I have been trained in England and have fought in several battles, and they do provide married quarters, which may not be salubrious but we could make them nice," said Hector.

"I know that the military life was not for you Hector, but the little I know of the American army it is a very different and more relaxed way of life, but there are constant dangers unlike over here. I know you have heard of the traumas that Liza experienced on many occasions with her previous husband, would you want to put Estelle through that?" asked the Major.

"If Estelle agrees to marry me then she will be under no illusions of what an army wife would have to endure, but I have always been lucky and I don't think that my luck is going to run out for some time to come," said Hector.

"What if she still refuses you Hector, have you thought about that?" asked Jennifer.

"I don't think that she will, but yes, I have thought about it and I will still move to America and join the army and try to forget her, which will be virtually impossible, and concentrate on whatever the army throws at me. I can't stay here with her around, I would have to go somewhere far away, and America seems as good a place as any," said Hector.

"Have you told your mother what you are planning, or Anthony?" asked the Major.

"No, I haven't yet, but I will before I leave. They will not be happy, but it is not their happiness that I am looking for. I wish Jamie and Liza were here as I want to tell them of my decision before turning up on their doorstep. I did promise Liza that I would not bother Estelle and give her the time to come to a decision, but if what I want to do goes according to plan then I must tell Estelle before she returns, so I want to travel as soon as possible," said Hector.

The Major and Jennifer were very quiet. They both could see difficulties with Hector's plan, but life was full of difficulties.

"You haven't said whether you approve or not," said Hector.

"You don't need our approval Hector," said Jennifer. "You need our support, and you have that."

The Major looked at Jennifer and smiled. "I am going to be so sorry to lose you Hector; I felt a little closer to my son through you. I want to tell you to stay with us, but you will never be happy here and I do wonder whether Estelle will ever be truly happy here again. Follow your dreams Hector, I did."

"Liza would tell you to do that, I'm not sure that Jamie would but he should be reminded of what his dreams were, and they finally came true for him. I wish you well Hector and hope that it all works out for you, I really do," said Jennifer.

"Have you planned how you are going to travel?" asked the Major.

"Yes, and I hope it will work out. I'm going to travel on the 'Amelia'. I won't be able to afford the luxury of first class, but I can cope with that for a fortnight and with what I am planning, probably third class will appear to be luxury. I know that Liza is planning to return three to four weeks after my arrival, so I should have time to sort out everything and I have to say that what I am hoping for will mean that you will need a new teacher for your children. I am sorry about that, but I really hope that it is the case," said Hector.

"I can step into that role for the time being," said Jennifer. "We are really going to miss you and I hope that we are also going to miss Estelle. Are you going to see your family now?"

"Yes, I had better get that over with, and then I'll return and collect my belongings from here," said Hector.

"If you like I'll pack what I can for you Hector. Do you know when the 'Amelia' is sailing again?"

"I believe that it is in three days' time, but I must also get my things from Anthony's house and from Jamie's. I really haven't put any roots down since I was rescued from Portugal, have I?" smiled Hector.

He left to face his family and he was under no illusions as to how they were going to take his news.

Anthony and Diana were at home and Rose was visiting. Little Thomas shrieked with pleasure at seeing his Uncle Hector. Anthony frowned seeing the look on Hector's face and he knew that he had something important to tell them.

"Can you take Thomas up to his nurse please Diana," said Anthony. Diana nodded and Rose looked warily at Hector.

"What is it that you have to tell us Hector?" asked Anthony.

"I'm going to America," said Hector starkly.

"I thought that you had promised that you would give Estelle time to come to the right decision," said Rose.

"I suppose you want that right decision to be rejecting me, Mother," said Hector bitterly.

Diana quietly slipped back into the room and looked worriedly at Hector and then at Rose.

"Of course, that would be the correct decision for her to make and you know it," said Rose.

"What will you travelling to America now achieve, Hector?" asked Anthony.

"I'm not just travelling to America, Anthony, I'm going to live there for good," said Hector.

Rose drew in her breath; "I suppose that woman has put you up to this. Anthony, tell him that it's a ridiculous proposition."

"Estelle doesn't know what I am proposing; she will be as surprised as you. Life over there will be much easier for people like us, we will both be accepted. As I said, Estelle doesn't know what my plans are and even if she still refuses me, I want to live there and start a new life. That is something that I need to do with or without her, but I do hope that it will be with her," said Hector.

"I suppose that Liza has encouraged you to do this," snapped Rose. "I bet she's funding you and giving you a job. It just shows her class also."

Anthony rounded on his mother, "Don't you dare say anything like that. You know she has done everything to help this family and I know that she is the one who told Hector to leave Estelle alone. If you ever say anything like that again you will be left to lick your wounds alone."

"I will never understand why everyone is so concerned about class and that is something that I won't have to worry about in America," said Hector. "Liza doesn't know that I am going to America, so she will not be funding me, nor will she be giving me a job. I'm going to join the American army and ask Estelle to become an army wife and hope that she accepts."

"Do you mean that you are going to enlist," said a shocked Anthony. "You will just be an enlisted man! You can't mean that Hector, you're better than that."

"Well perhaps they will see that and promote me quickly," said Hector.

"You must love her very much Hector," said Diana quietly. "You're giving up a great deal for her."

"She's worth it Diana and you must remember that she would not allow me to give up anything for her, but she will have no choice now as I will have already given it up and I'm happy to do so," said Hector. "I hope that I will go with my family's blessing."

"Well, you're not going to have mine," said a furious Rose.

"I'm sorry about that Mother, I had hoped that you would understand how I feel," said Hector. "I'll pack my few belongings and get out of your way now. I will say goodbye before I leave."

"I'll help you Hector," said Diana.

"Thank you, Diana. I appreciate that and I would like to say goodbye to my nephew," said Hector.

"Of course Hector," said Diana as she left the room with him.

She helped him to pack, telling him that she was going to miss him, and she was sure that Anthony would also. She felt sure that his mother would come around and wish him well.

"I doubt that Diana; I've known her longer than you and once she has made up her mind, she rarely changes it," said Hector.

"Give my love to Liza when you see her. I don't think that she is going to be very happy with you turning up unannounced; she will think that you have broken your word and she sets great store in people keeping their word but she will soften when she knows what you are planning," said Diana. "I wish you a safe journey Hector and hope that we will meet up again some time in the future."

They then went into Thomas' room where he was taking his afternoon nap. Hector looked at him for a long time and asked Diana to say goodbye for him, and he quickly left the room and made his way down the stairs. He went into the drawing room where Rose was still seated with an enraged look on her face. Anthony looked across at Hector sadly.

"Goodbye Anthony, thank you for all that you have done for me. I know that I have not been an easy brother to have and I'm sorry that I have embarrassed you on so many occasions," said Hector. "Goodbye Mother."

Rose did not answer him, and he sadly made his way to the door. Anthony followed him. "What plans have you made for getting to America?"

"I've got to get to Southampton and I'm going to ask one of Jamie's drivers to take me as they know the way so well. I'm then going to get passage on the new fast ship. It will be more comfortable than the hold of the older ones, but that's how it is."

"I'll take you to Southampton Hector, when are you leaving?" asked Anthony.

"I was going to make my way to Jamie's tonight and then on tomorrow morning, but if you want to take me I'll sleep at the Home tonight and perhaps we could call in at Jamie's for the rest of my belongings tomorrow before going onto Southampton," said Hector.

"Of course, and we can stop at the bank on the way because I'm not having my brother travelling any way other than first class, it may be the last time that you experience any luxury. I envy you Hector; you have an adventurous spirit and I do hope that it all works out well for you. I'll pick you up tomorrow morning and we'll have to stop at one of the hotels on the way," said Anthony.

"Thank you, Anthony, and I'm sorry that I'm leaving you to deal with our mother alone," said Hector.

When he arrived back at the Home the Major and Jennifer were pleased that he would be staying the night as it was already getting very late and they were equally pleased that Anthony was taking him to Southampton.

"How was your mother?" asked the Major.

"It was a difficult meeting. I would have liked to have said goodbye to her properly, but she didn't give me the chance. I don't know why she started blaming Liza for what I wanted to do, but Anthony soon told her to stop such accusations," said Hector.

"She had no reason to think that Liza was involved, but you must appreciate that when people are upset they say and do things which they do not really mean," said Jennifer quietly.

Hector spent a disturbed night; his mother's attitude had upset him considerably. He was up early the next morning and whilst he was toying with his breakfast Anthony arrived and he had brought his mother with him. Hector stood as she came in and she held out her hands to him. He didn't say anything, he just went over to her and put his arms around her, an action that neither was used to, but it seemed the right thing to do at that moment.

The Major and Jennifer came in and they agreed to take Rose home when Hector and Anthony left.

Finally Hector's bags were placed in Anthony's carriage and it was time to leave. Both Rose and Jennifer were shedding tears, and the Major looked a little strained as he shook hands with him. Jennifer kissed him on the cheek and wished him well and then it was his mother's turn.

"I do wish you well Hector and I do hope that you find what you are looking for. Perhaps one day we will travel to America and be able to visit you. I do want you to be happy and I hope that Estelle loves you as much as you love her, and if she does then you will have a good life. Goodbye my son, have a safe journey and I didn't really mean what I said about Liza yesterday. It was just the heat of the moment and I hope you will give her and Jamie my love," said a very tearful Rose.

"Thank you, Mother, I will. I'm glad you came this morning. I will write to you," said Hector and he quickly got into the carriage with Anthony before he showed the emotion that he was feeling and made matters worse for his mother and Jennifer. Anthony thought it wise to quickly move off and they swept down the drive and were on their way to a new start for Hector.

They collected all his belongings from Jamie's house and carried on to a hotel for the night and the following day they were at the docks at Southampton where they organised a cabin for Hector on the 'Amelia' which was sailing on the tide in the early hours of the next morning. Anthony handed him a package with some money in it.

"You know I can't pay you back Anthony," said Hector.

"What was it that you said to Liza, 'friends never have to say thank you', with brothers it is even more so," said Anthony. "I'll say goodbye now Hector, and hope that we will meet up again someday, and I sincerely hope that you get what you want and who you want. Give our love to everyone over there and please do write to us."

"I will Anthony, that I promise," said Hector and Anthony turned and walked down the gangway and into his carriage whilst Hector watched him drive away.

He soon got over the initial sadness of leaving his family and the Major and all the children as his enthusiasm returned about his plans for a new life with Estelle. He felt that there was no obstacle to their marriage now and he hoped that she saw it the same way, he was sure that she would.

***

The voyage was uneventful but comfortable and when the New York skyline came into view his excitement grew. He knew that his best way to get to Liza's house was to find Henry at the Marchant & Fuller offices which were somewhere on the docks. He was watching as they came into port and of course he should have known that the largest building was the one he was looking for.

He arranged for his baggage to be brought dockside and he paid a porter to bring it with him to the Marchant & Fuller offices. As he was about to enter the building, he was stopped by a young man who asked who he was and what he was doing there. Hector remembered that there had been a problem last time Liza and Jamie were in New York and he assumed that this was one of their security guards.

"I'm Hector Ffoulks and I'm here to see Lord and Lady Edgeworth and Mr Fuller, I know that Mr Mahoney will point me in the right direction," said Hector.

"You know Mr Mahoney then?" said Walter Anderson.

"Yes I met him when he visited Liza and Jamie last year," smiled Hector.

"Well, Mr Fooks, if you'll wait in the lobby, I'll tell him that you are here," said Walter.

It wasn't long before Hector was being ushered up the stairs and into an office where Henry was standing and looking puzzled at him. "I didn't know you were visiting, Hector."

"No, neither does anyone else but I don't think that they will be displeased to see me," said Hector.

"You think not?" said Henry. "Peter is here, I'll call him for you."

It was not the welcome that he had been expecting, but of course it was probably known that he had a problem with Estelle and that he should be giving her time to make a decision.

Peter walked in frowning, "What on earth are you doing here Hector. I thought you were waiting for us in England."

"I needed to come here Peter, and you will know my reasons when I have seen Jamie and Liza and Estelle of course," said Hector. "This is not just a whim on my part; it is a serious matter that I need to discuss with them."

"I'll take you there," said Peter. "I'm sure Liza will make room for you, but whether she will be pleased to see you could be another matter."

Peter's carriage was brought around and they both climbed aboard having already had Hector's luggage put in place. It was a quiet journey as Peter was not known for small talk.

"Where's Lord Edgeworth?" Peter asked of Bridget when they arrived and was told that he was somewhere in the grounds with the boys.

"Lady Edgeworth is in her study, Sir," said Bridget. Peter was beginning to understand her, but Hector was totally lost with her accent.

Peter ushered him along the hallway and knocked at a door and entered before anyone could answer.

"You have a visitor Liza," said Peter.

"Oh, I didn't expect you home so soon Peter, who is it?" asked Liza.

Suddenly Hector felt like a naughty schoolboy being hauled in front of the headmaster for punishment, but there was no escape, so he walked into the room without giving Peter the chance to say who he was.

"Oh Hector, you know you shouldn't be here," said Liza tiredly.

"I'll see if I can find Jamie," said Peter who really didn't want to be in the middle of an argument.

"I should be here Liza, I have made a major decision which I had to talk to you and Jamie about which may or may not concern Estelle," said Hector.

"Sit down Hector, you look too nervous standing there," said Liza. "You know I'm always pleased to see you, Hector, but this is what you promised not to do."

"I've come over here to live Liza. I'm going to enlist in the army and I'm going to ask Estelle to become an army wife," said Hector. "You know that this will solve all the perceived class problems which I have always thought of as stupid."

Liza sat and blinked at him and finally said; "but you left the army Hector; you found that you didn't like that life. I'm sure you won't like the rigours of the American army."

"I would do anything to have Estelle with me and if she still decides against me then it is a life that would help me forget. I can't stay in England with her there and I'm not able to be with her; that would be the cruellest thing that could happen to me, so I have made the decision to leave that country no matter what the outcome with Estelle is," said Hector.

Jamie slowly came in shaking his head, "Oh Hector," he said. "You do make life awkward for everyone, including yourself."

"Hector has decided to leave England and stay in America. He feels that a life here, with or without Estelle, would be preferable," said Liza. "He has the mistaken belief that an army life would suit him, but you and I know that it would be the worst career that he could have, especially as he is considering becoming an enlisted man."

"What?" exploded Jamie. "Why the army?"

"Because I must have a means to earn and if I have a wife to keep it will also give us a place to live," said Hector.

"There still is a class hierarchy here Hector, although it is not as hardnosed as in England and mostly I have found that there are those who think they are better than others rather than actually being so," said Liza.

Hector laughed, "So you play with them then Liza, and they never realise it."

"Maybe I do, but it's still there, although I doubt that it would worry you and I don't think that it would worry Estelle overly," said Liza.

"She is going to be surprised to see you Hector, and I'm not so sure that initially she is going to be that happy, but before you do anything stupid like enlisting in the army, I suggest that you have a long conversation with her and see if she loves you enough to give up her family, her homeland and career for you. You may be giving up a great deal for her, but she also would be doing the same," said Jamie.

"She is out with Adam and April at the moment, and I'll get you settled into a room for you must be tired after your journey. Did you come on the 'Amelia'?" asked Liza.

"Yes, Anthony paid for my passage so that I could have a little luxury on the journey. He said that it would probably be the last luxury I would ever experience, but he was wrong because he obviously has never seen your house," said Hector.

"How is your mother?" asked Liza tentatively.

"She was not best pleased with me and said some terrible things, but she came to say goodbye and wished me well on the morning that I left," said Hector. "Diana was very sweet and understood exactly how I felt about Estelle; I found it difficult to say goodbye to little Thomas."

Liza rang for Bridget and arranged which room should be made ready for Hector. They could hear people arriving back from their trips to various places and Liza and Jamie ushered Hector into the sitting room where he was greeted with surprise by everyone.

"It's nice to see you Hector," said Miranda, "if somewhat surprising. Are you staying long?"

"For as long as it takes for me to get settled," said Hector which caused the raised eyebrows of all those who really didn't know what he was talking about.

Liza decided to change the subject and asked everyone what they had been doing that afternoon and mostly they had been shopping. Wendell and Amelia appeared and were ready for their afternoon tea.

"I heard you were here Hector," said Wendell. "Did you have a good trip over?" Liza thought how wonderful it was that Wendell could make this surprise visit appear so normal.

"I came on the 'Amelia' and it was very comfortable," said Hector.

"I thought you must have done with the time factor since we last saw you," said Wendell. "I'm glad you found it comfortable. It is a good ship."

Amelia just smiled at him; she was also astute enough to realise that his arrival was rather awkward, but she was also making it appear unsurprising.

Peter came in and went to sit with Grace and they started a conversation about the places that she and her father had visited that day.

Bridget knocked to say that Hector's room was ready, and Jamie said that he would show him the way and they left the room. Liza asked Bridget if Adam and April had returned yet and was told that they had just arrived. Liza excused herself and went with Bridget to where Adam, April and Estelle were having tea in the staff dining room.

Estelle looked up as she came in and said that she had heard that Hector had made the trip over to America.

"He has something very important to tell you Estelle; so important that it negated his promise to leave you to make your own decision. It is up to him to tell you, but if you don't want to see him then that can be arranged," said Liza.

"I can be with her," said Adam.

Liza nodded but Estelle said that Hector was not a dangerous man, just a little persistent and much as she appreciated Adam's concern, she would see him alone and find out what he wanted to tell her.

"Do you know what it is that he wants to tell me," said Estelle to Liza.

"No matter whether I know it or not, it is not up to me to tell you," said Liza. "It is up to him only. Shall I tell him that you will see him?"

"Yes, please. Where will I find him?" asked Estelle.

"Nobody is in the library at the moment, so would you like to go there, and I'll bring him to you," said Liza. "You look annoyed Adam and I can understand that, but don't forget that Estelle is in control of this situation and I'm sure she will handle it well."

Liza took Estelle to the library and then carried on to Hector's room and knocked on his door. He answered and she told him that Estelle was waiting for him in the library and she hoped that he was ready to see her.

"I'm nervous Liza. This is the most important conversation of my life," said Hector.

"I'm sure it is, and it is only something that you can deal with. I wish you well Hector. I would like to see you settled, although settled in the army is not quite what I would have thought was the wisest of decisions," said Liza and she led him down to the library and closed the door on them both.

The boys stormed in through the front door with Gabriel telling them to calm down. They were followed by Kate, Zelma and little Liza. Matthew stopped in front of his mother and said that he could see that something had happened.

"Uncle Hector has arrived unexpectedly, and he is in the library with Miss Reece, so please would you all be a little quiet and later I would love to know what you have been doing this afternoon. When you have all washed, I'm sure your tea will be ready for you, but I would be pleased if you could come back down quietly," said Liza.

Gabriel and Kate smiled, and Kate asked if this was the man that Estelle was making a decision about and one who had said that he would give her the time to do it.

"That's right Kate," whispered Liza. "We'll just have to leave them to sort it out."

"It's very reminiscent of how Jamie was all those years ago," said Kate and she and Gabriel took little Liza up for a late afternoon nap. Zelma just raised her eyes to heaven and Liza knew she was thinking 'Men!' She smiled and said that she would see that the boys were indeed washing before their tea.

Liza went into the sitting room and sat next to Wendell. "What's his decision Liza, because he won't have travelled all this way without a very serious motive?"

"He's decided to move to America with or without Estelle. Naturally he hopes that it is with her," said Liza quietly.

"And what sort of future has he planned for them both?" asked Wendell.

"He says that he is going to enlist in the army," smiled Liza.

"That would be a life that he wouldn't enjoy and would his love for Estelle make up for the hardships that it would bring?" said Wendell.

"He's made the decision and has left his family, his work and any friends that he had behind regardless of whether Estelle marries him or not," said Liza.

"I suppose it's fortunate that we will have serious work for him that will keep him occupied for a number of years," said Wendell calmly.

"We do think alike, don't we? Yes, we do have work for him, but he doesn't know that Wendell, and they must make the decision with what they are prepared to undertake at the moment. Let's see how this meeting maps out before we make major plans for him, or perhaps them," said Liza. "If she agrees to what he is proposing now, then it is truly a match made in heaven. It's so nice that you and I always think along the same lines. I wonder if Peter and Henry are thinking the same as us."

"I'm sure Peter is as I know that he was impressed with how Hector handled the work at both the Ffoulks House and now at Langston and when he knows that Hector is planning to live here then he will be happy that we have someone else who we can rely upon," said Wendell.

"Do you think it would be a good idea for Brendan to spend some time working here on the Daltons project?" asked Liza.

"He's on your payroll, so the decision is yours, but he did some very good planning work on the 'Amelia' and you know what he has done on your business. If you are really asking my opinion then I have to say that not only would it do him some good, I think that it would be good for our new project. We must sit down and when we have worked out exactly what is needed, we must decide which business handles which project," said Wendell.

"We must make it quite clear that Henry is in the overall driving seat; he has always been our eyes and ears in America and this latest project is totally down to his contacts. We must tell Hector and Brendan just how important Henry is to us; we want nobody getting above themselves where he is concerned," said Liza.

"Do you think that they would become overbearing in this?" asked Wendell.

"You know that Hector can have an unfortunately pompous manner which won't go down too well here but he always took instruction from the Major. However he must be made to understand that the American perception of an accent such as his could be taken wrongly. Brendan, on the other hand, thinks of himself as family, and sometimes such a thought can alienate others but I think that he will jump at the chance to come here and show us what he is capable of," said Liza.

The library door opened, and Estelle could be heard running up the stairs obviously in distress.

"It would seem that didn't go too well," said Wendell with resignation.

"Oh dear," said Liza. "Where do I start?"

She got up and looked into the library where Hector was on his knees in front of the chair that Estelle had been sitting in. He looked around and his face told her that Estelle had refused his proposal. She went in and closed the door after her.

"What were her reasons for her refusal Hector?" asked Liza.

"Everything. But all for my sake. I could not seem to get her to understand that I have left it all behind; she thinks that I can go back and pick up where I left off," said Hector. "I really thought that I had managed to take away every obstacle that was in our way."

"I think that you rather sprung it upon her," said Liza. "I think that I will ask Jamie to come in and see you."

She left and beckoned Jamie to her. "It didn't go down too well with Estelle then?" said Jamie.

"She still thinks that he can return and pick up the pieces. She really thinks that he would be better off without her," said Liza. "I'm just going to see her. Will you stay with Hector for a while?"

Adam was making his way along the hallway with a look of thunder on his face. Liza put her hand up to stop him. "I'm going up to see Estelle; Jamie has gone in with Hector. I'm sure she will want to see you in a little while but I must tell you that what Hector was proposing was a complete change of life for him, and hopefully for them both and he has already sacrificed a great deal to make that dream come true. It is, of course, Estelle's decision and she seems to have made that decision, which was not what Hector wanted."

Adam hesitated and then said that he would go to Estelle later and he returned down to the kitchen where April would be waiting for him.

Liza slowly made her way up to Estelle's room and she could hear her crying softly inside. She tapped on the door and when there was no answer, she took the decision to enter anyway. Inside Estelle was sitting on her bed holding a handkerchief to her face.

She quietly went and sat beside her on her bed and waited for her to calm down.

"We're from such different backgrounds for it ever to work," sobbed Estelle. "He can return to his life with no problems. I know that I will be able to find work elsewhere in England; I know you will give me a good reference."

"He's not going to return to his life in England. He's left everything and everyone for you Estelle, and you aren't prepared to do the same for him. I understand that," said Liza.

"He won't want to enlist in the army over here, so once again he is saying that he is going to make a sacrifice for me and I can't allow that," said Estelle.

"Let us take family, friends, jobs, in fact everything out of the picture. Do you love him? I don't have to ask him that question because I know he loves you," said Liza.

"It's because I love him that I can't let him carry out what he has in mind. It wouldn't be fair on him," said Estelle between sobs.

"And what you are doing is totally unfair on you. If you and he truly love one another then there is no problem that cannot be dealt with. He has solved all that he considers as problems, are you going to do the same?" asked Liza.

"I have Adam to think about," said Estelle.

"Adam has April; all you have to do is love him like the good brother that he is, and he would want you to be happy," said Liza.

530

"His family will never accept him because of me," said Estelle.

"He's dealt with that one; Anthony took him to the ship and funded his trip, Diana wished him luck and finally his mother hoped that he succeeds in all that he wants," said Liza.

"He would hate the army," said Estelle.

"Yes, he probably would, but is prepared for that especially if he had you to come home to," said Liza.

"I have my teaching career to consider; I can't let the children and the Major down," said Estelle.

"The Major knows that you may not be returning, and Jennifer would take your place until a replacement could be found," said Liza.

"You make it all sound so simple," said Estelle.

"It is very simple. You love one another but it seems to me that he has made every sacrifice possible and your sacrifice is the ultimate one. You are going to give up love for love," said Liza sadly.

"The way you say it makes it seem very foolish," said Estelle.

There was a light knock on the door and Adam came in, and walking over to Estelle put his arms around her and all he said was that she must do what will make her happy and not be concerned about anything or anyone else. He had done that, and he was now so very happy.

Liza said that she would leave them to talk and Estelle asked her to tell Hector that she would like to see him again after she had spent time with Adam.

She slowly made her way down the stairs and tapped on the library door and entered. Jamie and Hector looked up at her. "You know that she turned me down Liza," said Hector. "I have done everything to take away what was stopping her, or so I thought, I have to accept that she doesn't love me."

"Adam's with her at the moment, but she has asked me to tell you that she would like to see you again shortly," and Liza gave him one of her most reassuring smiles which Jamie knew so well, and Hector was beginning to realise had something to do with solving a problem and his heart leapt with hope.

Jamie stayed with Hector whilst Liza moved into the sitting room. Wendell and Amelia smiled at her knowingly and Miranda and Lucinda looked at her quizzically. David, Grace and Peter were discussing a trip that they would be taking the following day, although they were aware that there was a problem with Hector.

531

"Do they know that there is a possibility that he could be working with us?" whispered Wendell and Liza shook her head.

"I think we should get him to come to the offices before we spring that on him," said Liza.

"You're going to let them suffer a little longer then," said Wendell.

"It's not suffering, it's sorting out whether they wish to be with one another no matter what they have to do," said Liza.

"Why are you testing them?" asked Wendell.

"I'm not testing them; they are testing one another. It has nothing to do with me. Hector may not want what we will offer him, he may be happy to enlist," smiled Liza.

"Hmmm," said Wendell. "I think I'll go and rest before dinner. Are you coming Amelia?"

"No, I think I'll stay a little while longer," said Amelia who was anxious to see what else would happen with Hector and Estelle.

Wendell left the room and Roberts appeared miraculously to make sure that he rested comfortably. Jamie made his way back to the sitting room and went to Liza. "Adam brought Estelle down to the library and left her with Hector. What did you say to her?"

"Nothing very dramatic; I just made her realise that she was giving up love for love," said Liza.

"That was very profound and now it is up to them," said Jamie.

Amelia was disappointed as they had to get ready for dinner and Hector and Estelle were still in the library. A place had been set for him at the table, but he was still in the library when dinner was served, and nobody was going to disturb them. They were still there when everyone withdrew to the sitting room and there were a few questioning looks around the room.

At ten o'clock the library door finally opened and Hector looked around wondering where everyone was; Estelle pointed him in the direction of the sitting room and was going to leave him to enter alone but he grabbed her hand and pulled her along with him.

The room went silent as they came in and all eyes looked at them expectantly. Hector was holding Estelle's hand and he started to speak but choked as tears started streaming down his face; he gulped and wiped his hand over his face but seemed unable to speak.

Jamie took over for him, "I gather that we are to congratulate you Hector and you too Estelle," and they both just nodded.

"I would suggest that you go and tell Adam and April your good news and then come back here with them when you feel better and we will raise a glass to you both," said Liza.

"Well, thank God for that," said Wendell when they had left. "I don't think I could go through another trauma like that one."

"What did you say to her to make her change her mind," asked Amelia.

"I think you know me better than that, Amelia," said Liza. "I said nothing that had not already been said."

Within half an hour Hector and Estelle were back together with Adam and April and champagne was brought in and everyone toasted Hector and Estelle's engagement.

"When will you marry?" asked Miranda.

"As soon as I can arrange it," said Hector. "I have to organise our future together, so we can plan it as a married couple."

"Oh good," said Amelia. "I can help to arrange another wedding. I helped Liza and Jamie arrange their wedding and Edward and Nicole as well as Joseph and Lily, so I have a great deal of experience."

"Thank you, Amelia, but Estelle and I will not be having a lavish wedding. We cannot afford that. We will just have a quiet one as soon as possible and hopefully before you leave New York," said Hector.

"Are you still planning an army career Hector?" asked Lucinda.

"I'm afraid Estelle will have to become an army wife, but she understands that we have to make our own way in the world and that is one way to do it," said Hector. "I must find the recruiting office tomorrow."

"You'll probably have to find a registrar first, so that you can arrange a marriage, unless you want to wait until you can have a church wedding," said Liza.

"Do you still have to wait three weeks for the bans to be read if you have a church wedding?" asked Hector.

"I have heard that there are some ceremonies that just take place on the spur of the moment. I'm not sure if they are really legal," said Jamie.

"If you can get someone to register your marriage, I can always marry you," said David and he laughed. "I do have the power to do that."

"I had forgotten that you could do that David," said Hector.

Liza butted in, "I think that this has been a very exciting day and I'm so pleased with the outcome, but I think that all the plans can be made tomorrow when we have all had a chance to rest, and especially Hector as he only arrived this morning. We can sort out the wedding tomorrow and also your army career."

"Yes, I'm feeling my age now," said Wendell. "Congratulations to you both and I'll see you all tomorrow."

Wendell looked towards Amelia and she reluctantly took the hint and they made their way to their room. David followed and Miranda and Lucinda congratulated them again and also went off to bed. Peter and Grace seemed to still have things to talk about. Adam was at last relaxing; he had been very much on edge since Hector had arrived but as always when he looked at April his frown turned to a smile. Hector and Estelle were in their own world and Jamie finally said that he would be making his way to bed and he looked forward to seeing them both the following morning.

"Don't go running off to the recruitment office without Jamie or Adam," said Liza, "and finding a registrar is more important, once you've done that you will know when you can marry. I'm sure you'll sleep well tonight Hector, and Estelle you will too."

"I think I'm too excited to sleep," said Estelle.

"I'm sure you are Estelle, but you have a great deal to do over the next few days," smiled Liza.

Hector kissed Estelle and she left for her room. He then turned to Liza and thanked her; she shrugged and said that she had done nothing.

"Yes you did, you told her some facts which made sense to her," said Hector.

"She made up her own mind and realised that everything she thought of was to save you pain, but you had sorted all that out yourself," said Liza.

"I still say thank you," said Hector and he put his arms around her and kissed her on the head. "You've always been very kind to me Liza and I know that I have imposed myself on you without notice on so many occasions. Goodnight my friend."

Peter and Grace were still talking, and Liza went to Adam and asked him if he was happy with the situation.

"Estelle is happy, so I am also. She looked after our mother for a number of years to the detriment of her own life and career. What Hector is doing is going to be a big shock to both their systems, but if they truly love one another then it will all work out. I know that he had an army career in England, I just wonder how he is going to adapt to how the army operates in America," and then Adam smiled and said, "that is if he ends up in the army."

534

"You've always been very astute Adam, but there's a great deal to think about first. Tomorrow, if you are with him, I'd like you to visit our offices before you go to any recruiting office. Jamie may be with you; you'll have to make up some excuse. I know, I'll leave something behind that you know that I need," said Liza and Adam nodded.

Zelma was smiling happily, "They are going to be alright. He loves her very much and she would have given him up for love. They have very strong feelings for one another, she reminds me of you." She left the room for her bed.

Kate said, "She's right you know; she does remind us of you." Gabriel nodded in agreement and they both said goodnight and also went to bed.

When they had left, Liza told April that she would be up shortly, and she turned to Peter and Grace.

Peter looked at her and said, "I know you and my father were discussing something earlier and you haven't had a chance to talk to me until now."

Grace said that she would leave, and Liza told her that she trusted her confidence.

"Directly I knew that Hector was saying that he was going to be permanently here with Estelle or without her, I thought that it was a God sent opportunity for him to work on our new project. I have seen the way he handled both Ffoulks House and Langston House and although I know that Daltons is a much larger undertaking, I have no doubt that he would be able to help with much of its organisation. Are you going to offer him such a position?" asked Peter.

"We must discuss it with Henry first because it will all be under his direction, but Henry has also seen what he is capable of. It was very useful that he and Myra visited us otherwise they would not have realised his worth. I did not want to say anything to Hector because I wanted him to think of how he was going to survive without asking for a handout from us, and he did think of it and I'm pleased that he had a plan, albeit one that really does not suit him, but it would have meant money and somewhere to live. I know that we can do better for him and in return he will help us enormously," said Liza.

"I'll go into the office early tomorrow, will you be with me then," asked Peter and Liza nodded and said that she would.

"Your father and I also discussed Brendan," said Liza.

"That I know, and I also feel that it would do him some good and you know he is very good as piecing together exactly the best way to fit places together.

He really should have studied architecture, in fact his father should have sent him to school, but he has now studied well and is doing very nicely. Yes, he would also be an asset in this new venture, and he is another one that we can trust," said Peter.

"You know that I said that the first place needed in Daltons was a schoolhouse, it will give Estelle something to get her teeth into," said Liza.

Peter smiled, "You are always so keen to make sure that all children have the advantage of a good education. You're right, Estelle would be ideal to undertake that. Where do you think they will be able to stay initially? There won't be enough room at the general store."

"By the time we are ready, the hotel will be vacated. There will be enough room for Hector, Estelle and Brendan and anyone else. It will have to be cleaned and beds brought in, but we have the wagons for that. It will be ideal until they can build their own accommodation," said Liza.

"You love planning for your business, don't you Liza?" said Grace.

"Yes, I'm really envious. I would like to be in the thick of it and see it gradually take shape and come to life, but I have other commitments and they occupy me just as much," said Liza. "I must get to bed now as we have an early start tomorrow. Goodnight to you both."

***

When Liza came down the following morning, Hector was already at the table with a huge plate of bacon and eggs in front of him. He looked up and smiled at her happily. "I'm starving," he said.

"Of course Hector, you didn't have anything to eat last night, no wonder you're starving," said Liza. "Estelle must be hungry also."

"I've seen her," said Hector "and she's already eaten."

Liza sat at the table and was served breakfast by Bridget. One by one the men arrived for breakfast apart from Wendell who was allowed the luxury of breakfast in his room with Amelia.

"Are you coming with me this morning Liza?" asked Peter, knowing full well that she was.

"Yes, but first I have to collect up all my paperwork as I need it with me today," smiled Liza.

Gabriel looked at her knowing that she was plotting something which was probably to do with Hector.

"What are your plans Hector?" asked Jamie.

"I'll hopefully find someone who will be able to register our marriage," said Hector. "And then I must find the recruitment office. Adam is coming with me."

"That will be interesting, perhaps I could join you," said Jamie.

Liza got up and left the table, firstly going up to see the boys, telling them that she would be back later today to watch them practicing their cricket, and then she went into her study and picked up her papers and saw Jamie in the library where she arranged to drop one of her documents down by his desk.

Jamie smiled up at her and said, "Very subtle Liza, don't worry Adam and I will lead Hector to your office."

Peter put his head around the door and asked if she was ready and she said goodbye to Jamie and climbed into the carriage which took them to the office where they discussed with Henry the possibility of Hector assisting with the Daltons project and to their bringing Brendan over also to help.

"You will be in overall charge Henry, and they will be directly answerable to you. I think you know that both are capable of taking on the responsibility of overseeing the workforce in Daltons and making sure that you are kept informed of everything that is happening on the ground," said Peter.

"I have seen how Hector organised both the Homes in England, and I think that he is quite capable of taking on a larger project. I think that he would be very good at taking on the responsibility. My only reservation is the fact that he is so very English, and his accent could make the workers not take him as seriously as they should. He was a soldier once, wasn't he?" said Henry.

"Yes, and he was in command of a great many men and in a war situation. He was in the Crimea and wounded, but not seriously. He left the army after that as I know that he found it a futile war and unnecessarily cost the lives of many young men," said Liza. "Major Styles lost his son in that war and I know that the Major has a great deal of respect for him and relied on him quite considerably. He is going to miss Hector."

"Is Hector showing much interest in what we are planning?" asked Henry.

"He doesn't know about it; he doesn't know that we are thinking about offering him employment, not that we would do that without discussing it with you first Henry," said Liza. "He thinks that he will have to enlist in the army so that he can keep a roof over the head of his soon to be wife. We haven't said anything to him."

"I gather from that that Estelle has finally agreed to marry him. I'm pleased; she will be very good for him. Isn't she a teacher?" asked Henry.

"That's right, which will be very useful in Daltons," said Liza.

"Jamie and Adam are bringing him to the office later today on the pretext of dropping off some documents that Liza left behind and that apparently Jamie knows that she needs," said Peter.

"I see," said Henry. "So we are going to see if he shows an interest in what we are doing before offering him employment. Don't worry Liza, I'll play my part. We've done it before, haven't we?"

"What do you think about Brendan?" Peter asked Henry.

"I think that he is very good at designing and he will be an asset when it comes to making the best use of the buildings. I've noticed that once or twice he seems to feel that he has more right than anyone to be with both companies, but he comes down to earth quite quickly," said Henry.

"That is something that I will have to have a serious talk to him about," said Liza. "He thinks of himself as family and that attitude comes over to the workers quite often. Strictly speaking he is no blood relative, although he does have a tentative link. He is Patrick's stepbrother's son and before a few years ago we had no idea that he existed. However his father, Michael, runs my operation in Italy with great efficiency and Brendan helped to get that organised. I think that Brendan is still feeling a little insecure and therefore tries to make out that he has some power in the company.

"I think that you may find that by bringing him over here he will have any illusions of grandeur knocked out of him very quickly, and it would be useful to have someone who has vision," said Henry.

"So we will offer Hector overseeing employment and talk to Brendan about his ability to make the best use of a building," said Liza. "I had better set the scene in our Board Room. I'll need our large map of Daltons and the smaller ones where we have marked where some buildings could be placed. A list of some of the costs of materials would also be useful."

Henry laughed, "Do you think that you will be able to reel him in Liza?"

"I think we will all be doing that," smiled Liza as she and Peter carried the documents they needed into the Board Room and left them. Liza went into Henry's office to wait for the expected visit and they didn't have long to wait.

Henry's assistant showed Jamie, Adam and Hector into the Board Room.

"I can't stay here too long Jamie," said Hector. "I've got a lot to do."

"Don't worry Hector. Your most important mission today is organising your wedding and you will have plenty of time to do that. If you don't get to the recruiting office today, then tomorrow will be just as good," said Jamie.

Adam was playing his part well by leaning over the table and looking at the documents.

"Is this the new project that is being undertaken? It looks rather large," said Adam.

"Yes, it's the largest that both companies have taken on so far. They're very lucky to have been given the opportunity, but it's going to take some organisation," said Jamie.

"How many factories are they planning?" asked Adam.

"I have no idea, but it will be quite a number. That's where they are planning to put them," said Jamie as he pointed to the area on the map and by this time Hector was taking an interest.

"What are they going to manufacture?" asked Hector.

"Many things but of course the government wanted Marchant & Fuller and Bradley & Company to take on this project and they are prepared to put money into it also," said Jamie.

"Really? What's happening in the town, I see there's a map of that with alterations and additions to it?" asked Hector.

"I know the first thing that Liza wants to build is a schoolhouse. The townsfolk have nobody to teach their children and you know what she thinks about education," said Jamie.

Peter rushed in saying that he was sorry to keep them as he knew that Hector had a very busy day and Jamie handed him Liza's documents saying that he had found them on the floor by his desk in the library where she must have dropped them.

"I'll call her; she's just in with Henry. In fact I know that Henry wants to congratulate you Hector," said Peter and he called Hector again as he had obviously not heard him as he was concentrating on one of the small maps which was showing alterations to the hotel in Daltons.

"I'm sorry Peter, yes thank you," said Hector really not knowing what he was thanking Peter for.

Liza and Henry came in and Peter handed her the documents that Jamie had brought with him. "Oh, thank you Jamie, I was looking for those, where were they?"

"On the floor by my desk in the library," smiled Jamie and Adam had to look away.

"The walls in this hotel are in the wrong places, who on earth built that?" said Hector. "The owners didn't know how to make the best use of the space that they had. They won't have made much money from their business running it that way."

"I don't think they made any money. People only stayed once and I believe they left scratching," said Liza. "Anyway it's my hotel now, but it will have to be cleansed before it's used. It will be fine once that's done and initially it can be used for our overseer before the workforce arrives."

"Will you be building a bank Peter?" asked Jamie.

"That will be essential as it is going to be a main trading area. Any bank will be as our others are and we have many plans to choose from as we won't be adapting a building, we will be building it from scratch," said Peter.

"I suppose the safest way to build it would be to dig out and make an underground vault, what's the ground like there? Is it clay or stone?" asked Hector.

"It's light clay and an underground vault can be concrete and steel lined, because if it's easy to dig out for us, it would be easy to dig out for robbers. But we have yet to get somebody there to see if it would be practical," said Henry.

"Whilst you are building the factories, are you also going to rebuild the town? What's in the town?" asked Hector.

"There's a general store, a carpenter, a sort of dressmaker and of course a hotel. There are several places where shops once were and a couple of run-down houses, but they are occupied," said Liza. "There's also a church, but no school."

"Are there many children?" asked Hector.

"Not yet," said Liza.

The men stood back and watched Liza 'reeling him in' as they had called it.

"But there will be when the factories are up and running," said Hector as he was standing and looking at the main map. "That seems to be quite a large river running by. That will be useful for the factories. Wait a minute; is that a rail track running by?" He looked up at Liza in awe. "If that's the case and it's running to New York then you're onto something enormous."

"The word about the railway will be common knowledge in a couple of months' time when the work starts on it," said Liza.

"But you know about it now. Is that legal?" asked Hector.

"Well, we were told by the government and the government are prepared to back us because they know that we will use their money wisely and create work for the people. We will of course make money for ourselves, but that is what business is all about," said Liza.

"You already have an overseer then," said Hector.

"Yes, we think so, but it's not definite yet," smiled Liza. "We've yet to make him an offer. He arrived from England unexpectedly and he's somebody that I have had experience of and we have worked well together. He's somebody that I trust implicitly."

Jamie, Henry, Adam and Peter were smiling, and Hector looked at Liza and said, "It's me, isn't it? How did you know I was coming over here?"

"I didn't Hector, but directly you arrived I knew that you were what we were looking for. I discussed it with Wendell whilst you were with Estelle yesterday and with Peter later. This morning Henry agreed that you would be ideal having seen what you did with Ffoulks House and Langston. This is a great deal bigger, but you will have adequate workers to help you in every way. We are also going to bring Brendan over to assist in whatever way necessary," said Liza.

Hector sat down and looked from one to the other. He opened and closed his mouth trying to formulate what to say until finally he said, "I don't know what to say."

"Do you want the challenge?" asked Liza.

"Do I want the challenge?" he repeated. "Oh Liza, of course I would love the challenge. Thank you so much. I think I'm going to make a fool of myself again." He sniffed and took out his handkerchief.

"Don't worry Hector; you're going through a very emotional time at the moment and you are amongst friends," said Liza.

Hector looked at Jamie and Adam. "You two knew what was being planned, didn't you? You manipulated it so that you brought me here."

"We had an idea of what was going to happen," smiled Adam. "I was asked to make sure that you came here this morning and a means to do it was being planned."

"I don't have to go to the recruiting office; that's a relief, but I was prepared to have that life you know," said Hector.

"Do you honestly think that Liza and I would have allowed you to enlist especially as we knew that it was not the life that you would have enjoyed?

We would have found you employment of some kind, but we were both very impressed that you were prepared to do that to provide a home for Estelle," said Jamie. "When we arrived here we had no idea that there was the opportunity of business in Daltons. Liza would say that such things happen for a reason, and much as you are not the only reason, it has worked out rather well."

"Estelle could run the school," said Hector thoughtfully.

"Why didn't I think of that," muttered Liza and Hector looked at her and smiled knowing that it was one thing that would have been uppermost in her mind.

"May I make a suggestion Hector," said Henry. "You have to organise your wedding, so it may be an idea to go now and get that arranged and then go and tell your good news to Estelle. Perhaps you could return tomorrow morning and we will get down to the business of detailing your employment and making some plans for the start of the project."

"Yes we must do that Hector," said Jamie. "We must find a registrar and see what date we can make for your wedding. We will all then know what we are doing and when."

Jamie and Adam then guided Hector out to the carriage and on his way out he seemed incapable of stopping thanking everyone.

When they had left Henry, Peter and Liza breathed a collective sigh of relief. "I think that went well," said Henry.

"I'm pleased that it dawned on him that we had him in mind for the project and I was even more delighted that he was passing helpful comments on the Daltons buildings," said Liza.

"Father will be pleased that it's been sorted out and I know that he realises just how trustworthy Hector is. He has some strange ways, but I think that working over here will soon curb those. I wonder how the workers will react to his name, I'm sure there will be some not very complimentary variations on it, but I think he will cope with it well," said Peter.

***

Jamie, Hector and Adam arrived home that afternoon to find Liza being run off her feet to the amusement of the boys as well as the adults who had followed the noise that was emanating from the garden. Gabriel was helping the boys bowl and Kate was attempting, rather unsuccessfully, to field. Zelma was watching and muttering that it seemed a rather stupid game that exhausted everyone, even those watching.

Every so often the boys would go into a huddle with Gabriel and Liza was sure that they were whispering tactics to make her run around until she felt that she would collapse. *How do they always manage that?* she thought, *I'm going to have to say I can't go on much longer.*

Jamie stood watching her for a little while and then he whispered something to James who nodded, and Liza was bowled out much to her relief. She smiled as she received a round of applause from all the spectators and Jamie gently led her away from the area that was being used as a pitch.

"How do they do that? They always do that to me, and I have no idea how they manage to keep me playing for so long," she said and then she stopped. "They could have bowled me out a long time ago, couldn't they; they just wanted me to exhaust myself just for their amusement. Now that I know, they won't be able to do that again," she said triumphantly.

"You think not Liza?" smiled Jamie. "I'm sure they'll come up with something."

"Has Hector made his wedding arrangements?" asked Liza.

"Yes, and we'll still be here for it," said Jamie. "I suppose it will be held here. I know he's going to ask you if you would mind."

"I wonder how Estelle has taken his news," commented Liza. "No doubt we'll find out later. I'm going to organise a bath before I become offensive to everyone."

Jamie smiled and gave her one of his lecherous looks and said, "I'll come and help you if I may."

"That would be nice; we seem to have had very little time to ourselves since we came here, but I suppose that's my fault as the business seems to have taken over this holiday," said a slightly dejected Liza.

"It has rather got in the way of a relaxing time, but it was always going to be busy with everyone being with us," said Jamie. "Neither of us knew about Daltons when we set out, and we certainly didn't know that Hector was going to descend on us out of the blue. Now we have a wedding to consider because no matter how much he and Estelle say that they don't want a big fuss, with the number of people in this household, we are not going to be able to keep it very small. Amelia will be in her element, and I'm sure April will want to make it memorable for Estelle. My mother and Lucinda won't be able to ignore the occasion, so it's going to be much bigger than expected."

As Liza was soaking in her bath and Jamie having enjoyed washing her, she said that they really had an awkward situation to address.

"I know what you are going to say, do we invite Estelle to dine with us as she is now engaged to Hector, and if we do then Adam and April should also join us," said Jamie. "As our boys' tutor Adam was always entitled to dine with us, but he chose either to eat alone or in the kitchen with the staff."

"I'll go to see Hector and Estelle and get them to dine with us and I'll also ask Adam and April, after all we are in America and that is why Hector has moved here; he believes that there is no class differential," said Liza. "I wonder how it will affect Freda and Roberts, and the other staff. It is a problem, isn't it?"

Hector had solved the problem for Liza and Jamie, he and Estelle had already eaten in the kitchen when the boys had gone down for their supper.

"I was hoping that you and Estelle would have joined us for dinner, and Adam and April," said Liza.

"Liza I am well aware that I have created an awkward situation and I am the only one who can remedy it," said Hector.

"Well, I hope that you and Estelle will at least join us in the sitting room after dinner. I know that Amelia is going to be very disappointed that she can't quiz Estelle on what is happening for your wedding. When is it going to be Hector?" asked Liza.

"It will be the week before you leave here and thank you for letting us hold the ceremony in your house. We don't need anything lavish," said Hector.

Liza looked at him and said, "Do you honestly think that Amelia, Miranda and Lucinda are going to let you get away with that; and I'm sure Kate, Zelma and Grace will also want a hand in it. I will try to curb their enthusiasm a little."

"And will you curb your enthusiasm Liza?" asked Hector.

"Probably not Hector," said Liza. "Just you wait until Myra hears that you are getting married, Amelia won't stand a chance. What we must remember is that it is yours and Estelle's special day, not any of ours and you both must have exactly what you want."

"I'm really looking forward to overseeing the Daltons project; thank you for thinking of me; you know that I won't let you down," said Hector.

"Are you going to be able to have a small honeymoon?" asked Liza.

"No, we really can't afford to go anywhere; our honeymoon will be when we get to Daltons. I know that we will have a lot of hard work there, but it will be so exciting. We'll make the hotel as comfortable as possible until we have our own home and I know that we will have to travel with the wagons with all the initial essentials, which is really just as pioneers do," said Hector. "I truly believed that I would have to be an army man and you know that I was prepared for that; I would do anything for Estelle."

"I know you would Hector," said Liza. "I'll arrange for a nice room to be made ready for you both when you are married."

The talk around the table that evening was about Hector and Estelle's wedding and Amelia, Miranda and Lucinda were pleased to hear that they would be joining them after dinner and when they did they had to answer so many questions that Liza could see that their heads were spinning.

"Amelia," said Liza. "I'm sure Estelle won't mind if you, Miranda and Lucinda help with the decoration of the room that the wedding will take place in. Hector doesn't need to be bothered with the details; he'll just be so happy to be able to turn up to a beautiful room made even more beautiful by his bride."

"You really are a romantic, aren't you Liza?" said Miranda.

"I always like a happy ending which is really a happy beginning in this case," said Liza.

Wendell called Hector over to him and they spent a great deal of time talking and Peter joined them for a while. Liza presumed that they were discussing business.

Liza and Jamie were discussing with Kate and Gabriel what had been planned for Simon and Zelma was listening in and looking sad at the prospect of losing him.

"Simon will be happy with us Zelma; you know how close Matthew and John were to him and now James has also become his close friend. They are four boys who will always care for one another; they will never allow one to be hurt without defending him. Once Simon gets over the initial sadness of leaving his mother and father and you Zelma and of course his sister, he will settle in with the others and be very happy and you know that I will love him as my own, I have done since he was three years old. I'm looking forward to having him back under my wing. He's becoming a very good-looking young man; I suppose he'll be shaving soon. He's very like you, Gabriel," said Liza.

"I will have little Liza to love and look after," said Zelma. "But I will miss Simon; and so will Rachel, they have been inseparable especially since Matthew and John had to leave. I know that she will spend time with me because she will know that you keep in touch with me."

"I hear that Simon wants to become a lawyer. That's a very nice compliment for you Gabriel. If he is still of the same mind when he finishes university, will he study law here or in England?" asked Liza.

"Much as I would like him to be back in this country, I believe that it would be better for him to study in England. He would only then have to read up on the few differences between the law in England and America," said Gabriel.

"Well you know that whilst in England his home will always be with us," said Liza.

"Thank you, Liza, I hoped that would be the case. It puts our minds very much at rest," said Kate.

"It would seem that Hector and Estelle's quiet wedding is becoming bigger by the minute," said Gabriel.

"Don't worry, I'll make sure that they have exactly what they want, but allowing Amelia, Miranda and Lucinda to decorate the room will do no harm and will keep them happy," said Liza.

Hector came over to Liza and said that he must make his way to bed now.

"Of course Hector, you've had a very busy day and we forget that you only arrived yesterday," said Liza.

"It's not that Liza," said Hector. "I must be up and ready for my first day at my new employment tomorrow."

"Yes, there's a great deal to organise. I've started making a list of the goods that will have to be transported to Daltons and they have nothing to do with starting the businesses there; they are to make it habitable for our initial workers. You and Estelle will have to organise what you will need; perhaps you will be too busy, so Estelle will have to do it," said Liza.

"I have very little money left for our needs," said Hector. "I must get her a wedding ring and that will leave virtually nothing. I'm afraid I spent most of my earnings on clothes for myself; I know I should have been more frugal and I have brought virtually none of them with me as I assumed that I would be in uniform most of the time. I am hoping that a bed in the hotel can be cleaned enough for us and there will be some furniture that we could use; gradually I will be able to get her all the things that she should have, but at the moment we will have to make do and mend."

"Having seen the state of the hotel, I have already had burned all the beds, mattresses, pillows and bed linen. I wrote to Mr and Mrs Grant and asked if they could arrange for somebody to clear out of the hotel everything that could have something nasty living in it. I presume that some wooden tables and chairs are left," said Liza.

"Oh," said Hector. "I'll have to think of something."

Liza was quiet for a while and then told Hector that she had completely changed most of the furniture in the house a few years ago. "I had spent some time here happily with Patrick and I needed to close the door on that part of my life. I think you will find enough to make things comfortable for you and Estelle until you can make your own choices. Bridget and Mary will help you to sort out all that you need. Don't be shy about taking as much as you need as it is just gathering dust in storage and will never be used by me again. Some of it dates back to James' time, so you may find it a little old fashioned."

"Just looking at you Liza I can see that there is still a small crack in that door, are you sure you want to get rid of the past?" asked Hector.

"You are much more astute than you like to appear Hector," said Liza. "Yes, take exactly what you want. I'll also arrange for Henry to give you an advance on your salary. You'd better go to your bed now; you have an early start tomorrow."

Hector looked closely at Liza and said, "Friends never have to say thank you."

Liza smiled and said that he was right.

***

The house was plunged into wedding mania and Estelle was looking more and more confused. Hector was busy during the day which left Estelle to deal with Amelia, Miranda and Lucinda who seemed to think that the wedding was for their benefit alone.

Estelle had been delighted that she could choose what she wished from Liza's stored furniture and she and April spent a great deal of time rummaging in the storage area. She and Hector had been allocated a large wagon for their furniture and a smaller one to sleep in on the journey to Daltons. Both would be drawn by oxen which were slower than horses but could pull more weight and there would be a great deal of weight to be carried by all the initial wagons going to Daltons.

Liza stopped Estelle one day and asked her what she would be wearing on her wedding day and she replied that the dress she had been given by Liza and she had altered for Lord Carlton's dinner would be ideal. Liza still had the dress that she had worn when she had married Patrick for the second time and she seriously thought about letting Estelle have it, but then she realised that she just could not do that.

"Come with me to the dressmakers Estelle, I know that she keeps several dresses in stock and there may be something that would suit you," said Liza.

"I can't afford anything like that," said Estelle.

"I think you can. It won't be very expensive as they are made to show the type of dresses that she can make, and they are to attract customers. There's no harm in having a look, it won't take us long. I have one or two things to do before lunch so we can go directly afterwards," said Liza and she collected her hat and cloak and ordered her carriage and she called cheerily to Estelle as she left saying that she would see her later.

She hastily made her way to the dressmakers and told the owner to say that each dress she showed to Miss Estelle Reece was only a small amount of money and that she would make up the difference later. Estelle was probably clever enough to realise what Liza was doing, but hopefully the clothes would be so pretty that it would make her accept the gift.

April was in the hallway as Liza arrived back from the dressmakers and Liza asked her what she would be wearing for Hector and Estelle's wedding. She was going to be the matron of honour and Liza felt that she should have something nice for the occasion.

"Go and choose something from my wardrobe April. You know what I shall be wearing, so find something else that suits you," said Liza.

Estelle appeared and she and Liza went on their way to the dressmakers where they looked at several outfits suitable for a bride and they chose a cream dress edged in burgundy and it had a matching long over jacket. A hat and shoes finished the outfit off beautifully. They decided against gloves as she would have to remove them for the ring to be put on her finger.

"I will pay you back Lady Edgeworth," said Estelle. "I promise you that."

"There is no need," said Liza.

"Oh yes there is. I will not feel happy accepting this, in fact I won't accept it unless you allow me to repay you," said Estelle. "You're already giving us a wonderful start to our lives together; I don't really want to start that life owing you even more."

"Alright, whenever you can, but don't pauper yourself in the attempt. Now you are to become Hector's wife I think that the formalities can be dispensed with, my name is Liza," said Liza.

Liza was spending her time between home and the office and she could see the wagons being prepared for their journey. Hector and Estelle had chosen their furniture well and it was already packed neatly in one of the wagons. Their second wagon had a comfortable mattress for them to sleep on whilst travelling, and they would have their clothes and personal possessions with them.

Another wagon had another bed and mattress plus items which should also make Brendan comfortable when he arrived. One wagon was loaded with non-perishable food items and the rest had tools, and enough wood to build a few one roomed sleeping places for the initial workers who were to clear the site, some of whom were riding along with the wagons.

Walter came up to her whilst she was standing and staring at the wagons. "Well Liza, you look deep in thought."

"I was remembering a time that I travelled in a wagon. Kate and I did it for fun, or so we thought, but we soon realised what a hard journey it must have been for the pioneers who were travelling for months," said Liza. "I understand that we will be seeing you in a few days' time."

"Yes, Hector has invited my wife and I to his wedding. I seem to notice that his upper crust accent is easing a little, which is just as well in this country," said Walter.

"I am so envious of them. They will be building a town that has all but been deserted. There are houses that can be renovated, schools to be built, businesses to be set up, men to be catered for and that is without concentrating on the factories which must be built and manned. I would love to be in the midst of all that," said Liza.

"I'm going on the first trip with them. I must decide what is needed for the security of the project," said Walter and Liza looked at him.

"You could delegate that, but you want to go don't you, just to join in the excitement," said Liza.

Walter smiled and nodded, and Liza sighed and wished she was going.

She went up to Henry's office and Peter and Hector were with him.

"Ah Liza," said Henry. "We have some friends of yours arriving in a day or so."

"Do we, who might they be?" smiled Liza knowing that she would like the answer but was still mystified.

"I sent word to Cole and Jack to take the wagon train to Daltons; they are the most reliable of our men. However, I know that they won't like being in

549

New York, especially Jack. You know how he hates cities, and this is one very big one."

"He'll mumble and grumble under his breath, but he has a heart of gold, although he would hate anyone to know that," smiled Liza. "When are the wagons leaving?"

"A couple of days after Hector and Estelle are married; so they will not be having a very long honeymoon," said Peter.

"The rest of our lives will be one long honeymoon," said Hector and they all stared at him and Liza thought how different he had become.

"Yes, I'm sure bumping along in an ox driven wagon will be most conducive to an easy life together," smiled Henry, "but there will be comfort at the end of it judging by what you have in your furniture wagon."

"Where will Cole and Jack stay whilst they are here," asked Liza.

"Under the stars Liza; where else?" said Henry.

"I don't suppose they would want to stay with me," said Liza and Henry just smiled. "It's some time since I've seen them." She was remembering how she had persuaded them to take Mark Kendal to safety when he was waiting for his Court Martial after killing Felicity and Lieutenant Crown.

She suddenly felt very sad and before she showed those feelings, she said that she would go home. If she thought that those in the room did not see how she was feeling, then she was sorely mistaken.

"I've finished here," said Peter, "I'll come with you." He ushered her out of the room and down into the carriage before she could object.

Peter sat with her and said nothing for a while. He then said, "What is it Liza? Is the past catching up with you?"

"Why that should be now, I don't know, but yes I had such an overpowering feeling of sadness that it is still difficult to brush aside. I want to be with Patrick so much that it hurts and I know that it's very unfair of me because I have a good life with Jamie and he is so good and loving and I do love him, but it's not the same. I push Patrick to the back of my mind and get on with all that I have to do, but every now and again this feeling of want is overwhelming. Something must trigger it and I suppose setting up Daltons and Cole and Jack arriving remind me of my life in Benson and meeting Patrick and falling so much in love with him that I would have given up my life for him and in the end he did that for me," said Liza.

"I can give you no advice Liza," said Peter. "I'm afraid that you are just going to have to work your way through this but you know that I am always your friend and brother and you are allowed to cry on my shoulder whenever you wish. I know that you will never show this side of you to Jamie as you think so much of him that you would never let him know that you have such unhappy feelings. It would upset and worry him and would probably make him realise that you are not as contented as you appear, and you would never want that for him. You do have a good life with him, and your boys are so happy that you are together it would be a shame to put doubts in Jamie's mind. I think you realise that you lost the love of your life but it is precisely that, Patrick is lost and cannot return and you will do what you always do and that is make everyone happy, no matter how you feel."

"Thank you, Peter, I know that I can always rely on you for wise words," said Liza.

"My words may be wise, but just because they are wise doesn't mean that you can't tell me exactly how you feel whenever you wish, and nobody will ever know what you tell me," said Peter. "You know that you mean very much to me, Liza. I have watched you go through so many traumas and still manage to make a life for yourself and your boys and now Jamie and nobody should ever have to experience what you have. You are very strong, Liza, and I have no doubt that you will carry on and hide your emotions from the outside world, but please you never need to hide them from me."

Liza was now softly crying, and she hoped that she would calm down before she reached home.

"Come on Liza, dry your eyes, we have a wedding to deal with and three ladies of a certain age to stop flapping about it," said Peter. "I know that you will manage to make them feel that it is all down to them when you have it all arranged without their help."

Liza smiled and mopped her eyes and Peter said that she looked fine and nobody would know that she had shed a tear, and by that time they had reached home and Liza took a deep breath and marched up the steps to be greeted by Lucinda saying that she didn't think that there would be enough flowers to decorate the room properly. Peter just smiled as Liza said that she wasn't to worry and that she would look into it for her.

*＊＊

It was the morning of the wedding and there was an atmosphere of great excitement in the house. Amelia, Miranda and Lucinda had excelled with the flower arrangements for the room. Liza had managed to find enough spring flowers to keep them happy and to make a bouquet for Estelle.

Both Estelle and Hector were very calm, unlike many others in the house, especially Amelia who seemed to be running around in circles with Miranda and Lucinda following her. April was busy helping Estelle dress before she changed into what she would be wearing for the ceremony.

Adam would be giving Estelle away, and Jamie was Hector's best man. David was dressed in his robes ready to perform the important ceremony. Stephen had excelled with the wedding cake and indeed all the food for the reception as it had really been arranged at short notice.

The chairs had been set out in the sitting room ready for the guests and everyone began to take their seats. Myra and Henry arrived followed shortly by Walter and his wife. The boys were quite excited but Liza wondered whether it was more to do with the food than the wedding; they had studied the cake with great interest and expressed the opinion that it was a shame that it would not be cut until after the rest of the food rather than before.

Hector and Jamie walked in and both looked well dressed and very handsome. Hector stood nervously at the front and Jamie could be heard to whisper that he wasn't to worry as she was going to turn up, much to the amusement of those nearby.

The boys were on duty at the door leading into the back of the room and it was up to them to open it when Estelle and Adam drew near, which they did. Hector turned and his smile was something to behold; all his efforts in gaining Estelle's hand in marriage had finally paid off and there she was walking towards him and smiling happily at him.

David performed the ceremony well and the Registrar carried out his duties and Hector grinned as he was handed his marriage certificate. There were congratulations all around and everyone then went through to the dining room for the wedding breakfast, and it was the boys' job to show the guests to their seats and that also included all members of the staff.

Jamie stood and called everyone to order. "I have known Hector for a number of years; from when he was a young lad who always tried to join in with the antics of his older brother, Anthony, who happened to be my best friend, much to our annoyance; through his army career and bringing him home from the war and the distressing impact that it had on him. Much to our delight he became a much needed and much-loved helper to the children in

552

the care of our Homes, although his method of teaching cricket to the older boys left a great deal to be desired."

"I am not going to make a long speech as I know that Hector has a few things that he wants to say, all I will say is that it was love at first sight when he saw Estelle and I can only admire his dedication in what he has gone through to win her hand and I am so pleased that he succeeded as I know that this is a match made in heaven. I wish them both well in their new life together and in the venture that they are about to embark upon. To Hector and Estelle," said Jamie as everyone raised their glasses.

Hector smiled happily, stood, and looked around at everyone. "This is definitely the happiest day of my life and that is because my beautiful Estelle is now my wife. There was a time when I never thought that she would agree to marry me, and I know that I annoyed everyone by constantly bemoaning the fact that she would not have me. I want to thank Jamie and Liza for always having the time and patience to listen to my woes, but my perseverance paid off and finally today is a day that I shall remember for the rest of my life."

"There are just a couple of regrets that I have and they are that my mother, brother and his family are not here with us and that the Major and Jennifer also could not be here today, but I do have those with me who I consider close family, in fact those who have acted towards me and cared for me as family should. However I can now say that I have true family with us in Adam and April who today became my brother and sister. I promise you Adam that I will love and care for Estelle always."

"Later this week we will be embarking on the biggest adventure of our lives. It will be a challenge but one that we are going to enjoy together; we are going to build a life in a new place and I know that I am excited about it and Estelle has assured me that she is also. I want to thank my new employers for the opportunity," said Hector smiling at Liza, the Fullers and Henry. "And I want to thank Liza for allowing us the use of her house for our wedding and organising our reception. Thank you, David, for performing the ceremony, Amelia, Miranda and Lucinda for making everything so beautiful and Jamie for being my best man and for supporting me throughout my life. Last but most certainly not least, I want to thank Estelle for agreeing to put up with me until death do us part."

Everyone clapped and when that died down a voice could be heard asking if the cake was going to be cut soon. Of course that voice was Matthew's.

553

The rest of the afternoon and evening went well and after little Liza had been put to bed and the boys had eaten their way through copious amounts of food, finally they were tired enough to leave the festivities. Wendell felt a little exhausted and went to his bed with Roberts making sure that he was settled. Amelia was still enjoying the evening, as were Miranda, Lucinda and David. Peter was in deep conversation with Grace as was usual for them. Adam and April were spending time with Hector and Estelle as it was obvious that Adam was feeling a little sad that it would be some time before he saw his sister again once she had left for Daltons. Jamie was relaxing with Myra, Henry, Walter and his wife. Liza was spending her time with Kate, Gabriel and Zelma as she did not know when she would have the opportunity to see them again. She was also catching up on some of the Benson gossip.

Finally the day was over and Myra, Henry, Walter and his wife left for their homes. Miranda and Lucinda made their way to bed and David soon followed. Jamie joined Liza and they discussed Simon's future with Gabriel. Liza looked up and could see that Hector wanted to leave but didn't quite know how to go without causing embarrassment to Estelle. Liza went across to Estelle and April and quietly asked if she had seen the room that she would be using for the next couple of days. She hadn't and so the three of them went to the bedroom and April helped Estelle out of her wedding dress and hung it up whilst Liza admired the nightdress that Estelle had chosen for her wedding night. Both April and Liza kissed her goodnight and left her to get ready for bed.

They both then quietly joined the others and Hector frowned wondering where Estelle was; he asked Liza and she quietly said to him, "where do you think she is Hector? She's waiting for you," she kissed him on the cheek and said goodnight. He quickly made his way out of the room and went to find Estelle. Everybody tried not to notice, and no comment was made.

Liza went back to Jamie, who was still with Gabriel, Kate and Zelma.

"Well Liza," said Kate, "today went well. I think Hector and Estelle appreciate what you have done for them. It's been a very enjoyable day."

"I certainly did not expect to have to organise a wedding whilst I was here," said Liza. "I also did not expect to take on a new business project and I hope that I can at last put my feet up and relax for the rest of my holiday."

"You know that you enjoy what you do," said Jamie. "You're always happy when you're busy."

"I really wanted to spend more time with my family and friends, which was why we originally came here," said Liza.

"If you are worried that you have neglected us, then don't. We have managed to see a great deal of you all and it's been quite exciting knowing about the new business venture," said Gabriel. "It's also been interesting to witness the traumas that Hector went through and come out the other side of. We would not have experienced all that if we were not here."

Finally Liza and Jamie made their way up to bed. April and Roberts had already gone to their beds, so they helped one another out of their clothes; a task that they both enjoyed.

"I wonder what Hector and Estelle are getting up to," said Jamie.

"They may not be getting up to anything," smiled Liza.

"I doubt that very much knowing how much they are in love," said Jamie. "But I do remember that I was almost incapable of doing anything with you the first time we went to bed together, and I loved you very much."

"Well it didn't take you long to get over that," smiled Liza.

"You're right, it didn't, did it?" said Jamie as he slid into bed and then climbed onto Liza telling her that he still loved her very much.

Chapter 26

Liza and April were organising the boys to take them to the ice cream parlour the next morning and they were surprised to see Estelle and Hector descending the stairs dressed for work.

"You're up early," said Liza. "You've obviously got plans for the day. We're taking the boys to the Ice cream parlour. Do you want to join us?"

"It's a lovely thought Liza, but we have to make sure that we are organised for our lives in Daltons and also to make sure that we have all that is needed on this trip for the work that has to be undertaken," said Hector.

"Do you know the type of food that you need to take on the trip?" Liza asked Estelle.

"Not yet but apparently the wagon master and guide are arriving today, and they will make sure that we have what is needed," said Estelle.

"They are very old friends of mine. I'll be down to see them later after lunch," said Liza.

"I understand that they need another two drivers for the wagons, otherwise the wagon master and guide will have to take over that job," said Hector.

"Jack is used to driving wagons. He took over my wagon all those years ago when Kate and I went to Senor Valdez's hacienda. Jack laughed at Kate and I as we tried to cook and he told us to get out of the way as we didn't know what we were doing," smiled Liza at the memory. "He was right; we had no idea what we were doing. I've seen him since and even in my own place he wouldn't let me near the stove."

Hector was looking at her closely and he could see that she was reliving a very happy memory and then it was gone, and a flicker of sadness replaced it. She then smiled again and said, "He calls me girlie," and she laughed at the thought.

Adam came running down the stairs having decided that he would like to sample another flavour of ice cream and Liza waved Hector and Estelle on their way. She was about to usher the boys out of the door when Gabriel, Kate and little Liza appeared and wanted to join them. Liza took another step forward and Jamie quickly joined them telling them to be quiet otherwise everyone else would want to go with them.

"You're going to have to get another carriage to take us all," said Liza. "I'll take Adam, April and the boys and you will all have to follow on in another one. I'm sure you can creep around to the stables without anyone knowing."

She rushed down the steps towards the carriage and seven of them squashed into it for the short journey to the city. Liza laughed as she watched the others creeping around to the stables trying not to make any noise; she wondered whether they would manage it.

Liza, Adam and April were sitting happily with the boys whilst waiting for their various ice creams when Jamie arrived with everyone else and Wendell had joined them. Liza was surprised that Miranda and Lucinda were not with them and was told that the call of the shops was too much for them and they were getting ready to go shopping with Zelma and Amelia and that David and Grace were going to keep them company and probably they would all take lunch somewhere in the city.

Jamie looked at his sons and Simon and they would have hated the fact that he thought that they looked and acted like the little boys that he had first known as they happily sampled their various ice creams, and then he looked at everyone else and realised that the smiles of contentment on all their faces were just like those of children. It didn't take much to make them all happy he thought as he then grinned and put a large spoonful of ice cream into his mouth.

He asked Liza what she would be doing that afternoon.

"Cole and Jack are arriving today, and I must go and see them. It's been a long while since we met up and I also want to see how everything is going with the wagons. I also want to make sure that Hector and Estelle have everything that they need," said Liza.

"Judging by what they were moving out of your storage rooms, I don't think that they will be wanting for much," said Adam. "They're very grateful for that and I am also. Estelle has a good start to her life now. I'm not sure if Daltons is going to be her permanent home, I suppose that is something that nobody really knows."

"It's going to be an ongoing project as the factories will always be needed, but if another project presents itself Hector might be needed to organise that.

All I can say is that Daltons will need Hector for a great many years to come," said Liza. "I'm sure that the children will also need Estelle, although if all goes according to plan she will probably need some help eventually."

"I'll see Cole and Jack sometime tomorrow. Will you tell them Liza? It's a great many years since I saw them," said Wendell.

"Yes, I'll tell them Wendell," said Liza and after she had finished her ice cream Jamie said that he would see the boys home safely, although there were enough people there to do that. He went outside with her and called a cab to take her to the docks.

"I know you're looking forward to seeing Cole and Jack aren't you Liza?" said Jamie as he helped her into the cab.

"Yes, it's been a long time since I saw them but I also want to ask Estelle what she would need for teaching the children, although I could do that when she gets back home," said Liza.

"I know you don't really want to do that because it would be taking up the preciously short time that Hector and Estelle would have alone this evening," said Jamie. "I'll see you later; you'll be coming home with Peter, won't you?"

"Don't worry Jamie, I'll make sure that I'm safe coming home," said Liza and she kissed him, and the cab moved off.

The cab pulled up outside the offices and as Liza was about to go in, she was called by somebody and she looked around, but could see nobody.

"Lady Edgeworth;" came the voice again urgently and Liza looked towards the sound.

"Who's that," said Liza cautiously; she was remembering the attack on her a few years ago, when Zelma and Walter had been hurt.

"It's Gareth Jones," he said.

Liza went towards him and said with some annoyance, "What on earth are you doing here? I would have thought the sensible thing for you to do would have been to go to some small town and disappear. You put me in a very awkward situation; the authorities thought that I had helped Theresa to escape and I had great difficulty in convincing them that I had nothing to do with it. I don't want to get involved with anything to do with you both."

Liza moved away towards the offices again and she then heard Theresa calling her. Walter was rushing towards her with a very concerned look on his face and he came between her and Gareth.

"Are you alright Liza? Are these people bothering you?" demanded Walter.

"Thank you, Walter. I'm sorry they just frightened me because of what happened before. I do know them and obviously moving to New York has done them no favours," said Liza who was shaking with annoyance rather than fear, but Walter didn't know that.

"What do you want me to do Liza?" asked Walter.

"Can you take them to your office please Walter and I'll be along shortly," said Liza and she turned to Gareth and Theresa and said that they were not to worry, she would be with them in a little while and she asked Walter to get them something to eat.

"Do you really know them Liza," whispered Walter.

"Yes, but I wish that I didn't. They are two people who should leave New York as soon as possible for their own safety and mine," said Liza.

"Do they need an identity change?" asked Walter.

"No they just need to disappear. I'm so annoyed that they have turned up here, but now that they have, I will have to sort them out," said Liza.

She turned to them and told them to go with Walter who will get them some food and she would sort something out for them in a short while. She smiled to reassure them and as she was about to leave she asked Gareth if he could drive a wagon.

"I've driven carriages, would a wagon be so different?" asked Gareth.

"These wagons are ox driven. I suppose you could learn that quite quickly if you are used to horses. Oxen are much slower, what do you think Walter?" asked Liza.

"I suppose so," said a not very convincing Walter and Liza smiled.

Liza left them and went into the offices where she found Cole and Jack in with Henry and Peter and she found herself lifted off her feet and swung around by a very exuberant Cole with Jack grinning at her.

"Hey girlie, you're looking well. I hear you have a posh title now, it won't make any difference to us," laughed Jack.

"I wouldn't expect it to Jack. How are you both?" she asked.

They discussed Daltons and the route to it, the number of wagons and what they were carrying. It then came to the drivers that were needed. Ten wagons were going, and they had drivers for eight of them. Liza piped up that she thought that Walter had just seen someone who could drive a wagon.

"I believe he's experienced in carriage driving and I know that this is different, but beggars can't be choosers," smiled Liza. "I think it's someone who wants work when they arrive and is quite happy to settle there with his wife, but that's up to you to decide Cole."

She looked at Cole and he realised that he had no choice but to take whoever this person and his wife were as it was something that Liza needed to happen. Cole thought that they must be people that it was better not to ask questions about and as long as they could pull their weight, he had no problem with that.

Liza made her way down the line of wagons with Cole and Jack and Hector appeared and was introduced to them. Then Liza was introduced to a man who was going to manage part of the restoration of Daltons. His name was Carl Fairburn and his wife was Gwen, they had four children, so the two boys in Daltons were going to have company and Estelle would be starting her teaching career there sooner than she had expected.

At last she could go to see Gareth and Theresa who were sitting quietly in Walter's office. They had eaten and freshened up and looked a great deal more relaxed. She told them that she had arranged that they drive one of the wagons and suggested that once at Daltons they put down roots there as there would be plenty of work for them both.

"It is a town that has been all but deserted but we are investing in it and bringing manufacturing to it, so not only do we need workers to build the town and factories, we will need factory workers once they are completed. Other businesses will be starting up so there could be opportunities there. It's up to you to stay there or go, the choice will be yours and I don't want to know what that choice will be," said Liza.

"Thank you, Lady Edgeworth," said Theresa. "We appreciate that you could have given us up to the authorities when you saw us in England."

"Are they the only clothes that you have?" asked Liza and they both nodded. Walter butted in and said that he could sort that out for them.

"They are going to need some bedding for the journey and when they arrive," said Liza and she handed Walter some money and asked him to arrange that for them and then give them any change so that they could get some food.

"They can come home with me tonight; my wife and mother will look after them and I'll make sure they have what they need for the journey," said Walter.

"That's very good of you Walter, after all you know nothing about them," said Liza.

"I know that they are in some kind of trouble and need help and I remember you taking a chance with me and my family when I was in trouble, so it's the least I can do for somebody else," said Walter.

"Thank you, Walter," said Liza and she then turned to Gareth and Theresa, "I wish you both well and hope that you can now have a happy and relaxed life. You may wish to change your names although I don't think that it is too much of a worry for you now. Cole and Jack will see you tomorrow and allocate your wagon to you, follow what they say because there is nothing that they don't know about travelling that way. Walter is going on the first trip to Daltons, so that is somebody that you already know. I will see you before you leave, and you will also see my husband who will be around tomorrow. I will tell him that you are here, but he may not acknowledge you and I think you appreciate that I will also keep my distance. It is not because I disapprove, but to be over friendly would not be wise for either of us. I think that you would both do well in Daltons, but there would be nothing to stop you from going even further if that is what you wish; you both now have the freedom to choose what you want. Good luck to you both."

Theresa was quietly crying, and Gareth didn't look much better, and they were trying to thank her, but Liza cut them off and smiled at them and left with Walter following her.

"Was it serious trouble that they were in?" he asked.

"It's best that you don't know, all I will say is that you will not be murdered in your beds. She has had a particularly bad time and Gareth has helped her to his own detriment. I hope they can close the door on their bad luck and have a decent future," said Liza.

"I'll look after them," said Walter as he walked her back to the offices.

Peter was waiting for her to take her home. "I don't know what you have been up to Liza, and I think that it's best if I don't ask."

Liza looked at him and wondered how he always managed to know that she was engaged in something not quite as it should be.

"It was just a little problem that is now sorted out," smiled Liza.

"Hmmm," said Peter.

"You're later than I expected," said Jamie when she had arrived home.

"Yes, I had an awkward situation that I had to sort out. I want to tell you about it when we have a quiet moment," said Liza.

Jamie knew that it was something that he was not going to like, but Liza wanted to see the boys and the rest of the family before he would have a chance to speak to her.

Jamie had taken the boys on a carriage ride around Central Park accompanied by Wendell. Adam and April had gone in another carriage with Gabriel, Kate and little Liza and when they had finished, they all went back for lunch which included Adam and April. Later they had entertained the boys with a short game of cricket, obviously watched by April and Kate.

At last Liza went to their bedroom to rest before dinner and Jamie bounded in with a questioning look on his face.

"What has happened Liza? I could see that you were annoyed," asked Jamie.

"I had to make a decision against my better judgement, and I would have preferred that you were with me, but you weren't, so I had to deal with it myself. Just as I was going into the offices Gareth Jones called me and when I realised who it was I told him that I really didn't want to be involved and tried to walk away, but Theresa then came forward and it was obvious that New York had not been kind to them. I told them that they were foolish not to have left and gone to a more obscure place, which was when Walter came rushing up thinking that I was about to be attacked," said Liza.

"Good heavens, they must have realised that by keeping quiet about seeing them in Southampton we had done all we could to help them. What did they want? Was it money?" asked Jamie.

"I didn't give them the chance to ask, I just wanted to be rid of them, but they were in a very poor state. Anyway, I have organised that Gareth drives one of the wagons to Daltons and obviously Theresa will be with him. Walter is looking after them until they leave, and I've told them that once they reach their destination, I don't want to know whether they are staying there or going elsewhere. I think they would be wise to stay as there will be work for them both, but at least they will be away from New York, because although it is a big place, the authorities are always on the lookout for criminals and they have not yet the intelligence to protect themselves. They would probably end up in prison for stealing to keep alive," said Liza.

"We probably should have reported them when we saw them in Southampton, but it's too late to think of that now," said Jamie. "I hope they don't become a problem in Daltons; however it may be the making of them. I don't think that they are a disruptive influence and with any luck they will make themselves useful and be able to create a good life."

"I'm glad you think that way Jamie. I really didn't want to be involved with any of this. I hope that this is all that we have to deal with on their behalf," said Liza. "Tomorrow we'll both have to just acknowledge them the same as we will have to for all the travellers."

"Are Hector and Estelle aware of who they are?" asked Jamie.

"No. As far as they are concerned, he is just a driver and Theresa is his wife," said Liza.

"So we will put it out of our minds and enjoy our dinner with all the family and friends," said Jamie. "I have asked Adam and April to join us tonight and tomorrow night as a favour to Hector and Estelle and they have agreed."

"That really pleases me. We'll have to keep April away from the wagons as she may remember Theresa and I don't want to put her in an awkward situation," said Liza.

"Well this has certainly been a mixed holiday. A marriage, a business and runaways; surely there can be nothing more," said Jamie.

Liza just looked at him thinking that he was tempting providence by saying that.

Hector and Estelle looked very happy and relaxed at dinner that evening, as did Adam and April and Liza thought how well April had blossomed in the last few years and even more so since her marriage to Adam. She was going to miss her when Adam became the headmaster of the school and they both moved to the village. Liza often felt that Adam could do better than teaching at the school, but he seemed quite content at the prospect.

Numerous questions were asked over dinner about the trip to Daltons and Hector seemed to know all the answers. Estelle was quite animated about what she would be doing but Liza noticed that Adam was looking quite sad which was natural as he would not see Estelle again for a long while.

"I hear that we found another driver today Liza," said Hector. "Do you know if he has much experience?"

"All I know is that he has driven in the past, and as I have said before, beggars can't be choosers. We just need one more now, but if not, Jack is quite capable of undertaking that job," said Liza.

"I'm glad today is over," said Liza when she and Jamie finally went to bed. "It started off so happily, and I was pleased to see Cole and Jack, but it has ended with a heavy weight on my mind."

"I am annoyed that Gareth and Theresa have put this pressure on us. I hope that they keep out of our way as much as possible. I'll be relieved when they leave," said Jamie.

That night Liza snuggled up closely to Jamie. She was feeling a little on edge and Jamie recognised that she needed comfort that night.

***

The next day was passing quickly. Liza and Jamie had taken the boys to see the wagons and to see Cole and Jack who Matthew and John remembered. Adam and April had been given the day off to spend with Estelle who had everything organised for her trip, so they went with her to a bookstore. Liza had told her that she could choose exactly what she needed, and the company would cover the cost and Adam was delighted to be able to help her. Liza already had a list of school items that were not immediately available, but she was arranging for them to be ordered and they would be forwarded on to Daltons as soon as they arrived in New York.

Everyone was feeling a mixture of excitement and sadness because Hector and Estelle were leaving them. The boys had become used to Hector's ways and they thought that Estelle was very nice. They had become part of everyone's lives for quite some time and they would be missed.

The afternoon before they were due to leave Hector came to find Liza and Jamie.

"Are you ready for your new life Hector?" asked Jamie.

"As the time has drawn near my confidence has waned a little," said Hector.

Jamie smiled at him and said, "Hector I know without a doubt that you will regain all your confidence. I know that you will be arranging and organising everything and everybody. You have plenty of helpers to rely upon and don't forget that Brendan will be with you in around a month's time and he's somebody who you can talk to openly. You also have the wife that you have wanted for so long, you are very lucky."

"I know that I am. I have a great deal to thank you both for. You came to rescue me from Portugal and you, Liza, spent an enormous amount of money to get me out of prison and back to England. You gave me employment and I shall miss all the children in your care but now I have an enormous challenge which I shall enjoy. Most of all you have helped me to make the woman that I love my wife, and I can never repay you for that," said Hector.

"We're just pleased that you and Estelle are now happy," said Liza.

"You will never know how much I appreciated being able to stay with you whenever I wished. You made me feel very much at home and I shall miss you both enormously," said Hector.

"We're going to miss you too Hector, but I do envy you the challenge that you have. I would love to help with building up the town. Also the journey there is going to be fun," said a wistful Liza.

"It's all going to be enjoyable," said Hector. "And I want to thank you both for everything that you have done for me. I know that you had to put up with a great deal."

"Hector, you've broken your own rule that friends never need to say thank you because it's known without saying it," smiled Liza.

"I tell you what I won't miss and that's your atrocious method of teaching the boys cricket; now they will learn how it should be done," smiled Jamie.

"You have to admit that the boys enjoyed it," Hector grinned.

Dinner that evening was bittersweet. Hector was unusually quiet, and Estelle was sitting closely to Adam. It was agreed without exception that they would both be missed, but there was excitement that they were going on such an 'adventure' as Lucinda called it.

Everyone decided that they would see the wagons off on their journey the next day. Wendell especially wanted to be there as it was the start of another arm of his business. Liza was concerned that April would be there, but she could not stop her as Estelle was her sister-in-law and Hector was now her brother-in-law. She sincerely hoped that Theresa would keep out of sight until they were well on their way.

"You look sad," said Jamie to Liza when they were in their room that night.

"I'm not sad really, I'm pleased for Hector and Estelle and everyone else setting out on this 'adventure' as Lucinda keeps calling it. In a way I would like to be with them, but I want to be with you and our family more. I shall be interested to see how Daltons progresses over time and know that we'll be back in a year or two. Perhaps there will be a decent hotel there by then, or maybe Hector and Estelle will have a house big enough for us to stay," said Liza. "It is going to be very strange not having him turning up on our doorstep whenever he felt like it. I got used to him being there."

"You'll hear about what is happening often; Henry will keep you informed regularly, as will Hector, although I don't suppose Hector will have a great deal of time to write, but somebody will, probably Estelle," said Jamie.

"It's going to be awkward that April is going to wave them off, but it is natural that she would want to. I do hope that Theresa keeps a very low profile. Nobody else knows her from the past; perhaps April won't recognise her," said Liza.

"You didn't recognise her at first, so she must have changed, and it wouldn't be surprising with the life that she had to lead," said Jamie.

"I knew that I had seen her before, but it took me a while to remember when and where. April lived with her for some time, so I think that the chances of her recognising Theresa are quite strong," said Liza.

"I should think that Theresa would assume that April could be with us and she would keep her head down until they are out of sight," said Jamie.

"I hope that this is the last time we will be faced with a situation like this. I find it unfair that we had to get involved through no fault of our own. If we hadn't walked through the inn in Southampton at exactly the time that Theresa and Gareth were there then we would never have become involved," said Liza.

"Well tomorrow we'll just have to wave goodbye to everyone and wish them all good luck on their journey," said Jamie.

Liza found it difficult to sleep that night and she was up and ready for the day early. Hector came into the dining room as Liza was finishing her breakfast. Liza smiled at him and complimented him on his attire. "You look like a very casual American Hector; it suits you."

"Well I will be living in these for some days so I can't guarantee the condition they will be in when we arrive in Daltons," smiled Hector.

"That's how they are worn over here; you've seen Cole and Jack haven't you," said Liza.

"Cole is quite clean and respectable, I'm not so sure about Jack," said Hector.

"I seem to remember that Jack has always been a stranger to soap and water," laughed Liza. "I really am going to miss you Hector and so are Jamie and the boys. Who are they going to have to teach them bad habits?"

Hector laughed, "I'm sure you'll find somebody to keep them amused. You'll be in New York again soon won't you?"

"It probably won't be for at another year or so. We have a great deal to do for a while. We will see Anthony and Diana as soon as we get back, and your mother of course. Have you a message for them?"

"I have written to them and I hoped that you would give them my letter," said Hector. "Perhaps one day Anthony will be able to visit me."

"I'm sure he will and he'll be so proud of the success that you are going to make of this project, and so will your mother," said Liza as Hector got up and said that he would see her later.

Everyone was bustling around getting ready for the day. The boys had already had their breakfast and were making their way back up to their room to dress. Jamie came into the dining room commenting that Liza must have got up very early. To their surprise Miranda and Lucinda appeared dressed and ready to go to where the wagons were.

"We won't be leaving here until around ten-thirty Mother," said Jamie.

"I know," said Miranda, "we wanted to see Estelle and Hector before they left; we'll wait in the sitting room for them to come down."

Peter rushed in and had a very quick breakfast and he was followed by David and Grace who were accompanying him to the offices, and they would make their way to where the wagons were waiting later.

Adam was going early with Hector and Estelle and April would be with Liza, Jamie and the boys. Wendell and Amelia were travelling with Miranda, Lucinda, Gabriel, Kate, little Liza and Zelma and they would be leaving at the same time as Liza and Jamie.

Everyone was organised, at least it appeared so and hopefully all would go according to plan.

The wagons were packed and ready in the open land adjacent to the railway track which already went part of the way to Daltons and was now being extended. The drivers were guiding their oxen and making them ready to pull the wagons. Gareth was handling them quite well and Walter was helping him with Jack and Cole giving instructions to all the drivers.

Finally they were all hitched correctly, and Cole and Jack were checking each one to make sure that they were ready. Those who were riding their horses with them were patiently waiting and chatting. All the family and friends were there talking to the various drivers and some wives.

The lead wagon was going to be driven by Jack and he had a new driver with him, who would take over from him in a short while. The second wagon was Hector and Estelle's smaller one and that was followed by their large one filled with furniture and had an experienced driver. Carl and Gwen Fairburn and their four children came next and Liza wondered where they would all be sleeping as their wagon was filled with furniture. Gareth and Theresa were next; their wagon was filled with tools and also had a mattress and blankets. Liza didn't know the rest of the drivers and one or two also had their wives with them.

Wendell and Amelia were going around each driver and the workers who were accompanying them and were shaking their hands and talking to the women. Amelia was spending time mostly with the women. It was a very exciting time and the boys were fascinated by the oxen. Cole came over and said that they were nearly ready to move off and said that he would see them all in a couple of weeks or so.

Jack climbed down from the lead wagon and found Liza. "Well girlie, this is going to be a big thing that you're involved with. I shall be glad to leave this city and get out in the open. I suppose you'll be going back to your posh home across the sea by the time we get back, so have a safe journey and I'll probably see you in another eight years."

"Has it really been that long Jack? Where have those years gone?" said a thoughtful Liza.

"Yes it has, and it's been even longer since I saw your friend Kate," he said as Kate was walking towards him. Suddenly Liza had to leave them to talk alone because she felt close to tears and as she turned there was Jamie next to her; he always seemed to know when she felt tearful and needed comfort. He put an arm around her shoulder, and they walked towards Hector's wagon where Adam was helping Estelle put her final trunk in place.

Jamie turned around and Liza noticed a strange look on his face. He was staring at Gareth's wagon and Liza followed his gaze only to see April talking to Theresa and it was obvious that this was not the first time that they had seen one another. Adam stepped down from the wagon and looked around for April; he frowned when he caught sight of her with Theresa and clearly he had no idea who she was.

"I believe we now know how Gareth and Theresa knew where to find you," said Jamie between his teeth.

"If that's the case then I am very disappointed in April," said Liza quietly. "She only had to talk to me, I'm not an ogre, she's been with me long enough to know that. I hope we're wrong, but I have a feeling that we're not. She knew what happened with that mad woman last time we were here; how did she know that Gareth wasn't dangerous, or Theresa for that matter."

"I think she must have known the background of why Theresa was here otherwise she would have been open with you about suddenly seeing in New

York someone that she knew years ago in Belfast rather than hiding that both from you, and it would appear, from Adam," said Jamie.

"Well we might as well go and wish Gareth and Theresa good luck on their journey and new life, but we will treat them just like we treat all the others that we don't know," said Liza. "I do wish them well; however I don't really want to see them again."

April had returned to where Adam was with Hector and Estelle and he was obviously asking her who she had been talking to and he didn't look happy. Adam was very astute and he realised that there was a problem with April's friend, but he was not going to let it interfere with his farewell to his sister and Hector, he would find out what it was all about later.

It was time for them to leave and Adam was kissing his sister and then helping her up into her seat beside Hector. A shout went up and Jack's wagon started to move slowly on its way. Liza waved to him and shouted goodbye and then it was Hector's turn to move off and all the ladies were crying, including Liza. Jamie shouted good luck to them, and they started trundling away. The next wagon was Hector's and Estelle's furniture and they waved at the driver.

The four boys were keeping up with Hector's wagon and shouting to him and Estelle, whilst Liza and Jamie were waving to Carl and Gwen Fairburn and their children and then it was Gareth and Theresa and both Liza and Jamie nodded to them and waved and wished them good luck, just as they were doing to all the drivers and passengers.

Walter was saying goodbye to his wife, mother and children and Liza could see that his cousin and his wife were also enjoying the day. He came over and told Liza and Jamie that he was going to enjoy the experience, although he really wasn't sure what his duties would be once they reached Daltons, but he was sure that he could find something useful to do.

Cole had been talking to Wendell and Henry and then he rode over to Liza and Jamie, "Well Liza I hope that we'll see you again soon. I'll make sure that everyone arrives safely and then both Jack and I will be back, and the wagons will be filled again and we'll take them back to Daltons. After that I don't know what we will be doing but I know that Jack doesn't like spending too much time in towns or cities and I feel the same. I see that your boys are enjoying the day. Goodbye to you both, I hope you have a safe journey back to England." He tipped his hat to them and rode off to make sure that all the wagons were moving as they should.

Henry would be going to Daltons with the second wagon train and if the timing was correct, Brendan would be with the third one.

The last wagon was now disappearing into the distance and Wendell decided that he would like to go back to the offices with Henry and Peter. Liza was also going to accompany them as they wanted to discuss how the day had gone and to finalise what machinery would be needed for the factories. The funds had already been allocated by the government and were sitting waiting to be used.

Jamie ushered the boys into a carriage with Zelma, Gabriel, Kate and little Liza. Gabriel was looking at him quizzically but said nothing in front of the children; he had seen that both Liza and Jamie had been looking concerned at one point.

April and Adam were with Miranda and Lucinda in another carriage. David and Grace decided that they would also travel back and there was room for them also. Miranda and Lucinda were chatting happily about the events of the day, but David noticed that Adam did not look too pleased, but he put it down to the fact that his sister had now left.

As he travelled home Jamie became more and more annoyed at the situation that they had been placed in and especially at April's part in it. He kept trying to believe that she really had done nothing and that today was the first that she had seen of Theresa. It was bad enough that Liza had been put in an embarrassing situation where she had to help an escaped criminal. The alternative would have been to report Theresa to the authorities and it would have been obvious that both he and Liza had known where she had travelled to, therefore they would have had difficulty convincing them that they had no knowledge of the original escape.

He was also beginning to seethe because what April had done was expose Liza to a possible attack as both Theresa and Gareth could have been thieves and killers. She could not possibly have known that they were harmless as she may have been aware that Theresa had escaped from a transportation ship which was full of robbers and murderers, she had no reason to believe that Theresa was not a murderer, or Gareth for that matter.

Throughout his life Jamie's staff members had never gossiped outside the household, they would never have jeopardised their positions by telling any outsider the whereabouts of their employers. It was a matter of loyalty and keeping a confidence was expected of them. He knew that the phrase that was used in Liza's original household in Belfast was 'what happens in the household, stays in the household' and none of them would ever have divulged any information about Liza and certainly not where she was going and when she would be alone.

Liza would have to deal with it when she returned home. It was just another delicate situation that was landing on Liza's shoulders. Just as he thought that, April was ushering the boys up to their room and Adam was following thoughtfully. Jamie was so annoyed that he felt that he had to speak to April to make sure that he was correct in his supposition.

"April," he called sternly, "I want to see you when you've finished."

Adam turned and seemed concerned by Jamie's abruptness and when he looked at April he realised there was fear in her eyes. This had to have something to do with the people April was talking to. The boys were looking concerned and Adam took them into their room and told them to wash their hands and faces and then go down to the kitchen as it was supper time.

He then took April's arm and guided her to their room. "What have you done April? I can see that Lord Edgeworth is not happy with you and I could also see that Lady Edgeworth was frowning when you were talking to those people on one of the wagons. Who are they April? You always told me that you would keep no secrets from me, and you also know that there is nothing that you can't tell me. So I'll ask again, what have you done?"

"It was nothing really, I just met someone I used to know in Ireland," said April.

"And you thought not to tell me," said Adam. "Because you kept it a secret from me, there must be something about them that you are ashamed of. How did Lord and Lady Edgeworth know them?"

"I told them where to find her; they wanted to talk to her alone because they needed her help," said April.

"You did what?" shouted Adam. "What do you know of these people? Were they trustworthy?"

"I knew Theresa from my previous life in Belfast and I know she got into some trouble recently," said April.

"And you told her where to find Lady Edgeworth. You should not have done that April. I presume you also knew the man," said Adam.

"No, I'd never met him before. I don't know who he was," said April.

"He could have been a murderer or a rapist, and you told them where to find Her Ladyship when she was alone and vulnerable. No wonder His Lordship looks furious," said Adam. "I can't say that I understand how and why these people are now on their way to Daltons; all I do know is that both Lord and Lady Edgeworth were not pleased that they were there, and they certainly were not pleased that you were talking to them."

"What am I going to do Adam?" asked April. "I'm frightened. Lord Edgeworth wants to see me now and he's probably going to sack me. What's going to happen to you? I didn't think about it clearly. I'm so sorry, I put somebody else before us and that was very wrong."

Adam looked at her but not unkindly and said, "If you are sacked then we will manage April. I can always get work, but it would be a shame to have to give up my position just a year before the boys go to Cambridge. I'll go with you to see him."

"He hasn't asked for you Adam. I'll go alone. He may not be as annoyed as we think," said a tearful April.

"I'll walk down with you," said Adam gently and he took her hand and they walked down the stairs together and knocked on the library door. Jamie barked "Come in" and a very nervous April entered and closed the door behind her.

Jamie was standing and looking out of the window and he slowly turned and stared at April.

"First of all April, will you tell me whether or not you told those people where to find my wife the other day?" he asked.

"I'm sorry Sir, yes I did," said April quietly.

"Well at least you're honest. How long have you been with my wife April, is it six or seven years, and she relies on you completely. Our boys have grown up with you and they love you. We have never doubted your loyalty to us, until now," said Jamie.

"I've always been loyal Sir," said a very distressed April.

"Do you remember what happened last time we were here? Do you remember somebody attempting to stab my wife, and Zelma and Walter Anderson were hurt?"

April nodded.

"We assumed that Theresa and Gareth found Her Ladyship just by chance the other day; we did not think for one minute that anyone within our household would tell such people where she would be so that they could accost her for their own benefit. The characters of these two people are unknown to us and their past history is cause for concern. My wife was alone and had no idea whether they were there to harm her; even you did not really

572

know that they did not want to take revenge on a supposed wrong that had been done them. She could have been hurt, or worse she could have been killed by them and that would have been down to you entirely. We are fortunate that it was not the case," said Jamie.

By now April was crying quietly.

"We are both sorely disappointed in you April. I have calmed down somewhat, and I now think that it was just a case of thoughtlessness on your part and a desire to help others less fortunate than yourself. However to tell others of our movements was a gross betrayal of trust and I hope that it will never happen again."

"It won't I promise you. I am so sorry Sir. Adam is also very annoyed at me. He had no idea that I had met Theresa and that I had told her that she would probably get some help from Her Ladyship, he told me how foolish I had been and he believes that I will lose my position within this household, and therefore he will also have to lose his position," said a very tearful April.

"No doubt Her Ladyship will have something to say to you when she returns. She will probably be surprised that I have spoken to you, but it is a subject that affects us both," said Jamie. "I do not believe that she will sack you April, but the choice will be hers. You had better go now as Adam will probably be waiting for you."

She left the room and Jamie could see that Adam was outside waiting for her. *This will be the first test of their marriage,* Jamie thought. It wasn't long before there was a knock on the door, and it was Adam to see him.

"You know that both April and I have been very happy within your household and I want to spare you any embarrassment by tendering my resignation, and April's, rather than you having to sack us. We are both aware that no details of what you are doing or your whereabouts should be divulged outside the household and I know that we have breached that confidence, therefore it is better that we leave but I do assume that you will allow us to continue until we return to England," said Adam.

Jamie gave a wry smile, "That's very noble of you Adam; I really do not think that either Her Ladyship or I were contemplating dispensing with either April's or your services and I would like you to wait and see Her Ladyship before you take such a drastic decision; unless, of course, you really want to leave us."

"I think you really know the answer to that Sir," said Adam. "April is convinced that she has caused us both to lose our positions and I'm not sure that she's wrong."

"Well, let's just see what Her Ladyship has to say; she will be back shortly. I believe that April has learned a serious lesson and I do also believe that she did not think clearly about what she was doing. I have calmed down quite considerably, but where my wife's safety is concerned, I am naturally cautious," said Jamie.

"I understand what you are saying Sir and you are right that it was foolishness on April's part, and you know how sorry she is and how sad she would be to leave you and especially the boys, as would I," said Adam.

"You have a good marriage with April and today that has been proved. As I said, let's wait for Her Ladyship to return and I have no doubt that she will be displeased with what has happened, but whether she feels that it is an offence that warrants sacking, I do not think it is likely. April was originally employed by her, so it is her decision to make," said Jamie.

Adam left and Jamie could hear the boys making their way down to the kitchen, but without the usual chatter emanating from them. In fact there was quite a sombre mood throughout the house and that was what Liza walked into a little while later. She frowned and decided to find Jamie as something was obviously wrong.

She found him in the library. "What's happened Jamie? The house is very quiet. I can't hear the boys at their supper and the sitting room door is closed tightly. Is it to do with April?" she asked.

"I'm afraid it is Liza. I have had a word with April and unfortunately, she did tell Theresa and Gareth how they could find you when you were alone, and she admitted that she had no idea whether they were dangerous or not. That side of what she did had not occurred to her," said Jamie.

Liza wanted to tell him that she felt that it was a situation that she would have preferred to handle, but Jamie had spoken to April and she knew that he had done it out of concern and she was not going to criticise him. So all she said was, "Oh."

"Adam came to see me when I had finished with April and offered his and April's resignation, which I have not accepted as I asked him to wait until you had spoken to them, although I did not think that you would deem it an offence that warranted sacking," said Jamie.

"No, we all make mistakes, and I believe that this is the first one that April has ever made in the time that she has been with us," said Liza.

"She compromised your safety and that had to be made clear to her. I don't think that she thought about the fact that Theresa was an escaped convict,

574

and I don't believe that she knew that, so it is something that I did not mention," said Jamie.

The boys could be heard going back up to their room. Liza smiled at Jamie and thanked him for looking after her she then called out to the boys and followed them up the stairs and saw them into their room.

"Is April in trouble?" asked Matthew and all the boys looked up at her expectantly.

"Not really, she just made a small mistake and it will all be forgotten soon. There is nothing for you to worry about," said Liza.

"Is Mr Reece going to leave us?" asked Matthew.

"Not to my knowledge," said Liza. "I'm just going to get changed and I'll see you later."

Liza went out and knocked on April and Adam's door and called out that she needed April's help to change. She walked along to her room and left the door open and waited. A very tearful April appeared in the doorway.

"Come in April. I need some water for a bath, and I need you to help me choose what to wear tonight. Can you organise the water for me please?" asked Liza much to April's surprise. She ran down the stairs and gave instruction for hot water to be brought up to the room and then returned.

The maids brought up the water and filled the bath while Liza started to undress and when the maids had left, she lowered herself into the bath with a loud sigh. April was in the bedroom looking in the wardrobe and making suggestions over what she should wear that evening and when it was decided, she pulled out the dress and underclothes ready for when Liza had finished soaking in the bath. Liza stepped out of it and dried herself and then donned her underclothes and dressing gown with April's help.

Sitting at her dressing table with April combing her hair Liza started talking.

"I knew who Theresa was, April; I knew from when I visited her in prison in Belfast and I decided not to tell you of what had happened to her as I felt it would upset you. I pleaded with the judge for her life as she was due to be executed and the judge saw my point of view," said Liza.

April was looking shocked and then asked if Theresa was one of the people who had burned down the Home.

"She didn't hold the torch, but she knew that it was going to happen and did nothing about it. I didn't feel that execution was just, but that was up to the courts and the courts felt differently to me. However at the last moment her sentence was commuted to transportation for life," said Liza.

"I knew that she had been in trouble, but I had no idea how serious it was. I thought that she must have been stealing and had to leave Belfast quickly," said April.

"I think that you appreciate that what I am telling you is in confidence. Of course there should be no secrets between husband and wife, but I have always relied on Adam's discretion," said Liza. "When she was moved to the transportation ship in London, His Lordship and I visited her and gave her some clothes and money to help her; we also gave her some books and paper and writing implements so that she could practice and be a useful member of the Tasmanian society."

April was now sitting on the bed and listening intently.

"That is the last that we thought we would see of her. We did hope that we would receive a letter or two from her to let us know how she was surviving. When we went to Southampton to meet Mr and Mrs Mahoney, I was surprised to see a young man in the hotel where we were staying. The last time I had seen him was when he had been serving tea and biscuits to us and the captain of the transport ship. The look of fear on his face made me suspicious and then I caught sight of Theresa looking around also in fear. I put my hands up and just said that I didn't want to know anything, and I went up to our suite where His Lordship was waiting. He also had seen them," said Liza.

"You didn't tell the authorities then," said April.

"We should have done, but we didn't. We decided not to get involved because if caught, it is doubtful that she would have been returned to the transport ship, she would probably be in court again with the original sentence of execution being imposed and that I would not want on my conscience. I always bore in mind that if I had chosen Theresa instead of you all those years ago, her life could have been so different. I never thought that she was a bad person, I just thought that she had not had the opportunities that others had and that she had no alternative when she was dragged back into the life of abuse," said Liza.

"So you are saying that she could have been me," said April.

"That is exactly what I am saying," said Liza. "I saw the pair again the next day and they were waiting to board the ship to New York, and I chose to ignore them and hoped that I would never see them again. As you may remember an inspector and his sergeant visited us twice accusing us of helping to break Theresa out of the prison ship, and in all honesty we could say that we had no idea how she broke out of the ship; we had no idea where she was being held on board. I was asked about the fact that I had spoken to Gareth and I said that I had spoken to many people that day as there were many who I knew by sight because of the company. Luckily that eventually satisfied them."

"You helped them get away," said April.

"I pretended that I had never seen them and hoped that I would never see them again," said Liza. "I was very frightened when I was confronted by an escaped convicted felon and her partner, who I knew nothing about apart from the fact that he had helped her escape and was therefore also a felon. I assumed that it was a chance meeting and they were just hopeful that I would turn up there at some time. What I had not contemplated was that a member of my staff had told them where I would be and when without considering that these people could be dangerous. You know what happened last time I was here, that should have given you enough of a warning."

"Why did you help them go to Daltons? I don't understand that," said April.

"It was a means to get rid of them and stop them getting into more trouble by stealing or worse. I certainly didn't want them to be arrested and shout about where they had come from and who they had seen and helped them in a small way. They had no work and nowhere to live and that makes for trouble. His Lordship agreed with my decision because I have no secrets from him. We both believe that if they have work, they could become good citizens of this country, but we have been wrong about people before," said Liza.

April was quiet and thoughtful.

"I do not believe that they are dangerous, but that day I had no idea of their intentions and I was indeed frightened that they were going to hurt me; luckily Walter turned up and stepped between them and me and I was very relieved to see him. You could have come to me and asked for help for Theresa, but I suppose you thought that I would do nothing. If you had asked, I would have been given the opportunity to make a decision without being placed in a position where I had very little choice," said Liza.

"I did not know that she had escaped from prison. I'm so sorry that I could have put you in danger," said April. "I am so very, very sorry."

"Well April, you know my secrets about Theresa and Gareth; are you going to tell everyone about them? Or are you going to carry on as you always have done until now and keep quiet about what happens in this household and the people within it?" asked Liza.

"I did have second thoughts about telling them, but it was too late. I thought about telling Adam what I had done but knew that he would be annoyed and probably feel that you should know. I heard nothing about them and presumed that you had not seen them and it was only today when I saw them on the wagon that I realised that you had helped them and I was so pleased for them. When Adam asked me who they were and I told him how they must have got to go to Daltons, he was horrified and pointed out the dangerous position I had put you in," said April.

"This has been a very upsetting day for you April, so I would suggest that when we have finished here you go and spend the rest of the evening with Adam. I won't need you later; I can manage. Get a good night's sleep and let's start afresh tomorrow," said Liza.

"Adam has tendered his resignation to His Lordship and so have I," said April.

"You and Adam will be leaving us to take up the position at the village school in around a year's time and none of us are looking forward to that day. I would be very sad if you both left before that time and so would the boys. You have both looked after them so well over the years and I know that you would protect them with your lives. His Lordship and I respect you both very much and the boys love you unconditionally. If you really want to leave us then there is nothing that I can do about that, but we all would prefer that you didn't. We are all human and we all make mistakes, luckily this one had no lasting effects," said Liza.

April was crying and Liza put her arm around her, which made her cry even harder.

"Come on April, dry your eyes and go and poke your head around the boys' door because they know that something is wrong and that it involves you. Will you reassure them that all is well, but first I suppose you should see Adam and you both must make the decision whether to stay or to go? I hope it will be for you both to stay."

"I'll help you into your dress first," said April. "It will give me a chance to calm down. You are very kind; there are not many mistresses who would understand that mistakes can happen."

"His Lordship also understands that, but he is always concerned for my safety. There have been several life-threatening occasions in the past and he wants to protect me as much as he can from any further dangerous situations," said Liza.

They left the room together and April went to her room where Adam was waiting and Liza went into the boys' room and they were sitting quietly reading, or attempting to.

"Is everything alright?" asked Matthew.

"Yes, it's fine. Just a misunderstanding and it's all sorted out now so there's no need to worry. April will be in later to see you. Did you enjoy your supper?" asked Liza.

"It was very nice," said James, "but everyone was quiet and on edge. Is April alright?"

"She'll be in to see you in a little while," said Liza and she went around each boy and looked at what they had been reading and discussed it with them. Finally she left them and went down to see Jamie who was just about to get changed for dinner and briefly told him what had happened with April and hoped that he approved and that he could persuade Adam not to leave them.

"I'll go and see him before I change and hope that he will be happy to stay with us and the boys," said Jamie. "I don't think April will dare open her mouth to anyone ever again."

Liza went into the sitting room and was assailed by many asking whether everything was alright, to which she answered that everything was perfectly alright and that it had just been a misunderstanding that was all cleared up now.

Wendell and Peter both looked sceptically at Liza, both realising that the problem had been to do with the couple that April had been talking to as the wagons had left that day. Amelia also had a suspicion that it was the case and she would ask Liza about it at some other time.

Jamie knocked on Adam's door and it was opened by April and Jamie smiled at her and asked to speak to Adam. She said that she had to go to the boys so she would leave them to talk.

"April has probably told you that we would be most unhappy if you both were to leave us now. You have both been part of our family for a long time and life would not be the same without you, so please I am asking you to reconsider your decision to leave. Not only would Liza and I miss you both considerably, but the boys would suffer immensely if you were not there to continue with their lessons and I know that there have been times when you have put them before yourself," said Jamie.

"April did not realise who she was befriending, and she will be very cautious in the future, especially if she meets somebody from her past. I believe that she has learned how to have a kind heart from Lady Liza, therefore she did not think clearly about what she was saying to who she thought of as a friend. It won't happen again," said Adam.

Jamie laughed, "So what you are saying is that it was really my wife's fault."

Adam laughed also. "Yes, well her kind heart does rub off on others. I would like to withdraw my resignation and that of April and get back to how everything was before. You can rest assured that we are both as loyal as we ever were, April just did not realise the implications of what she had done."

Jamie carried on to the bedroom where Roberts was waiting for him, having already sorted out the clothes he would be wearing for dinner that evening.

Meanwhile April had gone in to see the boys and by the time she had helped them get ready for bed, they were all smiling happily, as was she. It was a crisis that had now passed and although she would always remember it, she felt that she could get back to where she was before. She had nearly cost Adam the job that he loved, and she had also thought that she would have to move away from this family that she adored.

***

The household settled down after the exodus of the wagons to Daltons. Marchant & Fuller and Bradley & Company each took on assistants answerable only to Henry when handling all business concerning the Daltons project. Also another foreman was employed to oversee the goods essential for the building of the factories and workers housing. The machinery for the factories was on order but it would be some months before it was needed.

With everything well in hand for Daltons, Liza was spending much of her time with Gabriel, Kate and Zelma. She was going to miss them, and she was envious of their life in Benson, but it would never be the same for her and she now had a good life with Jamie that was different but nonetheless happy. Gabriel and Kate had decided that they did not want to wave Simon off on his journey to England from the dockside; they were going to leave for their home two days before the Edgeworths were to take the 'Amelia' back to Southampton. Liza had written many letters to the people in Benson for Kate to take with her and it was noticed that Simon had spent a great deal of time writing to Rachel.

Zelma spent most of her time with the boys and the remainder she spent with Liza. They talked of old times, which unfortunately brought memories back to Liza which she had thought were well and truly buried in the past. There was, however, a great deal of laughter because of their memories. Apparently Bandor was spending much time with Zelma and Liza assumed that he relaxed when with her as he really felt that he neither was in the white man's world nor in the Cherokee world and Zelma accepted him for who he was, as did many in Benson.

Wendell and Amelia spent many hours talking to Kate and later they admitted to Liza that Kate was no longer the young woman that they had known in Belfast. She was still a dear friend, but she had changed in many of her thoughts. Liza told them that it was understandable, but they must appreciate that she had been to hell and back for many years, however it was wonderful that she and Gabriel had found one another and little Liza was the icing on the cake, although Simon was much loved by them both.

"Yes," said Wendell, "you can't expect her to be the same Kate that we knew and spent time with over seventeen years ago. Her life is so different, but we are pleased that she is now happy. I can see that she is going to miss Simon and that shows that she became his mother and he thinks of her as such. I know you will look after him; you've done it before, and I can also see that he thinks a great deal of you Liza. He's going to enjoy living with Matthew and John again and he also gets on well with James. They are going to be a force to be reckoned with. When Nicholas and Richard come to stay you are certainly going to have your hands full until they all go to university."

"I know," said Liza. "I'm used to children, but Jamie only had James when we first met and now he will have four boys under his wing and another two when Bella leaves her two with us."

"You only had Matthew when you first came back to Belfast; your responsibility for children has also increased over the years," said Amelia.

Liza acknowledged what Amelia was saying, "I did look after Simon for some years before I had to leave Benson and I did also teach at the school, so I was well used to the way children thought and acted."

There was a great deal of speculation as to how Hector and Estelle were getting on and many were envious of the adventure that they had embarked upon. Liza had Hector's letters to his family safely in her keeping.

Several trips to the ice cream parlour took place as did many cricket practices. Adam and April had settled back into life with the family and nobody mentioned the misunderstanding that had taken place, although Amelia would have loved to have known what it had all been about.

Finally the day came when Gabriel, Kate, Zelma and little Liza were to leave. All the boys were quiet. James was the only one who had not lived with Gabriel and Zelma. Simon was trying not to show that he felt like crying, or indeed when he was alone he was crying. Kate and Zelma were also crying and behind Gabriel's stern exterior was a sadness that he had not experienced since the death of his first wife and Patrick's death six years before.

"We will look after him as if he was our own, Gabriel," said Jamie. "All the boys are good friends and that will help him settle with us and you know that Liza already loves him. The trip on the 'Amelia' will take his mind off leaving you; it will be exciting for him as he has not travelled across the sea before. I hope that you will be able to find the time to visit us."

Jamie went with them to the station and smiled as they said that they were not looking forward to the meat stews when they took the stage on to Benson. He saw them into their seats and said that one day they would be able to do the complete trip on the train. They all knew that Liza did not like farewells, she had said goodbye that morning in the privacy of her home and then waved to them from the front steps, quickly disappearing inside to find Simon.

The boys were sitting together in their room and all were looking miserable. April was trying to cheer them up by suggesting some of the games that she knew that they liked.

"I suppose a trip to the ice cream parlour is out of the question," said Liza.

"We could do that, it would be nice," said John. "We haven't been there for over a week. Would you like to do that Simon?"

"If you like," said Simon.

"That's a good idea, it will take your mind off things," said Matthew.

April and Liza made sure they were ready, and Liza wondered whether Adam wanted to join them which he did. Wendell was behind his newspaper, but Amelia said that she needed to go out. Miranda and Lucinda were going shopping again. Grace was dealing with some of Liza's correspondence and David said that he would join Wendell in the library as he knew that several newspapers had been delivered.

A very sad contingent arrived at the ice cream parlour, but the boys soon cheered up at the sight of their ice creams being made for them. April and Adam had returned to their normal happy selves and chatted to the boys about their various flavour choices. Simon was beginning to relax but he wanted to sit next to Liza, he naturally thought of her as the next best thing to his mother and father. Jamie turned up having been informed of their whereabouts and he nodded to Liza intimating that all had gone well at the station. He would tell her the details later. He stood trying to make up his mind which ice cream to choose; finally it was a strawberry one that he decided upon. Amelia was amusing the boys by trying to hide that she had managed to drop some of her ice cream onto the table, but she was pleased that it had missed the front of her dress.

Adam and April said that they would take the boys to the park, so Jamie, Liza and Amelia drove home together to organise finalising their packing. Roberts and Freda had most of Amelia's and Jamie's trunks packed. Liza wanted to sort some of the dresses that she would need to wear on board the 'Amelia'.

The house seemed very quiet without the boys and Liza felt very unhappy that Gabriel, Kate, Zelma and little Liza would not be returning. She sat on the bed and stared into space thinking of all the times she had enjoyed her friends in Benson; she could see the main street and imagined herself waving to Kathy and Joe in the general store, Charlie Penn and his wife from next door; Caroline's dress shop, the Bank and on to her printing works; Jake and his sheriff's office and out of the town and along the road to the fort to see the Colonel and the Captain, with Ben at his desk in the office and on to see Ada and Bea. She had to stop those thoughts because otherwise she would see Patrick taking the parade, and she had to shut that out of her mind.

Jamie came into the bedroom whilst Liza was still staring into space and he recognised the look of deep sorrow on her face; he hadn't seen that look in a long while and he hesitated before finally moving towards her and touching her on the shoulder. She jumped and looked up at him in surprise saying that she hadn't heard him come in.

"You were in deep thought and you looked very sad Liza," he said.

"I'll get over it Jamie. I'm just sad that Gabriel, Kate and Zelma have gone, and I don't know when I will see them again. I enjoyed their company although I don't think that I spent enough time with them," said Liza.

"I believe that they don't see it that way. We only spent a couple of days away from them and I know that you had to spend some time at the offices, but you would have done that anyway. They enjoyed seeing the wagons go on their way, in fact I believe they enjoyed every minute of their trip. The only sad part was their leaving Simon behind, but they know that he will be well looked after," said Jamie.

The next day the 'Amelia' came into port and Jamie and Liza took the boys to see the ship. Simon was fascinated as he had only seen sailing ships before, and he was looking forward to travelling on this steamship. They also took the boys to see Henry and Peter in the offices and then went back home for lunch with the family. Although the boys always enjoyed eating in the kitchen, they liked being with the adults on occasion and they were allowed to join in the conversations as long as they did not shout.

Everyone was packed and nearly ready for their departure the following day. Wendell and Liza were going to the offices that afternoon just to make sure that everything was signed and sealed for the Daltons project. Myra and Henry would be dining with them that evening and Myra would be bringing certain documents regarding the charity for Liza to sign.

The conversation around the dining table ranged from Daltons, to the functions that they had attended. Also they wondered if the weather would hold for their trip back to England. The prospect of war with the South was touched upon, but everyone felt that it would be such a foolish move that once again it was talk rather than action. Finally Myra and Henry left for home saying that would see them off on their trip the next day and they all then slowly made their way to their rooms. The boys were still awake; they were obviously excited about the start of the voyage the following day. Jamie looked in on them and wished them goodnight, and Liza went in and smoothed each head and kissed each one saying that she would make sure that they were up early ready for their trip. Simon smiled up at her and she realised that he was remembering that it was something that she did to him when she was living in Benson.

"I think I shall now be pleased to get home," said Liza when she was in with Jamie.

"I'm pleased that you think of it as home Liza," said Jamie. "I suppose the cricket matches have started, that's something to look forward to. I wonder if Simon knows how to play."

"I think he will soon learn; he's very tall for his age and I believe he's quite fast on his feet, so he will make for a good cricketer," said Liza.

"I wonder if he's as fast as John; if he is Derek might choose him to take his runs," said Jamie.

"He might, but I think that Derek and John have made themselves a permanent team," said Liza and she yawned and moved close to Jamie.

"I thought how sad you looked yesterday. It's a long time since you seemed so sad. I suppose it was because Gabriel and Kate had left," said Jamie.

"Yes, and it brought back some memories of my early days in Benson when I was setting up my home and Danny was there. Kathy and Joe were so good to me, as were the Colonel, Ada and Bea. Edward had arrived in time for Christmas that first year. Angus and Ben also were with us for Christmas lunch. Of course Edward had fallen for Felicity by then and he couldn't wait to leave and go for tea with the Colonel and Ada," said Liza reminiscing.

"Edward and Felicity became a disaster. It's a wonder you didn't realise what she was like, I wouldn't have expected Edward to because anyone in love just doesn't see a problem, but I would have thought that you could see through her exterior," said Jamie.

"I really didn't see her very much before she and Edward married, but once she had I was under no illusions that she disliked me, but you know all that," said Liza.

"I remember that you told me that she had said that she knew that you would not be welcome at home in Belfast, and you believed her, which I find hard to believe," said Jamie.

"Jamie, I was alone and pregnant and the society in Benson was much more relaxed than the society in Belfast. I know that Edward was shocked when he saw that I was expecting and it was suggested that I visit when Matthew could be left behind as he would be an embarrassment," said Liza.

"Oh Liza, you must have felt so sad. Felicity really was an evil woman. When you think about the fact that she had an illegitimate child it is difficult to understand how she could think that you would not be accepted. But no matter what you thought others may think, you made your way to Belfast with Matthew and you were welcomed with open arms. It must have been a great shock to you to find that your home had been taken over by Edward and Felicity," said Jamie.

"Well, it's a long time ago and poor Felicity is hopefully at peace now. She was not mentally stable, although there were times when she appeared quite sane. It was all very sad and now it's wonderful to see Edward so happy with Nicole and little Edward," said Liza. "I want to just think about us getting home. I've enjoyed my time here, but I want to get back to normality now. New York is lovely but it is a little surreal."

Chapter 27

Copious tears were shed by Bridget the next day, along with unintelligible words, as they prepared to leave for their journey. Mary was helping April organise the boys and Liza was making sure that all the staff were happy in their employment so that there would be no problems whilst she was not there.

Adam was being particularly caring of Simon and was making sure that he had everything that he needed and finally the time had come for them to leave the house and make their way to the docks where Henry and Myra would be waiting for them. Liza was sad that she would not be able to say farewell to Walter, but his cousin would be there to make sure they were all safe.

Myra was mopping up her tears as was Amelia; Miranda and Lucinda were sad to say goodbye but were looking forward to getting back to their own home, as were David and Grace. Peter was finishing paperwork in the offices and Liza joined him just to make sure that she was not needed for any last-minute decisions.

"I think that we have covered everything whilst we were here," said Peter. "You go on off and I'll join you presently. I can see that you are torn between staying in America and returning home, although I believe that New York is not where you would choose to be, but life moves on, doesn't it Liza?"

"It does and I'm not sure that it's wise for me to return to America too soon; I seem to have been dwelling on the past too much on this trip and that is not good," said Liza and she left the office and joined everyone on the dockside.

Their trunks and cases were being taken on board and April, Roberts and Freda were directing where they were to be placed. The captain and the first mate were coming down to greet the passengers and Wendell was pleased to see that it seemed to be a full passenger list. All the cargo had been safely loaded the previous day. The captain immediately went to Wendell and Amelia and grinned welcoming them to the 'Amelia' and the standard joke about two beautiful Amelia's being at the dockside. Wendell said something to him, and he turned and smiled at Liza and moved towards her.

"Mr Fuller thought that I had forgotten you, but how could I do that. You were just out of sight for a moment," he said as he kissed her hand and Liza smiled at him thinking not only was his charm unnecessary, it probably was as false as his smile, but she took it well and let him believe that she had not realised it. Jamie also smiled and Liza assumed that he was thinking the same as she was.

The captain and the first mate began to guide their party on board with Myra and Henry following. The boys went to their cabin, anxious to show Simon where they would be, and this seemed to brighten him up as he had been a little anxious. April and Adam followed them to make sure they were happy.

They all found their cabins and April, Roberts and Freda had done a wonderful job sorting which cases and trunks went in which cabin and it then just left time for them to say goodbye to Myra and Henry. With kisses all round they left the ship and stood on the quayside for a short while and then Myra climbed into her carriage and was gone. Henry stayed a little longer talking to Walter's cousin and then he gave them a final wave and went back to his office.

Within the hour they cast off and slowly the tugs pulled them out into the main stretch of sea. They picked up speed and were on their way to England. Liza and Jamie and the boys were watching the New York skyline disappear. David and Grace joined them and commented that they had enjoyed their stay but were now looking forward to the journey home and finally arriving at their house. Wendell and Amelia were resting, as were Miranda and Lucinda.

They dined most evenings with either the captain or the first mate. The other passengers realised that they were the owners of the shipping line and at first they treated them with caution, but within a few days it was realised that they were just as human as the other passengers. Liza did find it strange that there were other passengers on board as she had been used to just her family sleeping in the two cabins available and often the captain and first mate had to relinquish their cabins.

One day they were sitting on deck when Wendell came to join them. "I miss reading a newspaper. That's the only downside to this voyage. I made my two papers last until this morning. Amelia has some books, but I don't think they are my type of reading."

"It's always good to talk to you Wendell, we will find something interesting to discuss," said Jamie.

"I'm sure we will," said Wendell. "We managed to carry out a great deal in New York considering we had no idea that we would be offered a project such as Daltons, as well as sorting out the love life of Hector and Estelle. It worked rather well that we needed somebody to live there and manage what we have in mind. It's good that we managed to get enough people to drive the wagons; I believe that one of them was more luck than judgement, yes it certainly was not judgement."

Jamie and Liza stared at him and waited for him to continue.

"If a court case comes up that I am interested in I make a point of attending such a hearing," said Wendell.

Both Liza and Jamie closed their eyes knowing that he had something else to say.

"How did she get away? Did you both help her?" asked Wendell. "If you did it was a very foolhardy thing to do, and I think you know that she deserved punishment for what she did."

"No Wendell," said Jamie. "We had nothing to do with her escape, although the authorities thought otherwise at one time. But I can assure you that we knew nothing of her disappearance from the transportation ship."

"So how did she end up on one of the wagons going to Daltons?" asked Wendell.

"When we went to meet Myra and Henry at Southampton, we saw her there with the man who was the transport captain's assistant," said Liza. "We chose to say nothing as we did not wish to be involved and also if she was dragged back she would quite possibly have her transportation sentence changed back to execution and neither of us would want that on our consciences, so we ignored them."

"April obviously recognised her, and I know you were both very annoyed at her and she and Adam felt that they should resign over it," said Wendell.

"April knew nothing of her sentence or crime, nor did she know that she had escaped from the transportation ship, but she did know that the woman had avoided the law. What she did do was tell her where she could find Liza alone to ask her for help and that was a serious breach of confidence," said Jamie.

"Good heavens," said Wendell, "Surely April knew what happened last time you were in New York. You could have had your throat slit. No wonder you were so annoyed at her, and I realised that Adam was too."

"Walter came to the rescue, but I admit I was frightened by suddenly being accosted by someone who I knew was a felon. As it turned out they were no danger to me, they had nothing, no work, and no place to stay. If they had been left like that they could have fallen into all sorts of evil, and who knows what they would have admitted to the authorities," said Liza.

"Why would that bother you?" asked Wendell.

"Because they knew that we had seen them at Southampton; in fact we received a thank you note from her which we were unhappy about and we destroyed it," said Jamie.

"So, you needed drivers and people to work in Daltons and you arranged a job for them to get them out of your hair," said Wendell. "I trust they are not going to be harmful to anyone. Does Hector know who they are?"

"No, I may be wrong, but I have a feeling that they are going to become exemplary workers and citizens, taking advantage of the opportunity to put their lives in order. April came from the same house as Theresa and she put her life on track; she was given the opportunity and she grasped it with both hands; I believe that Theresa and Gareth will also. I'm sure Walter will set them on the right road," said Liza.

"Walter knows their background then?" asked Wendell.

"I have no idea what Walter knows. If they told him then that was their choice, all he knew was that they needed help, and you must admit that we needed a driver," said Liza. "We had hoped that Southampton was the last that we would have seen of them and we thought that the sensible thing that they could have done would have been to leave New York and go to some obscure town where they could forget their pasts and make a good life for themselves, but obviously they did not have enough money to move, nor did Gareth have a job. Anyway, it's over now and I hope they make the most of Daltons. I have suggested that they move from there when they have accrued enough money to set themselves up somewhere else. America is a big country, and it is full of people trying to hide from their pasts."

Wendell was thoughtful for some time. "Well, I hope you are right and that they don't upset anyone in Daltons. Walter will probably make sure they stay on the straight and narrow."

"Yes, he will do that alright," said Liza smiling.

Wendell's eyes narrowed as realisation swept over him, "Ah," he said. "Walter is one of your protégés. How did you come across him?"

"Walter has been a good and loyal employee for many years, and he doesn't need his past raked up, if indeed he has a past to rake up. He has kept our company and its properties and goods secure making it more profitable than it was before his time. Nobody needs to know what he did before, and you know that he would not jeopardise his position by taking anything. Do not forget that he was stabbed because of me, that is what loyalty is all about," said Liza slightly annoyed at the questioning.

"There's no need to get peeved with me Liza; I do have an interest in the company, and I do have a right to know if there is something that could cause us difficulties. Just because I had a slight stroke does not mean that I can't be informed of such decisions. Did you tell Peter that you were placing known criminals on our payroll, or Henry?" said Wendell.

"No I didn't Wendell," said Liza, "and with all due respect you know as well as I do that our payroll is probably already full of criminals, it's just that we don't know about it. That's the only difference," said Liza.

"I take your point Liza, but if there was any chance that there could be a problem, then at least Henry should have been told," said Wendell.

"Walter is aware, and I think that is sufficient and I can assure you that there will be no trouble," said Liza. "They need the work too much to create any difficulties. You've never questioned my judgement before Wendell."

"No, I haven't, and I shouldn't have started now. I'm sure you're right and these people will turn out to be exceptional workers and citizens. You have dealt with people before who have been just this side of the law, but I knew that the girl was a criminal and I also knew that she should not be where she was and should have been well on her way to Tasmania, so I think I had the right to question your judgement," said Wendell.

"As far as staff is concerned in America, Henry has the last word and he interviewed and employed all the wagon drivers. Two drivers were needed at that time and he offered one of the positions to Gareth and I really think that we should finish this conversation now as it is just going around in circles," said Liza. "But you are right, next time I get put in an awkward position; I will let you know."

"If we had not ignored seeing Theresa and Gareth in Southampton and instead reported them to the authorities, we would not have had all these difficulties and you and Wendell would not have been crossing swords," said Jamie. "But we both made that decision mainly to save someone from the gallows; we did not dream that it would come back on us both in England and

America. I don't like to hear you two speak to one another like this and I'm sure you don't either."

"You would be surprised at the number of times that Liza and I have argued. Sometimes I persuade her to my way of thinking but mostly I believe that she persuades me; there are, however, times when we have agreed to differ and perhaps this is one of them," said Wendell.

Liza smiled and nodded her agreement and that was the last time that the subject was mentioned by Wendell.

***

The rest of the voyage was uneventful but nonetheless enjoyable. There were only a couple of days when the sea was choppy, and several passengers took to their cabins, but all the Edgeworth passengers did not succumb to sea sickness. Adam and Liza made sure that the boys were well occupied, and they also were able to join in some of the deck games that had been organised.

The boys were enjoying every minute of the trip and especially Simon as it was all new to him. He was finding it very exciting and that was helping him to not miss his family quite so much. They were not the only boys on the trip and they teamed up with two boys from Wessex and it made for a more interesting journey for all of them.

It seemed no time at all that Southampton came into view and unfortunately that meant that they would part company with Wendell, Amelia and Peter as they would be staying on board until the 'Amelia' reached Belfast. They were going to spend a while on dry land before the onward journey, so they all made their way to the hotel and enjoyed their last few hours together. Liza always found it difficult to say goodbye to Wendell and Amelia. Jamie and Liza went to the dockside to see them safely back onto the 'Amelia' and Grace was with them to wave Peter off also. It seemed hard to believe that the weeks had gone so quickly but they had achieved a great deal in that time.

Finally the ship left port and Jamie, Liza and Grace made their way back to the hotel and found the boys having their supper, being well supervised by April. Simon said that he was looking forward to reaching what was now going to be his home. His American accent was quite pronounced but it certainly was not unpleasant, and Liza noticed that both Matthew and John had slightly slipped back into their American accents.

Their three carriages arrived later that evening ready to take them back to Surrey early the next morning.

"Are you looking forward to getting home Liza?" asked Jamie. "I know that I am."

"It will be good to settle back into a more normal life," said Liza. "I suppose Bella will turn up at the weekend. I'm going to miss the fact that Hector will not be turning up without notice; he became part of the family. I wonder how he and Estelle are getting on; they have a great deal of work ahead of them."

"I know they'll manage and enjoy doing so. I suppose we will have to replace him and Estelle also," said Jamie.

"We're lucky that Jennifer is capable of filling in until we can find Estelle's replacement. With Hector we are not going to find it so easy," said Liza.

Jamie smiled, "We're back talking about English problems rather than American ones."

"I think that when we go to America again, we'll go south and visit Charles," said Liza.

"Everyone's talking about war with the south, I wonder whether it would be wise to go there," said Jamie.

"They have been talking about cessation for so long now that everyone will be surprised if it happens, but obviously we wouldn't go if there was any chance of war," said Liza. "We've only just got back so I don't want to go away for a long time. I would like to see Charles' plantation though and meet again some of the people that I have come across before. It would be very interesting."

"I'm sure Charles would love you to visit him. I'm not so sure that he would want me to be with you," said Jamie with a smile.

"He's like that with most ladies; it's his southern charm," laughed Liza.

"If you say so Liza," said a not very convinced Jamie.

They were all up early the next morning and managed to reach their home by evening. Mrs Frances had the house organised for their return and Matthew, John and James couldn't wait to take Simon up to their room and they could be heard telling him that they had always made sure that there was a bed for him both at Edgeworth House and also at their house in Belfast.

Mrs Price had moved her family back into their home in the village and Mrs Frances said that she had made sure that they had enough furniture to make them comfortable. She also informed both Liza and Jamie that the work on their house was really well done. Liza said that she would visit them the next day and no doubt the boys would want to join her.

Bernard was still with them as his vicarage was under construction and he was continuing to hold services in the cricket pavilion, and it would take some weeks for him to be able to move back.

Miranda and Lucinda as well as David and Grace would be dining with them shortly while their trunks and cases had been left at their houses. Nobody was going to change for dinner, but first the boys went down for their supper with Simon wondering where he was heading.

All the adults congregated in the drawing room and Bernard was anxious to hear about their time in New York and was interested that a new venture had been undertaken.

"I see that Hector is not with you," he said and smiled when told that he and Estelle had married and that he was now employed to totally oversee the project at Daltons.

Before dinner Liza couldn't resist visiting the boys in their beds and all four looked very comfortable and she went around and kissed and made sure that each one was covered and when she came to Simon's bed she kissed him and he put his arms around her neck and said, "goodnight mummy Liza."

She smiled at him and the years fell away, and she saw Simon as the tiny boy that she loved dearly. "Goodnight Simon, God Bless and welcome home."

Jamie followed her into their room and chatted to them for a short while telling them that it was nice to see the fourth bed with Simon comfortably in it.

Dinner was a little subdued as all but Bernard was very tired after their long journey and Jamie apologised to him for making his first dinner with them so quiet.

"It's very unusual for this household to be so silent, but I understand," smiled Bernard.

"Tomorrow we'll see how the church and vicarage are progressing," said Jamie "and I know that Liza wants to visit Mrs Price and the family. I'm sure that the boys will want to go also."

"She's very happy with her house. The builders have done a really good job and the decorators finished it just ten days ago. Mrs Frances made sure that she had everything that she needed. I know that she told her that all the furniture had been discarded and was due to be thrown away, as well as the furnishings, but I know that was stretching the truth. But Mrs Price has her pride and she needed to be told that," said Bernard.

"Nearly everything had been destroyed and replacements were beyond her current means. She has worked so hard all her life under very difficult circumstances; it's about time she was given a helping hand," said Jamie.

Liza smiled at him as it had not been in his nature to comment in such a way even if he thought it. It was nice that he was beginning to voice such opinions.

"I'll come with you tomorrow; I would like to see Mrs Price's house and also how the work is progressing on the church," said Jamie.

"Of course," said Liza. "The boys are looking forward to seeing Derek and introducing Simon to him. It might be quite noisy tomorrow."

"I'm sure it will be," smiled Jamie.

Immediately after dinner Miranda and Lucinda along with David and Grace went to their homes and Bernard went to his room leaving Jamie and Liza to make their way to their rooms. April was waiting for her and she could hear Roberts in with Jamie and when they had left Liza quietly made her way to Jamie's room.

"I do enjoy sharing a room with you Liza and our room in New York has all the luxuries that we could wish for, but to be back here and have you come into me at night excites me just as much as it did the first time we were together," said Jamie.

"I'm very comfortable here Jamie; I've always loved being in your room and in your bed," said Liza as she settled down next to him.

***

Mrs Price was at home when they called the next day and Derek and Susan wanted to hear all about the trip to New York once they were introduced to Simon. The house had been well repaired, and the family were very happy and comfortable in their home. Derek was now walking with the aid of just one walking stick.

The boys stayed with Derek and Susan whilst Liza and Jamie visited Mr and Mrs Rogers at the Inn where they caught up with what had happened in the village whilst they were away. When they collected the boys, they made their way home and stopped at the church to see how the work was progressing and it was obvious that Bernard would be with them for some time to come, but it was all taking shape nicely.

When they arrived home Grace was in Liza's study going through all the correspondence that had arrived whilst they were away and had set aside the letters that only Liza could deal with, which took the rest of the day.

Their plan was to visit Anthony the following day and they would also call on the Major and Jennifer and see what was needed now that both Hector and Estelle were no longer with them. They decided to call on Anthony first as they felt it was important for them to know what had happened to Hector as soon as possible and they expected it to be a happy meeting as Hector had told them how even his mother had wished him well.

The boys would have liked to accompany them but Liza felt that much of the time would be devoted to discussing business with the Major, so she arranged a picnic for them as it was a beautiful day and Adam and April were going to enjoy the time with them. Miranda and Lucinda may join them and so may David and Grace, although they were still settling back into their homes. No doubt some form of ball game would be organised for them.

Liza and Jamie left soon after breakfast, making sure that they had Hector's letters with them. They arrived at Anthony's home mid-morning and were greeted warmly by the family, especially little Thomas who was now talking quite well but still asked for 'Maffew'.

"I'll send somebody for mother as I'm sure she would like to see you and hear all the news," said Anthony. "I see you have some letters."

"Yes, one for you and one for your mother," said Jamie, "And of course for the Major. We'll visit him after we have finished here."

"I see," smiled Anthony as he took the letter. "Excuse me while I read my letter, I'm sure Thomas will keep you occupied whilst I read what Hector has to say."

"Of course," said Jamie and Anthony was right, Thomas did amuse them by showing them his toys whilst Diana stood next to Anthony reading the pages as he had finished them.

Rose rushed in and welcomed them back to England and said that she hoped that their trip had been successful, to which they replied that it had. Refreshments were brought in and Liza handed Hector's letter to his mother.

"Did he persuade her to marry him?" asked Rose abruptly.

"Well, the persuasion was indeed considerable, but she finally relented and agreed," said Liza. "She really thought that she would be ruining him and that by her refusal he could turn around and be accepted back into the family fold. But he had no intention of returning, he was going to join the army with or without her and if it was without her, he would try to forget her, although he doubted that he would be able to."

"So, what happened?" asked Rose.

"Why don't you read your letter mother; it will probably tell you everything you need to know," smiled Anthony who had now finished his letter and Diana was still reading the last page.

"Yes, of course, I'll go to your library Anthony and read it in private if you don't mind," said Rose.

Diana came to join Anthony bringing the letter with her and they were both smiling.

"So you let him believe that he would have to join the army no matter what the outcome of his proposal to Estelle and when she finally accepted she believed that she would have to become an army wife and he believed that he was going to enlist and that was what their lives would be. And when did you tell him that you had a very important venture for him?" asked Anthony.

"Not until the next day," smiled Liza. "I knew that it had been love at first sight, but they seemed to need to prove that to one another. It was a wonderful experience for us to see when he realised that we had such a situation for him; I wish you could have seen it."

"How did you convince Estelle that she would not be ruining Hector's life?" Diana asked Liza.

"She realised that he was not returning to England regardless," said Liza.

"That isn't strictly true, is it Liza?" said Jamie. "I believe that Liza told Estelle that she was giving up love for the sake of love. I remembered what you told me you had said because it seemed so very profound and very apt."

"You've always found the right words, haven't you Liza," smiled Anthony. "He's going to make a wonderful life for himself, and when Thomas is a little older, we can travel to America to see him and Estelle and who knows, may be their child or two."

"It's not going to be an easy life; it will mean a great deal of hard work for them both, but they'll manage it happily together," said Liza.

Rose marched into the room and it was obvious that she was furious. They all turned and stared at her, but her eyes were only on Liza.

"I was right; you have interfered once again in our family. He would never have stayed in America if he really had to join the army, so you created a position for him. I'll never forgive you for that and I suppose you also pushed that Estelle woman into his arms. How could you do that; you are as cheap as that woman. I've always said that your class will show up no matter how much you try to appear as a lady. You are a disgrace to your title," shouted Rose.

They all looked stunned and little Thomas started crying.

Jamie was the first to recover and he stood and said, "How dare you speak to my wife like that. Thank you for your hospitality Anthony, come on Liza we have other people to see who do appreciate what you do for them."

Liza stood up rather unsteadily and took Jamie's arm.

"No," shouted Anthony. "Stay. You get out Mother, and don't come back until you have calmed down and are ready to apologise to Liza. Obviously your letter appears different to mine, because if it was the same you would never have said such things. Go on, get out."

Diana was comforting Thomas and she also had a shocked look on her face. Rose hesitated until Anthony shouted for her to leave immediately, which she did.

"Please don't leave," said Anthony. "I am so sorry; what my mother said was totally uncalled for. You have both always done everything to help Hector, and quite honestly I never believed that he ever appreciated either of you, until I read his letter. He always imposed himself on you and I now know that he liked being with you both and aimed to be just like you. He says that he knows that he can never repay you both for what you have done for him and he does not mean financially, he means by making him a much better person than he ever was."

"Hector was always, and still is, a good person, he would just have hated anyone to know it then, but now he will have Estelle to make sure that he is appreciated for all the good that he does," said Liza. "The Major knew what he was really like and was happy to treat him like a son. He's going to miss him; he made up a little for the son that he lost."

"We'll leave now Anthony," said Jamie. "I think you have family matters to deal with. I will not have Liza spoken to like that, but my annoyance is not with you and Diana, so I know that it will not sour our friendship."

"I had thought that my mother-in-law had accepted what Hector was doing; she went to see him off when he left for his trip and she wished him well and hoped that he achieved all that he wished for," said Diana. "Obviously she had dwelled on the situation and wished it were otherwise. I am so sorry Liza; you always seem to be on the receiving end of unkind words."

"I'll get over it," said Liza. "Will you be able to spend the weekend with us? We now have Simon with us until he finishes his education, which may go on for some years as he is going to study law after university."

"You're just making conversation Liza," said Diana.

"No Diana, I would like you to spend the weekend with our family; I know little Thomas would. I will warn you that Bella and her boys may turn up. I never have any warning of her arrival, but their rooms are always ready, including a nurse and her maid," smiled Liza who really never felt less like smiling.

"I hope that you will join us, but I will not have your mother within our household. It is a shame as I know that my mother and Lucinda enjoyed her company, but when they hear that she has been less than kind to Liza, I know that they will not wish her in their house," said Jamie.

"I'll make sure that your rooms are ready and if the weather is as good as it is today, it's going to be a cricketing afternoon," said Liza with a smile. "We must go and see the Major and Jennifer now. We must find out how they are getting on with replacing Estelle. I'm afraid Hector is going to be hard to replace, but there must be somebody out there who will be suitable."

Jamie was still fuming as they climbed into their carriage. Liza smiled sweetly as if there had been no problem and waved saying that she would see them at the weekend.

"Oh Liza, you always do everything so right, but get accused of doing everything so wrong. I am so sorry and so annoyed that you are once again the target of ignorance. I will not have you spoken to in that way without there being some repercussions," said Jamie.

"I cannot believe that Hector said anything but kind words which obviously Rose somehow took the wrong way. No doubt Anthony will sort it all out," said Liza trying to cheer herself up but with little success.

"It will be sorted out Liza, and if Anthony cannot do it then I most definitely will. Try and cheer up Liza, you mean everything to everyone else and we're now going to see the Major and Jennifer, and the children who will all be pleased to see you," said Jamie.

Jamie was right as not only were the Major and Jennifer pleased to see her, but the smaller children were all around her. The older ones were smiling but carried on with what they were doing. They discussed with the Major that they would have to find a new full-time teacher and they all felt that a female would be better as most of the children had been hurt by men and they would feel more comfortable with a woman.

"At the moment we can manage without Hector. He has the Langston House well organised and I can finish that quite well but no doubt you and Jamie will be able to help with that," said the Major.

"Of course we will," said Jamie. "We don't have any other Homes in mind yet so we will be able to deal with Langston, but we will soon have to start arranging interviews for staff."

"Perhaps we could all go there early next week and plan exactly what and who we will need," said Liza.

"Young Lord Langston and his sister have been very helpful," said the Major. "They have settled nicely into their house and the wall separating them has been completed and they fully understand why that had to be. Lord Langston would be delighted to encourage those who may be interested in art. I believe that his sister would also like to help in some way."

"Well, as you know there's always something for people to help with; I'm sure she can be of some use to the children. You seem a little overcrowded at the moment," said Liza.

"The authorities arrested a large group of abusers and we had to take a dozen youngsters all at once. Luckily most are young enough to be helped, but we do have a couple who are aggressive and seem to want to go back to their previous way of life. We watch them constantly as we don't want them to influence any of the other children," said the Major.

"You'll join us for lunch I hope," said Jennifer. "You can then tell us all about Hector and Estelle."

Liza and Jamie told them the complete story of Hector and Estelle, and the new American venture in Daltons that they would be organising and overseeing.

When they had finished Jennifer said that it would probably not please Rose as she was sure that Hector would never enlist in the American army and if he did it would only be for a few months. She was convinced that he would be back within a short while.

"Jennifer is right, Rose was hoping that he would return and she was even prepared to accept that Estelle would be with him, although what Estelle's life would have been like with Rose's attitude I would not like to say," said the Major. "Oh, I can see from your faces that you've spoken to Rose."

"It was more the case that she spoke to Liza," said Jamie. "She was obviously delusional; if Hector had enlisted then he would have been in the army for at least five years. I'm afraid she blames Liza for Hector not coming back. I'm sure she believes that Liza planned it all. It has caused a very serious rift, but I am sure that Anthony will be able to calm the situation. If he doesn't then I will, because I will not have Liza abused the way she was this morning."

The Major and Jennifer could see that Jamie was very annoyed by the situation, and they had heard some of the things that Rose had said about Liza in the past.

"She is very silly because she will alienate her own family by taking that attitude. I hope that it will all be sorted satisfactorily," said the Major.

"I'm sure it will be," said Liza and hoped that they could leave the subject alone. She really wanted to make plans for Langston House. "Will you be able to stay with us overnight when we go to Langston?"

"I think we should be able to do that, thank you," said the Major.

"You'll be able to meet the fourth member of our pack of boys," laughed Liza. "Simon will be with us for quite some years to come. When he finishes at Cambridge, he will go onto law school before returning to America. He wants to follow in his father's footsteps and that will take some time."

"You seem really pleased to have another boy in your care Liza," said Jennifer.

"I've known him since he was tiny, and his father came to Benson to practice law. His mother had died having him and for many years he was like another son to me. He and Matthew were inseparable and when John came to me it became a gang of three, and now they are reunited and James completes the gang of four. They all get on together really well, and his bed has been waiting for him since before Jamie and I married," said Liza.

"Four boys all of around the same age are going to be quite a handful," said the Major.

"When you have three boys all planning to play tricks on you, what's another one? I'm sure Jamie and I, as well as the other members of our household, will have to try to be one step ahead of them, but I'm sure we are going to be caught frequently," said Liza.

Jamie laughed also and said that he was sure that they would be caught, and he warned the Major and Jennifer to watch out for them when they came to stay next week. It had lightened the day which had started out so badly for Liza and soon they were in their carriage and making their way home.

"This has been both a good and a bad day," said Jamie. "I can see that you are still upset at Rose's comments and so am I. They were grossly unfounded and totally untrue; I will make you feel better. We have our four boys to go home to and they always cheer us up, as do all the rest of the family. Are they all dining with us tonight?"

"No, it's just you and me tonight. Bernard has been invited to dine with David and Grace this evening and I think that your mother and Lucinda don't want to be left out and they have invited him tomorrow evening," smiled Liza.

"I know that I have said it before, but it's not many years ago when I had no mother and no uncle; it was just James and I echoing around our house. I don't remember smiling very much, even with James. I talked to him and sometimes read to him. I always said goodnight to him whenever I was home, but there was very little laughter in the house," said Jamie.

"I suppose you do find it a little overwhelming at times, I know that I do so you must find it quite hard," said Liza.

"Good heavens of course I don't. If I want to have some time alone I have my study and my bedroom. The house is large enough to accommodate everyone. I like the fact that the house has constant sound; I don't find it offensive; I find it quite comforting. I also find it entertaining that I never know who I am going to bump into. I will miss Hector; the way he used to just turn up and make himself at home amused me greatly. I like having a large family. I even enjoy Bella turning up out of the blue with Nicholas and Richard and just assuming that they are welcome. I love every minute of our life; I wouldn't change it for the world. I know that we have to attend functions when we would much rather be at home, but that's what we have to do and we do it together which makes it more enjoyable than it otherwise would be," said Jamie.

"I wonder if we will ever see Rose again, I do hope so. I thought that all her prejudices had disappeared, but obviously she has been hiding them well. I don't want it to affect our relationship with Anthony and Diana, but Anthony must have loyalty to his mother," said Liza.

"I just hope that she has calmed down and sees reason. She naturally was upset that Hector is now living and working in another country and had to blame somebody for it and unfortunately it had to be you. She knew that you could probably employ him, and she didn't want that. She knew that he would not like the army and stupidly thought that he could enlist just for a few weeks and then run home again to lick his wounds, but there is no excuse for what she said to you and it will have to be a most sincere apology before I will allow her in my home again, or near any of my family. I've known Anthony a long while and I'm sure that he will be able to adequately smooth the situation. Of course, even if she apologises you will have to feel that you can accept it. So we will see what happens and I hope that you won't let it worry you too much and I will try to make you forget it all," smiled Jamie as he pulled her even closer to him.

"I don't think that we should tell the family what happened because I couldn't be sure that they would not show their displeasure, and you know that your mother and Lucinda enjoyed having her stay with them. I think that your uncle and Grace would not show their feelings quite so easily," said Liza.

Bernard was there when they arrived home and he asked how there day had gone at the Home, which they told him was very good and said that it was not going to be easy to replace Hector, but they also would now have to find staff for Langston House. He asked if he could accompany them when they went there during the next week, and they had no objections.

The boys were happy to see them and told them about their picnic that day, they had just finished their supper and joined them in the drawing room. Matthew pulled a slight face when told that Thomas would be visiting at the weekend and the other boys laughed apart from Simon who also found it amusing when told how much little Thomas followed his idol 'Maffew' around.

"He will grow out of it, Matthew," said Liza. "In fact he may well have already."

"You always taught me not to tell lies, Mother," said Matthew imperiously but with a sly grin.

"I'm not lying Matthew; he could well have altered his fascination for you, and it could now be James, or John or when he meets Simon, he could start following him around. I hope you won't become jealous if he does," smiled Liza.

The next day was Friday and nobody would have known from Liza's countenance that Rose had hurt her so much. One or two did notice that Jamie was a little tight lipped but when spoken to, he smiled and also spent a great deal of time with the boys. Lucinda asked if Bella would be bringing her boys to them that weekend and Liza had to admit that she had no idea if she was, but Anthony and Diana would be visiting with little Thomas.

"I suppose Rose will also be with them, so we had better get her bedroom ready," said Miranda.

"I'm not sure if she will be coming; I know that she had one or two other commitments, but you never know so it's best to be prepared," said Liza.

Miranda looked at her with a frown, but Liza still smiled and Miranda whispered, "So Hector's marriage and work did not go down too well with Rose."

"You are very astute Miranda, but she will calm down and may well be with them this weekend. Please don't say anything to Lucinda as I know that she would be very upset if she thinks that this family has been insulted in any way and I also know that she would defend us very adamantly and probably create a further rift. There is no rift between us and Anthony and Diana and I don't want there to be an atmosphere for them this weekend. The forecast from the farmers is that it is going to be beautiful weather so a keen cricket match will be played on Sunday afternoon and I'm looking forward to it as we have missed out on many so far," said Liza.

During the afternoon Anthony and Diana arrived without Rose. They were introduced to Simon and little Thomas trailed after them all as they played in the grounds. Adam and April were never far away from them as the rest of the family sat in the garden near the house having afternoon tea.

"It's a shame Rose couldn't join us this weekend," said Lucinda and Anthony nodded and said that she had plans for this weekend but was sorry that she was going to miss out on a family weekend. David stared at him but said nothing.

The four boys suddenly appeared followed by little Thomas whose loyalty had remained with 'Maffew' but as he was getting bigger, he was not such a problem to Matthew, and the other boys also included him when they could.

Rose wasn't mentioned over dinner that evening; it was as if everyone realised that it was a subject not to be touched upon, but their trip to New York and Hector and Estelle were the main topics, along with the new venture that Liza's businesses were entering into in Daltons. Anthony said how exciting it sounded and he was proud that they had chosen Hector and trusting him enough to handle the project.

Later that evening when Miranda, Lucinda, David and Grace had left for their homes, Anthony told Liza and Jamie that Rose was now very embarrassed about how she had reacted towards the news of Hector's marriage and his position within Liza's companies and did not feel that she could face anyone, although Anthony had tried to persuade her that all would be forgiven once a sincere apology had been given.

"I told her that Liza was not one to hold a grudge, but also she was not one to take too many insults like the ones that she had thrown at her. She realises that Liza had nothing to do with Hector's decision to go to New York and persuade Estelle to marry him; he had already told her that he was going to stay in America no matter what and really when she thought about it all, she realised that Hector now had a very important and responsible situation which he would not have had without Liza. She also knows that his employment with the charity was something that had brought him out of the doldrums and back into the real world," said Anthony.

"There is no doubt that she will now be boasting to her friends about how important he is and that Marchant & Fuller and Bradley & Company could not survive without him," said Diana.

"Hmmm," was all that Liza said.

"You know that I was so annoyed at her," said Jamie. "It seems to me that if something isn't as some want it then Liza always gets the blame. I am really fed up with the criticisms that she receives from others when I know that she only tries to make life easy for everyone."

"Oh, Jamie," said Liza. "There are times when I have to make decisions to the detriment of others, but for the good of the majority. It's not easy and does warrant criticism on occasion."

"Well Liza, you've just said it yourself; you sometimes have to decide for the good of the majority," said Anthony.

"I'm glad that Anthony and Diana are here this weekend," said Jamie as they were in bed that night. "We have been friends for so long that I would not have wished to have a rift, however I can live without Rose as I cannot tolerate her attitude towards you. I knew that both Anthony and Diana did not agree with her, I could see that from the looks on their faces the other day. It must be very difficult for them as they now have divided loyalties, although it does seem that Rose has realised that she was wrong."

There was a surprise the next morning when a carriage drew up and a very sheepish looking Rose stepped down. Liza was the first to catch sight of her and she ordered one of the servants to take Rose's bags to Miranda's house.

"I presume that you would like to stay with Miranda and Lucinda," said Liza as she acted as if there had never been a problem between them.

"Well, if they'll have me," said Rose quietly.

"They got your room ready just in case you could make it this weekend," said Liza.

"I need to talk to you Liza," said Rose.

"Yes, I know you do Rose. Shall we go into my study? I'll order some tea for us," said Liza.

Jamie suddenly appeared and nodded to Rose, but he realised that Liza had it all in hand and he was not going to interfere unless it became necessary.

When they were alone Rose said, "I was so foolish the other day Liza. I really know that you had nothing to do with Hector's decision to go to America and stay there no matter what the outcome was with Estelle. Anthony explained to me that you let him think that all he could do was enlist in the army and Estelle agreed to marry him when she also thought that it was how their life was going to be. I know that she is not a money grabber, or she would never have agreed to be with him as she knew that he had no money. The opportunities that you have given him, not only in the past but this new project, are absolutely wonderful. You obviously have a great deal of faith in him and I am so very proud of that."

"He is going to do very well now," was all Liza would say.

"I don't know how to apologise to you Liza. Sorry is so inadequate. There has to be something that I can do to make things better between us," said Rose.

"Just by having the courage to turn up this morning is enough. I think that Jamie will take a little convincing, but you have known him a very long time and he really wants no rifts between our two families and neither do I. You drew him into your family when he really had no one of his own, and that has always meant a great deal to him," said Liza. "He's not going to shout at you Rose, but he will listen to you quite calmly."

"Will you arrange for me to see him soon please Liza? I'd like to see him before I go to Miranda's," said Rose.

"Stay here Rose and I'll find him for you," said Liza.

He wasn't far away and when he went in to see Rose, the door closed and Liza did not know until later what they discussed, but they both looked quite happy when they emerged from the study and Jamie decided that he would escort Rose over to Miranda's. Liza breathed a sigh of relief and she could see Anthony and Diana peeping out of the drawing room as Jamie left with Rose.

Later that day another carriage drew up with Bella, her boys, Nurse Dawkins and a maid. It was not surprising, but Liza knew that there would be many questions which could be awkward now that Rose was also with them.

All the boys were delighted to be together, and Nicholas and Richard were quickly introduced to Simon and they went off to do whatever it was that boys of that age do. Luckily little Thomas was having an afternoon nap, so he would not be bothering them until later.

Diana had been right, Rose spent most of the time over dinner boasting about how necessary Hector was to the operation in America and that he was chosen for his intelligence and organising skills. She continued that there was nobody else that the company could have found to carry out such important work.

"Is Hector in charge of the whole operation?" asked Bella of Liza and before Liza could answer Rose chimed in.

"Yes, he is the one who is arranging all the buildings for all the workers and then for all the factories. He has a great deal of responsibility," said Rose triumphantly.

"You do have a manager in New York, don't you Liza?" said Diana.

"Yes, Diana, we do, and he has been with us for a great many years and is very loyal to our companies," said Liza. "He is in overall charge of our American operations."

"Ah yes, but this is a new and very large undertaking which has to be handled with great skill," said Rose.

"Did he marry that lovely girl?" asked Bella. It went very quiet around the table.

"Yes, he did," said Liza. "And they are both very happy embarking on a new life. It's going to be hard work for them, but they'll manage it beautifully."

"I dare say it was very exciting for them both going off on a new venture," said Bella.

"He had many people helping him, and Brendan will be arriving shortly to help with the project," said Jamie.

"I suppose Brendan will be a good assistant for him. He'll have so many decisions to make that he will need someone to carry out the day to day running of the business. Hector has always been the very intelligent one of my boys," said Rose.

"Rose for heaven's sake," said Jamie. "Both your boys are intelligent. Anthony runs the estates wonderfully well; it takes a great deal of thought and organisation to keep them financially sound. Hector went into the army and went to war; he was just more outgoing than Anthony which is not a measure of intelligence. He showed his superb organising skills since leaving the army and working for the charity."

"I always thought that Anthony was more intelligent than Hector," said Bella in her usual tactless manner.

Liza decided that it would be better if she kept out of the discussion, feeling that no matter what happened she would probably get the blame for it. Others around the table were showing a mixture of amusement and discomfort.

"Will you be playing cricket tomorrow David?" asked Liza.

"No, I'm afraid my bones tell me to rest, but you will have enough people to make for a good team. I shall watch and cheer on of course. I presume you will be showing your cricketing skills tomorrow Anthony," said David joining in the change of awkward subject.

"I wouldn't miss it for the world. Liza tells me that your farmers are giving us a good weather forecast for tomorrow," said Anthony. "I suppose John will be taking Derek's runs as usual."

"No doubt he will," said Liza. "Derek is walking with just one stick now. I think that soon all he will be unable to do is run. He is looking so much straighter, but it's been very hard and painful work for him."

"You got a specialist for him, didn't you Liza?" said Diana.

"Jamie organised it for him when he realised how incapacitated Derek was," said Liza.

"To my shame Liza realised it before I did. I am so annoyed that nothing was done about it soon after the accident happened because it may have meant that he could have walked sooner. He has dealt with it all so very well over the years," said Jamie.

"Young Simon is a very good-looking boy," said Bella.

"Yes, he takes after his father; I think that he is going to be very tall. I'm pleased that he's with us; I've known him since he was a tiny little boy. He has a very nice nature, but he likes to play tricks on us, just as the others do," smiled Liza. She was so pleased that the subject of Hector's intelligence as opposed to Anthony's had been changed successfully.

"Next time you go to New York I think I'll come with you," said Bella. "I'm sure you have plenty of room for us all."

"We are thinking that we will travel to the southern states next time we go to America. We have friends there and would like to see somewhere different," said Liza.

607

"I hear that the north and the south could be coming to blows in the not too distant future," said Bernard.

"I know that they have been threatening that for quite some time and then it all dies down again. Naturally we would not go if the threat becomes more serious," said Jamie.

"That sounds quite exciting. Is it Charles Enderby's plantation that you would be visiting?" asked Miranda.

"Yes, we would go there and visit other places both on the way and on the way back. It will be quite an adventure," said Liza.

"You'll probably buy it," said Bella.

"That is not my intention. I don't need any more investment in America. Daltons is a big enough project and is going to take a while before it begins to pay off. No, I need nothing more in America," said Liza.

"Well if you do Liza, I know that Hector would be able to run it when he has completed Daltons for you," smiled Rose happily.

The pleasure that Jamie, Anthony and Diana had because Rose had come to apologise to Liza was slowly being eroded and true to her nature Bella decided that she had heard enough of Hector's brilliance and said that because of the excitement of their New York trip, if she heard any more about it, her enthusiasm for her trip would be clouded by knowing too much detail at this stage. She just fell short of telling Rose to be quiet, but she was bordering on doing so. Nobody knew whether Rose understood that she was telling her to change the subject.

Once again there was a mixture of amusement and discomfort from those around the table and Bella started a conversation about how her boys had missed coming to meet up with Liza and Jamie's boys and had shown keenness to meet their new American friend.

At last dinner was over and David smiled at everyone and suggested that he was still getting over their trip and he would leave them now and offered to escort the ladies to their home, which they were happy to do. Grace also said that she would leave then and looked forward to meeting up again the next day.

"Yes, I've also had a very tiring day," said Bernard. "I think I'll go to my room and finish my sermon for tomorrow."

In the drawing room Bella flopped down in one of the chairs and said, "Well I don't know how you all managed to keep as quiet as you did over dinner. I have never known Rose praise Hector before; she has always been very critical of his way of life and of his abilities. I have to say that is one of the most boring dinners that I have ever experienced in this household. The food as always was superb, but the company left a great deal to be desired."

"Bella," said Jamie. "You have to remember that she is a mother and is probably missing Hector very much and she copes with it by building him up greatly in her mind."

"Well, let's hope she calms down over the coming days, or months, or years. I don't know that my patience would stand much more of her prattle," said Bella.

Anthony and Diana stayed quietly looking at her and wondered how they were going to change the subject and also how not to show that they agreed with Bella without being disloyal to Rose.

"Come on now," said Bella, "Tell me exactly how you got on in New York and what you got up to, of course without how wonderful the brilliant Hector was throughout it all."

This brought some light relief to everyone and the rest of the evening was filled with conversation and laughter. Bella's attitude had changed dramatically and as always, she had a wonderful sense of humour when she was in Jamie and Liza's home.

"Well Liza," said Jamie when they were finally in bed. "This has turned out to be an unusual day. Rose really got on everyone's nerves over dinner; I wonder how my mother and Lucinda are getting on with her."

"I think that both your mother and Lucinda will be able to handle her," said Liza quietly.

"You don't seem very happy Liza. I would have thought you would have been pleased as Rose turned up and apologised to you. I know that you did not want any rifts between our families," said Jamie.

"I just wonder how many times I have to forgive people and accept apologies. I'm tired of getting the blame for everything that happens. It started when my parents blamed me for living when my brother had died and has continued right up to now. I have to smile and say that I understand, and I don't understand. Why don't you get blamed; not once did Rose accuse you of anything, just me. Hector's marriage and employment was all down to me but in a negative way, certainly not a positive one. Just for once I want someone to say 'thank you Liza, that was a very good decision and has helped whoever it is'. It's all very depressing," said Liza.

Liza was lying on her side and pouting, and Jamie loved seeing her that way. It reminded him of a child and Matthew in particular. He put his arms around her and told her that he never blamed her for anything, and numerous people knew what she did for them and whether she knew it or not, they thanked her every day of their lives.

"You never mention your parents; do you know if they are still alive?" asked Jamie.

"No, I have no contact with them at all. The last that I heard was from Wendell years ago. Apparently my mother wanted me declared dead when I had been missing for a while. Wendell refused telling her that I had to be missing for seven years before I could be declared dead and besides, she wasn't named in my Will," said Liza.

"Are you telling me that she was laying claim to your assets? Did she show no concern for your welfare?" asked Jamie.

"She wasn't concerned for my welfare and apparently she thought she was going to benefit from my death. Wendell gave her some money and sent her on her way. In fact he had no idea whether or not she was named in my Will. He had summed her up correctly; he remembered that James had to pay her for me in the first place," said Liza.

Jamie watched her closely. "There has to be somebody in your family who had a nice nature, otherwise you would not be as kind as you are. There also must have been somebody who could use their brains successfully. You ought to investigate your family. We looked into mine and look who turned up. We have a wonderful grandmother for our children and a cousin and uncle for them also; not to mention a surrogate grandmother in Lucinda. You might find someone that you like."

"No Jamie, all my family are here now, and I have Wendell and Amelia and their boys who became my family many years ago. I neither need nor want any other family. They have not bothered with me over the years and I am happy not to bother with them now," said Liza.

"If your mother was that mercenary all those years ago, I'm surprised that she has not contacted you recently. Your name is mentioned in most newspapers when we are attending functions for the charity; she must know who and what you now are," said Jamie.

"She must therefore be dead then," said Liza.

"I have rarely heard you sound so harsh Liza," said Jamie.

"She sold me Jamie; I was lucky that James was so kind, but she didn't know that. I could have had a terrible life for the sake of money. Forgiveness in those circumstances would be impossible," said Liza.

"I can understand that," said Jamie, "and I see why you concentrate so much on making our boys happy and let them play their tricks on us and give them more freedom than other children have."

They both lay in bed quietly thinking and Jamie noticed that Liza's pout was back, and he leaned over her and kissed it away. "There's no need to pout Liza, you are very much loved in this household and very much loved by me." She smiled at him and her green eyes sparkled amazingly.

***

They went to the church service at the cricket pavilion the next morning and all the boys met up with the village children and Derek managed to keep up with them quite well once the service was over.

The pavilion was then reorganised ready for the cricket match that afternoon and finally they all went back for Sunday lunch which as always included the boys.

Simon had enjoyed being with Nicholas and Richard and was pleased to meet some of the village children. He was looking forward to the cricket match and remembered playing a form of it at the fort when his Uncle Patrick was still alive. He wondered whether they still managed to make mummy Liza run around so much that she nearly collapsed; Uncle Patrick had taught them to do that.

Luckily at lunchtime Rose had ceased with her praises of Hector to the exclusion of all else; Liza assumed that Lucinda, or perhaps Miranda, had told her that not everyone wanted to be told how wonderful her second son was, and that nobody believed that he was wiser than his elder brother who had kept the Ffoulks family fortune intact over the years and a roof over their heads through difficult circumstances.

Simon was very polite over lunch but he wanted to know everything about the afternoon they were about to spend at the cricket pitch and Jamie, Anthony and David went to great lengths to tell him the correct rules of the game and the boys told him of how they took Derek's runs for him, but that he was a very strong and accurate batsman.

"The food is wonderful; it's lovely pies and bread and salad, and cakes and puddings. We all love the afternoon and we meet up with everyone from the farms and village," said James.

"We take it in turns to play between the older men. They really are the Edgeworth team, but we all join in and we learn to get better that way," said Matthew. "It's like we used to play at the fort in Benson, but we are much more organised and skilled, it's still fun though."

"I'm looking forward to it," said Simon. "Do you play every Sunday?"

"If the weather's good we do," said Liza. "There's a great deal of disappointment if it rains; but sometimes we still go to the pavilion and eat all the food."

"I hope we don't have to sit on the grass," said Rose.

"Don't worry Rose," said Miranda. "We will make sure you are provided with a chair. You don't honestly think that Lucinda and I would be grovelling on the ground, do you?"

They left for the cricket ground about an hour after lunch and during the course of the afternoon Simon proved that he was an extremely good player. Some of his tactics were a little different to the normal rules of English cricket but he was forgiven for being American, much to everyone's amusement, but he did enjoy playing.

Derek now stood to play, but still fell with every ball that was bowled. John still took his runs and Adam and David were on picking him up duty, which sometimes meant that they too still ended up on the ground. It was, however, marvellous to see him standing to bat and as always he was heartily cheered when he left the pitch.

Everyone had built up an appetite for the afternoon tea and it was a time for the players to analyse their game so far. They had been practicing well and were looking forward to a match in a month's time which would be between the Edgeworth team and one from another village. It was going to be held at the Edgeworth home ground and they were all looking forward to it. The boys would not be playing on that day, but they would be there in force cheering on their home team.

The second half went smoothly and finally all the leftover food was packed away and everyone made their weary way home and soon after they arrived, the boys made their way to the kitchen to see what was left for their supper. Everyone else went to rest before dinner, which would consist of a very light meal which would be set out so that they could all just help themselves to as much or as little as they wanted.

The fresh air, the game and the food had made them all very sleepy and it wasn't long before they all made their ways either to their homes or up to their rooms.

"Do you feel a little better tonight, Liza? You were very depressed last night, and I hope that I made you feel a little better. Rose seems to have calmed down over Hector," said Jamie.

"I do feel better Jamie; Rose hardly mentioned Hector today, which I believe was a relief to everyone. It's a shame because we had a great deal to tell everyone about him and his job is really very important just as she has said, but we daren't touch on the subject whilst she is around," said Liza.

"I think we are going to do rather well when we play the next village. Our team has become very professional. Do we have white cricket clothes for them all?" asked Jamie.

"Yes, Mr and Mrs Lambert and Mrs Frances have made sure that everyone knows what they need and if they haven't got it then they have arranged it for them," said Liza.

The cricket match with Sandown village was the highlight of the season with the Edgeworth team winning by eighty runs. It had been hard fought but enjoyable and Sandown were not bad losers. It created a wonderfully happy atmosphere and a return match was to be arranged for the following year. The analysis after the match was that the Edgeworth team were not to be complacent as the 'Sandowners' were a force to be reckoned with and no doubt they would be practicing hard over the course of the coming year.

Chapter 28

At the end of September they decided to visit Belfast for a few weeks. They would only be taking the boys with April, Adam and Roberts. Peter needed Liza to help with some of the decisions for Daltons and both she and Jamie thought that it would be a good idea for Simon to see where Liza and Kate had spent so much time before going to America all those years ago. The boys were a little disappointed as Adam would still be tutoring them during that time.

Simon was finding his life quite exciting as since being with the Edgeworth household he had been to New York, had a comfortable and happy life in Surrey and now he was going to meet everyone in Belfast and stay in yet another large house. Liza hoped that it wouldn't spoil him for when he finally returned to his father and Kate in Benson, but she had commitments and it was nice that she could take her family with her.

The journey to Belfast was uneventful but it fascinated Simon and he loved the bed in the room that the other boys had planned for him.

Hector had sent extremely detailed reports on what had already been achieved in Daltons as well as lists of goods which were still needed to make the town workable and much to Liza and Jamie's consternation, he was singing the praises of a couple called Jones who were showing that they had the dedication and ability to take some of the responsibility. Brendon's designing skills were of extreme value and Hector had taken it upon himself to adapt were necessary. Estelle and someone called Tess Jones had taken over the hotel and all the rooms were now habitable, although in the future they would reorganise it to make best use of it. Garth Jones was working closely and successfully with the overseer, Carl Fairburn. When Jamie and Liza heard this, they knew that Tess and Garth Jones had to be Theresa and Gareth.

"They haven't been very clever with their change of names," said Jamie. "Hopefully whatever they are doing won't create too much notice for them."

"I had hoped that they would just keep their heads down, earn a little money and then move on to another location. However it seems that they are becoming indispensable in Daltons," said Liza. "Perhaps Daltons will become so large that they will be able to lose themselves, especially if any authorities come sniffing around."

"I'm sure that there will be a great many people working in Daltons who are hiding from the law. Gareth and Theresa won't be the only ones keeping a low profile," said Jamie.

Liza laughed, "Jake, the lawman in Benson had crossed over from the wrong side of the law to the right side of the law. I am quite convinced that it does sometimes take a thief to catch a thief. I'm now going to ignore what we know and just believe that they are both new to us."

"Your friendly security manager in New York is one of your protégés, isn't he? He seems to be one step ahead of any criminal problems. I suppose it is useful to have someone on your side who knows the criminal world," said Jamie.

Liza just smiled and said nothing.

Whilst they were there, they made plans for Christmas. Wendell and Amelia decided that they would travel to Surrey and Peter said that he would join them just for a few days over the holiday. Edward and Nicole still had to decide whether they travel with little Edward to be with the family. As with the previous year, Joseph and Lily would be with the Major and Jennifer.

Every day Liza spent time at the office. They had increased their staff as was necessary with their large commitment to Daltons, but they were not feeling that the investment was too great as the American government's contribution towards the set-up had been received. All talk of war between the north and south had ceased for the moment and it was felt that it would never come to fruition any time in the future.

They spent many hours at Liza's house mainly because Simon wanted to know and see where his mummy Kate and mummy Liza had lived all those years ago. He often went to Kate's old room and just sat quietly looking around. It was as if he felt that it was part of his heritage. He enjoyed Belfast and certainly enjoyed being accepted as part of the Fuller family. Edward and Joseph were fun, and Simon could see why John liked Peter so much; he was calm and would always explain anything that was needed. Simon could sense that he would protect mummy Liza's family above all else. He also admired the way he appeared so businesslike; it was very much how his father acted.

Joseph and Lily approached Liza one day whilst she was working in the office which had been James'. She always thought of it as his office although she was the only one who ever used it now. She looked up surprised and realised that they had something important that they wanted to talk to her about.

She smiled up at them and invited them to sit. "What is it that I can do for you?" she asked.

"Liza, I know that I am not like Peter or my father as far as business is concerned, but I am honest and am quite capable of keeping accounts. Also one of my assets is that I love children and can never bear to see them hurt," said Joseph.

"I know what you are Joseph, you are a good and solid person and I have seen how you are with children but what is it that you would like Joseph?" asked Liza.

"Lily and I would like you to consider us to run the Langston Home. I know we are quite capable of doing so, especially as the Major is in overall charge of the project and we will be able to learn so much from him, but initially I know that we can make the children happy. Lily is able to teach them to read and write and I know that I can keep them safe and encourage them to have a much better life than they have at present," said Joseph.

Liza sat back and frowned. This was something that she had not bargained for; she had thought that Joseph was contented in the work that he carried out and she was not sure that he had the acumen to run a home like Langston.

"You know that Langston must be run like a business and not a charity, although it is one. You also know that we are answerable to our benefactors; we are no longer run just as a Marchant & Fuller charity, we are much larger than that now and have very lofty people studying everything that we do," said Liza.

"Do you not think that we are up to the task then Liza?" asked a very disappointed looking Joseph.

"I believe that you could be more than capable, but you may be overwhelmed to begin with, and I have to admit that I would have liked to have an experienced person in charge to start with. However, where would I find someone who has had experience running such a Home? Even the Major had not run such a place before, but he had been used to commanding men in his army career which helped considerably," said Liza.

"I would help all that I could also," said Lily sadly.

"Of course you would Lily, and I know that you would be very good with the children's education. It would be quite an upheaval for you both to move from here to Langston; you would miss your family Joseph and they would miss you very much," said Liza.

"But we would be near you and near Lily's mother and the Major. I love my family very much Liza, but you are just as much family as they are, and I know that my mother and father will travel to see us frequently. I'm not so sure about Edward and Nicole now that they have little Edward and Nicole's sister is here, but I really would like to have such a challenge. I often feel that because I am the youngest Fuller I am overlooked for anything that has responsibility. Hector was totally irresponsible when he came back from Portugal and he turned his life around. I am not irresponsible and would like to be given the opportunity to prove it to everyone," said Joseph.

"Have you spoken to your father or Peter about this?" asked Liza.

"No, I wanted to talk to you first as I know you would think about it and not just throw the idea out as my father and Peter probably would," said Joseph. "They do not give me credit for much."

"Oh, I think that they do Joseph," said Liza. "You do realise that we must discuss this with the other members of the board of which you are a member."

"I would much prefer that you discussed it with the others without me being there and then they can say what their thoughts are without embarrassment," said Joseph.

"As you wish Joseph," said Liza. "I'll find an opportunity to talk to your father, Peter and Edward and give them my recommendations. Jamie should also be at the meeting as he is also on the board of the charity, but I don't think that we need to go further as what is really being suggested is the employment of staff."

"You know that we will work hard and do everything that we can to make the children happy and ease them back into a world that is safe for them. We would not let you or the children down," said Lily who was very near to tears.

"I can see that doing this work means a great deal to you both, but even if we agree to it, we must consult with the Major as he will be in overall charge of Langston house. Have you suggested your idea to him?" asked Liza.

"Only in passing last time we saw him, and he thought that such employment would do me some good," smiled Joseph. "I believe that he thinks that I could do with some responsibility."

"I'll try and convene a meeting for this afternoon at your father's house," said Liza. "Or if that's not convenient then I'll arrange it for tomorrow morning."

"Thank you, Liza," said Joseph. "I know you'll do what is right for the children."

"The Major would be working with whoever we were to take on at Langston for quite a while. The Ffoulks Home runs very smoothly now, so much as he is needed there, it is not quite so essential now," said Liza.

When Joseph and Lily had left Liza sat and the more she thought about their request the more she could see merit in it. They would be inexperienced in running a Home, but who wouldn't be; the Major and Hector had had no previous experience when they worked on the Ffoulks Home. It was fortunate that Hector had organised Langston House until it was so very nearly ready to receive children. It could well be the making of Joseph.

Liza managed to arrange a meeting at Wendell's house with Peter and Edward and on the way she stopped at Jamie's house and he also joined the meeting.

Liza outlined what Joseph and Lily would like and then asked for everyone's opinion.

Both Liza and Wendell sat back and waited to hear what the others had to say. Edward thought that it was a good idea as Joseph sometimes found that quite often he was kicking his heels at the office. Peter was a little sceptical as he felt that Joseph may not be able to handle the business side of the Home but appreciated that he would make the children's lives very happy. Jamie agreed with Peter although he felt that as the Major was in overall charge then Joseph could learn a great deal, and they were nearby in an emergency.

Wendell smiled at Liza and she nodded back to him. "I believe that it would be the making of Joseph; we probably have never given him the opportunity to show what he is made of. He is as honest as the day is long, he loves children and Lily is very intelligent. If the Major is willing, then I think that Joseph could learn a great deal and become a very efficient manager," said Wendell.

"I don't think that we will have a problem with the Major, but it will be courtesy to ask his opinion as he will have to be in charge of Joseph. Lily wishes to work also, and she is leaning towards teaching the children and I believe that she is strong enough to command respect in the classroom," said Liza.

"So in principle we all agree that Joseph should be given the opportunity to manage Langston House, subject of course, to approval by the Major," said Wendell. "Joseph has not interviewed many staff in the past. Will you undertake that for him Liza?"

"Of course, but also the Major will probably undertake that to start with," said Liza.

"His mother is going to miss him," said Wendell. "One of her chicks will be leaving Belfast; she will probably cry for a while."

"She'll see that it's a good opportunity for him," said Liza. "I'll write to the Major tonight and send it first thing tomorrow. We should have a reply in a week, which is well before we have to leave here."

The Major's letter arrived before the week was out and he said that he would be delighted to have Joseph and Lily managing Langston House. He had a few reservations as he would with any new manager but knew that Joseph and Lily's hearts were in the right place and that he was quite capable of keeping an eye on and training Joseph, who he knew would eventually become an efficient overall manager and would care for the children above all else.

Wendell had been right; Amelia was shedding tears at Joseph and Lily's departure. Joseph remarked that it was useful owning a shipping company as they could move their furniture with little difficulty.

"Are you sure you want to move everything immediately?" asked Liza. "What if you don't like managing Langston and want to move back?"

"Is that your tactful way of saying that I may be no good at managing Langston?" asked a worried Joseph.

"Oh no Joseph; I think you will do a very good job. All you are lacking at present is confidence and that will come to you quickly," said Liza.

Lily and Joseph would be travelling with Liza and the family and staying with them until their accommodation at Langston House was ready for them in a few weeks. It was hoped that the Home would be fully staffed by Christmas but would not be taking any children until after the worst of the weather, which should be during February. Liza had already written to Mrs Frances warning her that there would be two house guests for the foreseeable future.

All the boys were happy that their Uncle Joseph would be with them as they presumed that their uncle would be spending all his time entertaining them. They were going to be disappointed as Joseph and Lily had a great deal of work to carry out.

"I find it difficult to believe that I am planning Christmas again and making sure that we are prepared for a winter which hopefully will not be as bad as the last one," said Liza to Jamie one evening.

"Yes, this year is racing by and you know that in September next year the boys will be leaving us," said Jamie.

"I know that they are looking forward to it, but I really don't know how I'm going to cope without them," said Liza.

"The house is going to be very quiet without them. Once they have settled perhaps we could take the trip we talked about to South Carolina; that is if they are not at war," said Jamie.

"It will give us something to think about," said Liza.

Amelia came rushing in and Jamie felt it prudent to leave her alone with Liza as from the look on her face it appeared that she wanted to cry on Liza's shoulder quite literally.

"Joseph is my baby Liza; I'm going to miss him so much. I try to protect him as he is the youngest," said Amelia with an audible sob.

"I know you do Amelia, but Joseph needs to know that he can stand on his own two feet; it's very important to him," said Liza. "You will be with us for Christmas and you will be staying until the worst of the weather is over, so you will see him almost every day, which is probably more than you do now."

"I know that I'm being silly, and you are right, Joseph does need to know that he can take on important responsibility and he has Lily by his side," said Amelia.

"Let's just think about how Joseph is going to be so successful and we are going to have a wonderful Christmas all together at our house," said Liza.

"I'm not sure that Edward and Nicole will be joining us," said Amelia. "So I may not have all my brood around me."

"You didn't last year Amelia and you know that all your sons are of an age where they can make their own decisions, sad as that is," said Liza. "Let's go and see if we can help Lily with her packing."

Nicole was already at Lily's helping her organise the move; little Edward was asleep in a cot and of course both Liza and Amelia spent some time watching him sleep.

"We'll have all our furniture organised well before we leave for England; we'll have to stay with you Mother, if we may," Lily said to Amelia. "Are you sure you have room for storage at your place Liza?"

"Yes, we have plenty of room for that. We'll make sure it's all safe and secure, especially during the worst part of the winter," said Liza. "Then the Home will be up and running and you'll have your own private quarters. You'll enjoy getting that ready for you to move into; it will be exciting for you."

The good news was that Edward and Nicole had decided to spend Christmas and into the New Year with Liza and Jamie. Arthur and Annalise could not afford the time away, but they would be spending the day with Anthony, Diana and Rose who were still going to Belfast for the Festive Season, although Anthony was not going to risk staying too long and getting caught away from England should the weather turn as fierce as the previous year.

"Will Bella and her family be with you this year?" asked Amelia and Liza just looked at her and shrugged her shoulders.

When they were all due to leave, Amelia shed her tears and as always did not want to go to the docks to see them off. Liza had comforted her by saying that in a very short while they would see her in Surrey with all her family.

The journey home was a little trying as the time of sailing meant that they had to stop twice at hotels on the way back, but at last they came up the drive and were relieved to see the smiling faces of Miranda and Lucinda to greet them. Grace was in Liza's study working and David suddenly appeared having been enjoying a quiet time in his home.

The sadness of leaving their home in Belfast had turned to excitement for Joseph and Lily and they were looking forward to settling and seeing Langston House and planning their new life. They were hoping to see Jennifer and the Major the next day.

It did not take long for the boys to find their way down to the kitchen for their supper and they could be heard laughing and letting Mrs Lambert know that they were enjoying what she had cooked for them. Liza smiled at Jamie and told him that nothing really changed in their household.

The atmosphere around the dining table that evening was lively; it seemed that Joseph and Lily's excitement had rubbed off on everyone else. They had settled comfortably in their room and nobody could deny the sparkle in both their eyes as it was obvious that they could not wait to get started on their new venture.

At last Liza was able to make her way to Jamie's room that night and surprisingly he lifted her as she entered and carried her to his bed, lay her down and covered her with the bedclothes until only her eyes were showing. He laughed and told her that she looked warm and cosy. He then climbed in beside her and snuggled down, putting his arms around her.

"Have I made you comfortable my Liza?" asked Jamie.

"Yes Jamie. I'm very warm and comfortable and have been dreaming of being here for the past few days. I could just go to sleep now, but I think you have something else in mind for me, am I right?" grinned Liza.

"When I'm just as warm and comfortable as you, I do indeed have something else in mind for us to enjoy," said Jamie.

***

The Major and Jennifer arrived the next day; they were going to stay for a few days and during that time they would be visiting Langston House with Joseph and Lily. Liza and Jamie decided that they would accompany them on their first visit.

Joseph and the Major spent most of that day in the library discussing what needed to be carried out initially at Langston and preparing for the interviews for the various members of staff urgently wanted before the house opened. The Major had many letters from those wanting such employment and he had arranged that they came to Langston over the course of the following days. Lily and Jennifer discussed how their quarters were laid out and how their furniture would fit.

Liza stayed out of the way and let them enjoy planning their future without her interference. She had a great deal of correspondence to catch up on and she and Grace worked together in her study for many hours. Jamie made the rounds of the tenant farmers with his overseer.

Bernard's rectory had finally been completed whilst they were away, and he had moved back a while ago. The church was nearly finished and although it was looking very attractive, the parishioners were sad that it no longer had a spire to guide them. Services were still being held in the cricket pavilion, but they were all looking forward to it being ready in time for the Christmas services. Liza was going to arrange that Bernard joined them for Christmas lunch and he could stay for the night if he so desired.

Derek was back in the schoolroom with the boys and he had now truly perfected his descent to the kitchen sliding down the banisters. Joseph caught sight of him, laughed and commented that it was ingenious under the circumstances, Liza wasn't sure that he would not try it himself.

Lily and Jennifer went straight to what was going to be Joseph and Lily's living quarters at Langston House the following day. The Major, Joseph and Jamie looked around the rest of the building and talked to the builders who were still on site. They chose the room that would be most convenient to conduct interviews which would be starting the following day. They had some tables and a few chairs but that would be enough to make the interviewees comfortable and they would have to appreciate that the House was not quite complete. The Major and Joseph asked Liza to also be with them when they saw the prospective employees.

"Certainly, if that is what you would like, but I know that you are both more than capable of undertaking that duty yourselves," said Liza.

"They are mostly women Liza, so they may feel more comfortable if you are there," said the Major.

They called in to see Lord Langston and his sister to introduce Joseph and Lily and it became obvious that they all seemed to like one another. Randolph Langston reiterated that he would be pleased to guide any child who had a leaning towards art and Lady Penelope said that she would also like to assist with the education of the children, or indeed in any other way that might be necessary.

"When will you be moving in?" asked Lady Penelope of Lily.

"Well Lady Penelope," said Lily. "Our furniture should be arriving tomorrow, but Liza and Jamie will be storing it for us for a while. We will probably be with them until after Christmas although there will be some things that I can do immediately, such as organise curtains and other furnishings. It's all very well arranging our accommodation, but we have to concentrate on what has to be put in place for the children."

"My name is Penelope, or Penny for short, and this is Randolph. We will be working closely together, and we would prefer not to stand on ceremony, especially in front of the children. We don't want them to feel that they should be in awe of us, and I hope that you and I are going to be good friends," said Lady Penelope.

On the way home Lily and Joseph said how impressed they were with Penny and Randolph and how down to earth they seemed to be despite their lofty titles.

"Randolph is not really happy having a title, he gained it through the deaths of his two older brothers; one in a riding accident and the other in the Crimean war," said Jamie.

"That's very sad," said Lily. "He did look very unhappy, but he seemed to liven up when he talked about giving art lessons to the children. For his sake I hope there will be some who have leanings in that direction."

623

The next two days were taken up with interviewing people for Langston House and at the end of the time they had settled on enough staff to get the Home up and running. Most would not be starting before Christmas, but they would all be settled by the New Year. The House was now almost ready and beds and other furniture were arriving daily.

Liza and Jamie had to attend two important charity functions on the following days, so they were unable to help Joseph, Lily, the Major and Jennifer to organise much at Langston House. They were delighted that Penny and Randolph rolled up their sleeves and also pitched in to help. Jennifer and the Major would not be returning to Ffoulks House until after the weekend and Lily and Joseph would accompany them to see what ideas could be brought back to Langston House.

Saturday morning arrived and so did Bella with Nicholas and Richard. As always she brought Nurse Dawkins and her maid. The boys were pleased to see one another; they were all growing up and mostly they read or discussed what they had been doing as well as what they would be doing in the future. Adam encouraged them to talk about their future; he always spent time with them even though it was the weekend. As the weather was good all the men and boys practiced bowling and batting.

Bella always seemed to enjoy her stay; she happily joined in with the routine of the household and she was showing a great deal of interest in Langston House and said that she would like to help when it opened as she had done with Ffoulks House.

"What are you doing for Christmas?" she asked over dinner. "Are you going to Belfast as usual?"

"Not this year Bella," said Liza. "We will be here, and the Fullers are joining us. Our family has increased so much that to get everyone organised to travel to Belfast at wintertime is becoming more and more difficult."

"Isn't it just as confusing for Wendell and Amelia to come here?" said Bella.

"Wendell and Amelia can travel to us whenever they wish. Peter, Edward and Nicole will travel together, and of course Lily and Joseph are already with us," said Liza. "Will you and the Duke be joining us this year Bella?"

"That's very kind of you to ask Liza," said Bella. "I don't want to impose on you, but if you insist, we'd be delighted."

All those around the table smiled and tried to look everywhere but at Bella.

"It's difficult to believe that we are getting to that time of year again," said Liza. "It has gone so very quickly."

"If the weather turns as it did last year then at least we will still be safe and warm within your house Liza, instead of in our cold mausoleum," said Bella who sounded very relieved.

"Last year we had to amalgamate rooms Bella, so that we could close some parts of the house to keep everyone warm, so you may have to be prepared to 'rough it' along with the rest of us," said Liza.

Bella laughed and said, "That sounds like fun."

Once again Bella had surprised all those around the table.

"What will you do for Christmas, Jennifer?" asked Lucinda.

"We will be with our children for the morning and for Christmas lunch and then, if we may, we would like to come here and join you for the rest of the day," said Jennifer.

"We have enough room for you to stay the night if you wish," said Liza.

"Thank you, we would like that," said the Major.

"It's going to be an even busier Christmas than last year," said Bella.

"We'll all be under one roof, so it will be easier than last year. If you remember we were in different houses then," said Liza.

"Your staff won't be able to have their Christmas lunch like they did in Belfast," commented Bella.

"They will but they won't have lunch, they will have Christmas dinner at around six o'clock. We will eat at around midday, and once again we will have a cold supper set out when that is over and we can eat that if and when we are ready," said Liza.

When Jamie and Liza were alone that night, Liza commented once again that it was difficult to believe that nearly a year had passed since last Christmas.

"We've had a very busy year Liza, which has made it pass so quickly. We spent a long time in New York, and we've been some time in Belfast. It doesn't feel as if we have spent very long at home in Surrey this year," said Jamie.

"We will this year as it will be the last year that our family will be together all the time," said Liza. "I really don't know how I am going to deal with not having our boys around us. They seem to be looking forward to it, which I suppose is only right. They have to be away from their parents and stand on their own feet eventually."

"Well, that's nearly a year away, so we'll enjoy our time with them and they will be back home for Christmas next year, and that is going to be a time that we will really look forward to," said Jamie.

"Did you enjoy going home for Christmas?" asked Liza.

"Not particularly. Actually I don't think that I spent many Christmases at home, I mostly spent my holidays with either Anthony or Binky; I was included in their family festivities," said Jamie.

"That's very sad," said Liza.

"It wasn't Liza," said Jamie. "I didn't want to spend the time at home. I would have been alone and that wouldn't have been fun. I had some good Christmases at my friends' homes. Our boys have good Christmases at home and that makes me very happy. I enjoy seeing their faces on that morning and no matter how old they get I believe they will always experience the excitement of Christmas morning with us."

"We still have a couple of months to go before that time but with the number of people who are going to be under our roof, it will have to be planned meticulously," said Liza.

"I can tell that you already have it in hand," said Jamie as he yawned. "You gave that away over dinner."

***

During the course of the following weeks furniture was regularly being delivered to Langston. The house mother and chief cook were employed immediately and saw all the kitchen equipment in place. Randolph and Penny Langston were kind enough to allow them to stay with them as the Home was not ready to accommodate anyone until after Christmas.

Joseph and Lily spent every day there helping to make the house comfortable and ensuring that all the furniture was in good order as it arrived. They were very keen to move their own furniture into their quarters but resisted the temptation as they knew that their concentration had to be on the accommodation for the children. Their friendship with Randolph and Penny grew as the time went on and several times they stayed the night with them.

Wendell and Amelia arrived during the first week of December; they brought Freda and Finley, who was Wendell's valet. They both would be needed to help when Peter, Edward and Nicole arrived with little Edward, as Wendell had felt that it was unfair to make so much extra work for April and Roberts.

Liza thought it best that just Joseph and Lily were with Wendell and Amelia on their first trip to Langston as she did not want to 'steal their thunder'.

The Major and Jennifer visited on many occasions just to make sure that all was going according to plan and the Major confided to Liza that he was more impressed with Joseph than he had previously thought he would be.

"I know that Joseph felt that as he was the youngest brother he was always treated like the baby and never given the responsibility that he craved. I have to admit that I never gave him the credit for the abilities that he so obviously has; he deserves all our support," said Liza.

"Lily has been very good for him. It's lovely to see a young couple so enthusiastic and working well together. I'm lucky to have Joseph as a son-in-law and I think of Lily as my daughter. I hate to admit that I have a great deal to thank Lady Evelyn Edgeworth for. If she hadn't treated you and young James so badly, we would never have met and I would not be happily married and have worthwhile employment," said the Major and he and Liza laughed at the irony of it all.

Liza arranged with Mrs Frances that every bedroom in the house was prepared and fires lit during the week before Christmas as she wanted to make sure that should there be a few surprise guests then they would not be caught unawares. Liza still had a vivid memory of the unannounced arrival of the Duke of Berkshire and his valet the previous Christmas in Belfast.

Three days before Christmas, Peter, Edward, Nicole and little Edward arrivedmuch to everyone's delight. On the same day a letter arrived from Lady Redfern asking if she and Lord Carlton could spend the holidays with them, especially as her daughter and grandchildren would already be guests for the festive season.

Liza went rushing into the library where she knew that Jamie would be. He was reading his newspaper with Wendell and David. The three newspapers dropped slightly as she entered, and she smiled once again at this familiar ritual.

"I've just had a letter Jamie," said Liza and all three newspapers dropped a little further.

"Have you Liza?" said Jamie. "It must be important or you wouldn't be telling me."

"Yes, it's from Lady Redfern," said Liza. "She wants to spend Christmas with her daughter and grandsons."

"I presume that it means that we will be having the pleasure of her company for Christmas," said Jamie.

"Yes, and Lord Carlton also," smiled Liza as the newspapers were now on their laps and all eyes were on Liza.

"It would seem that we are not being given a choice," smiled Jamie. "Isn't it just as well that you have organised extra rooms to be made ready and I also presume that you have made arrangements to have enough food to feed everyone."

"I didn't think you knew we'd done that already," said Liza.

"I couldn't really miss the rushing around that has been taking place this week in this house," said Jamie. "I suppose they will also be bringing their staff with them."

"She didn't say, but I presume so," said Liza.

"It must be nice to be as popular as you apparently are," commented Wendell as he lifted his newspaper up again and David nodded his agreement and followed suit.

"Thank you for telling me Liza. I presume we won't be having any further surprise house guests this year," smiled Jamie.

"I'm afraid I can't guarantee that, but I really can't think of anyone else. Unless of course Anthony and Diana failed to travel to Belfast and decide to turn up on our doorstep," said Liza thoughtfully.

"Don't worry Liza; I know that they have left for Belfast. They should actually be there by now," said Jamie.

Liza laughed as Jamie smiled at her and lifted his newspaper again. She left the library and found Mrs Frances down in the kitchen with Mrs Lambert.

"We were right to plan for unexpected guests Mrs Frances," said Liza. "Lady Redfern and Lord Carlton will be with us for Christmas and I presume they will be bringing a maid and valet with them. Hopefully it won't mean too much extra work for you Mrs Lambert. I presume you are well organised for your staff dinner on the day; you'll probably have at least two extra mouths to feed also."

"It certainly will be a house full, but we'll manage. At least all the rooms are organised already and I'm sure Mrs Lambert will manage and have enough food for everyone," said Mrs Frances and Mrs Lambert nodded in agreement.

"I'm afraid Lady Redfern failed to mention exactly when she would be arriving, but I presume at the same time as the Duke and Duchess of Berkshire," said Liza.

There was a thundering sound coming from the hallway and Liza assumed that Mr Lambert and several helpers were struggling in with the large fir tree that was going to be placed in the stairwell ready for decorating that afternoon.

Liza dashed up from the kitchen to supervise exactly where the tree should be placed and also to ask Grace to quickly write a note to Lady Redfern saying that they would be delighted to have her company over Christmas as well as Lord Carlton's. She was to arrange for the young stable boy to take it immediately to her.

The boys decided that they would also help to supervise with the placement of the tree, as did nearly everyone else in the household and whilst they were doing that Bella and her boys arrived with Nurse Dawkins and her maid.

"I think we have arrived in the middle of chaos," laughed Bella. "Are we in our usual rooms?"

"Yes, Mrs Frances will show you," said Liza.

"No need, we know the way. I presume Nicholas and Richard would prefer to stay here and help with the tree," said Bella.

"Is the Duke not with you today? And I don't know when your mother and Lord Carlton will be arriving," said Liza.

"I didn't know my mother was joining us for Christmas," said Bella. "Obviously she won't be needed at the Palace. The Duke won't be arriving until tomorrow; they probably will get here together."

Mr Lambert was now leaning over the banisters tying the top of the tree securely in place, whilst others were filling the large base pot with earth. The tree was giving off a beautiful aroma and the boys were sorting out the decorations that had been used the previous year in Belfast. They also had made new baubles and Amelia, Miranda and Lucinda had made green and red bows to be placed on the tree. David and Wendell had been given the task of placing candles safely in holders. John had had the idea of cutting thin strips of shiny silver material which would be placed gently over branches so that they hung down and could move with any draft, he said that it would bring the tree to life. He also had added to the previous years' star for the top of the tree also with shiny silver material.

It was Jamie's job to place the star on the top, which he successfully did but not without choruses of "left a bit. No right a bit. Straighten it up. That's right".

The top decorations were put in place by leaning over the banisters, Mr Lambert climbed a ladder for other high ones, and all else were within reach from the floor.

Everyone was joining in and luckily Lily and Joseph arrived back in time to help. Tea, lemonade and cakes were brought up from the kitchen and they all stood around eating and drinking while still decorating the tree. The final baubles were the strings of beads which they had made the previous year and they were draped across the branches and caught the light from the fire in the hall and the lamps as did the silver material strips.

Finally they all stood back and had to admire their handiwork. Mr Lambert came in with baskets of holly which would be placed over pictures and anywhere else that could hold a sprig. Edgeworth House was now ready for Christmas.

By that time the boys had organised themselves for their supper and they could be heard going down to the kitchen chatting happily. David and Grace were dining with Miranda and Lucinda that evening and somehow Peter managed to gain an invitation also, which took a little pressure off the kitchen. Amelia was in her element with little Edward and Wendell could be seen smiling like the doting grandfather that he was and this allowed Edward and Nicole to meet with Joseph and Lily to hear all about what they had been doing over the past few weeks.

Jamie was enjoying sitting at the head of his table that evening; he felt happy surrounded by his family and friends. Liza was at the foot of the table which was where she always sat when they had many guests. She assumed that the next evening would also have the Duke and Lady Redfern as well as Lord Carlton at their table.

Presents were now mysteriously appearing at the foot of the Christmas tree; it was going to be an exciting and interesting Christmas morning.

Two carriages drew up the next day and they were carrying the Duke, Lady Redfern and Lord Carlton along with their staff that consisted of a valet and a maid.

"I trust we haven't arrived too soon Liza," smiled Lady Redfern really knowing that she had not.

The Duke and Lord Carlton were admiring the Christmas tree; they both turned, and Liza was engulfed by the Duke who asked how it could really be a year since they had spent Christmas in Belfast.

Mrs Frances and Harper showed them to their rooms and their staff helped them settle in, but they were soon down and once again standing and admiring the tree. Jamie had been out with his overseer when they had arrived, and he greeted them warmly on his arrival home.

The Duke smiled his greeting and said, "I understand that Bella and our boys will be staying with you until the worst of the winter weather is over."

Jamie was a little taken aback but recovered well. "I believe it has been discussed," said Jamie and the Duke nodded knowingly.

Liza butted in, "at least Bella won't have the indignity of trying to hold onto her stomach on board ship this year. It was rather a trial for her last year."

The Duke smiled at her and was about to say something just as all the boys came down from their rooms ready for their supper. Jamie introduced them to Lady Redfern and Lord Carlton who they had not previously met. They each said, "Good afternoon" politely and of course Matthew said his usual greeting of, "Good afternoon Lady Redfern, I trust you are well."

"Yes, thank you young Master Edgeworth, I am quite well," said Lady Redfern with a smile.

The boys continued on their way to the kitchen and at the same time afternoon tea was served in the drawing room. Bella appeared and kissed her mother saying that she was pleased to see her but had not realised that she would be joining them until Liza had told her the previous day.

"I have not experienced a Christmas with my grandchildren since they were babies and as I was not needed at the Palace, I felt that a Christmas alone was rather depressing. Liza and Jamie have kindly welcomed me to their home to enjoy the season with you all. I must say I am looking forward to being here, everything seems so very friendly. I can see why you like to spend your free time here Bella," said Lady Redfern.

"I shall be staying until the worst of the winter is over. I know that we were snowed in last year and we were so cold in our house that I was determined not to go through that again this year, so I shall be here as long as necessary," said Bella.

"The forecast is not as bad as last year I'm pleased to say," said Jamie.

"That's a pity because it sounds such fun what you had to do last year," said Bella.

"What did you do last year Jamie?" asked Lord Carlton.

"We closed some of our rooms, especially in the east wing. We all moved in together. Some had to share rooms, but that made it cosier for everyone. We were concerned that our fuel would run out before the winter snow had gone. We were not so worried about food, but it was so cold that it was difficult to keep the house completely warm, so we managed to use and keep fires going in just about half our rooms," said Jamie. "It worked out very well and we managed to enjoy the experience."

"Yes, my boys told me that it was quite an exciting time for them, but you say that this winter will be better," said the Duke.

"Apparently so, according to my farmers and one or two of the villagers," said Jamie. "They were right last year, and I have no reason to doubt them for this year. But don't worry Bella, we will get some snow which will make it difficult to travel, so you will get your wish and get blocked in with us for at least a few days."

"Will you be staying also?" Liza asked the Duke.

"I doubt it Liza," he said. "I have one or two business commitments that I must take care of early in the New Year."

"And you Lord Carlton? Do you also have commitments?" asked Liza.

"No, Liza, I don't, and my name is Douglas and I would prefer that you call me that," said Lord Carlton.

The next day was Christmas Eve and Miranda and Lucinda were anxious to show Lady Redfern, the Duke and Lord Carlton their home and they would be entertaining them for lunch along with David who was then going to show them his house. Grace and Peter were going into the village for last minute shopping. Wendell and Amelia had offered to look after little Edward so that Nicole and Edward could have some time to themselves. Joseph and Lily were lunching with Penny and Randolph along with the Housemother and the Cook for Langston House. Bella was going to rest for most of the day, especially as she had agreed to attend the midnight service with everyone else. The boys were spending the morning with Adam and during that time they were also wrapping the remainder of their presents; they would be allowed to accompany everyone to the midnight service, so they had been encouraged not to play anything that exerted them too much. Liza and Jamie decided to relax in Liza's study, which was a room where she was rarely disturbed.

"It's going to be a very busy day tomorrow," said Jamie.

"It's all organised; I don't think we are going to be overworked, unlike our staff," said Liza. "Your mother's staff will be here to help so hopefully they all will be able to enjoy the day as much as we will."

The midnight service at the renovated church was beautiful. It was the first service to be held there for nearly a year and the church was crowded. Bernard looked so proud to be conducting such a service and David was asked to assist.

After the service Adam, April and Nurse Dawkins hurried the boys back to their beds, although they would probably be too excited to sleep quickly.

There was a slight fluttering of snow as they chatted outside the church and Bernard confirmed that he would be delighted to join them for lunch the next day and a note on his door was sufficient to tell parishioners where he would be staying that night should he be needed. As most of his parishioners were at the midnight service, he did not believe that it would be a very long service the next day.

David and Grace went straight to their home as did Miranda and Lucinda and their staff, which left all else to have a nightcap before retiring ready for the next day.

Before Liza could make her way to Jamie's room, he came to her. "We have a great many people relying on us to make sure they have an enjoyable time tomorrow," he said. "But I do like being surrounded by family and friends. I'm sorry that Anthony and Diana aren't with us this year, and of course Hector and Brendan were with us also last year."

"I don't think that anyone is relying on us to make them happy tomorrow, they will do it themselves. I know the boys will be happy and so will your mother and Lucinda. Peter will be happy because Grace is here. Amelia and Wendell will be happy because they have all their family with them and especially little Edward. I don't know why Bella will be happy, but I know she will be. The Duke will be happy because everyone else is and so will Douglas and Lady Redfern for the same reason. Your uncle loves being part of this family; he'll probably take a little time out to visit Holly. The Major and Jennifer are always happy, but they will be more so because their family will be here," said Liza. "So we don't have to do anything to make them happy and we don't have to do anything special to be happy ourselves, because we already are."

The adults seemed to be just as excited as the boys on Christmas morning and half the presents were handed out after breakfast; the other half would become part of the after-lunch entertainment. Bernard arrived in time for lunch and Mrs Frances took his overnight bag to his room.

As always when they had a large gathering, Jamie sat at the head of the table and Liza at the foot. She had arranged that the boys were interspersed with the adults but made sure that they did sit opposite one another.

It was a lively and happy lunchtime and Jamie looked up to find Liza smiling at him. He had seen the look on her face before which was when Patrick had

633

turned up unexpectedly and she had looked at him with such love that no words needed to be said and Jamie realised that he had at last achieved that same feeling from her. He had known that she loved him since before they married, but to be able to know what she was saying by just looking at her was something that he had always wanted, and it was happening now.

Wendell looked up and was about to ask Liza a question but stopped realising that something significant was happening between Liza and Jamie. He too had seen how she had reacted to Patrick and now Jamie had that same love. *It's taken a while,* he thought, *well done Jamie, you've been very patient, and it's paid off.*

Jamie tapped his glass and stood up; Liza hadn't realised that he was going to make a speech.

"I am so very pleased to have you all here today. A few years ago I had my son, James, as my only family and much as I loved him, we were a lonely pair and then into my life came Liza and her sons, who are now officially Edgeworths and it makes me very proud to have three sons. We also have Simon with us who will be like a son to us whilst he is here. I have my Mother and Lucinda and my Uncle David and Cousin Grace to complete my family."

"However, around this table are friends who are just like family to Liza and I. Wendell and Amelia and all their family are also our family; we cannot imagine a Christmas without them; nor would we want to. Nicholas and Richard have become regular visitors to this household, and we will miss all the boys when they go to university next year.

"It's nice to see you back at our table Bernard, we have missed you and I am so pleased that the Duke, Bella, Lady Redfern and Douglas have joined our family and have been so supportive of all that we do."

"There are those who are not with us today, but I would like to mention them as they are important to us. They are Liza's and my friends from Benson, namely Simon's parents and sister who are Kate, who lived with Liza in Belfast at one time, and her husband Gabriel, together with their daughter, little Liza. There is Liza's great friend Zelma who has saved her life on many occasions; also the Colonel and Ada; Marshall and Bea and their children. And we must not forget the Reverend George Prior and Angela and many more from that town. But I must not miss mentioning Kathy and Joe who were amongst the first people to help Liza find her way back to us."

"We were sorry that Anthony, Diana, Rose and little Thomas could not be with us today; they are good and close friends of ours as are Annalise and

Arthur. Hector and Estelle have set out on a new and exciting life and we wish them well on the adventure and Liza's nephew Brendan was with us last year, but he also is in America working on the Daltons venture. The Major and Jennifer will be joining us later, after they have made sure that all the children at the Ffoulks Home have a wonderful Christmas and we look forward to seeing them."

"I spent many a Christmas in the Redfern household in my youth and I will not forget the kindness that was shown towards me when I was such a lonely figure at that time, but now I would like you all to raise your glasses to those who are not here with us today and I know there will be those I have not mentioned, but I wish them all well, so the toast is 'Absent friends'."

Everyone stood and raised their glasses saying, "To Absent Friends."

They finished their meal and left the dining room to Mrs Frances and her staff to clear the table and when that was done food was brought up and covered for their later supper. Mrs Lambert was now concentrating on Christmas dinner for all the staff and they would be left alone to enjoy their time together.

In the drawing room the boys had gathered up all the remainder of the presents and their second gift unwrapping time had begun. When that was finished the annual Christmas game was spread out on the floor and all the boys were on their knees setting it up. Liza was determined to leave it to them this year, however she soon noticed that Edward was standing and watching followed by Joseph and eventually they were both on their knees joining in. Peter was talking to Grace but was slowly making his way across and if Wendell had been a betting man, he would have put money on Liza joining in and he would have won.

The room was now filled with shouts and accusations of cheating. Douglas was next to get on his knees and play and Bernard decided that he could help. As always Jamie and Wendell watched together, *there it is again,* thought Wendell, *that look that says it all; at last she's happy.*

Peter could be heard telling Liza to be sensible and play properly, with Liza replying that she was not the only one who was playing that way and why wasn't he telling Douglas to play properly or Bernard as well. She was told that she was encouraging the others to play badly, and she looked up defiantly telling Peter that as everyone was enjoying themselves her way, perhaps he had always been wrong in the way he played. Peter grinned at her and admitted that her way was more fun and with that the Duke got on his hands and knees and joined in to the cheers of all those playing.

The Major and Jennifer arrived in the middle of all the chaos and after all the greetings Liza took them and their bags up to their room as she did not want to disturb Mrs Frances who was enjoying her Christmas dinner.

It was then time for supper, much to the delight of all the boys but they knew that it was their duty to make sure that they did not push in front of any adult and Liza and Jamie were proud to see that they offered to assist anyone who may need their help to carry plates to the table for them.

Lady Redfern and Amelia spent much time together and Bella was very happy in Nicole and Lily's company. Miranda and Lucinda always enjoyed themselves in any gathering. The Duke, Douglas, David and Bernard spent most of the time laughing and helping the boys to enjoy the day as did Edward and Joseph. In between joining the boys, Peter spent the rest of his time with Grace. Wendell was pleased to meet up with the Major and Jennifer again and Jamie wandered around making sure everyone had everything that they wanted. Liza found that she did not need to entertain anyone as they were all entertaining themselves.

"I hate to admit it Liza," said Lady Redfern, "but this is the first Christmas that I have spent with my grandsons since they were babies. They certainly seem to be enjoying themselves and it's nice to see how well all the boys get on. Bella tells me that they are all going off to university together and that your boys' tutor recognised that Richard is much brighter than first thought."

"Both the boys are bright," said Liza, "but Richard is very intelligent for his age."

"As is young Matthew I understand," said Lady Redfern.

"He's been taught with the others without bothering about age," said Liza.

"I happen to know that your tutor gave both Matthew and Richard lessons for children above the age of the other boys. What is the tutor going to do when the boys leave for university?" asked Lady Redfern.

"The headmaster at our local school is retiring next year and Adam will take over from him. In fact the headmaster should have retired last year but he extended his time waiting for Adam to be free," said Liza.

"I'm sure there would be many a family who would like to employ him; I can think of several who would appreciate his way of teaching. He seems too intelligent to bury himself in a village school," said Lady Redfern.

"I have queried that with him; I told him that he could land himself with very lucrative employment elsewhere, but he wants to give the local children the best start in life. He has been with us for many years and this village is now his village and that of his wife. He is very happy with what he is planning, and I must say that the village children will do very well under his guidance," said Liza.

Mrs Frances, Harper and several maids appeared to clear the table and Liza asked them if they had enjoyed their Christmas dinner to which they replied that they had.

By that time the boys were very tired, and Nurse Dawkins and April appeared and guided them to their rooms, whilst the adults sat back and chatted about the day whilst enjoying their choice of nightcap.

"Well Liza and Jamie, you've done it again. You've given us all a very happy, enjoyable and entertaining Christmas," said the Duke.

"No Duke, you've done that yourselves; all we did was provide the venue," said Liza.

"Come on Liza; you're too modest. I've had one of the happiest Christmases I've ever experienced and that is down to you both," said Douglas. "And I have to add that the antics of your children and your way of playing your game gave me one of the best laughs I have had in years."

"I'm praying for lots of snow," announced Bella. "So I hope you are going to help me Bernard. I want to stay here through the winter and stay warm and if we get snowed in then I'll get my wish."

"Well you know you're welcome Bella," said Jamie.

"You may get your wish Bella," said David looking out of the window. "It's snowing a little now."

"I'm afraid I don't think it's going to settle very much," said the Major. "It's a little early for heavy snow, but you never know. Does anyone know what is being forecast?"

"The farmers are saying that we are not going to have such a bad winter as last year, I'm pleased to say," said Jamie. "I know you would like it to be different Bella, but many people suffered last year, especially the livestock farmers. We were lucky; we did lose some animals but not as many as some farmers. We lost one villager. Sadly he refused to leave his inadequate home and move in with others and paid the price for his stubbornness."

"Well, I'm not needed at the Palace for at least three weeks," muttered Lady Redfern.

"Yes, I don't have any commitments for a while," said a thoughtful Douglas.

The Duke was smiling at both Liza and Jamie. "I think your guests are planning to stay with you for some time and they seem to think that it is their choice rather than yours."

"You know that we would never turn anyone out into the cold," laughed Jamie.

Gradually tiredness overcame them, and Peter and Harper saw Miranda, Lucinda, David and Grace to their homes as the others made their way to their various rooms, until it was just Liza and Jamie left in the drawing room.

"The day went well Liza," said Jamie. "Everyone seemed to have a very good time judging by how they all seem to want to stay a while."

"I know that Peter doesn't want to stay longer than necessary, and Edward also has business to attend to. I'm not sure whether the Duke has commitments, and the Major and Jennifer will get back to their charges at Ffoulks House shortly. Everyone else seems to be fairly flexible. Wendell and Amelia are staying until the first signs of spring; we may well travel to Belfast with them for Easter, it will be their choice," said Liza.

"I know that will make you very happy," said Jamie. "Shall we go up to bed now?"

"Yes, I'll check on the boys first," said Liza.

"You mean the young men, don't you?" said Jamie.

"That's rather sad for me," said Liza. "They're not my little boys anymore."

"They'll always be your little boys Liza and they'll always love you, but they have to be allowed to grow up and sadly through next year they will definitely become independent young men," said Jamie.

"Well, I'm going to enjoy the time with them before they go to university; I'm not going to travel anywhere apart from Belfast, I'm going to stay close to them," said Liza.

"Which means that you will probably get on their nerves," smiled Jamie.

"I know but I'll try not to," smiled Liza and they both went into the boys' room and stood looking at their sleeping family before making their way to their rooms where April was waiting for Liza and Roberts for Jamie.

Jamie came to her room before April had finished but she went quickly leaving them alone.

"This is the second night you have come to my room Jamie; do you prefer it to yours?" she said as she smiled up at him.

"No, I just wanted to be with you as soon as possible," said Jamie. "The look you gave me today told me exactly how you felt, and you are doing it again now Liza. I know that you have shown me in so many ways how much you love me, but your look now tells me something more; it tells me that there is no past, there is only now and the future and that I am the only one in your heart. You are making me feel so wanted and loved and you tell me all that without the need for words."

"You obviously don't realise that you are doing the same and you have put into words exactly what I feel; it's very special between us isn't it, Jamie? It's a shame that it took us so long," said Liza.

"I'm going to arrange to have our portraits painted because I believe that we now are so happy that I would like to capture how we feel. I've had one painted before, but I certainly don't look happy in it," said Jamie.

"I haven't seen it; was it that bad? You've hidden it away, haven't you? Did you have it painted with Evelyn and is there one of her?" smiled Liza.

"Yes, I did, and I've had both portraits stored in the loft, but I want one of you which will hang in pride of place with all the other Edgeworths," said Jamie.

"Who will you commission for this?" said Liza.

"I wasn't too happy with the artist who I had before; I suppose there are a number of people who could undertake it," said Jamie.

"I've seen young Lord Langston's work and his portrait of Penny is quite outstanding, perhaps we could approach him and see if he would be willing to spend the time with us," said Liza.

"We'll go and see him when we are a free of all our guests," said Jamie as he guided Liza towards her bed where they showed each other just how much they loved and wanted one another.

Epilogue

"I will have to make arrangements to move Liza into our family crypt and lay her next to Jamie Edgeworth. I believe there are formalities relating to disinterring somebody. I'll see our vicar to find out what he knows," said Jamie.

"Liza arranged that for Holly Edgeworth, David's wife," said Ellie Fuller. "I suppose it was relatively easy in those days. I have no idea what it involves now."

"Holly Edgeworth had only been buried less than two years when she was moved, Liza has been buried for over one hundred and twenty years, so it may not be that easy," said Eddy.

"No matter, she must be moved to be with my ancestor. That is where she should be and I am going to make sure that she is put in her rightful place," said Jamie. "I still wonder why their son, James, agreed to his mother having her moved because he loved her and pleaded with Evelyn to allow his adoption by Liza. It's a very strange turnabout on his part."

"No doubt it will all come to light in time," said Ellie. "The boys are about to start university and I know that she and Jamie are planning to visit Charles Enderby in South Carolina and their timing over that could not be worse. They also end up in Benson for a while."

"I think that the time has come for us to go to America," said Jamie. "Can you both afford the time to do that?"

"I can afford the time but being able to afford to be out of work for much longer is going to create problems," said Ellie.

"I could take just a few weeks away from my business," said Eddy, "but as far as funds are concerned, we could sell Liza's jewellery, it's worth a lot of money."

"We can't do that Eddy, you know that she has said that it isn't ours to sell," said Ellie. "I can get my job back in New York and keep on researching her life in America. It will take longer but we will do it eventually."

640

"From what we have learned about this family, it was Liza who guided the Edgeworths to keep their money invested wisely, so I think that as we are working on her life we should use some of her money to help with that research," said Jamie.

"That's very kind of you Jamie, but we started this because Liza was regarded as a member of our family and she came to us for help," said Ellie.

"May I ask what happened to the Marchant & Fuller fortune?" asked Jamie.

"I'm afraid it's a long story but the outcome was not a happy one. Liza left all her shares to the Fullers and unfortunately in time there was no one left with the business acumen that Wendell and Peter Fuller had, and Liza as well of course. The company was split into various sections and each was eventually sold but for a fraction of what it had once been worth," said Eddy. "We just have the offices and a couple of warehouses still within the company which are currently on the market. That is where I found the old safe which had Liza's journals and jewellery in it."

"You have a business don't you Eddy?" said Jamie.

"Yes, I'm in the salvage business and it is now becoming quite lucrative, but it has taken a few years to get to this stage," said Eddy.

"And you worked for the New York Times, didn't you Ellie? It sounds rather glamorous," smiled Jamie.

"Sadly it was not as glamorous as it sounds. It was exciting to live in New York and I wish I had known more about Liza whilst I was there. There were several old houses still there and I wonder if hers was one of them," said Ellie.

"I wonder if all her money came to us," said Jamie. "I would have thought that she would have left some to Matthew and John."

"You forget that Matthew and John became your family by adoption and possibly the children's charity benefitted in some way," said Eddy.

"There is so much more to find out about Liza," said Jamie. "Just when you think you have found out everything about her, another question comes to mind which we need to find the answer to. We need to travel to America and possibly to Italy also. I need to go to Belfast just to see where much of Liza's and Jamie's life was spent."

Ellie and Eddy were quiet as they knew that they could not afford to travel as Jamie would like. They both felt frustrated and Jamie realised what they were thinking.

"I have a fund put to one side for travel, but I have never used it. I need to know what happened to my ancestor, Jamie, and that must include his wife, Liza. I cannot do this alone; I need you both to help me so please accept that I can afford to pay for your travel and accommodation, if you can afford the time to assist me," said Jamie.

"If it was not to do with finding out about Liza and Jamie, then naturally we would not accept your offer, but I think you know that Liza wants us to do this and much as it sounds strange, we must carry out her wishes and hope that it will lay her to rest," said Ellie.

"I also feel that my ancestor is not resting peacefully, and I owe it to him to set the records straight," said Jamie.

"I do have to return to Belfast before we start out on the next phase of our journey," said Eddy. "So it will be a few weeks before I can set out."

"Whilst you are making your arrangements in Belfast, I shall be finding out what has to be done to move Liza to her rightful place and when I have done that I shall be in touch as I'm sure you would both like to be here to see that done," said Jamie.

"Another chapter in their lives is just starting," said Eddy. "Do you think this will be the last one Ellie?"

"I don't know," said Ellie, "but I do know what Liza would like the title to be."

"Don't keep us in suspense," smiled Jamie. "What is the title to be?"

"On many nights, in my dreams, I have heard a man's voice saying the words "Pride of Place" and I wondered at the meaning but felt that it could be significant to the next chapter in Liza's life. Perhaps I was being told what the title should be, and this time it was not Liza telling me. I have toyed with other titles, but this one keeps coming back to me. It may be your ancestor telling me that Liza should be given the respect that she was due, and the fact that he was so proud of her."

"You could be right Ellie," said Jamie. "I would no longer dispute that we are all being guided by those who have gone before us and we should be proud of all that they achieved. We have already given Liza pride of place in our drawing room and we are going to place her in her proper place next to my ancestor. I believe he will be proud that we are doing that, so I think Pride of Place has two meanings and will be a wonderful title."

***